LOVERS, BUILDE[RS]
THE DREAMERS W[HO]

HANNAH EICHENBERG — [...] lence and personal tragedy to become one of the most powerful women in America, she would sacrifice it all to achieve her most sought after goal — revenge.

MARK NORTHERN — He used his fists to rise from waterfront brawler to real estate baron. But his ultimate triumph eludes him — the heart of the woman he loves, the woman who curses his name.

VICTOR OAKHILL — A modern Icarus yearning for the skies. But his betrayal of a gangster's daughter could cost him his wings . . . and his life.

EVANGELINE GRANT — Heart-stoppingly beautiful but rebellious and cruel, she thrives in a world of depravity and evil . . . until one final degradation plunges her into insanity's abyss.

BENEDETTO SERPA — The charming but deadly Sicilian-born underworld kingpin. Hannah's ruthless protector, he will destroy any and all rivals for her affections.

JANA OAKHILL — Sensuous and manipulative, she will use her irresistible sexual allure to enslave any man — including members of her own family.

FORD STRYKER — The proud and determined mulatto, a stranger in the white man's world. Born into a powerful family that did not want him, he could eventually prove its most valuable asset.

JUSTIN OAKHILL — Impetuous and child-like but afire with dreams of greatness — dreams that could be shattered by the most forbidden love of all.

THE FINEST IN FICTION
FROM ZEBRA BOOKS!

HEART OF THE COUNTRY (2299, $4.50)
by Greg Matthews

Winner of the 26th annual WESTERN HERITAGE AWARD for Outstanding Novel of 1986! Critically acclaimed from coast to coast! A grand and glorious epic saga of the American West that *NEWSWEEK* Magazine called, "a stunning mesmerizing performance," by the bestselling author of THE FURTHER ADVENTURES OF HUCKLEBERRY FINN!

"A TRIUMPHANT AND CAPTIVATING NOVEL!"
—*KANSAS CITY STAR*

CARIBBEE (2400, $4.50)
by Thomas Hoover

From the author of THE MOGHUL! The flames of revolution erupt in 17th Century Barbados. A magnificent epic novel of bold adventure, political intrigue, and passionate romance, in the blockbuster tradition of James Clavell!

"ACTION-PACKED . . . A ROUSING READ"
—*PUBLISHERS WEEKLY*

MACAU (1940, $4.50)
by Daniel Carney

A breathtaking thriller of epic scope and power set against a background of Oriental squalor and splendor! A sweeping saga of passion, power, and betrayal in a dark and deadly Far Eastern breeding ground of racketeers, pimps, thieves and murderers!

"A RIP-ROARER"
—*LOS ANGELES TIMES*

Available wherever paperbacks are sold, or order direct from the Publisher. Send cover price plus 50¢ per copy for mailing and handling to Zebra Books, Dept. 102, 475 Park Avenue South, New York, N.Y. 10016. Residents of New York, New Jersey and Pennsylvania must include sales tax. DO NOT SEND CASH.

TOWERS

NORMAN STAHL

PINNACLE BOOKS
WINDSOR PUBLISHING CORP.

PINNACLE BOOKS

are published by

Windsor Publishing Corp.
475 Park Avenue South
New York, NY 10016

Copyright © 1988 by Allison Knight

All rights reserved. No part of this book may be reproduced in any form or by any means without the prior written consent of the Publisher, excepting brief quotes used in reviews.

First Pinnacle Books printing: April, 1988

Printed in the United States of America

For the saints who put up with me.

GENEALOGY

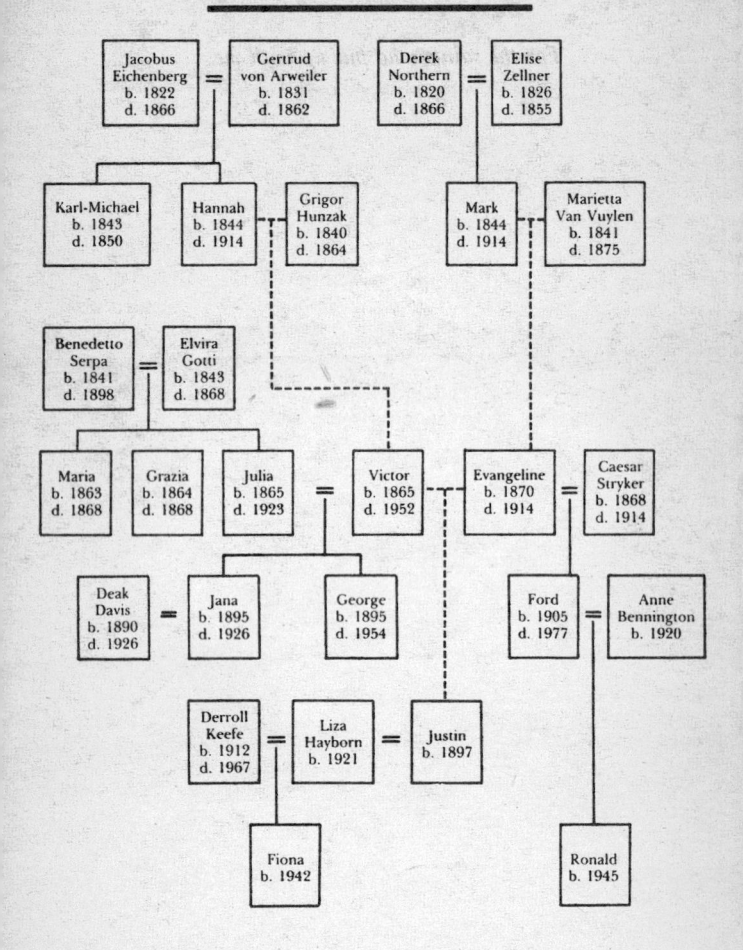

- Jacobus Eichenberg (b. 1822, d. 1866) = Gertrud von Arweiler (b. 1831, d. 1862)
  - Karl-Michael (b. 1843, d. 1850)
  - Hannah (b. 1844, d. 1914) ---- Grigor Hunzak (b. 1840, d. 1864)
    - Victor (b. 1865, d. 1952)

- Derek Northern (b. 1820, d. 1866) = Elise Zellner (b. 1826, d. 1855)
  - Mark (b. 1844, d. 1914) = Marietta Van Vuylen (b. 1841, d. 1875)
    - Evangeline (b. 1870, d. 1914) = Caesar Stryker (b. 1868, d. 1914)
      - Ford (b. 1905, d. 1977) = Anne Bennington (b. 1920)
        - Ronald (b. 1945)

- Benedetto Serpa (b. 1841, d. 1898) = Elvira Gotti (b. 1843, d. 1868)
  - Maria (b. 1863, d. 1868)
  - Grazia (b. 1864, d. 1868)
  - Julia (b. 1865, d. 1923) = Victor (b. 1865, d. 1952)
    - Jana (b. 1895, d. 1926) = Deak Davis (b. 1890, d. 1926)
    - George (b. 1895, d. 1954)

- Derroll Keefe (b. 1912, d. 1967) = Liza Hayborn (b. 1921) = Justin (b. 1897)
  - Fiona (b. 1942)

A PREFACE

This nation rose on the genius and audacity of a handful of great builders. The members of the two families here portrayed never lived, but their great deeds did. Flesh and blood people no greater in number than those who live in these pages achieved them. The people and their loves are fiction. Their visions in steel, glass and concrete existed, as real as the earth and the heavens they touch today.

Chapter 1

EYES CLOSED, standing jubilant and naked in the hot wash of the June sun, Hannah Eichenberg missed the glint of metal from the hazy treeline a mile from her window. If she had held the woods in her sight instead of in her mind she would have seen it, because she missed nothing on her land.

The servants knew all about Hannah and her window. They had heard the laments of her father when she asked him to profane the ancient design of the tower to let in the grand southern sweep of Golden Fluss. But Jacobus Eichenberg understood her scorning the stunning western view of the broad Bistritz River, shallow but swift-running and lovely, for the sight of her trees and hills. She wanted the wall of glass so she could look even further upon the endless acres that she rode so long every day. Never mind that the icy winter gales would roar out of Russia, cross the low hills of Bohemia and knife through the panes to crush the heat of any fire. Hannah must see and smell her land when she could not touch it.

Hannah could see a young gardener pushing a barrow across the broad lawns to a group of sculpted hedges. If he turned, he could see her, but she did not immediately move. For the past weeks something in her body had whispered a need to be seen by a man. She wanted to feel male eyes on her now so she would be ready later. She feared seeming overwhelmed, stupid and girlish when the moment came to show herself to the love that had come into her life so quickly, and from such an inconvenient quarter. Ashamed at last, and overcome by the brooding certainty that her body could never please any sensible man, she stepped back into the cool shadows of the room.

The tall mirror to which she turned showed her the sad basis of her doubts. She was as far from pretty as a twenty-year-old woman could be.

Her belly was as flat as a sheet of iron. Her ribs had not an extra ounce of luxuriant female padding about them. About her bosom, things got worse. They were not there in endless volume to be pushed upward in the kind of mountain that would silence a ballroom. The breasts stood hard and high, no more than a big man's hand could hold, she blushed to think.

Not able to end the viewing of horrors, she turned in profile. Hopelessly long, her legs stretched as lean as those of any of the kicking café dancers she had seen when she slipped away to explore in Vienna. Not a fashionable fold in sight. No lover, holding in his mind the billows of the great statues and paintings, could find comfort in her meager lap.

But she could conceal her body, at least, in the ballooning clothing of estate society. Her slim hips and high, tight bottom might hide from men's eyes under shameless padding. It was the face that offered no hope.

While her eyes, violet and large, and her skin, white and without a freckle, could stand with the best, the rest was peasant shambles.

The nose, instead of a great, bridgeless sweep filled with heft and character like a Hapsburg's, was the merest servant's button —turned upward and pertly rounded where it should have sharpened and reached out to command respect.

As for the lips, the thin, noble line that would have told there was nothing of a low, sensual nature in the owner was not in the least present. She bore a broad, curving flower whose natural redness did nothing to downplay her shame. When she smiled she might have been, with all her breeding, a welcoming ale-maid in the coach inn on the road to Sadowa.

He would never stay with her. When he got over the calf-love and shyness of these early years and saw the real women, the full-bodied, eagle-featured nymphs of Vienna, each of them fit for a ceiling mural, he would be gone.

But meanwhile, the green glades outside the windows and their early-summer perfumes rose to fill her heart and sent her to her riding clothes with resigned courage.

As she pulled on her boots, her lowered eyes again missed the glint from the trees, whose tops rolled restlessly in a nervous mid-morning wind.

Grigor Hunzak had raped before. By keeping it in his own low class of peasant and by staying clear of women with men as strong and quick with a knife as he, he had remained free and healthy. Today would be a much different thing. He had even bathed in the Bistritz to the hoots of Bauer and Metz.

Hunzak growled and wrapped a couple of broad leaves around the brightwork of the bridle of Bauer's horse. The sun falling wrong on a thing like that could give you away from thousands of yards. He wished he were alone. Metz was an idiot and Bauer only half as smart as that. They drank too much. Talked like women. Serfdom might be dead for a few years, but no one believed the peasants who worked these old estates needed a trial, or even a jail, when there was a crime of any size. A throat was presented by the master to the felon's fellow workers in the fields for a knife or rope.

He remained mounted to maintain the view of the enormous house. By Jesus, he thought, it is the most beautiful in the valley. Golden Fluss had first appeared on the Bistritz, a north-swinging branch of the Elbe, seven hundred years before, the old stories said. The wars had leveled it a dozen times, but the hardheaded holders of the land had rebuilt it more and more grandly. The present house had gone up just a hundred years before in the golden years of middle-European design. It escaped all hints of the fortress and stood on the river as a hundred yards of grace and glory, with three grand wings of yellow-stuccoed stone. The house was not quite as large as the house of Hunzak's own master, but stood more handsome in every way. Hunzak knew that Lord Northern—the dog—felt shamed by this, and that it pained him to have his own bleak pile of stone seen side by side with Golden Fluss by traffic on the Bistritz.

The wing that held the stables held the steady watch of Grigor Hunzak.

Not allowed to bring his bottle, Metz had turned sullen. "More pogroms in Russia, the priest says. Moravia, too. They take care of their Jews in the east. No one cares. Here we sneak and hide. Why should we?"

Bauer could read perhaps a hundred words, so he could hold forth. "The power is in the land. When they let the Jew hold great lands, they give him great power."

Hunzak stood in the stirrups to better his view.

"Eichenberg is an *English* Jew, remember. The English queen makes Franz Joseph shit in his pants. I think our emperor would like to be an Englishman himself."

"Eichenberg hardly sees England," Metz said.

"It's the same with the pig Lord Northern. But in his house too, the language is English. The old title, the old tongue. Our land is good enough, but not our ways."

Grigor Hunzak thought about lying with Hannah Eichenberg. She might be a Jew, but he could think of her in no other way but as a grand lady. She had passed close by him in open coaches, and he saw that she bore herself with the best of the landed bitches. She was spare of flesh for his taste, but she had escaped that bloodless horse face, and her eyes were the sky itself.

What he now had to do put him off. To grind one of those fine whores into the dirt, with no fear of the rope, should have come to him as a joy. With her, somehow it did not.

He had made up his mind that if Metz or Bauer tried to touch her beyond what was needed from them, he would break their arms. He had told them so. They were afraid to ask why.

Would she think him handsome? Hunzak found himself wondering. He hoped so. The girls of the fields thought he was. In dozens they had gone into the barns with him at the first asking. French blood flowed in him, an old woman in the village had told him. Perhaps it had been noble, a man fleeing from the great French revolt. He was as proud of his broad, elegant nose and high cheekbones as he was of his strength and balance in a fight. But for the blackness in his eyes and his lack of height, he thought, he might have passed for a Frenchman. She would like a Frenchman.

While the others looked away, he drew a comb, stolen from the great house, through his dark, heavy curls and his newly trimmed beard.

"Marriage is the weapon for this Queen Victoria," said Bauer. "Through it, she will take the whole countryside. Englishmen have the two best estates in the valley now, eh?"

"They make better masters, at least," said Metz.

Hunzak called him a barnyard name. "Because they beat us less? When we were serfs the old-time bastards had to allow us bread, and maybe held us in a little regard because they enjoyed our mothers warming their feet now and then. As workers for Englishmen we can't even count on that. And we must do these things for them."

"Grigor, is this the way they begin to drive out the yids?"

"Metz, don't you know by now it's the land? Northern is as mad for it as Eichenberg. With their women dead there is nothing else for them. It would be no surprise to see our fine Englishmen flop down during the plowing and get their hard cocks into a furrow. Our noble lord has tried money, crooked titles and fences moved in the night. Now he can try guns. He'd *kiss* a yid for an acre of ground. Or kill for it."

Through the trees, Hunzak, with the sharp eyes of a woodsman, made out the figure of a tall woman in riding clothes coming through the lofty doors of Golden Fluss. She strode down the long verandah toward the stable wing, stopping to speak to a gray-haired man who sat at a table.

"She comes," Hunzak said.

14

* * *

As always, Hannah did not look at the tin horse, and, as always, it burned into the corner of her vision as she swept by. The hideous toy standing on its wheels, eyes rolling and insane, nostrils flaring like a demon's, had stood on the broad, long verandah of Golden Fluss for fifteen years—since the death of Karl Michael, its last rider.

She had not killed her brother. Indeed, she had run harder than she had ever run before from the yellow boathouse on the Bistritz to scream to the servants. Karl Michael's little punt, a novelty made for placid pools, not swift-running rivers, had gone over and Karl Michael, burdened by many layers of clothing, was being swept away. But she had the awful and certain memory of feeling joy upon being sure that her best efforts would not succeed. And when the body of the seven-year-old boy had been grappled to shore, his face no less cold, no less mocking, than it had been in life, she had felt no sorrow. For this reason, and no other, she had broken and wept for a week. For solace she brought back the thousand spites and taunts of Karl Michael—the way he would seem to offer his friendship, love and trust, and then snatch them away at the cruelest moment and turn upon her with uncaring glee. The way he mocked her every effort to be pretty or bright or good at her lessons returned to her, and she despised him for it as though he still lived. She was appalled by her talent for hate that would not fade.

As Hannah approached Jacobus Eichenberg, who had placed the tin horse upon the verandah and saw that it was painted freshly each year, she was sure she had come by her unforgiving ways through her father. For while Eichenberg had not doubted for a moment she had run as hard as she had been able, he had seen the flicker of gladness in her eye. And now, set firmly next to the deep love he held for his last child was a thing he would not forgive. The tin horse was there to softly proclaim it, and she understood.

Eichenberg rose from behind the silver tea service. "Don't go. Take a cup with me."

15

"One cup. Then I must ride." They hugged briefly. "You have newspapers from Vienna, Father?"

"They mean nothing. It's the papers from Berlin I read."

"Bad?"

"Fatal, I think. The Prussian tiger is hungry. Schleswig and Holstein were too small a meal for Herr Bismarck. He won't share Germany with Austria now."

"But we fought Denmark together."

"To him it was just a thrust of Austrian power to the north, where he doesn't want it."

"We're stronger. The Austrian cavalry are the greatest fighters in the world. Everybody says so."

She was sure he was proud of her interest in the world outside the valley, and she kept up her reading.

He pressed her into a chair and poured her tea, waving off a servant. Hardly into his middle forties, his cheeks had hollowed and the Arabian darkness of his hair and beard showed broad streaks of white since the death of her mother two years before. "I traveled in Prussia last month, Hannah. They're ahead of us. Our officers hate staff work. We think it's all a matter of heroism in the field, at the expense of precise obedience to orders. Meanwhile they've formed a general staff with a genius for war. It's working out dispersed-formation tactics to make use of their needle gun against our muskets and packed masses of troops. It won't be pretty if trouble comes."

"Father, we have General Benedek."

"And they have a cold, beardless piece of mutton named von Moltke who has turned a conscript army of clerks and cow-milkers into a killing machine. Benedek is a brave clod who should command a company, not an army. Drink, Hannah. Drink up."

"That's the way you always hounded Mother. I don't know why she didn't float away the way you kept forcing that stuff into her."

Eichenberg smiled. "I never gave a damn for the tea. It kept her close to me for a half hour a couple of times a day. And now I sit out here with two cups in place and try to pretend she'll be along to take hers. The damned typhoid. It was in the drains."

Hannah wanted to ride for the woods but stayed a while longer to distract his pain.

"I heard shots again last night."

"Northern's men came across our fields. Looking for stray stock, they always say. Then a barn burns. A couple charges of birdshot keeps them moving, but there's no way to keep them out of three thousand acres, is there?"

"If they burn my new cottage on the north hill, they'll get more than birdshot from me."

"Why worry?" Eichenberg teased, trying to hide his concern from her. "You've got a half-dozen others scattered about, and who knows how many gazebos and rain shelters. About time somebody thinned them out."

"I like to see things built. Pretty things. Useful things. Needlework and painting don't do a thing for the way people live. Buildings do."

"Then let me get you an architect."

"Then there's nothing of me in it. Buildings should tell about the builder."

"Well," Eichenberg said, "save a good cottage for us. We may end up living there."

"You fight too much with Lord Northern."

"More and more every year. And there's our fine government, too. Now that your mother has taken the respect of her name and her Catholic protection to the grave, they won't be angry at what drives a Jew off their good Christian land."

"They know you haven't been a Jew for years."

"You never stop being a Jew, Hannah. They know that as well as God. Yes, I dropped the practice after some sellout rabbis in Budapest let them slaughter my grandparents for their farm without a warning or a chance to run. But the Almighty I curse for making men like that is still the God of Abraham."

"Mother always knew that."

"Of course. We did what we had to so we could marry in the face of her Church. But she never asked me to give her more than my heart and my name. How we loved, Hannah. How we loved."

For all his sad remembering, Hannah knew he was no destroyed, sentimental dreamer. He would not tolerate Northern's incursions for much longer. An attack upon his land was an attack upon his family, and she had seen his rare but terrible rages when anything he loved was slighted. He had gone against a cousin contemptuous of her mother with swords at dawn in Marienwald, all but killing him.

"I must go, Father."

He stood with her and drew her to him. "They say I married Mother for these lands. But I tell you I'd have married her for the first smile she gave me."

"She'd have lost it all without you to take the debts."

"But a Jew couldn't have held it without her."

"It's your land as much as hers, Father. Always."

"When we sat around the fires, the old people talked of the acres the family had lost going back a hundred years. They mourned every one of them as though they had names and faces. The only fires I want my great-grandchildren to sit around are the ones in Golden Fluss. The Eichenbergs have lost their last acre to the thieves and butchers. I promise that with my life."

Hannah walked rapidly for the stable. She was eager for what waited in the woods.

The men who had taught Hannah to ride at the age of seven had been given their orders by Eichenberg: "She is to ride like a man." The keeping of a great estate was the work of a rider who could push a horse a long distance over the meanest ground. The clumsy riding habits, sidesaddles and team-drawn rigs favored by women wouldn't do for the future mistress of Golden Fluss. Her father saw to it that her outfits were spare, if ladylike, allowing an easy straddle and a steely grip of the guiding calves.

With the slightest pressure of Hannah's spurs, the big bay broke from the stables in a strong, easy gallop. Eichenberg would be following her with his eyes, so she used the terrain to break contact. She cut behind a row of hillocks and began to use the lines of shrubs and small copses to shield her ride from the eyes of the people working the fields to the south.

Popping open the watch pinned to her lapel, she saw that the tea had made her late. But then, she thought, there had never really been an hour set. And she had always been there first by a good margin. Still, she cracked the crop against the horse's surging flank and soon came around a rocky ridge to find the treeline close before her.

The thick woods marked the start of the Northern estate, Himmelberg. The steady heightening of bad feelings between the landholders gave the low stone wall between the properties a new malevolence. Without hesitation she took the horse over it with a graceful bound.

The trees were immense, ancient, their trunks huge. Although the thick canopy of late-spring leaves shut out most of the sun, bright shafts cut downward in bright, white lines in the forest mist. The trunks were far enough apart for Hannah to sustain a good gallop on the trails, but she was moving away from the trails to the place that had come to be her whole world.

Bright birds sang and chattered all around in a frenzy of spring mating. Two deer guided her for some minutes before they lost themselves in the tangle, heading for what she thought must be a day of endless passion.

All about her the sounds and sights became benign, part of a magic world holding her, and soon another. So the other horses, ridden by men who knew this wood as well as she, were not in her eye or mind.

At last she was there. She rode the bay between a steep cut of rock and a huge pile of deadfall and came into the glade she had found as a child. It had been her own place for most of her life. She thought there was no way it could make her more happy. But since she had begun to share it, its raptures grew greater each day.

From a steep hill above her, a waterfall tumbled down a shallow-sloping wall of granite into a silvery brook that the horse crossed in a single step. The trees, thinner and closer-growing here, arched upward to form a cathedral above the clearing. The floor was a soft, green cushion of low ferns, lush moss and a riot of vivid wildflowers.

She climbed off the horse and listened for him, but the rushing water masked all the subtler sounds.

Hannah unpinned her hat and hung it on the saddle. She looked at the ground and thought about the two of them on it. Not sitting with their backs against a trunk, talking and laughing and feeling the sweet things of a new, young love as they did. Not kissing chastely, as always, and letting their hands travel trembling, haltingly down each other's neck and back. For one bold moment, she saw herself writhing beneath a body about whose very anatomy she could not be sure.

Hunzak and his men quietly entered the clearing at three places, making a semicircle to pin her against the rock that let down the torrent.

Finally seeing them, Hannah gasped. She didn't have to ask them who they were—she knew: Northern's men. The neverending skirmishes along the borders of the estates had brought the Eichenbergs into ample contact with all of the Northern men strong enough to fight and steal. The one at the center, the one who looked like a statue left coarse and unfinished, had always been a leader of trouble. He had stared at her on roads and at local festivals as if he might fall upon her. Hannah saw that he looked at her that way now, at a time when she did not have a pair of Golden Fluss men at her elbow.

She was back on the horse before they could speak. "Stand aside," she said crisply, trying desperately to remain and sound calm.

Metz rode forward quickly. "Get off there, you Jew bitch. If you want to mount something we'll find you a nice stallion right here," he leered, grabbing his crotch.

"Metz, you ass," Hunzak snapped. "Shut your mouth. *Stay where you are—*"

Metz's horse had taken one step too many, so it no longer blocked the trail behind him.

20

Hannah raked her spurs and drove her massive bay against the flank of the smallish mare Metz was riding. The impact rocked him half out of the saddle, and she rode under the swipe of his arm as he tried to catch her by the sleeve. In an instant she was streaking down the trail, a chorus of curses and a commotion of tangling horses behind her.

The speed with which they broke out on the trail behind her told Hannah they had been picked as riders. A peasant growing up as a stable boy could outride many a baron.

But she had other problems, too. This trail led away from Golden Fluss. Even if she could stay ahead of them, when she broke from the woods she would find herself on a wild part of the Northern land.

She was furious with herself for having ridden to the glade at close to a full gallop. They must have been waiting for hours, and their horses were fresh and strong. Hers would not last much longer at this rate, even if the land had not begun to slope upward. She had to reverse back to Golden Fluss, and she couldn't do it on the trail.

Before she got so far from the Eichenberg land that she no longer knew every tree and turn, she swerved into the brush. Away from the trail, sharp branches tore at her clothing and knee-high tangles grasped at the legs of the pounding horse, but she dared not slacken his speed.

Her hope that the men behind wouldn't know her way soon faded. Shouting through the trees, they fanned out and prepared to cut her routes of retreat. They were chasing her toward ground that funneled her toward them.

Hannah cursed to herself, trying to maneuver. She raced to pick up a narrow trail she knew to be ahead, making the chase a duel of speed and horsemanship.

In an odd way, she realized that she was not frightened. The headlong flight from a tough enemy thrilled her as much as anything she had known. But, for all her superb riding, she was losing her race.

The bay began to founder and stumble at almost the same

moment that the dim shapes of the other horsemen showed up in the trees to the right and left. If she had had a horse under her with five more minutes left in him, she would be away.

The perfect rhythm of the hard-running bay broke. He staggered in the turns and his shoulders were streaked white.

The leader of the pack, riding like a devil, broke out ahead of her on the trail just a second before she reached it herself. He jerked his horse sideways to block her, and she reined in so sharply that the exhausted bay went down. She swung her leg clear of the crushing weight and rolled away. A second man rode at her.

Hannah ducked the first grab and scrambled back to her saddle. Her hat still hung on it. She had the long hatpin in her hand by the time Bauer jumped down and lunged at her.

The pin ran straight through his upper arm, nicking the bone nicely. The weapon broke as she tried to pull it out for one more thrust.

Bauer screamed and swore while he tried to pull the pin through the other side of his arm. Metz tried to snatch her hair from horseback, but she grabbed his sleeve and bit his thumb so hard that the nail came off.

Then a strong arm came from behind to clamp her, and it was over.

Hunzak, on foot now, held her tightly, but not punishingly. He waited a few struggling seconds until her efforts drained the last movement from her.

Metz and Bauer were beside themselves. They glared at their wounds as though they would bite off the injured parts like rabid wolves. Roaring, they lurched at Hannah, their hair filthy, their stubbled faces twisting in rage.

Grigor Hunzak jerked Hannah away from them. His clubbed elbow took Metz on the point of the chin, sitting him down as if he had run into a tree. A thick boot shot into Bauer's ankle just short of hard enough to break it, and the man quickly sagged down next to Metz.

A big knife with sawteeth filed into one edge appeared next to

Hannah's face. She was wondering how to pray when she realized the blade was for the cowing of those on the ground, at least for the moment.

"If you two pigbrains make one more mistake, I'll send you home in small, dripping pieces. Get up. We begin."

Hannah screamed with anger, clawing and biting at the arm around her. Using the butt of the knife, Hunzak hit her hard where her head met her neck. After that she could only drift in and out of the things that happened, some seen through a thick haze, others seen as sharply as in the clearest of nightmares.

The bed they laid her upon was pine boughs, soft and sweet-smelling. Hands held her wrists from above and her ankles from below.

Hannah felt a distant surprise at how gently Hunzak removed her lower garments. Nothing was torn and she was hurt in no way.

"We were *all* supposed to have her, Grigor, damn you. I'm getting mine—"

"You'll get your stones sliced off and put up Bauer's ass if you bruise her."

Bauer, bearing down on her wrists, felt the pain in his arm and spit in her face. "Now you'll find out what Jews are missing—"

Hunzak's look silenced him. Hannah watched a big hand come down and wipe her face.

Her eyes were frozen on his. She didn't understand the misery she saw mixed in his desire.

He released his belt and uncovered himself. She sobbed with fury and tried to roll over, but he pushed her hips to the ground.

He was huge and she was dry. The pain pressed in like a glowing coal. The sneers and chuckles of Bauer and Metz tightened her with humiliation, making her agony worse.

She screamed for him to finish or to kill her, but he kept on thrusting, tearing. Yet, there remained a strange caring behind the blazing black eyes. And there was pain of his own—a man who had found what he had lived for just a moment before its end.

He convulsed and a rising sigh breathed out of him as he shot into her. He rolled away, but the hot knife of shame that she felt stayed inside.

"Do we get invited to the wedding, Grigor?" she heard Bauer sneer.

Hunzak rose and fastened his clothing.

"You look as though you just caught your cock in a door," said Metz. "Was she that bad?"

"Shut that sewer. Bauer, get her horse up. She should be able to walk in a half hour."

Bauer remained squatting. "What? I'm supposed to play servant to some Jewish cunt—"

A big paw reached out and jerked him up by his wounded arm. *"Get her horse. Then ours."* When Bauer had gone off whimpering, Hunzak pulled Hannah's skirt down over her belly and thighs.

Her eyes were open, but she had drifted far away. The back of her neck throbbed, and her head weighed more than she could lift. She couldn't raise her cheek off the boughs. The trees floated in a film.

As Metz and Bauer gathered the horses, shouting back and forth above the loud chatter of birds and insects, one of the trees began to move, quickly growing larger. She watched it numbly. Abruptly it came bursting toward her in a roar of crackling brush.

"Watch out, Grigor—"

Bauer's choked cry was drowned by a thunderous spurt of orange. Hannah's eyes swam clear. Mark Northern was there, reining and wheeling the familiar gray Arabian to bring a long pistol to bear.

Her heart broke as his eyes went to the piled undergarments.

The slender rider dismounted frantically and ran to her. "Hannah . . . *Hannah* . . ."

She had thought nothing could cloud the sunny beauty of the face above her. But now she saw the delicate features break into an ugly wolf-mask of fury.

All she could do was weep with anger.

Metz and Bauer had begun to sweat at the warning shot. Hunzak was without fear. He stepped back and motioned Mark to him. "We'll talk." When Mark came menacingly forward to place the muzzle against his breastbone, the peasant dropped his voice.

24

"It would be best if you rode on, sir. Your father would want you out of it."

"My *father?* What?"

Hunzak affected a puzzled air. "Sir, is this a game you're playing for the woman? She has charms, for a Jew. I feel it myself. But I beg you not to abuse good Christian men—"

Mark thumbed back the hammer. "I'm going to see to it that you're all hung by the feet from this tree you're standing under. Then I'm going to skin you with my own hands and gut you like the pigs you are."

The power of the landed families was such that Hunzak had no reason to doubt the promise could be carried out. Now his peasant temper began to rise. "By Jesus, twenty-two years old and still a fool. Lord Northern thought you would at least have the sense to stay out of the way—"

"What are you saying?"

"Are you blind? Deaf? Or just stupid? You must see your father hiring men good with guns while the Jew hires men good with plows. Why do you think it is?"

Mark's tone became low and deadly. "Why?"

"Don't try to tell me you don't know that the state has no interest in a yid's right to the land."

"Go on—"

Hunzak looked at Hannah and took his voice still lower. "There's no worry here. She'll go to her father with this. Or, if she doesn't, we'll tell it in the taverns that she came to us. They'll believe it. You know how Jews are. Eichenberg will hear either way. He'll come after us. And what is a good master like Lord Northern to do but protect his men. We'll be rid of the Jew in the fight. And then you, sir, will have new estates to ride, looking for poor people to threaten and new Jews to fuck—"

Mark hit him with a backhand swipe of the gun barrel.

The earlier gunshot had silenced much of the woods. Hannah had heard every word. She felt a sudden revulsion, a rising wave of horror and disbelief that she was powerless to thrust back.

There was a whirl of lightning motion.

She had heard often of Hunzak's fame as a knife-fighter. Now, as Mark's second blow landed, she saw the reflexes that made that fame. Without a thought of what it could cost him, the peasant snatched the sawtooth knife, dropped under the gun's muzzle and slashed at Mark's belly. The move would have laid open a man without a lifetime's training with the foil and saber. Mark had the bright snake's-tongue of the blade in view before it cleared the belt, and his darting feet shifted and danced him away before his mind could stir. He retreated in perfect balance and jerked the trigger. The gun clicked in a misfire.

"*Now,*" Hunzak roared as Mark spun the cylinder of the revolver to clear the jam.

Metz and Bauer, sensing this was the last chance they had to save their lives, ran wide of Hunzak and dove for Mark. Hannah saw Hunzak flip the knife in his hand so the blade fell into his fingers. She had watched her own fieldhands hit a tree squarely at twenty feet with a thrown knife, and this man was stronger and quicker than any of them. As his arm shot back, she squirmed on the ground and kicked into the back of his knee. The leg collapsed and Hunzak fell by her side.

Bauer got to Mark first, but caught the butt of the revolver straight on the temple as he came in. The thin bone collapsed with a crack, and he was dead before he tumbled. Then Metz was on Mark's back, choking with one arm and snatching for the cleared pistol with the other.

Mark shot him in the elbow and he jerked away screaming.

On his knees, Hunzak started to slash backward at Hannah. With a split second lost he flipped the blade to throw again, but Mark's bullet caught him just below the breastbone and passed through his spine. He toppled sideways, the black eyes as wild as ever, but quickly dying.

With an arm dangling, Metz vaulted to the saddle of a horse and plunged off the trail. Mark was onto the Arabian before the man was ten strides into the forest.

Hannah sat up but couldn't find the strength to move further. There was a bubbling laugh as Hunzak, fallen on his side, the red hole pumping thick blood, spoke to her.

"Does he think I'm so easy to kill?" He drew himself to his

elbows, the knife still in his hand. "From this distance I could put this through your neck with my eyes closed."

"You'll die just the same."

"Yes. Lord Northern saves himself a small house and a few acres."

Her tongue felt thick and dry. "There's no use lying anymore. Everything you said was false, wasn't it? Save your soul. Swear—"

He laughed at her. "I don't swear on a God that doesn't exist."

"Please—"

There was a gunshot from back in the forest. Hunzak looked to the sound. "Metz will be there to meet me in the other world, I think."

Her voice quavered. "Swear he didn't know."

Somewhere inside he was drowning. "For one kiss, I might." He pulled himself toward her on his elbows, moving in painful inches.

"You must swear."

"You must kiss me." More blood came from his lips. He kept moving closer. "Then you'll know."

He had pulled one final time with his elbows and turned up his sweating face to hers, when Mark burst out of the trees, riding hard. All he saw was the knife in Hunzak's hand. He fired straight down as the horse reared, the two bullets going through between the shoulders to explode the heart of Grigor Hunzak and its hopeless dream.

"Stop waving that knife and control your tone, or I shall call Ulrich to remove you."

Lord Derek Northern was the perfect man to handle a sudden, shocking confrontation. His slack cheeks and jowls held features as devoid of emotional movement as one of the stiff-faced paintings that lined the oak-paneled wall behind his chair. His voice never rose above a sibilant whisper or betrayed the slightest change in breathing. Mark recalled through his rage that when his father had beaten him with all his strength, or ordered him beaten by people with more power in their arms, he had spoken in tones no louder or more urgent than he used when ordering more pudding.

"Peasants are liars. Peasants are rapists. If we arrested everyone accused there would be no one to work the fields. They make their own justice among themselves with knives just like that one. The wardens find the pieces along the road and in the forests all the time. When I send them to sweep up the garbage you say you've left, they won't think it worth talking about over their beer.

"The Eichenberg woman knew what dangers were in that forest. If she rode into it, perhaps it was what she was looking for."

"Sir," Mark shouted as loudly as before, "if you speak against Miss Eichenberg again, you'll fight me with any weapon you please."

The threat was not empty and not without effect. Mark's temper was well known to his father and there had never been any pretext of love between them. But there was no fear for his life in Lord Northern's consideration of the threat. He had fought a dozen duels, and, for all his apparent softness, had shown himself as deadly with a sword or pistol as any who challenged him. Indeed, Mark owed much of his own great skill with those weapons to his father's harsh teaching. What Northern feared where he feared nothing else, Mark knew, was leaving his lands and name without an heir.

"You love this Jew, I must take it."

"Yes."

"Shocking."

Mark's frustration tore at him. The stone face before him, the manner that never changed, had allowed Northern to hear Mark accuse him and to deny it all without having to act out any of the false shock and outrage that might have betrayed another man.

"I'll go to her now," was all Mark could say.

"Are you going to stay on here with me?"

"No, Father, I'm not."

Northern motioned for him to wait. "Will you believe I was no part of this if I tell you how to save Eichenberg's life?"

"He's in danger?"

"Mortal danger. His men will look for the girl soon. If they hear the story you told me, from you or from her, he'll come for blood without waiting to hear more. He'll fight, alone or with men. He'll lose. He'll die. You know that."

"Just what you want."

"But not without you to hold the land."

"What would you do, Father?"

"Talk to her now. Tell her how it must be."

"How must it be?"

"She rode into the middle of some of our men who were settling accounts with one another over some gambling debt or family insult. You were trying to calm things before it got out of hand. She was knocked off her horse while they were fighting. She wasn't hurt but, of course, quite shaken. The men killed one another. You brought her here to look after her until she could ride. A good neighbor."

"You're afraid of the law."

"There is no law here for a Jew."

"We won't lie for you."

"She will if she wants to save her father. And you will if you want to marry her."

Jacobus Eichenberg joined Mark on the verandah as the sun started its plunge over Golden Fluss. "She's asleep. The doctors say there's no sign that the fall hurt her."

"Thank God," Mark said, afraid Eichenberg would see the shame on his cheeks.

"I'm surprised to see her so upset, even by such terrible things. She's very brave."

"I know." He had not meant to say that, but it opened the door for him.

"You've seen Hannah before, then?"

"Many times. We met riding months ago. She's very charming. We've been together quite a lot, really."

"She never told me that. Unlike her again."

"Well, we can't pretend there aren't bad things between our families, Mr. Eichenberg."

"Yes, and it's a damned shame."

"I agree, sir."

"Hannah owes you a great deal for today. And I, too."

"Then may I call on my friend?"

Eichenberg, off balance, was silent for a moment. "If that's your wish," he finally said.

"That would be my most devout wish. Good evening, sir."

In the weeks that followed, Mark found himself with a Hannah he didn't know. Her body came back quickly. But her spirit, always the strongest part of her, seemed dragging, crippled. She wouldn't get back on a horse or even visit the stables where she had once spent hours helping with the grooming.

Her old interests dropped away. Eichenberg showed Mark the room that held her drawing table, where she covered the wall with the designs of the small buildings she had scattered over the estate. Yet even when Mark told her that he shared such an interest, that he had supervised the building of the best barns on Himmelberg and helped with the design and construction of public buildings in Sadowa, she wouldn't take him to the room to talk about her work.

Mostly they sat at a far end of the verandah taking cool drinks in the summer heat, or strolled aimlessly on the lawns that stretched down to the Bistritz. Mark thought that Eichenberg might have told him by now that the visitor had seen quite enough of the recovered Hannah. But the man must have seen that his daughter still needed healing in some dark place that no doctor or father could reach.

Neither Mark nor Hannah had been able to speak of what had happened in the woods, and he could see her cheeks burn when she thought he might. And when he went to touch her beyond the taking of her arm, she drew back. So they strolled and talked of everything but said nothing, and the fear of somehow losing her started to rise like a rock in his throat.

For a time he resolved to wait, no matter how long, for the wounds in her mind to heal, letting her heart come to him when it would. But the day came, as they were standing at the river rail of the yellow boathouse, when his fears would let him wait no longer.

"Hannah," he said suddenly, "I can't bear such coldness. All my life, from the very start, I didn't know what it was to feel loving arms around me. My father enjoyed having me beaten and cursed by the dozen tutors trying to make me the kind of man a Northern should be. He'd let down my pants in front of them to give lessons in flogging when I hadn't done well with the foils or the riding or the numbers."

"But what about your mother?" she murmured.

"It didn't take her long to see that if he could have gotten his lands and an heir without her, he would have done it."

"Didn't she fight him?"

"He terrified her. She wasn't strong. She finally moved into another part of the house so she wouldn't have to see what she couldn't help. When she died," he said bitterly, "he would have mourned more for a favorite dog." He gripped the railing. "He made failure the greatest terror of my life. I swam the Bistritz, both ways, in the spring floods when I was six years old. I made it only because I was sure father's swimming master would cross over into the world of the dead to flog me if I drowned. And the scorn was worse than the whip. There were languages—five of them—music, classics, an endless string of things that made a perfect Northern. When I faltered in any of them he told me what hopeless filth I was in words you can't imagine."

Tears were in her eyes. "And you were all alone. How could you live?"

"I lived on crumbs of affection, Hannah. Whenever a word of praise or an admiring touch out of anyone was tossed my way, I would banquet on it for a week."

For the first time since the awful day, she put her arms around him.

"That's the story of a man who can't bear to be thrown away again, Hannah. You must tell me where I stand in your feelings."

She stepped back from him, forcing herself to speak. "I can't get out of my mind what . . . that man said . . . that day. I heard."

"I didn't know, Hannah . . . In honesty, I don't know if the man was lying. All I can say is that my father denies everything. And that on my sacred love for you, I was no part of any such treachery."

"I brought you to those woods, Mark. To that spot. No one else knew about it."

"They followed you."

"Or you brought them."

"I killed them for you, Hannah. They would have killed me, too."

"Because they saw you were going to murder them." She faltered in her attack. "Perhaps you cared something for me. Perhaps it made you weak for a moment, and you spoiled it for them. Then you had to be rid of the embarrassment."

"Hannah, I *love* you—"

"So you thought your first path to Golden Fluss might be best after all. You could marry me."

Mark could not answer her for a long time. "Hannah," he said finally, in a broken whisper, "I love you past my power to tell it. Yes, I had it in my heart to marry you. But I won't let you live in such shadows. I'll leave you now, and you won't have to worry about me marrying or betraying you."

"But I do, Mark." Her face broke and she stepped into his arms, clutching him and weeping without control. "There's going to be a child."

He felt her need for him fighting her distrust. He held her for many minutes, joy alternating with misery. The thought of Hunzak's child in her body was like a knife in his breast.

Then, unexpectedly, her glistening face turned up to his. He saw the doubts had not driven away her love for him. Her heart struggled to ignore her mind. Slowly she brought her lips to his. . . .

Together, they told Jacobus Eichenberg the next day.

He struck Mark. Not the slap of an outraged gentleman, but a sweeping blow with a closed fist that swelled and discolored the cheek. He might have struck Hannah too, but Mark stepped between them and told him he would protect the woman he loved.

Eichenberg retreated to his rooms for a week.

Hannah bore his fury with dignity.

When he was himself again, he called for her and Mark. "I can't pretend that I forgive this. But there is a child to think of, and we will do what we must." He never apologized for his behavior to them.

"He's like me," Hannah told Mark. "Once you've hurt him, he never forgets."

But the next morning Hannah walked on the verandah and found the tin horse was gone.

Jacobus Eichenberg had never talked to Derek Northern except through various representatives of the law. Now they met on an empty road outside both estates. Each man remained in his own open carriage, parked wheel to wheel with the other, while the drivers were sent away.

They talked more easily than Eichenberg had thought possible. His own polite charm and natural ease, even with the most formidable people, and Northern's schooled correctness and ever-quiet manner were enough to reach a quick accommodation.

"I will handle the Church, Eichenberg. My wife's family connections let me do that very well. It will be made clear to them that Hannah's records are to show that she had the Sacraments, and the ceremony is to stand as binding in this world and the next as any ever done in the Austrian Empire. You have no objections to the Roman ceremony?"

"Great objections, sir. But we do what must be done."

"The chapel at Himmelberg, I thought, since yours, I hear, has not been in use."

"That's satisfactory."

"It will be pleasant for you to have your daughter in a house you can see from your lands. You must feel free to visit us, of course."

"That's generous, Northern."

33

"We must set our old feeling aside and look to the advantages in this. The child brings together what will be the greatest estate on the Bistritz."

"Can our lands ever really be one?"

"If our families can be one—"

"For people like us, our land is part of our soul."

For a moment Eichenberg thought Northern might smile. "Then," said Northern, "we must find a way to win your soul."

The birth of Victor Northern in the very early spring of 1865 gave rise to none of the joy and celebration usually raised for the coming of an heir who would someday join two mighty estates.

The baby was broad and heavy, making a difficult birth. Although the fierce presence of Northern kept down the whispering, the servants did not miss the shortness of the months since the wedding, or the appearance of the child. "His hair, Sara. His eyes. His skin. Where'd all the blackness come from? Where's the Northern in him?"

Victor doubled in size and energy every week. He was quiet and seldom cried, but when he called out, it was with a big, brassy horn of a voice that caught the attention and held it.

None of the faces thrust before him put him off. He took to doctors, nursemaids, callers and all the hundred hefters of new children. While he never smiled, his nature was sunny enough. And the quick, dark eyes were never still, looking not so much for amusement as for new things to puzzle over in a mind he seemed determine to fill as quickly as he could.

Mark had not known what he would feel at the birth of this son born out of his wife's horrible injury. But from the moment he first held him, he knew that Victor Northern, whoever his father, was never going to know the cruel, loveless abyss that had been his own life. He began to pour the affection he had so desperately missed onto the child. "My God, Ulrich," a nursemaid said. "I'm afraid to touch that child, even for changing, when Master Mark is there."

Hannah seemed glad of the way he felt. He watched the instincts of a mother and a loving, caring soul warring with the memory of shame and humiliation that rose when she touched her son. She would fret fearfully when he seemed feverish or in pain, but she also seemed unable to kiss him or play with him. "Of course I love Victor, Mark. I just don't like to talk about him. I'm very happy for your feelings for him. It relieves me."

But there was more than that to trouble Mark.

Hannah had apologized to him a dozen times for the things she had said at the boathouse. Yet, it was as though she tried to convince herself he was no longer under suspicion. When she overcame her doubts for a moment and held him, he could feel the burning of the old love rising in her to match the heat of his own.

"Do you truly love me, Hannah?"

"Just as I always have."

But always the curtain between them would fall again.

She had taken a separate room at Himmelberg after their marriage, a decision he for a time respected, first out of her recent injury and then for the last stages of her difficult confinement. It was not until weeks after the birth of Victor that he realized with dismay that she had no intention of allowing him into her bed.

"You wouldn't want me in that way if you knew how those men left me feeling."

"You're sure it's only them?"

"Time is what I need. I'm trying, darling, with all my heart."

The harder he tried to believe her, the less he succeeded.

As Hannah painfully progressed, Mark finally realized Bismarck's dreadful intentions. The joint administration of Schleswig and Holstein by the conquering Austrians and northern Germans was plainly not going to last. The Iron Chancellor had a flaming vision of the endless scatter of German states—Saxony, Hesse, Bavaria, Hanover and the rest—united with the sword under Prussia, with Austria's power in the Confederation ended. He seemed unaffected by the promise of many states in the German Confederation to throw their armies in with Austria's magnificent units against his own conscripted, untested divisions. As always happens at the approach of any great war, the baser urgings of greed and bigotry began to take the field long before the first reserve was called up or the first cannon fired. Men came from the government to talk to Jacobus Eichenberg.

"You've come under suspicion, Eichenberg."

"Of what?"

"We have it on the best authority that you may be one of a cabal of Jews pretending loyalty to Austria while committing their wealth to the victory of Bismarck."

"And why?"

"To be rewarded with the lands of loyal Christians in the event of a Prussian victory."

"The name of my accuser, please?"

"We protect our witnesses, Eichenberg."

"Get out of my house until you have that name on your lips. Get out before I run you out with the flat of a saber."

"We might return with soldiers."

"You will need many. Paul, when these visitors are gone, burn the rug they are standing on. It's been soiled with the scum of the earth."

Things deteriorated rapidly at Golden Fluss. The fields and stock were raided by men who had the look of Vienna street toughs. Barns burned and Hannah's cottages were vandalized.

Little by little Eichenberg's men, mostly farmers with no stomach to fight, left. He could get no one from the surrounding estates to replace them. There would be no crop unless he could find help.

Debts were being called in as mobilization loomed, and he desperately needed the crop money. If he could get a tough, dependable core of men to protect the property, he might get others to work. The needs of the armies would drive up the crop prices and remove the pressure on him if he could hold out. But he saw no way to hold out alone.

Then the offers to buy Golden Fluss began to come in. They

all came through Vienna agents, and none of them offered more than a quarter of what the estate was worth. Eichenberg could see the millstone grinding toward him, and it was too heavy to turn aside. With the greatest misgivings, he went to the only man he could.

"Yes, Eichenberg, I could let you have some men. And I could help you get some farmers to get your crop in, but it wouldn't help in the long run." Northern, seated in a wingback chair that dwarfed him, smoked a fragrant Caribbean cigar.

"Why not?"

"Because nothing helps a Jew when the government wants his land for some special friends."

"Your own family has a hereditary claim on that land now, Northern. And you're powerful."

"As long as they pretend their target is a traitor, I can't bring that power to bear."

"Must I then lose everything? I'll burn Golden Fluss first. I'll slaughter the stock and sow the earth with salt."

"No, dammit. It's *ours.*"

Eichenberg went stiff inside to hear him refer to his Golden Fluss as *ours*. "Can you lend me money? Make the rate what you want."

"I'm stretched until the harvest."

"Then there's no help here, Northern." Eichenberg sent the rest of his brandy sizzling into the fireplace.

"But there *is* help, Eichenberg. Listen to me. You will sell me Golden Fluss. A token sale. Nothing permanent. The papers, though, will be perfectly in order so they can't suspect collusion in the family. You leave the land. Take the servants you need and move to Vienna. With the lands in my name, with my influence in the government, they won't touch the estate. The war will be short. No one is going in with Prussia. Benedek will smash them after all. Sanity will return. Stability. Law. Respect for property."

Eichenberg saw the steel-tooth trap he had been run into. He was asked to place everything he loved into the hands of the only man on earth he had ever truly loathed. Ultimately his trust had to be in young Mark, whom he had quietly grown to like and respect despite the earlier trouble. And family ties and honor must mean something even to a man like Northern.

The decision was easy only because there was none other to make.

"How will I live?"

"I'll work the estate. Send you what it brings in. When things are clear, after the harvest, I'd say, you return my token and you come back. We build the land side by side for our children. And Victor. We'll command the river."

There was not another thing to do. "Done," said Eichenberg.

"Ah, yes," said Northern. "Done."

"I'm going to Vienna with you."

"I forbid that, Hannah. I want my blood holding this land. Hold our claim with your husband and child. My going for just a while will make things better perhaps."

It happened just as Northern had said. The pressure against Golden Fluss vanished with the Jew. Depredations ceased, offers dried up, workers returned and the fields came to full production in time to promise a good crop for the year.

Jacobus Eichenberg went to Vienna with the best of his servants and rented a small villa at the outskirts, writing to Hannah every day. He tried to rekindle the interest in theater, café life and museums that he had held as a young man, but earth that was not his did not rest comfortably beneath his feet. Walking each day in the broad parks, he strove to regain the feeling of the soil and things growing. Traveling to the Danube, he sniffed at the river air and listened to the rush of the flood, looking for the sublime feeling he had known walking his own shores along the Bistritz. He talked to old friends, far fewer now, looking for the intellectual clash that would waken his mind again to a world that had gone by him.

But it was all alien. On Golden Fluss he had been reborn, a different, simpler, better man. To him, his small garden plot outside his own verandah was worth all of the Vienna woods. The little Bistritz was mightier in heart than the grand Danube. He wrote Hannah that he would have traded all the museums, cafés, theaters and learned debates for five minutes of talk to some fieldhands on a high ridge overlooking Golden Fluss as the night lifted purple out of the hollows of the sun-touched hills.

"The only comfort I find," he wrote, "is the thought of the hour when I will return to the place in the world that is mine, and the peace that lives only in its soil."

In some ways 1865 was the happiest year of Mark Northern's life. Hannah was his, and he had a lifetime to make her forget her wound and overcome her doubts. If she still kept him from her room, she was now growing more at ease with his touch. She had begun to laugh and to exchange feelings with him again.

They discovered a shared love of music and singing and would sometimes go alone to the piano, where she played like an angel and he sang in the clear open-throated tenor he had never let ring free since the awful days of his voice lessons. Often they played duets and set out to master Liszt's difficult *Legendes* together.

To bring Hannah out of herself, Mark went against his principle of asking his father for nothing.

"Father, we haven't had entertainment here since before mother died. Hannah is lonely. Could we have some people? Some music? I'd want the young society from Vienna, and from the estates around us."

"We must make our new family happy, mustn't we, Mark?"

He was surprised that Northern not only obliged, but did so with style and alacrity. And to his further surprise, and somewhat to his puzzlement, the gatherings were held not in the ballroom at Himmelberg, but in the one at Golden Fluss.

Northern, though, explained that the room at Golden Fluss was larger and more elegant than his own. Furthermore, the cleaning and preparations would help keep the place up to standards beyond what its skeleton staff could hope to maintain.

There was also the matter of Hannah's morale, Northern said. She might be more at home where she had danced as a girl.

Indeed, she was. And Mark showed her he could dance as elegantly and excitingly as any of the captains of cavalry in the Vienna ballrooms. As they swung to the mighty waltzes, her color heightened and he was certain that her breathlessness had less to do with her exertion than with her feelings for him.

But there was uneasiness, too. Watching his father circulate through the ballroom and the corridors of Golden Fluss, Mark saw a man who was more than a guest under a roof not truly his own. Hannah's look told him that she had not missed it either.

Soon Northern took a huge, sunny corner room at Golden Fluss as an office, moving furniture and some pictures from Himmelberg. Later he established a bedchamber and brought many of his own horses to its stables. Mark thought that his father had begun to spend as much time at Golden Fluss as he did at Himmelberg. Certainly he rode the Eichenberg lands far more than he did his own.

"It's as though he can't get enough of what's been forbidden to him," Hannah said to Mark.

Mark grew to love little Victor more than ever as the child began to walk. He had not brought Hannah closer as Mark had hoped. Even though Victor was her own flesh, he seemed poisoned to her because of his conception. She was intelligent enough to see her feelings and sensitive enough to deplore them, and tried hard not to let the child feel her drawing away. Her care for his well-being was intense and endless. Mark sensed that she longed to give her whole heart to them both but could not . . . yet.

By the winter of the year, Jacobus Eichenberg realized the squeeze on his funds was quickly becoming critical. His spoken agreement held that Northern would forward to him the price of his Golden River harvest minus expenses. Harvest and stock prices had been better than he could have hoped after the trouble in early '64, and '65 sales had been better yet. But the money from Northern, never much more than a trickle, had now all but dried up.

At first there had been letters, and excuses—pest damages,

stock disease, exorbitant demands on fieldhands as the army sought men, uncertain prices because military buying was distorting the market, losses in shipment—were represented in profusion.

Eichenberg's polite requests to see the account books of Golden Fluss were readily acceded to, but when they arrived he couldn't believe his eyes. The accounts of the two estates had been rolled together for convenience and it was impossible to separate the estates' production. Also, Northern had found Eichenberg's bookkeepers incompetent compared to his own and discharged them. The Golden Fluss accounts were in such a muddle that it would take extra weeks to sort them out and copy them separately.

As the excuses grew thinner, Eichenberg's communications grew sharper in tone. Northern's letters stopped entirely.

Even so, Eichenberg might have held on until the protracted political crisis resolved itself a bit more, except for his speculations. They had seemed prudent during the happy years when he had made them—railroads and new German steel-making techniques, mostly. But the investment in rail systems that might be chopped to pieces and in manufacturers that might become part of an enemy power were not good things at times like these. Moreover, his bankers, all longtime lenders to him, had suddenly become doubtful of funds anchored by lands with only a promise of restoration. There were no legal papers to back Eichenberg, because Northern, beyond deeming them not necessary inside the family, thought it dangerous to have lawyers witnessing documents created to confound the authorities. The only documents were the ones guaranteeing Northern's title to Golden Fluss.

Now Eichenberg's payments to his banks were late, his credit was at high risk, and he had no hope of raising more money by arranging terms on his land.

Although he preferred to believe that Northern was merely mismanaging, as his many excuses indicated, Eichenberg's rigorously suppressed doubts began to grow. As far as he had been able to see, Northern had been greedily acute in the running of Himmelberg in the past years. The troubles were not accidental.

Eichenberg determined his course and wrote of his decision to both Northern and Hannah. He would return to reclaim Golden Fluss, with all the risks of that, while he still had the small amount of money he must give back to end their agreement. He still didn't know if he had enough power to hang onto his lands, but he had seen again what any peasant in the field could have told him. Without the land he had no power at all.

The husky servants Northern had stationed outside the door of his new office in Golden Fluss did not prove necessary. Jacobus Eichenberg took one look at the papers pushed at him by Northern's fat, pockmarked lawyer and knew immediately what had happened. He also knew that no amount of raging, begging or threatening would move the rocky face and heart before him to alter a single detail. The huge unpayable price, a thousand times larger than the token Northern had paid in the first exchange, would remain as it was, and another Eichenberg would find himself as landless as the Jews that fled the pharaohs. No power on earth would have caused him to demean himself beyond the depths his trust and stupidity had already sunk him. And his rage was not the hard, hot kind that would not be contained, but a cold, jagged block where his heart used to be. He said only one thing to Northern.

"Wherever your blood goes, from now until a thousand years from now, I pray that the land will bring the same pain it has always brought to my blood. I can think of no greater curse to call down for the cruelty and treachery of this theft. But the Northerns will not keep everything that they stole from us."

When Mark returned from business in Linz three days later, Hannah and Victor were gone. His bewilderment turned into fury when he tracked what had happened to Northern's fat lawyer, who sought to impress him with how smoothly they had taken the Jew's land for themselves.

This time Northern needed his servants. Mark was coming for

him with a saber when they waylaid him. After he no longer struggled and shouted oaths, his father spoke to him in that obscene calm.

"Listen to me, Mark. It was God, not I, who decreed in heaven itself that Jews were to wander landless. It was an abomination to have one on the grounds won by the blood of Christian knights. And don't bring to me your squeals about theft. Any Jew, by the time he is old enough to grow that foul beard, has stolen more than I could in ten lifetimes. That I had the strength to take back what belonged to Jesus Christ, to someday hand it over to a son who will serve Him, does not damn me."

"You and everything you ever touched are damned," Mark shouted. "This land will be mine, you say? Good. Then I can give it back to the people you stole it from, while you're rotting. And I tell you, Father, I'll not have you buried in this soil. I'll throw you to the dogs."

Northern's voice held as firm and calm as ever. "You don't care about the old Jew any more than I do. You are a Northern. You're as hungry for the land as I am."

"Never—"

"It's still that girl, who gave you her bastard but not the hole he fell from. She saw her purpose in all this quickly enough. She's less of a fool than you are. Or perhaps Jews just understand these things better."

Mark struggled against the servants again. "Tell me what she heard from you—"

"The worst, my boy. Now let me unmake this unholy marriage. With Golden Fluss inside our fences we can have any match we want. We can have an heir of your blood, unpolluted, and give him immense lands to join to these."

"I'll go to her—"

"She'll spit on you. She'll tell you that you only want her because she holds an heir to contest these estates. No matter. Denounce the child for what he is."

"Never. I'll have them back."

"I think not. Read her last words to you." He handed Mark a

slit-open letter. The handwriting was unmistakably, heartbreakingly Hannah's. He read:

> M—
> Your cruel and savage work, successful though it now seems, will not be permitted to stand in Heaven. I only thank God that I found out before I gave you any more of the love I once longed to pour out to you. That I will never look upon you again is the one happiness that remains in my life.
>
> H.

A snowstorm closed the roads for a week. By the time Mark reached Vienna, Eichenberg's villa was empty. The people who knew Hannah and her father had heard their tale by now. Even when Mark laid hands on some of the men, they refused to tell him where his wife and child had gone with Eichenberg.

Twice he picked up the trail where Eichenberg had tried to effect legal remedies. But the man's pleas had been shut down so quickly that he had not remained for longer than a single night anywhere. Finally, in Prague, to his rage and despair, Mark lost them entirely and returned dispiritedly to what had been his home.

He had at first determined to leave Himmelberg and the father whose sight he could no longer bear. But what if there was word of Hannah and Victor? There was no other place the news could come to him. He was caught on the land that had destroyed all he had ever wanted.

"I'm moving into Golden Fluss, Father. I trust you will have the decency to remove yourself and stay away from me as much as you can."

"If that's what it takes to keep you on your own land. And don't worry. You'll forget her."

The man had never known love or suspected in the least that it could last forever. Mark meant to teach him something about that.

44

The months moved by in a haze of misery. Each dawn brought him a flicker of hope that today he would hear something, today she would return with Victor. But his sinking soul knew that even if she did, there weren't words enough to make her believe him or to turn aside her hatred.

But now, far to the north, Bismarck moved at last to unite Germany in blood and iron.

Chapter 2

THE LANDOWNERS in the country along the Bistritz began to gather together like sheep at the first howl of a wolf pack. Maps appeared on walls, personal riders brought dispatches from Vienna, newspapers were devoured and telegraph offices haunted.

"With just a little bad luck, gentlemen," Northern said quietly, "they'll be fighting this war on our doorstep."

As long expected, the Prussians moved to command the captured duchies of Schleswig and Holstein alone. Prussia was on its way to Bismarck's dream of a great Second Reich uniting the fragmented empire. An empire in which Austria was no longer to share power.

The move was, of course, calculated to goad Austria into a fast, decisive war, and that arrogant country hastened to oblige. In April of 1866, Austrian mobilization began.

The fond expectations that the north German allies would be an effective part of the alliance to crush Prussia came to a fast, sad end when the blue-coated, brilliantly-led formations of von Moltke, maneuvering with a precision and ferocity that were to change war forever, tore the brave armies of Hesse and Hanover to shreds and turned south as though they had brushed away a swarm of annoying flies.

"The Saxons are falling back in good order to join us," a government official told Mark. "Together, we'll mince those Prussian clerks."

In the early maneuvering for the decisive engagement, von Moltke split his forces, sending half in from the west and the rest in three columns through the mountains in the northeast. The potential pincer held a hideous danger for his forces. The Austrians could fling their strength against one or another of the divided armies and annihilate each in turn. But brave, stupid General Benedek never even considered the danger of the flanking force, much less the opportunity it gave him. He decided that the Prussian mountain forces would circle to join the second force for a united attack from the west, and strung his main defensive forces along the east bank of a river—the Bistritz.

Mark watched the plumes of dust building on the roads behind Golden Fluss, and after two days the glorious Austrian armies appeared in all their unstoppable, magnificent might.

Towed by mighty teams, artillery batteries clattered thunderously down the roads and cut across the fields to the high points that would command the battleground. Squadron after squadron of magnificently uniformed cavalry rode through, one group of regimental colors more glorious than the last.

The infantry arrived finally, marching crisply, their supply wagons bristling with digging tools. They threw up earthworks everywhere and went into the forests with axes to gather what they needed for a series of *abatis,* groups of trees felled with their branches sharpened and turned toward the expected enemy advance.

"One finds oneself feeling sorry for the men that must move against such fortifications manned by these disciplined and courageous forces," a French correspondent wrote.

Soon the artillery pieces had been brought into line and the hammering of measuring rounds began to be heard through the day. The artillerymen would know where each round would fall, waiting only a formation of Prussians to cross their target square.

In Salzburg, Hannah watched her father's torment. From rumors, newspapers, talks with officers and from his own instincts, Jacobus Eichenberg saw where the ultimate battlefield must be. The land was no longer his but it would never pass from his heart. The thought that Golden Fluss was in the path of danger while he was in no position to help defend it drove him to the brink of insanity.

For Hannah it was worse. She shared every bit of her father's commitment to the lost land, and she also had the misery of Mark. While she had thought often, in the days since his betrayal had been confirmed, that she would welcome his immolation, the threatened fact was quite another thing. Over and over each night she saw his body torn and blood-soaked on the field. She saw him dying in agony, with the only memory of her that last malevolent letter. Guilt and regret seared her.

He won't stay, she told herself. If the danger moved closer, he would do the sensible thing. He would leave the lands until the battle swept through. Even as she tried to put this comfort into her mind, she knew he would never go. He was a Northern. He would die on the ground that was his. The war inside her grew as fast as the one von Moltke was sending to the south. She saw that she was desperately in love with a man she must send away if he came through the door in answer to her prayers.

An old friend of Eichenberg had newspaper connections in England. For British correspondents, he supervised a circuitous telegraph and observer network meant to get around military censorship. He permitted Eichenberg and Hannah into the house at the outskirts of Salzburg that contained the chattering telegraph as the Austrian disaster began to unfold.

With his knowledge of the terrain, Eichenberg could gauge the flow of the battle better than any of the professional observers around him. The flat maps could not tell the others the depth of a stream, the thickness of a wood or the height of a hill. He knew where what looked like an hour's march would be a day of hard slogging.

The battle began a few miles west of Golden Fluss, with the estate squarely in the path of the Prussian advance. Fortunately, the heart of the Austrian forces blocked the way.

Eichenberg did not like the way the Prussians moved straight forward at the center of the Austrian defenses. For one thing, it indicated that von Moltke's conscripted army of tradesmen and farmers had leadership, courage and discipline far past what had been thought possible. And for another thing, it was not like the Prussian legions to go for a straight-ahead breakthrough against prepared positions. Theirs was an army of maneuver. The only way their frontal attack made sense to him was if it were meant merely to pin the Austrian forces in combat while a second force fell upon them from the flank. Trying to convince himself that all would be well, he kept telling Hannah that the Austrians were strong enough to stand under any direct assault on the Sadowa front. And that their northern flank, anchored on the towns of Nedelist and Lochenitz, would hold against any attack from a second force until reinforcements could stabilize the situation.

But Prussian bravery and stubbornness began to force Austrian mistakes.

The Prussian Seventh Division got across the Bistritz and gained control of a small wood running up to higher ground. The Austrian command began to fret that this high position threatened them unacceptably, although this was far from true, and swung their flank-protecting forces from the north into battle in the west. Eichenberg instantly saw what Benedek couldn't. One infantry brigade and a light cavalry division were all there was left to stem a second Prussian force in a move from behind. The Austrians had given away their flank in an incredible display of tactical stupidity.

What Hannah saw developing in her father's face terrified her. It was the face of a dead man. She woke in the middle of one night to answer a cry from Victor and found that Eichenberg had gone. The note that he left her had little of his stately script. She could hardly read the agitated scrawl.

49

> Dearest Hannah:
> I do a dishonorable thing leaving you and Victor alone at this troubled moment. I could not face you, whom I love so very much, because I could not then have brought myself to do what I must.
>
> Although Golden Fluss bears our name no longer, I cannot think of it taken by a ravaging army. Even the foul Northern will defend it with his blood, and I can do no less.
>
> I have left the ready money in the writing box on my desk. There are sufficient deposits in our Vienna banks to keep you modestly but comfortably. You must never stop pursuing our claims even if Austria falls.
>
> Sell what remains of my effects if I do not return. All I have taken is two favorite hunting guns. Don't mourn in any case, because I will have died where I wanted to.
>
> All my prayers and love, Hannah, and my regrets for having failed you in so many ways.
>
> > Your adoring Father

By mid-morning, with but a single traveling bag in her hand and Victor in her arms, Hannah had found her way onto a supply train bound for the front. If her father's train was delayed in the chaos that had descended upon the rails, she might still overtake him to dissuade him from his hopeless cause.

Mark, near the center of the battle, understood far less of what was happening than Eichenberg, even as he rode each day to watch the debacle unfold.

Now, on what must be the final day, Mark watched the enormous pressure thrown against the Prussians. Two crack Austrian corps, the Fourth and the Second, came forward again and again. It was inconceivable that the hugely outnumbered invaders could hold against the reckless gallantry of the attacking Austrians. But the thunderous rapidfire of the Prussian needle guns, pouring into the massed formations called for by the Austrians' outmoded shock tactics, piled the dead into appalling mounds.

Mark rode back to Himmelberg, passing through carpets of dead, hurtling past batteries whose guns still stood in perfect ranks above the torn corpses of the gunners and animals that had served them.

He supposed that the Prussians didn't know how little remained to oppose them as the day died. It wouldn't be until the next morning that they rolled forward and tried to finish their retreating foes. He hoped that the Prussian breakthrough along the river had remained here to the north and that the estates below had been spared.

All along the way he saw the flames of burning houses. Whether they had been destroyed by Austrians to keep them out of Prussian hands, or by Prussians to clean out pockets of resistance, he couldn't tell.

When he rode out of the high wood and saw the stirring sweep of Himmelberg and Golden Fluss before him, every building magnificent and intact, his heart almost burst with gratitude. But just across the river he could see the fires of a Prussian camp beginning to wink in the dusk. They would be treating their wounded, resting for the next day when they certainly would cross the Bistritz.

The camp was not a large one. He could make out in the dying light the glint of helmets and breastplates. It was the mauled remnants of a squadron of cavalry. Yet, even reduced as they must have been, they were a huge host compared to what lay before them.

Austrian soldiers were visible, but they were a straggle of stumbling wounded, unhorsed cavalry and dazed infantry separated from their decimated units as the main body reeled backward. They would present little problem to the disciplined unit across the Bistritz, who still greatly outnumbered them.

Northern heard his son's report and realized that the main body of the Austrian army was gone from before him. He had supposed as much, watching the retreat clog the roads around him. And he had not shrunk from what he had to do.

Somehow, beyond reason, the workers of his fields, the sons of men who had worked the grounds as serfs, felt the threatened ground was in some way theirs. So when Northern sent them to gather arms and ammunition discarded in the rout, many of them actually returned with the muskets. And they wielded shovels and picks to throw up shallow pits and hasty earthworks along the broad lawns of Golden Fluss, opposite the Prussian encampment across the Bistritz.

There was no one on the east bank of the river who did not see the hopelessness of the position. But as the peasants dug in and raised the log barricades, many wandering soldiers drifted out of the woods and across the fields to join them.

Bloodied officers laid out the fields of fire, passing along instructions for the loading and aiming of muskets. The less badly wounded pulled the ones who could not walk into firing positions. These men would ease the sting of their defeat in the only way it could ever be eased.

This would not be a battle to appear in any regimental history, but a skirmish forgotten after the last wound had healed. Except for the dead, it would be of no importance at all.

"No man will burn my house or have my land while I hold a breath," Northern said to Mark. "But perhaps this can be regained afterward. Go. The records are in Vienna."

Mark shook his head, completely willing to die on the soil that had grown him. In Northern's immovable mask, Mark thought he saw the faintest twitch of approval.

Behind a rough barricade of logs, Mark spent the night next to his father. It was the longest stretch of time they had ever spent together and would probably be their last night alive. But Northern never spoke. He looked unblinkingly on the outlines of Golden Fluss and Himmelberg against the reddish summer sky as though his love for them could hold them safely there forever.

52

Whenever Mark fell into a restless doze, he saw Hannah again and felt a rush of happiness and relief that was dashed at every fitful wakening. His only desire to survive the day came from his hope of finding her again and making her somehow see that his love and loyalty could never falter.

Bugles called him out of the night's last sleep. He pulled himself up behind the logs and watched the Prussian camp across the Bistritz come to life. In the first slanting rays of the morning sun he saw the remains of the cavalry unit. He estimated that they had lost half their number. Wounded lay in long ranks, tended to by other wounded, their bandages visible even at this distance. A few of their officers galloped up and down parallel to the river, some dressing the ranks of an assembling formation, others trying to make out what they faced across the shallow ford.

Rapidly the disorganization in their ranks disappeared. They wore polished helmets and breastplates, and these, glittering in the sunlight, arranged themselves as straight, solid lines of silver as the cavalrymen prepared an advance. What Austrian officers remained on the west bank rode about on horses they had caught wandering from yesterday's battles. They brought their men into position and rallied their spirits with crisp commands and bold encouragement. Peasants felt like hussars and enjoyed the heady power of a killing implement in their hands. Veterans, still half in shock from the defeats of the day before, were eager to pay back the Prussians for their wounds and humiliation.

The defenders of Golden Fluss drew back the hammers on their muskets and awaited the Prussian assault. But first there was a brief conference among the mounted officers on the other bank.

A single Prussian detached himself and rode across the stream, a white scarf fluttering from the tip of his saber.

Northern and Mark rode forward with an Austrian captain to meet him on the bank.

The Prussian was tall and well made, bearing himself with the easy arrogance of the titled officer. "Good morning. I am Major von Krieger. You must be aware that your brave forces have been defeated and have fallen back everywhere. Your resistance here will accomplish nothing, even if you had enough forces to resist effectively. Give up your arms, come out of your positions and surrender to me."

There was a roaring clatter from the Prussian camp as part of a light artillery battery arrived, the teams of horses dragging six cannons into line. The swarming crews began to unlimber them speedily.

"Sir," said the Austrian officer, "I am Captain Falkenheyn."

The Prussian eyed his uniform. "Black and Yellows. You gave us a fine fight."

"And must continue to do so. My last orders were to hold this line in the face of any enemy advance."

Von Krieger scowled. "All we want is to make sure that the land, the stock and the houses are of no use to your forces."

"Then you must take them with our blood. And yours," Northern said.

"Surrender, Falkenheyn. See it as a soldier."

"I see it as an Austrian."

"I understand." Von Krieger saluted, wheeled his horse and splashed back across the stream.

By the time the Austrians had returned to their positions, the artillery battery was in place on the other side of the water and the gunners were loading.

Mark placed a half-dozen muskets behind him and looked to their priming. As he worked, his eyes strayed upward to the road from the east. An open carriage careened into sight, a single man at the reins. The carriage never slowed at the entrance to Golden Fluss. As the driver took in the scene before him, he swung out of the driveway and headed across the wide lawn. It took him just seconds to cover the ground to the defenses. He pulled the frothing horses close behind Mark's position, gathered a couple of fine sporting rifles from behind his seat and leaped from the carriage.

"Sir, you must get out of here," Mark shouted at him.

"I might ask the same of you," Jacobus Eichenberg said. He was dressed in expensive traveling clothes but left no doubt as to his bloody intentions as he took his place at the barricade. "The Almighty knows this ground is mine, even if you do not. I will defend it."

"If I had my servants here," Northern said, "I'd throw you off."

"Hannah, sir?" Mark pleaded. "Where is Hannah?"

"I left her—" His words died as he followed Mark's stare. A second carriage was coming up the driveway to the house, driven as hard as the first. "Oh, God. She's followed me—"

They had started for her when the flat, air-splitting crack of von Krieger's artillery shattered the morning.

Geysers of earth and flame shot a hundred feet into the air across the breadth and depth of the defense-studded lawn. From across the river came a ragged cheer and the staccato song of a bugle. And then the swish of a hundred sabers drawn out of their sheaths. In another instant the first line of the Prussian cavalry bolted for the Bistritz and hit its shallows in white, churning fountains.

Falkenheyn scrambled to the top of an earthwork and flashed his saber above his head. *"Fire."*

Thin but persistent sheets of flame began erupting from the scattered Austrian positions, the sound having nothing of the concentrated authority of fire by massed units. But a half-dozen pieces of the advancing wall of flesh shuddered and catapulted forward into the stream, and the defenders gathered voice for a whooping cheer of their own. The oncoming horses, in water to their breasts, were seriously slowed for the moment and the defenders enjoyed what was sure to be their only moment of command in the engagement. The more direct hits by the musketry from the near bank penetrated the bright breastplates, and more riders toppled into the waters.

Between his father and Eichenberg, Mark loaded and fired desperately. Behind him a hellfire of shellbursts raked the vast lawn between him and Hannah. The defenders who rose and tried to scurry to better shelter were sliced to bits by whirring fragments.

A gust of breeze parted the smoke before the house, and he saw Hannah, out of the carriage now, carrying Victor. He thanked heaven that she had the child, or she would surely be trying to come to her father.

Now a servant ran to her from the house. He sheltered her in his arms and pushed her up the steps. The carriage she had come from dissolved in a flash of orange and flying splinters, a wheel turning gracefully in the air.

"Run, Hannah . . . run," screamed Mark.

In the distance, the hurrying figures disappeared through the huge doors of Golden Fluss. Mark and Eichenberg had hardly time to release their breath in relief when a shell, aimed high and wide, struck those doors squarely, slammed through the wood and exploded inside. The tall, magnificent stained glass window that soared for three stories above the doors lifted outward in a million brilliant fragments. The roof high above lifted like the top of a music box, hung suspended, then fell back into a maelstrom of collapsing beams and masonry that stripped open the center of the building and left its inner floors gaping to the outdoors. A hundred tons of rubble descended and the dust of it billowed upward to obliterate the center of the great house.

Mark's bellow of pain and anguish could not be separated from Eichenberg's. They stood with what little was left of their world vanishing in that dirty, rising cloud.

When Northern said, "They're across," Mark turned to meet a death he welcomed.

The tattered force of separated soldiers and stubborn peasants got in one more good volley before the Prussian horsemen scrambled up the bank and regained the momentum of their charge. Then, furious at this lethal annoyance after their victories of the day before, they thundered up the slope with enraged cries and waving sabers.

They rode wide to flank the rude barricades and rifle pits and then swept down on their tormentors, slashing and howling. With muskets empty and no time to reload, the defenders rushed out of their positions, swinging their weapons as clubs, or trying to use the bayonets against the mounted men.

Mark, Northern, Eichenberg and Falkenheyn soon found themselves the last men standing.

A swearing, sweating knot of cavalry disentangled from their last sweep and formed a line to take the position on the open side. Before they could spur their mounts, von Krieger rode out to block them and called to the men behind the logs.

"Surrender, damn it. There's no point in this."

Northern, using one of Eichenberg's exquisite rifles, shot him out of the saddle. The cavalrymen, screaming like men driven mad, swept forward.

Hannah, the blood matting her hair, Victor wrapped squalling in her arms, stumbled from the crushed facade of Golden Fluss in time to see them all cut down. The Austrian officer tumbled the lead rider and Mark got another with his gun muzzle almost touching the man's chest. Then the Prussians were on them in a fury. She could see the silvery sabers rising and falling in the soft sunshine, the horses thrusting in, rearing, pounding with their hooves as though the men being killed were to be not just slaughtered, but buried in the earth by the weight of the charge.

A blazing pain in Hannah's head reached down into her heart. She just had time to place Victor on the ground before the flagstones rose up to hit her.

The stars were high when Mark woke, but he didn't see them. They were paled by a sky still glowing red from the flaming shell of what had been Golden Fluss. The embers blew across the heavens in clouds. Signaling Hannah's soul set free, he thought bleakly.

He reached up to wipe the blood out of his vision and found the left side of his face a ruin. Touching the wound, which somehow did not yet hurt, he felt a furrow that ran from below his left temple up into his forehead. He estimated that the saber stroke had been delivered more with the flat of the blade than the edge, so the wound had been spectacular without being fatal. As he probed further in the wreckage of his cheek, he found that he had lost his left eye.

When he tried to rise he thought for a second that he was paralyzed but soon found it was the hacked, heavy body of Falkenheyn, fallen across him, that held him down. When he rolled the captain away, the fearful wounds told him that the officer had absorbed a score of blows and thrusts undoubtedly aimed at the man beneath him.

Northern and Eichenberg were there, run through repeatedly but not greatly mutilated. Their staring eyes were both turned to the flaming house. His father carried to the other world the same dead face he had worn in this one.

Fearing to see, Mark forced himself to look to the south. As he knew it would, the blazing glow of what had been Himmelberg lit the night.

He attempted to get to his feet now, but he hadn't gotten away as clean as he thought. A saber had gone in below the ribs on his right side and emerged from his back. He estimated it would be enough to kill him, and lay back to await the darkness slowly closing about him. . . .

Chapter 3

THE SUMMER of 1867 was late but hot. Hannah welcomed the heat and couldn't absorb enough of the sunshine. She remembered almost nothing of the previous summer after the day of the battle. Her grief and shock had darkened every hour until the winter. And then the cold snow seemed to be just an extension of her soul, and she didn't know if she was shivering from the bitter drafts that blew through the ancient rooms of the von Krieger *Wasserschloss* or from the chill that never seemed to leave her heart.

At her side, Kurt von Krieger slept in a long chair. The light breeze blowing across the high turret ruffled his thick, white-blond hair in the sun. Even after a year, the infection in the bullet-shattered arm crept through his body and drained his strength. He wore only a loose shirt, and she could see the bandage, changed that morning, had become wet with suppuration and stained the sleeve.

Hannah didn't even notice the smell anymore. Indeed, she insisted on changing the dressing herself, because she owed everything to Kurt.

She walked to the battlement and rested her elbows on the

warm stones. Below, stretching for miles, the lovely green hills of Bavaria reached out in all directions. The red-tiled roofs of distant towns were oases of peace in a silent paradise. On the Munich road, a string of haywagons seemed to be carrying heaps of gold to market in some fairytale come alive. She supposed that the wagon drivers thought much the same things as they looked toward this small jewel of a castle set in its picturebook lake.

Her mind was at last clear enough to begin to piece together what had happened since that morning when the world exploded inside Golden Fluss.

Old Gerhard had saved her life and Victor's when he had shoved them underneath the huge oaken table that stood in the entrance hall. The splinters of the shell and the rain of rubble had not been able to overcome the six inches of medieval hardwood. The fragment that killed Gerhard had raked her scalp slightly, but she had never lost consciousness. In just a few minutes she had been able to dig her way out.

For the thousandth time she cursed the weakness that had struck her down when she had seen Mark and her father fall. She should have been there to see to their proper burial. Kurt had sent men back later on, but the fallen who belonged to no army unit had been hurried into open graves because of the heat.

She would carry the agony of the loss of Jacobus Eichenberg to her grave. Against the loss of Mark, she could at least call up his foul betrayal as a defense. And while she still wept for him on the darkest nights, she had hopes that he would someday be swept from her heart.

Hannah wondered with a chill what would have happened to her if Northern's shot had killed Kurt von Krieger. Or if the wounded major had let the agony of his mangled arm distract him from caring about the woman and child brought to him by his men in a roundup of the injured.

He had been a popular officer. When a Prussian surgeon directed him to a field hospital for the removal of his arm, the men who were taking him bowed instead to his wish to be brought to his castle near Munich. There was a doctor in the city who might save the limb. If it went rotten and killed him before he got there, so be it. He didn't want to live on as a cripple. He had also insisted that Hannah and Victor be taken with him.

Later on she had tried to believe it was entirely due to his gentleman's kindness. Injured, her wits dulled, her home in flames, and burdened with a child, she was marooned in a ruined, lawless countryside peopled with desperate peasants and soldiers. Heaven knew she was an object of pity. But the way he had looked at her when they first dragged her before him told her insistently that it was more than generosity.

To be sure, he had never been anything but courtly to her. In the rough, fast trip by coach he had used all his strength to rouse himself against the opiates to speak reassurance. She heard vaguely through her grief that his was a great landholding family. Their estates were far to the north, on the Baltic. The *Wasserschloss* to which they traveled was a winter place, not terribly far from the warmth and pleasure of Italy. He liked it, and as a bachelor remained there alone for a good part of the year in times of peace.

The arm had been a near thing. The sour doctor from Munich had pronounced it hopeless to save, but he went to work with inspired surgery and special drugs and poultices to do exactly that. However, fragments of the bullet remained unreachable in the bone and caused the elbow joint to infect and reinfect. Progress was miserably slow.

Hannah had her own suite of rooms where she lived with Victor in the full attendance of the von Krieger servants. New clothing in the latest Paris fashions had appeared, along with books and the latest music for the piano.

A special nurse had been assigned to Victor, who had come through the ordeal with a fearless curiosity and fortitude she had never seen in a child so young.

She was not a prisoner, she knew. But widowed, penniless and with no way to contact any of the far-flung relatives of the Eichenbergs—none of whom was well enough off to help in any case—she did not know how to leave. If it hadn't been for Victor, she might have gone into Munich to try to make her way in a world of work she had never known. With him to feed and shelter, she didn't dare chance it. And there were Kurt's intentions to consider.

He had never said that he loved her. Yet, from the beginning, there was no question that he did. It shone out of him every time he came to see her.

They always talked in great circles. She had told him as little as possible about her life before, because to speak of it was unbearable to her. He knew only that the house he had burned was hers and that her father and husband were among those his cavalry had killed. One of their escort had told Hannah of Kurt's attempt to save them and of Northern's deadly response, so she bore him no ill feelings.

Kurt moaned in his sleep, and she went to wipe the sweat of pain from his forehead. In spite of his body being broken, perhaps because of it, she felt a physical pull to him and it filled her with shame. Did she desire to give to him what she had not been willing to give her own husband, and so soon after that husband's death? In her awful loneliness, though, she was susceptible. And why should the love of a man who had never deserved her love stand in her way?

She blushed at her presumptions. He was the Baron von Krieger, and neither he nor his relatives were likely to look kindly upon his marrying when they learned she was the daughter of a Jew.

As she ran her handkerchief over his brow, the pale blue eyes opened. With the high color of a slight fever and the little boy's ready smile he was a nearly irresistible man.

He took her hand. "My nurse. My friend. My angel . . . And soon you must be more."

"You mustn't take advantage of me."

"I would never do that. I want you in marriage, Hannah. Nothing less."

There it was. "You don't know enough about me, Kurt. And I have nothing to bring you."

"But I have much to bring you. And that's all that's important. Especially now. I've heard from the attorneys."

Hannah stiffened. "About the lands?"

"They're gone. Everything you and your husband's family ever held. Part of it is the Prussians. They're punishing all the owners who stood against them. Part is your own government. Since they must punish you for Prussia, why not reward themselves? They'll break up the estates and sell them, and the money will fall into their pockets."

She flared. "They can't. They can't do that."

"Governments do what they please."

"Not everywhere. There must be a place where your own country won't steal the ground from under you."

"I'll put more ground under you than you can see from a tower higher than this. Our estates in the north take two days to ride across."

His arm slipped behind her shoulders, and he drew her down to him. There was not so much strength in the movement that she could not have pulled back gracefully, but she went to his lips and felt a shock of wanting that she hadn't expected. She stayed on his mouth until his hand moved gently down and found her breast.

She pulled away, cheeks flaming.

"I'm sorry," he said quickly. "That was wrong and stupid."

"I think I wanted you to do it, Kurt."

"May I write to my family?"

"No. I must think."

The moon rose that night as a silvery slash and hung outside her window in a sea of stars. From her pillow she watched the constellations march by for sleepless hours as she searched in herself.

The great, melting tenderness and longing she had felt for Mark before her rape was nowhere in her for Kurt. Still, feelings like that had probably died with the youth that had ended forever last year. She wondered how much of what was compelling about Kurt had to do with the lands he held before her. The feeling of drifting above the soil, rootless, had been unbearable to her since the day she left Golden Fluss.

One thing was undeniable. The undercurrent of desire that had been missing since she rode into the dark woods to Mark a year ago had suddenly returned, and she was seldom free of its insistent tug.

A soft knock sounded at her chamber door. If she had been asleep she would have not heard it. Whoever knocked had counted on her being awake. She lay, not stirring a muscle, until the sound came again.

Hannah slipped from her bed and crossed the thick, soft carpet. There was no way her step could have been heard through the heavy door. But the voice that whispered on the other side must have known that she now stood inches away.

"Hannah . . . Hannah, my sweet love . . . I must hold you . . . I must hold you. Now . . ."

She had to hug herself with both arms as tightly as she could to keep her hand from going to the latch. The memory of Mark, the day in the woods, her loneliness and weakness churned in her head.

"Hannah, please . . . I need you . . . I love you so much . . ."

She remembered Kurt's body as his men had stripped him of his fever-drenched rags in the coach. His skin had been as white and soft as a woman's, but the muscles were sleek, chiseled ripples. His manhood had been a graceful arc against his thighs, topped by a soft cushion of golden curls. She had never gotten it completely out of her mind.

Hannah pressed her hands against her belly to drive out the fire that was growing there, but it slowly spread and she began to shiver even as the sweat of midsummer rolled between her breasts. She watched the big clock on the mantle, struggling against the rising tide in her as the minutes inched by.

A long shudder rose in her and she heard herself moan. She spun and tore open the door. The corridor was empty. Half devastated, half grateful, she sagged back against the wall. It was some time before she should bring herself to close the door again.

Well, she thought, the knock would come again.

But the Countess Clarissa Schoenbruhn arrived the next morning.

It had taken four large coaches to bring her, her maids and her baggage. The wheels ground on the courtyard cobbles like the sound of doom itself. The petulant, headlong impatience of the drivers echoed what was in their passenger.

Everything that Hannah had ever wanted to be was there in abundance in Countess Clarissa. She was no older than Hannah. Her waist nipped down to a handspan, while the sweep of her hips and bosom blossomed enchantingly above and below. Her sharp voice was held in utter control. Her eyes had the fashionable bulge of fine breeding, and her nose fell from forehead to tip in one grand sweep. The best shops and hairdressers of Berlin had turned her out so stunningly that not even a week in a jouncing coach had been able to wilt a hair or thread.

And there was no question that she loved the young Baron von Krieger and considered him very much her own.

From her window, Hannah had watched them in the courtyard at the moment of her arrival. No lady so well bred would have displayed such emotion in front of coachmen if she could have controlled it. She hugged Kurt and kissed his cheek and hand, lamenting tearfully at the sight of his damaged arm.

Good manners, rigorously introduced from an early age, can overcome anything, Hannah thought at dinner that night.

Kurt had told Countess Clarissa the simple truth, stopping just short of the complete truth, letting her make of it what she would. It had not taken Clarissa Schoenbruhn more than three seconds to see what she had before her, and to begin, with the greatest sweetness, to deal with it.

"I told Kurt that all those guns and horses and bad friends would bring him to grief," Clarissa said after the mandatory polite fencing. "All the army has ever been is a place for wild young men to ride, drink, fight and put off their obligations."

"The baron must have a great many obligations, Countess."

"The first of which is to join our houses in a marriage. That stupid war has put everything behind. My father is very impatient."

"Clarissa," Kurt said harshly, "Would you've had me sit home while my countrymen were dying? Would you rush me to the altar with a rotting arm?"

Clarissa could hardly believe the words had been said. "My darling, you could scarcely have expected us to know what a bloody thing the war had been for you. You hardly wrote, and said almost nothing when you did. 'Just a scratch,' you said. 'Home in a month . . . I'll be there soon . . . Rest . . . Business . . .' I recognize it was very good of you not to want us worried, not to want to let us see you until you were whole. But was that fair to us? Or to Mrs. Northern? She had to take the brunt of caring for you that should have belonged to the people who love you. I'm sure she'll be happy to be able to get away now."

"Mrs. Northern will be my guest until we can straighten out her affairs, Clarissa. She suffered great material losses in the war that took her family."

"With my gratitude as great as yours," said Clarissa. "I would consider it an honor to contribute to the future well-being of Mrs. Northern and her child."

"As I said, Clarissa, many arrangements must be made. It will take some time. More wine?"

The summer wore on, Kurt chafing more and more at the presence of Clarissa, and Clarissa smoldering at the presence of Hannah. The countess's stay was to have been for two weeks. But letters flew to the east and three more coaches arrived with her clothes. She would not leave the castle undefended.

Hannah now had time to put the lid on the dark, boiling kettle inside her. There were no more nighttime knocks at her door. Clarissa hovered everywhere, her great jealousy as carefully hidden as the small twinge felt by Hannah.

Even so, Kurt came to Hannah when he could and made it plain that he wanted her for his own. "I never loved her, Hannah. I've never loved any woman . . . until now . . . Never wanted to and never expected to. Yes, I would gladly marry Clarissa because I owe that to the future power of the von Kriegers. But never, as long as there is a chance to have you, will I sacrifice my love in exchange for some soil. You must give me an answer, my sweet girl."

Each time he asked her, Hannah suspected she would finish by saying yes. But when it came time to speak the words, she found herself putting him off.

Mostly it was Mark, and the love that would not go.

Yet, there was more. There seemed a corner of Kurt von Krieger that she had not yet been able to look into. Laid low by his wound, he had shown her nothing of the wildness she sensed in the cut-short stories of his years as a young soldier in a notoriously dissolute officer corps. Of course, she realized, most of those stories had come from Countess Clarissa.

Hannah met the countess one morning near the stables. Clarissa seemed relaxed and happy.

"I have a marvelous surprise for Kurt," the countess said. "He needs a holiday from the exclusive company of women. I met some of his friends, the wilder ones, when they visited from the barracks a couple of years ago. They're not to my taste, but apparently I was to theirs. We got on famously after a while. And they're coming here. For the rest of the summer. The heat is awful in the cities, they say, and most of them answered my letter with a very hearty yes. Especially when they found out that the entire old bunch had been invited."

"But if they're not good for Kurt—"

"Who is to say what's good for Kurt? I only know that he's tired and on edge. He needs a touch of the old vices, don't you think?"

The old friends, none much older than Kurt, arrived inside the week and were distributed among the ground-floor bedchambers. There were five of them, all now separated from the army, and they were every bit the tonic Clarissa had predicted.

For the first time since Hannah had been there, the *Wasserschloss* rang with life and laughter. The young men, not so much handsome as open-faced and attractive in their raw vitality, were everywhere. If they were spoiled and too noisy and overdressed, that innocent arrogance was half the fun of being sons of the gentry.

They got Kurt up onto a horse almost every day and took him for yelping gallops over the hills. Often they dragged him into Munich and were gone for two and three days at a time.

In the evenings they lingered for long hours after the meal, which they took without the women after the first days, and drank enormous amounts of good wine. They swilled and played cards late into the night, though careful to hold down the louder obscenities.

Once, in the dead of night, Hannah heard whoops and splashes. She found a window that showed her the whole bunch of them splashing naked in the lake. Kurt was among them, paying no attention at all to the dressing on his arm.

From that day onward, the arm began to heal itself rapidly from within, and soon the bandage was gone and he exposed the scar to the sun. He now had full use of both hands on the reins of a horse.

While Hannah could appreciate their chaotic, childish exuberances as a much-needed diversion for Kurt, she could maintain no high regard for the youths. She was glad that they all but ignored her and that she could put the time dutifully to Victor's upbringing.

Clarissa, though, for all her claimed distaste for the men, was frequently in their company. They were flattered by the attention of such a grand lady and soon, when they saw they would be welcomed, sought her company with or without Kurt. Hannah could see Clarissa's power over them rising.

But Kurt had not forgotten Hannah. He began to find ways to elude Clarissa. He became almost feverishly insistent in his suit. The correctness of his behavior toward the countess deteriorated, and he was at times almost brusque. The great lady's composure never faltered, but she must have known she was running out of time.

Riding alone one day toward the end of August, Clarissa came to Hannah as she walked the shores of the lake. For the first time she spoke with directness, unsmiling.

"I can give you enough money to send you away comfortably."

"If you choose to insult yourself by making such an offer, I choose not to insult Kurt by considering it."

"Mrs. Northern, you are a clever woman. You serve yourself best by holding him back. Your intention is to inflame him, and you've succeeded nicely. All that remains in your plan is for me to leave."

"You're quite wrong, Countess. I'm glad you're here. It gives me time to think about what I want."

"Time to decide? That's amusing."

"Think anything you want."

"I think, Mrs. Northern, that you are a conniving little Jew. Kurt was too much of the gentleman to pry into what you were. But I don't have such scruples. Your father made a nice try at scrubbing the family blood clean, but even a single drop shows up, does it not? You stand there trying these lands on for size. And dreaming about so much more, like so many money-grubbing kikes before you."

Hannah's expression never changed. "Why didn't Kurt come to tell me all this himself? He could have brought my things and pointed out the road."

Clarissa rattled a cold laugh. "It was too late for me to tell him. I am sure you know that very well. He loves you so much that he would hate me for trying to turn him away from you."

"If I marry him, Countess, I will have the honor of telling him beforehand myself."

Loathing twisted Clarissa's face. "I wish women fought duels."

"They do, Countess," Hannah said. "They do."

By the first week of September, Hannah had reached her decision. She was now sure that the wound left by the death of Mark was too great ever to be healed, but Kurt's sweet nature and manliness were things she needed, and perhaps his tenderness would eventually stir feelings of love in her.

The young men were to leave within the week, as was the countess. Kurt had become so dismissive that her pride would not let her stay longer. Hannah would give herself to Kurt and become the Baroness von Krieger as soon as Clarissa was gone.

This determination brought a certain peace to Hannah, and she began to sleep better. But several days later, long after midnight, she was roused by roistering from below. The open windows of her room were just above and across from the flung-back windows of the hall where Kurt and his friends were having, she supposed, a drunken farewell. The wine-soaked laughter seemed more a series of animal barks and howls than sounds made by civilized men. There was an occasional smashing of glass as a goblet hit a wall or the fireplace. Somebody started to sing a bawdy soldier's song. Immediately, a bawling chorus of thickened voices took it up.

Hannah listened, trying to understand, trying to be patient. At length, she detected a new voice. It belonged to the Countess Clarissa Schoenbruhn, without a question.

So out of character for her, Hannah thought, to have forced her way in on the men. But then, the departing comrades were after all great friends of hers. Kurt couldn't very well freeze her out if she had come as the guest of his guests.

The din subsided for an hour, and then, suddenly, the courtyard was in turmoil. Hannah sped to the window to see the cobbles below splashed with the light of a dozen lanterns. A group of stablehands, bleary and half dressed, led a cluster of horses clattering out onto the stones, while more hands strove to finish saddling and bridling the moving animals.

Other horses had been made ready, too. These were large draft animals from the barns outside the walls. Hannah could see them through the open gate. Their riders, men she recognized as being among the bigger and rougher servants, were already mounted. They carried torches, and the rear quarters of their animals were strapped heavily with canvas carrying-bags into which were thrust many implements. She caught the distinctive shapes of shovels and pickaxes.

The revelers were all directly below her now, and the Countess Clarissa too. The men, draining their bottles and smashing them under their feet, were too drunk and wild to glance up at who might be watching. The countess, Hannah saw, was not drunk at all, and looked up at her with what might have been a smile.

What was happening and why, Hannah could not fathom. But Kurt was leading the expedition, and in the highest good humor.

"Come on, boys," he cried. "They've been waiting a long time." He leaped to his saddle, wheeled once around the square to gather his forces and led them out the gate with a series of whoops that were echoed and reechoed by the riders who thundered out after him.

Hannah at the window and the countess below watched the winking torches grow smaller as the band disappeared down the road.

Again, Clarissa looked up at Hannah. "Riding is such fun, don't you think?" she called in a clear, hard voice. "We must do more of it ourselves. Perhaps tomorrow."

Close to morning, Hannah heard the horses come back into the courtyard again. The men were quieter now. They spoke little, and what laughter there was sounded growling and mean.

She watched them dismounting slowly, exhaustedly. Their clothing and shoes were caked with mud. Some had scarves wrapped around their hands. One wore a long coat, stained and falling to pieces. It was far too large and obviously he had picked it up somewhere. What had seemed a joke when he was drunk seemed to have palled terribly on him, and he snatched the garment off and flung it at one of the servants, who jumped back from it and let it fall.

The tools came off the carriers. The sledges, pry-bars, picks and shovels were clumped with the same gray mud that was drying on the men.

For once they didn't go together for a drink or a meal after their riding. Each seemed to want to be alone. Kurt tried to call after them with some cheer, but the words fell heavily, and he, too, made his way into the castle with leaden steps.

Puzzled, Hannah waited until she heard his footsteps in the corridor and opened her door as he was passing.

He told her with a look that there would be no questions. His smile fell apart. "When I drink too much you can get me to do anything, I'm afraid. I'm all right, though. Just some fun. But I'm going to sleep until tomorrow night."

Before Hannah had finished dressing next morning, Countess Clarissa was at her door in riding clothes. She greeted Hannah easily. "Did you think I was joking about our ride, Mrs. Northern? It's a beautiful day. I'd love for you to come. I'll send one of my girls with what you need. And I'll have the horses brought around. You do ride?"

"Not for a long while," said the surprised Hannah.

"You might enjoy seeing what mischief our friends were up to last night. It's only five or six miles. In the court in an hour, shall we say?"

A disquiet was building in Hannah. But the thought of a long ride was pleasant. "Thank you, I greatly look forward to it."

The countess rode as well as Hannah. The horses were magnificent animals and took the rolling terrain in long, easy strides.

It was the first time Hannah had been out of the shadow of the walls since she came, and her spirit lifted out of her and opened itself to the world as it had in the old days. Ribbons of clouds scudded along with them, seeming to race the galloping horses across the blue. People waved from the roads and hilltops, and the riders cheerfully waved back. Hannah felt the sun painting the color back into her cheeks and thought at last that it might be good to be alive.

It became apparent that their destination was a middle-size

town across a wide valley. The cozy cluster of red roof shimmered in the heat haze, the sun filling with silver the winding river that ran nearby.

They didn't ride into the town. Clarissa avoided it and swung wide. On the circling road were more people than one would have expected on a morning that was not part of a market day. They had the bemused air of a crowd who had just come from a carnival whose exhibits had exhausted them. Some laughed, but most seem depressed, even angry.

The cemetery was walled. It was not large, lying at the bottom of a bowl of low hills. A few more townspeople straggled out. Some wept, some could hardly drag their feet, some moved so quickly they almost ran.

Hannah and the countess dismounted at the gate. Now Hannah could see that the letters above the entrance were Hebrew. It was an ancient cemetery, one of the remnants of once-flourishing Jewish communities that had dwindled or vanished.

When Hannah hesitated to enter, Clarissa smiled, took her hand and drew her inside.

A gruesome, fetid stench came forward, turning Hannah's stomach. The desecrators had worked with savage enthusiasm. Hardly a headstone stood upright or unsplit. Crypts had been broken open and coffins pulled to the floor to shatter and spill their ghastly contents.

Some of the fresher graves had been excavated and their occupants brought back into the daylight to show the horrendous effects of time in the earth. Arms, legs and heads had been hacked off and rearranged sportively on the bodies. Heads sat green and grinning, gaping mouths accusing, empty eye sockets staring furiously.

One large corpse was propped on a stone bench, a newspaper thrust into his rotting hands. Unlike the other men, he wore only the remains of shirt. His long coat was missing. Hannah remembered the man throwing the coat in the courtyard and was immediately, explosively ill.

As she staggered out of the cemetary, she read a newly chalked message on the side of a crypt: *Juden Heraus.*

73

* * *

Before Kurt wakened, Hannah was gone with Victor.

In her purse she carried two steamship tickets ordered a week before by Countess Clarissa. The rail tickets to Bremen were also paid for and there was an envelope of money inside her clothing. Nothing nearly so munificent as she might have expected if she had taken any of Clarissa's previous offers, but enough, she hoped, to keep her and her son for a month once they had reached the barbarous shores of America and the godless hellhole that was the seaport of New York. She sagged with despair.

Victor stood solemnly at the window of the train. Hannah noticed that during the trip his eyes never wandered backward to linger on some interesting sight that was passing. Always he looked ahead, his eyes alert and hungry for some change on the horizon.

CHAPTER 4

IN BREMEN, Hannah went to the wharves to see the ship that would confine her for the next weeks and knew that her days as a fine lady had ended even earlier than she thought they would.

The *Dortmund* was a hybrid packet pushed by both steam and sail and not suited to either. In hard use in the emigrant trade, she had not aged well and her passage prices had fallen to the bottom of the lists. There was one class, and it was abysmal. The Countess Clarissa had taken what little revenge she could. She had even booked the passage in the name of Eichenberg, which suited Hannah perfectly. She wanted to move away from all memory of the Northern family.

Hannah moved decisively. She took the cheapest room she could, commensurate with safety, and hired the landlord's young daughter to look after Victor. Then she put on her best dress and had two trunks of the fine clothing Kurt had bought for her carried to a bustling market square she had seen from the train. There, having drawn a fine crowd with her queenly air and appearance, she sold everything, including the trunks, in a single afternoon at good prices. The next day she used the money to buy the sensible clothing and accoutrements she would need to prepare her and Victor for a new and harder life.

When the *Dortmund* cleared the Bremen breakwater two days later and hooted a double blast of farewell to Germany, Hannah, on the foredeck, followed Victor's example and kept her eyes resolutely on the horizon ahead. That a roiling storm was gathering there did not bother her at all. She was ready for the gusts of wind and rain to cleanse her.

The puzzled cheer that rose from the more rustic elements of the *Dortmund*'s passengers three days into the voyage was premature. What they took for New York and a miraculously quick passage was Queenstown, Ireland. The owner of the *Dortmund* had been presented with an opportunity to pick up seventy-five Irish emigrants stranded by the breakdown of an English packet.

The ship, already crowded, now became almost unbearably overloaded. It was almost guaranteed that money had changed hands among the maritime inspectors to permit it. An extra few hundred pounds of rations were rushed aboard, but the already dismal fare plummeted in quantity as well as quality. Hannah had brought an extra bag of nonperishable foods to supplement the ship's supplies, or she would have feared for Victor's life.

As the *Dortmund* made her way into the open Atlantic, the suffering of the poorer passengers became extreme. Those people who had not been able to buy their way into the few comfortable enclosures on the ship were stowed beneath the deck in airless holds stuffed with makeshift bunks and a few rough benches and tables. Steam, noise and heat poured in upon them from the engine spaces. Swearing stokers, hammering pistons and scraping shovels overcame even the endless babble of several hundred unhappy, seasick people.

Not surprisingly, most of the passengers moved to the decks and stayed there day and night, even against the piercing chill of mid-Atlantic nights and an occasional drenching storm.

Hannah had paid her way into a cramped box that had been the ship's charthouse. As small as it was, she and Victor shared it with five others, and they filled every inch of the space. Four of these were sullen Polish miners who remained stunned and sick for the entire crossing. The fifth was a moon-faced man of middle years named Frank Chumlin, whose worn and ragged clothing did not seem to justify his endless enthusiasm. He was an American inching his way home on the dregs of one of his many failed business ventures, this one having gone under in Dublin. He was delighted to find that Hannah spoke English, and he could not speak glowingly enough of her opportunities in the country of his heart.

"The streets are not golden, Mrs. Eichenberg. That gold is a hundred feet down under hard rock. But the ones who have the heart to dig deep, they'll find it."

On days when the swell lessened and the sun shined warmly, Hannah left Victor asleep in the charthouse and walked among the crush on the decks to stretch her cramped legs. Mostly the people were frightened and stuck clannishly with their own groups. Conversation was short and muted, the emigrants seeming to save their strength for the brutal travails they knew to be ahead. One Irish family made an exception:

The parents were as square, plain and strong as a stone church, and a hundred times as noisy and cheerful. Though scarcely forty, they had produced an uproarious and laughing band of ten children who churned endlessly in an area behind the foredeck. All shared the same broad-nosed, wide-eyed, big-toothed face and bellowed with voices like cavalry bugles.

The father, whose name was Patrick Hanratty, spoke to all he could catch for as long as he could hold them, even when they couldn't make out a word of his brogue-wracked English. Patrick's handsome wife, Moira, had the same propensity for friendly blather, but had to subordinate it to the care of the terrible ten and her husband's determination to command the stage. "He'll make your ear bleed, but his heart's a sweet one."

"As I see it, Mrs. Eichenberg," he said, the vowels becoming transformed musically into *ays* and *oys*, "the same amount o' scrabblin' at the ground in New York as I done in Kerry should raise up a five storey buildin' instead o' ten pounds o' potatoes. And if I can't get work, at least there'll be more to steal."

By the second week, the close quarters and bad sanitation had a chance to work on the health of the weaker passengers. Many sickened and made the living spaces dreadful with their emissions.

Three old people and as many children were slipped over the side of the *Dortmund*. Two of the Hanratty children appeared suddenly at death's door. Their father prayed in a roar, bullied medicine out of the captain and tended to the care and comfort of the fallen with every ounce of his strength. But his love of his sick wife and the two little ones made a hole in his courage that nothing else could have accomplished. "I've killed them all," he said repeatedly.

Before he could disintegrate completely, Hannah stepped in.

"Get to the rest of the children and stay out of my way," she told him.

She got hold of a medical volume from the captain and devoured the pertinent parts. She brought her own blankets and made a sensible schedule of doses for the medicines the man had obtained.

Quickly, the family began to gather around Hannah. She spent whole nights with the sick, slipping away when she could to take care of Victor in the charthouse.

For one dark, terror-filled night, with green waves sliding over the deck and sending cascades down onto the people in the holds where the hatches had been propped open to prevent asphyxiation, the feverish Hanrattys clung to the ragged edge of life. Hannah bathed and massaged and administered until she fell asleep across the father's lap. When she awoke near nightfall, all the fevers had fallen and a tearful Patrick Hanratty was feeding the younger victims. "It'll take both Jesus and Mary to thank you right, Miss Hannah." He kissed Hannah's hands until she had to pull away and run.

As she moved quickly through the clumps of people, she collided explosively with a huge man who had risen from behind a winch. It was like running into a pile of rock, and the strong odor of a male long-unwashed rose up from the ragged clothing to strike her as powerfully as the physical impact. The face she looked up into sent a cold wind through her heart. The glaring black eyes held her own image, as though he had captured her soul with the first glance. About the face there was nothing of the noble world she had left. The brutal peasant handsomeness was overlaid with the casual arrogance of a Roman legionnaire. The wide mouth smiled, but it was with the warmth of the winter sun.

Hannah had half fallen. The hand he offered her, broad and powerful, was strangely soft. The nails were trimmed and clean, and the fingers graceful as they moved over hers.

If his voice was graveled, it was also remarkably gentle. The accent was one she had already learned from her shipboard listening. It rose from a rough Sicilian dialect of the sort heard in the northern cities of the island.

"Signora, it makes no sense to move faster than this chamber pot of a ship."

She wanted to break the brooding interest in those eyes. "I have to get to my child," she said.

"It is not wise to leave your own blood to help others."

Hannah flushed, remembering how often she had left Victor.

"My own son was well, thank God."

"Jesus Christ will think well of you and send you many blessings. But the Irish can never pay you back."

"I don't help people to be paid back."

"That, too, is not wise." He smiled more broadly than ever, his teeth brilliant against the dark stubble on the strong chin. He touched the ruined peak of his cap in a goodbye.

The fog rolled down upon them in thick banks on the day the *Dortmund* edged down the Narrows, entering New York Harbor. The sails had been furled since the wind failed the day before, and the creaking paddle wheels splashed ahead so slowly that it appeared to Hannah she could stop them with a hand.

Knowing where they were, the passengers crowded onto the deck and into the rigging to catch the first view of the new land where they expected to live and die. Chumlin had fought for a place at the starboard rail for Hannah and himself. But only a cottony world of white was there to be seen.

Toward midday, a flap of lines and a singing in the stays announced a crisp wind from the southwest. The hanging fog began to swirl and speed past them. The sun became first a yellowish tint on the mist, then quickly a luminescent ball set into a sky of purest blue. With increasing speed the curtain began to roll up to reveal a scene of such splendor that it would never leave the mind of any who stood this day at the rail of the *Dortmund*.

Ahead, under the last wisps of fog, low against the sun-jewelled waters of the bay, was a magnet that seemed to draw a thousand ships. Their white sails and smoke belching funnels all seemed to bear down on an arrowhead of shoreline that was one continuous mass of slips and wharves flanked by two mighty rivers. Except for a green slash at the tip, there seemed not a tree or hill. Only a scattering of lofty church steeples broke the sky, into which streamed the smoke of a hundred-thousand chimneys.

The grandeur and freshness of the scene restored the voices of the suddenly-recovered passengers of the *Dortmund*, and they sent huge cheers and wept greatly.

"There's already 900,000 souls here," said Chumlin. "You don't hardly need the rest of the country."

The figure staggered her. "Where do they all live?"

"Down here at the bottom, mostly. Where the Dutch started. It's just farms and squatters up north on the island. Beautiful in some places. Especially up around the Harlem Flats."

"It must be terribly crowded."

Chumlin's sunny face clouded. "Mrs. Eichenberg, unless you have a lot of money I don't know about, the *Dortmund* is going to seem like an empty plain to you. The rich live on Fifth Avenue in palaces. The poor live six-and-seven-hundred to a building."

"So they'll run out of space someday, and that will be the end of New York, Mr. Chumlin."

"Unless somebody finds a way to hang people from the clouds, Mrs. Eichenberg."

The noonday guns cracked out a salute from Forts Hamilton and Wadsworth flanking the Narrows, and Victor yelped. Chumlin hoisted him to the rail to better see the fairy city. The dour little boy sent forth an uncharacteristic shout of pure pleasure.

The *Dortmund* anchored off the tip of Manhattan. A red paddle wheel tug soon appeared, towing a string of four gray barges. Into these the passengers were transferred on precarious gangways, their baggage following from the rail in a perilous rain.

"You'll come in at Castle Garden," Frank Chumlin told Hannah. "They'll need something bigger pretty soon, but it's quite a place. A fort first. Then a summer garden. They gave General Lafayette his farewell grand ball there in 'thirty-two. Jenny Lind sang in it when it was a concert hall, before the Emigration Commission got hold of it."

Castle Garden proved to be a processing center from which would-be entrants could still be turned away.

A bald clerk with a Scandinavian accent wrestled with names, ages, nationalities, destinations and vessels, all delivered in a dozen thick tongues. At his mountain of paper since early morning, whatever patience he had owned was long gone.

"Name and ages."

"Eichenberg. Hannah, twenty-one, and Victor, two."

The man tried to write the name faster than she could spell it for him, so it ended up a blotted shambles. Swearing under his breath, he scratched a line through it.

"Lady, do yourself a favor. And me. You sound English. Why mess yourself up with a heinie name that makes you sound like a greenhorn? What's that handle of yours mean in English?"

"Eichenberg? . . . Oak hill is close, but—"

"Oakhill it is."

The protest she was forming faded away as he boldly entered the new name. Nothing remained from her old world except Victor. The feeling this gave her was surprisingly pleasant.

In stalls, surgeons checked for the most obvious signs of serious disease and coldly turned back the most stricken to die on another shore. Other inspections turned away paupers, the crippled and the mad.

Hannah's attention went to a small, tattered man with a twisted back. His pinched face seemed entirely occupied by darting eyes. He scuttled through the crowds, questioning in Italian, searching the faces of the arrivals with an alarming intensity. Behind him, a large policeman, bored but ready, walked ponderously. The twisted man occasionally tugged him by the sleeve toward whatever group he was preparing to inspect.

Hannah was ready to claim her luggage from the customs men. Rail tickets were sold in the rotunda, and she was beginning to think of what her destination might finally be in the vast land.

Then Victor, walking at her side, was snatched suddenly from her hand. She whipped around and saw her son was now sitting in the arms of the huge Sicilian from the *Dortmund*. Her cry was choked off by a deadly glare from the man.

The Sicilian's voice was low and steady, his smile even. "Signora, I must implore your pardon. Another wretched traveler needs your kindness." He motioned with his head. "You see that fellow with the policeman? He is known to me from the other side. Pasquale Lupo. A jackal who eats the flesh of his brothers."

"Please give me back my son," Hannah said, fighting back her panic, "or I'll call that constable myself."

"To hurt where there is no honor is something I would not want on my soul. Or yours," the Sicilian said, a tombstone in every word.

"What do you want of me?"

"With *our* son in my arms, I am the husband of an English lady. I have never seen the yellow hills of Sicily."

"As soon as you speak—"

"I will not speak." He loosened the dark bandanna about his neck and showed her his throat. A long, thin scar, still fresh, ran from the center of his neck almost to his ear. "As I could not for a long time after this."

"I don't see how—"

"You are quick. You will manage." He turned his attention entirely to Victor, becoming a loving father who pinched and kissed the boy's cheeks incessantly.

Victor seemed surprised but enjoyed the affection he seldom received, especially when the Sicilian handed him a closed but spectacularly large clasp knife to play with.

The new couple were halfway across the floor of the rotunda when Pasquale Lupo and the policeman overtook them. The little Italian scurried in front of the Sicilian and stared up at him, fear and triumph fighting in his face.

The twisted man's accent was not as thick as his prey's. "Ah

... ah ... ah ... Let me see. The mustache is new. The fine clothes are gone. He is older. But ... yes ... That's *him,* Signor Carmody. Yes, this is Benedetto Serpa. The worst of a family of thieves and killers. Palermo was almost in their hands. But he kills one magistrate too many, Signor Carmody. His friends break the code. Si. *Benedetto Serpa.* Twenty-five dollars for this one. That's fair. Don't starve my children."

"Shut up, you damned guinea," the policeman said as his hand wandered in the neighborhood of the back pocket where he carried his revolver. "Maybe we better have a word, bucko," he said to Serpa, who superbly mimed confusion.

Hannah stepped angrily in front of the policeman. She became the grandest of English ladies. "What is this Italian saying about my husband?"

The officer looked bewilderedly from Hannah, splendid in the one fine dress she had kept from the Bremen market square, to the Sicilian in the soiled, ragged suit that had not been off him since the *Dortmund* sailed. "This is *your* husband?" he muttered in surprise. "Well . . . I'll ask him some questions if you don't mind, madame."

The Sicilian seemed to be trying valiantly to speak in his defense, but only growls and croaks came forth.

Hannah pulled away the cloth at his throat. "August fought for Austria at Königgratz. That wound means that he won't speak again for many months. Or perhaps ever."

"*Lies,*" Lupo spluttered. "That was where the Lonardo brothers opened his throat. I heard of it. He made the butcher hang pieces of them in his window."

Taller by almost a head, Hannah stared down at him. "How long since you saw this . . . Benedetto Serpa, was it?

"Thirteen years. Since I left. But I don't forget—"

"So you thought you might get twenty-five dollars from the police because my husband's face called back a dim old memory? Did this Serpa have a son?"

"Girls, I thought, but—"

"Did you hear he was married to an Englishwoman?"

"I heard nothing—"

She directed herself back to the policeman. "We've lost everything. Our estate. Our money. My husband's health. We sold what little we had to come to a country where the police protect the rights of the people. Are you going to send us back on the word of this friend of criminals?"

"She protects the assassin, Signor Carmody."

"Constable, do I look like one who would protect an Italian, much less *marry* one?" She caught the policeman in a grin and saw he was becoming uncertain. More barges had landed with passengers from another ship, and the registration desk was inundated with jabbering arrivals. It was time to gamble. "We can settle this. The gentleman at the desk was quite satisfied that we were Mr. and Mrs. August Mueller of Vienna. Let's all make our way through to him and have him find the papers. It will be cleared up in half an hour."

The policeman looked at the milling masses and pulled her back after her first step toward the desk. Abruptly, he stepped up to Victor and tickled the boy's nose with a fingertip. "Hey there, young fella. Where's your Daddy? C'mon. Show me where your poppa's at. This ain't him, is it?"

Bright, quick Victor knew more words than most two-year-olds, but he didn't share them easily. He set his lips in a hard line and, remembering the Sicilian's short moment of affection, threw his arms trustfully around his neck.

The twisted man was becoming frightened now. "Signor Carmody. You must send him back. This ain't his wife. This ain't his kid—"

"Look at them, Constable," Hannah said as Victor turned his face alongside the Sicilian's.

The officer saw the same dark skin and eyes, the same thick, curling hair. And, most of all, the same look of souls that could not be bent. "Ahhh, that's his daddy all right. Can't miss it. Sorry to trouble you, madame."

"Look at *her*, damn you!" Pasquale Lupo screamed, with the petrified look of a man watching his coffin lid come down. "Signor Carmody—"

The strong hand of the policeman closed around his arm and dragged him off.

After that the looming figure did not leave Hannah's side. He waited with her for her trunks, and when they appeared he swung them on his back with his own suitcase as though they were matchboxes.

"Are you that . . . Benedetto Serpa?" she finally asked him.

"The name of my father and his father," he said.

"If you can just get these to a carriage there will be no need to wait."

"What may I call you, signora?"

"Mrs.—Oakhill."

"And your son?"

"Victor."

"Respect me, Mrs. Oakhill. Don't shame me by refusing my gratitude. Victor is my son now, and you are my sister. I protect you and keep you until Signor Oakhill arrives, if it takes a hundred years."

"My husband is dead."

He offered no condolence, and the wintry grin brushed his lips again. "Then I must defend you as more than a sister."

She watched him trying to put together enough coins for a carriage. "You're going to have enough to do looking after yourself, Mr. Serpa. I have a little. Perhaps I could lend you something."

"*Never,*" he said, raising his voice for the first time since she had known him. Then, almost kindly, "They say this is a terrible city for the poor and for women alone. You are a fine lady. You will not survive it with the child."

"You have a place?"

"Yes," he said. "Of course, the people who now occupy it do not yet know that they are in our beds."

A disreputable-looking rig driven by a black man wearing remnants of a Union Army uniform drove by. Frank Chumlin, sprawled like a grand duke upon a jumble of baggage, rode at the rear. He spotted Hannah and bawled for the driver to rein up.

"Mrs. Eichenberg—"

"Mrs. Oakhill now, if you please, Mr. Chumlin."

"Oh, yeah? They wanted to call *me* Chambers. Listen. You won't find a cheaper hack than this one. Where are you going?"

She looked to Serpa, who produced a greasy piece of paper with a scrawled address. Chumlin glanced at it and whistled. "Tough country. Right on the East River." He cast a wary look at Serpa. "He going with you?"

"Yes," said Hannah without embellishment.

"This isn't far out of my way. Climb on." The rig plunged into a city that was half fairyland, half cesspool. There was an absolute premium on leather lungs, because one had to be heard above the maddened clang of horse-car bells, the melodious imploring of ten-thousand street peddlers and the roaring grind of a hundred thousand steel rims on cobbles. Garbage and debris grew everywhere in malodorous mountains, but they seemed more the shed shell of a furiously-growing insect than the detritus of decay.

Hannah recognized the rows of what must have been the original Dutch and English buildings from pre-revolutionary times. But these were being pulled down everywhere by twos and threes and replaced by structures whose only design object appeared to be the enclosure of the requisite space quickly and cheaply, and with as bland a facade as possible. Huge, snorting teams of dray horses hauled gigantic loads of brick and lumber, turning every other intersection into an uproarious nightmare of tangled traffic. The unending ring of hammers and rasp of saws, and the spiderwebs of construction scaffolding on every block indicated that growth was exploding in every direction.

For a while they moved down a street that shadowed them with a lofty trellis of steel supporting a single track. Submerged in the other din, a roaring locomotive, spewing sparks and cinders on all below and towing a string of cars, was upon them. It flashed by overhead before Hannah had a chance to think of all the hurtling tons so flimsily supported.

"That's the new elevated railroad," Chumlin shouted over the hubbub. "All the way from Battery Place to Thirtieth Street. Day's going to come when you can ride anywhere in the city on one of those things."

As they angled across the island, heading east, Hannah became aware that the passage of a single block could place one into what seemed another city. Before long the handsome and ornate buildings grew low and mean, and the streets narrow, angled and stinking. The boiling energy and purpose of the preceding turmoil faded away. Filthy, dangerous-looking men loitered, and the work of gin and beer was seen crumpled in the doorways and alleys.

Hannah at last began to worry. The children she saw were little more than hills of filthy rags, and she tried not to think of Victor, immaculate in her arms, as one of them. But it was the dwellings that outraged everything in her being.

"We're just about there, I'm afraid," Chumlin muttered.

The driver refused to venture into the alley that held their destination. He pointed into the darkness and set about removing the baggage with all the speed he could. Hannah noticed that he had opened a couple of extra buttons on his coat to expose the hilt of a sheath knife.

Chumlin tipped his hat to Hannah without stepping off the conveyance. "I wish you the best of luck, Mrs. Oakhill. And you, sir. Perhaps we'll meet another time."

When they had gone, several loungers arose and drifted closer. Serpa paid no attention and filled his hands with the baggage. They had barely started into the alley when one of the men, rat-faced and missing his front teeth, cut them off. He thrust out a hand and spoke a few menacing words in Italian before he switched to a crippled English. "Help the poor."

Without a word, without spilling a trunk from his shoulders, Serpa swung an oaken knee into the man's side. Hannah heard the ribs break, as did the other loungers, who froze where they were. The man dropped and Serpa kicked him in the mouth. There were no more teeth to lose, but the blood was considerable.

The Sicilian nodded his head in the direction of Hannah and Victor and spoke to the men in short, guttural Italian words. They backed away another step and took off their hats to her, mumbling sullen apologies.

Hannah followed the broad shoulders to the end of the alley, where a low door, defaced by chalked obscenities, had painted upon it the number she had seen on the piece of paper. As she clutched Victor closer to her side, Serpa kicked at the lower panel so the heavy wood shuddered at the hinges.

A fat, scowling woman jerked open the door and immediately whimpered the names of several saints. She started to run back inside, stopped in terror and managed to motion them in.

"Rendino," Serpa said to the woman.

They went up a staircase so narrow that their heels brushed each side. In the room at its head, eight dark men, each eye wilder, each mustache fiercer than the next, sat at cards in the fading light from a grime-caked window. They were in their undershirts, but several wore high-crowned hats. Three feral-looking women sat in the shadows along the walls.

The men stared at Serpa, unwilling to believe what their eyes were telling them. Then, one after the other..., "Serpa... Serpa ... *Serpa* . . ."

Hats came off quickly. The women scurried away. Some of the men came hesitantly forward and took the trunks from his back. Several kissed his hand, one his cheek.

From where he stood, Serpa now spoke to them in Italian. The words came for a long time, all bearing an edge that could have drawn blood. Only by watching the faces of the listeners, who spoke not a single sentence in return, could Hannah have any notion of what he told them.

Whatever it was, it was eventually reassuring. The naked fright began to be replaced by hope, then anxiety, then cautious relief. Some smiles were attempted. Women were called. Wine was poured and harsh barks brought a rattle of utensils from an unseen kitchen.

Through all of this Hannah had stood as though invisible. Finally, Serpa pressed Hannah gently forward with the flat of a huge hand. "Signora Oakhill," he said, and then pointed at the child. "Victor." The men nodded and mumbled some greetings. "When you speak to her, it will be in her tongue. They are as my family. If they are hurt or insulted, you will answer. Tomorrow we will walk on the street so all will know I am not dead in Sicilia after all. They will see Signora Oakhill and her son. You will make them know that I protect her. I will be sending to find many people I once knew. They will be told as well. And, most important, my enemies must be informed."

He then switched back to Italian and issued a string of orders. Several of the men flushed and were on the verge of an objection, but they pressed it back into their throats. A flurry of movement occurred. Several more women appeared and hurried to a door leading off the room they were in. After some commotion they came out carrying mounds of clothing, sheets, mattresses and personal effects. Then the luggage was snatched up and taken inside the emptied room. Serpa motioned Hannah inside, followed and pulled the door shut behind him.

His voice took on a sincerely apologetic tone she had never heard pass his lips. "Signora Oakhill, I burn with shame to offer you such a miserable place. You must understand I was driven from Sicilia with little more than what I wore when I ran from the hills."

"Mr. Serpa, it's not the misery of these quarters that concerns me. It's that I am moving those people out. There must have been at least six of them using this room."

"These people have suffered their awful poverty because there has been no man of respect to lead them, to keep the wolves from eating them. They have had to turn against me to remain alive. It has damaged their honor. Now I am here to restore it. They are happy to pay what they owe me, as I am happy to pay you."

As he finished speaking these words, he opened his suitcase and began to stuff the drawers of a large bureau with his belongings. "There is plenty of room in here for your things, and even a closet."

There was only one mattress on the floor. For all of them. Hannah knew she should seize up Victor and whatever little she could carry and run, but with dead weariness the strength and courage had all come out of her by now.

At dinner, Hannah counted thirteen people around the big table. There could not have been more than five rooms in the narrow flat, and all these were crammed into them.

For all her exhaustion and despair, Hannah found herself ravenous after the grim fare aboard the *Dortmund*. She fell upon dishes drowned in richly spiced sauces and found herself drinking wine that wouldn't have been used to scrub the drains of Golden Fluss.

The women were silent, the men all business in their talk, all of it in their own tongue. There were two words spoken that she understood as Serpa all but spat them onto the table. *Pasquale Lupo*.

As the men talked and the women cleared, Hannah excused herself unheard and saw to bedding down Victor. Not knowing when Serpa would come through the door, she hurried through her preparations for bed. She had taken a knife from the table, but doubted that it was in her strength to kill him if he tried to take her by force. And to kill herself would leave Victor alone. She removed the minimum of clothing she could to make use of the washstand and resolved to shed nothing more than her skirt, shoes and bodice, despite the grueling discomfort of the heat. Victor she placed on a corner of the mattress, leaving all the room the big Sicilian would need. For herself she chose the corner farthest away and shielded by the bureau. She spread a coat on the worn rug, curled upon it and tried to sleep, but her eyes would not close. The bright fan of the kerosene flame held her mesmerized.

As sure as she was that she had not slept, she did not hear Serpa come in. The first intimation she had that he was in the room came when the essence of him filled her nostrils and powerful arms slid under her shoulders and knees and lifted her from her cramped corner. The chest that brushed her cheek was bare, the sharp ripple of lean muscle sending a shock through her that she had never before known. The unfightable force she felt in that tree-like body told her that cries and resistance would bring her nothing. But the stuttering in her breast, she knew, had little to do with fear.

A moment later she was lowered to the mattress. Victor murmured in his sleep, inches from her face. She had not stirred and Serpa could not have known that she was awake.

His breath was softly audible just above her. A drop of hot sweat fell upon her cheek. She willed her hand to go to the knife she had hidden at her hip, but her fingers would not close. But he was gone anyway.

Somewhere during the hours, the oil burned out of the lamp. The flame grew small and dim and then was swallowed by the stifling darkness. The window on the airshaft was a barely perceptible patch on the wall.

In the morning Serpa was asleep under the window, the long muscles in his back glistening with sweat where the sheet in which he had wrapped himself had slid away. Hannah dressed quickly, gathered up Victor and slipped out of the room.

The days that followed were not easy for Hannah. She was not a prisoner in the cramped, crowded flat, but something worse. To the previous occupants she was an unwanted, distrusted stranger. The men saw her as Serpa's alien spy. The women, brutalized by their husbands and in virtual bondage, resented her protection by the fearsome man who cowed their own men. To her surprise, she did not really mind their sneering innuendos delivered in Italian. She began to know for the first time in her life the heady uses of physical power. Still, she tried to help with the work of the house for a long time before she knew that the women's rebuffs would never end.

Serpa, she saw, was having a difficult time with his plans. One of the children, Leo, was a boy of fourteen or so who had a fractured but ready command of the new tongue. He was arrogant and talked to her incessantly when he was not observed.

Hannah learned that Serpa had been sending money and people from Messina for several years to establish himself in a country where the opportunities for his business would be limitless. But his enemies had realized they must be rid of him before the base of his new power was established. They had used the murder of a magistrate, engineered by themselves, to turn an army of police against him. His supporters had melted away under a barrage of bribes, arrests and intimidations. His money and properties were seized and he was pursued up to the north German coast before the stranglers had lost the trail.

Well aware of what was happening in Sicily, his American lieutenant, Bartolemeo Abruzzi, had taken the business for himself. What men retained residual loyalty to Serpa were frozen out or worse. As men unused to the sweaty, low-paying work of the standard immigrant, they were being slowly enticed back to the arms of Abruzzi when Serpa arrived. It was a place of shadowy allegiances where Abruzzi had most of the men and all of the money.

Serpa began to disappear into the streets early and return long after Hannah was in bed. He said little to her, but what he said was courteous and solicitous. "You look well, signora. Stay with God."

A night came when Serpa was helped home by two of his men, one leg of his trousers torn and bloody. When the cloth was cut away, there were two ragged holes where bullets had passed through soft flesh without getting the bone. He would have no doctoring other than what the women could apply, and his peasant vitality had him back on his feet in two days.

On the third day, the police fished a large cotton-sack out of the river. In it, tied together but otherwise unharmed except for being dead by drowning, were three of Abruzzi's dripping lieutenants. Hannah was in the crowd that gathered on a pier and stared at the wide-eyed corpses with the gaping mouths, and watched the faces of the neighborhood as it turned to sneak looks at Benedetto Serpa. She knew that an important corner had been turned.

The battle was far from over, but Serpa began to make himself felt in the business that no one spoke of. As the months passed, money began to appear in the flat. The men blossomed into modish clothes, and the women bought exactly the food they wanted. New furniture appeared, including a real bed for Hannah and a smaller one for Serpa under the window.

The smaller gangs began to take sides. There came a knock on the door one morning in late winter. Hannah answered and was greeted by a smiling, well-dressed man who handed her a paper bag tied closed with a string. "To Signor Benedetto Serpa with respect from the D'Ambrosia brothers, Signora Oakhill."

She was alone for once, the rest having gone to attend a neighbor's funeral. Seeing that a spot of blood had worked its way through the bottom of the bag, she suspected it might be something perishable for the freeze box hung outside the window, so she slit it open. Onto the table fell an awful, purple thing the size of a small fist, one end ripped and ragged. With a deep retch she realized it was a tongue. Through a hole in the tip, a man's silver ring had been tied. The initials were *P. L.*, and she knew that Pasquale Lupo would speak no more to the police at Castle Garden.

Serpa was deeply distressed when Hannah avoided him as much as she could over the following week. One night he broke the rule he seemed to have set for himself after the first evening: He came into their room before she was asleep. He carried a lamp and knelt by her side. There was pain in his words.

"Signora Oakhill, you have been shown a terrible thing. I am horribly sorry. I know it will make no difference to you that I did not do this thing myself. It was done in my behalf, though truth be told I have done worse. It will also make no difference when I tell you that worse has been done against me. But I beg you, do not turn away from me so coldly. I fight for my life in the only way I can. And for yours, and the child's."

"Mr. Serpa, I will never be able to live with such things. I must go from here."

He grasped her hand unexpectedly. She could not have freed it if her strength had been a dozen times what it was. "I owe you my life, so all your commands are mine to obey. And I would never press myself forward on your affections against your wishes. Yet, I implore you not to go. Not simply for your sake, but mine. To know you were alone in this savage place would destroy me."

"We mustn't be together anymore," she said, made breathless by his intensity.

"I have been wrong. I kept us here in this place beyond the time I had to because it fills me with excitement just to sleep in the same room with you. But now we will be more apart. There is a house down the street, fine and almost new. Two floors. You will have the top for Victor and yourself. I will have below."

"No."

"Remember, Signora Oakhill, that it is thought that you are my woman. You cannot leave my protection."

"I'm suffocating here, Mr. Serpa."

"You'll have more than the rooms. You'll have money of your own. And you'll be free to move about. I'll send a man behind. See this city as I have seen it. It will excite you as nothing you have imagined."

"You must not . . . speak to me except as a friend. Ever."

"Upon my heart it is sworn. But I ask something."

"Anything your great kindness deserves."

"Signora Oakhill . . . this life is a horror of loneliness. My family, my brothers, the people I trust are thousands of miles away. I can speak to no one. Every ear may belong to an enemy. I ask you. Let me come to you as a loving companion, and no more. We will have some wine. And we will speak of what is, what was and what might be."

The wretched loneliness she heard in his words moved her. Against all good sense she answered, "My door will never be closed to you as a friend."

Before a week had gone by, Hannah's life had changed hugely. The house was bought, and Hannah whisked to the best furniture stores to tailor it to her taste. Filomena, a wide-eyed young maid, cook and nurse, arrived to care for it, and the first of the weekly envelopes containing a hundred dollars appeared in Hannah's mailbox. A breathtaking fortune.

Even before Serpa had moved in downstairs, a handsome but deadly looking man named Nello appeared across the street, occasionally relieved by an older counterpart named Gino.

Then the routine began. After Filomena had cleared the dishes and washed them each evening, she would leave promptly. Never more than fifteen minutes later, Benedetto Serpa would knock at Hannah's door. He would be scrubbed and dressed in his finest suit and would carry a hat even though he had gone no further than the stairs. Often he would bring her a small gift, such as a book.

Hannah would make him a cup of the strong espresso that he favored, and they would sit at the table in the kitchen, separated by its width, and talk for precisely one hour.

To their mutual surprise, they became easy with one another very quickly. When he was relaxed, his voice modulated beautifully and expressively, and the big, finely manicured hands shaped his points with the grace of a great sculptor.

He told her of his early life in Sicily, lingering happily on tales of village life with mischievous playmates and loving family. Eventually he told her of his courtship and marriage. A farmer with good lands had died in the next village, leaving a sick widow and a handsome daughter. Her father had been saving the daughter for a first-class marriage, but now that he was gone, the riffraff came crowding in. Using what legacy he had, size, ready fists and a dark charm, he had plunged in to win the hand and the lands he needed.

His new wife, Elvira, had turned out to be sensitive, proud and hardworking. But she scorned the learning that her husband sought everywhere, and proved herself cool, sour and, in the long run, tedious. She had borne him three fine daughters in rapid succession, his love of them finally overcoming his disappointment at his lack of sons.

Meanwhile, hard times had come to Sicily and farmers starved everywhere. Those who had courage, families to feed and a gun or two banded together and went after the properties of the great and oppressive estate owners. The original case against injuring the pillaged except when necessary faded when the owners brought in heavily-bribed government forces to murder brigands and their families without the nicety of trial. There were networks of informers, who had to be disposed of in the most drastic ways. This inspired a code of silence and a tighter banding together of the outlaws.

Serpa had been among the first to see that the way of the gun alone was doomed, and that the sun-blasted villages had not enough wealth to sustain a decent life even with the most energetic theft. He gathered the best and most loyal of the men of the local bands and went to the cities of the north, concentrating his power in Messina. He found the groups who had their hands deepest in the pockets of the city and joined with them at first. Then, improving their methods and squeezing himself into power as bloodlessly as possible, he became the youngest of the powerful leaders. The old leaders were kept around in positions of honor if they saw the wisdom of passing the reins. If they did not it was on their heads.

He did not smile or appear ashamed when he told her that his business was an honorable one in the slime pit of Sicilian political and economic life. And he had already seen that New York was no cleaner in these areas.

Hannah understood that he did her great homage by speaking to her of these things that he would not have spoken of with his own mother. He was putting himself in her hands to show the way he trusted her.

For her part, Hannah resisted opening herself to him as long as she could. Obdurately she kept the images of the drowned men in the sack and the grisly thing in the paper bag in front of her. She told herself that she would stay with him for only as long as it took her to save enough from the money he gave her to get a place in a far distant part of the city and to train herself for work that would support her and her son.

But on some nights as they sat talking, the hooded lamp painted his half-beautiful, half-evil face with something deeply compelling. She found herself having to fight to resist an unreasoning intimacy. She remembered their first moment on the *Dortmund*, when she had felt pulled into his soul though those black eyes.

When it came time for him to leave each evening, he moved to go like a man headed for execution. She would not admit to herself that she often wanted him to linger, much less that she wanted more than that.

There was never a moment she did not know he was another order of animal, a prowling thing whose inner law came out of a jungle into which she could never venture. He lived by dark power and sudden death. Yet, along the narrow path where his honor held, it held unshakably. Hannah could not have stood for a moment against his want, except that he owed her a debt that gave her a power over him none else owned.

She often wondered if he felt anything for her beyond the raw, animal focus that she felt for him. . . .

Hannah made immediate and widespread use of her new freedom to roam the city. Since the burly, eventually affable Nello was to be an unwanted shadow, she decided to make him helpful. She gave him the name of Frank Chumlin, remembering her shipmate from the *Dortmund* had said he did not live far away, and asked that the tentacles of the Serpa organization be put to work finding him for her. There would be uses for a businessman, however inept, who knew New York and its ways. Next, she asked Nello for a map of the city.

No general ever planned a great campaign more carefully.

To begin with, she had to learn this island, all twelve miles of length and three miles of width, as well as she had known the bright lands of Golden Fluss. She must know its people, its wealth, its buildings, its land, its future. From here on, her fate would come out of her wits, and it was on this footprint in the river than her main battles would be fought.

With Nello always trailing a dozen steps behind her, often with Victor sitting spellbound on his shoulders, Hannah Oakhill, twenty-three years old, began to explore the grand sprawl of Manhattan in the early months of 1868.

As she progressed, her natural adventurousness and curiosity, her suppressed sense of joy and anticipation, came crowding back into her.

The south of the island, at the Battery, was a tangle of narrow, randomly running streets twisting to the whims of the original Dutch settlers. And while the views of the glorious harbor were breathtaking, the building plots were stultifyingly narrow. Her interest in these plots was far more than academic, for she was determined to have her name on land of her own again. The money that Serpa gave her was not going into clothes, carriages and furnishings, but into a bank near City Hall. At the first moment that she could, she would have her property and her own life disentangled from Serpa.

Her savings, enormous though they seemed compared to the going wages, were nothing when placed against the price of a foot of ground on the lower island. If she was to find what she needed, it would be elsewhere on Manhattan.

By the time she was ready to make a sweep of the riverfronts, she had a knowing and congenial companion, for Frank Chumlin had been found. That feckless fellow was working as a salesman of horse-car equipment. His presence not being required at any desk, and most of his business bought by bribes to the traction companies, he was free when he wanted to be.

Hannah listened to him patiently, often eagerly, but having heard his opinions she was likely to amend them.

When Chumlin told her that the city's true wealth was in its magnificent harbor with dockage on two mighty rivers, she didn't completely agree with him. And his notion that this town would someday be the industrial hub of the world struck her as totally wrong.

"These waters that you see as a roadway, Frank, I see as a barrier. The people on this island are prisoners of a fleet of ferries that can't even begin to connect them satisfactorily with either the mainland or Brooklyn. Waterways might still be everything in backward countries, but Father told me that the next fifty years will belong to the locomotive. This country is going to be paved over with steel rails before long. Nothing else can haul such bulk at such speed. And how does a rail cross a river? How do industries grow up where a city is hundreds of miles away from the coal to power them. Don't you think that the industrial cities will grow where the coal is and where the rails run straight to the center?"

"My heavens, Hannah, it's strange to hear a young lady thinking like that," he said a bit condescendingly. "That would mean Pittsburgh would get all the factories. I'm sure that important industrialists will be surprised to learn that New York has no future."

"Oh, I never said that," she laughed. "But the most important goods that those ships will bring in, Frank, are *people*. New York will collect the sweepings of Europe, keep the best and send the rest to a slower place. The people with farmers' minds and miners' souls will move on. The people who can think and sell and build will be here. This will be a city of the mind and spirit. It's happening already. Can't you see it? Can't you smell it and feel it?"

"Ow, you're digging into my arm, Mrs. Oakhill."

She told him of her dream to hold important property again, and her enthusiasm quickly enlisted his full cooperation. He told her all he knew.

The margins of the city were a perilous sinkhole almost everywhere. The clipper ships, already relics barely twenty years after they had set their seemingly unbeatable records around the Horn, crowded the East River where the winds to help them maneuver were fresher. The West River, or Hudson, held the new steam packets, whose screws and paddle wheels helped them flout the winds and tides. Beneath the miles of piers, sharing space with rats the size of terriers, were the river gangs. No man, police or otherwise, ventured into their hellish dens. They ventured out at night in skiffs and rafts, pirates who swarmed silently upon craft moving and anchored. The lucky sailors lost only their cargo.

"The East River on a foggy night is more dangerous than the North Atlantic, Mrs. Oakhill. The Hudson is no better. Mr. Barnum has no need to go to Borneo for his savages. Give the riverfronts and all who find their living there a wide margin."

"There's quite a tide," Hannah said. "When it's out, there's an awful lot of land that sits there. I wonder if it's possible to buy it."

Chumlin looked at her as though she were crazy. "I don't know. Who'd give a dime an acre for a lot of wet mud and a cut throat?"

"Somebody who thought river property was one day going to be worth a lot more to people than it was to ships."

"I think we'd better start looking uptown, Mrs. Oakhill," he said uneasily.

Down the spine of the island the wide avenues ran with wealth. From 23rd Street north the homes and buildings were new and impressive. Millionaires whose names were beginning to be legends even in the capitals of Europe were plundering the old world of architecture, artists, stone and furnishings even as they plundered the new for the wealth to do it. Fifth and Madison were magnificent, if somewhat monotonous in the similarity of the mansions, and would soon be streets for London, Paris and Rome to respect.

Chumlin showed her the street where the Dutch had walled off their New Amsterdam against the Indians two hundred years before. She was a bit amazed at how leisurely the northern frontier had advanced. Above 50th Street, there were wide-open tracts of hundreds of acres, some still bearing the outbuildings of the farms they had been not long ago. Her guide pointed out the problems of filling in the numerous streams and ponds that crossed and dotted the hilly island. It was an endless heartache to builders.

Each day they penetrated farther north. She left earlier and came home later, with Nello always trailing in near exhaustion. Serpa worried, but he saw her new happiness and said nothing.

Above 60th Street there were wonders. The new Central Park, even in the grip of a snowy winter, was a vast delight of rambles, bridges, fountains, and frozen lakes set like jewels in the snow-covered hills. Swirling hordes of laughing skaters of every age and rank, all made shapeless by their bundles of clothes, covered the ice everywhere. The horsecars bore flags with a red ball to announce when the ice was strong, and there was skating by lamplight. Hannah's quick eye noticed that even among the poorest there was a sense of vibrant life and boundless hope that was missing always in the class-divided world that lay behind her.

She tried to imagine beautiful buildings around this happy place, visible above the trees, where dwellers could look down on the pleasant sight at all hours and fill their hearts. But she knew that the brutal nature of travel from the south, the long slog by foot and horsecar, would keep people out until the elevated railroads arrived many years in the future. But arrive they would, and then . . .

Her travels steadily took her over most of the map by the time the first green haze of spring had begun to appear. It was at this time that she first set foot on the heart-filling Harlem Plains.

Although this rich land was so far north that it was not really considered to be part of the city, it was as bucolic and well-favored a suburb as could ever be wished. Chumlin informed her that in this fresh, untainted countryside the finest citizens had always made their homes. He took her past Alexander Hamilton's old estate, still standing in good repair.

Hannah learned that in the summer the cool trees and gorgeous vistas brought picknickers and strollers in fashionable profusion. Those who kept homes or summer cottages here were careful to give Harlem addresses, which were thought much more elegant than any home in the city. She allowed herself to dream that she might herself someday own such an address.

A burning summer and another bitter winter went by. By the spring of 1869, Hannah knew the city as well as anyone. And she also knew that the thousands she had saved from Serpa's money, an unbelievable treasure to those who filled the brawling slums, were nowhere near giving her money enough to compete with great landholders like the Astors, who were there always before anyone with a bit more money. At last her spirits began to droop.

Victor and Benedetto Serpa were the only people close to her now, Chumlin having married Katie, one of the numerous Hanratty children he had met on the *Dortmund*. She was a pretty girl, who set about nagging her happy drifter of a husband into a more productive provider, and he was soon all but lost to Hannah.

Victor began to grow broad and strong very quickly. Hannah saw all too plainly the sullen good looks and earthy strength of Grigor Hunzak in him, and she was less able than ever, as she remembered her shame, to love him as a true mother should. When she realized this she would redouble her care and buy him more presents.

The child, at four, seemed not a child at all at times, except for the energy that exploded out of him. Victor was most comfortable in the company of adults, not children. He talked seldom, but when he did his vocabulary was far beyond his years. If Hannah was colder to him than she should have been, the child, seeming to feel it, returned the sentiment. She sometimes felt she was with a cool, tiny adult patiently waiting to be free of his child's body and his caretakers so he could get on with important things. Then he fell in love with heights.

Hannah supposed that it had begun when the ever-trailing bodyguard, Nello, had begun to play with the boy while she detoured into some lot or alley, seeking property. A game had developed where Nello turned Victor into a small acrobat. Skillfully manipulating his grip on the little hands, the Italian swung Victor between his legs and high over his head in swift, swooping arcs. The man had the reflexes of a master juggler and quickly passed his extraordinary sense of movement and balance to his delighted, diminutive partner. One afternoon, far on the other side of a wide lot, Hannah watched Nello tossing her happily shrieking son a full five feet into the air, catching him beneath the arms a foot off the ground. She had screamed for the man to stop, but thought that the game had gone on a long time undiscovered and would continue to be played outside her vision.

At any rate, Victor's chunky, spring-loaded thighs, always churning, began to carry him onto window sills and fire escapes, up steep staircases and to the top of the highest heaps of rubble he could find. He didn't crawl or move tentatively as a child might, but ran upright, full tilt, with the unthinking agility of a young Alpine ram. All of Hannah's angry shouts and vigorous spanking could not change a thing.

Hannah's more important concern for Victor involved Benedetto Serpa. As the child gained reason, the Sicilian began to spend more time with him. The little mouth began to form Italian phrases as easily as English. Hannah suspected that the bond being formed was to a purpose that had not altogether to do with his genuine affection for the boy. It was a way to get more hold over her, and she could not allow that to happen.

Outwardly, the nightly meetings at the kitchen table seemed what they had always been. Hannah, however, had come to know the meaning of every glint in the dark, unblinking eyes as the lamplight struck them. The man was taut with pain and yearning, although always as proper as a Boston judge. Finally, feeling the pull of him more and more, Hannah resolved to begin to turn him away.

"When will you see Signora Serpa and your children again?"

"When God wishes it," he said shortly.

"I can't believe that God wants a man to be separated from the fruit of his heart and body for as long as you have been separated from yours."

"Abruzzi would war on those who are dear to me."

"But, Benedetto, Nello tells me that all of you are very careful with the safety of each other's families. Surely you don't war on Mr. Abruzzi's women and children."

"You don't know him. Snake's blood runs in his veins."

"You protect me. You could protect your own."

"Are you not happy with me, Mrs. Oakhill?"

"I am comfortable and very thankful for it."

"Can you feel nothing for me?" He spoke like a wounded man.

"There is no sense in discussing what must never be."

"You are stronger than I."

"You must send for Signora Serpa. And I would be in your debt if you would not be so close to Victor. You are not his father and should not seem so."

"You mustn't turn away from me. It is not necessary . . ."

"But it is. It's very difficult for me to say this, but we should not visit in the evenings anymore."

He looked as if he would die. "That would make me very sad."

"And me. But I must be gone. There's no longer a need for either of us to live in this terrible neighborhood."

"The police do not penetrate here. And I must be close to my people and my enemies. I will help you find a place—"

"I can do that myself."

"Again you do not respect me."

"Would you not have me respect *myself*? Good night, Benedetto."

Serpa respected her wishes completely. But the expected release of the tension that had been building inside her did not take place. She waited every evening for the soft knock she had commanded not to sound. What should have been gratitude for his compliance was something like disappointment. The flaring temper he had shown the man in the alley on their first day here could have splintered her door in a moment. He could have fallen upon her with fists or bitter words and cut the ties that had been permitted between them. She would have welcomed that.

As she searched through the streets for her new place, she would come across Serpa as though by accident. He would be passing on the street as she emerged from looking at rooms, or he would walk into a restaurant where she had stopped for lunch. He would pause for only a few words. There was no sign of the usual bodyguards, who might have seen his helpless despair. Always he seemed to be waiting for her to take his arm or ask him to her table.

Away from her, she heard from Filomena (who saw passion as easily as others saw flesh and blood), he had become a wounded lion, snapping at all who came close. Leo reported that he had begun pursuing his enemies with a ferocity that appalled even the hardest of his men.

Late in the fall, a period of endless rains began. It was as though all the billions of gallons of water that steamed out of the surrounding rivers in the broiling drought of the summer had returned to drown the city. The streets ran ankle deep, the garbage of the Five Points sweeping by more swiftly than a man could walk.

The ancient, poorly built structures began to surrender to the deluge. Roofs, the dried tar weakened and shrunken by the months of pitiless sun, yawned with cracks that sent the water streaming down the walls and through the ceilings. Piles of plaster grew on the floors, and cornices that had clung for a hundred years plummeted down to the pavement below. At the foundations, some built on only two courses of bricks, the floods raised the levels of long-filled streams and set them to work at the mortar that had been inadequate since first laid a century before.

In the late hours of a Saturday night, when Serpa had crossed into Brooklyn by ferry to avenge a wrong, and Hannah lay sleepless, a new sound began to make itself heard above the relentless rush of the rain on the roof and windows.

At first it was as though a series of distant artillery pieces had gone off, echoing their muffled reports across the river. These sounds had no sooner died than a crackling rumble came, low at first and then building until the windows rattled in their frames and the bed beneath her shuddered. Each time the rumble seemed to be fading it began again, louder than before, until four separate shocks had been felt. The last filled the sky outside like summer thunder and was followed quickly by the chilling, unmistakable cries she knew so well from the battlefield at Golden Fluss. Horrified, she knew that somewhere nearby pitifully maimed people were dying.

Hannah dressed with desperate speed. A glance out the window told her that her nighttime guardian, Gino, had wisely taken himself out of the empty, rain-filled street and gone to bed. It was only after she had reached the street and was running toward the waterfront beneath a blanket thrown hastily around her that she realized she had forgotten to tell the deep-sleeping Filomena where she had gone.

She sped beneath the spectral fingers of a hundred bowsprits toward the sound of the cries, meeting no one but a few confused drunks trying to puzzle out the commotion that had wakened them. At last she saw what it was and pulled up sharply.

What streetlamps there were to penetrate the blowing sheets of rain showed a stark and ugly gap in the line of buildings that faced the river. From its location she remembered the buildings as crumbling tenements being used as an overloaded warehouse for ship's stores. The homeless would elude the caretakers on nights like this and slip through the loosely boarded windows in dozens. Now at least four adjoining buildings had collapsed from three stories to a splintery pile not much higher than a tall man could stretch.

The rain was drowning the last of the fires that had started when the contents of scores of glowing kerosene lamps had been sluiced out onto the kindling of floors and old spars. But this small blessing was not heeded by the terrified who were crushed and trapped under the fallen tons.

She ran three blocks to a brothel. *"Come out. Come out and help me—"*

By the time a significant force of police and fire brigades had arrived, Hannah, leading a team of rescuers she had swept out of the streets and dragged out of nearby saloons and dwellings, had been working for an hour pulling rows of dead and injured into the streets, where many of the survivors were in real danger of drowning.

"You can go home now, madame," a policeman said to her. "This work is for men."

"Then why aren't there any more of them here?" she asked. "I've got three prostitutes doing more work than all of you."

She went on working until her clothes and the skin on both her hands were in shreds. Time became blurred. She tottered with fatigue but went on as more cries rose from far beneath the rubble where still others were coming to their senses.

Hannah became the focus of the effort, its spirit, its energy. A husky force of firemen fell in behind her and put their backs to whatever work she led them to.

At an hour of the night when the rain had become a solid, punishing wall that the weary workers pushed against, a slanting tunnel was gouged down into what had been the building's basement. The opening snaked between fallen columns of brick. Its walls bristled with nails, glass shards and vicious splinters. In answer to heartbreaking moans from below, one fireman after the other tried to make it down to the bottom with water and bandages but never got close. "It's too damned narrow for any of us."

Hannah was half the size of the smallest of them and knew what she must do. She had the packet of rescue materials tied to her small waist and was gone into the opening before anyone could move to stop her.

"Get out of that. We've got enough dead people—"

Down she went, crawling headfirst, trying not to let the terror of the hellish passageway reach her. She had snatched a fireman's sheath knife. Each time her clothing caught, she slashed backward until she was free. Again and again she felt her flesh tearing, and the lantern flame grew dimmer with every minute. The sound of her labored breathing thundered in her ears. Suffocating panic crowded closer.

Suddenly the rubble beneath her gave a huge lurch and the artillery blast she had heard from her bed exploded in her ear. The bottom of the tunnel fell away even as the top began to crush down onto her back. The lantern twisted out of her hand, and she was falling through the air alongside it. A cry had hardly started in her throat when the air was driven out of her by the force of her landing. Heavy, tearing things were coming down all around her.

The next minutes were nothing more than battling for her next breath in a choking dust that was heavier than the air she was trying to draw in.

With a huge effort of will she brought her wits back together and began to gather her senses. She was lying on heaps of thick, coarse canvas. Sails, she thought. They had cushioned her fall. All her limbs moved. Nothing was broken. The cries that had drawn her down began again, but now they were so close she heard the indrawn gasps that preceded them.

She had tumbled into the basement as a shift of the wreckage sealed her passage. In a split second she had gone from rescuer to one of the hideously trapped.

From far above, muffled by the newly packed debris, she heard the frantic shouts of the men she had left. She knew they were calling to her, but she was unable to collect enough wind to shout back.

By a miracle the lantern still held a dim light. She found the knob, turned up the flame as much as she dared in the bad air and crawled slowly about her prison. One by one the blackened, wild-eyed faces came into view. The lantern showed her that blood flowed freely, limbs bent at impossible angles and bone poked through skin. There were nine men in all, six still alive.

A single look at their pathetic state was enough to chase the last of her terror. The strength she had thought entirely gone flooded back into her one more time. She braced herself in the debris and moved beams and clumps of brick that would have taxed the power of any man.

It took every bandage she had brought to stem the bleeding and close the wounds. A canteen of water was quickly sucked dry. When she had done all she could for the people physically, Hannah talked to calm and reassure them. Sometime the next day her voice failed, and she fell back unconscious.

She dreamed she was in hell, doomed to be forever in pain and at the point of asphyxiation. When her hopelessness had reached its greatest depth, she began to perceive a spot of light. It grew larger and brighter, and the sound of the upper world began to filter in. In a glowing halo, the figure of an angel suddenly loomed and she raised her leaden arms to him. A great, unexpected happiness began to pour into her. *"Mark,"* she called, and there was a delicious gust of fresh air.

Her eyes opened and she looked up into the desperate glare of Benedetto Serpa as he lifted her toward a bright blue sky. There were deafening cheers. The faces of the men she had been working beside an eternity ago pressed in a circle above her.

She was riding in Serpa's arms as he kissed her bleeding face and murmured to her, gently, endlessly, in soft, crooning Italian.

Afterward, from a thousand miles away, she heard a doctor saying that she was not badly hurt. She could be looked after at home. Trying to ask about the injured, she found she was too tired to form the words. Sleep came crushing down upon her.

When she awoke, she knew the clock must have spun many times. It was night and she was in her own bed. A lamp turned very low cast a weak glow from a nearby table. Its light sculpted the haggard, stubbled face of the Sicilian. In the features there was a love, an anguish she would have thought impossible in a soul so fierce. He was kneeling at her side, his eyes moist and unwavering upon hers. Seeing her awake he tried to speak, but his voice caught hopelessly. He took her bandaged hand to his lips and held it there for a long time.

"Benedetto—" she whispered. "Thank you for pulling us out."

He was trying to steady his voice. "They said you were dead in that heap. I screamed at the saints for mercy. I brought all our people. Even some of the Abruzzis joined us. Tell me how you are."

Painfully, she brought herself up on one elbow, moving each part of her in turn. There were shocking twinges. But other than the sting of abrasions and minor cuts, there was little more than a crippling stiffness to remind her where she had been. "I feel good, Benedetto. But look at you. You haven't been out of those clothes in days. Have you slept at all?"

"If you had died, I would never have slept again."

She placed her hand against the rough cheek. The skin burned as if a preternatural fever lived beneath it. The heat seemed to draw the loneliness up and out of her long-frozen soul. His love drew her. Hannah pulled away her covers. "Come . . . come and sleep."

His breathing all but stopped. She thought she saw a shudder move down the thick frame.

He began to undress, not turning, not hiding himself in the shadows. From under the sweat-stained shirt an iron torso came into view, the muscles of the belly a jagged ladder of strength. The arms writhed with sinew as he undid the rough trousers.

Hannah, too, did not turn away. She watched the enormous, gleaming arch of his erection appear above the falling trousers. Where the pillars of his thighs joined, the black fur fanned thick and wide.

He eased her out of her flannel nightgown, she raising her hands unhesitatingly to allow the removal. She had a glimpse of her own pale body covered everywhere with blue bruises and dark cuts, and thought that revulsion must now seize him and send him away. But then she was locked into his arms with his mouth sucking the breath out of her. Her arms went around his shoulders, and she let her hands wander down the swelling ridges of the awesome back.

He was at first slow, gentle, awed. His fingers moved into her and found sensations in places she never knew to exist. Her fear that some suddenly intruding memory of the forest might overcome her faded forever in a rising surge of want.

Another being now slid out of Benedetto Serpa, one that did not know the soft ways of creatures that walked on two legs.

He slammed inside Hannah with a force that thrust pain and pleasure into one flaming cauldron. The wounds of her body he forgot. He guided her limbs and her flesh with irresistible urgency, determined to know every one of the thousand haunting delights that must have tortured his dreams over the months.

Hannah was hurtled along until her own white flame flashed inside her and she matched him thrust for thrust.

Something unspeakably beautiful blossomed into her center. He smothered her cries and his own by covering her mouth with his. Their tearing gasps rose and died together.

Afterward, they clung together.

So quietly that she could hardly hear the words, Serpa said, "Who is Mark?"

A great emptiness appeared in her heart. "A man I will never see again."

Her exhausted body asserted its claims again, and she slept past noon the next day. When she awoke, Benedetto Serpa was gone. Not just out of her bed, but out of his rooms and out of the city. The word was that he had returned to Brooklyn to finish the business that had been at hand when news of Hannah had reached him. But he had left no note, no promise of a time to return. Days passed without him.

Hannah was at least half glad. What she had let happen was unbelievably stupid. She had turned loose a giant she could not hope to control, and to whom she must at all costs not become a possession. It was only when she went to her bed on the subsequent nights and lay upon the warm embers of what had happened there that she had to fight against a wish for him to return.

Serpa's people seemed different. They had apparently seen him before he left and knew that something had changed him.

There was fright in their faces, tension, a nervous waiting for things unknown.

Even the faithful, easygoing Filomena was quiet and withdrawn.

"You have troubles, Filomena?"

"No, Signora Oakhill. But in the night I worry for you."

"Why?"

"You have no God, signora."

"My God has not been kind to me."

"Come with me to Father Alleghieri. He has no church yet. Just an empty store. But the Holy Flame is there. Show yourself to him and to God. We will pray together."

"For what, Filomena?"

"For shelter from the storms that come across the sea, signora."

The rains were finally gone. The snow had not yet come, but the first days of hard winter fell upon New York beneath dazzling blue skies. Hannah awoke one morning with her strength fully returned and an urgent restlessness to prowl on her own. She watched from the window until Nello had vanished to answer a call of nature, wrapped herself in her warmest coat and slipped into the streets.

Realizing that she had never seen the site of her desperate labors by daylight, she crossed down the bustling street beneath the bowsprits and came to the collapsed buildings.

The novelty had worn completely away, and whatever crowds had come to view the disaster had melted. She was surprised to see no one at work clearing the debris.

As she explored, it soon came to her attention that the buildings on each side, the same sort of tenements turned into warehouses, now stood empty.

A policeman, grown too old and stiff for more rigorous duties, patrolled the street in front of the tangle, shooing away children who would have enjoyed playing on the fascinating mountain. He quickly recognized her as the heroine of the collapse and was happy to tell her all he knew.

"The inspectors finally came around to see what happened,"

he said. "They couldn't nail anybody because the owners were all inside and they're dead as a buzzard's dinner. Somebody said there was some heirs, but they live across in Newark and there's no luck findin' 'em yet. That's why the city ain't movin' in to clear the mess. If it's somebody else's property, let 'em pay to get it done. The buildin's on both sides are condemned now. There was nothin' much to hold 'em up but the walls that fell down."

"Do you mind if I climb up on the heap?"

"If you had the sand to go down in that hole you can go anywhere. Holler if you get stuck."

Hannah made her way up the crumpled wreckage and finally clambered onto what had been a second-story fireplace. It stood well above the level of the rest of the debris and afforded her a superb view of the river as well as of the devastation around her.

Standing higher than the hulls of the ships, Hannah could see the fleets of ferries battling their way slowly against the stiff current. Soon the ice would return and thicken, making the broad passage a nightmare for both the pilots and their passengers.

Yet, the problem had only begun. As New York filled, its workers would increasingly have to live away from Manhattan. The city of Brooklyn would be the bedroom for the metropolis, and the hundred-and-thirty miles of Long Island stretching to the east would be a garden to feed the New Yorkers. There would have to be an unimaginable number of ferry crossings on both sides of the river.

Before she started to climb down, she took one more long look around, her hair whipping in the wind. The gap in the waterfront facade seemed to her a great gate, waiting a connection between two rapidly growing worlds.

Watching the commotion and energy on the street below, she suddenly knew that there was nothing that this new race of many races could not beat. They would solve the vast problems with vast ideas not yet dreamed. She had read in a newspaper that a Union Army engineer named Roebling had created miraculous bridges during the war. And that he thought that using new kinds of suspension-engineering and cable-spinning techniques, it might just be in the reach of man to build a great New York bridge across to Brooklyn. The reporter had rashly predicted that such a wonder might rise after the next fifty years, but he was wrong. They would need such a bridge long before then, and this was a breed who would never learn to wait.

Shading her eyes, she squinted across to the other shore. She knew nothing of the nature of the river bottom or the structures that must give way to enable a bridge. But as a matter of distance between shores and access to major streets, this spot would not miss such a crossing by a hundred yards.

A rotting beam let go somewhere. Below her the rubble groaned and shifted. Looking straight down into the basement she saw bedrock. This island, this spot, could hold a building a hundred stories high if it were in the power of men to design and construct it. Hannah's mind swirled with ideas and resolutions every step of the way home.

Something was happening at the house. From down the block she saw a group of people clustered near the front steps. A carriage was parked at the curb, and the driver was disappearing into the building with trunks on his shoulders. The people were Serpa's. But they were different. They were shaved and had ties and fresh, white collars. Shoes were brushed of the filth of the streets and in some cases shined.

The nervous murmuring stopped when the people saw Hannah. A path to the steps opened for her. Something colder than the day brushed her heart. Were the women preparing something torn and dead in a back room? Had the dark alleys of Brooklyn sent home one more package for the ground?

She saw Filomena, stiff-faced, frightened, and went to her. "Benedetto?" she asked.

Filomena directed her up the steps with a touch, following her fearfully.

The passage to the stairs up to Hannah's second-floor rooms passed wide sliding doors leading to the Serpa flat. These would have stood open if the house had been used by a single family. Serpa had kept them closed always. She had never looked into his living space. Until now.

What she saw in a dark, sparsely furnished front parlor was a handsome, clear-skinned woman somewhat older than herself. The visitor bore the weariness of a great journey. Her hat was in her hand. There was a pile of worn baggage behind her. Sitting on a trunk in a prim line were three pretty little girls, the youngest no older than Victor. Their shyness barely held their excitement in check.

What Hannah read in the woman's look told her more certainly than any introduction that this was Mrs. Benedetto Serpa.

"Signora Oakhill?" she said in a voice that thrummed with the unsaid.

Hannah nodded. "Hello, Mrs. Serpa." She supposed that she herself was the only one within a mile who hadn't known.

A phalanx of women in black began to file in behind the new arrival. From inside, Benedetto Serpa appeared, filling the opening. He looked at Hannah with immense sadness before he reached out his hands to bring the doors closed, leaving Hannah alone at the foot of the stairs. As she climbed quickly, she knew that this roof was no longer hers.

There was no sleep for Hannah in the next two nights. The path she was preparing to walk would decide the rest of her life, and her son's. She thought step by step through what she must do. At the center of her reasoning lay the thickly tangled codes of the Sicilians. Leo and Nello had talked enough for her to begin to understand and fear.

She had seen new faces. People who had come with Elvira Serpa. Aunts and uncles, she guessed by the look of them. Relatives whose eyes spoke of deadly pride and grimly kept promises. Their every glance whispered that they had been told of their family's dishonor. Not even Serpa's terrifying presence could keep her safe for long. She must be away soon. But she must not make the move to go herself. He had to come to her, or she would never know her dream.

On the day he once again mounted the stairs to knock at her door, it came as no surprise. The clamor of rioting children and arguing adults that had gone on for days below had been quiet all morning. Only one of the black moods of Benedetto Serpa could produce such quiet. He had unpleasant work, and his family was wise enough not to cross his path as he prepared to do it.

He was dressed in his finest, as in the old days, his hat cradled in his arm. She had never seen such misery on a man's face.

"Come in, please, Benedetto. You have such a lovely family. I would like to meet your children."

He spoke so softly she hardly heard. "Every day I thought I would tell you. Every day the words would not come."

"Why? You only did what I asked."

"It pains me so to think of you having to go."

His debt to her had been repaid a thousand times. But he must not be permitted to see that.

"Then I am being sent away?"

His discomfort was becoming unbearable. "There is nothing else to do. But you will leave with no worry. There will be another place. Better than this. And money for you."

"That's not enough."

This hit him as unexpectedly as she thought it would. "Signora."

"Am I to forget what happened between us? Are you to forget?"

He reddened. "It is in the blood of my heart."

"You owe me more than you offer," she said steadily, although dying inside for having to say it.

"Don't be angry."

"Is all the honor only to be on your side?"

"I will give all I can. But Abruzzi is not beaten. The cost is high. The officials must have their piece of the carcass. But I will give you more when I can—"

"I'll make you free of your debt now, Benedetto. If you help me to get something."

"Anything. Anything."

This poor man, she thought. But, she had a dream . . . he was her only hope. "Those fallen buildings and the ones against them. I want that land."

Bewilderment crossed his face. "It's a ruin."

"I want to build on it," she said with determination.

"Women do not build, Signora Oakhill."
"Not even one who was Benedetto Serpa's woman?"

It turned out to be easier than Hannah thought. Serpa had lawyers now, good Irish clubhouse men. They found the missing heirs in Newark, three tired old German brothers on the brink of poverty. Frightened at the tales of the expenses of clearing the wreckage of the collapse, they were happy to settle for enough to carry them comfortably through their few remaining days.

The talkative Leo was used as a messenger in some of the dealings, and he told Hannah that there had been interest by several individuals and companies with far more money to spend than Hannah Oakhill. But they had been visited by both the Irish lawyers and the glowering Rendino. Serpa's name was no longer unknown in the city, and the would-be buyers became convinced that any projects on land in which he showed interest would be dogged by atrocious misfortune.

In a similar way, certain construction enterprises that were not as busy as they could be learned that their futures could be considerably brighter if they turned their hand to Mrs. Oakhill's project. Profit would come at a later date, as it always does in repayment of kindness.

What Hannah had chosen to build was the best saloon on the waterfront.

It would contain fine quarters for her and Victor, and be called the Golden River, both a salute to the waters that flowed outside its door and a translation of Golden Fluss.

Her decision was not made lightly or alone. On days when she had been able to ease Frank Chumlin away from his busy life with Kate, she explored with him her choices of commercial enterprises that might rise upon her land.

The boundaries of those choices were clear. The place must suit itself to local clientele. It must be straightforward enough to be understood by a woman without a scrap of business experience outside of estate accounts. Its stock-in-trade must be nonperishable, quickly consumable, easily obtained and desirable to any man of any class, It had to be better than anyplace like it within two miles. And it had to produce enough money to buy more buildings rather quickly.

While Frank Chumlin's description of his business failures told her she must rely on her own wits in matters of money and planning, she was sure she could have complete faith in him in all manners of expertise in human frailty.

Having once been driven to Argentina on a wool clipper thanks to the close pursuit of creditors, he knew the simple needs of sailors. One day he took time off from the tack shop he had now opened, and sat her down on a dock piling to give her his notions. As they spoke they could watch a stream of wagons hauling away what remained of the fallen tenements. To the cheers of delighted crowds, teams of draft horses pulled down the tottering walls of the condemned buildings, and whole floors tilted and fell in explosions of brown dust.

"Now, Hannah," Chumlin said, clearing his throat uneasily, "talking about what sailors need doesn't always belong in any lady's ear."

"I understand that."

"Then here I go. First there's the size. The best sailor places are *big*. Not just long, but wide and high. You can't understand how tight it is on a ship. For months you're sleeping and eating where you can hardly ever stand up straight or swing an elbow without splitting your head or knocking somebody over. There's not even room for a good fight."

"How about a room three stories high?"

"Yeah, Hannah. You could put galleries up around the second and third floors. Wide enough for tables for cards. And . . . rooms off the galleries."

"For lodgings."

"Yes . . . lodgings . . . too."

"You're thinking of easy women?"

"A sailor ashore will first drink, then eat, gamble, go with a woman and sleep. If they never have to leave your roof for any of it, you'll put the rest out of business. But they might get together to burn you out."

"Let it be heard around that Mr. Serpa will look upon that with considerable displeasure."

"They understand that kind of Italian. But you'll need somebody tough to run a place like this. Maybe one of his apes."

"No, no," she said firmly. "I don't want him in this any more than he is. And it has to be a man who knows the business. Who?"

"Dirtyface Doyle."

"Tell me about him."

"Meanest man on the waterfront, once. No great brain, but he ran the best joint on the west side before he lost it betting on his fighters."

"Fighters?"

"Barge fighters. He keeps a string of 'em. Bare knuckles. All the referee does is make sure they come to the mark without any knives or broken bottles. They all end up dead, crippled or with their brains turned into oatmeal."

"Barbaric."

"That's why they fight on old barges in the river. Even the rottenest parts of the city ashore won't put up with such scum and the crowds they draw."

"Why do they do it?"

"Money. A great deal of money for the best. Men like Doyle take bets on them and give them a good part of the winnings. But he's getting old for that mob. I think if I put it to him right, you could get him."

The Golden River soon began to rise. Hannah took temporary rooms in a top-floor flat overlooking the site so she could watch every step of the construction. She was totally engaged from the first moment. If she had dreaded to watch her belly swelling with Victor, this was a pregnancy in which she exulted. Each detail had its own fascination, and she learned it thoroughly and filed it away in her mind.

Victor's first real toys were bricks, hammers and nails. His first games were building little houses of scrap. His first worry, learned from the grimy, cursing giants he walked among, was whether it would be too cold to mix mortar and pour concrete. "It's too goddamned cold to pour," he would pipe, to the horror of the faithful Filomena, who had been sent with Hannah.

By the time the Golden River stood completed in the spring of 1870, little Victor was fatally infected with the same exhilarating malady as his mother.

But Dirtyface Doyle was not to be the manager. "You can't get him, Hannah," Chumlin told her. "He's found himself a new fighter. Best in the last ten years, he told me. We'll have to wait until one of those gorillas kills the new fella."

Chapter 5

THE BARGE was a big one, once used to haul coal across the Hudson. It was now more useful as an arena in the East River. It had been decked over to make a roof to keep out the rain, the snow, the gaze of policemen and nonpayers. Fifty cents a head was a stiff entrance fee, but when something in the order of a thousand admissions had been collected, and the interior of the barge with its roughly made benches was crammed to capacity, there were still several hundred disappointed men left topside or on the pier.

The fighters prepared themselves in a canvas shelter at the wharf-front end of the barge. A stinking kerosene stove did little to cut the chill, although the wind had died to almost nothing. The two fighters waiting to go below for their match shivered. The line of lanterns strung overhead showed the gooseflesh on their naked torsos.

There was a savage roar that came straight up through the deck, and Mark Northern knew that somebody was down. There might be a round or two to complete the annihilation, but he would soon be down in that pit himself.

He turned up the flame of the closest lantern and studied in a

119

hand mirror the healing cuts of last Tuesday's bout. The one over the right brow was deep and still scabbed. The thick stitches were still in place, but they would open up in minutes. The slices in each cheek were almost a month old and would hold up with some luck.

"Take a good look, Gentleman Jack," his opponent said, "because you ain't never gonna look that good again."

The man, Bluejacket Dunne, was a brute who had spent his youth in the topyards of a Black Ball clipper. He was said to have been the hardest fighter of a hard-fighting line. Good enough to leave the sea and try his fists to get a stake for a bucket shop on some waterfront. His shoulders were twice as wide as Mark's. He was nearly seventy pounds heavier. He had so many scars on his face that it seemed to have been knitted rather than born out of whole flesh.

Mark was so used to the name of Jack Grant—Gentleman Jack, the crowd called him—that he would probably have neglected to respond to his old name. Dirtyface Doyle had named him. Jack was the kind of unfancy handle a sporting man could warm up to. And Grant was the name of the general who had beaten Bobby Lee and saved the Union.

"Save your words, Dunne. They're all you'll have to eat after the fight. Except maybe for some teeth." Mark's voice was one his own father would not have recognized. The clear tenor was gone forever, replaced by a husky growl that was the result of a blow to the throat in a fight that had taken place over a year ago.

The face he studied in the mirror was an ever-changing mystery, even to himself. What the saber-slash had started had been added to by almost eighty vicious slugging matches.

The lid of the empty left socket had been sewn shut, a grisly interruption of the white scar that ran from his forehead down his cheek. It was well that an eyepatch masked the sight when he was in public. His short, newly grown beard hid the bottom of the old wound, but the hair showed a white streak where broken tissue ran beneath. Both dark brows were by now split a dozen times, and the tissue had reformed into a perpetual scowl. His teeth had somehow survived, but the lips were delicate no longer. As for the

Mark said nothing and let his grim half-dream go on: He arrived in New York with barely enough money to keep him for a month. He took a room in a rundown hotel, deciding he would not liquidate the second earring until he could use it as the capital that would reestablish him on the land.

This took some determination, because when his stake was gone he found how hard this big, cold city could be on a man without a trade and without contacts. He was too slight and elegant to compete for laborer jobs with brawny Italian and Irish immigrants, and too unknown and inexperienced to go into a business establishment. He had found work as a waiter in a good restaurant where his accent, bearing and manners made him valuable, but his soul had died inside him and he sought desperately for something else.

Wandering the meanest streets of the eastern waterfront one night, he had followed a drunken, rollicking crowd to his first barge fight.

At first the primitive, blood-spattered spectacle had revolted him. But as the matches wore on he felt the fierce freedom, the wild courage in these gutter warriors. They stood alone, as arrogant, brave and proud as doomed kings. They bore the pain, threw back the taunts and gloried in the cheers with roaring gusto. No agony could have caused them to carry a cup of turtle soup to a contemptuous rich man in a restaurant.

After the last bout, some of the burlier and more inflamed patrons had challenged the winning gladiator, backing themselves against him with their own money. They were hoping either that the exhaustion of the long fight had brought the professional down to their level, or that their own prowess in street brawls made them the match for any man. Whatever their estimation, they were wrong. The veteran, who had gone seventeen punishing rounds a half-hour earlier, returned to demolish a pair of amateur challengers without breaking a hard sweat, taking their money as an easy bonus. Mark saw that this could be his way in.

For some weeks he attended every fight he could, getting to know the battlers, their styles and their stamina. Some would have pulverized him in moments. Others were vulnerable. They smoked big cigars up to the moment the hammer clanged on the bell to begin. They often fought with liquor in them, and the fat poured over their belts. He would start with these weaker foes and work his way upward with experience.

Even so, he barely survived his first bouts. Under the fat was iron, and an inbred fierceness fueled their bodies far beyond what their condition promised.

Still, he won and collected the bets on himself at long odds. And better than that, he stole the imagination of the crowd. In his first brawls he weighed barely a hundred-and-sixty pounds. His English accent and stylish ways, his eyepatch and his dazzling speed were something not seen before on the barges. Always an enormous underdog, he drew the money of the wilder bettors looking for big odds and rewarded them stunningly when he won. These winners talked him up in every bar on the waterfront, and soon patrons were coming to see him in the post-bout fights as much as they were coming to see the main action.

That the rules were few and far between he had learned quickly. Thumbs, elbows and knees were thrown to maim. Headlocks and direct kicks with heavy boots were forbidden and booed, but far from unknown. Short lengths of pipe were discovered in fists. Blood flowed, spurted and splattered, with only the worst wounds closed with black tape after having been rubbed with dirt and spat into to promote healing.

He found that he could punch with surprising power. But so could they, and he evolved techniques for staying far outside the range of their butting, grappling and savagely thrown uppercuts, slicing their faces to ribbons and exhausting them. When they were blinded with blood and rage and charged forward heedlessly, he would strike as he sidestepped, becoming rapidly famous for his ability to dislocate a jaw with a punch that traveled no more than six inches.

Dirtyface Doyle had been only one of the men who had offered to back him. But he had waited for Doyle to ask because he had been told he was the best. Not only did he bet the biggest and share the most, he had the toughest fighters and held them to remarkable standards. They could smoke no more than five cigars and drink no more than a single bottle of whiskey a day, all to be consumed before noon when there was an evening fight. Better yet, he trained his men. He had taken the rear of a popular brothel, the Dream of Heaven, pushed the beds and dividing sheets back during the daytime hours when the establishment stood idle, and fashioned a rough gymnasium. Here he gave drills in bare-knuckle fighting that only a twenty-year veteran of the trade could develop. It was at the Dream of Heaven that the hulking Irishman taught Mark Northern to stay alive.

The name Dirtyface had come to Doyle from the thick, blue stubble that no amount of shaving could scrape off his enormous jaw. The bones of his nose had long ago crumbled and been swallowed, and the cartilage was randomly distributed. Even at sixty he was a great-bellied figure that few would cross. But he was fair in his way and practiced what could easily pass for kindness to some of his old fighters who had lost control of mind and limb.

He had liked Mark from the beginning and hadn't up till now overmatched him with any of the huge assassins who were being brought from out of town to take on the best of the New York barge fighters. The best in the country were a far cry above the best on even a waterfront as predatory as this one.

Mark's drifting mind snapped back to the moment as an icy breath blew in on him.

"Close that damned canvas before I knock you into the river, you steaming pile of shit," barked Bluejacket Dunne at the rouged dandy in the silk hat and evening clothes who had pulled aside the canvas flap.

The man turned to call to someone. "Here it is, Marietta. Here's where they chain their mad dogs now."

Other faces appeared at the flap, dressed as he was and tittering drunkenly. They were very moneyed and completely out of place.

"This one looks like he was harpooned off New Bedford," said one of them, wrinkling his nose at Dunne.

"I thought they sliced off the blubber," said another.

As Dunne prepared to come off his stool after him, the dandy let his coat fall open to show a small silver revolver in his waistband. "I would really enjoy shooting you in the knee."

They turned their attention to Mark. "Ah, that must have been a pretty boy once."

"He has a fine figure, doesn't he? Like the Michelangelo David."

"Too bad the hammer slipped when he was doing the face."

"Look at that marvelous eye. Hatred enough in it for two. There's something attractive in its wildness, I think."

"Will you come home with me after your fight, for fifty dollars? A little blood will be all right."

"I like him and I don't intend to be outbid by the likes of you." This man, larger than the rest but as soft as a pudding, shouldered inside and ran his fingers down Mark's cheek. "I'd like to suck his—"

Without rising, Mark grasped him low in the groin and twisted. As the man went flat on his back screaming, Mark stepped over him and hit the closest face at the flap. Its owner disappeared backward into the night. The carrier of the silver revolver took a second too long in thumbing back the hammer. A knee came up under his wrist as the heel of a hand came down, squirting the weapon into the air. Catching it neatly, Mark placed the muzzle against a wide, terrified eye.

"Now, my good man," Mark said to him evenly, "I am going to make a very careful shot here, because I want you around to share the joys of being a one-eyed man."

"Marietta! *Marietta!*"

"I might change my mind if you would apologize to Bluejacket here, on behalf of your friends."

Those friends, except for the one still writhing on the deck, had disappeared.

"I'm sorry. Truly sorry. Very sorry. Sorry indeed."

The canvas flap drew back again. A woman appeared, who five years earlier must have been the most beautiful in New York. She had the eyes of a hunting cat, sparkling brighter than the broad band of diamonds about her neck, and though she was smiling, there was a twist of cruelty that never left the lips.

"You are soiling one of my favorite toys and making him smell frightful." She sniffed distastefully at the evidence of loosened bowels.

"They soil *us*, madame," Mark said, not lowering the gun. "They have insulted Mister Dunne, and that scum on the floor laid a filthy hand on me."

"He's never been on a farm," she said. "I'm sure he thought it would be all right to stroke the pigs."

Dunne pulled her roughly inside, ending her struggles with the embrace of a thick arm. "That necklace'd make me a lot less sore."

"She'd have the police on you by morning."

"Then mebbe she can pay me another way."

He stooped and swept his free hand under her dress. There was no question about where he was holding her, but she never flinched or even lost her deadly smile.

Without thinking, Mark swung into Dunne's kidney. He bellowed in pain and dropped to one knee, releasing the woman, who made no move to flee. "What the hell—"

"I killed a couple of men for something like that," he said.

There was a touch of surprise in her voice. "Ah, yes. Gentleman Jack. Of course. I've heard about you. And you're every bit the posturing fool I thought you would be."

"What has fallen out of your friend's trouser leg is cleaner than any of you, madame."

She turned to Dunne. "Do you want to earn this necklace, Dunne?"

He almost forgot his rage at Mark. "Who do I have to kill for it?"

"Him," she said with a toss of her head at Mark. "In the fight, of course."

The bull-shouldered man gave a toothless and terrible grin. "No trouble, ma'am. I was fixin' to do that anyways. And I ain't lost in two years. I'll whip him proper."

"That's not enough. I want you to smash him so he'll never be able to stand up again, much less fight. I want that other eye closed for good. Hard men should turn away when they have to look at him. He shouldn't be able to remember his name for the rest of his life. Is that plain to you?" She unhooked the necklace and dangled it in front of the man's eyes. He turned to Mark.

"Grant, I never liked you and your uptown bullshit anyways. Better find yourself a tin cup before we go below. You're gonna be needin' it."

The fallen man struggled to his feet, his face as gray as cinders, quivering with loathing. "Shall we make our bets?"

"Oh, yes," she said. "Everything you're carrying. Put it on the whale."

"The odds aren't good. He's a strong favorite."

"On the whale. And get five thousand on credit. Doyle knows me."

"A pleasure," he said, and followed her out, trying to wipe himself with a scarf.

A prolonged roar from below told Mark that a man had been destroyed. It would be his turn to fight in a few minutes. He had reckoned his best chance against Dunne to be the man's lack of motivation. For a cut of an ordinary night's betting he would fight mightily, but with enough pain, cuts and frustration he would finally lie down to wait for someone easier. With those diamonds before him, he would endure to the death.

Dunne flexed his huge arms as he prepared to leave. "You won't slip away on me now?"

"Not if you had a gun in each hand."

"Haw! She's got your balls."

"Has she?"

"You saw the way she looked at you before you opened your big yawp. She wants you in the straw. You feel it."

"I'd rather be in the straw with you."

"Haw! See you below, Grant. Say hello to Jesus for me."

Dirtyface Doyle intercepted Mark before he started down the ladder into the bowels of the barge. They stood aside as the battered, unconscious hulk that was the loser of the previous bout was hoisted laboriously topside to the jeers of the sporting crowd as they packed in for a closer look.

"Blood of the saints, Jack," said Doyle, "What the hell's going on? It's seven to one against you and the money's pouring in anyhow. It'll break me if you go under."

Mark told him quickly what had happened in the shelter.

Doyle swore savagely. "Slip off the ladder on the way down. Sprain something. A little break'd be better. Two hundred for your trouble."

"They'd hang us up on bale hooks. Now tell me who that witch is?"

"Marietta Van Vuylen. Old family. Knickerbocker Dutch. They owned half the ferries to Jersey. The yellow fever got her people in Philadelphia fifteen years ago. It all came to her. House the size of City Hall. A devil. A bitch. A whore. She's been coming down here off and on for years. Likes blood. Likes pain. Likes fighters, too. Takes them home sometimes. Even the black ones." He spat. "Cunt."

"She's still beautiful. She could have anyone."

"You saw who she was with . . . fuckin' lilacs."

"Let's go."

Bluejacket Dunne had covered his wide expanse of naked torso with whale oil to gain an advantage in the close-in grappling that was one of his favored tactics. Mark expected this would be a mistake. He had no intention of closing with the much heavier man, and the oil would interfere with the cooling of the body, important in the late rounds.

Marietta Van Vuylen and her simpering followers had paid their way to the edge of the platform. They stood watching, insolent and loud. Her eyes remained on Mark, filled not with hate, but something much more disturbing. She waved the necklace and the mob thundered. Dunne winked and waved.

The crowd hardly heard the bell over the tumult. Bluejacket Dunne moved forward, and one of Mark's hopes immediately dissolved. He had expected that the great prize would bring his man out in a series of bulling rushes and wild swings. But the wily giant had not gone undefeated for two years because he was not wise in the ways of the ring. He would move slowly, relentlessly forward, absorbing whatever of the lighter man's blows he had to, not swinging until he could land, because he knew a missed blow cost twice the energy of a hit.

They closed. Dunne plodded forward, his body square to his opponent, the huge, ready fists held in front almost in a line.

Mark shot a hard right hand between the big paws. Dunne's nose split down the center and sent a gout of blood down his chin and into the hair of his chest. The pig eyes hardly blinked. Twice more Mark sent in the best he had and the thick neck absorbed the blows. A bone shifted in his hand on the last swing and sent a fiery twinge of warning. If he broke a hand on that oncoming rock of a brow he was as good as obliterated.

Dunne backed him into a knot of spectators on the platform and landed his first blows. Again Mark was shocked. He blocked every fist on forearms and twisted shoulders, but he had never felt such punches. The man was a pile driver on legs. After each impact Mark felt his arms go numb for a moment, purple swellings appearing in moments. After several rounds of that he would be unable to raise his fists, much less throw them.

From the crowd a hand hooked his elbow for a split second. Dunne lashed at the opening and a sliver of agony went into Mark's side as a lower rib cracked. Mark brought back an elbow and felt the wind go out of someone. A tree fell on his neck as Dunne struck again. Down on one knee, Mark focused just in time to see the thumb coming for his eye. He slipped out of its way only to meet a knee at the temple. The crowd cheered and whistled. The referee snarled. The flaring torches wavered and whirled as Mark went down.

Sitting, he found his face inches from Marietta Van Vuylen's, her cheeks blazing, her lips drawn back over glistening teeth. As the bell sounded, she called him a name he had never before heard in the mouth of a woman.

At that word, something furious and urgent returned his strength and he was able to get to his stool.

"That's one tough bastard, Dirtyface."

"Anything gone?"

"Rib and some of the left hand."

"Go for his shin or his kneecap."

"This is his crowd. They'd default us."

"Then bleed him. But it'll take a lot longer."

"Maybe longer than I can stand up to those sledgehammers."

Through the next nine rounds it took every bit of Mark's speed to avoid the heaviest of Dunne's pulverizing punches. Mark opened up the split nose further, both brows and under both eyes. Also, he had caught Dunne while he had his tongue between his teeth and opened a great wound in it. In addition to adding spectacularly to the flow of gore that now reddened the bigger man to the waist, the tongue swelled and cut into his breathing. But none of it was working.

The vision of the necklace dangling in the hand of Marietta Van Vuylen transferred strength and ferocity. And while Dunne landed only a single blow to every one of Mark's half dozen, those few were doing impressive damage. Mark's stitched brows had opened again and the flowing blood was more of an impediment to his single eye than to Dunne's two. The sailor's knuckles felt as though they were sheathed in iron. Dunne had learned in his years of brawling that bone was as vulnerable as flesh if it were hit hard enough. Seeing that Gentleman Jack's agility made face and body elusive targets, he went to brutally bruising the bones of the arms that were raised to oppose his punches. Repeatedly he struck the elbows from the side and the forearms from below where the muscle did not cover thickly. He blasted between the shoulder and the bicep. Mark felt the snap and precision beginning to seep out of his punches. He was fading faster from his pounding than Dunne was fading from bleeding.

The woman had a fine feeling for pain. She could sense how quickly it was weakening him. He could hear her bloodthirsty screeches above all the other uproar.

When he sagged down onto his stool at the end of the fourteenth round, he knew it was only time before his guard went down and the pressing crowd on the platform prevented him from dancing away from destruction.

"Listen, Dirty. How many more of those torches can you get your hands on?"

"Must be a hundred of them in a bin over there. Why? There's light enough to see you gettin' killed real good, Jack."

"Tell your boys to get as many going as they can. And get the hatches closed."

"You won't be able to breathe down here in a few rounds."

"You've got the point."

By the nineteenth round the temperature in the hold of the jammed-full barge had climbed fifteen degrees, and the air was fouled and gritty with pitch. The spectators, crazed with the whiskey they carried and the blood that spattered the ringsiders, hardly noticed. But to the men in the ring, pushed to the end of their endurance and fighting for each breath, every added degree of heat and every poisoned gasp drew away more strength.

With the thought of the necklace obliterating all else, Bluejacket Dunne knew only that the fires of hell burned more brightly in the hold.

The sweat poured out of Mark until his torso glistened as brightly as Dunne's with all its whale oil. The oil was slowing the cooling perspiration. The sailor could feel himself weakening and tried to finish Mark quickly. An apparition in scarlet, he pressed forward, clubbing with all he had left.

The crowd smelled the end and pressed forward, screaming. The fighters' circle narrowed again and Mark had nowhere to dance away. A fist thrown from the shoulder rammed into an elbow and the arm fell of its own accord. He could see the other fist coming but could not lift a forearm to block it. It caught him on the side of the head above the ear and the world exploded.

He didn't remember getting back to his stool but knew by the sound of the kill-hungry crowd that the fight wasn't over.

"C'mon, Jack. Drink this and pour the rest over your head. You won't be able to get your hat on for a month. Will you be able to stand?"

Mark couldn't quite think of Doyle's name. Everything seemed dim and doubled. "Maybe . . . What about him? . . ."

"His face is redder than the blood and he's stranglin'. Christ, I'm half faintin' myself. But he'll put out all he's got left this round. He smells that little saloon of his."

"... Rib's ready to let go. Can't punch with the bone the way it is ... If I ... don't wear him out now ... it's over. Got to make him go with all he's got left ..."

"If he lands one more—"

"*Got* to stand ground with him ..."

The bell sent them out. It was the twenty-second round.

Some of the spectators had gone down from the heat and bad air by now. The woman had thrown away her hat and torn the lace away from the top of her dress. The sweat ran down in rivulets between her breasts. Her hair was wringing wet and plastered to her cheeks. The chilling smile had grown wilder than ever, and she cursed Mark at the top of her voice.

As it sometimes will with men in close and deadly battle, Mark and Bluejacket Dunne became one driven mind. Each, as though he had been inside the other, knew that this was the last of it. There was no thought, no more maneuver left in either of them. There was only what was left in their wolves' hearts to propel their broken bodies to the end. The dying flames of their strength surged up and they stood brow to brow and hammered.

Dunne had two good arms, but the heat had pulled the bone-crunching power out of them. Mark could only paw with his damaged arm, but the other he fired into the raw, red-streaming flesh in front of him with metronomic fury. White bone showed at the cheeks and forehead.

But the crimson covering his arms was not all Dunne's. His own face was opening to pounding fists.

The screams in the thousand throats around him seemed to be coming out of his own to shrill his agony.

"His *eye!* Get his *eye,*" he heard the woman shouting until her voice broke.

Dunne's thumb hooked out at him. Mark was barely able to duck his forehead and catch the thrust on the bone. The thumb snapped at the base.

It was all instinct now. Mark staggered in a circle away from Dunne's good arm until his huge opponent began to wobble with exhaustion, a matter of moments. Then, with the flaming torches beginning to tilt, and the heat smothering the last of his wind, he aimed a short punch that carried in it all the hatred he felt for the shrieking woman. It landed, and the jaw broke off its hinge.

Bluejacket Dunne dropped face first onto the deck, his demolished face splashing a red circle.

The crowd howled its madness as Doyle ran forward to lead Mark out of the maelstrom that closed around him. If thousands of dollars had been lost, it had been paid for with the joy of being able to tell grandchildren what they had seen this night.

"You just made us rich, Jackie lad," Dunne yelled in his ear.

"Not rich enough," Mark gasped through a thickening fog. "Get me on deck before—"

Marietta Van Vuylen stepped in front of him. He had only seen such a look on maddened barnyard animals. Her white dress was flecked everywhere with the blood that had splashed. Now she pressed herself to his dripping chest.

"Very amusing, Jack Grant."

She pulled his face down to her and kissed his torn lips a moment before he felt himself dropping backward into Doyle's arms.

Mark woke with a low afternoon sun warm on his face. His muddled mind tried to guess in what bed he lay. Neither his threadbare rooms near the Hudson nor Doyle's tenement flat had a window that let in the sunshine at any moment of the day. When he tried to move, the pain that shot through his body everywhere caused him to gasp. He felt bandages on his face and found one arm to be resting in a sling. A vicious headache made him afraid to move his head.

When he began to look around cautiously, his heart skipped in his chest. For a fraction of a moment he thought that the last years had been nothing but a long nightmare and that he was back in Austria in some great house where he had spent the night after a fine day's hunt.

Above the huge bed, whose headboard was exquisitely polished and carved, was a high ceiling into whose plaster had been cast a roistering population of cherubs and garlands. The furniture was massive European antique, and the carpet was of the same Persian magnificence he had known at Himmelberg. Squinting against the sun, he made out through the tall windows a row of marble mansions opposite.

He peered under the covers to check his huge, purpling bruises and found that he was naked. There were men's clothes hanging on a rolling valet on the other side of the room, but they were not his. He would have cried out if he had any idea who it was he should call for.

When he thought he had gathered enough strength, he pushed aside the covers and slid his feet to the floor. As he tried to stand, every punch that Dunne had landed hit him again. He dropped weakly back to the edge of the bed.

There was a small sound outside the heavy, paneled door. The brass handle twisted and Marietta Van Vuylen came in carrying a basin. There were washcloths and towels over her arm. She walked to him and looked him up and down.

"You look like you should be hanging on a butcher's hook."

"Why am I here?"

"They couldn't wake you up on the barge. That filthy man you were with didn't seem to know what to do, and some of the losers wanted to just drop you into the river. After you'd earned me more than seventy thousand dollars, the least I could do was bury you in a nice spot. But my doctor found you were still alive. The place I had picked out in the garden will just have to wait."

He covered his lap with a corner of the blanket. "Are you saying you bet on *me*?"

She removed the blanket. "How could I resist those odds after our sweet little talk?"

"That was a stupid bet."

"Not at all. A furious man always beats a greedy one. Get back into that bed, Jack."

He did so to get away from her staring at his nakedness. "Just as you say . . . Marietta."

"Ah. So you were a little interested."

"Doyle told me some things."

"Then you won't be surprised that I'm here to wash you."

"I can do that myself now."

"Not the way I can."

She set the basin down on a bedside table and dipped the washcloths. "If you please."

Mark had not thought about another woman since he had lost Hannah. It had not yet occurred to him that he might someday want someone else. But now he found himself uncovering himself for this creature who barely tried to hide her madness.

She sat on the side of the bed. The water was warm and her hands were as soft as the satin of the sheets. The cloth moved over his shoulders and down his chest slowly, teasingly.

The sun was lower, blood red now through the window and splashing the walls and the beautiful demon's face. She leaned closer to his belly and washed there.

"So, Jack Grant. You're not as badly hurt as we thought."

After a time she put aside the washcloth and traced the iron slabs of muscle with her fingertips. She appeared contemptuous of Mark's arousal even as she added to it.

"You are ugly," she said. "Grotesque. A trained gorilla. A gargoyle." Then, with her eyes resting on his, she bent and took his penis into her mouth. She didn't play, but went as swiftly as she could in her devouring, pulling out in a dozen explosive seconds what had been dammed in his body. What she had taken in she spat upon his belly before she moved up to cover his lips with hers. When she stood to leave, it was as though this were one of a pile of small bills she had to dispose of as part of a tiresome day. "Stay for a month if you like. Those stitches in your face are the work of the very expensive Doctor Maurice Duplessis, and he's extremely proud of improvements he's made on some of your more hideous scars. He'll be furious if I let you get away before he's finished with you. With that arm, you won't be fighting for a couple of months."

"I wouldn't want to become tiresome."

"Oh, it takes at least *three* months to become tiresome. And I do want to visit you when you have the use of both arms."

Everything inside Mark told him to run from this house, naked if he had to. But he heard himself saying, "That might be nice." He looked to the valet. "Those clothes are not mine by any chance?"

"In fact they are. I had you measured. They're not custom, of course, but good of their kind. There's a card on that table with the name of an excellent tailor. I've written on the back that you're to have what you want. Meanwhile, feel free to use the house as your own."

"I'll be lost wandering around here alone."

"You won't be alone very much. I have a great many friends."

"When will I be with you again?"

"When do you sleep?"

"Between eleven and six."

"I'll see you between eleven and six."

By the time Mark dressed she was gone with the carriage. The house proved as expensive and enormous as he had guessed from the appearance of the bedroom and from what he had seen from the window. Marietta's house sat on the upper reaches of Fifth Avenue and was by no means the least of the marble palaces around it. He met eight different servants as he limped around during the day, and there were rooms for others.

During the afternoon there was a commotion at the front door. After much loud conversation and, finally, shouting, a well-dressed young man in a silk hat was ushered in and escorted upstairs by two large butlers. He was admitted to a room a few doors down from the one Mark had been given, and he emerged soon after carrying several suits and a silver comb and brush set. The clothes had something of the cut of the ones that Mark now wore. The man passed him as he left and looked him over. "Be careful, my friend. She'll take things away from you that you didn't know you owned."

Mark fell quickly in love with the house. It was the work of a wonderful architect, its proportions classic and perfect, its materials impeccable, its appointments in a taste that could not be questioned. The rooms, especially the grand salon with its ornate bandstand, brilliantly polished floors and string of eight magnificent crystal chandeliers, were huge, but so beautifully scaled that the viewer did not feel small or intimidated. But something sat on his spirit.

For the first time he was looking at wealth on the scale that it took to be among the rulers of this new world. Even Himmelberg and Golden Fluss, for all their venerable and handsome design and furnishings, seemed little more than exercises in rural pretension next to this. What chance did he have to generate a scintilla of the cash he needed to establish himself on the land except as the owner of a rent-grubbing hovel or two?

He remembered what the visitor had said, and he thought about it for the best part of a day. If she was one to take, the property and power he saw around him said that she was also one to be taken from.

That she would tire of him quickly, there was no question. He must find a way to stay in her favor, in her presence until he could gain what he needed from her.

Reviewing the cards he held, he found a single ace. It would have to be played boldly and quickly.

He returned to his rooms and retrieved a metal box from a small safe he had bolted to the floor at the back of a closet. From it he took a thick roll of bills and the earring he had taken from Himmelberg.

From an aloof butler he learned the name of Marietta's jeweler, and it was there he took the stone.

The store was a palace in itself, and the way the owner—brought from his imperial office by the mention of the Van Vuylen name—looked at Mark's clothes told Mark he must get to Marietta's tailor quickly.

The examination of the earring was another story. The jeweler's face melted into an astonished smile. He screwed the loupe so deeply into his eye that Mark feared he might destroy the vision. "Extraordinary. Truly extraordinary. There were only two cutters who did work like this. Father and son. And they've been dead sixty years. The stone is perfect, of course. More than perfect. It has the sun and the stars in it. But the cutting. It's immortal. The technique lost. What a pity that the other is gone. What a tragedy. I recommend auction, if selling is what you wish. You would get a fine price—"

"Could you set it into a ring?"

"A *ring*—what a remarkable idea. I don't know. An earring has a shape that may not make a ring. And I wouldn't touch this cutting for a million. But wait... I think it can be done... Hmmm ... Yes... *Yes* ... It can be done *very* handsomely, perhaps." Mark supposed it was the first excitement the man had felt in thirty years. "But the setting must be something incredible, from another universe. You must not stint."

Mark handed him the roll of bills. "Work with that."

"Is Madame Van Vuylen to know?"

"Not until I give it to her. Then she should know from you what she has. So it will get all the care that such a stone and such a setting deserves."

"That might not be necessary. Madame Van Vuylen has quite an eye for jewelry and has looked for work by these cutters. I would be surprised if she didn't recognize it. And, needless to say, I know her taste in a setting very well indeed." He beamed coyly at Mark. "This will win you a heart."

"You are supposing, sir, that there is a heart to begin with. I bid you good day."

While the stone was being prepared, Mark began to know Marietta. She came to him at night, as she had said. It would be evident that she had come from some long debauch. There would be much wine on her breath, although she seldom slurred a word or wandered in thought. Often there would be something else, which turned her light eyes into pools of blackness and caused her to be sometimes indolent, a cat coming to be stroked, and sometimes wild, jittery, a prowling leopard.

She would carry in a candelabra and begin without a word. He slept naked and ready, and she seldom had the patience to fully undress herself before she was onto him. In the bedside table were incenses, unguents, lubrications, devices. She used them with precision, skill and in elaborate sequence.

For all his plans to stay aloof, he soon found that he could not have enough of her. He found himself waiting for her as eagerly as he had once awaited Hannah, although the fires burned in a different place.

From the first he had known that Marietta's appetites consumed many men concurrently. The room on the other side of hers from his own often held someone for the evening. And he heard exactly when it did. For when Marietta reached the peak of her ecstasy, she moaned, she yowled, she cursed and sometimes screamed. The servants, he had learned from a delivery man, were the best paid in the city, and so never heard a thing.

When the cries came in his own bed, they were exciting past anything he could have dreamed. He was a Viking pillager taking a woman as wild as himself. But when she was with the others, he knew how far down she had pulled him. He thought of the dead Hannah and was glad she was not in the world to see what he had become.

Eventually she began to speak to him after she had finished. No matter what time she arrived, no matter how she had punished her body before and afterward, she remained alert, agitated. The day was for sleep behind sealed doors. The night was to feed her endless voracity. She was often as hungry for his talk as she was for his body.

"Take that patch off your eye. I can tell more looking into that horrible void than the good one tells me. And it makes me shiver less. Tell me who did that to you."

"If a woman like you even *knew* about what my life was once, it would be poisoned."

"Was it so wonderful?"

"In some ways."

"Was there a woman who brought more of the devil to your bed?"

"There was a woman."

"Tell me her name so I can spit on it."

"Why? You don't care about me, Marietta."

"I do when you're inside me, in all those dark, wet, stinking places. I do when you're tearing a man with your fists, and you've become a hyena. I do when the blood is running out of you and the pain is taking you places that I can't go."

"Really, I'm touched."

"I'm with you too much. I'm neglecting the other people, Jack. The other pleasures."

"The fights?"

"Yes."

"Your friends with the rouge?"

"Let me take you to bed with them. It's a new taste."

"I think not."

"You'll become tedious soon, Jack. Then I'll turn you out. But I'll try to have word of where you are. So when you become paralyzed and insane with the punches, and you're sleeping under the docks, hauling slops for the river gangs, I can find you with my friends. And then we can laugh and give you a dollar. Soon, Jack. Soon."

It was time for the diamond.

He gave it to her one night after she set down her candelabra and stepped out of her clothes, but before she had touched him.

"Marietta, I like the stitches you had put in my face so much that I thought you should have something as nice."

"What does this celebrate?"

"A kind woman who has promised me a dollar when I'm in need."

She recognized the store from the box and opened it with mild bemusement. The ring hit her as powerfully as he had hit Bluejacket Dunne. Her eyes grew moist with longing, as she removed it and turned it in the light. The jeweler had been right. She knew exactly what she held. "So hard. So cold. I would want my heart to be like this. To never lose its fire." She pulled it onto her finger. "I've filled three drawers with diamonds, always looking for the one that could blind the world and speak to my soul." She pushed him back onto the bed and straddled him. "And now it's been given to me by a man who has the wrath of the devil in his face and who is going to die in the mud and be eaten by river rats."

"I would like to have you prevent that."

She reached down and pressed him into her. "Perhaps I can delay it, Jack."

It was not until after the pink flush of dawn that she had finished with him. For the first time since he'd known her, she slept with her arm about him. But it seemed to him that her skin was a degree or so colder than any he had ever felt.

Mark found himself the center of Marietta Van Vuylen's glittering underworld. He became a sullen pet of a society that he could not have guessed existed. His dangerous manner, his tiger's grace, his spectacularly scarred face, proved irresistible to his new acquaintances.

He knew many of their names from the society pages. But these were the sweepings of the great families. These people rose up like werewolves as the sun set and prowled to places whose depravity they accepted and added to eagerly.

Mark witnessed men in evening dress drawing on opium pipes as young boys drew them to red-painted rooms. He saw women kissing other women with their tongues and selecting black men in harem costumes by genital heft. And always he saw Marietta at the core of it.

As far as he was able, Mark stayed at the edges of this yawning cesspool.

"Come on, Jack. A day in that room and you'll never be the same man again."

"I'm already not the same man."

But he could not stay out of her degeneracies entirely. He had to follow Marietta, gaining her attachment in the only world she knew. He learned her body as a great musician would learn his instrument, and he played it with an immense talent long undiscovered. The day came when she preferred him above all the rest, and it was only he whom she took into the rooms heavy with brocade and sweet smoke, to ingest through the night.

"Let yourself fall, Jack. It's sweet."

But always he held back the last morsel of himself, and her appetite for him sharpened by the day.

If he at first felt guilt for abetting her debauchery, it soon vanished. The demon in her fed upon all that was unclean and unleashed a fearsome energy that gushed out of her.

By the beginning of the summer of 1871, seven months after he had come to Marietta's house, it was taking all his strength to hold himself clear of her strange sorcery. He found himself making love to her with a concentration so fierce that it would be as though he had fallen through the shell of her body and was trapped there fatally.

His wounds had long since healed, but the steel machine that was his physique was beginning to rust. If he was not to be destroyed with her, he had to complete his move.

"I want you to own me, Marietta."

"No one can do that, I've found."

"As a fighter, I mean."

"You'd go back as you were before?"

"No. Bigger. With your money behind me. And the money of your friends. Bring Doyle right here into the house to train me. That barn of a salon would make a fine gymnasium."

"Allow that filthy man into my house? Have professional fighters under this roof?"

Mark drew back a curtain to afford a view of Fifth Avenue and the other mansions. "Think of what they'd say."

She smiled at that. "Whatever it was, it would be marvelous."

"The idea will be to get away from the fifty-cent-a-head fights. Raise the stakes to the sky. Get the word to the best fighters that can be found anywhere. Stay on the barges. But fill them with silk hats. Seventy-five dollars a ticket, finally. With Doyle's help I make the matches."

"What makes you think I need that kind of money?"

"*I* need the money. You need the excitement."

"You'll be killed."

"And what could be more exciting?"

"Well spoken, Jack."

Mark began the next day. He found Dirtyface Doyle and told him the proposition: They would have Marietta's full backing to set the fights. She would pay to bring fighters from wherever they were and board them in New York. And, most important, she would use her connections. She would whisper in the right salons, reach the right journalists, pay the right policemen. She would make Gentleman Jack Grant a million-dollar property, if he lived.

Within three months Dirtyface Doyle, living in an unused maid's room by night and in the gymnasium with Mark by day, had rebuilt the conditioning that had crumbled, adding new layers of muscle and technique.

Restless and ready after his return, Mark demolished his first opponents in the early rounds. Jim Fisk, the millionaire roisterer, won $300,000 betting on him, and some of Marietta's friends did almost as well. The word spread rapidly and Mark went from prince of the barge fighters to king of underground New York.

"Hey, looka me, I'm Gentleman Jack," the little boys in the streets cried as they flailed happily at one another.

"C'mon boys. Delmonico's for a steak, and then we'll let Jack Grant earn us a new carriage," the brokers called across the floor at closing time.

Mark's need to maintain his body enabled to him to escape the worst of Marietta's depredations, but she no longer seemed to mind. She was always on his arm now and the crowds were hypnotized by the ferocious pair. Suddenly Mark was known well past the boundaries of the waterfront. And Marietta was welcomed into the great houses where her parents had once been welcomed. Dinners were given in their honor, and the best young names in New York asked if they might come to watch the great fighter train in Marietta's salon. Indeed, the party of the season was held in that salon, with the equipment still in place and Dirtyface Doyle and several other barge fighters stuffed incongruously into evening wear, present for dangerous color.

The racier young ladies of the ruling class dreamed of an evening with the brutally attractive monarch of the ring.

"Jack Grant can loosen my corset anytime, Cora."

"Have you ever seen anything like that eye? It makes me go limp."

"He's prettiest when he's cut, don't you think?"

For two years, through 1872 and 1873, the fighters got better, the bets got bigger. Always knowing that there would be no more chances to get his stake, and that the capricious Marietta might tire of the game at any time, he was more than ready for whatever they threw at him across the circle. His willingness to maim and be maimed became absolute. When one of his opponents died in the twenty-eighth round from injuries and exhaustion, his fame took yet another bound upward, and the bets upon him became astronomical.

Marietta's cadaverous banker, Hollis Roper, came to all the bouts, often with an expensive prostitute on each arm. His reputation as a man as ruthless in pursuit of a financial killing as Jack Grant was of a killing in the ring brought Mark to him. Mark's share of Marietta's bets, several hundred thousand dollars before long, went straight to Roper for investments, and those investments prospered grandly. Mark spent almost nothing, letting the money grow. When he returned to the land, it would be in the way he had dreamed.

But while he fought less often than in the first days, the fights, against increasingly savage opponents, were infinitely more damaging. Mark worked harder and harder to stay on top, even as his body paid the cost. He tore a muscle in his left shoulder and another in his chest. Fighting too soon afterward, he caused the injuries to heal incorrectly and they sent hot nails into him when he swung thereafter. A kick delivered to his right knee by a falling opponent left him with a painful grating in the joint. It swelled miserably at the end of a long fight, even after hard binding.

But there was more than this to tell Mark that the end of his days as a fighter might not be far off.

The reckless madness displaced by her attention to him was returning to Marietta. Her lovemaking was as wild as ever and still confined to his bed, but there was a new cruelty to it. Her teeth and nails drew blood almost every night, and she invited the same and worse from him. "Pain excites you, too, Jack. That's why you're so good at what you do."

"I can do without it."

"Well, I can't. And you're getting uglier than ever."

Slowly, perhaps taking their cue from Marietta, the society that flocked to the barges began to change. The crowds and bets were larger than ever, but now both were turning against him. Syndicates were formed to back other fighters who drew their own followings. The mob had tired of the old king. Although he was barely thirty-one years old, he seemed to have been enthroned forever. New, tough, relatively unmarked young men began to appear, and when they were doing well the cheers rang for them as they once had for Mark. And when they went down, as they always did, a good part of the spectators turned sullen.

At the beginning of 1874, Dirtyface Doyle came to the gym with a face collapsed in worry. "They've got Ripper McCoy comin' in."

"I heard he wasn't interested in this kind of fighting. I heard he wouldn't leave San Francisco for anything."

"A new syndicate. They're givin' him twenty thousand to show and backing him with seventy-five, with a half share to the fighter."

"It doesn't make sense for the syndicate, Dirty. There's not enough in it for them. He'll be the favorite. The odds will be short. It's more than the money. Who's backing him?"

"I can't tell, Jack. Usually they're blatherin' all over the place about a thing like this. Now everybody's clammed."

"I can't take him. McCoy's a mile out of my class. He's beaten ten men I couldn't touch."

"It'd be stupid to fight him. You'd never be the same."

"Oh, I'll fight him all right."

"Why? You wouldn't be dumb enough to bet."

"Not on myself."

Doyle's face fell. "I didn't think you'd drop for anything."

"I'm not going to drop. I'll only go down when he hammers me down. I'll do my best. My former friends will get their money's worth in blood. And that will be the end of Gentleman Jack Grant."

"Don't. You've got plenty with that banker fella."

"Only half of plenty. I didn't hold up as long as I thought. When's McCoy coming?"

"April, Jack. Only two months."

"Cancel the other fights. Get me as ready for this one as any man can get, and talk it around town how I'm going to dump him. I don't want those odds too short"

Mark had an arrangement with Marietta's banker, Roper, where he was able to borrow against his nonliquid investments for his bets. He cautioned Roper against telling anyone, even Marietta, and bet the full value of his investments. Roper himself, for a cut of the winnings, would get the bets down without any of the hawk-eyed waterfront crowd seeing that Mark was going on McCoy.

Ripper McCoy arrived a week before the fight. He was twenty-four years old and had been fighting for eight years with spectacular success. He worked out at one of the exclusive men's clubs at the invitation of its president, a secret fanatic of the barge fights, and Mark went to watch.

This was no fat, slow-witted Bluejacket Dunne, taking all the blows that could be thrown while he tried to score with his own. Nor was he one more steel-bodied farmer or miner who let rage and hate direct his fists. His face showed damage, but nothing like Mark's. He would have technique in abundance.

He was bigger than Mark, though not by as much as it seemed at first. The difference between them was mainly in the thickness of bone. Ripper McCoy had the framework of a man fifty pounds heavier that he actually was. His wrists were as big around as the upper arms of many lesser men, and the fists below them like shipbuilder's mauls. Everywhere on his body the taut muscles were thick and tightly bound into where the huge bones joined. The sense of strength was overpowering.

By now Mark knew the physical configuration of a quick, deadly puncher. And from the sharp downward slope of Ripper McCoy's shoulders, from the muscle compressed in their comparatively narrow width, and from the circularity of the deltoids above the biceps, he knew this fighter could batter down a brick wall. The blows would come harder than anything Bluejacket Dunne had thrown, and with a speed that the ponderous Dunne never knew existed. To these deadly gifts he added one even more terrible: intelligence. When Mark was pointed out to him he came over and stuck out his hand.

"I heard about you, Jack. Good things. That's why I came. Outside of the money."

"Thank you. I heard about you, too. I was hoping you'd stay away until I was through."

"I couldn't have people thinking that any barge fighter could break up a real professional. Especially me."

"Of course."

"You're going to be surprised."

"I expected that, McCoy."

"I can't let up, no matter how bad you're hurt."

"Look for the same from me."

"You've got sand, Grant. Listen. Watch out for yourself. Sometimes all the punches don't come from in front of you."

McCoy nodded and returned to his training, leaving Mark to puzzle at those last words. He decided to see to it that Doyle had men placed around the platform to prevent sneak attacks from the pressing crowd.

Admission had gone to $125. And if the staid burghers of the city knew nothing of what was happening on the waterfront on this night, the "sporting crowd" knew little else.

The crush was intense, with the pier alongside the barge an impenetrable jam of bookies, spectators and fine carriages discharging the gentry from uptown and the grifters of city government from downtown.

Marietta was there early with the lowest of her friends. A special box had been built for them at ringside to hold away the crowding. They were already drunk and the center of the uptown contingent that swirled about them handing around bottles and cigars.

The rouged men, who had not been much in evidence over the past two years, had returned in a state of highest glee.

"Florian, I have a wonderful rug to sell you after the fight."

"What sort of rug?"

"It's a genuine Jack Grant, complete with eyepatch."

"From what I hear, darling, that's going to be just a bunch of small scatter carpets."

Already in his black tights and stripped to the waist, his hands soaking in brine to toughen the skin over the knuckles, Mark waited alone in the foredeck shelter. Ripper McCoy was being prepared in a huge and sumptuous carriage on the pier. It belonged to the owner of the city's largest piano factory, a man who at one time had vied to be in the shelter to loosen Mark's back muscles with his own hands. That didn't disturb Mark. The continued absence of Dirtyface Doyle did. He had not seen his big-bellied handler since the middle of the previous afternoon.

Ordinarily Doyle would have been with him every instant of the last day, reassuring, checking arrangements and working out last bits of tactics. But now he was gone without a word. A great, grim aloneness began to settle on Mark. He tried to fix his mind on the fact that this would be the last time he would have to face this dehumanizing butchery.

Doctor Duplessis, the portly, muttonchopped physician who had nursed him back to health for Marietta, dropped by. "I hate to see all that good work come undone, Jack."

"You'd better not let her see you talking to me, Doctor. Things are changing."

"I won't touch her anymore. There are things that turn a doctor's stomach. Where's your man?"

"Only God knows."

"You have no one behind you?"

"Not that I know of."

"I have my bag along. It would be an honor to help you."

"Many thanks, Doctor."

Duplessis was hardly gone when the flap of the shelter opened again.

"Look what I found, Grant." It was Hollis Roper, the banker. He pulled Dirtyface Doyle through the opening. "He was wandering around on South Street. I thought you might like to talk to him. Enjoy the fight."

Roper gave the rumpled, fog-eyed drunk a push forward and was gone.

"Good God, Dirty, what happened?"

Doyle's reddened eyes couldn't meet Mark's. His standard genial roar was hardly a whisper. "Jesus, Jack, I don't know how to tell it to you."

"What? Come on. We've only got five minutes."

"She got me. First with the whiskey, then—"

"*Who* got you?"

"That devil in skirts."

"Marietta?"

Doyle nodded miserably. "She had me up in her bed most of the day yesterday. And last night. I've been in some pretty bad houses on Water Street, but I've never been with anything like that."

Mark gave a short, hard laugh. "You mean you were in the room right next to mine all that time. And I thought she was leaving me alone to save my strength."

"I'm real sorry, Jack. I couldn't stand up to her. I know you two—"

"What whores we're with shouldn't concern either of us, Dirty. Forget it and let's get ready." He knew Doyle could see how much it bothered him and how little he had expected it to.

"There's something else, Jack." Doyle could hardly speak. "There's the bets."

Mark went rigid. "Roper got them down, didn't he?" "

"Yeah. But not on McCoy. The money's all on you."

Mark grabbed him by the beard and pulled his face down to his. "Who told you?"

"She did. She was in it with Roper."

"Why? *Why* did she do it?"

"For the same reason she slept with a bag of shit like me. To grind your face in the dirt while she said good-bye."

Mark tried not to let the huge emptiness in him show. "No matter."

"No *matter?* You'll lose everything you bled for."

"If he beats me, I won't be alive to mourn it. Goodbye, Dirty. I don't want you with me."

McCoy came out of his corner with grace and deliberation. The pandemonium of the crowd might have been taking place on another planet for all it disturbed his concentration. He established quickly that he was not a toe-fighter who stood at the mark, and took his chances with strength, hand speed and a rock chin. He circled and feinted, patient and deadly.

Mark tried his best move, a combination of blows delivered with more speed than strength, with the purpose of separating the opponent's upraised fists. It worked and Mark's uppercut landed full force on McCoy's chin. A trickle of red appeared at the corner of his mouth, but the great column of his neck absorbed the impact almost completely and the eyes remained clear and hunting. The very next time Mark tried the move it didn't work. McCoy had taken the previous blow into his instincts and was now impervious to the technique.

After a series of light blows, McCoy seemed satisfied that he had divined Mark's basic maneuvers. In short order his own blows begin to land.

If the fists of Bluejacket Dunne had been sledgehammers, Mark thought, those of Ripper McCoy were rapiers. They came slicing in through openings created with a blurring series of feints and landed with exquisitely concentrated impact. If McCoy didn't make the bone itself crumble, as Dunne had, he found the precise spots where a nerve center could be crippled or the arch of a cheek collapsed.

Using all the speed he could muster, Mark kept the other fists just a half-inch off center. But he knew they would begin to find their targets when he started to tire in the face of his younger, beautifully conditioned opponent.

By the fifth round Mark found he could hardly land a punch. McCoy read his every preparation to swing in an eyeblink and slipped the blow with a move of his head almost too subtle to be seen.

Marietta shouted to Mark from her box. "Come to the back door after our parties. You can dance for scraps, darling."

Her friends took it up. "Fifty cents a night to keep me warm, Gentleman Jack."

"If you'll put a bag over that awful face."

Halfway through the thirteenth round, the exhaustion caused by the many missed punches began to have its effect. McCoy sensed the dropping of Mark's guard by perhaps a half-inch and began to unleash his blows straight from the shoulder, their impact doubled, their speed blinding. The image of a rapier cutting him apart flickered through Mark's mind again, followed by a simple, desperate notion.

He emptied his mind of the ring strategies that had failed to serve him, and he became the formidable fencer he had once been. He abandoned the upright, square-to-the-opponent stance that had been the staple of prizefighting since its first days. He turned his body sideways to McCoy, catching its weight on bent, springing legs, the front one coiled to thrust or retreat, the rear one maintaining balance with small, sliding steps while poised for explosive thrusts forward. Now his right hand became his weapon, sliding into openings, driven by the legs and torso as well as the extending muscles of the arm. The tactic stalled the attack of Ripper McCoy until the end of the round, his adjustments failing to thwart it.

Doctor Duplessis' coat and vest were soaked through as he worked on Mark, stitching and sponging. The face and torso were again a gory slaughterhouse. "I think you can hold him off that way."

"For a while. But I can't hurt him. The right hand can only jab. No power. That's something I didn't have to worry about with a foil."

"Can you make any other adjustment?"

"I'm going to have to," he said as he answered the gong.

It came to him quickly. The fencer's stance, torso turned, right hand forward, left held back, presented a great coiled spring. At the next opening produced by his lightning maneuvering, he spun his torso around the axis of his spine and propelled the left fist with the entire force of the turning shoulder behind it. For the first time in the fight McCoy stumbled backward and a film crossed his eyes. The fight-wise crowd did not miss the change and almost split the planking with their roars. Twice more in the round Mark jolted the younger fighter, filling the air with flying sweat and blood. He was now holding his own, but he was terribly afraid his strength would not hold out long enough.

"I can jolt him, but I can't put any combinations together," he said to Duplessis between rounds. "Even though I'm hitting him harder, I can't follow up to finish him. He's too good. He'll outlast me."

"How much have you got left?"

"Seven, eight rounds, maybe."

"Coming low out of that stance, Jack, can you take him in the chest?" There was a sudden edge of excitement in the doctor's voice.

"The chest. Yes. But why—?"

"Because that's where the heart is, Jack. I had a workman brought in last week. A brute. A crank flew loose on a winch he was winding, and the flat of it took him across the chest. Not a bone broken. Not even much of a bruise. But he died on me. I opened him up before they hauled him to the morgue. His heart was where the bruises were. It's just like any other muscle. Pound it enough and it functions less and less well, and finally quits."

"I'm sure as hell not getting anyplace with his chin."

"Patience now. Three inches above the tip of the breastbone."

The crowd didn't like it at all. As far as they were concerned, any blow that didn't land somewhere on the head had been misdirected. After all, it couldn't make you bleed or knock you unconscious, and was as exciting as watching a baby being spanked. They sensed McCoy's frustration and bafflement.

"Send him back to dancing school, Ripper."

"He's no woman, Grant. Stop going after his tits."

There were boos after two rounds, and McCoy showed signs of losing his professional patience. Having lowered his hands to defend against the low-flying smashes, his own attack was faltering. He realized Mark was weakening faster than he was, but he had brought his reputation from San Francisco. How would it look if a common barge fighter, almost ten years older, had to be finally beaten by exhaustion? Mark could tell the moment that McCoy decided to accept the painful but apparently harmless pounding to his chest in exchange for a chance at a knockout.

An exchange of thunderbolts began, Mark hoping that the crushing fists exploding upon him in blood would be just enough off center to enable him to complete his own vicious tattoo above the breastbone.

Time after time he pivoted his shoulder with all the twisting fury of the muscles in his back, driving his knuckles into what seemed ironclad muscle and bone. The badly healed muscle above the bicep stabbed its pain through him without mercy, and his torn-up knee swelled, throbbing beneath its bandage. His eye was all but closed, and all of Doctor Duplessis' work was unable to do more than slightly slow the flow of blood into it. More of McCoy's jolts landed as he failed to pick them up. Only the fact that the chest before him was a large and undefended target enabled him to fight on. Four rounds later, he was wobbling to his stool.

"It's not . . . working . . . Doctor . . ." He could barely find the breath to speak.

The words were not out of his mouth before McCoy teetered sideways on his own stool and fell to the deck, supporting himself on one elbow. His startled handlers lifted him back and began dousing quickly with buckets. McCoy managed a sick smile and waved weakly to the crowd, most of whom had missed the moment.

"The hell it's not working. If your eye was functioning a little better you could see the man is positively blue. You're damaging his circulation. Badly."

"He's damaging more than that on me."

Duplessis hesitated before he spoke. "Would you take a chance on killing him?"

"*Killing* him?"

"He's leaving his throat open to you. One good blow there, with his breath almost gone as it is, and he'll be through fighting. But he could die."

"How?"

"There's a little bone in the throat that the right kind of pressure can break. The tongue can fall back into the windpipe, and you've got a dead man in an hour or less."

"God. No other way?"

"Not as quick, Jack."

The gong sounded.

"My life is bet on this," Mark breathed. "It will have to be the same for him."

McCoy was fighting on nerve and instinct, but in a man like him that was still a formidable partnership. A crushing jolt to Mark's temple told him that a single misstep could still stretch him out. He went back to pounding the heart.

The center of Ripper McCoy's chest was one spreading, purple bruise, and it was for here that Mark still saved his hardest punches. But he was watching for an opening low in the blocking forearms. It didn't have to be wide enough to allow a sweep to the chin. All he wanted was the throat.

Mark's legs had lost whatever spring they had, and his arms screamed to be allowed to fall. Thirty-one years made a young man at a desk, but it made an old man in the barges. He didn't know which swing would be his last. But McCoy was going almost as quickly. His whole body had gone gray in the torchlight. His desperate attempts to draw another breath could be heard above the din.

The realization that the fight Ripper McCoy should have won ten rounds ago now hung in the balance changed the tone of the roaring. Bets were momentarily forgotten. The mob swung back to the man from their own waterfront.

"Send him back to Frisco in a box, Jackie boy."

McCoy had become a stationary target. Mark slid in and out of range, giving no openings, sending all he had left into the swelling bruise that now spread from shoulder to shoulder on his opponent.

He ducked away to wipe blood out of his eye, and when he focused again, McCoy's elbows gaped wide. As Mark coiled to unleash the bleeding rock of his fist, he saw the head above him loll back in exhaustion. The stretched throat was there, motionless and undefended, its veins pounding with blood. McCoy's eyes, dimming gray lights in his streaming face, caught Mark's and flashed their pain and hate and understanding.

The finishing blow never landed. Something long forgotten in Mark swung it wide, and he finished clumsily.

Like a reptile whose teeth slash instinctively even after the head is severed, McCoy caught him on the angle of the jaw with a lashing left fist. A blazing light grew and spun in Mark's head. He ducked and covered, stumbling sideways, fighting the jelly in his knees. His eye opened to watch McCoy's culminating onslaught, but the San Franciscan still stood where he was, his chest heaving in horrible, strangling wheezes.

Mark got to him. The hit he aimed at the blurred features would not have staggered a child, but it seemed to break the last slender wire of will that held Ripper McCoy together. He didn't merely melt downward. The agony in his body gathered in a last spasm that lifted him and threw him to the bloody deck with convulsive force.

There was no need to bother with a count.

The interior of the barge became a world of men gone mad. They tried to hoist Mark on their shoulders, but he used the last of his rage to fight and curse them off. Duplessis came to lead him away. "You're coming back to my office. If this is the face you're going to take out into the world, we've got to put it together so it won't stampede the horses."

On their way to the ladder leading back to the deck, surrounded by the laughing, cheering people who had been calling for his maiming an hour ago, they found themselves confronting Marietta. Mark had only seen the look she now wore during their most depraved lovemaking.

"Come. Come home. We'll do very special things."

"Move away."

"The sunshine of Rome is a good place for us to heal you."

"I'd sooner be in hell."

She stepped forward and tried to kiss him. He slapped her so hard that she almost fell. She smiled and tried again, and he hit her again, this time knocking her into the arms of one of her followers. She would have kept coming, but the man held onto her. Her fixed grin was terrible.

"I have something for you, Jack. Something awfully interesting."

He pulled himself up the ladder, a lost soul fleeing Satan's darkness.

Mark did not heal quickly. The surgery performed by Doctor Duplessis stretched over several months. At the end of it the face, while far from pretty, had taken on a strong and rugged symmetry at least. The pulling and puckering had been taken out of the scars and the worst clusters of ruined tissue excised. Even the nose, after some clever work with what remained of the bone, regained a touch of good looks. But his appearance was even further removed from the features he had brought from Austria.

"Your mother wouldn't know you, Jack," Duplessis said. "But at least she wouldn't scream and faint."

The bookies had to struggle to pay him his enormous winnings, but pay him they did. If Gentleman Jack Grant had not been given every cent due him, their reputations would have been forever destroyed. He at last had the money to begin to build his dreams.

He took fine rooms in Chelsea and opened accounts at the best men's stores. A handsome carriage and team were bought and sheltered in a nearby mews. Rigorously avoiding anything and anyone he had known from Marietta or his days on the waterfront, he became every inch the gentleman his fine manners bespoke.

When it came time to contemplate returning to his rightful name, he found he could not do it. The agony he had known as Jack Grant had pounded the new identity into his bones. It would do very nicely in his new life, he decided.

One thing he had found, Americans preferred doing business with Americans. He worked on changing his speech. His musically trained ear was excellent, and he quickly picked up the rhythms and inflections of American English, salting in local colloquialisms and dropping those he had brought with him.

Mark had not been idle in the pursuit of his dreams over the past two years or during his convalescence. He had carefully scouted the properties for which he wished to begin to negotiate. He had taken much care not to reveal his interest to the owners, doing his investigating in the most clever and inferential ways. There was no way he could have all of what he coveted, of course. Not at once. But he was confident that there were not a dozen properties in the city better placed to appreciate than the ones he had on the list that never left his pocket.

Near the summer of 1875, when his face and spirit were sufficiently healed for him to begin to show himself in public, he hopped aboard the first electric streetcar in New York City and looked toward his first purchases.

He suffered some disappointments.

The two properties he had explored most diligently, and for which he held the highest hopes, had already been picked off by a buyer as perceptive as he and a bit quicker.

"It's a Mrs. Oakhill," one of the previous owners told him. "From downtown. Been nosing around here for years. Finally came up with something besides a lot of questions. About a month ago. Pretty smart for a woman. And tough. Got plans about a thousand times bigger'n she is."

"Thank you," Mark said, hiding his annoyance. "I guess one has to move a bit faster if he is to be there in front of the Oakhills of this world."

"Damned good looking, she is, too, Mr. Grant."

"That is of very little interest to me, sir. Good afternoon."

Chapter 6

THE HEAT waves vibrated off the littered sidewalks, and Hannah's dread increased. The ancient tenement loomed six stories above her, the grime of fifty years lying in black layers upon its crumbling bricks. Pieces of sill and cornice had fallen from the sagging upper reaches, much of the debris still lying below where it had fallen years before.

A Polish family was being evicted, the mother moaning with her children, the father screaming at the landlord's men in the old language. Furniture blocked the steps, so Hannah went through the mangled iron gate that lead down to the basement, from which she could gain the stairs from inside.

Only yards away, begrimed, emaciated men and women lined the walls, asleep, drunk, unconscious and perhaps dead. Sweepings of the street, they were allowed these unlovely quarters for five cents a night, although they often lay through the daylight hours, too.

As she climbed upward on the trembling stairs, the heat grew relentlessly. She could have wrung out her underclothing, she was certain. Almost as shocking as the building itself was the brutal crowding that swirled around her. She knew these old buildings well enough from plans she had studied, although she had never had occasion to enter one. They were endless in length, perhaps two hundred and fifty feet long, and only twenty feet wide. The six awful floors might hold over a hundred families, as many as six hundred people crammed into the structure. A racing, shrieking ant colony of children swarmed by her, flowing past patiently climbing peddlers and mothers crushed with their burden of offspring. "One in the hand, one on the arm, one in the belly" was a saying of the streets, and it was precisely accurate.

Squeezing past several rag-stuffed fruit boxes containing naked, sleeping infants, Hannah came to a door upon which the name *Hanratty* had been lettered neatly on a shirt cardboard. She drew a deep breath of the fetid air and knocked.

Moira Hanratty opened the door. Hannah recoiled when she saw what this decaying hell had done to her. The blooming cheeks, robust frame and laughing eyes of the woman on the *Dortmund* were gone. The sallow wraith before her had the habitual squint of longtime miners once seen in Alsace. A look into the flat behind her told why. Without a window anywhere, the lamps burned dimly all day, their choking emanations hanging sulfurously in the unmoving air. It would not have been possible to read in the present gloom, Hannah estimated.

"Miss Hannah, you shouldn't be here. No decent person should." She embraced Hannah quickly. There were rosary beads wound through her fingers.

"Can I come in, Moira?"

The Irishwoman's cheeks reddened against the paleness. "I'd as soon invite a friend into a hogsty," Moira said as she stood aside.

Even in the near darkness Hannah could see that the place was as immaculate as scrubbing and picking up could make it. But the peeling green paint and cracked, crumbling plaster were past the powers of any housekeeper.

Several post were boiling on an iron coalstove, raising the heat to a level still more unbearable. Only the four smallest children, the ones too small to be entrusted alone to the streets or even to the older children, were present in the inferno. They lay panting and unmoving on a sweat-drenched mattress in the corner.

"How did you ever find us in this snake's nest of a city?"

"Your Katie married a friend of mine. Frank Chumlin."

Moira brightened a bit. "Ah, yes. A sweet man, that. But he's after movin' his mouth too much. What's he been sayin'?"

Hannah could see that Moira's pride might get in the way of this mission, but she had to confront it. "He said that Patrick's been killing himself working three miserable jobs eighteen hours a day to keep the family together."

"Hanratty's not afraid of a bit of work."

"Where is he, Moira? I have to find him."

"He has the flux for the five days past. It makes him too weak for the work. He's stuck to the bed, the Saints help him."

"May I go in? Please."

Where there was this sort of heat, no ventilation, only a trickle of water and bowel sickness, there had to be the sort of smell that choked the room in which Patrick lay. Hannah picked her way through the half-dozen disintegrating mattresses that filled the floor until she stood above where he sprawled with closed eyes.

Shock swept through her. The burly Irishman seemed half the size of when she had seen him last. Only the drenching sweat told her that this was not some corpse shrinking with decay.

"Patrick . . . Patrick, it's Hannah . . . from the ship."

The sunken eyes opened slowly. By some superhuman effort the apparition on the mattress worked up the old grin and even managed a parody of his old cheerful bellow. "Bedad, look how fine you are, standin' there in the clothes of a duchess." With a huge effort he pushed himself into a sitting position with his arms and supported himself by leaning against the wall. His eyes went ashamedly to the slop jar covered with newspapers and flies. "Jesus, what a place to be seein' you. Kate's bucko, Frankie, tells me you been doin' real good."

She knelt by him and wiped his face with a handkerchief. The horror on her face was plain. "Good enough to need a man I can trust. Remember how you talked about how the same amount of scrabbling that would raise up ten pounds of potatoes in Kerry would raise up a five-story building in New York? Well, I found out you were right. I'm doing it. I'm learning how. Come learn with me. I'll pay you what you need."

"That's your soft heart talkin', Miss Hannah. I'm just a thick-skull and a strong back. And the back is flat on a mattress now."

"Why didn't you let me know how bad things were? Why didn't you let Frank tell me before now?"

"What could anybody do for us when we have to live in the likes of this? Moira's fingers are bloody twistin' them rosary beads all day. Listen . . . listen, Miss Hannah. You can hear the death right through the walls."

He was right. Hannah heard a ceaseless staccato of coughing and hawking rattle through the thin plaster. "Consumption," she said, shuddering.

"Filthy, no sun, bad air, jammed on top of one another like fleas on a dog. It goes from chest to chest like the lightning. And that's without the typhoid and the diphtheria. They carry 'em out of here most every day. 'Specially the kids. Half the people love 'em until they smother 'em, the other half ignore 'em so they won't grieve so much when they go."

"Yours?" Hannah asked fearfully.

His feverish eyes closed with shame. "None yet. Because we started shuttin' our eyes when the big ones came home with the milk and vegetables they stole to keep us strong enough to live another day with clean lungs. I know it ain't right, Miss Hannah. But it ain't right either that a man in a golden land has to live in places like this. And I know this ain't the worst."

"Patrick, we're getting you out of here. And quickly."

"What are you talkin' about? I can't get the rent here, down as I am, even with what the kids can find and what Moira has with her washin'. There's just too many of us to feed and cover. It'd be no better anywhere else."

"You're coming to the Golden River. It's not a place for children, but you won't be there for long, I promise you. There are rooms upstairs I've been using for other things. We can fix up a kitchen and a water closet."

Patrick shook his head with what vigor he could muster. "No, with thanks. I can't be acceptin'—"

"Yes . . . yes, we'll go." It was Moira, glaring at him with round fierce eyes. She clutched a half-conscious baby, who cried weakly in her arms. "If your damned-to-hell pride will let the children die, mine won't. I love you, God knows, Patrick, and I promised before God to obey you. But I'll leave you there for the flies if that's what it takes to save my kids."

Sliding again to the mattress, Patrick Hanratty stifled a sob and then managed to nod.

"I'll send a wagon by tomorrow," Hannah said. "I'll have a doctor here today."

As Hannah hurried away down the suffocating corridor, she understood that what she had seen and learned in this sad place would stand with her as long as she lived. The greatness that lay hidden in even the meanest people could never shine out while they were sheltered in places that slew the soul. Alone among the creatures of God on the land, man, without fur, scale or feather, cannot huddle, burrow or perch. His body and spirit perish without the proper home in which to raise and love his family, in which to restore his body and accumulate his wealth and learning.

Whatever else those who build upon the land might do, she thought, they must never forget that even the greatest building is there for the uplifting of individual men.

She realized, too, that the power to shape the walls between which a nation lived and worked was the power to shape that nation itself.

The Golden River had proved as bounteous as its name from the moment of its opening. The section that ran up the greatest profits had nothing to do with what went on at the bar or in the endless galleries above. At a rear corner were the four-room offices of Oakhill Development.

Determined from the first that the Golden River was to be no more than a supplier of flowing cash for real estate acquisitions, she had built the offices into the original plans. In addition to her own office, there was a design room where four architects worked at drawing tables, a communications room where teams of runners and lawyers kept reins on properties purchased or sought, and an accounting office to keep the money marching to its best uses.

While she had not hesitated to seek advice, she found that her instincts for the business had usually brought her to the same place as the experts, with notable improvements.

Her basic method of operation had at first upset her excitable little lawyer, Ezra Brogan. "Mrs. Oakhill, you simply must not sell properties so quickly. Why get rid of something for eight thousand dollars when people on the inside know it will be worth twelve-thousand in two years?"

"Because, Mr. Brogan, I can use that eight thousand to buy eighty lots uptown that will be worth eighty thousand dollars in the same time."

"That land will be wilderness until the twenty-first century."

"There are beginning to be some smart people who don't agree with you, sir."

"No one respectable, madame."

"Mr. Jack Grant might not be respectable, but he has more foresight and courage than anybody else I've seen buying land."

Brogan smirked. "I heard he was buying mud, among other things."

"Tidal land is something I mean to acquire myself. He's just beaten me to it."

"Getting in your way is he, Mrs. Oakhill?"

"Just as I have gotten in his way now and again, Mr. Brogan."

Hector Augustine was the youngest of her architects. He was a bushy browed Argentinian of great flair, within whom none of the old prejudices had a chance to harden. To him she had given the assignment of designing the prototype of a new tenement, one that would establish the model for all future tenements.

At length he had unrolled his drawing before Hannah, and she saw his main idea at once: When placed against a similar building, the new building added an appreciable space between walls for windows and cross ventilation. The unworkable length of the old design had been cut way back, allowing two structures per plot, with back windows to let in still more air and light. Also, the stairway pattern had been changed to open a clear shaft from the first floor to the roof. The rising heat was sucked away by rooftop ventilators of ingenious wind-driven design, and skylights filtered illumination down into all the previously black interior corridors. The water closets were moved from the basement to each floor, ending one of the oldest horrors of tenement living.

"Mr. Augustine," Hannah said, "a lot of people who will never know your name will owe their lives to these lines of ink."

Patrick recovered quickly at the Golden River and helped to build the rooms where his family would live. He learned with prodigious energy, was a tough, commanding presence with ready fists, and was quickly raised to foreman on subsequent projects.

Partly because she mistrusted the ability of the public schools to deliver the kind of education she wanted for Victor, and partly because she felt the guilt of not being able to love him without the shadow of his ghastly origin moving over her heart, she decided to educate him at home where she could be close to him. And since home and office were one, most of Victor's early schooling was given in the confines of Oakhill Development. It was an education that would benefit him for a lifetime.

The unseen but ever-busy Jack Grant began to gain more of Hannah's grudging and annoyed admiration. He had formed a company with the grandiose name of Grant Majestic and had brought something new to the commerce of buildings in the city. With him the cut-and-dried business of acquiring, constructing and selling was not enough. He seemed at times to be more salesman than builder.

A casual reader of the newspapers that flooded New York would have supposed that Grant Majestic was about to depose the Astors as the leading power in city land. Story after story reeled off the golden promise of this or that modest Grant property as the only place to live, do business or prosper in the future, giving many assurances that only the rich or famous would be permitted inside the walls.

Brogan laughed as Hannah showed him one of the more lurid pieces. "It's well known that he has set aside a good sum of money for each of his properties. This he considers a cost as necessary as the upkeep of a roof. He distributes the cash to the most unscrupulous of the newspaper writers, along with a page or so of what he would like to read. Except as an exercise in conceit, I fail to see any good purpose."

"Well, I do. Mr. Grant senses that a reputation comes too slowly to a man or to a building project if he waits for merit to assert itself unaided. He helps things along. And I'll bet he moves properties more quickly and at better prices than we do."

"He's had considerable success in a short time. I daresay a lot more people know the name Grant than the name Oakhill," Brogan said grudgingly.

"Let's give him a faster horse to chase. Find out who he pays and give them more. Twice as much if they skip his pieces. I'll write our material myself. And have somebody keep an eye on him. I like the way he chooses parcels to buy. No reason we can't have some help beating him to the table."

She was smug about this last action until one day she realized that the same portly gentleman wearing the same green-checked suit had been loitering across from the Golden River for weeks. He had been following her wherever she pursued a deal. Jack Grant was ahead of her again.

The dealings of the two antagonists were a spit in the ocean of New York real estate, but so imaginative and spirited was their rivalry and self-promotion that they became known well past what their size might have predicted.

When Grant hired Negroes with double-width advertising signs to walk where his prospects where thickest, Hannah bought space on the delivery wagons of the city's biggest breweries. When he took to meeting the better class of immigrant ships with transportation to his rental properties, she took to meeting them with a ride and a free lunch. Her offer to name a new building after the principal tenant was matched by his promise to name it and subtract the first month's rent.

Times were good and the banks bet on energy and innovation freely. The two were stretched to the limit, but their bets kept paying off for themselves and their lenders.

Several times Hannah went to affairs where she had heard Jack Grant would be present, but always he had just gone or canceled late. So after many months she had still never set eyes on her rival, whom she had heard was a New York river ruffian for all his put-on airs, and a spectacularly ugly one at that. But her concerns with Grant were pushed aside abruptly one evening late in the year.

Hours after the Golden River had closed, Benedetto Serpa came to her in her office. The pale mantle of an early snow was melting on his shoulders and the hat he held in his hands. She had not seen him alone since she had left his house after the arrival of his family.

"Signora Oakhill, again I put myself in your hands."

"Just tell me what you want and consider it done. Please come in."

"Bartolomeo Abruzzi has sworn to have my life. He has become insane in his hatred and his methods. I do not wish my family to stay with me, nor with any man connected to Sicily. The loyalties are too tangled to trust. You are the only one I can turn to."

She could see his hunger for her had not changed. Mrs. Serpa appeared in the doorway behind him. Her feelings had not changed either, the jealousy pouring out of her eyes. The three children, looking sleepy and hastily dressed, clung to her skirts. "You wish me to shelter your family, Mr. Serpa?"

"Yes. You have enough rooms to keep them comfortably, and others for my men who will watch. High up in the third galleria would be good. Two long flights of stairs to come up, all in open view. The same for the stairs outside. I will pay you well for what you lose on the space."

"You know perfectly well that's not necessary. I'll take them up now. I'll take care of the food and anything else they need."

"It will be weeks perhaps."

"That's all right. I'll have the rooms cleaned out and furnished properly in the morning."

He smiled and took her hand in both of his. Mrs. Serpa spoke angrily in her own tongue at this, but he turned and silenced her with two guttural words.

"Tell her she can trust me as much as you can, Mr. Serpa."

Hannah installed Serpa's family in the rooms adjoining hers.

Once a day, if the weather was fair, the refugees were taken for a walk at an unpredictable hour. This was the only occasion when Hannah saw Mrs. Serpa, and the Sicilian woman pointedly never spoke to her or looked at her.

On one night a week Benedetto Serpa came to the Golden River to visit. Through the wall Hannah would hear the happy shouts of the children as they played with their father, and much later on when it was very quiet she imagined she could hear the squeaking of the brass bed next door as he fulfilled his conjugal duties. It did not hurt her, but she remembered their night together. He would leave in the morning before first light.

During one of these exits, a man with a rifle was seized on the wharf opposite. After that there were Serpa people in the rigging of the ships when he visited.

Another problem crept into Hannah's affairs. The lawyer Ezra Brogan left the city and his family without notice. His wife was terribly upset, unable to guess his whereabouts. The police were oriented to street crime, not extensive investigations of vanished middle-age men. A constable confided to Hannah that most such disappearances could be traced to involvement with a woman, and when the men did not return they were often not only safe, but happy. This position seemed verified when Mrs. Brogan received a substantial sum of money in the mail, with no message but certainly from her conscience-stricken wandering husband. There was further reassurance in the appearance of a lean, clear-eyed young Irishman named Dennis Lawson, who parted his fair hair straight down the middle. He presented to Hannah his card as a practicing attorney and announced he had been sent by Brogan.

"Mr. Brogan, who was known to me through professional associations, came to me a week ago and suggested that his good client, Oakhill Development, would be needing a new lawyer very shortly. He was good enough to think that I would make a reliable replacement for him."

"Based on what?"

"On my experience in real estate transactions, my excellent references from the school of law at Yale University and the recommendation of colleagues who will cheerfully provide what further assurance you wish in writing."

Lawson had not the first idea of what had befallen Ezra Brogan.

"With several negotiations coming to a boil," Hannah said, "I'll be glad to take you on a trial basis."

In a short time he proved himself to be every bit as capable as Brogan was said to have thought, and as convivial and cheerful a companion as a man engaged in serious business could be.

They worked at first in her office during daytime business hours. But the constant stream of interruptions eventually shifted their contact to early evenings and, inevitably, late evenings. They worked well together and eventually were able to accomplish their work with efficiency while they chatted animatedly.

"You never go into the saloon, Mr. Lawson. Do I gather that you don't approve of such places?"

"In fact, I don't. I promised my father I would stay away from bars when I left for law school, and it's been a good policy."

"Then you can't approve of me."

"Quite the opposite, Mrs. Oakhill. I believe that educated, intelligent women are a sadly wasted resource. It gives me great pleasure to see one such as yourself making her way in a man's business. Doing your work, I can see plainly that the Golden River is only the beginning of your plans, and I'm most impressed at the way you've gone about it. The contracts you've scratched out yourself are as good as mine except for the small details. Also, I believe you could give your bookkeepers lessons on the proper handling of finances."

"Is your wife inclined to business?"

"If I had a wife, I imagine she would be. I don't have much patience with hollow-headed chatter and giggling. At thirty-six

I've about given up hope of finding a woman interesting enough to be around. May I tell you, Mrs. Oakhill, that being here with you is far more pleasure than it is work."

"What a gallant thing to say, Mr. Lawson."

"Don't you know me well enough to call me Dennis?"

"Only if you know me well enough to call me Hannah."

From this moment on, Hannah became acutely aware of how badly she had missed the company of an attractive, easygoing man whose interests were the same as her own. The few male colleagues who didn't look upon her as a freak trying to be a man were shallow in their outside concerns and in any case not inclined to spend time with a young woman who seemed better at their job than they were.

"Are you ever free on Sundays, Hannah? I thought I might prepare a picnic for us on the Harlem Plains."

"That should be the woman's job."

"Let's leave the battle of man and woman to more important arenas than who will prepare the picnic basket. One o'clock, then? Dress warm. It'll be chilly until the wine gets to doing its job in us."

"Am I to assume that I've said yes?"

"And that I've charmed you completely."

It was on that Sunday, bundled and laughing, seated on a blanket spread on a huge flat rock, with a bottle of good burgundy warming the delightful cold meats and sweet cakes inside them, that he leaned forward unexpectedly to kiss Hannah. He took both cheeks first, a bit shyly, gauging her inclination go further, and then her lips. With no one to observe them under the denuded trees, they were soon embracing and adding new kisses.

"Hannah, I'm making a sad mess of the rules of proper business behavior."

"I can't understand how you were able to deceive Mr. Brogan about your character," she said with a smile she did not try to hide.

On the long ride back they said little, the high color in their cheeks put there perhaps more by embarrassment than cold. But the people who watched the carriage go by saw what looked to be two very happy people.

Two more days went by, during which they worked closely, saying less that did not pertain to the work than they had since their first week together. Dennis did not mention the small pleasures of the flat rock, and Hannah felt foolishly awkward. However, his eyes and his smile told her that he had not forgotten, and that he had plans for the future that she would have to wait to learn.

On the third night, the first really heavy snow of the season began to fall. She prepared a booming fire in the office fireplace and laid out the evening's work on her two-sided partner's desk, his pile opposite her own.

He ordinarily arrived by nine o'clock, but by ten-thirty he had not yet appeared. It was completely understandable. The wind was blowing strongly down the avenues. The drifts would have closed many streets hours before. Probably he had tried gamely to make his way from his rooms far across town, being finally forced to return home. No harm done, she tried bravely to tell herself. They were well caught up and could finish on the following day.

By eleven, though, she had the full realization that she was thoroughly disappointed and miserable that he had not appeared. She had come to expect and need his pleasant presence. All attempts to play down the possibility that a handful of awkward outdoor kisses had kindled something significant in her met resounding defeat.

At nearly one o'clock, as Hannah sat sadly watching the last of the dying fire, he came through the door, the brisk jingling of the entry bell an incredibly happy noise.

He looked exhausted, with icy clumps frozen into his hair and across his shoulders. He was breathing hard, his voice husky. "Do you mind if we don't work, Hannah?"

She went to him, her arms going quickly about him. The ice she felt numbing her arms through her sleeves was in delicious contrast to the insistent heat she felt in his lips. "Come. Please come with me."

Her hand took his and she drew him through the door into the cavern of the Golden River. The saloon had closed early. Just a few lamps remained lighted on each of the three levels of galleries circling above, so Serpa's men, scattered below, could keep their watch.

The men would see, but she wanted Serpa to know that his power over her had ended in still another way. Under the sullen eyes of the guards standing deep in the shadows, she brought Dennis up the stairs. Only she and the trusted Filomena had been allowed to the third level where the Serpas lived, but her hand in Dennis's told the watchers that there would be a new visitor from now on.

"I've never had a man look at me that way," Dennis said with a mock shiver.

"They won't interfere with you," Hannah said with a backward glance into his eyes.

"And I've never had a woman look at me that way either."

With Victor asleep in his own room she brought Dennis into hers. There was none of the frightening intensity she had known that day with Benedetto Serpa, but a deeply satisfying communion with a gentle, caring man whom she was not afraid to let into her heart.

They undressed each other slowly, kissing and caressing as they went. He knelt before her and touched his tongue to her nipples, and they thrust out hard. Then he licked downward and into her until she felt her legs going weak.

He was in complete control of his ardor, leading her gracefully from peak to peak. What Serpa had taken in irresistible plunges he softly led her into, igniting her own urges and letting her complete the penetration herself as she was lifted on a quickly growing flood of want.

"Don't hurry," she whispered. "Please don't hurry."

"I won't, Hannah. I don't want to miss any part of you."

Dennis did not come to her every night, nor did he pursue her hotly in any way. Each day he worked with her, and on Sundays they would walk or ride widely in the city, remarkably attuned to each other's thoughts and feelings. He would often leave her at her door with an unhurried kiss and a quick turn away. But when her need for him had grown unbearably, it seemed to touch off the same spark in him, and they would mount the stairs by twos and ransack one another's bodies.

She did not question him about his intentions because she already knew that he was a man who moved slowly but certainly.

They knew by the arrival of extra gunman around the Golden River when Serpa was to visit. On these nights she sent Dennis home early. She had seen the stricken look on the Sicilian's face when he had caught the lawyer leaving her office. It was best that she did not torment the man with Dennis's presence in her rooms while Mrs. Serpa was being visited.

Dennis was uneasy. "I don't want to know what was between you two, Hannah, but I know it was important to him. A man said something about you at the bar a couple of nights ago, a policeman told me. Somebody caught him outside later and worked on his toes with a hammer. He's dangerous, Hannah. To everybody. Ask him to take his wife and children and leave."

"I can't do that, Dennis. I owe him far too much."

"Maybe too much for your health, my love."

Dennis Lawson slowly increased his attentions to Hannah. He became more quiet, more intense, more sentimental, sending a thoughtful stream of flowers and bringing gifts for the smallest occasions.

"I can't let you surrender any more of your reputation for me, Hannah. We must do something soon about our situation."

"If you think that would be best," she said, her quiet smile hiding a rising excitement.

"Hannah, I think your birthday might be a special one this year."

He brought her present a week early. The package was large enough to fill his arms and heavy enough to cause him to be sweating slightly as he carried it in from the winter chill. The wrappings were brightly festive with bows and artificial flowers, and she expected that he had done the work himself.

"If you open this before it's time, I'll never do another contract for you," he laughed.

"But will I have to leave it right here on my desk for two days?"

"Follow me upstairs. I just had a thought."

In her flat he marched to a back closet in Victor's room, cleared a place at the back and pushed the present inside. Then he turned the skeleton key in the lock and dropped the key into his breast pocket.

"You're a wicked, suspicious man."

Benedetto Serpa visited two days later. But this time Dennis was not inclined to go home. He found excuses to go over papers and add things to leases, his mischievous smile telling her that this was one of those evenings when he would like to make the long climb with her.

"It wouldn't be wise, Dennis."

"No. Only fun."

"Tomorrow," she said, kissing him lightly.

"Tonight," he replied, kissing her considerably less lightly. "He's already up there. He won't know. And I promise you I'll be gone before he wakes up."

"You hate getting up in the middle of the night."

"Not as much as I'd hate to go home."

One more long kiss broke her down. They went quietly laughing up the outside stairway, and he was onto her almost before the door had closed behind him.

There was a special abandon in his lovemaking this time. He reached a high, steady peak of excitement that she had not seen in him, giving and taking pleasure more lavishly than he had in any previous evening. He didn't stop until she had to grab a corner of the pillow to muffle her climaxing moan.

Afterward he did not lie down. He cradled her in his arms as always, but remained propped on one elbow, watching her with the tenderest of smiles until she was asleep.

It was a call from Victor, low and sleepy, that woke her. "Mother. Mother, can I come in?"

Hannah was relieved to see that Dennis was gone, although she wished he had wakened her to kiss her goodbye. She was uncomfortable with him when Serpa was just beyond the wall, and Victor was of an age when she didn't want him to see her in bed with a man.

Turning up a lamp, she opened the door to the child who stood looking up solemnly in his nightshirt.

"Did you have a nasty dream, Victor?"

"No, Mother. There's a bad smell in my room. It woke me up."

"Then we must see what it is."

She took the lamp in one hand and stuck out a finger of the other for him to hold.

Before they had crossed his threshold she caught a pungent whiff. Fire? No, it was not the straightforward sharpness of natural materials burning. There was something chemical and alien to it. And she remembered it from somewhere. Yes. The big Fourth of July celebrations, when the streets crackled with fireworks and the night skies pinwheeled flame.

At the back of the room a flicker caught her eye, brilliant and sputtering. It came from the closet, whose door stood open an inch or two. With surges of alarm beginning to move through her, she let go of Victor and rushed to pull at the knob. Below her she saw her gaily wrapped present from Dennis. But now there was a tear in the bright paper, and a hissing, sparkling cord, shortening rapidly, protruded from the hole. She grabbed for it and she jerked back with burned fingers. The cord was burning fast . . . too fast! Attempting to drag the box out into the room, she found it was far heavier than she imagined.

"Outside, Victor," she shouted. "Run outside."

With his powerful little legs churning, he beat her to the door to the gallery. She unlocked it and pushed him through, pointing to the stairs. *"Run down. All the way to the bottom."*

In the saloon below, alerted by her shouts, four bodyguards appeared with shotguns, looking up into the galleries.

"Get my son to the street," she cried. *"And get out yourselves."*

Once she had seen Victor's curly head disappear down the first flight, she ran to Serpa's door and pounded on it with both fists. *"Wake up. You've got to get out of here. Wake up. Wake up."*

Elvira Serpa got to the door first. The red light of a flickering votive candle showed Hannah the distrust and anger in the hard face above the white woolen nightgown.

"Signora Serpa. Get your husband . . . Signor Serpa. Quickly. Please. You have to leave *now*. Right away—"

Elvira did not understand her words. Her look mingled confusion and dislike. Julia, the youngest of the children, a serious wide-eyed girl of Victor's age, appeared behind her mother.

"Benedetto," Elvira called, but did not otherwise move.

Hannah yelled through the open door, *"Mr. Serpa. You've got to get out of here. Hurry. Please—"*

She heard Serpa's voice in an unintelligible answering shout from a back room. The bodyguards had reached the third gallery and were running toward them brandishing their weapons. Everyone was running in the wrong direction.

Serpa came into view, naked and bleary eyed.

"The children. Get the other children—"

He, too, hesitated bewilderedly "Signora Oakhill, what is—"

Hannah grabbed the child from behind Elvira and scooped her into her arms. *"Into the street everybody—"* She ran for the steps past the confused guards. There was a scream from Elvira, and bare feet were running behind Hannah. The woman still didn't understand.

At the head of the stairs Hannah turned to take her hand and lead her down, but the fury of the frightened mother and jealous wife was overwhelming. Elvira's frantic grab for the child only succeeded in pushing Hannah over the edge of the first step, and she went somersaulting down the long flight. Instinctively she hugged little Julia tighter in her arms, protecting her from the worst of the fall. But her own head cracked into every step, and when she rolled onto the landing at the second gallery below, she found herself, numb, completely unable to cry out or move. The child clung to her tightly and began to cry.

Serpa was racing down the stairs. He raised Hannah up him, gently prying the hysterical child away. His voice trembled with concern. "Mrs. Oakhill . . . Hannah . . . Hannah, my sweet love . . ."

Over his shoulder, far up at the head of the stairs, Hannah saw Elvira Serpa stagger with despair. The other children were with her now, holding to her. Then one of the bodyguards was trying to guide Elvira and the children back to their rooms.

"No. *No* . . . *no*—"

The billow of flame and whirling splinters shot across the Golden River a split second before the thunderclap concussion of the bomb. Hannah's vision attained complete clarity for a moment. A bodyguard seemed to fly out into the void three stories above the floor of the saloon as a vast glass skylight vanished upward into the night. All the walls and vertical columns smeared and became jagged, their strength running out of them before they began their howling collapse.

The long beams she had watched being set into the roof so lovingly were descending hammers now. They rotated on their axes as they fell, taking what little remained of the top gallery with them. Two more guards who had run inside from the street at the first shouts had time for one mortal shriek before they were ground out of existence.

Serpa swept Hannah and the child beneath his gigantic body as the roof, the galleries and a side wall roared down into the central void that had been the Golden River.

Less than a minute later, the last of the debris had fallen and settled. After one weak cry of a man's voice somewhere in the wreckage, there was complete silence. Snow filtered down through the now open roof, the wind swirling it and sending in a deadly chill despite the fires beginning to burn all around them. Hannah saw that the second-story landing upon which they lay was the only fragment of the gallery structure that still clung to a wall. The framing of an enormous chimney behind them had prevented the falling roof from crushing and carrying them down with the others.

The child whimpered. Serpa whispered to her gently in Italian and assured himself that she had not been hurt. Then he had to turn and look down into the remains of the obliterating avalanche that had pulverized his wife and other daughters. He screamed his grief and fury hopelessly at the sky.

Later, half-mad with her guilt, Hannah poured out to Serpa what her blind and trusting stupidity had cost him.

As he towered over her in her hospital bed, she could almost feel the room vibrating with his anger. Yet, she could not be sure whether his rage was directed more against her culpability or against her having been in bed with another man not ten yards from where he had slept.

"So I have betrayed you after all, Benedetto. Like the worst of your enemies."

Within the gruffness of his voice there was still enormous caring. "You saved me before. Now you have saved me again. And my sweet daughter. You were the one betrayed."

At the thought of Dennis Lawson, tears of bitterness started in her eyes. Why had the stinging lies of Mark Northern not taught her the misery that followed giving away the heart? "I don't know what made me such a fool."

"You loved him, Hannah?"

She was startled not so much by the question as by the use of her first name again, a signal that there had been a subtle, irreversible shift in their relationship. He had moved quietly above her. In his terrible code, despite his assurances to the contrary, she now owed him the lives of his lost family. He would move to claim repayment. The currency would not be her life, but her heart. "Yes. I loved him."

He covered her hands with his. "Victor will remain with me and my daughter, Julia. Filomena will be there. I have taken new quarters. You will come with us when they let you out of here in a few days."

"The Golden River is all gone."

"I will build it for you again."

"No. That part of my life is over. Did my office burn?"

"It was saved. I have your papers. All of them."

"My people will know what to do with those. Tell them we'll start again soon. Bigger than before. And find me a lawyer. One I can trust."

"A pleasure. But there is the matter of the old lawyer."

There was a note in his voice that frosted her heart. "I imagine we'll never see him again."

"He can go far on what Abruzzi paid him. But I think not far enough. Now I must go examine my debts." He bent to kiss her forehead. She felt the cold lips of a man who hungered for a death.

Again under the close protection of Serpa's men, Hannah gathered her staff into temporary quarters and carried her business forward. She had insurance on the Golden River—at Lawson's insistence, she remembered wryly—and would be able to rebuild handsomely without dipping into her land investments. This would be not a saloon, but the first major business offices to intrude on the waterfront. Oakhill Development was going to have quarters as impressive as its future.

As she worked, a brutal war was being fought for the Five Points. Bartolomeo Abruzzi, his plan to be rid of the leadership of Serpa thrown back, committed all the forces he could muster, including the worst that could be gotten from Philadelphia and Boston. The police patrolled in pairs, and were effective mostly in the promptness with which they carried away the shot, stabbed, drowned, brained and otherwise savaged soldiers.

Despite the herculean efforts of the tireless Filomena, Hannah found herself becoming the mother of Julia Serpa, who was at the Oakhill house as much as her own. The little girl was not pretty except for her lustrous hair and bright black eyes, but she was already tall, well formed and graceful, and her seldom given smile always reached the heart. Perhaps because she was as quiet and devoid of childish nonsense as he, Victor accepted her as his first playmate of his own age. She was at his bedroom door waiting for him when he rose in the morning and trailed him everywhere during the day.

Hannah increased the pay of Victor's tutor, Frau Wendt, who spoke perfect if teutonically tinged Italian, and the delighted Julia took her lessons with Victor. She admired Hannah wholeheartedly and worked hard to pattern her English after hers rather than accept the hard German edges in Frau Wendt's. She made rapid and effortless progress in all departments, chattering with Hannah about anything that would allow her to hang about for a while. Julia missed her mother, sometimes weeping in the night, but Elvira, Hannah learned, had been a harsh parent and her daughter reveled in Hannah's gentle ways.

Concentrating on her business, Hannah began to try to put Dennis Lawson out of her mind. That he had come to her treacherously and murderously was not questioned. But she wondered what terrible coercion wielded by the malignant Abruzzi might have been brought against him.

Of all of Serpa's vicious men, one she had met on the first day, Anthony Rendino, chilled her as did none of the others. He was short, with delicate hands and feet, yet he had the head, neck and shoulders of a bull. His eyes were tiny specks of malevolence, and a straggling mustache hid a toothless mouth. It was said that there was none faster killing with a knife, and, when he wanted, none slower. Hannah had quietly made it clear to Serpa that she wished to be with this man as little as possible. So when he appeared behind her on South Street one day, popping out of the crowds of men pushing iced fish in carts, she knew there must be a grim and special reason.

"Signora Oakhill," he said in his oddly high-pitched voice, "You must come with me to the Ships." There was menace in his voice that told her no objections were possible, and she followed him silently.

The voluble Leo had told her of the Ships. Early in the century, when the shoreline cut in much further at places than it did now, the hulks of ancient sailing ships, sunken and embedded in the mud, were built over as the new waterfront rose. Now, lost beneath street level, interconnected by passageways that were little more than burrows, the decaying holds and cabins remained with their moldering frames and ports still discernible. These rotting chambers held life and deeds that did not dare the light of day.

Rendino led her first into a lantern-lit basement where sailors sprawled on burlap sacks and smoked pipes that filled the air with sweet-smelling smoke in gagging clouds. Their eyes were the vacant windows of abandoned dwellings. At the rear—under an alley, she imagined—a filthy piece of sail hung across a passage hammered through the brick. It led almost straight down into the earth. When Rendino lit a stub of candle, she saw that railway ties had been set into the dirt as a crude stair, and she trailed behind him on these as he descended.

Where a hole had been cut through thick, moisture-weeping timbers, they entered the first of the Ships. As she moved through she understood why the police never penetrated to the wooden caverns. If there had been vessels to ferry the damned to eternal fire, these would have done nicely. There were bunks and chests everywhere. Upon and under these, silver candlesticks and cutlery showed, with expensive-looking rugs and rude sacks of fine clothing. Bewhiskered, bowler-hatted men with eyes that never rested spoke to wiry, stocking-capped figures who looked like they might be descended from the rats who had inhabited the bilges of these holds.

At length they arrived at what must have been a stern cabin, its door still sagging on rusted hinges. Two men she knew to be Serpa's flanked the entrance. One stopped Rendino with an upraised palm and motioned her through.

Serpa sat at a table before a seeping, mud-clogged expanse of what had been windows looking upon broad oceans. A single guttering candle threw the only feeble light. The outline of his face writhed in the flickering shadows, and his eyes burned brighter than the flame. "Signora Hannah, I ask you please to seat yourself and be brave." He waited until she eased herself warily onto a chair. "Let me show you what we have."

She could see the hot wax running down his huge fingers as he picked up the candle. He carried it before him into the shadows near the bulkhead, where she saw the torn, terrified package that was Dennis Lawson. The eyes that had gazed into hers with such tenderness as they made love were now white-rimmed circles of a terror brimming on madness.

"Hannah . . . Thank God . . . Hannah—"

At the sound of his voice, the ice around her heart threatened to melt away completely.

The gravel in Serpa's words showed the effort he was making to contain himself. "This man has done unholy things. To me. To my family. To you. He has lost his right to call himself a creature of God. He is the spit of Satan."

Dennis tried to writhe closer to her. His hands and feet were tied so tightly that blood was visible on the rope. "I truly loved you, Hannah. I had gambling debts to Abruzzi. You should have heard what he threatened. I'm not brave. It's too late to say how sorry I am. But at least believe I loved you."

"What about the four children in that building? Did you love them, too?"

"I didn't mean to . . . I didn't have the strength to do anything else." He was weeping.

She turned to Serpa. "Did you bring me here to give my blessing to what you're going to do? Or did you think I'd enjoy it?"

"In truth I hoped for those things, but I did not expect them."

"Then tell me what you want from me, Mr. Serpa."

"You told me you felt love for him."

"Yes, I felt love for him."

"It is for this reason he is not yet feeding the crabs. My every bone calls out for his pain and blood. My honor screams for it. But if his death will bring you pain or hatred for me, he will live no matter what my people say. You must tell me now what to do with him."

Dennis Lawson's battered face opened into desperate hope. "Remember how it was, Hannah. So beautiful. So happy. I felt it just the way you did. Don't let my weakness make you forget. You're good. So good. It's why I started to love you—"

"*Shut up,*" Serpa snapped. "She will speak." He seated himself to wait.

Hannah was thunderstruck. She had imagined Lawson as a dead man as soon as she had seen him in Serpa's power. It had been out of her hands. No guilt, no decision of her own. She could tell herself she was horrified at the forthcoming execution, her hands clean. She could let herself be certain that she would have spared him if it had been her own judgement. The vengeful, unforgiving streak that had caused her all her life to fear for her soul could have gone unchallenged. Now she had this chilling choice.

There was something else hanging in the foul air. If Serpa spared this betrayer the fate that Sicilian honor demanded, Serpa would be finished forever as a leader. He could no longer be trusted to preserve the secrets of the code. He would soon die as quickly and disgracefully as Lawson.

The thought of a love that would pay such a price jolted her. She had once felt it in his body, now she felt it as a molten thing pouring out of the core of him.

"Take me with you, Hannah. Take me home," Dennis called.

Whether Serpa's unsolicited passion now tore forth her own for him, or whether that bitter, pitiless thing in her again failed to forgive, the words were quickly on her lips. "I have no right to answer for my own wishes. I do so in the name of Mrs. Serpa, for her blood and the blood of her children."

"Hannah . . . *No* . . . *No* . . . You *can't* . . ."

She was near fainting in the coffin-breath air. "Promise me it will be quick," she said to Serpa.

"A hard promise. But I will keep it."

"Pity, Hannah . . . Have some *pity*, won't you—"

"Rendino," Serpa called.

Hannah had to squeeze past her erstwhile guide as she hurried out. There was a small clink as he drew a short length of rusty chain from a pocket. Behind her Serpa hissed some short Italian words.

Before she was out of earshot she heard the last of what the earth would hear from Dennis Lawson, a half scream, half gurgle snapped short in the same throat that had spoken to her such beautiful words of love.

What she had breathed in the Ships lay poisonously in her chest and could not be cleared. A fever rose in her before she was home and raged for nearly a week, its fire mercifully and permanently blurring the sharpest outlines of what she had lived beneath the ground.

Serpa's mourning was long and scrupulous. He spoke to Hannah only in greeting and stayed alone in his rooms when he was not out in the prosecution of his business. And that business arrived at a long-sought success when Bartolomeo Abruzzi died with his inner council in a burning building in which all reachable exits had been nailed shut a short time before. The fire brigade's engines having been blocked by a tangle of beer wagons, their plight was hopeless.

By the following day, all the defectors to Abruzzi who had seen their error had repledged their fealty to the forgiving Serpa forces. The few who did not return to him were soon back in Sicily or bumping uneasily on the bottom-sands in the swiftly moving currents of the East River.

Serpa now held illimitable domain, and he expanded his power. Before Hannah had finished commissioning the drawings for the new offices of Oakhill Development, a major construction company was clearing the fire-ravaged ruins, unbidden and unpaid by her. An owner of several fine houses offered her a choice of them at terms that were unbelievably generous. The things she had dreamed of on the *Dortmund* were happening, but at the cost of an irresistibly mounting debt.

In time, his mourning period ended, Serpa came to her. There was no sweeping her to his bed, but a courtly, formal courtship in the most stately traditions of the Sicilian countryside. One of the scowling aunts who had arrived with Elvira was always present during his parlor visits, unoccupied and watchful. She trailed behind during their walks and rode with them in Serpa's new carriage. That they had already shared a bed mattered not at all. Things were to be done correctly when the end of it was to be a marriage in the eyes of the understanding God who made special allowances for the children of his most troubled island.

If Hannah had known what panic was, she would have felt it now. There was only the baffled Filomena, by now completely devoted and a deadly keeper of secrets, with whom to discuss her misgivings.

"Signora, not even the American President Ulysses brings respect like Benedetto Serpa. Your enemies will smile and put away their harm. You will not have to go to a business like a peasant in Castelamare. He will take the cares of your office to himself, and place good men to make it prosper."

"Filomena, I respect the Sicilian ways. But they would kill me more quickly than one of their chains around my neck."

"Signore Serpa will honor you like the Virgin Mother and love you like a desert lion."

"Your women dress in black and sit together in their work. They only do and talk about the things of wives. Their men come to them only at the table and in bed."

"And so they are the happiest and most blessed of women."

"To my taste they are damned, Filomena."

The servant's eyes widened at an unthinkable thought. "You would refuse the respectable offer of Benedetto Serpa?"

"I must."

"He did . . . not please you?" The flabbergasting thought caused Filomena to blurt the question that torture could not have pulled out of her at a more guarded moment.

Hannah stifled her smile. "I'm sure that no woman could fault Mr. Serpa in the discharge of any of the duties of a gentleman. But the love I feel for him is . . . less than he deserves."

"Ahhh, there will be misery."

"You don't think he will respect my wish to be his lifelong friend outside of marriage or his bed? Tell me truly."

Filomena picked her words slowly. "He will honor any of your wishes. But he will make it very hard for another man who desires to lie down with you."

Hannah lost little time putting Filomena's thesis to the test. She selected Harold Lisle, a shy and handsome banker with a fine wave to his hair, for a chaste dose of her charm. She had not missed the fond and admiring looks of this pleasant bachelor as they did their business, and was not incorrect in her guess that his previous residence in Charleston had kept him ignorant of the reputation of her formidable suitor.

Exactly when she knew he would, Lisle dropped in upon her in her new rooms near Chatham Square and asked leave to call in the future, which was granted. For a short time he took her riding in his carriage in the park and to fine dinners. His company was as far from stimulating as company could be, but he was a pleasant enough stalking horse.

Soon, Harold Lisle vanished. Not from the face of the earth, she was relieved to learn, but from her life. He never called upon her or wrote to her again.

The omniscient Leo, after much prodding, confided that Harold Lisle one night had his trousers removed in his own closed carriage, after which he had endured a lengthy and humiliating conversation with the earthy Rendino, who disparaged his private parts and held a straight razor close to them. Lisle had been persuaded that prolonged communication with Mrs. Oakhill was unwise in the extreme.

So there it was. She might hold Serpa at bay indefinitely, but while he was about there were to be no other men who might be interested in her as a woman.

To some degree there was comfort in that. Her two experiences with love had been disasters that made her feel she would invest no more of her heart. However, she knew by now her own untrustworthy body. This was the weakness that Serpa sensed as he waited.

She sometimes thought that if all he wanted was to have her in his bed, she might have been weak enough to do it. His riveting black eyes and panther's body sometimes made her squirm beneath her clothing. And no matter how hard she tried to shut it out, there was a certain shuddering thrill in being touched by a man capable of the ultimate touch. But he wanted more than her flesh. To give it would imprison her forever in a world that was not hers. So she relied on what remained of the memory of Dennis Lawson's last gasps when she felt her defenses slipping, and plunged into her work to the exclusion of all else.

If it had not been for a growing restlessness, a need for respite from her repetitive days, she might have made a sullen peace with herself. Her unwanted, unexpectedly vivid dreams of searching for Mark Northern were growing fewer, if no less devastating.

CHAPTER 7

"I DON'T know, Jack," Duplessis said with a worried shake of his head, throwing the letter back on Mark's desk. "The man is more things than a businessman."

"But he builds, Claude. My God, how he builds."

Since he had become the personification of Grant Majestic, Mark Northern's instincts had been all but perfect. In five years he had made his company a name to be respected and consulted. Riding the rising crest of the post–Civil War boom, he used the bloody dollars he had earned on the barges to phenomenal effect. His ability to pick properties that could be turned for fine profits was growing into a legend. And, of course, he helped this along with a still-burgeoning flair for promotional dazzle.

He gathered up a double handful of the papers that obliterated the surface of the huge desk and heaved them into air, letting them fall heedlessly. "This is not enough, Claude. It's not land, it's paper. It's not building, it's clerking. Do you know, I never went inside the last three things I bought. Eventually I won't look at the outside either. I'll sit here at this desk making numbers and chicken scratches like a pawnbroker."

"It's everything you wanted, you idiot." After the final fight,

Duplessis had become Mark's only close friend. He was educated, bright and easy to be with, never withholding an abrasive opinion.

"Deeds and contracts, contracts and deeds. I'm smothering in seedy landlords, droning lawyers and ten-dollar rents. I need to do something big enough to let me breathe."

"Well, then, Jack, Mr. Guy Cutts is exactly the medicine for you. He will be uncomfortable as long as there's a dollar or an acre in the country that doesn't belong to him."

Mark laughed at the comic look of distaste on Duplessis' face. "The man has done honorable things, Claude. His banks sold millions of government bonds to finance the war."

"Nobody doubts his ability to sell," Duplessis said. "It's *what* he sells and *how* he sells it."

"His idea to promote a railroad to connect Lake Superior with the Mississippi was a good one."

"Especially since he happens to own a good piece of a port town called Duluth that would boom with a railroad to the river."

"If the country waited for philanthropy to build it, it would wait as long as Africa. He makes things *happen*," said Mark.

Duplessis looked at the letter again. "He writes that 'ten leaders of the New York investment community' will be there with you. I wager that includes every thimblerigger, highbinder and widelooper east of the Hudson. And when did Gentleman Jack Grant, for all this early success, become an investment leader?"

Mark laughed and nodded. "When indeed. I can't believe Cutts is silly enough to believe all my promoting, as inventive as it might be. But at worst it's a lunch at Delmonico's in interesting company."

With a glance at his gold repeater, the doctor grimaced and waved him out.

The traffic on Lexington Avenue was all but impenetrable, so Mark walked down to 23rd Street. He guessed that in fifty years they would have to devise a second layer above these streets for the use of horse-drawn vehicles. Perhaps, if it wouldn't be too frightening for the animals, they could move between the passenger-hauling locomotives of the elevated railways that seemed destined to black out the sun.

Mark liked Delmonico's. The fine, ornate restaurant attracted the dynamic, wealthy business class of the city, leaving the stuffy rich to their uptown clubs. Yet it was a fine place to take a lady for a dinner, the afternoon crowd having giving over to a more sportive set.

He had begun to see women extensively for the first time since he had lost Hannah. His heart remained with his dead wife, but his needs as a man had to be met finally, and he was positioned well enough to have feminine company of the best sort. His rakehell fame as the fierce battler Gentleman Jack had helped rather than hurt his status as an escort. An evening with him was worth a month of talk in the front parlors as well as a blissful night, and the fact that some of the most respectable families were dealing with him in his lucrative business brought him a rapidly growing acceptance.

As for his looks, although he would never make a portrait over a fireplace, there had been more improvement. There were no longer fresh livid scars, and Duplessis' work, now free from swelling and further disturbance, restored much smoothness and symmetry. With the fine clothes, the carefully trimmed beard, the hair now permitted to flow long, his eyepatch was now regarded as more rakish than sinister.

As he made his way through the elaborate entrance to the restaurant, two escorted women smiled at him discreetly as they went by, and he touched his hat with a slight nod. He filed them into his memory, for he kept his circle of feminine acquaintances wide and uninvolving, and he might call on them sometime if they crossed his path again.

"Mr. Cutts is waiting for you with his party, Mr. Grant," a waiter told him. "There's a special table at the back."

Approaching the huge round table, Mark was surprised to see that one of those seated was a woman. Her back was turned to him, but she was marvelously dressed in the latest mode and had captured most of the attention at the table.

The escorting waiter approached the table's central figure. "Mr. Grant is here, Mr. Cutts."

Guy Cutts exploded from his chair, his height not increasing appreciably. He was a square stove of a man, his mouth so lost in muttonchop whiskers that only the presence of a long, unlit cigar held clenched in his teeth gave proof that he owned such an orifice. A clear excess of shrewdness around the eyes was balanced out by a like amount of good-humored zeal. "You know about me, Grant. And, by God, I know about you. If you recognize any of these pirates, say hello and save me some introductions."

Mark knew four of them immediately facing him. Two were people with some power, and with whom he had dealt before. And two he knew from his time with Marietta Van Vuylen, having met them on the barge the first night he had been with her. They glared at Mark with loathing.

"You don't have your pistol this time, I pray, Mr. Grant. I don't care to be threatened by a thug again," one of them spat.

"I believe that was your own pistol, sir. The one you use to shoot people in the knee, I recall," Mark answered.

"I still have a scar under my eye where you struck me," the other one said.

"It becomes you. And it won't interfere with the transaction of business, as you can see from my own case."

"We don't approve of your choice of colleagues, Mr. Cutts," the first man said. "And what does he know about business on our scale?"

"He knows things that we don't, and that we need very much. Mr. Grant and Mrs. Oakhill have something more important than their money to contribute."

The woman turned and smiled at Mark. The stone walls he had built against the grief in him crumbled in a delirious, unbelieving shock of pure joy. His chest constricted around a heart he feared would burst, choking off all hope of speech.

"I have been hoping to meet you for many months, Mr. Grant," she said, as irresistibly beautiful as the last time he had seen her.

"Can't blame you for looking like that, Grant," said Cutts.

"Mrs. Oakhill makes the rest of us look like warthogs in suits, doesn't she?"

As Cutts quickly introduced the others, Mark could feel Hannah's eyes upon him. In another moment she would rise and scream her hatred at him, and nothing he could say would ever turn it aside.

"Sit down, Jack. Right here next to Mrs. Oakhill. We'll set the mood with a bit of champagne."

Every bit of him raged to cry her name, to take her into his arms and kiss her until his strength was gone. His desire to drink in the look of her until the parched years of loneliness were slaked was almost too great to bear. Yet, seated directly at her side as he was, he could not turn to her except to speak, and there wasn't a thing in the world he could say.

The champagne was poured. Cutts extended his glass. "To the people to whom God has offered the chance to weld an empire of the Atlantic to an empire of the Pacific, to make the greatest nation ever dreamed. And to the people who will create the glories of Solomon . . . and all his wealth."

They drank, and Cutts began a stream of easy banter to bring the group together as the meal was being served. "Business can wait for the cigars, if Mrs. Oakhill will indulge that male vice later."

"She will," Hannah said firmly, "and she will join you then in a very large brandy."

"More than fair enough," laughed Cutts.

Hannah now turned to Mark and examined his face with great directness. "Do excuse me, Mr. Grant. I don't want to be looking at those fascinating features of yours out of the corner of my eye. I think if I were a man I would want to look as fierce as you."

She had said it to put him at his ease, he realized, after she had seen his great discomfort. Her laughing mouth was not a foot from his; the lips he had coveted, the eyes that filled his nights, were so close that he could have kissed them before she could move.

"It's kind of you to tell such a sweet untruth," he said, his shattered voice hoarser than ever with what was seething in him.

Then, with wakening wonder, he began to understand that she had truly failed to recognize him.

The huge mirror opposite confirmed that recognition was impossible. His gray-flecked hair and beard, the scarred and repaired features beneath the eyepatch, the added weight and brutalized voice had done their work. But most of all it was the setting, three thousand miles, seven years and a whole world away from the battlefield that had burst them apart.

How should he tell her? When? As he contemplated this, he began to dread what must then occur. Her friendly brightness, now washing over him so gloriously, would fade in an instant. He would watch the angel's face convulse with abomination, and he would lose her again just moments after he had found her. His instant of joy after his years of despair would just serve to make the remainder of his life even more unbearable than what had gone before.

"I can see why they call you Gentleman Jack. You speak like one."

"I was born in Boston, Mrs. Oakhill," he was saying before he realized the words were out of him. "My people were English, and they had a lot more breeding than they had money or standing. English gentlemen don't fight on the barges, I promise you."

And so he found he had made a decision. Mark Northern would remain despised in death. Whatever Mark had been to her, Jack Grant must be something else. He prayed that Guy Cutts might pave the way for him to be part of her life every day.

At the end of a sumptuous meal, Cutts hunched himself above an enormous brandy snifter and began. "For the benefit of Mrs. Oakhill and two or three of you who are not of this country, I will review the relationship of the United States government to the railroads."

"They are using them as a tool to open your West, are they not?" said a man with a French accent.

"Just so. The war has been an enormous drain on this country, in lives, treasure and lost time. Some of the richest land the world ever knew stretches from the Mississippi to the Pacific in the northern latitudes. But it's largely empty, with no prospects of it filling up quickly enough. It is not inconceivable that foreign powers could make claims on that land if they beat us to the settling."

"So the government pushes the building of transcontinental railroads," a Spaniard said.

"What better way?" Cutts asked, with a great swig of brandy. "The towns grow along the tracks just as the cities grew on the rivers. The people spread out from the towns. The railroads supply them and branch out, the cycle repeating. It's a growth machine."

"If this is a railroad scheme I am not qualified, Mr. Cutts. Railroads are outside my experience—"

Cutts chopped him short with a wave. "Señor Alfonsin, I wouldn't touch this if it was only about trains. This is about *land*, my friends. More land than you ever imagined."

"Whose land?" Hannah asked.

"The government's . . . and *ours.*"

"How much of it will be ours?" Mark asked.

Cutts took a deep breath. "Get a grip on your hat, Mr. Grant. The government is giving my Superior Pacific Railroad *forty-seven million acres.*"

The people around the table sat stunned.

"That's more land than there is in the six New England states."

"A bit more, actually."

"I don't understand," said the Frenchman, dabbing at his lips with a napkin.

"What happens," Cutts went on, "is that the United States will *give* us alternate sections of land running ten miles on each side of a track running from Duluth, Minnesota, on Lake Superior to Puget Sound of the Pacific. It's a wonderful scheme. As we open their country for them, the value of their land multiplies along with ours, and they share in the fruits of the expansion without it costing a dollar in taxes."

"What kind of money are we talking about for profit?" one of Marietta's friends asked.

"Bearing in mind that we paid nothing and that prime land in the West was going for a dollar twenty-five an acre a little while ago, I estimate that we could sell dirt along our track for between six dollars and ten dollars an acre."

The Frenchman looked dubious. "This is a bit too good. Please tell us what is not so good."

A touch of reluctance stole into Cutts' manner, but he spoke with candor. "The charter wasn't given to me, it was issued to one Josiah Perkins in 1864. It called for him to start construction within two years and lay a minimum of fifty miles of track per year. The trouble was that there was a little thing called the Civil War going on at the time. Very expensive. He couldn't sell the bonds and stock to finance construction. He petitioned Congress a couple of times for extensions, but now his time has run out."

"So you're taking over to raise the money and get things moving?"

"I have a very good reputation for getting things moving, Mr. Grant."

"I would hesitate to say that you had a very good reputation for anything, Mr. Cutts," said the more unpleasant of Marietta's friends. "We are respectable men. I think it would damage our reputations permanently to be associated with a town jobber." He spat out the last words. "A town jobber is what you are at the end of it, is it not?"

"The term to me is not a dishonorable one," Cutts said with an edge in his own voice now. "The dream must precede the reality."

"Tell me what a town jobber is," said Hannah.

The unpleasant man answered her with relish. "His method is elementary. He obtains land at a likely site, such as a fork in a river or, in this case, on a proposed railway line. He hopes for financing on long-term notes backed by men with good names. Then he hires architects to lay out a magnificent city on the land. Unless I'm mistaken, that portfolio behind Mr. Cutts' chair is filled with such figments of the imagination. May we look, sir?"

Not a bit abashed, Cutts untied and opened the hand-tooled leather cover of a large portfolio and drew out several enormous, incredibly detailed drawings of what was evidently the street plan of a metropolis on a large body of water. A railroad track ran through the center of town, terminating at the waterfront in an impressive series of roundhouses and storage yards.

Waiters came forward to clear the table at a signal from Cutts, and in a moment the surface was covered totally with the drawings. "This, good friends, is what the future of the American West looks like."

Most of the viewers were awed despite the warnings of the unpleasant man, who continued from where he was interrupted.

"Isn't it wonderful there on paper? Streets, squares and public buildings, all completely and beautifully named. See Abraham Lincoln Plaza and the Thomas Jefferson Courthouse and—clever—here is Oakhill Street not at all far from Cutts Boulevard. And look at the wharves on this fine waterfront that shames that of New York City. They are neatly numbered so one might sort one's way through the invisible fleets of merchant ships without confusion. Also, don't miss the parks and churches, and even the monuments to the nation's leading figures. Especially those who might have money invested, eh, Mr. Cutts?"

Cutts cocked an eyebrow at him. "All people with vision deserve to stand upon pedestals."

"What is it you ask of us, although I can very well guess what it is."

Spreading his hands and turning his palms upward on the table, Cutts was a raffish gambler showing he had nothing to hide. "In fact, I need many things from you. Money, of course. What you can put in yourselves and what you can get from the powerful people of this city. But mostly courage, imagination and dedication to nothing less than doubling the populated area of this great nation. You will have the blessing of those pioneers who will people a new paradise, as well as the blessing of God Himself for opening His proudest gifts to His children."

"Paradise?" the Frenchman huffed. "Your General Sherman said that much of the area is as bad as God ever made, or anybody can scare up this side of Africa, if my memory functions."

"The natural pessimism of a military mind sees land only as battlefields and opportunities for fortifications." He pulled a letter out of his coat. "Let me read you some of what a respected colleague wrote to me after he carefully inspected the land from Lake Superior to Puget Sound."

The unpleasant man rolled his eyes. "Oh, yes. Do let us hear a bit of that."

Cutts read excerpts: "A vast wilderness waiting like a rich heiress to be appropriated and enjoyed . . . There is nothing on the American continent equal to it . . . Such timber, such soil, such orchards, such fish, such climate, such coal, such harbors, such rivers . . . There is no end to the possibilities of wealth here . . . The soil sustains a growth of firs and cedars two hundred feet high . . . Salmon are not caught here, they are pitchforked out of the streams . . . ."

"What, no cities cut from rubies?"

"I hear, sir, that you are obtaining Superior Northern stock at ten cents of the dollar from the previous leadership," someone said.

"And that you own half the land in Duluth."

"Not quite ten cents and not nearly half. But what of it? A personal stake lends zest to the game," said Cutts.

"A good swindle to kite the value of your property would lend even more zest."

Cutts seemed immune to anger. "I tell you plainly that the difficulties are large. I must mortgage all the notes I sell—only a bit of cash down is required—to get the railroad moving nicely on schedule. As the tracks extend, I sell land for more new towns on the line and get the old towns to issue their own bonds to buy my stock. So it's always a race to sell bonds and then sell land to retire the bonds."

Mark interrupted him. "But you're always selling that stock on the prospect of the future business of an uncompleted railroad."

"It's a worm reaching backward to haul its tail forward," said Hannah. "Any serious breakdown in the cycle and—"

Any mention of difficulty set fire to Cutts' enthusiasm. "To make sure that no such breakdown occurs, we must have the cooperation of people far more influential than ourselves."

"How can we reward them for their interest in our success

when it's all you can do to raise money for bonds for the construction?"

"With forty-seven million acres at our disposal, it would be niggardly not to extend a few thousand acres to a friend who might like to build a woodland cabin, or perhaps a small town of his own," said Cutts.

From this moment, Guy Cutts was transformed. With eyes blazing belief he whisked his visitors across the dreamscape that sprawled over the table. Minutes spun into an hour, and still there appeared no dam strong enough to stem the torrent of florid descriptions. "Not New York and not Chicago will be the central commercial diamond of the United States. That city, destined to be the greatest that the world has ever known, will be Duluth. As the great port on the freshwater sea that will be joined to the saltwater sea at Puget Sound, this metropolis, linking the South by way of the Mississippi and a short extension of track, and the East by the Erie Canal, will be the keystone of the greatest transcontinental communications and hauling system ever accomplished."

As well as anyone in the room, Mark was able to separate the hyperbole from the real. He was in no way unaware of Cutts' reputation for a sharp deal. But something else had now become plain. Cutts, perhaps in spite of himself, believed with all his heart in the possibilities of this dream. Yes, he wanted the money before any of it, but what thrilled him was *building,* the pushing into the unexplored, the spreading of towns and then cities across the plains, like the flowers of an explosive prairie springtime. Mark looked at Hannah and saw the same realization wakening in her. Like him, she was feeling the fertility in the rich soils of the West and longing to bring it to fruit.

"Think of it. Your own names on towns yet undreamt."

"More likely those names will be above newspaper columns that describe our being led away in chains," someone said.

Cutts never swerved. "Our first effort must be to raise five-point-six million dollars to push the line from Duluth to the Red River. Land profits are the lure. So we establish a wholly owned land company called Northern Mountain. I suggest a fifty-six thousand–dollar package, divided among Northern Pacific stocks and bonds and Northern Mountain stock. And perhaps a bit of stock representing holdings in the city of Duluth. That alone will one day surpass the original investment by many times."

From somewhere beneath the table he pulled forth sheaves of contracts ready for signature, a fistful of pens and an ink bottle that he wrenched open with a loud pop. "The details we can niggle about in the offices of some bank. But by making our commitment right here and right now, we make ourselves convenient to the finest champagne and service for our celebration. And we may toast farewell to our small lives and fame as we enter an era where our names will be honored upon ten, twenty, fifty million lips. At this table will be not merely investors, but the guiding hearts of the Superior Pacific. Yes, I picked some of you for your access to wealth, but before that for your energy and spirit." He dipped a pen and held it forth. "As the first signer of the Declaration of Independence found greater glories than those who signed behind him, I invite one of you forth to be remembered eternally."

There had been whispering around the table for the past half hour. Cutts must have known that his crusade hung in the balance at this moment, but his eye and hand held as unwavering as a lion tamer's.

Marietta's friends stood first, thrusting their hands pointedly into their pockets. The unpleasant man spoke for them. "While all of this has been put very carefully and sharply, we sniff the pervasive stink of a great crime here. If we did not fear for the reputations of several of the more upstanding people here who might be foolish enough to throw in with an economic ruffian, we might feel compelled to warn the authorities and potential investors. Not that those reputations will not be destroyed in all cases as their owners go forward. In so saying, we bid you all good afternoon."

There was a diminishment of Cutts' obdurate sweetness of tone. "You have succeeded in making me think less well of Mr.

Grant, sir. He was clearly incapable of hitting you half as hard as you deserve. It makes me wonder if I might do better."

The two considered for a moment the reckless nature of the short wide man and the capable look of the thick hands, and then walked speedily away.

But whatever spell Cutts had cast had been broken. The others did not leave or refuse so abruptly, but with evasion, vague promises and carefully explained refusals they were all gone within the hour. The pens and contracts lay untouched. Only Mark and Hannah still sat.

Cutts was working somewhat harder now to maintain his good cheer. "You must excuse me for bringing you to a table with such a sorry collection of withering daffodils. But, you see, this is the fifth such meeting I've had this month, all of them with no more luck than this. We're getting down to the scrapings, I'm afraid. I would have been to you two earlier, but I hadn't fathomed how badly I needed your unique powers until recently."

"My unique powers?" Hannah said with a slight smile. "And here I thought you needed my money, and I was quite prepared to give you a good deal of it."

"As was I," added Mark.

The purchase agreements appeared before them so quickly and smoothly that Cutts might as well have waved a wand. "All evidences of heartfelt commitment accepted gratefully, of course. The real treasure you bring to me, though, is flair for *selling*. Your imagination. Your willingness to break outside of the way it's always been done before."

"You're a fine model for that, Mr. Cutts."

"Thank you, Mr. Grant. But I must turn my hand day and night to keep the financial side of this leaking ship afloat. The bankers drink my time as if it were fine Madeira. I need you to push the sales. I will pay any expenses, support you with contacts in any way I can and double the shares of whatever you buy."

Hannah shook her head. "Shares are paper. So is money. I want land. Ten thousand acres, shall we say, for every million dollars sold?"

The surprise that flickered across Cutts' face was immediately supplanted by delight. "Now that's the woman I've been looking for all my life. You shall have it." He swiveled around to Mark. "The same good enough for you, Mr. Grant?"

This was much more than business to Mark. He quickly calculated all he knew about Hannah and made his gamble. "No, of course not. As a man I will be doing all the negotiating and traveling. I will make use of Mrs. Oakhill's ideas, naturally, but I must have double what she's been given."

So instant and violent was the rise of color in Hannah's face that Mark thought he might have pushed her too far. She didn't speak until she had regained a measure of composure, cutting short any answer Cutts was about to make.

"Mr. Grant, all your opponents on the barges were men, and you were able to beat them all because you had more strength, more skill and more endurance. Possibly you were lucky that you never tried a woman."

Cutts roared with glee. "By God, Mrs. Oakhill, you look like you could take us both right now."

Mark pretended to try to calm her. "Please, Mrs. Oakhill, I only meant to—"

The words hit like bullets. "Let it be understood I will not be one more of your silly investors with nothing to say beyond what I can titter from behind a fan. I mean to be standing at your side, Mr. Grant, whomever you are facing and wherever you are facing them. I will be heard and I will be respected. I've beaten you enough times in previous dealings for you to know that I can support my words."

With considerable effort, Mark managed to keep the relief out of his voice. "Very well, then, madame. If you are so certain you can carry your end, let's guarantee our harmony by making our work something of a partnership. We'll take offices separate from our businesses and work together. As for the land arrangement, we can split what I just proposed if Mr. Cutts agrees. Fifteen thousand acres each for every million dollars sold."

Bursting from his chair, Cutts quickly circled each of them with an arm and drew them happily to him. "Say *yes*, Mrs. Oakhill. Say *yes!*"

Mark's lips almost brushed her cheek as the exuberant Cutts squeezed. "I'd like that very much," he said as he breathed in the lost sweetness of her. "And it will say that you forgive me."

She spoke tonelessly. "I will indeed say yes, Mr. Grant. But you will find that I forgive very slowly, but mostly not at all."

From the first day, they worked together as if they had been doing it all their lives. Mark suspected that something instinctive in her, something far out of the sight of her mind, responded to what they had been. An immediate openness sprang up between them that would ordinarily have taken months to develop. If she wondered at this unexpected rapport, she never put it into words.

However, there were times as he worked when he was sure she had stopped her pen for a moment to stare at him from beyond his central vision, searching for something that tugged at her elusively. Once, as they were shuffling through papers side by side, he caught her staring at his hands as though on the verge of a recognition. She reddened and resumed her work. "They must have been beautiful once, Mr. Grant, before you broke them up so."

His greatest difficulty was in containing his raging curiosity to know all that had befallen her. Being unable to tell any of the truths of his own life, he was loathe to question her directly and invite her own curiosity. In any case, she was stubbornly closemouthed about her past. It appeared that even the slightest thought about what had occurred in the years before she arrived in the United States caused her pain that she was completely unwilling to face.

On a day when he overheard her speaking German to representatives of European interests, he was able to get her to say that she came from Austria, but she went no further. At the back of his heart he held the terror that he would someday hear her reviling her dead and scheming husband.

As they began to put together their plans of operation, they made use more and more of the administrative people from their own organizations. These moved freely between their regular offices and the new ones taken downtown under the name of Grant and Oakhill. From Hannah's employees Mark slowly, gratefully put together the most important of the missing pieces. When he found that little Victor was alive and prospering, he had to excuse himself to wipe away tears. And the relief at learning that there was no Mr. Oakhill in Hannah's life, that her new name was one of the standard Castle Garden changes, made him feel like singing at the sky.

In the matter of Serpa, the facts were learned sketchily but with essential accuracy. "You know Benedetto Serpa, Mr. Grant? Well, Mrs. Oakhill does, too. They say they're not cozy, but anybody who gets close to her might not have anything to use his fly for."

On the one hand he was grateful that her ominous protector kept suitors always at bay. On the other he worried endlessly what the dreaded Sicilian might force upon her or, worse, what she might willingly, happily accept.

The man's deadly presence in no way threatened to turn Mark away from what he must finally do. Regain Hannah.

In the early days with Hannah, there was only one single minute when Jack Grant almost became Mark Northern for all to see.

Working at the two-sided partners' desk where they did the bulk of their work for Guy Cutts, he heard Hannah come into the larger outer office. She was intercepted by some clerk, the music of her voice delightful even through the closed door.

Then there were head and shoulders visible at the bottom of the smoked-glass upper panel. The brass knob twisted and the door opened cautiously. A handsome and sturdy child peeked in, his black, luminous eyes unchanged in their seething curiosity since Mark had last seen them.

"Hello, Mr. Grant."

"Hello, Victor," Mark said, adding much gruffness to cover what was threatening to undo him. "I've been waiting a long time to meet you."

The boy pulled off his cap, and a dark, glistening mound of

curls fell about his forehead. The vigor and strength of Hunzak were there plainly in the chin and broad cheeks, but the well-remembered sweetness and sensitivity of Hannah softened the oval features and made them impossibly dear.

"Mother is busy. But I didn't want to wait, sir. I used to hear the men talking about your fights. While they were building. Can I . . . sir, can I shake your hand?"

"Yes . . . yes. If you'll do one thing." He walked slowly toward the boy from behind the desk. "You must never call me Mr. Grant again. We're going to be very close friends. And my close friends call me Jack."

The child's face split into a rapturous grin. "Oh, *Jack*, that's *slick*." He marched forward with his hand stuck straight out in front of him.

Mark bent and shook it once and then found himself on his knees with the child crushed in his arms.

"Wow, Jack. You're *strong*. I bet you could've *killed* those guys if they made you mad."

Mark made himself back away. "I always wanted a little fighter like you to handle. Maybe I can show you a couple of things sometime."

"*Wow! Jack. Wow!*"

Hannah walked in.

"Victor, that's no way to introduce yourself."

Victor turned to her without loosening his grip. "Mother. Jack Grant's going to teach me *fighting!*"

"How about building, instead?"

"That's good, too."

With his lost family so suddenly together with him, Mark felt that if he could also have drawn Hannah into his arms, his heart might have stopped with happiness. "Certainly," he said, standing up with Victor still wrapped about him. "I'll have a little drawing table and a cut-down set of tools put in here. We'll have good men working on what our railroad towns are going to look like. They'll teach you fine."

"*Wow, Jack!*" He kissed Mark and instantly grew quiet. There was a slightly puzzled pursing of his lips, as though something banished and forgotten had begun to be called back by that touch.

Mark lowered him quickly to the floor. "How old are you now, Victor?"

"I'm seven, Jack. But I'm strong. I think maybe my father was strong. Was he, Mother?"

Hannah's expression went dead and she led the child out of the office.

The shocking word came in a note from Dirtyface Doyle:

> Dear Jack:
> Marietta is killed. Ripper McCoy done it drunk in her bed with a busted bottle last week. She took up with him after you. He got clean away. Hope you still don't keep a grudge on me after nearly four years. They will bury her in Green-Wood Cemetery in Brooklyn this afternoon. I will go for old times and because everybody else run out on her. Also I want to talk to you. You should catch a ferry and come also. Three o'clock. I hope Eddie the bookkeeper wrote this good.
>
> Truly yours, F.X. Doyle

Except for Central Park, Green-Wood Cemetery was the most beautiful place Mark had seen since he had stepped ashore. A tall, beautifully ornate arch led into an enormous expanse that was more a charming woodland than a metropolis of the dead. Paths wound gracefully beneath lowering and ancient trees. Graceful benches hid in shady copses among charmingly imaginative monuments and mausoleums. There were strollers and young lovers everywhere. The living brought their happiness to leaven the sadness of those who slept away eternity.

As Mark walked deep into the endless expanse, carefully following the directions Doyle had penciled on the back of his note, the warm sunshine that had marked the ferry crossing began to fade. What had been fast-moving clouds scudding swiftly across the blue coalesced into swollen, sluggish billows. The thin warmth of the day vanished entirely. A damp chill settled into the air. Between the trees Mark could see strollers everywhere beginning to turn back toward the gate.

Within fifteen minutes the gloom beneath the leafy canopy was so profound that it appeared to Mark that a sudden, unnatural night had fallen upon the middle of the afternoon.

Finally he stepped onto a rutted path, longer, wider and straighter than the rest, and saw some of the landmarks Doyle described. At the distant end of the dark tunnel of trees, whose leaves were beginning to show their undersides to a wind soon to bear rain, he saw a hearse, its horses drooping their plumed heads. With a confused sinking of the spirit, he turned toward it.

He hardly knew why he had come. Or why Doyle had written to him. The ceaseless cruelty of the woman left no room for feelings of tenderness. Although he did not like to admit it, he knew it was those nights, so many of them, when she had come to him like a frighteningly beautiful dream of hell. When a man was touched by a fire like that, he decided, there could be no complete healing. She would always lie with him unexpectedly in the night, joined as tenaciously to his darkest soul as she once had been to his body. Even now he felt her close, hovering, wanting. In some way that he dared not face, he mourned her.

He passed the hearse and came into a dreary clearing into which the descending clouds began to drop mist. An ornate mausoleum and many heavily carved headstones, all bearing the name *Van Vuylen*, clustered inside a low rail of marble sculpted in a motif of draped urns. Many of the dates went back to Dutch Colonial times.

Just as Doyle had written, Marietta had been abandoned. Only the black-clad men of the undertaker and the soiled, puttee-wearing squad of gravediggers were in evidence. There was no clergyman. Whoever of the distant family had arranged the burial had provided the fine hearse and coffin, but not himself, his grief or his respect.

By the time the casket was being lowered into the ground, a miserable rain, surprisingly icy for the time of year, began to fall. Two silent reporters, probably from the sensational tabloids and looking to spot the murderer of this fallen socialite peering contritely from the trees, arrived late and scribbled sketches and descriptions into notebooks. They talked to no one, quite capable of creating any number of juicy quotes all by themselves. They left as the first clods were thumping down onto the box.

Mark stood at the grave's edge, wondering if the occupant of the disappearing coffin was going to a world any more tormented and evil than the one she had known here.

It occurred to him that he had not seen Dirtyface Doyle. He looked about unexpectantly, his eyes sweeping the gloom through which the rain was now beginning to blow.

Doyle was right behind him, not five steps away, water streaming from the brim of his hat to drown the cigar he held clenched in his teeth. "Hello, Jack," he said. "I'm glad you came."

His long coat was thrown over his shoulders like a cape. Mark could see that he sheltered something beneath it, a bundle that he held in one arm.

"Hello, Dirty. I don't know why you're here. But then I don't really know why I'm here either."

"Maybe you don't care much for me these days, Jack. But I had somethin' I had to show you."

Doyle opened his coat so Mark could see the child he held. In the face of the little girl, who was not more than five years old, he saw the part of himself he would never be able to see in Victor. A stab of pure brightness shot through the gloom, and Mark made out the shimmering fire of the magnificent ring he had given to Marietta. It hung on a chain about the girl's neck.

The thud of the falling clods in his ears, Mark stumbled closer to her, a sudden lightness in his head.

"Her name is Evangeline," Doyle said.

She was shockingly beautiful. The features were Mark's, but she looked at him through the cold blue eyes of Marietta, clear windows through which the dead mother looked out from her damnation. The tears that ran on the pink cheeks might have been crystals of ice. And if the lips were his, they were also Marietta's in their cruel, near-sensual set. There was a seething intensity about her that was close to frightening. Yet, the small hands held to Doyle desperately, and a stifled little sob overcame Mark's faint misgivings quickly. He brushed away the tears with a gentle fingertip.

"What happened, Dirty? Everything, please."

"She took on McCoy before your bed was cold. There was nothin' he wanted here. He wanted to get back to Frisco. Had a wife and a couple of kids back there. But you know how she was when she wanted somethin'. She put the hex on him. He stayed on, gettin' drunker and drunker. Then he got into the opium pipes and the powders. He wouldn't be worth a fart in a real ring anymore, so she said she'd back him on the barges, like she done with you. That's a different world from the one he came from. He found that out with you. So she kept me on in the house to train him."

"When did you find out about the baby?"

Doyle evaded his eyes. "Before you were gone. When she was drunk in bed with me that time."

"Why in God's name didn't you tell me?"

"She said I'd end up part of the foundations of the new courthouse if I did. And she had a look that told me she meant it."

"Why? What difference could it make to her?"

"Only a devil like her could hatch such a scheme. She planned it the whole way. It was a baby she was after. Your baby. She said you was the best man she knew."

"For the child's sake I might have married her, for all the witch she was."

Doyle snorted. "That's the last thing in the world she wanted. I caught onto that quick enough."

"I don't understand."

"She wanted to raise herself a kid outside all the rules. Her way. In her kind of life, without you around."

Mark's blood tingled. "My God. How bad was it?"

"As bad as it could be. This girl already knows things that respectable women go to their graves without knowin'."

"Is it possible that Marietta couldn't even love her own child?"

"Ah, she loved her all right, and the girl loved her back. That only burned in the terrible things deeper. The only blessin' is that the black creature didn't live longer, Jack."

"Why is it that you have Evangeline?"

"Because there's nobody else that wants her, is why. River rat I might be, but I couldn't let her live these years with no one sane to look out for her. I took her when I could and tried to hold off what was happenin'. One time I beat hell out of a steamship line president I caught undressin' her. The thing is, I got kind of attached. But I tell you, Jack, there's somethin' in her that scares me, too."

"What about Marietta's people? There must be somebody—"

"Sure there's somebody, but those fancy people don't want nothin' to do with a whore's bastard, you can bet. They took the money, the jewelry they could find and the house quick enough. But they won't even offer the kid a ride to the orphanage. I thought I might take her in myself, but with the life I live I'm not much better for her than Marietta. There's only you, Jack. Will you have her?"

"Nobody will care?"

"Nobody who's not in hell."

Mark reached beneath Doyle's coat and brought the child into his arms. She was shivering and the rain sent the bright golden curls streaming down her forehead.

"Why didn't they get the ring? Or you, Doyle?"

"Marietta hung it around her neck before she died. Dragged herself to the kid's room to do it. It's a witch's ring now. Nobody wants it. Even me."

"Say goodbye to her, Dirty."

The big-bellied man bent close, as though he might kiss her, and then shied away. He nodded to Mark, set his dripping hat more firmly on his head and slogged away.

The force of the rain increased again. Mark saw that Marietta's grave was now filled, the loamy mound above it washing away in the downpour.

The child called out unexpectedly, "I hear you, Mother. *I hear you.*"

They rode out of the cemetery in the hearse, and as it bumped down the long, gloomy path beneath the dark, overgrowing trees, Mark felt a depression settle upon him that would continue unrelieved for days.

For many reasons, the coming of Evangeline could not have occurred at a worse time. The preparations for the Guy Cutts project was draining the hours out of all Mark's days and most of his nights. Now, at the moment that this unanticipated child of his needed him most to undo the fearsome damage of Marietta, he would have to be gone for days, weeks, perhaps months at a time.

And there was the matter of Hannah. A short time ago Evangeline could have entered his life unobserved by anyone he cared about. Now she had to be explained in some way to the woman whom he dreamed of keeping in his life.

For several days he hid Evangeline in his home as he sorted through his feelings. He hired another expensive housekeeper to look after her needs, but spent all the time he could close to the child.

Evangeline did not understand the concept of play or the notion of affection. The games and toys that Mark bought for her she examined carefully and discarded as soon as she ascertained their purpose. Mark's hugs and kisses were treated in much the same way. She handled them as curiosities to be tried on at first, later to be merely endured as they failed to produce any pleasing effect in her.

Although she often laughed, it was at odd, inappropriate times. The mortal discomfort of a goldfish fallen from its bowl and flopping on the carpet delighted her. But when she had enough of its pain she placed it back into its water and fed it solicitously thereafter. When the housekeeper burned her hand on the stove, the woman's wail of pain was matched by Evangeline's cry of joyous excitement. Still, she appointed herself the woman's "nurse" and fussed with the dressings every day. Damage had been done, Mark thought, but what was gentle in her blood had been not quite entirely overcome by what was not.

Mark could hardly keep his eyes off her. Sitting by a window in a pool of sunlight, she seemed to catch and multiply the rays in a dazzle of burnished hair and glittering eyes, like the diamond she wore about her neck. Her beauty might have been spun out of the falling shafts of light. Hour by hour, he began to feel a father's love for her building, heating his heart and generating intensity and tenderness. There were times when he suspected that this rapidly expanding warmth reached into the cool marble of Evangeline and caused her to begin to be drawn to him. But with her, he expected, he would never be sure.

"I'm your father, Evangeline. You must begin to call me that."

"I heard about fathers. Mother had lots of them."

"I don't want you to talk about those others anymore. I don't want you to talk about your mother, either. Not with me. Not with anyone."

"Yes."

"Yes, Father, you must say."

"Yes, Father."

"Will you kiss me, sweetheart?"

She kissed him strongly on the lips. "Mother's fathers used to kiss me—"

"Evangeline!"

"Yes, I mustn't talk about them to anyone."

Mark told Hannah that Evangeline was his. He told his partner only that the child's mother was dead, leaving the rest open to speculation. He was grateful that Hannah accepted his need for privacy as willingly as he accepted hers.

"Say hello to Mrs. Oakhill, Evangeline."

"Hello, Mrs. Oakhill. Do you have a father like I do?"

"Not anymore, dear."

"Are you allowed to talk about him?"

"Yes, I am. Why?"

Evangeline looked at Mark. "I thought maybe you couldn't talk about dead people."

Hannah Oakhill understood almost nothing about Jack Grant. Especially the affinity she felt for him almost from the moment they had been introduced.

As his crosstown rival, she had been trying to meet him out of nothing more than admiring curiosity for many months. It was only after having heard that he was one of the men invited by Cutts that she had decided to go to Delmonico's to talk business with a man whose reputation caused people to hang onto their wallets and false teeth while he was in the room.

She had, of course, known that Grant came off the barges, and she came prepared not to be surprised by any amount of physical damage or barbarity. She expected that the Gentleman Jack appellation came from gaudy dress and the fact that he didn't eat his mashed potatoes with his hands. So she had several shocks during that first introduction.

His clothing had been immaculate, tasteful and in the highest fashion. Although any expensive tailor might have accomplished that for a few hundred dollars, only a lifetime of familiarity could have caused him to carry his clothes the way he did.

The beard and the eyepatch could not hide the savage battering of his face, but the bone structure was intact and marvelous. While scarred and plainly repaired, the nose had never been large and assumed its own rugged, not unattractive character. Most fascinating was the eye that remained. The slices around the brows had certainly affected its shape, but it concentrated the strength and turmoil of its owner in a way that made her gasp quietly. The same sort of golden brown in Mark's eyes had reflected peace and tenderness. In Jack Grant the color snapped out so hungrily, so boldly, that she could almost feel it against her skin.

If his voice was hoarse and broken, his words were precise, cultured, well chosen and always assured. He would probably never lose the thick shoulders and tigerish movements of a fighter, but there was appealing grace in him.

Until his story of a genteel Boston upbringing, she was surprised at the scrupulous perfection of his manners, which were in some ways more polished than those of the half-drunk dandies around the table.

She was grateful when he angered her with his doubts about a woman being able to function effectively in business. It reminded her that men existed to wound and scorn women, and that she invited them into her merest affection at deadly peril. Not that he sought such affection. After his first mesmerizing stare he seemed to have seen quite enough of her. Seated right at her side, he appeared determined not to look at her directly, for the most part. When he finally faced her for their confrontation after the other investors had gone, she found herself oddly pleased to have at last regained his attention. And, without knowing why or being certain that she liked him, no force on earth could have made her refuse his offer to work together.

The intensity of their work side by side was such that she had little time to contemplate the inner life of her harmonious new partner. But when her mind did find a moment to drift toward him, she found her curiosity and fascination growing. Ideas seemed to flow out of him full-blown, complete in every detail. Yet he listened to her own ideas carefully and modified his without a quibble. An unspoken, mutually respectful rivalry grew between them, and it was his dynamic example that caused her to reach deeper inside herself than she ever knew she could, to match and often surpass him.

Across the desk, he seldom raised his head to speak or stopped his writing. But she thought she heard pleasure in his voice when he talked to her, something relaxed and pleased that she didn't see in him elsewhere.

She wondered if he, like her, allowed the hours of work together to stretch out because of the pleasant company as much as the urgency of the tasks at hand. And she enjoyed how Victor talked about his friend, Jack, as though a new father had appeared for him.

Now the sudden appearance of Evangeline had changed the rhythm of their lives. Hannah was annoyed with herself at the relief she felt to learn that the woman who had borne her partner's daughter was out of the way. She also recognized the tiny twinge of jealousy that there had even been any other woman.

There were moments when she longed to ask him to tell her every detail of what had gone before in his life. But seeing the intensity of his need for privacy, she always held back.

What she was able to deal with far less well was a sudden, sharp cut in her hours with Jack Grant.

"I'll try to make up most of it at home, Mrs. Oakhill. Evangeline needs more than a housekeeper now. I have to be with her as much as I can."

Instantly Hannah saw Jack Grant's problem as a precise echo of her own, and the answer sprang into her mind with startling clarity. "Might I make a suggestion that would solve a problem for both of us, Mr. Grant? I'm building a new house for myself and Victor. It's quite large, with plenty of room for the help. Frau Wendt is a superb teacher and Filomena is a wonderful, loving Italian mother for any child she comes near. Why not move Evangeline in with me? I'll be there for her, and Victor could become her big brother. They both badly need the company of other children. The house would be open to you at any time, of course, and I could have a room set aside for you when you wish to spend the night with her."

His delight was obvious. "That's a marvelous notion, Mrs. Oakhill. Thank you."

"We can make it more marvelous still. There was to be a big drawing room. I'd have little use for it. It's very well situated for an office. We could do much of our work there when we're not traveling. Perhaps all of it, so we'd have more time for the children."

"I'd like to share in the cost of the building."

"Nonsense, Mr. Grant. There's something about Evangeline that makes me feel she could have been my own daughter." Until she said those words, Hannah hadn't realized that she had made that odd observation.

"If we're going to be a bit like a real father and mother," he said, "maybe it's time we called each other by our first names."

She had been looking for a way to say that without appearing forward. "That would be fine, Jack."

"Should we shake hands on it, Hannah?"

The feel of his hand in hers gave confirmation to her heart that she had made her proposal with the chief and shameless purpose of having him near to her as often as could be managed.

In the short time it took to complete the new house, the work of the Superior-Pacific Railroad rose to swallow them up. Nonetheless, Hannah was able to see that their new arrangement was a success. Victor soon stepped outside his nature as a miniature adult and adopted Evangeline, first as a toy and then as a playmate and friend. He took her intermittent screaming rages, replete with kicks, scratches and bites, as a challenge to the patience and understanding of a grown-up seven-year-old. He never shouted angrily or struck back, but coaxed her out of her redfaced furies with teasing games that soon had her laughing again. Then things would go smoothly for days, until she would smash one of his toys for no apparent reason or bite him in the midst of a smile, as though to warn him that there was a wildness in her as deep as her bones, inbred and untamable. Yet, Hannah thought, the first tastes of new, gentle love were also having their effect. If Evangeline turned upon the people who now offered their affection, it was because any amount was short of satisfying her raging hunger for it. The death of her mother had been a cruel desertion that had left the child in hostile, uncaring emptiness.

If her instability was a trial, the child's sweetness in her tranquil moments was a marvel. Her harsh, nervous laugh was soon supplemented by a shy smile that was the essence of sunshine. And when she bestowed it, it became impossible to remember that she had ever misbehaved, even while waiting certainly for the next outburst.

She was capable of great loyalties, and of switching them like lightning. For weeks she would be at Victor's side from sunup to sundown. Then at midday she would switch to Grant, crawling into his lap and getting underfoot until it was tempting to tie her down. Hannah and Filomena also had their turns in her revolving adoration. When she inevitably returned, it was as though she had never defected. Evangeline became a treasured member of the strange little household, her charm being sought all the more for its being so elusive.

As for Grant's relationship with Victor, Hannah watched it develop and become loving and steadfast so quickly that people who did not know them assumed completely that they were father and son.

Though it took some time for Grant to begin to use the room set aside for him, he thereafter became a regular overnight guest. And soon he was in Hannah's house as much as in his own.

Not forgetting her injuries from men, Hannah refused to impute his growing presence to anything but his devotion to the children. That notwithstanding, she was glad to notice that he seemed happy to be spending more time close to her.

The attention of Serpa could not be forgotten. He had viewed her new associate suspiciously from the first. And when he had learned that Grant was now a frequent overnight guest, he had Filomena taken off the street as she shopped at the fish market. She later told this story to Hannah:

The housekeeper had been brought before him, her terror only slightly lessened by the presence of the gaunt, unsmiling parish priest, Father Alleghieri, who stood holding a Bible.

"Filomena," Serpa said quietly, "the soul of your mistress, whom all of us so admire, may hang in the balance above terrible sin. You miss nothing, so I am certain you know all. I also know that you fear God greatly. For the sake of Jesus and Mrs. Oakhill, do what Father Alleghieri asks."

The priest came to her and placed her hand upon the Bible, after which he pressed her to her knees. "At the risk of your immortal life, tell me what there is between Mrs. Oakhill and the man Jack Grant."

Filomena almost burst with relief at having to tell no soul-damning lies that would have been given away instantly by her impossibly guileless face. "With Jesus as my loving witness, they sleep apart. They do not embrace or even touch. Their words are only the words of business, except when they speak of the children. I swear it."

When she went to rise, Serpa held her down by the shoulder. "I believe you have spoken truly of what has come into your eyes and ears. You are a woman. What is in her heart?"

She found the courage to look up at him directly. "A woman injured by men is like a dog kicked too many times. No one can say when they are ready to be petted. But I would say that she is not."

When she had told her mistress all, with shivery misgivings that Serpa would learn of it, Hannah hugged her gratefully. "Thank you, Filomena. But Mr. Serpa is going to have to do his worrying from a distance very soon, and without your sharp eyes. Mr. Grant and I will be going west for several weeks to serve our business. You will be staying home with the children and Frau Wendt."

"You will be careful, Signora?"

"Of Mr. Serpa or Mr. Grant? Or Indians?"

"For you, Signora, all these men are dangerous."

Hannah and Grant had gone as far as they could in their work for Guy Cutts without setting eyes upon the lands about which they would be required to rhapsodize. So early one morning in April they rode the rails west to Chicago and progressed from there to Duluth. From that port city on Lake Superior they would proceed along the route of the Superior-Pacific, whose tracks ended all too soon to the West, to Puget Sound. They were not alone.

"The group we want to bring isn't cheap," Grant had told Cutts the last time he and Hannah had visited his office in Washington. "Photography isn't a science, it's an art, and Saul Bruderman is a Tintoretto with a lens. He's worked out a way to process the plates, that will make the camera see better and more excitingly than the eye. I've seen his pictures of the deserts and the Colorado canyons. They capture all of God's beauty and more.

He'll get the spirit of that magnificent northern wilderness in a way that will have people fighting to be first in the new towns along that track."

"He'd better," Cutts said. "Nobody wants a piece of land on a railroad going through no place to nowhere unless we can give them something to dream about. And that land money is as important as the share money. Pay your camera genius what you want. Now why do you need the artist too?"

Hannah unrolled some landscape pictures she carried with her. They were inks and watercolors, quick sketches many of them, but done with such evocative power that the viewer could smell the miles of grasses, sense the rustle of the lush trees and hear the rush of the broad rivers. "If Ernst Trier can hang work in some of the best museums in the country at the age of twenty-eight, I think he might just be good enough to fill in the spots along the way where the camera is a bit too truthful. The art of the pen will reproduce in the newspapers, too. And it's the newspapers that will make us in the end."

"Indeed, Mrs. Oakhill. And words can sometimes make prettier pictures than either the pen or the brush. I certainly don't have to ask you any questions about Crunch O'Meara."

Mark strewed a large bag of books, pulp novels, magazine stories, pamphlets and essays on every imaginable subject across Cutts' desk. "O'Meara writes like other people breathe. He has at least three dozen different styles, going from biblical to what would make a barkeep blush. All of them punchy enough to knock you off your chair. We've got to restrain him, though, or every blade of grass will become a redwood tree. And we've got to hold him to a bottle-and-a-half a day. But he can describe a cow pie so you'd want one for your mantlepiece."

"Don't be gone too long, you two. We need you to get those sales going."

"We'll move like lightning, Mr. Cutts," said Hannah. "You'll see us again in less than four months."

Somehow, the madly disparate explorers made a convivial if unlikely team. O'Meara, a ferret barely five feet tall, had only his addiction to the pen to keep his addiction to the bottle from destroying him. His incredible facility for producing words on paper drew away his need to speak, and he was largely silent as he scribbled wherever he sat, stood or lay. He had his perfect counterpart in the lean young Danish artist, Trier, who sketched and painted as avidly and silently as O'Meara scribbled. The two prisoners of their art became inseparable, often developing prose and pictures simultaneously. Not far behind them in their rambles was Bruderman. The photographer, no longer young and a sartorial nightmare of competing plaids, was a learned man who lectured seamlessly on any subject that crossed his path. He required no answers or discussion beyond an occasional nod or smile, and thus served as a constant, gentle entertainer and educator for his reticent colleagues.

The result of the cohesive nature of their staff was to leave Grant and Hannah alone together enough of the time so their intimacy might grow between grueling work and travel.

Meanwhile, the two partners were forever unable to conclude whether Guy Cutts was an even greater charlatan than had been advertised, or a man of vision and destiny who outstripped even his most overblown estimates of his own abilities.

Their first view of Duluth, the earthly paradise so often described by Cutts, was a great and sobering shock and inclined them to believe the former.

The metropolis could not possibly have mustered two thousand souls, and these were huddled in a disorganized clutter of shacks and stores distributed among streets that somehow remained quagmires although the last snow had melted weeks before. Except for the town's location, where its decrepit, ice-ravaged docks could put lake cargo ashore with some convenience and access to roads west, the dispirited struggle would not have existed for an hour. What attempts had been made to throw up a civic structure or two as a center were being rapidly confounded by an element of accelerated disintegration that could not be explained by any available law of physics.

As for the citizens, although ready to fight to the death with rusty knives at the suspicion of an insult, they were otherwise cowed by the succession of icebound winters, fly-tortured springs, drought-blasted summers and mud-choked autumns, and seemed as devoid of spirit as men tortured too long. Hannah thought, as she took in a breath loaded with clouds of tiny, stinging flies, that the flotsam of the New York waterfront might upgrade the spirit, breeding and intelligence found on the waterfront of Duluth. The railway gangs who returned to town from the wilderness for a drink, a fight and a visit to the house of excessively soiled doves seemed glad to flee back on the next handcar.

"So this is the coming Rome of the American West."

"Now, Hannah. All it needs is a good sacking and burning. And then a railroad and some towns for it to go through."

In short order their guide, a shaven headed mute named Dummy Bowes, appeared in buckskins and led them out.

Whatever depression they had acquired in Duluth was speedily dissipated once they reached the end of the westward reaches of track and proceeded by cart, coach and horseback along the trails of the most overpowering country they had ever seen.

Bruderman and Trier were no strangers to the vistas of the opening West, but even they were awed by the well-watered richness and majesty of the terrain. O'Meara scratched away so rapidly that he forgot to drink for days, and the others feared he would write his way through the mountains of notebooks he had brought. No horseman at all, he still managed to keep his seat and direction while he wrote using both hands.

To Hannah, whose idea of an immense overland journey had been one from Vienna to Paris by rail, the distances were beyond anything her imagination could handle. On a clear day they would top a high rise and look out upon an expanse of plains, trees and rivers that would have made up an important nation in the old world, and here there was not a house, a farm or even a distant rider to be seen.

"Jack, it makes me want to cry."

"They're fighting bloody wars somewhere for land that's not half of what you can see from here."

"For the first time I feel this job might be too big."

"Hannah, I think that's the first lie you ever told me."

Day after day they rode under skies bluer than any they had ever seen and breathed air as exhilarating as priceless perfume. Armies of clouds grew fat and lean, raced and loafed across the sky, met and clashed in dangerous, freshening storms where electricity made hair stand and nostrils tingle.

The travelers grew brown and hard, becoming closer and more respectful of the God in these endless skies as they became mindful of what specks they were, moving across the rolling, stunning infinity.

Their camps were picked by Bowes, who was often riding miles ahead, and he looked expertly to their comfort with an amazingly eloquent assortment of whistles and hand signals. He seldom motioned for help, and his deft, tireless gun, ax, knife and frying pan produced snug shelters, instantaneous campfires and a deliciously fried assortment of small game, all seemingly without effort.

Bruderman, Trier and O'Meara subsided with the sun every day, asleep almost as soon as they had eaten the last of the evening meal. This left Grant and Hannah to sit before the sparkling fire with Dummy Bowes. The cold was often considerable, and they all pulled in close to the flames, each wrapped in a blanket from head to toe. Bowes invariably sucked sweet tobacco out of long-barreled Indian pipe. The endless alertness of his expression, even at these relaxed moments, made his companions forget for a time that he was totally deaf, and that conversation might be carried on to his utter indifference. But little by little they began to speak to one another comfortably in his presence.

Mostly they spoke of their day and their plans for the Superior-Pacific. Sometimes they shared their hopes for their businesses in New York, each poking awkward fun at the other's sharper deals. It was when they touched on Victor and Evangeline that it became obvious to Hannah that they remained apart in many ways. Neither was ready to go deeply into the past. Although there were times that she suspected he was attracted to her, she began to doubt that he would ever approach her as other than a business partner. She supposed that he had loved someone long ago. And that memory would hold him away from anyone else. She was annoyed with herself for the regret this caused her.

There came a night when they were camped beneath towering pines on a high plateau below the Dakotas. Although well into June, the weather turned biting, sending a freezing sleet. As night came on, they built a fire sheltered by an overhanging ledge and ate a cheerless meal. As usual, O'Meara, Trier and Bruderman turned in immediately afterward, but their curses and moans said that around the fire was a better place to spend the night than in the canvas shelters. The others decided to spend the night where they were, feeding the flames by turns.

The leathery guide who sat with them was as always immune to all swings of temperature. But he saw that Hannah shivered despite the fire and that Grant wasn't much better off, even after they had taken several considerable pulls on a jug of fiery rum. So after a time he got to his feet and came to them. He signaled for them to move shoulder to shoulder. Then he removed their blankets. He placed the thick woolen wraps one on top of the other and draped the doubled covering over the seated pair. Now they had twice the protection plus their body heat to warm them. They nodded their thanks.

Bowes, a comic and crafty look in his sharp eyes, waved an unexpected goodnight and gathered up his gear. He motioned that he would build another fire on the opposite side of the sheltering rock and sleep there.

When he had gone, Hannah found herself savoring this first physical closeness to her aloof partner.

"I'm sure we both know why he did this," Hannah whispered to finally break the thick silence. Bowes' rum was working in both of them.

"He meant no insult to you, I'm sure. It's a natural thing in his world. Don't be angry with him, Hannah."

"I think it was a terribly kind and thoughtful thing. Will you think poorly of me if I stay here with you?"

"Nothing could ever make me think poorly of you."

She hesitated a moment before she spoke. "Not even if I told you I wish I were Bowes' kind of woman right now?"

"Hannah," he said wonderingly, "You don't know me—"

"And it's my guess that I never will. It won't stand in my way if it won't stand in yours." There was no going back now.

He turned his face away so she couldn't read anything there. "The wilderness does odd things to civilized people. Especially mixed with the lightning in that jug," he said.

Under the blanket she found his hand and pulled off his glove. She twined her fingers through his. Her cheeks felt hot against the freezing wind. "If this surprises you, I assure you it surprises me even more."

His hand didn't move in hers. What if he was disgusted, and she had simply made a drunken fool of herself? Then she would have not only destroyed forever their growing closeness, but any chance of their continuing to work comfortably together on their enormous task.

"Please understand," he said softly. "Since the first day I saw you in New York, my one wish has been to have you. In every way. But I hoped that by then you would love me as a man whom you were certain about. I couldn't stand it if one day you turned away and said, 'You never let me see what you really were.'"

At last his hand began to tighten on hers. A great hope grew in her. She spoke slowly to hide her nervousness. "Are you now assuming that I love you?"

"God, I'm sorry, I—"

"What I'd like to assume first is that you love *me.*"

"And if I did, Hannah?" She had never before seen him so little in control of himself.

"Then I would demand that you give me a full three seconds to tell you the same before you did anything about it."

He turned to her, his face in the firelight suddenly beautiful beneath the scars. As he tried to compose himself to say something, he caught what she knew was in her eyes. His open mouth came down on hers and drew her quickly to him.

The chilling sleet blew in over the fire, carrying with it clouds of hot embers. Under the blanket they were wrapped in long, bulky coats of canvas so thick and stiff that buttons could hardly be undone in the best of circumstances. Beneath the coats were layers upon layers of shirts and vests. And, nicely illuminated, they were easily in the view of any of the men in the tents opposite who chanced to waken.

They considered none of it for a moment. Shivering, breathless, they worked furiously at one another's clothing, each grudged loosening of a buttonhole, each hard-won falling open of a garment driving higher the unstoppable desire that was expanding in their bodies.

Hannah had only a fractional moment to feel the lash of the sleet and the sting of embers where the clothing had been torn back from her breasts and thighs before Jack Grant covered her, the knotted muscles of his fighter's belly visible for the flicker of an eye before he arrived enormously inside her.

All the convulsive heat she had felt with Serpa was there, but there was something new that carried her past that peak. Here there was no dark overlay of rutting bestiality, but a running sheet of brightness that leaped from her skin and lightened the world to the treetops.

He arched upward upon his arms, pushing, twisting, quickening his thrusts. "Oh, Hannah. You'll never know how long I've loved you."

"It could never be long enough."

He cried out and pulled backward. Hannah felt the hot streaks of him jump across her belly. He bent and kissed her. "Forgive that, Hannah. We'll have our children when all this is done. At the right time, after a fine wedding."

While her body screamed to go on, these words so filled her mind with joy that she almost forgot the long shivers running through her.

They were not together that way again for the rest of the journey to Puget Sound and the return. The nearness of their companions was too unrelenting and the accommodations unendingly brutal.

But a pact had been sealed with their bodies, and its sweet reverberations were with them always in the long weeks, the thought of new sweetnesses a distant, shimmering certainty.

Now, seen with the eye and spirit of a lover, the spectacular glories along the route of the Superior-Pacific completely enchanted Hannah. The sunshine might have been a rain of gold, the rivers the tears of angels. She wondered whether her senses could be trusted anymore.

But she saw that the rest of the party was as swept away as she. A whole pack horse appeared to be loaded with little except bags of sketches and exposed photographic plates produced by Bruderman and Trier. Even the reticent O'Meara broke his silence on certain evenings when what he had seen in the day had especially captivated him. He would read his more inspired descriptions aloud as Bowes prepared the evening feast, and the listeners knew that even though the words were all overblown by three times, there was more than enough truth to make the group believe in their cause more strongly than ever. At home these words would sweep away doubt like an avalanche. Somewhat disturbingly, O'Meara continually revised, pumping in new and even more florid adjectives and leaps of fancy. But with wonders like these, who could exactly determine where fancy left off and dishonesty began?

Cutts welcomed them back like a conquering legion returning to Rome. He had gotten every nickel he could from the banks without more land and stock sales. They had arrived not one moment too soon.

After a brief but fervent reunion with their children, when they had sorted out what they brought back and made some sense of what now had to be done, they realized it might be many months before they had a chance to carry forward their own happy plans.

"Can we wait, Jack?

"No, Hannah. We can't."

"We'll have no real life together until this is over."

"We did a good job for Cutts. Perhaps we could just tell him good-bye now."

"We could do that. He could find someone else after a while."
"Do you want to?"

She hugged him. "Opening up half a continent. We wouldn't forgive ourselves if we weren't there. Our wedding will be an extra prize at the end of it. A reward bigger than all the others."

As they kissed she felt a flutter of doubt. Was it unnatural to love the land so well that it held her—however briefly—from a love she had despaired of finding ever again? She might have told him that she had thought better of the delay, but his lips stayed on hers so long that all else left her thought.

The printing presses turned unceasingly, cranking out an ocean of luridly illustrated brochures and flyers. But literature alone would not be enough. There had to be speaking tours complete with magic-lantern projections and uniformed bands. Cutts produced a voluble corps of respected names who were ready to proclaim their complete belief in the project, describing the prodigies they had seen with their own eyes. Hannah doubted heavily that the people were indeed respectable, or that the land had really been bought or really been seen, but Cutts assured her that they were just a half step ahead of a stampede of actual purchasers ready to present similar testimonials.

"There's too much ground to cover for us to stay together," Hannah said to Grant. "You work north up to Boston. I'll work south to Baltimore. Then we'll each move west."

"Did you ever speak to an audience Hannah?"

"I never had anything I wanted to speak about."

"I sound like a damned bullfrog."

"They'll come to see the great fighter who's going to bring them glory, land and money. Make sure you have a reception afterward so they can all shake your hand and faint at your scars."

"This face will set them climbing out the windows."

"There will be wives and rich widows and maiden ladies. They'll feel what I felt. Just don't let them get you in front of a fire while they're rummaging for their money."

To her pleased amazement, Hannah was a superb speaker and

an even better organizer. Her trips were planned and carried forth like major sieges.

First there was a prolonged preliminary bombardment of mailed and hand-distributed literature, followed by an escalating secondary barrage in the newspapers, this evenly divided between openly paid advertisements and glowing features obtained by discreet gifts to the most important editorial writers. Rather than trust to the unreliable prose of provincial scribblers, she had Crunch O'Meara prepare sample pieces where the great writer's winged prose might be tailored with a scissors to local needs and space.

She found soon that the people of this young country best grasped what they were being presented if a verbal "handle" were first attached. So the Superior-Pacific became the "Railway to Destiny," and the country through which it proceeded, happily available for sale, "The New Eden." Guy Cutts was identified as "The Hope of Landless Millions." All these terms were soon common currency in print and in parlor conversations.

After the fortifications had been suitably softened, Hannah arrived with her army. Not all of it, of course, she and Grant having split the forces between them, but there were more than enough. Grant had taken Bruderman, the photographer, to the more sophisticated and hardheaded New Englanders, who were more likely to be convinced by the solid evidence of scientific photographs. Hannah took Trier, the illustrator, whose not truly accurate, but infinitely colorful and exciting composites were much more to the taste of the more emotional and hot-hearted southerners.

The sons of Dixie liked their rhetoric well embellished, too, so she prevailed upon Crunch O'Meara to accompany her expedition south, and his eloquences found a home. Hannah quoted liberally from his notebooks, letting the dusty, dirty, tattered journals be seen in her hands for naked authenticity. Since each lecture was widely reported in the local newspapers, she tried to have new material each evening so no eye-popping fact would be missed in any town.

O'Meara wrote fanciful reams of connective tissue for the scattered descriptions in his journals, neatly distorting the framework of time, place and distance. He could place crashing breakers on the Duluth waterfront, with the sun setting gloriously in the east over Lake Superior. He could place giant trees on treeless plains and lush farms where no farmers had yet appeared.

So debased had the currency of land descriptions become, Hannah soon comprehended, that an utterly truthful rendering would amount to condemnation. Her twinges of conscience soon subsided.

Her delivery style was natural, impressive and quickly polished. She had a clear, ringing voice that cut through to the rear of the largest halls, and her elegant European accent disarmed and bewitched her audiences.

"There is no question that upon this pulsing artery of growth, reaching into a goldmine of natural resources and intersecting trade routes that will make the caravan roads of old Cathay seem poor, there will rise a dozen cities to rival and beggar New York. To the few men with foresight, these future metropolitan engines of wealth will represent fiefdoms not seen since the day of the feudal baron. From the railroad, from the towns and cities, from the timber, the mines, the fish, the farms, great fortunes will flow. Our terms are long, our offer unprecedented. Come forward to me, and, whether or not you are ready for riches, let me embrace and thank each and every one of you for your kind attention."

Face to face, holding them in her arms, her perfume all around them, her wonderful eyes and red, smiling lips inches from theirs, Hannah found the cavaliers who had come up to express regrets often departed as buyers.

From the north came reports that Jack Grant was having a similar success. The showmanship he had begun in New York flowered. He soon appreciated that his harsh, almost frightening voice and battle-scarred face were assets in the winning of attention. His cultured speech and ways were in exciting contrast to his rough background. Boston Brahmins, intrigued in spite of themselves, came forward to shake the hand of the great bareknuckle fighter and lingered for brandy and buying.

Cutts delightedly checked the figures for the first swing and found that he was for the moment oversubscribed and that five million dollars to begin the new construction was in hand. He sent both Grant and Hannah a foot-square box of soil with a thousand dollars in gold coins seeded through it. The message read:

Heartiest congratulations. This is the first of the new ground broken on the Superior-Pacific Railroad. The eventual worth of every foot of land along our right-of-way is included. Joyfully, Cutts.

Hannah immediately made the box of soil and gold an exhibit in her travels, and she caught and landed many a fish lingering by it.

But there were troubles. Cutts met the two in Chicago and addressed his concerns. "Cash is our problem, friends. Our subscribers pay in installments. They have ten years to come up with all the money, but we, unfortunately, do not. To keep building at the required pace we must have more. Ideas, please."

"Famous men are what we need now," Hannah said. "There are not enough of them in the world for their money to make enough difference, but the money we can raise on their names can be considerable."

"Good," Grant added. "It won't make any difference if they don't have the cash. We can make them very special terms, or even give them land for their help."

Hannah was warming up. "Not just businessmen. Theatrical people, clergymen, government figures, even figures of athletic reputation. Jack has shown that can be important."

They worked carefully, spreading the impression that not just anyone was to be allowed to participate. A list was leaked to one of the newspapers. It cataloged many notable people who had been found unsuitable for inclusion, and a minor stampede developed among those who didn't want to be overlooked.

The vice-president of the United States, the chief justice of the Supreme Court, President Grant's private secretary and a horde of governors, congressmen, judges and actresses were soon in the fold and writing paeans to the scheme.

One especially rewarding sale came out of a trip to Brooklyn. An omnivorous reader of the city's scandal sheets, which often produced tidbits to be used with advantage, Hannah had learned a great deal about the fabled hellfire minister, Henry Ward Beecher. His congregation was enormous and loaded with the city's financial and political leaders. He seemed to have one weakness: the inability to remain aloof to the ankles of a pretty woman, and all above.

So there came a Sunday afternoon when Hannah sat alone with the great man in his sun-filled front parlor in Brooklyn, having her fill of his tea, his sweet cakes and his rumpled, stentorian, middle-aged charm.

"Mrs. Oakhill, as distressing as it is to learn that you were tragically widowed so young, it is also an inspiration to a truly romantic heart such as mine."

"I have done some reading where perhaps I should not, Mr. Beecher, and your romantic heart is well known."

He set down his cup and edged closer to her on the brocaded sofa. "The service of God is the loneliest one in the world, my dear. It's natural that other lonely creatures sense that affinity and cry out to me as they cry out to God for all the blessings and comforts of close companionship."

"And do you not agree that one such comfort of close companionship would be God-sent advice on how to increase their fortune by a great amount?"

He was now close enough to take her hands in his and clasp them to his breast. "I believe in the future of the Superior-Pacific Railroad as firmly as I believe in the great hereafter, Mrs. Oakhill. My gratitude to the heavenly powers that enable me to share its bounty on such excellent terms as you have offered me is boundless. But my gratitude to the earthly powers is also considerable. I would be happy to bring my poor gifts of tongue and pen to bear on the financial betterment of my congregation. But the exact wording and degree of fervor in such work can be greatly increased by long and relaxed discussion. Through those sliding doors is a large, comfortable bed, and a cabinet filled with fine port and sherry. Comfortably reclining and free of the raiment despised by Adam and Eve, we might profitably speak of our business."

"Mr. Beecher, your words tug at my heart, but they must not tug at my garments. I would, however, find it delightful to feel the Divine warmth on my cheek through your lips, so that I can speak of it discreetly but with great titillation one day."

"A kiss on even so lovely a cheek as yours is a small beginning for so great an endeavor."

"Not if it seals an additional promise of five percent for you on each Superior-Pacific package purchased by your flock."

"Sometimes the flesh is more profitably mortified than gratified," he said, but nonetheless, with speed belying his soft roundness, claimed both cheeks and her nose.

Again sales surged forward nicely, and again the gigantic appetite of the extending tracks ate at the money too quickly.

"The big capitalists are not coming in," Hannah said. "We have to go to the one place that can supply it quickly. The government in Washington. It's shameful that we don't have a subsidy."

"That was because of the size of the grant," said Cutts. "There were people in Congress howling about plundering the public domain."

"We must show the United States government how greatly it was mistaken," said Hannah.

Cutts paved the way. He got the attention of many more key congressmen, including the Speaker of the House of Representatives, by spreading shares and making loans without collateral. Then, climbing on their backs, he made his way to the upper echelons with his whirlwind lobby. "It is your duty to open the golden West to waves of settlers. To remove the threat of the murder of these people by savage Indians, there must be a railroad to quickly carry soldiers and supplies and establish a line of forts. And then there are the minerals, iron, gold, silver, much of it on the land the United States would retain in its own sections. And this is not to forget international considerations. Can you doubt, Mr. Congressman, that the brown, papist plotters of Mexico scheme to regain their rich lands in California and the whole Southwest? Or that a United States stranglehold on transportation and communication through the northern states will eventually compel Canada to accept our dominion and join its vastness to ours?"

Mindful that any bill to benefit the Superior-Pacific eventually needed the signature of the President, they did not neglect him.

"A thousand dollars for two fishing poles, Jack?" marveled Hannah.

"It beats the blazes out of me, too," he said, flicking the long, exquisitely made rod. "Never caught a fish in my life. But the people who know tell me that these are the equivalent of the word's most desirable woman to a fisherman. With a flick of the hand it's supposed to send a hook half-a-mile down into the deepest lake and speed it into the mouth of the biggest bass in residence."

"But a thousand dollars—"

"The creels are included, Hannah. And if President Grant and his son are the fishermen they're supposed to be, they might take up the invitation of the donors to wet a line together."

"Jack, presidents aren't fooled so cheaply."

"No, but they're often fooled so thoughtfully."

Within the month, deep in the Adirondacks, a boat bearing Ulysses S. Grant, his son Jesse, Jack Grant and Hannah Oakhill floated on a clear lake on a perfect day. The President had a bottle in the bottom of the boat and had consumed half of it. A dozen husky bass flapped in the creel, and the President held the pole that had conquered them as if it had been sent from heaven.

"You've got us spoiled. After fishing with these, a regular pole is going to feel like a crutch."

"How would you like to get it going in one of those streams in the Northwest where nobody but the bears have fished, Mr. President?"

"Don't tempt me. This damned job has little enough to hold me. Vicksburg was clean and easy compared to the no-quarter fighting I see in my office every day."

"You're going to be glad about those notes you signed for Mr. Cutts. It will help establish a future for your wife and Jesse."

"Yes, I appreciate the advantageous terms. You also know, I presume, how important I believe the railroads—especially yours—will be in the opening of the Northwest frontier. But there are problems in meeting your needs."

Hannah watched a flight of ducks winging low over the trees

and settling down into the sunset-splashed water. "I can well imagine that, Mr. President. But surely your personal involvement—"

"Don't smear the bear grease on me, Mrs. Oakhill," he said, and the fire in the man's eyes reminded Hannah she was speaking to the man whose armies had burned their way down the Shenandoah. "I've done all I can. There will be no subsidy for your railroad."

"I'm sorry, sir. I understand."

"Good. Now will you settle for a congressional resolution that authorizes a mortgage on the land?"

They exchanged guarded grins. A mortgage was as good as the money itself.

"We'll settle."

"Watch your line, Jack. I think you just snagged a big one there."

The railroad and the people pushing it went through a period of impressive progress. The announcement of the mortgage passing the Senate sent the value of land in Duluth rocketing, and Cutts added still more to his holdings and bought some for his associates. And, of course, his own bank was selling the bonds and receiving a fee of twelve percent.

Hannah began to see that what they had thought of as important wealth in their New York development businesses was the smallest of change in both coin and excitement compared with this. Their love fed on that excitement. Although they were apart almost all the time, they met when they could in New York to be with the children and saw one another for a day or two at meetings with Cutts when their paths came close. They held one another and kissed when they were alone, speaking breathlessly of what was to be.

The night in the forest had awakened the heat in her body once more, and she waited with hopeless impatience for him to take her again. She was sure she felt the same unbearable tension in him, but he made no move to her bed. Still blushing at the thought of her inebriated advances under the blanket by the fire, she could not quite bring herself to risk his respect by repeating them.

As the magnitude of what Cutts was bringing off became more apparent, opposition sprang up everywhere. Rival banking houses and newspapers used words such as "robbery" and "carnival of corruption" freely. Even some of the members of Congress who had benefited from support of the Superior-Pacific became hostile.

President Grant's notes were quietly destroyed.

"Ideas," Cutts demanded from behind three empty champagne bottles at Delmonico's. "Where are the ideas?"

Grant and Hannah were out in front of him.

"Europe," Hannah said. "We've got to go to Europe. It's fresh territory. They're crowded and they're disgusted. And enough of them will come if we make the right terms. There's no other way to get the momentum back."

Cutts lighted up. "Perfect. You're Europeans. Polished. Successful in this country."

"And we speak the languages," Grant said. "We took the liberty of buying steamship tickets."

A cloud crossed Cutts' face. "Can we spare you for—how long?"

Grant shrugged. "As long as it takes. It could be our last chance, and it could be our making."

"Yes. It's like being trapped on a damned treadmill. We have to sell bonds to build the railroad to drive up the value of the land, then sell the land to retire the bonds. If we can stay afloat to sell whatever's left, it's El Dorado. And if we can't—"

"We'll do it."

"That's a long time to leave your children."

"We thought about that, Guy," Hannah said. "They're coming."

"Why not?" Grant said. "Their tutor can come along and they can have all the excitement of traveling."

"They'll be in your way."
"That's exactly what we want."

The long, idle days of the Atlantic crossing were agony for Hannah. Victor was in her suite and Evangeline in Grant's. But the children slept soundly and there were doors to be closed in the suites. She waited for his knock in the night, her yearning throbbing as steadily as the soft vibration of the engines, but he did not come to her.

As they neared England one bright morning, with a single night at sea remaining, she came to him at the rail where he looked over the choppy sea. "I don't miss the sleet of that night, Jack," she said. "But I miss everything else."

"No more than I do."

"Come to me tonight."

His evident pleasure at hearing the words was at once clouded by some confusion she did not understand. He held her gently. "You must never, never think that I held your honor lightly, Hannah. You must allow me to look after it a while longer, and not tempt me to do what I so want to."

"There's always either too much honor or not enough."

"I want you to be sure that with me it was always too much."

"I understand, and I love you for it," she said reluctantly but truthfully. "Forgive me for throwing myself at you."

"I do. And I love you for it."

They arrived in London. Their first stop was at a house in Belgravia, the residence of the financial editor of the London *Times*, where a long meeting concluded satisfactorily.

"I'm very glad, Mr. Lexford, that you were able to see what unfair damage the *Times* exchange agreement with the Philadelphia *Ledger* has been causing."

"Yes, indeed, Mr. Grant. You've shown me in the most convincing way that the stories they have sent us on the Superior-Pacific were complete slanders."

"We don't expect retractions, of course."

"Oh, no, old boy. It will be more effective to have our readers realize slowly, as I myself will realize, that the grand representations of Mr. Cutts are understated, if anything."

Hannah smiled sweetly above her teacup. "What an honor to have your support not only in word, but in deed. Your purchase of such a large amount of bonds is very heartening to us."

"As your financial terms were heartening to me, Mrs. Oakhill. Stretching the payment until nineteen-forty will certainly be a convenience."

"When we learned that on your salary as financial editor you had managed to accumulate four hundred thousand pounds, we knew we had an astute investor who would appreciate the small advantages."

Immediately thereafter, the views of the London *Times* toward the prospects of the Superior-Pacific Railroad became so radically enthusiastic that the features extolling its glories sometimes spilled off the financial pages into the editorials and front columns. By the time the Superior-Pacific representatives reached the continent, they were able to point truthfully to a brisk upsurge in sales and positive sentiment in England.

In a stop at the French Bourse, they invoked leading members to visit the New Eden at Superior-Pacific expense to ascertain for themselves that any other investment then known was the equivalent of throwing money away in handfuls.

Stopping in Berlin, they got as far as the outer office of Bismarck himself, proposing a tour of the Superior-Pacific route, promising it would certainly result in land purchases on a scale that would represent nothing less than an expansion of the German Empire into the richest parts of the New World. For a pittance, and without committing a soldier, his nation could share in the greatest natural and commercial wealth that would ever be generated. They even pointed out that a magnificent city-to-be had been laid out in the rich Dakotas and given the foresighted name of Bismarck.

As expected, the great men and their institutions declined with elaborate replies. These were edited just a bit to make it seem that but for a war, a panic or a revolution or two the leaders would be even now emptying the national treasuries to buy Superior-Pacific bonds and land.

To the banks, to the newspapers, to royalty they went, paving their way with land that lay four thousand miles behind them. The names Cutts, Grant and Oakhill were known everywhere. Even so, Cutts sent word that the land sales were still not massive enough to retire the sea of bonds.

The voyagers took three days in Switzerland to think and rest.

As she watched Victor and Evangeline at play against the cloud-shrouded mountains, Hannah had time to realize that shortly this would be a family. Grant arranged separate rooms, but alone in her big feather bed with the outrageously refreshing Alpine air pouring through a window with the moonlight, she knew that all her happiness depended on being with him very soon for the rest of her life.

"I want this to end, Jack."

"So do I, darling. And soon it will. We need just a few more months and some ideas as big as these mountains."

In Hamburg, on their way to Stockholm, they stopped at the offices of the North German Steamship Line, where they left behind several thousand acres of Minnesota and a short conversation with the directors:

"Your kind and wise decision to establish preferential fares for Scandinavian emigrants bound for Superior-Pacific lands will make the fortunes of many starving families."

"And of several families not starving, it is to be hoped, Mrs. Oakhill . . ." a director said optimistically.

It was hardly autumn, but the wind came down unimpeded from the Arctic Circle and left thick frost on the brown stubble of the Swedish plain.

"Look at them, Hannah. They won't get through another winter here. By heaven, while there are times that I feel like a thief in this business, there are others when I feel we're doing God's work."

The people had come seventy-five miles in wagons pulled by emaciated horses and cattle. The Swedes were gray-faced and frozen. Nevertheless, their threadbare clothing was their best, their hair was trimmed or neatly braided and they were spotlessly clean, as befitted people considering the transaction of the most important business of their hard lives.

"Will they have the money, Jack?"

"Most of them will. The fare is almost nothing now. And they have furniture and livestock to sell. They save, too, like no people you ever knew, Hannah. It will be a scrape, but if we sell them, they can do it."

The wagons creaked to a halt and the people climbed stiffly down, their eyes all turned toward three houses whose outlines of pale, fresh lumber showed vividly against a background of dark evergreens. An excited muttering began to run through the assembling ranks of transported farmers.

A gaunt, somber man whose eyes were circled with black and whose hair might have been either white or blond, came to Hannah and Grant. His English was good. "I am the pastor, Claus Soderstrom. I had your letter and your literature. We had three meetings and decided to come to see for ourselves what you have. Are we the the first?"

"No, Pastor," Hannah said. "There have been dozens. More are coming tomorrow."

"And nearly all have bought, sir," Grant added. "I have their names and their towns. You'll know many of them. But that's later. We have food for everyone now."

"Their bellies are hollow," Soderstrom said, "but they're hungry for more than food. Let us go to the houses, Mr. Grant."

"Will you translate for us?"

"Yes, but what they see will speak louder."

They led Soderstrom and his flock, perhaps a hundred people, up the gentle slope to the three distant structures. The farmers moved spellbound, excited but not hurrying, savoring their walk toward an impossible dream.

The siting of the houses, up the slope and at a distance, had been Hannah's thought. She had said, "Putting them against the pines will duplicate the setting Mr. Trier has drawn for the brochures. Putting them far up the hill will whet the appetite, let the imagination do its work and bring the vision slowly into focus."

A platform had been built before the central and most impressive of the houses. Hannah let Grant and Soderstrom pull her up to it with them. She would speak at length before the people were permitted inside.

After introductions, Soderstrom translated as she spoke, becoming more excited as the listeners did, until his earlier impassiveness entirely vanished.

"The three houses you see before you, my friends, are precise copies of the homes in which you will live in the New Eden of North America. Never before have people had the opportunity to see, to touch, to walk through a dwelling bought at a distance of four-thousand miles.

"You will notice there are three models, ranging from cozy and comfortable to large and luxurious. The prices range from two hundred dollars to one thousand dollars to give you a choice that will fit your ability to purchase."

The eyes of the assembled people danced at the sight of the buildings. Hannah was proud of the designs, which had come out of her office from the talented hand of Hector Augustine. They were solid and beautifully proportioned, with even the smallest of them overflowing with all of the gingerbread and scrollwork that any heart could wish. Handsome weathercocks sat on every roofpeak, and window boxes were colorbursts of artificial flowers.

Once Hannah had finished detailing the marvels of the houses themselves, she let Grant take over to declaim the mechanics of sale, purchase and construction. Soderstrom was hard-pressed to keep up with the tumble of wonders pouring out of the hoarse throat:

"To guarantee the satisfaction of the home buyer, the Superior-Pacific Railroad Company has pioneered techniques that are the ninth wonder of the homebuilding world.

"Once in the United States, your fare to your lands will be deducted from the purchase price of any additional acres you acquire. And the houses that rise will do so in a way that is a miracle of speed and efficiency: As you already know, the Superior-Pacific tracks run through the most magnificent logging country in the world, with trees that make these that tower above us here seem like matchsticks. There will be sawmills all along the way where the parts of the house you choose will be cut to exact size from the specifications of plans drawn by the most brilliant New York City architects. The parts will be shipped to your building site absolutely free on the cars of the Superior-Pacific Railroad. Building plans so simple they could be read by a child will be put into your hands for a beautiful home you can build yourself with nothing more than strong arms supplied by you, and hammer and nails supplied by us.

"And so you will come to live in a land so fresh, so pure, so abundant that the only threat to your health will be a feverish overindulgence in that abundance. I bid you to hold back in such abandon. And now your homes are open to your inspection."

By now the sales would have been assured even if the people had found the houses stuffed with plague-infested rats. As it was, the milling, pathetically eager customers discovered a cornucopia of design amenities and found that the comfortable furnishings were incredibly and unexpectedly included in the price.

"Greed can work in wonderful ways sometimes, Jack," said Hannah. "It's beyond their comprehension that it so serves our needs to get them on our land that we can make little or nothing on this end. But it rebuilds their world."

"While it rebuilds ours," Grant said.

Soderstrom had not even gone into the houses, being content to watch the joy in his people's faces as they hurried from one to the other, exchanging stupefactions. After he watched for a while, he spoke without turning. "I will lead them out."

"What is the name of your town?" Hannah asked him.

"Lindblom."

"I will write ahead to have the sign carved for the railway station—New Lindblom."

By the time they had duplicated their success at a score of other locations in Scandinavia, dozens of ships were sailing with their settlers, many of them beating Hannah and Grant back to New York.

In the city they found Cutts in fine fettle, thriving on the assaults of a growing horde of enemies, vanquishing worry with startling reserves of optimism as he was pushing the Superior-Pacific relentlessly westward.

Victor and Evangeline were returned to the house with Frau Wendt, remarkably broadened by what they had seen and both inclined to consider themselves part of a true, complete family. Their parents caught up on the business of their own New York firms as best they could and left to observe firsthand the changes in Duluth, Minnesota.

They could not have imagined the magnitude of those changes. It was not so much the increase in population, which even now hardly numbered five thousand people, as the framework that was rising. Duluth was a city of surveyor's stakes and strings, open foundations, chalk lines and building skeletons. Nails were more numerous underfoot than pebbles and a sharpener of saws or seller of hammers might have earned enough to buy half the town. A thousand people were expected to arrive each and every month from here on, and the preparations, frantic as they were, lagged considerably. Every day the phantom streets were staked farther out into the wilderness, the nonexistent buildings bordering them enjoying roaring sales.

One morning as Hannah and Grant crossed a wide boulevard of the future, presently running between clots of tents and rude shacks, she was delighted to see a broad, bright young face with an unmistakable stamp. "Michael," she called. "Michael Hanratty."

The oldest son of the legion first encountered on the *Dortmund* was hurrying along with a duffle as large as he was on a sturdy shoulder, and a pretty, tough-looking carrot-top of a girl on his opposite arm. When he saw Hannah he abandoned both and welcomed her with a handshake that almost wrenched off her arm. Already the music of Ireland had become muted in the harsher tones of New York City. "Jesus and His Saints, Miss Hannah. Are you settlin' in here, too?"

"Not exactly. I'm with the Superior-Pacific. This is my colleague, Mr. Grant."

Michael switched his assault to Grant's hand. "It's a sacred honor to take the hand that put a hundred men dreamin' on the deck. My hat's off to you, Gentleman Jack."

"I'm working with better kinds of dreams now, Michael."

Hannah saw the swelling in the middle of the red-haired girl who now trailed up. "Is this your beautiful wife?"

"Mary Dawson this is, now Mary Hanratty. An American all the way, but a good hand with the cabbage."

"I know all about you two from Mick," the girl said, "and I am pleased to acquaint." Her accent hailed her from the city of Brooklyn, where a corruption of early Dutch and English had a fascinating but murderous effect on all vowels. "We would be pleased to have you visit our place if you are free to come. It's not much yet because we been busy and we been here only six days."

Unwilling to lose track of an old friend in a new place, and curious to know how a man who was more than a faceless signature on a deed was going to fare in her heavy schemes, she nodded and they followed the new Hanratty couple through the illusory streets of Duluth.

"Are you staying at one of our reception houses, Michael?"

"Ah, that was a nice thought, Miss Hannah. But they was filled up weeks before we ever got here."

Along with her satisfaction that Duluth was booming past all their hopes, Hannah felt a twinge of guilt that they had brought so many struggling people so far with promises that in too many cases would finish far short of fulfillment. "What about the food?"

"Just like they said. Plenty of it, all of it good and not costin' any more than it cost them. The free doctorin' is there, too." He pulled up a trouser leg to show an extensive bandage around his calf. "Ripped the bejabbers out of myself on a nail stickin' out of one of them shacks. The doc did a good job. Wouldn't take any handout to move people up on the line, either."

Everywhere there were *For Rent* signs on "buildings" that were as yet no more than a couple of uprights, and the builder-landlords spent as much time accepting payments and setting terms as they did sawing and hammering.

At the outskirts of Duluth, which is to say a full half-mile from the closest fully completed building, they came to the Hanratty lodgings. The builder, who was for the moment nowhere to be seen, had been a bit more thoughtful in his early labors than some of the others. The floor had been completed and so had the roof. So even though there was not a trace of a door, window or completed wall between the uprights, the lucky tenants would be up out of the mud and relatively safe from rain.

"Well, how do you like it?" Hanratty asked, pointing to a spot perhaps ten feet square that had been separated from the other rooms by a chalk line on the floorboards.

"We thought we might chalk in some furniture after awhile," said Mary. "A bed, a table, some fine chairs, maybe a nice stove for me. But I wouldn't want to be puttin' on any airs."

"You have to admit the ventilation is wonderful, and the views are just marvelous," said Michael.

Their fellow tenants, mostly rough-looking men alone, but some in families with small children, were settling into their spots, keeping inside their lines and not talking across the chalk lines, pretending, Hannah supposed, that they were plaster a foot thick. "You'll freeze to death here at night. Even in the summer sometimes. I traveled this country. I know it."

"Look," Grant said. "No matter what our literature said, this is no earthly paradise. It's a brutal climate much of the time and killing work all of the time. Somebody who's done this kind of work and knows life on the land can make it go and even prosper. But for city people it could be failure, heartbreak, sickness, even death."

Hannah nodded her agreement. "I could never face your father again if anything happened to you and Mary. Look. I'll pay your fare back to New York, return your money and give you something for your trouble. I'll give you a note that will get you a job at Oakhill Development—"

Michael raised his hand to stop her. "Whoa, Miss Hannah. I'm not such a dreamer as you think. I can tell poetry from the truth, and there's nothin' here that surprises me or scares me."

"If we die," said Mary, "it's not goin' to be in some stinkin' rathole in the Five Points, right, Michael?"

"Right indeed. Remember that day when you come to get the old folks out of that hell, God keep you? Remember that heat? Well, I had enough of that to enjoy walkin' across the North Pole in my underwear. My bones are baked permanent."

"But there's a living you have to make—"

"Maybe you forgot it, Miss Hannah, seein' what we become, but we Hanrattys are farmers. We scratched at the ground like ants from last star to first, and the landlords come through and stomped us when they wanted. We didn't get enough out of the ground to feed us and a sparrow. Funny thing, though. The less the land gives a farmer, the better he gets to know it, the better he gets at the work and the more he loves it."

Mary took his arm and held him to her. "My granddad had a fine farm in Brooklyn, he did. I know my way around a plow, and a cow, too."

"How will you find the land you want?"

Michael dug into the duffle and brought out a deed. "We found it already. We were out on horses one day after we got here. We rode way down the track, and every place we put a hoof the ground was a thousand times richer than all the land I walked over all my life in Ireland. We found a spot where the land is flat for good plowing and so rich it'll take an ox to peel back the sod to get at the topsoil. And that topsoil goes down as deep as your arm. There's good water and good wood, too."

"How many acres?"

"Fifty, Mr. Grant. Seven dollars an acre. It took most of what was left from the money I won in the card game that sent me out here."

"If the land is that good," said Hannah, "you can't settle for fifty acres." She scrawled on a pad. "Give this in at the Superior-Pacific land office and you'll have another fifty."

"If I can pay when I can." He took it without hesitating. "I wouldn't take it if I didn't know this ground could get it back to you in no time at all."

"We will always remember you, Miss Hannah," Mary said.

"The train will drop off our house. I'll keep this piece of chalk on the mantle to remind us of our first room on the prairie."

"I hope we're worthy of your trust, Michael. We sometimes say too much."

"Miss Hannah," Michael said. "I'm sure the people doin' this are no better than they have to be to get their dollar. For all of that, I wish all the treasures of heaven to them." He looked at the deed in his hand as he would a sack of gold coins. "They put me on good land that can feed my children and my children's children. They gave me stars and trees, and fresh air and good work. What man could be so brassy as to pray for more?"

Hannah could feel the warmth of their happiness, and it spread into her own heart and thawed away many more doubts about what she had done.

They had not been back in New York many weeks when Mark saw that the dark clouds were beginning to build faster than the gusts of new money could blow them away.

The excesses of promotion that had been carried through by Cutts while his partners had been in Europe had brought ridicule to the operation. Hardly a newspaper or a magazine published had an issue without a scathing satire of a Superior-Pacific brochure.

In spite of this, Mark did not completely despair. He was now convinced that the promised wealth was not only there for all who had invested to gain it, but there in measure that beggared his promises. If Cutts' scheme was threatened by its headlong pace, it was inavoidable because the scope of the operation demanded nothing less. What was actually failing was the vision of the small-hearted institutions that could not see on the scale needed.

More work, doubled and redoubled schedules, were the only hope, and Mark and Hannah did not flinch. Their only happiness and relief came when they were able to do their work together for a couple of days and enjoy late, exhausted dinners at Delmonico's.

He was glad of the exhaustion that helped quell the temptation to forget his highflown vows of honor with her. There was no instant when her body was completely out of his mind.

One agonizing note continued to sound in Mark's mind. His masquerade as Jack Grant had become not less successful but more so. The flinty, mercurial businessman he had become removed him from the sheltered boy that Mark Northern had been more effectively than even the cataclysmic physical changes. The longer she knew Jack Grant, the deader Mark Northern became.

But there was no getting around the fear that a long, intense intimacy would find him out. A muttered word while sleeping, a careless memory, an unmistakable trait and it would be over. And then any hope of his regaining her would be lost more surely than ever. He would be guilty in her eyes of a great and completely indefensible deception. Worse, it would be an admission that Mark had been part of his father's treachery. As this ran ever in his mind, he had to stifle the impulse to end his wearing and guilty deception.

Hannah appeared to have read his inner turbulence incorrectly. His occasional distances, he suspected, she saw as lingering doubts about what they had planned. All his words of love and assurance could not completely satisfy her. "Most people are married several years before their thoughts drift so far," she said.

Soon it became evident to him that she was enticing him to go further and faster. Alone and in public she sat closer and held tighter. She spoke less of business and more of their future. More than that, when they were alone in the night she offered herself as delicately as she could.

He thought the whole world could see him weakening.

Always restive when Hannah was away, Mark tired of his house one evening when she had remained in Boston, and went to a favorite restaurant just outside the Five Points. Called the Roma, it was far from grand. But nestled below grade on the bottom floor of a commercial building, it was cozy, dimly lighted and served marvelous Italian food. The waiters were from the owner's horde of children, and the atmosphere, loaded with seductive aromas, was always soothing to a beleaguered soul.

He ate delightfully and chased the food down with several glasses of good, home-pressed wine. He was lingering over a cigar and a cup of powerful coffee when one of the proprietors broke off in the middle of a soft ballad he had been strumming on a mandolin. His eyes were on the door, and they grew wider.

Two men had appeared inside, one heavily mustached, with a huge head set on bull shoulders, the other as thin and cold as a knife blade.

"Bon giorno, Signor Rendino, Signor Malatesta," the mandolin player quavered.

The one he had called Rendino thumbed him out of the room. When the boy had gone, Malatesta called in Italian through the door behind him. A third man now appeared.

Benedetto Serpa came to Mark through the shadows and stood before the table. "Please excuse my interruption, Signor Grant. I tried to wait until you were through with your meal. May I sit with you?"

The other two had remained at the door, well out of earshot. Long ago in the ring Mark had lost the ability to feel fright. But he knew there would be menace in this meeting and idly regretted that the waiter had taken away his knife with the plate. He pointed to a chair with his cigar, and Serpa sat himself.

The Sicilian wore a wide-brimmed hat that he did not remove. The lowness of his voice excluded the intense agitation that showed itself in his face. *Odd,* Mark thought. *That's fear I see.*

"I won many dollars betting upon you, Signor Grant."

"I'm happy I avoided disappointing you."

"I hope that you can avoid disappointing me once again."

"In what way, Mr. Serpa?"

"I have a great regard for Signora Oakhill."

"No greater than mine."

"I offend a fine woman by speaking her name behind her back, but things must be said."

"What things?" said Mark.

"I have watched. Here. In Europe. In the West and in many cities. Always I had a man."

"Watching me with Mrs. Oakhill?"

"And without. I had hopes that you would go with other women, or perhaps with other men. I could have found ways to let her know that you were not worthy. But you have behaved with honor always."

"Then you know that I behave with the same honor with Mrs. Oakhill."

"I know well, Signor Grant, that your rooms are separate when you travel. And Filomena sometimes is unwise enough to speak to Leo, and I know that Mrs. Oakhill still does not share the room you keep in her house. But it is not things of the body that weigh heaviest in my heart."

"What then?"

"The love that I could not find is now there in her. For you."

"I devoutly hope so, Mr. Serpa. And I return that love. Why will you not give your blessing to her happiness, even if you can't give it to mine?"

"No matter what you have heard, I am not a completely uncivilized or uncaring man. Or even a stupid one. I have waited long for time and separation to ease the hot knife in my heart, I promise you."

Mark knew there was a back entrance through the kitchen. The only weapon close to hand was a nearly empty wine bottle. He estimated the speed with which he might use it to disable Serpa. Then he might sprint for the outside, hoping the men at the door might delay to attend their leader. "So you mean to kill me."

"I have thought about little else for a long time, Signor Grant. But I cannot."

"Because she would know it was you no matter how carefully you did it. And you'd be finished with her for good."

"That is right. So you must go of your own will and continue to live in health. But the parting must be cruel and final, so she will not mourn you. So she will hate you. And her hate can be as strong and enduring as mine."

Mark knew better than he how true this was. "Why should I do this, Mr. Serpa?"

"You wish to have the lands of this city and build upon them. I will make it so that all who stand in your road fade away. You will have the best prices, the best opportunities. I will give you a city of your own."

"There is not a city in the world worth the loss of Hannah. You understand that."

It was not especially warm in the room, but the front of Serpa's shirt was soaked through, and he had to wipe the sweat from his eyes with his fingertips. The words came as though they were being pulled from him with hot tongs. "Then she must die."

Of all the things Serpa might have said, this was the one with which Mark was not ready to deal. "What are you talking about?"

"I cannot have her hate me. I cannot cause her pain. And I cannot have her with you. There is no other way."

"You *love* her. How could you?"

Now the wetness on Serpa's cheeks was tears. "It will be suddenly with no blood and no hurt. The grief I will feel until the last day of my life and through eternity will be my punishment. But she will be with God, and not with you."

Mark gathered himself desperately. "You'll die before she does."

Serpa glanced to the men at the door. "And Rendino? And Malatesta? And sixty others? The orders are given. My death is nothing."

"This is a bluff." The other's eyes told him nothing.

"No."

"You're not human, Serpa."

"But you are, Grant. You *are*."

A thousand bloody plans surged through Mark's brain, the hatred for Serpa rising in his throat like the vilest vomit. One by one those plans fell away as his terror for Hannah's life unmanned him. No matter what murder his rage urged him to, he knew he could never risk what was in the heart of the deadly and unmovable Sicilian.

In winning his desperate, impossible dream to have her again, he had lost her.

"There will be a special hell for you, Serpa. I'll be in it waiting for you."

* * *

So precisely did the meeting with Serpa coincide with the beginning of the death throes of the Superior-Pacific Railroad under Guy Cutts, that Hannah did not attribute the sudden change in Jack Grant's behavior to anything but the pressures of the moment.

As though everything in his world was destined to end at once, Mark watched the edifice of the railroad slowly crumbling. The tracks had reached the Missouri River by now, a stupendous feat against high odds, but the money had dried up and there were no other worlds or politicians to go to for more. Many of the more blatant gifts to newspaper people and senators were surfacing in the newspapers on both sides of the ocean, and scandal fed upon scandal.

With the gigantic potential of the wealth that would one day be created by the railroad, which was physically as intact as ever, farsighted banks represented the only thread of hope. They might stretch themselves to complete the building and go for a long but certain payoff. In Mark's presence Cutts said to J. P. Morgan, "In ten years your bank will have whatever you put up returned to you fiftyfold."

The bulky figure with the diseased nose shifted in a huge chair on the other side of a sea of mahogany, an earthquake waiting to destroy a country. "In a shipwreck, Cutts, the money is in salvage, not lifesaving. Good day, sir."

The boom after the war had sucked up money in enormous quantities, and the bottom of the vault was visible. Interest rates were heading sharply upward. A nervous stock market was turning downward and the pungent whiff of disaster was in the breeze. The banks were beginning to call in loans. The bonds and stocks of the Superior-Pacific were rapidly losing value as collateral.

Cutts displayed the only bit of optimism. He gave a grand party in Philadelphia with President Grant in attendance. The guest list was gilt-edged and glittering despite the barrage against Cutts in the press. Indeed, many members of the press deemed themselves fortunate to be invited and saw champagne and truffles in unparalleled abundance. More impressive was the calm and assurance of Cutts as he moved among the giants of finance, none of whom seemed to entertain a worry in the world.

Cutts spoke to the newspapermen over cigars and the finest brandy. "Anyone who assumes the ascendance of scraps of paper over forty-seven million acres of soil to be built upon, farmed and mined, is a fool."

The journalists were seated at their desks early the next morning writing moving accounts of the confidence evinced by the nation's financial leaders in the Superior-Pacific when word came through that Guy Cutts had closed the doors of his bank.

Mark took the news to Hannah. "It's all going. Cut your financial exposure in any way you can."

"The land?"

"I can't hold all of it. But I'll hold as much as I can. You should do the same. It will come back as surely as the sun."

"I'm not even sure that the sun will come back anymore, Jack."

Seeing that she was about to extend her arms to him, he turned and hurried away, feeling as though his belly had been ripped open.

Hannah found herself hoping for the quick demise of the doomed railroad. Only the quick removal of its weight from Grant's spirit, she felt, could make things as they had been. He had not spent a day with her or a night under her roof since her last trip to Boston. All the ease they had developed together was gone. He shrugged away from her embraces of welcome or departure, and his lips, when she found them, were suddenly cold. If it had not been the chaotic moment that it was, she would have felt something like panic. But she was sure that once they had cut their losses and got back to their businesses to ride out the approaching storm, he would be sweet and apologetic, and their life together would at last reach fulfillment.

The failure of Cutts' bank brought down not just the Superior-Pacific, but the nation. The dream of wealth created by greed and forty-seven million acres had spread its paper everywhere, replacing iron, brick and mortar in the economic system. Other banks failed in quickening progression. The stock market went into a plunge so precipitous that the Exchange had to be closed. Panic grew and reigned.

In a single day the work on the Superior-Pacific came to a complete halt. The hammers, picks and shovels that the workers laid down as they walked away unpaid were soon lost in the weeds that grew up along the roadbed. Locomotives stood empty at the end of the unfinished rails, waiting for the hand of some banker to shovel the coal and open the throttles.

As the railroad faded, the farmers along the right of way saw their access to supply and markets fade. Their hopes drooped. Many pulled out to beat the winter, hoping to catch the east-moving trains taking back the rail workers and the citizens of Duluth, Minnesota.

The population of Duluth fell from five thousand to close to two thousand in a few weeks. With the railroaders going, the merchants had no hope of remaining in business. They liquidated their stock for pennies on the dollar and followed.

The half-built houses remained as they were, to slowly crumble back into the ground, the chalk lines that once delineated "rooms" fading slowly.

Towns along the tracks, with the proud new pioneer names destined to grow with the centuries, were abandoned before their second birthday.

One of the farmers did not leave. He bought all the supplies he could at distress prices and another hundred acres of land whose cost was now reckoned in pennies. Michael Hanratty wrote to Hannah that he and Mary, with their new son Daniel, would ride out the snows on their land in the house he had built from Superior-Pacific lumber, and they would be there to plant in the spring.

And everywhere up and down the line thousands of Norse farmers, with their escape lines to Scandinavia cut forever, turned to do the same, making sons and daughters in the cold to work in the new land.

Hannah was not destroyed. While the value of her land plummeted, she still counted it as her greatest wealth. At Oakhill

Development there was little building in the great financial crash, and only a small treasury for the speculations of the future. But the rent rolls were solid and the buildings there to sell in better times. She would weather the passage.

She was sure it was much the same with Grant, but he had not seen her to mention a word of his manipulations. How much longer could this thing hold him away from her? She must talk to him very soon.

They were to see Guy Cutts one more time. The blocky little man called them to Delmonico's, where it all began. It would be Hannah, Grant and all those who had stuck through it until the end.

Again, the champagne was copious, and anyone glancing across the room at the toasting Cutts would have thought it was the beginning of a spectacular enterprise rather than the end. "My friends. Our endeavor has achieved more in failure than most achieve in their wildest success. If the wealth did not flow to us as we had hoped, it flowed to this nation and the brave souls who remain on the prairie. The vultures will have their feed, all right. But the Superior-Pacific will be indigestible. It will pass to new hands and be built. The work we began will be finished and Lake Superior will open on the Pacific, with all the land in between forming a spine of prosperity. We will see the great fortune gathered just as we promised, taking satisfaction even though it is not ours."

As he spoke, most of Hannah's attention had shifted to Grant. Coming late, he had sat not at her side in the seat she had saved, but at the opposite end of the table. He never caught her eyes or even glanced at her. His face appeared scarred and ugly for the first time since she had met him. She imagined the killer's scowl it now held had been what his opponents had seen on the barge, moments before he hammered them to bits.

Cutts completed his toast. "So this is to the bravest, most resolute and resourceful people it has ever been my privilege to join. I'm proud of every one of you."

To laughter and applause, the toast was thrown down.

"What about you, Guy?"

"What's next?"

If he was heartbroken, there was no sign of it. "I needn't tell you that my name will not be eagerly sought at the head of an important scheme for quite a time. I will say frankly that I was the greatest customer of your brilliant selling and have lost all except my holdings in Duluth, which my creditors do not find worth collecting. I will go there for a time to sit upon my land, fondly expecting that it will keep me during old age. I understand, because I commissioned it, that there is a statue of me lying in a basement in Duluth. I will wait the propitious moment to erect it."

There was more applause and some heavy pounding on the table.

"Invite us for the dedication."

"We'll charter a car on the Superior-Pacific."

The little man grew serious and waved them silent. "The odds for it are not good, but if I can ever again put together something worth the efforts of this magnificent crew, I would like to believe that you would be with me to a man. Excuse me, Hannah. And to a woman."

Hannah rose first, filling her glass. "The woman is *in*."

The men immediately joined her, and they all disrupted Delmonico's with their cheers and agreements. One by one they jumped up.

"To the death, Mr. Cutts."

"Till the rivers run dry."

Then they noticed that Jack Grant had remained in his chair, his expression unchanged from the mask it had been when he arrived.

"You will not stand with us, Jack?"

He got up stiffly. "I will rise only to take my leave. I must tell you that this entire business has left a very bad taste with me. I have been bamboozled into taking part in some very dubious things and feel disgust with myself for being so taken in. All of you, it seems, have no qualms at all and would cheerfully repeat this. The best of you would do so in the fearful naïveté that has been so disastrous to our attempts, the rest from a weakness for larceny that can never be improved. I don't know what the rest of you are pretending, but I have found this a very expensive way to waste my time in company that cares little for its own reputation and less for mine." As he said this last, he looked directly at Hannah for a moment. "This is an experience I do not intend ever again to be part of, and I might say the same for the people in it.

"This city no longer welcomes me. And I wish to undertake things without consulting partners less capable than myself. So I will take my daughter and move to Philadelphia, where I can begin new undertakings. I hope, as part of a new and far more blameless life, to find a good woman to marry and be the mother of my child. Please excuse me if I have been unforgivably harsh, but the truth is that I wish to forestall your forgiveness. I hope you will live prosperous lives with more honor than you have up to this day. Goodbye, gentlemen. And goodbye, madame."

He was gone before the assembly could close their mouths. So stunning was the stiffly delivered torrent of words that they remained silently standing for several moments, their glasses still poised in their hands.

Some of them had over the months divined the man's special relationship with Hannah. They turned to her now for some explanation of the totally unheralded outburst, only to find her even more shocked than they, and as white as the snowy table-linen.

When Hannah returned home, less than an hour after she had left Delmonico's, all traces of Grant and Evangeline had gone from her home. Filomena had been given a generous parting gift, but no explanation of the sudden leaving. Grant had excluded her from his rooms since early the previous day, when he must have been packing. There was no question that he had planned this fast departure for some time.

"The little girl was very upset, signora, but he told her no more than he told me. I have never seen a man look more terrible."

For the rest of the day Hannah sat shocked in her parlor, trying to understand what was in Jack Grant's heart.

She had no inkling that their reverses on the Superior-Pacific had been affecting him so badly. In even the hardest, darkest moments of their struggle he had been a rock that broke the highest waves. His spirits were never excessively low until recently, and he had never blamed meanly or allowed his temper to fray. But it now seemed clear than the disaster had been eating at him inside and finally burst through his reserve. He was striking at anyone close, a man completely broken down.

Why hadn't he confided his agonies to her? She knew less about this man she loved than she knew about most of her employees. But how could he have hidden his feelings from her so well?

The cruelty of his departure from those with whom he had worked so nobly for so many months shook her. Most deeply disturbing was the way such a venomous streak could remain hidden for so long, even from eyes clouded by love.

Forcing herself to consider all that had gone before, she began to appreciate how little of the time of their association they had actually spent alone. In the United States they had been either in separate cities or under the eyes of the others in their wilderness party. In Europe there had been eighteen-hour workdays, with exhaustion at the end.

Had she taken the delirium of that one night in the forest to mean more than it possibly could? Yes, he had held her many times after that and spoken of love as often as she. He had been full of promises of what their life would be, and she thought she had seen in him a happiness as great as hers. But it all could have been a long, slowly fading echo of that moment in the wilderness when the tenets of civilization were momentarily suspended. After all, he had not come to her bed again, even when she had left no doubt about what she wanted. He could have realized long before she did that he had no desire to become more deeply entangled in what was to be a temporary dalliance. As to his protestations of love, she supposed that she had all but demanded them of him with her own fervent declarations. What passion she imagined she had seen in his eyes could have been nothing more than reflections of her own hot dream.

Humiliation began to grow inside her fear.

Through the night and all through the next day, as a storm drenched the streets, she sat waiting, hoping for word from Grant. Watching from the window, she yearned to see his compact, explosively agile body leap from a carriage and bound up the steps three at a time in his eagerness to apologize. Her longing put his racing words of contrition into her ears until she could swear she had heard his voice.

The rain stopped by evening and a pounding wind followed it, shaking the windowpanes and sending ash barrels clattering down the street. The temperature plunged ten degrees in an hour. And suddenly the wind and chill were sweeping terribly through her breaking heart. "I'm going out, Filomena," she called through the servant's door as she struggled into a hat and coat.

"No, no, Signora," Filomena said, hurrying out. "It is the middle of the night. There are no carriages—"

"I don't need a carriage."

"It is too far to Mr. Grant's house," Filomena said, not having to be told Hannah's destination.

Dazed with worry, Hannah hurried through the wind-whipped streets. High above the earth the clouds were being ripped to bits and blown away in rags made silvery by a full moon.

Somewhere along the way her hat was torn from her, and she let it skitter away as her hair was whirled around her head and tumbled down about her shoulders. She lost track of the time she had been walking, the long blocks melting away beneath her hurrying feet.

It was past two in the morning when she approached Grant's house. Alone among the other dwellings, its windows poured light.

There was a carriage and two large carts in the street, their horses standing sleepily in the traces, their drivers huddled bundles. The carts were heavily loaded.

Hannah summoned what was left in her aching legs and hurried to the door, sounding the big brass knocker thunderously. When no one appeared at once, she renewed her attack, the metallic hammering echoing out into the night.

Haggard and smelling of drink, Grant answered the door himself. His rumpled clothing was the same he had been wearing when she had last seen him at Delmonico's. "I have no time for talk. We're leaving inside the hour."

She slipped past him into the high vestibule and pushed the door closed against the curious glances of the men in the carts. "I want you to tell me why you're doing this, Jack."

"I made that plain."

"There were things between us I thought equally plain."

"You thought incorrectly. Perhaps we both did. I was weak and stupid, Hannah."

"You never loved me?"

"Of course I did. Very much, for a time. It's my way. If I never told you much about myself it was in part to conceal that dreadful habit. I'm afraid I've disappointed a great number of women in the same way. I believe I should have ended it sooner, but we were thrown together so closely that it would have been awkward, don't you think? I tried, at least, not to compromise you excessively." The words were costing him all his strength. He sagged back against the wall of the vestibule, looking as though he might fall.

She went to him instinctively. "You're sick."

"Too much drink."

She put her hand to his head. "There's a fever."

For a fraction of a moment her touch brought a flicker of relief to his agonized face, then he brushed her away. "Go, damn it. *Go.*"

She couldn't stop her sobs. "How could my heart lie to me so? Why does it still feel a love that's so plainly gone?"

"Hannah—"

As his face vanished behind her tears, she turned to go, fumbling blindly for the latch.

The strength of the hand that seized her arm was so much greater than what had been apparent in the drooping husk of Jack

Grant that she though someone else must have slipped into the vestibule. He pulled her to him with such force that the breath gasped out of her as she hit his broad chest. Before she could breathe again his mouth was over hers, the fever in him closing on her lips. They clung together as though all the world's yearning had run into their arms. Whatever words one of them tried to say were never heard, because the lips of the other were there to cut them short.

At this moment the door flew back with a startling bang. The cold blast of wind that suddenly filled the vestibule made Hannah think that a gust had overcome the latch. But when she turned there was a man standing there, filling the doorway. The vestibule was dim and he was framed in a streetlight. The wind flapped his cape wildly about his shoulders and he kept one hand pressed upon a bowler hat. The other hand clasped a cane so excessively heavy and brutal-looking that it might have been a cudgel.

He was unknown to Hannah, a thin, taut-faced man with a face ravaged by pox. There was a touch of Europe in his voice, which was coldly apologetic. "All my pardons. What an embarrassment to me." He leaned outside, seeming to check the number above the door, then closed his eyes to mime deep humiliation. "I have come to the wrong door, it seems. I thought there was someone with whom I had business here."

Hannah felt Grant's arms fall away. "What business it it that you do in the dead of night, sir?"

"There are many things that are best done in the darkness, madame."

"Please go."

"Yes. I will return to this street when I am more certain of my destination." He bowed and eased the door closed as he backed out.

"Did you ever see him before?" Hannah asked.

Grant battled for control of his face. "Maybe. On the street. I'm not sure." His voice was again as cold as though they had not touched. When she went back to him, he turned away. "But in any case, he has done us both a favor. Tears and a beautiful woman have always had a terrible effect on me. You're so damned lovely that I thought I might have you one more night, after all. That would have been unforgivable, wouldn't it?"

"Jack, my God—"

"You're a good businesswoman, Hannah. You have a great feeling for the land, one as strong and sure as mine. We should have kept it all business. That we didn't was my fault. I hope we can work together someday, all my unpleasant words at Delmonico's notwithstanding. You could give all those cigar-smoking monkeys lessons."

"Please, Jack—"

"If you don't mind, Hannah, I have to be in Philadelphia early in the morning." He opened the door and called to the waiting carriage driver. "Luther, you'll be taking Mrs. Oakhill home."

She broke away from his guiding hand. "Your soul is as scarred and disfigured as your face. And the wounds you've left in me will heal just as jagged and ugly. I'll have them to remind me that not even fists can tear and maim like love and trust. I'm very experienced with hating, Jack. But you will make me better."

He did not answer, but slowly closed the door upon her, his face like a figure carved on a headstone.

Chapter 8

VICTOR OAKHILL thought that the New York City of 1882 must be standing at the threshold of a glory greater than any that had ever arrived in the Florence of the Renaissance. He prowled its streets obsessively, letting its wonders reverberate inside him and lift his excitement higher every day.

At sixteen he could have passed for twenty. He had already been shaving for two years and was as thick through the shoulders and thighs as most of the men working the docks along the rivers. His broad, strong face showed the slightest upturn of the brown-black eyes, the feature so prevalent in the peasant bloodstock of eastern Europe.

If his physique was precocious, it was just a shadow of the maturity that came to him through his long love of the streets of the city.

As soon as he had become swift and cunning enough to elude the nimble and tireless Filomena and the fatherly shepherding of Nello, Victor had been off on his own. To be sure, a boy known to be the son of a special friend of Benedetto Serpa was likely to be treated with care. Indeed, some of Victor's most hair-raising initiations into the underlife of New York had come through the guidance of well-meaning ruffians of every age who thought that there was nothing too horrendous to teach a member of the Serpa circle.

Before he was into his teens he was known and welcomed in such hellholes as Bill McGlory's Armory Hall, The Haymarket and the Burnt Rag, all of which made the Golden River look like a convent.

"On the rare day that one patron does not shoot another dead in Bill McGlory's," one policeman said, "Bill takes on the job himself."

Victor's early physical development and dark-eyed attractiveness worked to doom his virginity at an early age. The women at the Burnt Rag and in the Water Street brothels had first used him to run errands, and then took to mothering and spoiling him outrageously. In his eleventh year he had been introduced to the charms of a comely Welsh girl of fifteen who had been on the street only two months and was known to be clean of disease. She awakened in Victor a vigorous appreciation of the possibilities of the loins, and began an accelerating parade of local professionals through his trousers.

He had found he liked strong drink and Henry Clay cigars but controlled those predilections enough to avoid the sharp nostrils of Filomena.

Later there had been new visitors in his haunts. The uptown rich had discovered the seedy delights of the downtown "hells," and the fasionable arrived in groups to spend the evening in the raucous, colorful and sometimes dangerous company of their inferiors.

Victor learned that when he came tan and scrubbed from swimming in the East River, his worn knockabout clothes riding nicely on his taut frame, he would have the calling cards of women, and sometimes men, slipped into his pocket. "Do drop in at the rear, young man. We'll find something interesting for you to do."

He called on the women if he found time on a lazy afternoon, and they were thrilled to be mounted by a good-looking young son of the slums, not ever knowing that his mother had built a commercial fortune that often rivaled all they had inherited.

* * *

Hannah was never far from his mind. He envied friends who took their mothers' love for granted, and who were not locked into an incomprehensible struggle that had no beginning, no end, no rules and no boundaries.

There was never a moment that he didn't feel he was part of some never-to-be-known sin against Hannah. The very intensity of her solicitude for his well-being and success only showed him her dismay at not being able to love him quite enough.

It had been best between them when Jack Grant had been there. In those two years his mother seemed gradually to have found a lost, loving and open part of herself. He could only understand later that she had loved Grant. And only when Grant had gone did he realize how feelings between two people could lift or destroy lives permanently. His own life had been wrenched and twisted by his hero's sudden departure.

Grant had brought them all together from the first day, Victor remembered, when the fighter had unexpectedly hugged his little visitor. From then on, whether anyone knew it or not, Victor, Hannah and later Evangeline were competing for the man's love. And he had appeared to bestow that love lavishly on each of them as the months went by. They had become in their secret minds a family, and that was the most important thing in their lives. The moments when they could be together were times of immense happiness.

Victor recalled a park in Stockholm where they had gone for a Sunday afternoon picnic. They had all dressed in white and were seated on a soft, white blanket. All the rest was the green of the trees and grass, and the rich blue of the sky, and Victor had thought that their family looked like a spot of pure, white happiness fallen from heaven. Then Hannah had taken him into her arms for just the joy of holding him, for the first time that he could remember. "Poor, dear Victor," she had said. "He deserves so much more love." And that day she had talked to him more than any of the other picnickers, even Jack Grant, and told him how she felt about things he never knew she thought about.

There were other close moments after that. And if she began to drift away, Jack was always there to bring her into the middle of things again, pushing them all together and trying to cement their closeness with his own affection.

There had been hope and laughter in their house that Victor had not known even in his dimmest memory.

Then Grant was gone and the moments of enchantment with it. Very soon Hannah was the same caring but unreachable creature she had been. It would have been bad enough if that had been all there was to it. But her joy in her business had gone, too. Her work was done in a spirit of efficient, aloof hardness. Her greatest successes were just dollars, not laughing triumphs as they had been.

"Good God, Mrs. Oakhill, aren't you going to celebrate? A Brooklyn Bridge coming through right where you said it would? Do you know what this will mean for your property?"

"All it will mean to me is more traffic to get through."

As Hannah had simply sheathed her feelings in iron, Victor had mourned openly. He had lost not only a father, but a sister. The difficult but often bewitching Evangeline had opened his heart to fun, wildness and exploration, and he missed her greatly despite her difficult ways.

Grant had written to him from Philadelphia and sent wonderful gifts. Several times they had arranged to meet on the streets. But Hannah had found out and put a furious end to their appointments. It was just as well, Victor thought, because the sadness of their new situation was too much for either of them to bear in such truncated reunions. The notes and gifts stopped except at Christmas, but Victor's yearning had never disappeared.

Irrationally, there were dreams that someday it would all happen again and the picnics in white would return.

There was another man who would be his father. Victor had known Benedetto Serpa since the day he had been scooped into those great arms at Castle Garden. In his small bed he remembered hearing the graveled voice from the next room as Serpa sat with Hannah at the table night after night, speaking of grown-up things.

Strangely, even as a child Victor had been able to understand his mother's feeling toward the Sicilian. They were so recognizable because they were so much the same as what he received himself. Serpa was held away, respectfully, sometimes even with a strong affection, but he could never come as close as he wanted. All the melting longing in his tiger's eyes could not win her heart.

It was not until after the streets had taught Victor what was possible between men and women that he comprehended that Serpa had achieved at least the physical part of his tortured dream.

Sometime not terribly long after Jack Grant had gone, Serpa had again become a steady visitor. The dimly heard talks weren't as quiet as they had been before, with the Sicilian often raising his voice in entreaty or frustrated anguish. Without understanding what it was about, Victor knew a long, subtle battle was being fought.

He supposed, later on, that Serpa had been the winner. Because at last there were nights when this awesome man, dressed as if going to a grand ball and smelling of toilet water, would appear with flowers. His voice would be hushed and he would be as close to docile as such a man could be. Then, Victor knew, he would follow his mother into her room and spend the night. Sometimes Victor heard him call out quietly to God, but from Hannah there was never a sound.

The new accommodation changed few things. But the worst of Serpa's chronic petulance seemed to lift slightly, and he quietly let Victor know that their own relationship had changed. Another type of family had begun, one that would not have come from heaven.

When Serpa had tried to draw Victor more closely into his world, Hannah had stepped in to block him. So to Victor, Serpa remained only a loyal, solicitous uncle who venerated and sometimes slept with his mother. Victor accepted that decision by Hannah and managed to take Serpa at his best. He did not dislike him, but his heart could not go out to the man.

Hannah, Victor eventually came to see, had not been entirely the loser. There were nights when Serpa came with his flowers that her eyes awakened and gave back much of the dark flames that were there in the Sicilian's. On such nights her son was sent early to bed. Victor sometimes discussed this relationship with Julia Serpa, who had quickly become his playmate and, as her quick intellect hurriedly mastered English, his confidante.

"Julia, do you think your father will someday marry my mother?"

"No, because she will not have him. I sometimes hear him praying out loud in his room for God to make her come to him with her heart. Leo says he never stops being angry because your mother will not let them be together all the time."

"You know what it is they do in bed, don't you, Julia?"

She had laughed as only a ten-year-old could. "Victor, in Sicily you are born knowing things like that."

As Hannah had drowned herself in her work with the departure of Jack Grant, so had Victor. His painfully developed sense of playfulness was largely lost, and his mother's budding permissiveness was cut off as well.

Victor's education had then become serious business. Frau Wendt's superior work had laid solid foundations, but now he was beyond her. The tutors arrived three or four a day, always in a room set aside at Oakhill Development so Hannah could make sure the effort was going forward with full speed and efficiency. In exchange for his acquiescence to languages, music and the classics, he was able to get for himself the very finest teachers of the disciplines of building. Geology, physics, mathematics, design, he devoured them all.

His greatest teacher was Oakhill Development. There were now two dozen architects and engineers employed, and many had known and loved Victor since he had watched their work as he stood on a stool at their elbow. There was no job that went through that he didn't learn something from the architects, and they sometimes let him try his own hand, often with impressive results.

In the same way as his mother, he was enthralled by the way

scratches on paper progressed from a hole in the ground to graceful structures that sheltered, warmed and made productive an animal that could no longer survive in the open.

As much as he enjoyed roaring around Bill McGlory's, his real delight came from watching buildings go up. He would read the newspapers to find where something interesting was rising, and haunt the site as work went on, bedeviling the foremen, architects and engineers with ten thousand questions.

As exciting as it was, though, he acquired a growing impatience with the process. He saw that each building was essentially built brick upon brick, floor upon floor, not much different than what he had accomplished as a small child with wooden blocks. It seemed to him that buildings should leap for the sky and grasp the clouds. Instead, they rose squatly and ploddingly, topping out where a resident of the top floor could see no farther than his neighbor's window across the street.

He watched the springtime weeds in vacant lots uptown. Thin, graceful, easily surviving the battering winds of the hardest thunderstorms, always firing upward to double the height of a man in two weeks. What nature could do, man could do, he thought.

His early love of the heights never faded and always threatened to take him into serious trouble. On some nights he slipped into the tallest building he could find and made his way to the roof. There he would mount to the parapet, enjoying himself more if there was a brisk wind, and race around it as fast as his legs could carry him. The fact that he could often hear the appalled screams of people in the streets simply told him that he had not gone high enough. Such daring and agility always eluded the tardily-called police and dared him to greater things.

Knowing that the towers of the great Brooklyn Bridge had recently eclipsed the steeple of Trinity Church as the tallest structure in New York, he would not rest until he made the top. On a stormy night, when the watchmen had been driven into their shanties, laden with ropes and a rucksack he made his way up the main cable. He was back before morning, but not without leaving the evidence of his stay. Hannah read in *The Sun* as follows:

MIDNIGHT DAREDEVIL SHOWS PLUCK CROSSING RIVER ON BRIDGE CABLE

Moving unseen in rain and darkness, a steely-nerved marauder last night crossed the uncompleted Brooklyn Bridge on its bare cables, which are at present unequipped with handrails or any other safety device. The dauntless fellow showed the skill and daring of a Swiss mountain climber, policemen at the scene said.

The evidence of the crossing on the swaying cables, from which will one day be suspended the 6,000-foot span, were two signs painted on bedsheets and depended separately from the east and west towers.

The enigmatic daredevil had written, "V.O. REACHED THE TOP."

No resolution of the bold climber's identity is expected. He is the first nonworker to have crossed the East River via the Great Bridge.

Hannah had confronted him, not able to completely hide either her fright or her admiration.

"Was it you who did this foolish thing, Victor?"

"It was the most wonderful fun I've ever had, Mother. And very easy. Don't be angry."

"Swear to me that you will never do it again in your life."

"I only did it because it was the highest thing there is. What in this city will ever be higher than the Brooklyn Bridge?"

He walked among the workers.

So much enamored of his city was Victor, that the thought of leaving it to go to Chicago for even a few months, as he soon must, distressed him. He drank in modern Manhattan as though it would be forever lost to him.

It was almost unimaginable to him that there were now one-and-a-half million souls on this island, a doubling of its population in just twenty years. Only through the wonders of science and engineering could such masses hope to function.

He remembered that only six years before, in 1876, the telephone had just been invented. Now every major business, Oakhill Development among the first, had a receiver, and the sky above was beginning to darken with wires strung from telephone poles with up to a dozen crossarms.

Elevated trains, their bell-funnels spewing ashes on all below, now ran on Ninth, Sixth and Second Avenues to haul the workers about their business, although omnibuses still made their way along the more elegant thoroughfares of Fifth and Madison Avenues.

There was an uproar as a steam fire-engine rumbled down the avenue, its powerful engine driving it forward at the vertiginous speed of four miles per hour, making it difficult for the fireman running ahead of it to clear the way for traffic.

At Madison Square he paused to gawk at the enormous arm of Bartholdi's stupendous statue-to-be of "Liberty Enlightening the World," looking for footholds for a possible quick climb.

A hot debate was being resolved in front of him. "Sure it would be more classic if she was nude. But this isn't Greece, damn it. It gets cold here. She can't be out standing in her birthday suit in a *snowstorm.*"

By dark his legs were heavy, but he forced himself onward to drink his fill of the wonders he would not see in Chicago, where his apprenticeship would begin.

On Broadway and on Fifth Avenue between 14th and 34th Streets the night was made day with the blaze of arc lights. As much as the sight moved him, he was more thrilled with the other potential of the waking giant of electricity. Its sparking wings would free the architect of chains to the ground worn since the first primitive had piled a stone upon a stone. It would replace clumsy steam engines and dangerous illuminating gas with compact, powerful devices that could go to any heights and take man with them.

He let his imagination fly free to a day when the squat eight- and twelve-story piles of masonry he saw around him would be eighty and a hundred-and-twenty stories, vertical cities in themselves that would expand the souls of men by the pure audacity of their assault upon the heavens. The electric lights in their crowns would be a string of diamond-studded lighthouses visible fifty miles at sea, signaling the placement of the greatest metropolis there could ever be and the bold genius of the men who built it.

New York would not be the greasy smudge on the horizon that was the mark of lesser cities, but a glory of cloud-piercing towers, a signature against the sky that would belong only to this place. And to Victor Oakhill.

As he turned toward home, he found he had built an excitement so uncontainable that he half-ran all the way. If he did not have to make his good-byes in the morning, he thought, he might have seized his suitcases and sped to Grand Central Station at once to watch for the arrival of the Chicago express.

His mother, still fully dressed, was waiting up for him in the drawing room that had never been anything but an office in the house since the days of Jack Grant. She looked perfectly in place amid the drafting tables, scattered rolls of blueprints and the framed elevations of completed buildings. One of the few things she shared with Victor was a love of this room and what it stood for.

Victor noticed the unexpectedly deep concern he only saw in her face when the primordial mother in her, the part that would not heed the mind, felt her son wandering into some dimly sensed danger. The look had last been there when she read of his stunt on the bridge months before.

"I finished packing for you."

"Thank you, Mother. You shouldn't have waited up, though."

"I made a mistake giving you this permission, Victor. I believe I'm going to wire Mr. Dunlop in the morning and withdraw it."

The look of utter dismay told his mother that there was no way to stop him short of shooting him. "Come on, now, Mother. You're almost as excited as I am at what Dunlop is doing in Chicago. They've even given his buildings a special name. Skyscrapers. After what they call a high fly in a baseball game."

"Come with me to the Adirondacks for the summer. I'll stay with you, Victor. Business is slow," she said, trying one last, hopeless time.

"You know perfectly well that's driven us both crazy when we've done it for a week. We end up sketching ideas for five-story log cabins." He didn't say it, but he also knew she was quite uncomfortable in his company.

"It's dangerous where you're going, and you'll make it worse scampering around like a monkey where it's highest. They're losing men every week."

"Because they're learning the new ways. The early mistakes are always the worst. It will make it safer for me later."

"It's ridiculous for a boy in your position to be working in the open with his hands for a whole hot summer. If I ask him to, Mr. Dunlop will take you into his office, and you can work with your head and wear a suit."

"For heaven's sake, Mother, that's the last way in the world to learn about skyscrapers. Dunlop himself can't do it from a design table. He's making up the technology as he goes along, solving problems nobody ever met before. A great architect or engineer can learn more about stresses and loadings through the soles of his feet than most of the others can do with all their numbers and tables." He had begun to stalk nervously among the drafting boards, examining blueprints at random, a boy addicted to structure.

"Your contempt for academic education won't do, Victor. If you just wish to buy and sell properties and employ technicians, as I do, what you've learned is likely to be enough. If you want to design the future yourself, you've got to have more schooling."

He swept an arm at everything in the room. "I want to do it all, Mother. You've done wonders, but I've seen your frustration. There's always a dozen small imaginations to slow up and bring down the big ones. There's more than construction to master. The inefficiencies of buying and selling and financing and operating have to be knocked in the head, too."

His mother was startled and impressed at this rare outburst of what was inside him. He thought that this might be the moment that he began manhood and partnership in her eyes.

"Is that what you really feel, or just a fancy way of telling me you're done with school?"

"I promise I'll get all the training I'm supposed to after I get back."

"Boston Tech, I think." It was the short name for the Massachusetts Institute of Technology. "You can get in at sixteen, and even as a second-year man if you pass the tests. Then you can set your own pace."

"Good," said Victor. "I've got only a couple of years to spare, Mother."

John Dunlop proved to be a spare, almost hairless man. His scalp shone indoors above the hatline as a white skullcap above a face burned almost black by endless forays on the high girders. As a man whose high-pitched voice tumbled out words about his obsession in endless torrents, he appreciated Victor's ability to listen quietly and absorb voraciously.

"I'm going to treat you like an idiot, Victor, with all deference to your mother as a respected colleague. Because I'm an idiot myself in what I'm beginning to do. I want it known that like any good idiot I will accept nothing as known and question everything now seen as a certainty. I will babble and rant out loud, so all can share in my confusion and help me resolve it. What we find true today we may find untrue tomorrow, and the contrary. I haven't been at this very long myself, so it won't take long to tell you where I've been. Any questions?"

"Yes, sir," said Victor, squirming on a stool in front of the master's desk on this first morning in Chicago. "When can I start?"

"Now. Start by getting out of that suit. You're going to be hotter and dirtier and more tired than you've ever been in your life. Pretty soon you'll be praying to be floating in one of those cold Adirondack lakes."

As the startled Victor started to slip off his jacket and tie, Dunlop was unfurling an enormous roll of paper and tacking it down. Then his pencil was flying across it. Victor saw instantly that separation from pencil and paper would have all but rendered him mute. His mind worked in pictures, the words merely describing what was already done.

"My grasp of the skyscraper came to me in the Philippines," he said, an amazing series of lines springing from his pencil. "In the poorer provinces they built huts of straw and bamboo. The concept of piling up stones had never caught on with them. It was too stupid and cumbersome for them to even consider.

"The structures seemed too flimsy to have stood for an hour. Yet, these huts that went up in a day or two at the most, thrown together by men, women and children who had no sense of mathematical or architectural training, withstood gales and even typhoons regularly. Ingenious combinations of flexibility and rigidity, obtained by an intuitive system of cross-bracing, gave fantastic strength per pound of materials used.

"And those materials were a story in themselves. Light enough to be transported in quantity over long distances using the most primitive transportation, they presented almost no bulk in the structure. The walls hanging on a light, strong frame meant there was no interior space lost to bearing-walls. All the room in the house was usable. The walls not being structural members, windows and doors could be cut into them anywhere for ventilation or access. And with the weight of materials being comparatively negligible, height was limited only by a willingness to climb.

"Why couldn't we have this beautiful, unshakable simplicity in our cities, I wondered."

Victor looked at the dozen ingenious huts that had materialized on the paper, as accurately done as any of the new cameras could have managed. "You can't have straw and bamboo in Chicago, sir."

"No, there must be the insulating factor of stone and concrete in cold climates, and durability for hard usage. But the bamboo of the Northern Hemisphere is finally coming. There are new furnace processes that will give us cheap structural steel at last. It will be here in abundance before the end of the decade, Victor. Then we'll have the physical flexibility we can't get in iron. We'll have buildings that can go a thousand feet high and sway in the wind without breaking."

Victor remembered the strong, slender reeds he had watched shooting upward in New York and marveled at how his own thought had toyed with these principles. "I can't wait, sir."

"You don't have to. Leave your fancy suitcases and your dude's clothes right here. I'll get somebody to help you find a place tomorrow. Let's get to the site now, so your mother won't think I'm letting you sit around not learning anything. I don't want her mad at me, because I want some commissions from her."

"You'll have to battle me for those, sir."

The hairless brows lifted at the cockiness of the sixteen-year-old's words, but he clearly liked Victor's serious ways, and how he was rolling up the sleeves of his shirt, cufflinks and all.

"Then let the battle begin," Dunlop said and drove Victor before him.

The site, at which they arrived after a short but harrowing but fast ride in a light rig, held the half-risen skeleton of the new Family Insurance Building. There was nothing at all awesome about its size. Indeed, it seemed a poor and spindly thing next to some of the huge piles that Victor had seen go up in New York, But it thrilled him as nothing had before, because it was the seed of giants. Dunlop saw the effect upon him and was pleased.

"It's not the first one I've built. I've been doing it since 'seventy-five. But it sure as hell incorporates all the learning I've had and I think we're ready to start going high."

"How high is this one, Mr. Dunlop?"

"Only ten floors. Hell, there are buildings more than half again as high. But think what they pay for that height. The bottom sections are maybe sixteen feet thick to support the weight of what's above, and the walls have to do the same sort of work. So those walls have to be where the building needs them, not where the people need them. And they can never be moved to accommodate a tenant. Because they have to maintain the integrity of the walls, the windows are small and deep, like the embrasures of a medieval fortress, and let in just about as much light. And that's not even talking about all the damned thick columns coming through everywhere you don't want them."

Victor didn't have enough eyes to see all that he wanted to see at once. "The foundations. They're not continuous."

Again Dunlop was pleased by what Victor knew, and by his perceptiveness. "We don't need those. The weight comes down off those vertical beams and goes straight into the earth on a concrete pier under each beam. Chicago is one big marsh underneath, and those piers are literally floating the building like some ship. In another place, like New York, the verticals might go down to bed rock. The continuous foundation is already starting to die."

"The walls bear no load at all?"

"Some. Our thinking is ahead of our materials. But the day will come when the walls of a building sixty stories tall might be nothing more than a tapestry of glass. The office worker who now sits in a dark rathole will be sitting in cheerful sunshine among the clouds, with no other illumination needed in the daylight hours. It will be a privilege to come to work."

"I was thinking the other day how electricity is going to help."

"Indispensable. The steam and screwjack elevators they have now are barely suitable for buildings of this height. They will be impossible for the real skyscrapers. Not to mention the impossibilities of getting gas to those heights, or water without pumps driven by a new force. But we can't stop while they're perfecting their machinery, can we? Peter Cooper designed an elevator shaft into a building before there were any elevators because he knew there would be. We, too, must think ahead."

Beneath the web of rising girders, Victor was able to look straight up at the sky. The old technique of completing each floor in turn, in effect stacking one building on top of the other until the permissible height was achieved, had been discarded. This frame could be taken up to completion before a single wall rose or any flooring was added.

"Your men are so young," Victor noticed. "A lot of them are not much older than I am."

"The older men got confused. They were used to the way they had always done it. They were used to having a full building under their feet at all times while they worked. Asking them to learn to run what these new boys call The Six-Inch Highway, with nothing but the street below, was more than I could ask, it turned out."

"They seem to be working well now."

"Because I let them work out the small mechanics of their jobs themselves. I'm learning from them as much as they're learning from me. They'll go on to other jobs, and the techniques will spread through the city, the country and the world. It will be no different for the architecture or engineering. Now, Victor, go up there and become part of it."

In the following deliriously happy summer months, Victor found that there was for him a direct ratio of delight to how many feet he was above the ground. Before the end of the first week he ran the high girders better than any man on the job. He learned that fear had a certain weight and mass. That it could unbalance a man as fatally as a carelessly carried bucket of bolts if that weight were not checked and rechecked a hundred times an hour.

One morning Victor watched a young man not much older than himself tip slowly, almost deliberately, into space from an eighth-floor girder. As he took a step just like the hundred before it, fear had lurched inside him and jerked his leg off center. Falling with his face to the sky, he only understood what had overthrown him as it announced itself halfway down in a shriek heard blocks away.

With the other workers, Victor had gathered in the circle around the red-soaked crumple of rags to renew his acquaintance with the killer, the better to know his approaching step. There were no philosophers in the grim onlookers, but they all understood that a jealous earth would increasingly demand its price as men broke away to reach higher. And they had agreed to pay it, although as slowly as they could.

So Victor came to feel the touch of a gust of wind a thousandth-of-a-second faster than people on the ground, and lean to it without breaking stride on a six-inch beam with eighty pounds of fastening plates on his back. He leaped across five-foot gaps in floor planking as though they were curbside puddles and rode swinging steel-beams up cables into the sky as joyfully as a little boy on a swing.

Dunlop had not lied about the brutality of the work. The sun blistered down on his shoulders like a burning torch while a relentless humidity produced sweat that puddled in the groin, glued trousers to knees and rotted shoes away. Every protuberance appeared capable of reaching out to slice, crush or tear. Fingers and toes were lost, arms and legs were broken almost without notice, as though the Family Insurance Building were a busy man hurrying over an anthill, heedlessly maiming.

Dunlop worked out a wonderful series of movable hoists operated by pulleys and steam, whereby the lifting equipment moved higher up in the steel as the building rose. But while this worked well for the lifting of the main beams, bricks and mortar, it was eventually the muscles of young men moving on the narrow beams that wrestled the material to its precise spot of installation.

Pushing a wheelbarrow leaden with wet mortar at the end of a ten-hour day, or battling a suspended, swaying, four-ton beam to line up its bolt holes in a capriciously gusting wind, sometimes made Victor feel as if both shoulders had been wrenched from their sockets and he would be crippled forever. But by morning the stretched, twisted ligaments and muscles had regained their snap and power and he shot up the ladders as though he would continue to fly upward after he reached the top.

His face blackened, his torso widened to a wedge of roped muscle and his thighs bulged against the seams of his trousers. Standing on the topmost girder looking out over the steamy, low-lying reaches of Chicago, he sometimes felt in his exuberance that he had the strength to reach down and pull the building up with him until everybody in the sooty city could see it.

Before the summer's end, still short of his seventeenth birthday, he learned that he could handle men.

It hadn't taken the other workers long to discover from Dunlop's special attention that Victor had not earned his position as fairly as they had. They abused him as steadily as they could without rousing Dunlop's attention, sending him up and down the iron for water and nonexistent tools until he was ready to fall and had barely time enough for his own work. The foremen sent him out on dangerous beam ends, trying to break his nerve and humiliate him in front of the others. When that failed he assigned him the labor of two men.

Victor never went to Dunlop, perversely exhilarating in the

challenge. He had something to prove to himself as much as to the men. He did what they wanted uncomplainingly until they knew he was doing it as well as the best of them. He was respectful to everyone, and so enjoyed the excitement of the new construction that his spirits stayed high during the worst of their efforts against him.

Despite themselves, half of the men found their respect for him growing. They took him into their gangs because they knew he would pull far more than his weight, defending him against other crews who would waste his time on exhausting errands. Unavoidably, there was bad feeling between those who thought he had earned an end to the harassment and those who didn't. Victor expected that he would soon be challenged by more than work and words.

The Zaworski brothers were short, thick and mean. There was a rumor that they had beaten two union men to death with iron bars when they had been dealing with strikes in Pittsburgh.

Gaswirth, the oldest foreman, slipped them a few dollars each week to keep discipline among the men who were too strong for him to handle himself.

"Watch out, Oakhill," a West Indian whispered to Victor one afternoon. "Gaswirth has bets that the Zaworskis will have you off the job by tonight."

Rather than fear, an icy satisfaction came over Victor. His patience with those who would not let him up had worn away. He did not underestimate the Poles as terrible foes, but he had never lost what Gentleman Jack Grant had taught him about using his fists. Those two years of priceless lessons had been put to practical use and honed in dozens of street dustups in the Five Points.

During the remainder of the morning he was aware that the Zaworskis were trying to box him in, and that the other men were watching it all as they worked. Victor knew he couldn't avoid them for long, so he picked the spot where they would catch him.

He brought his lunch pail to a spot between girders where three planks had been laid as a crossover. Sitting on the planks as he ate, there was a single plank of width for others to edge around him, but no room to advance shoulder to shoulder. As he ate, he watched the Zaworskis whisper about the problem and finally reach their decision.

One behind the other they started across the planks, ten stories above the street.

"Coming through?" Victor asked.

"Coming right through your ass," said Casimir, the heavier of the brothers, who walked in front.

When he reached where Victor was sitting, he hooked the toe of his boot behind the lunch pail, which was open at Victor's side, and sent it off the edge. There was a tinny thunk as it struck the pavement. "I don't like that guinea cheese you eat, Oakhill. It makes your breath stink," said Casimir.

"What you going to do for lunch now, skunk breath?" asked Stanislau, the one at the rear.

"Well, now," Victor said, coming nimbly to his feet. "Since I've got nothing else to eat, I thought I'd spend the time knocking the hell out of you two instead."

"That tickles us. How about the second floor? They've got a lot of planks down. Plenty of room."

Victor stood facing Casimir. Stanislau, behind him, was already turning to leave the narrow planking.

"I thought right here would be a good place," Victor said.

Casimir looked bewilderedly down into the great gulf on each side of him. "What are you talking about?"

"Get 'em up," said Victor, raising his fists.

"We need room, you crazy sonofabitch."

"I've got all the room I need."

The man started to pull a wrench out of a loop on his belt. Victor hit him solidly on the chin. The wrench sailed off into the air, and the planks danced beneath their feet as the falling man stumbled backward into the arms of his startled brother, who had returned in time to catch him beneath the arms. Stanislau just barely retained his balance on the swaying planks as the watching men gasped and shouted warnings.

Heeding Jack Grant's long-ago words about the ephemeral nature of advantage, Victor stepped forward and did what he had to. As Casimir hung dazed and sagging in Stanislau's grip, he caught punches that smashed ribs on both sides, then another, even harder, on the chin. There was now no question that without the arms circling his chest, Casimir would slide to the sidewalk below. His brother's face, exposed over his shoulder and grub-white, was locked in that position as long as he was supporting the load. So Victor began to hit the helpless face as its owner tried to inch backward off the planks. He struck selectively. He wanted the man's head to stay clear enough to allow him to stay on his feet with his brother. But inside the requirement, Victor wanted to do all the damage he could. So he split lips and brows, blacked eyes, bruised cheekbones and methodically flattened Stanislau's nose.

When backward progress had stopped completely and the locked-together Zaworskis had begun to totter, Gaswirth screamed. "Let up before you kill 'em both, you bloody idiot," and Victor stopped swinging.

It took Dunlop two days to find out what had happened. Then he fired Gaswirth and the Zaworskis and gave Victor a gang of his own to handle. Nobody objected, and before they were through there was no better gang.

The hardest part of Victor's work, though, came after he climbed out of the iron. With no chance to wash, rest or eat he was dragged to the office of the tireless Dunlop for sessions with the blueprints that lasted until midnight. Victor would stagger home to the one-room flat that did little more than shelter his unconscious body for a few hours, with an armful of the sheets Dunlop had filled with sketches, notes and numbers. When Victor had come to Chicago he had been bursting with pride at how much his hungry mind had picked up in New York. The long hours with Dunlop had quite deflated him. The more his luminous mentor taught him, the more holes he saw in his background. The promise to his mother of further formal education was not to be the empty one he had meant it to be. In any case, Dunlop's enthusiasm for building to match the mountains fed new fire into his own vision, and he several times startled his master with bold notions of his own. He was soon filling almost as many sheets with his sketches.

"Victor, if you were ten years older we could rebuild Chicago."

"I'll be back after I finish rebuilding New York," Victor said, as he scribbled.

No matter how jaded the builders, the topping out of a building, no matter how modest, makes a wonderful day. The crew set the traditional tree to the pinnacle girder and cheered loudly enough to be heard on the street. Whatever divisions there had been between Victor and some of the men vanished, and there was much embracing and handshaking.

Dunlop had joined them for the small ceremony, and he remained for a while with Victor. "This begins it," he said. "I feel it. They'll point to this little building and say, 'There's where it started.'"

"Then why don't you look happier, sir?"

"Because the exciting part, the going *up* is all over on this one. Now we just finish. Walls, floors, windows. The drudgery. And while I want to start a dozen of these right now, each one ten stories taller than the last, I have to wait for a commission. And the commission is as likely to be a henhouse as a skyscraper."

"That's the trouble being just an architect, isn't it? You're always waiting on the whim of someone else to tell you what to build, and when and where. If only somebody could control it all."

"Somebody can."

"Who?"

"Hannah Oakhill and her son, Victor."

Victor laughed. "Mother does things *her* way. You don't know her."

"I don't have to. I know you." Dunlop took his hand. "Go home to New York now, Victor. You're stopping at the best moment. When you hit the spot in the sky you were aiming for. And tell Mrs. Oakhill thanks for sending me a boy who became a man. One who's going to write his name on the clouds."

Victor, his shoulders bursting the jacket of the suit he had departed in almost four months before, did not expect to be greeted at Grand Central Station. But he was, and with completely unexpected enthusiasm.

Julia Serpa, a sweet-smelling blur of yellow taffeta, all brimming eyes and beautiful smiles, laughed her way into his arms. His joking greeting was cut short by a long, hard kiss, delivered squarely on his lips and held for a very long while.

He didn't think he could ever be flustered by someone he had known for so long and so closely, but he knew his cheeks had reddened.

"Oh, Victor, Victor. I didn't even know you were gone for the first month. Then I started to miss you in July, and August almost drove me crazy. And I think I've been standing on this spot waiting for you since the beginning of September. For God's sake, tell me you missed me, too."

"Of course I did, Julia," he stumbled. "I thought about you all the time." They had been as close as only people who had grown up together as children and never been far apart could be. After Evangeline had left with Jack Grant, Julia had been his closest friend, the one to whom he could confide absolutely anything.

It had been Victor who had slipped her out from under the deadly watchfulness of her father and her aunts to show her the joys of life in the streets. He had always protected her like a lion from harm and insult, every inch the big brother, although she was in fact two years older than he.

However, her life had been in no way as open as Victor's. The dreaded aunts had stepped in after the death of Elvira, and the easy romance that came to Victor was unknown to her in any way. If she regretted this, it was never permitted to show. She was trained endlessly to protect her virtue for the one man whom she would love and with whom she would mate for life.

As the son of Hannah Oakhill, Victor was allowed access to Julia that would have been unthinkable with anyone else. In fact, as the girl had grown to maturity, the aunts, having heard much of Victor's reputation in the streets, implored Serpa to bar Victor from her company until a nice Sicilian of suitable age could be found and brought across the sea. That Serpa refused such a sensible request gave rise to much bewilderment.

With his wants met more than adequately elsewhere, it had never occurred to Victor, biologically or emotionally, to consider Julia as more than a childhood friend and beloved sister. Aware of the nature of the Sicilian tongue and mind, he had gone through some pains in the late years to be seen with Julia only in the most public and innocent places.

They were not, however, completely unaware of one another's physical blossoming.

Julia had become a tall, striking girl. What she lacked in formal beauty she made up in clean-bodied grace, satiny skin and all the smouldering Sicilian fire of her father. She was much her father's child in her seriousness. But when the flame burned through her shell, she was a force of nature. Victor had not missed the way heads had begun to turn in the street, caught by her queenly bearing and darkly glittering eyes. He was as proud of her as any other brother would be. And when she had run her hands brazenly over his swelling arms and broadening shoulders, he had always thought it was a natural, sisterly admiration.

If there had been any more significant emotions stealing into Victor unseen, they had much to fight against. Victor knew the terrible rules of honor lived by the Serpa clan, and it had up to now never crossed his mind that he might break them. But perhaps it had begun to cross Julia's.

She spoke to him straight and unblushing. "I must have loved you the whole time, Victor. You didn't meet another girl in Chicago, did you? I couldn't bear it if you didn't love me back." Before he could answer, she kissed him again, harder than the first time.

The terminal being no place to carry such a conversation forward, Victor spent some of his hard-won Chicago dollars and they started for home in a closed carriage. They were no sooner under way than Julia pulled down the curtains and was upon him again.

"I'll keep this carriage going until Canada if you don't tell me you love me, too, Victor." There was still an intriguing little hint of Sicily in her speech.

"I love you more than any friend I ever had, Julia."

"Forget me as a friend. I want to be more. I want to be everything."

Overwhelmed, Victor tried to scrape some defenses into place. "That trip just knocked the blazes out of me. Let's uh, talk some other time."

"Take me someplace. I'll sleep with you."

"For heaven's sake, Julia—"

She took his hand and with strength and determination brought it high under her skirt. Up there she wore nothing. She clasped her legs on his hand, holding it on her wetness. For just a moment he tried to withdraw against the pressure, but then she kissed him again using her tongue, and he was routed. He worked into her first one finger and then many, not knowing which of her moans were pain and which pleasure.

She fumbled at his trousers and after an inexperienced but resolute manipulation brought him forth. "Oh, you *do* love me, Victor."

Reassured and elated by what she had felt below, she released her hold and circled his neck with her arms for a final barrage of kisses that drove him nearly flat on his back on the leather cushions. His hand was still quite trapped.

"Julia," he managed to say against every physical instinct, "this is not the place for this."

Her thighs released his hand and she sat up, a general pleased with the success of a well-planned lightning attack. "What is the place, then? What is the time?"

He had trouble reestablishing the containment of his trousers, and his brow was as wet as his hand. "I have to go away very soon. To school. To Boston. I'll be studying hard. There won't be time for anything for a long while."

She had smoothed her clothing. "Have you ever heard of The Ten Pains of Death?"

"No."

"It's a list of the worst things that can happen to a Sicilian. Do you know what is number one on the list?"

"No."

"To Wait for One Who Does Not Come."

"I'll be back. I promise. Everything I want to do is in this city."

"Is marrying me something you want to do?"

"*Julia.* These things take *time.* Your father would slice me up if he ever thought we *had* to do something. If your aunts didn't do it first."

"Of course we can't hurry the courtship. That can go as slowly as you want. But you can ask my father *now.*"

"I'm not Sicilian. He'll never—"

"He wants your mother tied to him in any way he can get it. He wouldn't care if you had fur and a tail."

"Julia, there's no way I can possibly think about this until after my school." He jerked up the curtains of the carriage and the daylight poured in.

She shrugged in the Sicilian way, smiling and shaking her head in rather good-natured exasperation. There was not another word on the subject. She took his arm and let him stutter his way through some of what had happened to him in Chicago. When he had finished, she sang softly in Italian, in a sweet, pleasant voice. The hand wound through his arm rested so lightly on his wrist that he could hardly feel it. But he wondered if he would be able to dislodge it using all his strength. His fingers tingled with the memory of her furry, delicious wetness. He found himself glad, for once, that his mother never came to meet him.

Safely in his own parlor, Victor never even thought of mentioning his brush with Julia. That would go away as did all girlish whims. Instead, he almost danced around the room as he told his mother of the wonders he had met in Chicago through John Dunlop, and how they had sent his dreams miles above the earth.

Business was the only language they spoke comfortably with one another, and he was overjoyed to see her eyes sparkling as brightly as his own.

"I found out that I know nothing, Mother. But now I've seen where I'm going." He vaulted to the top of a desk, no longer able to remain on the ground. "I have ten million ideas, and I'm going to need you and Oakhill Development and all the luck that God ever made. But there's no power in heaven that could make me see what I want any clearer."

"Good. Then my writing to Boston Tech in your absence won't be a waste of time. The tests for the next term are in two months. Time enough for the tutors to sharpen you up again."

"Wonderful."

She noticed something. "Victor, did they teach you to leave your trousers open in Chicago?"

He blushed, turned and buttoned. "No, that's something I learned in New York."

He tore through the two days of entrance exams to the Massachusetts Institute of Technology and entered as a junior. This was impressive but far from unheard of, there being several boys younger than he entering at that level.

He liked Boston for its gentleness and courtesy but saw little of the city. The school, a handsome, classical building standing isolated in Back Bay on Boylston Street between Berkeley and Clarendon, was hardly twenty years old and already acclaimed. It was all work. He took a room only two blocks away and never wandered far from it or his classrooms.

If he learned no hint of what was taking place in Chicago, he was nearly drowned in the basic grounding of architecture and in the importance of the classics in design.

The four S's, Stability, Strength, Stress and Stiffness, were things he had largely mastered in the office. But Geology, Stereology, Mechanics and Calculus were new worlds, and he conquered them happily.

Taught by truly gifted teachers, he discovered he had a fine hand with a pencil. His visualizations came stunningly to life, and if he was not quite as prodigiously facile in his drawing as Dunlop, he had a better feeling for the importance of a detail, the difference that could be made by setting and by designing so the changing light painted a structure with colors and shadings that vastly enhanced the stone and steel. He could take a building he had drawn and reshade it in minutes to emulate the effect of the sun at any hour of the day, any day of the year.

It was the school's attitude to classical architecture that filled him with dismay. His teachers, as good as they were, had almost no regard for American architecture of the present. Buildings were judged good to the extent that they hewed to the classical Greek and Roman designs. The instructors were appalled by the post–Civil War trend to English, French, German and Italian styles, especially when they were not suited to their setting and use. Except for advances in building materials and techniques, he might have been preparing to build for some Roman emperor.

It might have been better for him if he had found something exciting in Greek Ionic and Doric, the Roman Corinthian, the Tuscan and the Composite, but he didn't. The deadening processing of architraves, taeniae, cornae, friezes, abaci and echnia that flowed easily but tediously off his pencil seemed to invite a shutdown of progress and imagination. The classics, he decided, were there to fall back on when innovation failed, or when there was fear of criticism.

However, his experience with Dunlop had humbled him enough to wonder if the fault was his. Perhaps he didn't have the patience for details that the ancients and their composites demanded. Without a sense of the classical proportions, any structure, no matter how brilliant the engineering, would be an abomination. In school he soon realized that his idol, John Dunlop, was far more truly an engineer than an architect. No matter how bold the structural interior of the recently completed Family Life Insurance Building, its blocky aesthetics would never quicken the pulse of an onlooker or a person looking to give an architect a commission.

Setting his jaw, he resolved to try to mate the timeless proportions of the classics with his lofty dreams even as he felt the ghosts of long-dead Greeks and Romans trying to chain him to the ground.

As quiet as he normally was, he was unable to keep himself from becoming an outspoken nuisance in his classes. The more dogmatically a teacher stated a principle, the quicker he was to challenge it. "Sir, how can you talk about keeping the buildings of our cities in scale to man? Nobody has the wisdom to set a limit on such a scale."

"Mr. Oakhill, Michelangelo, admittedly without a shred of your talent, thought otherwise. He made a building as tall as your beloved skyscrapers by hurling the Pantheon on top of the Parthenon, so it doesn't loom but appears suspended from the heavens. The statuary inside the dome of St. Peter's is proportioned larger as it goes high so the building doesn't soar away from a man too small for it."

"With respect, Michelangelo couldn't be counted on to design all the buildings in New York. And man creates and recreates his own scale. His buildings should signal the size of his spirit, however tall."

"Controlling size controls crowding, the most dismal of human conditions, Mr. Oakhill."

"On the contrary, sir. The city *demands* concentration. The skyscraper, by spreading the load to the skies instead of the suburbs, creates a marketplace of disciplines and ideas. A man working in the shadow of a dozen fifty-story buildings—"

"And what a hideous shadow that would be—"

"—will be able to walk to and meet with more human knowledge and skill in one day than Aristotle could in a lifetime."

"Bravo, Mr. Oakhill. You have surpassed Aristotle and Michelangelo in a single afternoon."

During the two years of grueling learning in Boston, studying through both summers, Victor returned home infrequently. His mother, he imagined, did not miss him greatly, and he had no friends whom he wished to see or business that needed his presence. But on each short visit, usually at holidays, Julia was there waiting for him, her newly shown ardor undiminished. He had confidently thought that her dogged pursuit after the day in the carriage would fade away with his absence. He believed she would laugh at her outburst and ask him to forget it. But she had been simply assembling her forces for a longer siege.

Constantly she would propose some simple excursion to an innocent location and then try to charm him into an indiscretion that would increase her hold on him. Victor learned to sidestep these, but feared for when he returned home, when her enterprise might be carried on full time. This fear, however, had pleasurable aspects.

He had not by any means put his dear friend completely out of his mind on his return to school after her unexpected protestation. There was no denying that he found something thrilling about a promise of romance from such a surprising direction. Even as he avoided her thrusts, there was a delicious newness between them now. The distrust of the aunts, their prying eyes and rude questions had always been a matter of irritation to him. Now their watchfulness added some of the spice of the forbidden.

For the first time, he began to consider whether he might feel about Julia Serpa as she felt about him. It had never been possible to contemplate the idea of passionate love while physical union was not subject for thought. But now that he had touched her and stiffened in her hand, the mighty dam of friendship that had stood for years had distinct cracks. Every surge of new pressure widened that breach imperceptibly as his mind accepted more and more illicit images.

He thought much about Serpa and knew it would be wisest to turn her away, but something bred into her flesh in the hot hills of Sicily would not let him flee. Her body spoke to him separately from her words in small ways that lighted large fires. A thin line of sweat on the beautiful line of her upper lip as she leaned close, her graceful hand resting low on her belly, a slight widening and lifting of the eyes to remind him of what she had looked like in the carriage. All these things filled him slowly with wanting that made it increasingly painful to back off. But he tried. "The Beaux Arts in Paris, Julia. Everything they taught at Boston was a pale imitation of that. It's a school of architecture joined to a school of painting and sculpture. I can spend a couple of years there. I could see the great things in Rome and Florence. I'd write to you."

"I have a room, Victor."

Inside him, a gate started to swing closed. It was the last moment that he could escape through it. "Where? How did you manage it?" He had meant to say that it didn't matter.

"It's Leo's place," she said. "He's been keeping a woman there for a year. Now they've gone to hide in Albany because he hurt a union man for my father. The woman is good and she has eyes to see what it is with us. She slipped me the key."

"If she tells Leo we'd be lost. He has a mouth as big as the harbor." Victor couldn't stop saying the wrong things.

"She knows better. And they'll be gone until after Christmas."

All it would take, he knew, would be a firm shake of the head, a sad smile, a kiss on the cheek and a brisk, decisive walk in the other direction. Her pride would break it off for good, no matter what the pain.

"When?" was what he said.

She opened her hand to show him the key that been resting there.

They went to the room at the east end of 14th Street by separate routes. Hurrying through the mid-afternoon heat, tumescence already tugging at him, Victor thought he saw an aunt or a Serpa man watching him from every doorway. My God, wasn't that the squat Aunt Zia coming out of the sausage store? And that could be Rendino seated on that newsstand, his pearl-gray hat with the huge brim pulled down to hide his watchfulness.

Again and again he took extra turns, entered stores to watch the streets through the windows, and doubled backward. When he could worry no longer, he sprinted up three flights of a tidy brownstone showing the address he had been given and knocked low and urgently on the door bearing the whispered number.

It opened just wide enough for Julia to reach out and pull him in with a bare arm. In a moment of lusty playfulness, she was dressed only in her hat and shoes, and laughed at his astonishment. He had only time to see that she was wonderfully made in the hips and breasts before he lifted her off her feet with a hug and rushed her to the turned-down bed.

For all his wide experience, he was overpowered by the sight and touch of her. The sharp and special smell of explosively rising want rose out of her and his reason floated abruptly away. He found no time to remove his clothing or her hat and shoes. With his trousers ingloriously around his knees and his necktie firmly knotted, he went into the thick, pungent pelt of her and lost every doubt that he had always loved her with all of his being. "I love you, Julia. I love you, I love you, I love you."

"I waited for you, Victor," she said, eyes closed, her pelvis driving. "Leo wanted to, and a rich fish man from Genoa, but I waited for you."

At his pounding release he flew to a high, pure sunshine. Then he plummeted to a deep valley on the other side.

"Julia, what the hell are we doing? This can't be. I have too many things to do. Let's talk tomorrow."

Hobbled by the trousers around his ankles, he was not able to roll of the bed quickly enough to escape her arms. "By tomorrow we won't have to talk, Victor." She removed her hat and one shoe before her unslaked passion started up again and she regained a handhold that could not be denied. Her mouth took him in clumsily, but ultimately with compelling effectiveness.

He mounted her three more times, each entrance more imaginative than the last, and his appreciation of her increased successively, along with his anxiety. "I think I do love you, Julia," he heard himself say testily.

"Tell me that sometime when you have your clothes on," she said.

As the next days passed, he labored strenuously at Oakhill Development to concentrate on what must be done to win respect from his mother. Drawing on his newly honed skills, he enlisted some of the better architects to help him design his way to the stars. But all with whom he tried to work, Hannah included, observed in him a strange and uncharacteristic discontinuity. And soon even the densest of the workers knew that the cause was Julia.

Serpa's daughter, not seen at Oakhill since she was a small girl, now happened by every day. She visited with Hannah and with some engineers she barely knew through long-ago introductions, and always ended up at Victor's desk. No amount of whispered pleading could make her stay away.

It was dangerous enough to slip away to Leo's room. But now she took advantage of the physical thrall in which she held him to drag him into new terrors.

She brought him to her house, first in the afternoon for conversation and coffee before one or more of the glowering aunts, then far into the evenings for anisette and songs at the piano. Sometimes Serpa would pass through, fix them with a stiletto stare and pass by. For any other caller it would have been an unbreakable commitment, but for a childhood friend who was also Hannah Oakhill's son it could be less.

The mere proximity to Sicilian elders would have been petrifying enough without her dragging Victor down onto the rug when the army was lax enough to leave them alone for longer than five minutes. The naked fear was as powerful an aphrodisiac as could be found for their young and boiling blood, and by dispensing with undergarments they were able to complete an attachment before Aunt Zia had the espresso more than half done in the kitchen. Soon there was not a stick of furniture in the room that had not been accomplice to their rapid acrobatics.

Happily for Victor, who was now in love with Julia for whole days at a time, Leo remained in exile and his room could continue to shelter the bulk of their exuberant misbehavior.

Inside of three months, Victor's anxious sweating was considerably controlled, and Julia's body was an important and much-needed part of his life. As for the rest of Julia, she remained as good a friend as ever, and her paucity of education and unfortunate lack of humor could not obscure a fine, deep sweetness.

When Hannah asked him unexpectedly one day, "Do you love Julia, Victor?" he answered her without thought.

"Yes, Mother. I think I might." Then he added, "Maybe we should keep that to ourselves. I'm not ready for any commitments."

A little bit at a time, his burgeoning plans for his skyscrapers regained the primary position in his life and he stopped feeling so out of balance. He cut down on his time with Julia, but the moments he gave her were regularly scheduled, delightful and inviolate.

It was late one Sunday afternoon in early February that Victor got to Leo's room early. The former tenant had returned but had been persuaded to take his lodgings elsewhere. Victor supposed that had been the work of Julia, although she coyly denied it.

He turned up the flame of the kerosene heater until he felt its warming flow and then removed his clothing to wait beneath the down comforter of the bed. Julia's time of arrival could not be precise because she had to work her way free of the long, lingering conversations her numerous clan carried on over tumblers of wine after the big Sunday meal. Then she would go for her "digestion walk," and wend her way to two happy hours with her waiting lover.

Victor had brought a beautiful hothouse rose and he laid this on her pillow. The soft bed was deliciously comfortable, and as the heater's efforts spread through the room, his eyes became heavy and he began to doze, smiling to himself at the turn his life had taken and dreaming of its gloriously rising promise.

At last he heard the turning of the key in the lock, the door opening and easing closed. He half-sat up to see Julia, her cheeks sure to be rosy with cold and expectation, but saw instead Benedetto Serpa.

The towering chieftain of the Five Points was standing soberly at the foot of the bed in his Sunday best, his huge, black overcoat a square, looming coffin.

Whatever heat had stolen into Victor's body departed in an instant. The most lethal weapon convenient to his hand was the rose on the pillow at his side, although he knew a brace of blazing revolvers would not suffice to stop an aroused Serpa.

But Serpa did not seem aroused, to Victor's incredulous relief. He wore the same serious, dispassionately calculating expression he wore to church and business. When he spoke it was more quietly than usual, if anything. "I did not mean to upset you, Victor."

Victor, helpless, could only play the game. "That's . . . all right, sir."

"I have been meaning to speak with you of important matters. But during your time of work you are so busy. So I thought Sunday would be good, and this a fine, private place where we are not hurried."

"Yes, sir. That's fine." Victor felt ridiculous speaking from bed, but he wore not a stitch and his clothes had been hung neatly in the closet.

"As a father, Victor, and a man of respect in an ancient society, I cannot be as careless of my daughter's honor as some American would be. You understand that?"

"Yes."

"If I thought that the one precious possession God has seen fit to leave me was being badly used, I would have to judge harshly. You understand that?"

"I do, sir." Victor could hardly hear himself.

"But, of course, your position in my heart is special. So I will greatly stretch the terms of my judgement."

Despite his untenable position, Victor felt himself growing angry. "I'm not interested in your judgement."

Serpa walked slowly around to the head of the bed and sat down opposite Victor. He took the rose from the pillow and smelled it reflectively. "You do not have to be as long as you decide to do the respectful thing."

"I suppose it was Leo who told you."

"He did not have to. It was I who had him offer the room to Julia."

"You *sonofabitch*."

"I am honest with you, Victor, because I want you to understand how much I want this marriage."

"I understand how much, Mr. Serpa. I don't completely understand why."

"It is important to me to tie the Serpa blood to the Oakhill blood."

"You mean you want hostages—our children—to tie my mother to you."

"I seek the happiness of all."

"How could you use Julia like this?"

"That is a question I would ask you, Signor Oakhill." He broke the stem of the rose short and placed the flower in the buttonhole of his coat.

"I love her."

"I depend on that. Why did you not come to me like a man and treat her with honor?"

"I . . . have so many things I want to do now. I couldn't give her the time she deserves."

"Ah, yes. The tall buildings. Your mother tells me. That is more important than Julia?"

"No. Of course not."

"Julia would not come to you with a mule and a couple of goats and chickens. I would place a great value on this marriage."

"Mr. Serpa, I don't need your money."

"Perhaps your tall buildings will. You will come to me soon for permission?"

"There's nothing that can force me into this."

"Not even Julia, who loves you so that her tears turn to blood, and who will sit dishonored and scorned for all her life, sitting in black with her aunts?"

The thought shook Victor. "I told you I loved her, too. Give me a day."

"A minute is too long. I will be home in an hour. You will have the permission. Julia will be there, too. She came home early from her walk."

Victor fell back on the pillow, exhausted by the strength of the Sicilian. "Yes, sir. I'll be along"

Serpa permitted himself a wolfish smile. "Then we'll be a family."

"Sir, I'll make Julia very happy."

The smile grew harder. "You have made me a promise. And I swear I will help you keep it."

In the middle of 1883 Victor Oakhill married Julia Serpa happily enough. The ceremony was done before Father Alleghieri in a mighty Mass attended by almost as many powerful city politicians as there were swarthy and broad-shouldered men who offered their congratulations in Italian.

Hannah would congratulate neither Serpa nor Victor. "He has taken advantage of you" was all she said to her son.

Benedetto Serpa's gift to his daughter was a fine house near his own. His gift to his son-in-law was a visit from an oily little Irishman who worked for the city.

"Mr. Oakhill, we would be honored to help ease any of your future building projects through the municipal process. It can be very corrupt, you know."

Although a bit dazed by the speed at which his new family life had arrived, Victor found himself enjoying it. He found it wonderful, if somewhat less exciting than before, to roll onto Julia's voluptuous loins every morning and evening without the agonies of evasion. And with her obsessive pursuit over, his wife became very much her old quiet self, a good friend and refuge who loved much but spoke of it little. Victor found that he had more time than ever to prepare his schemes, although there was a quick, nasty interruption that took him away from his affairs for months.

Julia was pregnant so promptly that Victor wondered if her condition has preceded their marriage. She began to swell almost at once, and even her tall, strong frame was soon not able to stand up to the huge, swollen mass that spread her belly grotesquely. By the end of the fifth month her back muscles were in spasm and she had taken to her bed. Poisonous fluids built up in her despite rotations through the city's finest doctors, and the lovely, graceful woman that Victor had tumbled so joyously became a bloated, smelling heap, moaning ceaselessly in a tangle of sweated bed linen. Victor's heart broke for her.

Serpa raged and demanded to know if there was still life in her womb. The doctor's assured him that there was, if anything, too much life. They were now certain that she was carrying twins. What they could not be certain of was whether the constant, violent movement of the children in the womb was a sign of their distress or their vitality. In either case, the result was unbearable misery for Julia, so that Victor spent entire days at her bedside letting her dig her nails into his hands.

"Victor, the Devil is eating my insides. Call Father Alleghieri to protect me."

By the time the twin babies were born, Julia was a listless, dead-eyed shell who only roused herself sporadically to scream.

The children, a boy and a girl, were large and perfectly formed. Emerging to Julia's unending shrieks, they were quiet and alert, their eyes open almost at once and seeming to take in all around them with cold appraisal, although that was, of course, impossible. As they were being cleaned together on the table, their arms chanced to link, and the doctor had some small effort in prying them apart.

Victor, still burning at the humiliation of his bedroom meeting with Serpa, would have none of the tradition of Old World names for children born in the New. He called the boy George, after the dragonslayer, and let Julia name the girl Jana, after a friend.

George and Jana thrived as infants, but Julia remained ravaged, as if they had sucked all the strength out of her bones. Filomena changed households to help, but even her wondrous stores of energy were taxed by the ceaseless wants of mother and children.

In the nights, Victor rose to the childrens' cries and held them. They seemed incredibly tuned to one another, waking and sleeping at very nearly precisely the same moment, and sharing the same traits and temperament. They grew better looking every hour, their hair as dark as his and Julia's, but their eyes large and almost transparently pale, a legacy of some Viking raid in Sicily or along the Danube.

Victor loved his children and was proud of them, but he thought he saw in those pale eyes, even when hooded in half sleep, the same crouching coldness that lived in the eyes of Serpa.

While Julia was at last beginning to move back to health and Filomena was getting a grip on raising his children, Victor was meeting frustration in his grand designs.

To his mother he was a talented apprentice who would after a few more years of seasoning be ready to share in the running of Oakhill Development. To the staff he was a young dreamer, wasting time on grandiose, impractical plans when he might have been helping them in the day-to-day crush. The companies to which he showed his most daring work as he sought commissions had read a good deal about the heretical dangers being promulgated by John Dunlop in Chicago. They listened only apprehensively to his callow New York disciple.

His concepts and drawings in more conventional areas were impressive enough to bring several building commissions to Oakhill Development, but these again were ultimately the same—tedious stone-upon-stone structures that held no interest for him. In spare moments, trading on the Oakhill name, he went to the banks to try to interest them in financing a speculation on a steel-skeleton building of fifteen to twenty stories, extolling it as the most important construction investment of the next twenty years. They could scarcely have been less interested if he had proposed structures hung from the clouds or built of bananas.

"Oakhill, it says something for your skyscrapers that there are a dozen leagues against them before a real one has gone up in the city."

It was true. From what was heard and projected about the giant buildings, they were seen increasingly as a gigantic germ that devastated the civilized world more terribly than tuberculosis.

For the hundredth time he burst in on Hannah. "Mother, we're like a man I heard about a while ago. His father left him a thousand shares in a company that made wheels for Conestoga wagons. He made him promise to hold onto them for his grandchildren, because, he said, 'There'll always be wheels.'"

"We're just fuddy-duddies, are we?"

"The idea of building and buying a bunch of little rabbit nests and letting the rents carry them until the land appreciates enough to sell is going out with square riggers."

"There will be square riggers sailing as long as there are winds."

"All right, Mother, let's use your own favorite thing, holding the land and renting it. For the same land price that you put up a four-story building to rent out, you put up a twenty-story building. You get five times the rents, and when the building sells, it sells for five times the price."

"But it costs so much to build, Victor."

"When the steel mills begin pouring out those beams in volume, the prices will drop like rocks. And the technique makes for speed. Pour concrete by the ton instead of putting mortar on bricks a pound at a time. Everything goes faster when you get rid of stop and go. Everything gets cheaper because of the speed, and because you bring in each craft as you need it for a long, straight run. In go all the foundations, then all the steel and all the floors and all the walls. Efficiency instead of piecework."

"Slapdash instead of craftsmanship. And I read somewhere that the steel of the buildings that have gone up is already rusting inside the walls. In five years you could have skyscrapers lying all over the streets of Chicago."

"Nobody knows that's so, Mother."

"And nobody knows it isn't so," she said sharply. "Those buildings are untested in both their designs and their economics. They could break us. It's like flying one of those new airships while it's still being built."

He fumed and stormed out. A few skyscrapers managed to appear in New York, but he was not part of their creation. They were nothing to stir the imagination, but he went to stare at them, as though at a lost love.

Nine years after he had left John Dunlop and brought his great dream to New York, Victor trudged to examine a parcel of property on Madison Square for Hannah. He had no sooner come into view of it when he saw that he had wasted his time. The nondescript three- and four-story structures that sat on the land were old and of little value without major renovation. But the worst of the parcel was its shape. It was a narrowish triangle, only expanding to decent width halfway back on the rear lots. He could see why the city was contemplating taking the land, near useless for building, and adding it to Madison Square.

The unfortunate shape was a shame, he thought, because from 23rd Street down to 14th was The Ladies' Mile, a highly-fashionable shopping district for well-to-do women. The location would catch the eye of the elite if it were possible to place any decent commercial structure upon it.

In his mind he placed a simple four-story building on the site, wondering unenthusiastically if a single unit instead of several would take some of the curse off the shape. He was turning to go when the dumpy vision he held, refusing to fade, began to grow. It rose to six floors.

Then eight.

Then twelve.

It paused at fifteen, then shot in one grand surge to twenty.

And suddenly the ugly duckling was a breathtaking, long-necked swan gliding into to the future of New York. He brought out the sketchbook he always carried and filled it from cover to cover.

He was overjoyed.

Halfway back to the office to share his epiphany with Hannah, it came to him that he was going in the wrong direction. His mother would listen with that patient tolerance she reserved for him, praise the imaginativeness of the sketches, and ask him to consider just one more time whether that difficult corner might not be quite satisfactory for the show windows of a two-story millinery store.

He veered his footsteps toward the Five Points.

Benedetto Serpa kept his offices above a block-square cavern of screaming, booted men in bloody aprons, who laid out fish on beds of ice as vast as the Arctic. It was said that no fish dared swim into the Ambrose Channel without his permission.

The Sicilian was deeply engaged with a delegation of men who sat around a long, scarred table. They looked almost as hard and immovable as their rock-faced host. Victor anticipated waiting for as long as it took to finish their business. But he saw Serpa dismiss them with a backhand wave of his fingers when the guard at the door signaled through the glass partition that his son-in-law was waiting.

Serpa led him to his own leather chair and seated himself at the end of the table. "Tell me how I may help you, my son. Is it trouble? Julia? The children?"

"No, sir, it's about something you once said."

"If it was a promise, you already have what you want."

"You said you placed a great value on our marriage."

"And you never came to collect what was offered with such an open heart. It caused me to question your wisdom. Can it be that you will at last honor my wish to help you?"

"As you have guessed, it's my tall buildings that need the help." He flipped open his sketchpad and slid it to Serpa.

The iron eyes were impressed for once. "It is *very* big."

"There are bigger."

"But this is more. It's good for the spirit to see it. It's beautiful, but there are *balls* to it."

Victor smiled at the heartfelt simile. "Well, I wish you were the president of Oakhill Development, Mr. Serpa."

"Your mother will not like this?"

"Whether or not she likes it, she won't build it."

"It will hurt her business, perhaps."

"It could make her the most important builder in the city. Maybe in the world, finally. But she won't see it."

"You don't have to tell me she is stubborn, Victor. What is the cost?"

Victor scrawled a long number on the back of his pad and showed him. "Roughly that, to do it right."

"That is a great deal if you are not a bank."

"I've been to the banks. They're terrified of things half this tall and one-tenth as original."

"Many of the fish we control wear suits and watch-chains. Some of them swim around bankers' desks. I will spear some interesting things for you. In two weeks you will have money at good interest. If it is not all you need, you will have the rest from me."

"Thank you. If Mother sees that I can get it all, she'll come in with me. The only thing she hates more than being talked in is being left out. And I want Oakhill Development to be part of this, so I can go on."

"It is wonderful to get the best of your mother once in a while, is it not?"

"And very rare. Please don't speak to her about this until we're rolling. And I'd like to buy the property I need before the end of the week."

"But this is Wednesday, Victor."

"I don't want to see the most spectacular new building in the world become a line of benches in Madison Square. I owe you a great deal, Mr. Serpa."

"You are the husband of my beautiful daughter." He came to Victor and kissed him on both cheeks.

Victor let his mother enjoy his sudden apparent acquiescence to the routine and methods of Oakhill Development. He not only did his work on the buildings cheerfully and quickly, but spent half the day out of the office scouting what he assured her were exciting new things.

What he was about, of course, was the acquisition of his wedge-shaped parcel under the name of Triangle Building Company. In what few hours were left in the day, he worked at a drafting table in his bedroom.

He worked what they called *en momentum* at Boston Tech, taking his ideas at the spur of the moment and letting them spill onto the paper. Right from the first scratches he began to break the rules.

The skyscrapers he had seen so far were suddenly abominations. They seemed ashamed of their height, trying to hide it under a series of successively-piled smaller buildings, each with it own cornice and with classical ornamentation that spread the window lines and the eye horizontally. Since the skyscraper must eventually survive and flourish on its utility, that utility must be tuned into a beauty of its own. A philosophy of building tall must be evolved, and this was the moment to do it.

Everything he drew broke the eye loose from the ground and hurried it skyward in a breathtaking swoop. He meant for this structure to not appear shorter than it was, but rather taller. And the triangular shape that he thought he might have to strive mightily to overcome became not his foe, but his ally. The bold, unexpected angles would distort perspective giddily for the upward-looking, giving the vaulting stone sides and vertical slashes of windows a lightness that shot the eye past the top cornice as though anticipating flight.

Long before he was satisfied with the design, he sketched ground-level perspectives from every location on the street, often filling in the background buildings to view the contrasts. Each sketch sent his excitement trembling higher.

The last bank completed its assurances. He was ready to see Hannah Oakhill.

"The Triangle Building, is it? That's an interesting name, Victor. Every project needs a handle by which the mind of the public may pick it up and carry it away. And when the name exactly echoes the form, it's brilliant."

"Thank you, Mother."

He was quietly flabbergasted. The excitement had not only caught her on the very first drawing, but she had made not the slightest effort to hide it behind her usual facade of reserved, pragmatic contemplation. The deep pool of likely arguments against his plans seemed to drain dry as quickly as he had been able to outline his intentions. She had gone to her architects and laid out the sketches for them on every available surface, calling for their reactions and ideas as the work of the day languished for hours.

The crusty crew that Hannah had assembled in her design room were men who spoke their mind as bluntly as she did. The younger of them found themselves shouting their excitement. The older shook their heads in genuine horror. Hannah let the arguments rage without intervention.

As the controversy swirled, Victor saw that Hannah was taking in both sides without prejudice, weighing and planning. And he gradually realized that what he had thought for years was inflexibility was simply a determination not to go forward until she had a direction to which she could commit her forces with full enthusiasm. And he sensed her imagination had caught fire with the notion of the Triangle Building. It raised her color and sent her slim figure pacing with restless grace. It came to him that his mother, into her forties now, had become more beautiful with each year. What a fool Jack Grant had been.

When they were back in her office alone, she collected herself and became the cool businesswoman again. He made up his mind to match her.

"So you have all the land and money."

"Yes, Mother."

"But some of it would have to come from Serpa."

"About a third."

"It would be a very bad idea to have Mr. Serpa's money in this. He is far too good at collecting his debts."

He saw she was angling to where he wanted her. "I found that out just as you did, Mother. And I came here for more than your admiration."

"Good. I think Triangle Building is a terrible name for a company, even though it's a good name for this building. How long will it take you to change that to Oakhill Development?"

"I'll see to it this afternoon."

"I'll sell what I must to have what you need. We'll cancel all new work, and I'll reorganize the office to give the Triangle Building full attention. I'll let you know the details as I go on."

She was testing him, and he didn't fail her. "Take in some sail, Mother. Up to ten stories, Oakhill Development is yours. From there to the clouds, it's mine."

"By what logic?"

"Because you're the fox and I'm the eagle. You're brilliant on the land, I'm made for the sky."

"What if the sky falls, little eagle?"

Hannah had not forgotten the promotional techniques that had taken the Superior-Pacific so far into the wilderness, Victor saw to his great unease. But the deal had been struck and committed to paper. He had one third of Oakhill Development and all responsibility for steel-frame buildings. She ruled what happened on the ground, and that included publicity.

Some old contacts on the newspapers were still in place, and before long the pages of the *Times, World, Sun, Post, Express, Mail, Telegram* and *Graphic* were resplendent with fanciful drawings of the new giant rising on Madison Square. Any hope Victor had of easing past a disorganized and complacent opposition vanished. With every inch that the Triangle Building rose, a new horror was attributed to it, giving rise to a new committee formed in opposition.

A highly placed doctor at Bellevue Hospital led a delegation to the mayor. "Imagine a day in August when the health-giving sun has been blocked forever on the streets. People move in half-darkness as the wastes of millions of vertically stacked people overwhelm the festering drains. Without a breeze able to penetrate those fetid canyons to dissipate the miasma, malaria, yellow fever and cholera will decimate the population. This is a certain fact of medical science."

The Fire Department was next. "Your Honor, at the present our finest pumper and most heroic efforts can put water little higher than the sixth floor. Our nets can't be trusted beyond that. We ask you to consider the fate of terrified thousands trapped out of the reach of help on the high floors. They would be incinerated before they were halfway down a fire escape, even if one were possible and even if the masses of humanity would not cause it to tear loose. And anyone who has seen the heating effect of a tall lamp chimney will know all he has to about the speed at which such a structure would burn. We would need a hundred morgues to accommodate the victims of such fires."

The physicists had their say, too. "A thin dime dropped from an upper story of a skyscraper has the striking power of a rifle bullet. The imagination recoils at the thought of some vile anarchist achieving more carnage with a handful of thrown coins than he is now able to achieve with a large bomb."

All this trepidation spread even to the brave police force of New York. The commissioner told the newspapers, "The crowding that will be the result of dozens of skyscrapers in a small downtown area will totally paralyze all traffic. New York will cease to exist as a center of commerce. And when the quitting whistle blows and the workers head for the streets in a rush, we will have riots every week that will make the Draft Riots look like a tea party at the Astors'."

It was too late to turn back. The publicity fed upon itself and doubled its mass every week. The construction site became as much a crowd attraction as a baseball game. Some early risers brought their lunch and secured a good spot to watch progress through the day. Enterprising omnibus owners ran tours to Madison Square. It was possible at the scene to hear people detecting signs of collapse in a building that was as yet little more than a hole in the ground.

When the girders began to rise, so did Triangle fever. Although there had been a fair number of smaller steel-frame buildings in the city, high-iron workers became the new heroes, the daring equivalent of balloon pilots. They appeared with their massive wrenches in advertisements for overalls and cigars, and at least one was invited to speak at a Fifth Avenue luncheon about the dangers of his trade.

Oakhill Development achieved the fame that had eluded it to now, and Hannah and Victor became as well known at Delmonico's as Bet-A-Million Gates ever was.

Ominously, though, there was not yet a clamor of businessmen striving to be the first tenants, or of any tenants at all. But that would come, Victor was sure.

But there was a more immediate menace. He had been confident that the powerful real estate interests would link arms with him against the doomsayers, as it had before in similar attacks by the public. In fact, they turned upon the Triangle Building almost as one. Whether it was jealousy, fear of being left behind or genuine dread and concern, Victor could not tell. But the Architectural League of New York, soon supported by the American Institute of Architects, began to campaign for a bill to outlaw skyscrapers forthwith. A League official echoed the concerns of all who had spoken before him and added his own terrors.

"No less than physicians, architects are responsible for the health and safety of the people. But even more than that, they are the high priests of a sacred tradition of classical beauty. The proportions and designs handed down from Phidias to Bramante to Wren have not appreciably changed over millenniums because they cannot be surpassed. They are trifled with at peril to the public tranquility and the delicate balance of the human spirit to human works. To permit a structure that is the simultaneous rape of all the aforementioned is monstrous. To let this great City of New York submit to a design that sodomizes the classical scale and tradition, and makes us a laughing stock among the great capitols, is unthinkable. God, and our elected authorities, prevent it."

The governor and the state senate and assembly got together a bill for the ban and promised their full support, Serpa's influence notwithstanding.

However, Anthony Rendino, his English considerably improved, and his wife and five-year-old son in tow, took the overnight express to Albany. Then, through the intervention of an official who owed much to Serpa, he and his family had a short audience with the leader of the assembly in the halls of the capitol building.

"Mr. Rendino, I regret to tell you in the presence of your wife that I do not approve of your countrymen or of an association with them even as brief as this one. You have one minute."

"I just want my son to have a chance to again say hello to you."

"Again? What do you mean *again?*"

"Remember when you come to New York to talk to the bishop last year? Near Easter?"

"Yes, yes. I suppose so."

"And the little boy at the dinner who brings you cigars and mints?"

"My God, it is him, isn't it? What the hell is this about?"

"Nunzio, say hello to the nice man who take you in the bathroom and play with your prick."

The legislator recoiled. "This is Serpa's work, you bastard."

Rendino slapped him sharply. "Please, all those bad words in front of my sweet family. Not from a man who touches little boys. Not from a man whose throat I would like to slit a little at a time."

"This won't work," the man whispered.

"We have kept track of the little boys lately. They have much to say."

"I'll have you arrested before you're out of this building."

Rendino dangled a watch chain with an initialed fob. "Good. The same police can hear from the boy you give this to."

"Maybe I can buy that back."

The bill to outlaw skyscrapers was left in the Speaker's basket on the final day of the legislative session.

The Triangle Building topped out and the stonework began to sheath the frame. A new madness began to sweep the gawking crowds.

"It's *swaying*. I swear to God I saw the damned thing *sway* when that last gust hit it."

"You're *right. I* saw it, *too.*"

Chapter 9

The notoriety of the allegedly swaying building added to the crowds that gathered at a respectful distance whenever there was a good wind. Certain young rakehells were given to strolling casually not ten yards from suspect walls, inviting destruction and enormous admiration from the more cautious. But the thin stream of rental inquiries now dried up completely as the building neared finishing.

The fear of a building's collapse being nothing to a builder compared to his fear of not having it substantially rented as it approached completion, Victor began to fret seriously.

"I'm sorry, Mother. I thought it would go better than this. I really believed they'd be snapping up the Triangle. There are taller buildings doing fine. But this one has them terrified. Maybe because they know how it's made, and it's the first one that *looks* as tall as it is. And there's that damned hysteria about the swaying."

"I know you're thinking this is my fault, Victor. But publicity, even bad publicity, never hurt a building yet. And it won't hurt this one if we keep ourselves calm and watch for our chance to reverse things."

"Those banks will be watching for their chance to foreclose if we don't get some cash coming in. The building would stand while Oakhill Development fell."

"Victor, rush work on the top floor so you can move your unit in there. Who ever heard of a man who wants to sell skyscrapers cringing on the ground miles from his building. Skyscraper men belong in the sky."

Victor named the skyscraper division Oakhill Towers and moved it within the week into the twenty-second floor of the still-uncompleted building. He gave orders that the office be manned and the lights be left blazing night and day so passers-by —and renters—could see the triangular corona of lights to tell them there were men working high above the earth.

The daring move was noted and buzzed about, but the Oakhill workers came to be regarded as another breed of high-iron men, freakish bravos whose livelihood demanded foolhardy risk.

As the stonework neared completion, presenting more area to the wind, at least two prominent businesses within falling radius of the Triangle Building moved to safer quarters.

The *Sun* gave great prominence to the moves and published a full-page illustration of the results of a collapse, with the wreckage reaching almost to Madison Avenue. Three companies who had been in halfhearted discussions for space on lower floors canceled their negotiations.

On the week of the building's completion, the *Architectural Record* was predicting the prompt foreclosure of the building, and the banks were despairing over the imminent possession of such a worthless hulk. Plans were considered, it was said, to cut the slim, wavering Triangle down to a more stable size.

Then, by telegraph from the South, came word of the approach of the finishing blow. A killing, fast-moving gale was pounding past the Carolinas and thundering north. It was likely to strike New York City very soon with winds above ninety miles an hour. Untrustworthy structures were not likely to survive.

Headlines gave their warnings, the area around the Triangle Building saw a notable evacuation and excursions were quickly organized to view the cataclysm. Reporters rushed to Hannah Oakhill.

"Mrs. Oakhill, we hear that you have ordered the building kept clear during the gale."

"Do you think it will topple from the base or snap off halfway up?"

"If it snaps off, will you just roof what remains?"

"Do you have any hope that the knifelike shape of the building will cut the wind and enable it to survive?"

Hannah sat quietly at her desk for the sketch artists and photographers. Victor stood behind her.

"The new physical principles upon which the Triangle Building is constructed have already been proven elsewhere," Hannah began.

"Not in a twenty-two-story slice of pie that flaps in the wind," a man from the *Telegram* growled.

"Steel-skeleton buildings now standing," Hannah said, "will continue to do so until they are laboriously pulled down to make room for taller buildings made the same way."

"That's not what a lot of the biggest architects in the city say."

"There's only one architect whose word interests me. Victor Oakhill."

"Are you going up on that twenty-second floor tomorrow, Mr. Oakhill?"

"I will be there putting in a full day's work on future steel-frame skyscraper projects. And my entire staff, seventeen men, will be there with me."

There was a commotion and the rustling of pencils in notebooks. "What do their wives have to say about that?"

Victor paused to let the tension build. "The wives of our employees have given the work of their husbands the highest possible confidence. *They* will also be present in our offices during the height of the blow. And with them . . . will be . . . their *children*, including infants in arms."

The room became a bedlam and several of the journalists began to hurry out. "You're *crazy*, Oakhill. And so are *they*," one of them called back.

"Hold on, boys," Victor shouted after them. "There's more."

Everybody hurried back. "In the center of our offices we will hang a plumb bob, irrefutable scientific evidence of excessive swaying. I will invite *one* journalist to view the result, whatever it is. For those of you who do not have the sand shown by the Oakhill women and children, you can read about it in your rivals' pages the next day. Who will sign on?"

There was a short moment when nobody spoke or came forward, followed by frenzied shouts and a sea of raised hands as the dreadful specter of being scooped appeared.

The center of the storm swept down upon Madison Square close to noon. The clouds hanging close to the top of the Triangle Building were so thick and black that it might have been early evening. Through the gloom and cascading rain the upward-staring onlookers, braced for the ghastly fall, saw a necklace of lights around the topmost floor. At every window was a figure, many of them plainly women and children. They waved to the shuddering throngs below.

There was no doubt about when the heart of the gale struck. Umbrellas blew out and sailed away. The gusts struck like clubs, several of the less robust watchers being blown onto their backs. A huge omnibus tilted onto one wheel, then blew over with a crash that sent up screams.

Julia stood before a window with George and Jana, both children in sailor suits and as emotionless as stones.

"There's nothing to be frightened about," Victor assured his family.

"Father," George said without taking his eyes off the street. "Jana and I want to stay. So we can see those people down there drown."

Soon all the eyes in the street turned up to the rooftop parapet at the Triangle's apex. Incredibly, there were figures struggling with something. A thousand fingers pointed skyward.

High above, feeling as though their arms were being torn from their shoulders as they drowned, Victor Oakhill and two burly engineers slowly raised Old Glory to the building's flagstaff. He could swear that the wind brought the cheers up to him.

Before the attending journalist's account of how the plumb bob had proven beyond doubt the huge strength of the building, before the full-page illustrations of why steel-frame construction could withstand forces intolerable to stone, even before the streets were dry and the sun well-restored to the sky after the shattering gale, the first questing tenants were hurrying through the lobby of the Triangle Building to make their rental offers.

It so happened that all three of them wanted the top floor now occupied by Oakhill Towers. A lively, impromptu auction broke out. The highest story went for a price well past Victor's expectations, and the two below it at not much less.

The renters who waited for morning had to be satisfied with increasingly lower accommodations, although the competition for this prestigious location built rates to what the top floors had gone for. As for those who delayed until the afternoon, only the first dozen were put on the waiting list, the rest being turned away.

By the following day there was a steady stream of phone calls from the disappointed who had now developed foresight. When was the next Oakhill skyscraper going up, and could they reserve space for it now? They certainly could, was Victor's answer. If they sent along a good deposit with a letter of intent to rent. When these came in, he bundled them together and took them to his banks, who, on the strength of the demand, made known their absolute eagerness to be part of the financing, and perhaps the ownership, of the fruits of the lofty future of Oakhill Towers.

One season passed into another, and the Triangle Building joined the Brooklyn Bridge and the Statue of Liberty in the symbolic trio that exemplified New York. The unmistakable wedge appeared on postcards sent all over the world, in bronze paperweights, in a classic photograph by Bruderman and on half the keychains in the country. No tourist would dream of passing through the city without seeing The Great Sight, and at no moment was there less than two hundred faces turned to its heights.

Whatever the earlier architects' estimation of the skyscraper's damping effect on air circulation, the shape of this one created a constant small hurricane of its own. Street arabs gathered in its shadow for the express purpose of watching the skirts of young ladies fly high and betray the sweetest secrets of their knees and ankles—another addition to the building's legend.

Suddenly the city was too short for the mode-setters. Everyone wanted to be in a skyscraper, especially one of Victor Oakhill's.

Hannah watched her son transform a city while he himself was transformed. It struck her that what she had withheld from her brooding child had doomed him to be forever incompetent in close relationships. The bumbling unworldliness that had allowed the Serpas to lure him into a marriage to which he was so ill-suited was a sad case in point. Knowing so little love, when it flared it confused him like a moth around an open flame. So now Julia languished as he poured his passion into the steel and blueprints that he understood. Whatever chance he might have had to find some warmth in his two coldly brilliant children was lost in a thousand days in the high steel and a thousand nights at the drawing board.

George and Jana sat more and more by the side of Benedetto Serpa, hearing his stories of another world and taking in his harsh, softly-spoken lessons with unblinking eyes. When Hannah tried to reach them, to show them where their feelings lived, it didn't work—maybe because they sensed that her own feelings were dead inside her. She saw with dread that she and Serpa and Victor's children had come to form a family that lived only in darkness, while Julia, no match for the forces that boiled in the others, was increasingly left outside. Hannah feared for the children's souls, as she feared for her own in her malignant emptiness.

Over more than fifteen years she had never lost track of Jack Grant. Like herself, he had held onto enough of his Superior-Pacific land to profit mightily when the railroad, reorganized after the fall of Guy Cutts, pushed through to Puget Sound with all the spoils that had been anticipated.

He had dealt mostly in Philadelphia in the years it took the railroad money to materialize, and then come back to New York. He now pursued standard real estate speculation with his customary unique talent. But his wild verve for promotion had grown quiet, as if he could no longer muster the enthusiasm to raise his voice.

Hannah had recently run into Grant's old friend, Doctor Duplessis, whom she had known in the Cutts days. Duplessis talked of Grant with evident concern. "It's just work and his daughter. There's nothing else in his life. That might not be so bad if Evangeline weren't such a crucifixion for him. She slowly became uncontrollable after they left you and Victor. She's twenty-four years old and those beautiful eyes have the look of a woman of forty. One week she's sweetness itself, the next she could give lessons to the devil. He just can't handle her alone."

Hannah had learned that there was still no other woman. But also that he never spoke of Hannah Oakhill. She should have felt good about that because it kept the wall she had built against her feelings for him tall and strong. But she didn't. And if she could sometimes forget him for two days, she would then suddenly have him with her every day for ten. Her best defense was her memory of the bitter final afternoon at Delmonico's, and her night of humiliating begging when he had sent her away.

The part of Oakhill Development that Victor ran as Oakhill Towers had quite swallowed up the part run by Hannah. And if she still held two-thirds of the shares, it was Victor's triumphs that were bringing in two-thirds of the money.

Not that the money concerned him, except that it let him build more and build higher. His mother was perfectly welcome to all the earthbound pettifogging and its rewards.

The old hardness toward him threatened always to leak back as she began to feel useless in his shadow.

On a crisp, clear day in October, with the light beginning to turn golden and watery, Victor picked up Hannah in his phaeton and brought her to the Triangle Building, where he led her to the roof. "Let's take a walk, Mother."

They went slowly around the parapet, Victor never ceasing to point. And wherever his finger rested there was seen rising in the distance another tower. Some were the spindly outlines of rising girders, others the solid shapes of completed buildings.

"I'm doing it, Mother. I'm putting my name on the skyline. That one is mine, and that one and that one, and the whole group to the southwest. And even the ones being done by others are there because I lighted the fuse. It's just beginning, too."

"I have a feeling you've come to me for more than my admiration, Victor."

"That's so. I have a marvelous opportunity for us."

"You're working through the night now. One more opportunity will kill you."

"You've hit the point exactly. I've finally seen that there's too much to this business to go it alone. Adding staff can only take us so far. We still have to make the last decisions. And, most of all, we have to deal as adversaries with the banks, the little companies, the landowners and all the rest of it."

"You're looking for partnerships."

"More than that. I'm looking for a trust. There's a beef trust, a mining trust, a bank trust and a railway trust. Why not a real estate trust, Mother?"

"Who would you seek out?"

He was looking over the city, a man fearful that the upward explosion he had begun would forget its master and proceed without him. "I've done my seeking already. The National Realty Bond and Trust Company, the Attorney's Title Insurance Company and the East River Realty will all come in."

Hannah whirled on him. "In whose name will you enter into this agreement?"

Victor appeared startled, as though he had forgotten the molten steel that ran through his mother's veins. "In the name of Oakhill Development, of course. I thought you'd be as excited to be in this as I am."

"You also thought, quite correctly, that your Oakhill Towers holds only a third of the company."

He had grown red. "A third that contributes three-quarters of the profits, and which will soon contribute much more. You will not be injured, Mother."

"I am injured already by the way you've passed me by."

"This is beyond your depth. The world passes us all by sooner or later. We're almost into the next century"

"I'm a long way from fifty yet, Victor. I think I might be able to count to ten for another couple of years."

"You'll share in it as fully as I do."

"No, Victor. I'll share in it twice as fully as you do, because the division of Oakhill Development will remain the same. We might have negotiated, but you chose not to."

The expected anger did not appear in him. "I'm sorry, Mother. I upset you, and I never meant to."

"You'll find backers enough if you want to go it alone with Oakhill Towers. You're quite famous now."

"I don't want to go it alone. I want us to go together. We've been apart for too many things too long."

"The terms will not change because you're sorry."

"That's all right, Mother. Its not the money I need." He gazed up at the pale October sky. "It's getting up there near the sun."

"Well, then, I look forward to going with you."

"May I hug you, Mother?"

"That's not the sort of thing partners should do, Victor. I like the view of your buildings very much. I believe I'll walk home and see some of them from the street."

Victor's traditionally weak association with his mother deteriorated further after his thoughtless bypassing in the matter of the trust, even though it was a quick and powerful success. He retreated still further into himself and slowly came to see that the satisfaction of another finished building did not depend on his putting the lines on the paper himself, or on his developing a new way to pre-stress a foundation to allow for the uniform settling of a tower. Just as he was delighted to have his new associated companies handle the drudging details of negotiation, acquisition and financing, he began to discover the rewards of finding architects and builders more talented than himself who would use his pioneering as launching points for the classics rising under his name.

The press gave him a name, Skyscraper Oakhill, and the wealth and fame that went with it helped him to break that most impregnable of all bastions, New York society. Not the top rank at first, but his polished manners and interesting, south-of-the-Danube good looks took him higher quickly. He accepted only invitations that had also been extended to his mother. It was good for business to have her great intelligence and beauty moving in such circles, was one important reason. Another was that he never again wanted her to believe that he thought he had risen past her.

He noticed that men of high substance, some looking to add to their fortunes, and some with an eye for a fine-looking woman, paid her serious court. To their annoyance, she always slipped away nimbly.

"God, Broderick, I'd like to wake up next to that."

"And her bank account, Phillips?"

"Blast her bank account. She's fascinating."

"Well, discuss it with Mrs. Phillips."

"I might if she took me seriously. Or if she didn't run with that wop who might cut my heart out."

"He would go after something more southerly than your heart, dear boy."

It hurt Victor to see his mother spending her life in the cold wastes. "Give some of them a chance. It might spark something in you. Mr. Serpa can't own you anymore."

"Mr. Serpa is kind and constant and presents no complications. And a spark is no good where there is no more fuel."

Victor made it a practice to examine the guest list of any affair he attended for names that might be useful to the company, and he several times came across the name of Jack Grant. The man whom he once thought of as a father had established a lower-keyed fame of his own as a shrewd developer of new areas to the north. His wealth had been accumulated more gradually but over a wider spectrum, and was known to be considerable. He had built a handsome house on a good corner of Madison Avenue, where he lived with his daughter when she deigned to be at home. Evangeline was something of a well-known scandal in high places, having misbehaved with some important names.

At no party where his name and that of Hannah Oakhill were on the same guest list, was Jack Grant present. Victor thought that this was no accident, remaining as sad and confused as ever about the loss of the only father he ever had.

The society life was never more than a convenient business tool to Victor. New York was being pulled up toward the stars and it was his hand that was first on the hoist. And what was happening now was just the start of it. The first decade of the twentieth century would sweep away the last of the doubters. The old ways would be dead and there would be a race for the highest and grandest. He meant to win this race. So even though he had more than he could handle going up, he had his architects prepare the titans of the next century, including one of sixty stories. Once more he outstripped the technology and organization available, but all that would come along to catch up. The plans were filed in long special racks at Oakhill Towers, golden children waiting to be born.

His own children were far less in his life.

George and Jana reached the age of five and already knew that Julia, Filomena and their earliest teachers were no match for them. They looked upon mother and housekeeper as bothersome pets to be manipulated or ignored.

The remarkable beauty of the twins brought them much attention and many compliments. They accepted these gracefully, with the wonderful courtesy they had been taught. They knew just when to smile and how much, just what to say and wear and do.

But sometimes Victor caught them at their cruel mocking when backs were turned. No one else heard them saying things that were so shocking, so cold-bloodedly coarse, that he didn't know how to confront them. Yet they seemed always polite, sometimes even loving, in direct dealing with him. Even when they were frustrated in wants that Victor knew to be terribly strong, they held onto their composure, smiling with knife-edge thinness.

They had Victor's all-absorbing mind, and they disposed of their lessons with negligent ease. At play, though, they were strangely crippled. The children of their own age soon found that the chilly pair had no understanding of games. They couldn't grasp the intimacy raised between competitors, the patience of working through the rules, the cooperation of teams or the reward of a cleanly won point. The goal had to be theirs at once, by whatever rules they decided. Their dominance had to be accepted from the first, and they were baffled and furiously contemptuous when it was not.

And there was their eerie closeness. They would never consent to be separated for different teams. They were always together at the ball, even when it was wildly inappropriate, and personal injury to one brought instant, total retribution from the other. "Hurt my sister and I'll have your eyes out," George would say as a little boy, and he tried to do serious harm to children who didn't listen.

When George would dirty his usually immaculate hands, Jana would lead him to a spigot and wash them spotless in her little sand pail. "You're the loveliest brother in the world, Georgie, and you must never be dirty, because that's ugly."

They were bothered not at all when they were finally cut off by all the other children. They already had all they needed.

Victor would sometimes see them together, gazing into one another's faces for long moments, as if a conversation were happening that only they could hear.

Between Julia having fallen miles from his interests and the proper, superficial warmth that was all he could expect from the twins, Victor's occasional heartfelt attempts to build affectionate bridges to the members of his family came to little.

But, beyond his sparse home life, there was no other smudge upon Victor's happiness as his business and dreams grew bigger and brighter every day.

Then, one afternoon, he was sitting to have lunch at the Metropolitan Club and looked up to see, at a table near the window, the familiar profile of Jack Grant.

Victor saw that Grant was delighted to see him, almost overwhelmed for a moment. But although he leaped up to hold Victor when he approached, and immediately ordered the table set for two, Grant was still uneasy, a man embracing a priceless gift that contained a hissing fuse. Living in the same city for almost all of their time apart, they had last set eyes on one another eleven years ago.

"Christ, what you must think of me, Victor."

Grant was half gray by now, the beard darker than the hair. Like Hannah, his tight body and glowing energy took years off him. The scars overpowered whatever lines had been added to his face, but that face had taken a permanent set of sadness.

"I figured out later it was something with Mother. Then I understood a little better."

"She ordered me away from you, Victor. I couldn't go against that wish. I'm not sure this meeting won't displease her even now. But I missed you horribly."

"Do you want to know anything about Mother?"

Grant rasped out a laugh. "I know more about her than I do about the president's wife. I made it a point never to lose touch with Leo. Victor, you have made me very proud with your work. And very jealous."

"Grant Majestic doesn't have to blush in front of anybody, Jack."

"But you're pushing the frontiers. You're not just making money, you're making things happen. It took you to shake me out of my stodgy ways."

"You're onto something new?"

"Harlem, Victor. I'm onto Harlem."

They ordered lunch and champagne and Grant told Victor about his plans, some of the old urgent excitement back into his voice at last. "The elevated lines have finally pushed north. Three of them. The trip that used to take half an afternoon from downtown is just about an hour now.

"The Plains were the most beautiful part of Manhattan when Alexander Hamilton lived there, and except for some squatters they've only gotten better since Harlem became part of the city in 'seventy-three."

"I know. Mother thought about getting in there a good while ago, but she thought it was too remote. And I was taking everything for the skyscrapers."

"You can't believe what's beginning to happen up there. Will you take a ride with me after lunch, Victor?"

"Why wait for lunch? I'd rather look at a building than eat, anytime."

"So would I, come to think of it. We can catch up on things while we ride."

They tossed off a glass of champagne and canceled the food. On the way uptown behind a fast-stepping team, they took turns telling what had happened in the years apart. But Victor touched little on his family and Grant not at all on his. Victor's curiosity about his long-ago little friend, of whom he had many happy memories, finally caused him to question Grant directly.

"Jack, I heard some disturbing things about Evangeline. It's all right if you'd rather not talk about her, but I've been concerned for both of you."

Grant took off his hat to let the breezes sweeping over the open carriage brush through his thick hair. He looked pleased rather than annoyed by the inquiry. "In fact I've been looking for somebody to talk with about Evangeline for the past ten years. I don't know anyone but Duplessis close enough to share it, and he became sick of hearing about it long ago. He keeps telling me to turn her out and give my heart a chance to heal. God knows he's probably right. And she wouldn't lack for people to look after her."

"Wild children are almost the rule these days, Jack. There are going to be new rules in the new century, and the young people can't wait."

"I know the difference between high spirits and a disease of the soul, Victor. I welcome a bit of rebellion. But there are times when I know she's simply trying to see how much pain she can inflict."

"But Evangeline could be so loving. That can't be all lost."

"Oh, when she's had her own heart broken she can break yours with her weeping and her hugs. Then she'll be in your arms every day apologizing for all the hurt she's caused you and promising to make it all up. And she'll mean it, I don't doubt. All the bitterness you've built up against her gets swept away. Then she brings breakfast, fusses with the plants, plays her harp, comes to dinner right on time and goes to bed at ten. She's so gentle and sensitive that it makes it all the more miserable to have to watch the poison building in her again. It's almost as if she softens your heart so she can trample on it more easily the next time."

"She was always fickle and moody."

"You forgot to add cruel, Victor. Yes, she is very much as she was. But a child can't do the damage a grown young woman can. Not to others and not to herself."

"What sort of damage?"

"Do you know names like Cyril Panzer, Denby Keith, Horace Belding and Jason Coozer?"

"I don't usually read the sort of newspaper that would stoop to describing what they do. If they didn't have the money and power, they'd be in prison, if not hanged."

Grant's fists knotted so they almost burst his gloves. "They are her regular companions. You know her way from when she was a child. From one to another and back."

"My God, Jack, some of them are thirty years older than she is. Have you gone to them to drive them off?"

"I did at first. I was ready to beat them to death. It took me just a little while to discover that *she* might be corrupting *them*. They've met their match, at any rate. She's driven them half out of their minds. And, believe me, she's got the looks and viciousness to do it."

Victor was shaken by the vehemence of Grant's words. "Hasn't there been a good man in her life? Someone to protect her, to reason with her and show that a clean, honest love can change everything for the better?"

"No good man would put up with her for a month. And he'd put her to sleep. She seeks the worst and thrives on it. There's something that comes into her look sometimes, something so twisted and mean that I almost call her Marietta—her mother's name."

Victor had never known Grant to look so beaten and helpless. "Would she remember me, Jack?"

"You're the one she cried for most when we left. For a long time. And she's followed your success, I know, because she tears your pictures out of the papers when she finds them."

"They all make me look like I have indigestion. Perhaps I could help her. And you."

"Tell me how."

"Have us meet again. She needn't know that you've told me anything about her. We were close friends. Maybe we could be again."

"She's awfully hard to get close to."

"I'll do it slowly. Perhaps she'll see an old married man who wants nothing from her as somebody she can trust. Then I can take her around and work on her. Later, I can introduce her to a couple of good-looking architects."

"You're too busy already, Victor. And she's always complaining about people deserting her just when she's getting to like them. Forgetting that she skinned them alive, of course."

"Give me a chance, Jack."

"All right. She's just come back home after a month in Saratoga. Had some sort of an awful row with Belding at the races. Just starting to calm down. Why don't you come to dinner? Friday, say?"

"I'll be there."

"Eight o'clock. And you needn't tell Hannah."

"I understand. Then I won't tell Julia either."

"Let's talk about something easier to deal with now—Harlem."

Victor, trapped downtown in his work, had not been to Harlem in years. It was no longer so much the plains it had once been, but was in many ways more pleasant than ever.

They came to a wide, lovely street lined with some of the most handsome homes that Victor had ever seen.

"Excuse me, Victor, for being so taken with the work of another architect, but your friend Stanford White has outdone himself here, don't you think?"

The houses were not the marble giants of Fifth Avenue, but they were large, much larger than the run of dwellings in the downtown residential sections. They were graciously designed brownstones, with broad, curving driveways and spacious front gardens overflowing with colorful flowers. Though attached in rows, they managed the feeling of classical villas in many ways. Their elegance was not austere and standoffish, but inviting, warm, welcoming.

"Jack, they're incredible."

"White has designed dozens of them and dreams of many more. He's set the standard for what can be a paradise on this crowded, grubby island."

"And a paradise where you don't need to be a Vanderbilt."

"There you have it. There's never been a place for the prosperous middle class, the real backbone of Manhattan. They've been stuck in those dreary rows of old-line brownstones not much more spacious or exciting than the tenements they escaped out of."

"Can we see what they're like inside?"

"Absolutely. I already own three of them, and I'd have more if I'd been here in time."

They hitched the team and went into one of the houses. Victor beamed his excitement. "This is what America is about. This is the reward of the people who worked hard and came up. We've found our style and our dream. This is it."

The ceilings ran twelve feet high, and huge windows sucked in the light everywhere. The plasterwork was exquisitely ornate, the doors, fireplaces and window frames, not to say many walls and ceilings, were stunningly carved, with much paneling by the finest joiners.

"Fifteen rooms in this one, Victor. That's the end of doubling up, even if you have ten children."

"And maid's rooms. I thought you said you didn't have to be rich to live in these."

"In the prosperity that's coming, there won't be many people without a maid in this part of town."

"What are the rents for all this, Jack?"

"Steep enough. In a city where rents go now for about $170 a year, these get ten times that."

Victor whistled. "One thousand seven hundred dollars a year. I don't know."

"Well, I do," said Grant firmly. "You know how conservative I've always been outside my promoting? That slow and steady stuff is over. I'm going to take all I can lay my hands on out of what I've got and bring it up here."

"Dangerous."

"Dangerous is when there's no value under something. The railroad land sellers had to promise a bunch of New York Cities along the tracks. We've got our New York City already here. The best part of it is that people haven't caught on yet."

"Then you could snap up whole blocks. Two or three."

Grant reached up to flick a fancied grain of dust off a gleaming chandelier. "I was thinking more in terms of twenty blocks. More if I could get the right players."

"You're fooling me. Unless you've done a whole lot better than anybody thought."

"Oh, hell, I don't have the money for all that any more than you do. But I intend to get all the raw land I can and sell before the houses are completed. Then buy more. I might be selling at a four- or five-hundred-percent profit before the others are well started."

"Is there that much money out there?"

"If not in pockets, then in banks. When the lenders see how this property leaps in value, Victor, they'll be damned happy to be in on it. They'll know the buyers will be able to double their own money every five years or so. Unless somebody finds a way to make this island a lot bigger than it is."

Victor put his arm around Grant's shoulders. "It's good to see you breathing smoke again, Jack."

"As I said, you and Hannah made me jealous. Now listen to me. Tell her what's happening here. If it's all too short for Oakhill

Towers, it's an awfully exciting play for Oakhill Development."

"I'm afraid I've eaten into her holdings with mortgages. She's not very liquid."

"When every dollar can become a hundred in a few years, you find ways to get liquid. Shall we go?"

As Grant locked the big oaken, brass-trimmed front door with its cut-glass inset, Victor spotted a couple of well-dressed Negroes going into a house across the street. "Do Negroes live here?"

"Heavens, no. It's still beyond all but the wealthiest of them. Those are servants, you can bet. There's some cachet to black help in the old Knickerbocker Dutch families. Gives them the feeling of the days when slaves waited on the patrons, I suppose. I daresay, Victor, that Harlem is the one spot in New York where there's no serious Negro neighborhood inside a half-hour's drive."

Jack Grant had designed his own house, Victor knew, despite his lack of formal training. Victor's expert eye told him that Grant had a far better feeling for the classics than he himself did after his ardent stint at Boston Tech. There was a bit too much marble and not enough fine wood, but it suited its master's reserved nature well.

A uniformed servant took his coat and brought him into the library.

A cheery fire cut the chill that sometimes came off the rivers in the evening, and Evangeline was standing before the crackling logs as Grant stood up from his chair.

"Thank God you're finally here, Victor. Evangeline's been fidgeting so much waiting for you that I was afraid she'd fall in the fire."

"I haven't had anyone proper to play with since he left, have I?" she said.

Victor was overcome by the sight of her. She was small, much smaller than he would have imagined, and the angelic face of the child he had known was miraculously intact, having merely added degrees of perfection in maturity. "Evangeline, I missed my bright orange express wagon after you'd gone. Your father would never admit you had it, but I knew he was protecting you. It's why I've come."

"Of course I had it." She spoke with a husky lilt, an exciting voice bigger than she was. "I dragged it into bed with me and took it to the lavatory. So when you came for it, I would be right there to be rescued from this dreadful man here who had taken me away." She tossed her blond head playfully at Grant, although there was not much playful in her eye.

Victor pretended to search the room. "But I don't see it."

"Oh, when you didn't come I got furious with you. I took the hatchet off the kindling pile in the kitchen and chopped your wagon into very small pieces. It took me most of an afternoon."

"Ah, but look at the lovely fire it's made," Grant said, his eye uneasily upon her.

Now she went to Victor and kissed him vigorously on the lips as she always had as a child. "I'm tired of all the friends I have, Victor. And you're so much more fun and so much better looking. I want us to be just the best friends in the world again. Can I count on you?"

"Victor has responsibilities to his business and his family, Evangeline," said Grant.

"Those are duties, and all duties are boring," said Evangeline.

"Time must be made for friends. When do we begin?" Victor asked.

"Right now at dinner. We tell each other just everything. I'll flirt devastatingly, as I do with everyone, and we'll make plans for the entire month."

"Evangeline—"

"Be a darling, Father, and understand that Victor does not want to become like you. He can find some terrible drudge to look after his buildings for a while. And Hannah and his wife must surely have some mending of socks to do."

And so Victor found himself swept up in her churning wants at once, her outrageous selfishness made delightful by wit, charm and an appetite for enjoyment that he found irresistible.

Of course he was very much on guard for the first appearance of the vast weaknesses described by her father. He suspected he had caught her in one of her upward swings, and braced for the plunge downward. But during the next month, the happiest he ever spent, he saw no sign of the blackness.

She was thoughtlessly voracious of his time, keeping him going for three and four days a week almost from sunup to well into the evening. He was grateful that Grant had schooled him in the opportunities in Harlem, presenting him with a ready-made explanation for all the time he spent uptown. To Julia one of his jobs was much like the other and she saw little change in his away-from-home routine. To Hannah, he saw, the surprising break in his night and day love affair with skyscrapers was welcome. She happily took up a great deal more of their management routine and waited warily for him to discuss with her any plans he might be formulating for development in Harlem.

Evangeline soon decided that lunch and dinner and theater was a slow, dreary way for them to become reacquainted. "Victor, you have to learn the proper nature of a good time. From now on we'll do outings. We'll travel to the outdoors and stay together for a good many hours at a time."

She began by introducing him to coaching society. The Coaching Club of New York had been promoting coaching as a sport for almost twenty years. "A drag costs only twenty thousand dollars, Victor, and a quarter share is all you need. One of my friends will have you driving a four-horse coach in no time."

"I was actually thinking of an automobile before long. Perhaps a Dreyfus. Or a Benz. They both did well in the Memorial Day Race from City Hall to Ardsley."

"You will hardly be meeting the likes of Alfred Vanderbilt or Delancey Astor Kane in an automobile."

So Victor bought his share, learned his driving—to her delighted squeals—and joined the stately Sunday processions through Central Park and up Harlem Lane. He made some fine acquaintances, useful for business, and felt less guilty about his time away from the office.

Coaching was just part of their week, "Why is it that the men of New York think it attractive to wear a face that looks like a pot of paste? I went by one of your buildings one day, and the men on the beams were golden brown from the sun. It was a beautiful-looking peasant vitality. I want you to look like that. We'll be taking the boat to Coney Island."

No sooner had they boarded at The Battery than she took his hat away, scaled it over the side and marched him to the top deck for the length of the sail. By the time they arrived he was as ruddy as a fireman's shirt and she exclaimed loudly at his handsomeness. She liked the look so well that she removed her own hat for the day. The thousand glances that came her way were less for the breach of decorum, Victor thought, than for the mass of golden curls fallen carelessly on her shoulders, and the brash stare that she returned to any and all.

The first time they went to the Island she took him to the exclusive enclave at Brighton Beach. They sat sipping lemonades on the sprawling piazza of the huge, wooden Oriental Hotel, looking out over beautiful lawns and flowerbeds to the beach and sea beyond.

Strolling on that beach, she boldly removed her shoes, affording him an unabashed look at not just her lovely feet and ankles, but truly spectacular calves. She made him wade with her, careless of her expensive dress in the water and mud, and brazenly admired his own strong legs. "There's just no point in being young and pretty in this society, Victor. When our bodies are hard and exciting they're hidden just as completely as when we're fat and old. I think that one day, when the world is wider, there will be beaches where people go as unblushingly naked as Polynesians."

"That might diminish certain useful mysteries."

"Would you buy an expensive silver service unseen because it diminished the mystery? Run ahead of me. I like to see the muscles working."

If her conversations were sometimes saltier than quite proper for a young lady, her behavior was otherwise impeccable. When they took dinner on the Oriental's piazza, their separate rooms waiting upstairs, she was careful to offer no temptations. Indeed, she made Victor feel like an aged uncle rather than a friend just three years older, and he didn't altogether like it.

On their next trip to Coney Island she proposed something of a more riotous nature. "Piazzas and lemonade will be waiting for us when we're old. The Sheepshead Bay Racetrack is just a bit further on. They say every third race is fixed, and that's the one I bet on. I'm very friendly with some of the jockeys and owners."

Evangeline might well have said *all* the jockeys and owners. They called out to her from everywhere, took her aside constantly and were never done whispering in her ear. When Victor realized that they were spending as much time with her as he was, he was not above showing them a possessive glare. He was surprised at how often he got the same sort of glare back.

She took a good deal of wine with lunch, shouted at the horses in a way that was a bit past ladylike and generally proved herself even more of a delight than when she was being completely proper.

Betting heavily, once with her own money, bankrupting herself completely, and twice with Victor's, she brought them out ahead with some of her jockey tips.

"It would be wonderful," she said, "if we could bet everything we own, our lives even, on a race that would take a whole year to run. Then we could have this marvelous excitement for more than a glorious little minute."

Back in the city she broke him into the Broadway life. To Hoffman's for drinks, then to Rector's for dinner. The Metropole and its opening to the street for more drinks, and Bustenboys for breakfast.

In these places she began to run into what were plainly the friends of the life that Jack Grant deplored. Victor recognized Cyril Panzer and Denby Keith. Though physically dissimilar, the men were exactly alike in their slitted, filmy eyes, always on the alert to feed on a weakness.

They stood close to Evangeline, their hands thoughtlessly on her bare shoulders, their splendid clothing in contrast to their breaths made putrid by cigars and drink. They, too, whispered to her, and this time, Victor knew, it wasn't about horses.

He remembered now that he had not spoken to her in the way he had promised Grant he would. It had seemed up to now a ridiculous thing to do, her behavior being what would have pleased him in a sister of his own. Over wine at Knickerbocker's he opened the subject. "I wonder if you figured out that I'm here partly to help your father handle you."

"Oh, sure. Even hiding behind his beard, his scars and his eyepatch, Father has the most open face in New York. But I was glad to have you with me again on any terms. And I hoped I could make you like me even after all I'm sure you've heard."

"Have no fear that you haven't made me like you, Evangeline. It makes me furious to think that you were there the whole time, waiting uptown."

"You know perfectly well from Father that I was doing more than waiting."

"Jack loves you very much, you know."

"I love him, too, most of the time. He was the only one who would have me when I was at my worst. His are the only arms where I ever felt safe and happy for an instant."

"Then why do you torment him?"

The high spirits that had been with her from the first faded now. She put her hand on Victor's, as if afraid he would leave her if she became less entertaining. "Because I want too much." Victor noticed, as she spoke, that she was twisting the magnificent ring that she always wore. "I was just little more than a baby when Mother died, but she was so strong. She would come to me in the night and she'd talk for hours in that voice that was so hard and so soft at the same time. And as soon as I could understand anything, she taught me to want. To look for more no matter how much I had. She frightened me by telling me that the people who loved me would all hurt me someday, and to be ready for it. And to prove it, she'd hurt me. I won't tell you how. And she made me watch things. With animals, with people, that nothing could ever make me repeat. Sometimes I had to touch—"

"That's all, Evangeline. You don't look well. I'm sorry." Her nails were drawing stripes on his hand.

"I won't speak about it again, but I'll finish. She told me to hurt people before they could hurt me. I didn't want to believe it. I tried to love her so much that she couldn't do it to me. So she'd have to love me back always. But she didn't let it work."

"Your father must have been there to help you."

"He was. But it was only later that I saw how hard he had tried. With anybody else it would have been enough. But I have too much of my mother in me. In the blood. It beats me every time."

"It's not beating you this time."

"Yes, it is. I'm fighting it harder every day, and I'm losing."

He put his arm around her and drew her close. "Nonsense. You've been an angel."

"Because I didn't want you to go away. I never stopped missing you, you know. And when I saw you'd come back, I made up my mind I wasn't going to lose you again. I wasn't going to hurt you ever."

"You'll never lose me, Evangeline. I promise. We'll be better friends that we ever were. Even better than we are now."

"You should go back to your business and your children. I've taken too much."

Victor found himself amazed at how shocking the thought of leaving her had become. "No, no. I want to stay with you long enough to prove that it can be different with the right . . . friend."

"Can we go now? I think something is making me sick."

She took to her bed for two days, or so the voice on the telephone told him. When she again agreed to meet him, she wasn't interested in his suggestion that they visit a roof-garden restaurant. She asked him to take her to the Bowery. "Down there they know how to give you something that makes you want more," she said.

Victor was not especially shocked. Although the old street with its long strip of tawdry and often illegal amusements was known to be one of the toughest and most dangerous in the city, there was enough slumming by uptowners to make it vaguely respectable and secure.

He was afraid that she would be morose after her confession at the Hoffman and her illness, but it was just the contrary. Her laugh was louder and her eyes brighter than ever. Her restless prowling for new things to show him became more urgent.

She led him down past the brilliantly lighted saloons until she found a shooting gallery. "Buy me some shots, Victor. You see all those little white men to be knocked down. I'm going to pretend they're all the ones I knew before you." She then unleashed a fearful barrage, trembling with concentration, laughing her elation when one of the little men fell. She was remarkably sharp-eyed and a great many went down. But a few were left standing. She put down the gun and turned to Victor. "I'm afraid there will always be a few that slip by."

In a billiards parlor, she outraged the regular patrons and drew the attention of the owner when she insisted on a game.

"This is the wrong place for her, Mister. My regulars like to say all the words they want, if you get my drift. I don't wanna lose customers because of her."

Evangeline looked at the man sweetly and said in a very loud voice, "You are a shit-face sonofabitch and a bastard if you do not permit a gentlewoman to play a proper game in this pisshouse of yours. It might be that my friend here should break your jaw."

The owner's scowl dissipated in the uproarious laughter of his patrons. "Okay, ma'am, I guess there's not much *you* ain't heard."

She acquitted herself handsomely, showing a fine touch and an unladylike drive to win.

"If my wife talked like that I'd sock her," she overheard one of the other players mutter.

"Victor," she said, not looking up from her shot, "Show that filth that he can't speak that way to a lady."

The man reversed his grip on his pool cue to make it a better weapon. Victor grabbed Evangeline by her shoulder and led her out. "I suppose I have to be glad you didn't start something with somebody at the the shooting gallery with a gun in his hand. I think we should go home."

"No, there's one more place." Her cheeks were flushed, as if she had been hours in the sun. Her smile had lost its sweetness.

She brought him along a side street and down a flight of stairs in a decaying brownstone. A brutal-looking man leaned back against the door, through which came a muted babble of voices. "Hey, Miss Grant. Ain't seen you in a while."

"Hello, Duster. Any left?"

"You're in time for the last drop. Fifty of 'em."

Evangeline clapped her hands in glee. "Which dogs?"

"Cuba and Ducky Dick. It'll be close."

"Give him ten dollars, Victor," she breathed, and went in past him.

They found themselves in a large basement, in whose center stood a wire pen ten feet square and four feet high. The only lighting was from two large gas lanterns hung overhead, the light diffusing hellishly in the smoke of nearly a hundred cigars in the mouths of gutter-sweepings. The cries of men calling out bets and odds assailed his ears.

Boxes had been stacked, low in the front, higher back toward the walls, to make a rude amphitheater. From the scene and the words of the man at the door, Victor expected a fight between pit bulls, the ugly spectacle of specially-bred dogs fighting to the death. But a chilling squeaking, more audible through its awful pitch than its volume, came through to him. He squinted into the darkness at the rear and made out disorderly stacks of heavy-mesh cages, finally making out the quick nervous boiling of the hideous mass of gray bodies.

This was a rat pit.

"For the love of Heaven, Evangeline, this isn't for a woman. Or anyone else, for that matter."

She gave no sign of having heard him. "I want a hundred dollars on Cuba, Victor. I've seen him before. He's magnificent. Give the bet to Hotzberg there. He's practically honest. And give some of the men up front something for their places."

As soon as some money had changed hands, they found themselves in the front row of boxes. They were no sooner seated than a pair of Negroes, wearing gloves and thick, ragged jackets despite the heat, came into the pit carrying mesh boxes of squirming rats. The audience counted aloud as they reached through tight openings and brought out the occupants one at a time. Often the vicious, terrified rats clung by their teeth to the gloves and had to be slammed loose.

"*Fifty,*" the spectators shouted in unison when the requisite number had been reached, the floor of the pen now alive with a scurrying gray carpet.

To applause and whistles, two men, sweating and exuberant, appeared with cages of their own. Inside sat terriers, one white, one gray. These were as far removed from the benign companions of children as tigers from kittens. They were scarred everywhere, and one had a crooked rear leg. Their eyes held not the gentle beams of friendship, but death pure and simple.

"Your watch, Victor. In case it's close you don't want to trust them with the time."

The sentiment was a common one, other timepieces coming out around them.

"First go," one of the straw-hatted dog handlers said. "Ducky Dick." He brought forth his dog, the gray terrier, and suspended him above the pit until both dogs and rats were in a frenzy only matched by the watchers. Victor could not hear the command ordering the dog dropped, but dropped he was.

"He's good, Victor. Maybe we made a mistake."

Ducky Dick, seeming to know he was racing the clock, went to the rats. With admirable efficiency he went not for the ones that scurried away, but for the ones that stood and counterattacked, so he wouldn't have to move. His jaws snapped with speed that defied the eye. A single shake of the head was enough to snap the spine, and the bodies, often released on the upward shake, flew into the air, sometimes landing unheeded in the maddened audience. The squeaks of beleaguered rats were of the same tenor as the cheers.

Evangeline's face was now a horrid mask, the veins in her neck and temples standing forth. *"Kill them, kill them, kill them—"*

It occurred to the shocked Victor that this display was for the dog she was not backing.

"Two minutes and fifty-five seconds," the timekeeper bawled as the last rat snapped skyward.

A drunk, delighted with the brisk time, was embracing anyone he could catch. Before he knew what he was doing he had Evangeline in his arms. As he went to back off she kissed him on the mouth, then turned to Victor as if it hadn't happened. "Another hundred on Cuba, Victor. Please."

As terribly as he wanted to carry her out of this miserable spectacle, the madness in her face told him it would not be possible. He laid the bet and watched the removal of the bloody bodies and the refilling of the pit.

In a few minutes, the black dog called Cuba was suspended over the pit to even more pandemonium than on the first drop. This terrier was not as big as the other, and it was unclear how he would maneuver on a crooked back leg, but there was a taut lethalness to him that his rival had not owned.

"All right, Cuba, my love," Evangeline whispered. "Let's see them fly."

The dog was a killing machine. Moving with a crabbed, circling gait, he was there waiting for the rats whichever way they leaped, his head a black smear of motion. At times there were two rats in the air, and they never so much as twitched after they hit the ground.

As loudly as the men cheered, they never drowned out Evangeline.

"Two minutes and twenty-one seconds," the timekeeper said.

She threw her arms around Victor and hugged him to her with amazing strength. Her face was streaming sweat, her hair plastered to her forehead. "Kiss me, Victor. Kiss me now."

Numbed, he went for her cheek, but she moved and caught his lip in her teeth. The pain didn't register, but he tasted blood when she turned him loose.

"Buy me that dog, Victor. I want him."

"You can't have a killer like that for a pet—"

"Oh, yes I can. Buy him."

Cuba cost a thousand dollars, down from two thousand, and the cage was thrown in.

The night air cleared the maddening vapors of the rat pit out of Evangeline's head after a time. The wild glitter in her eyes quieted, and she soon became her laughing, proper self. "Oh, my, I hope I didn't forget myself too much. But what if I did? You understand me better than anyone, and you don't mind."

"Actually, I found all of it very frightening."

"Look inside yourself, Victor. You found it thrilling. It took the blueprints out of the corners of your mind for the first time in years, didn't it?"

As soon as she said it, he knew she was right. "Yes, I suppose so—"

"And you liked it. It woke you up. It excited you and made you want things you didn't want before. That's what really frightened you."

"Don't tell me what I'm feeling. I have to get you home."

"Look at those stars. Look at the size of that moon. Maybe you can leave them, but I can't. The *General Sherman* has a midnight schedule into the Sound tonight. It won't be back until dawn. I'm going to be on it. Will you?"

He thought of Julia, who always remained awake to tell him goodnight, trying to arrest their drift apart in whatever small ways she could. "Yes. I'll be with you, Evangeline."

The beat of the carriage-horse's hooves echoed through the empty, gaslit streets, Evangeline sitting close against him now as the late night chill began to roll in. He put his coat around her shoulders and circled them with his arm.

The *General Sherman* was one of those majestic paddle-wheel excursion steamers that sailed from the East River into Long Island sound. It ran on a daytime and early-evening schedule, but in the warm months it ran a Friday midnight sail.

The Sound steamers were magnificent vessels, already throwbacks to a more opulent age. All wood, with a Grand Salon soaring three decks high, the *General Sherman* was a palace afloat. Behind the towering side-by-side stacks, a walking beam drove gigantic side-paddles. As they approached her, every light aboard was ablaze, the only significant interruption of the darkness on the quiet waterfront. There was a jam of carriages along the street and on the pier as the restless and the romantic arrived to prolong the lovely day.

"Now, you old grind, isn't that the most beautiful thing you ever saw?"

"I have to admit that it is," Victor laughed.

They went up the gangplank and entered the Grand Salon that ran almost the length of the boat. Around its height, at the level of the second deck, were staterooms off a walkway. "It's like being back in the Golden River," Victor said. "The place my mother built."

"But she isn't here to send you to bed tonight."

The woodwork was teak and highly polished, the carpets thick and the lights electric. There was a dance floor at the rear, and the band had already begun to play. Victor took a table and ordered some wine, and by the time the *General Sherman* slid out onto the river, they were dancing on the upper deck, the music floating up from an open skylight.

They whirled about quietly for a long time, the stars taking hold as they moved away from the lights of the city. Another steamer glided by, returning, the sound of its own band floating across water silvered by the moon.

Victor could not have told anyone the exact moment that he became caught, but he suddenly knew he was. He danced her to the rail, stopped and kissed her, this time holding nothing back. Before he knew what he was going to say, he had said it. "There are staterooms downstairs. Do you think they're all booked?"

"I've never had any trouble getting one," she said.

Even as the words tore cruelly through him, he was glad that they could have the room. "I'll go below and take care of it."

She stopped him, hesitant at last. "No, Victor. Don't do it."

"You don't want to?"

"I brought you here because I did."

"You're afraid you'll want too much?"

"Yes."

He kissed her again. "Then I'll give you too much."

Later, as she stood quietly in the moonlight that reflected through the window, her voluminous clothing on the floor about her, he held her in his arms and understood for the first time just how small and delicate she was. He wished his body were not so broad and thick, fearing terribly that he would hurt her, but she showed no fear.

In the narrow bed, burning with a love that stole his breath, he carefully held from his mind all the excesses he had learned at Bill McGlory's and took her as reverently and respectfully as he could.

Her moans were soft, and except for clasping him tightly with her arms and legs, she lay quietly until he was done, which was far more quickly than he would have liked.

When they were through she turned herself to the bulkhead, away from him. And while she accepted his embrace from behind, she never said another word until she said goodbye to him at her front door. From the cage in her hand, Cuba gave a low, lethal growl.

Victor made his excuses to Julia in the morning, when he arrived home, changed and went straight to the office where he worked through the day. Afire with guilt, he managed to stay away from Evangeline for two days, burying himself in his neglected duties and making plans that would occupy him deeply. The clamor inside him to be with Evangeline had so begun to frighten him that he tried to break away before there were too many memories.

He cursed himself when he finally called her on the telephone, even though it was his avowed purpose merely to make an appointment to discuss discontinuing their meeting alone. But when a servant told him that she was taking no calls, he was so thoroughly disappointed that he broke the earpiece slamming it back.

The next day and the one after that brought the same results. He didn't want to speak to Grant, because he was sure that what was happening would show.

In the end he called on Evangeline at home at an hour when Grant would be out. He knocked at a side door, where he knew the downstairs maids to be more relaxed guardians of the gates than was the butler. A new girl, identifying herself as Ibi, answered the door. "I am Mr. Oakhill, a good friend of Miss Grant's. I thought I might inquire about her health. She has not been available—"

"Mr. Grant is not home, sir. I'll get Johnson—"

"That's not necessary. Is she confined to her room?"

The maid looked confused. "She's out sir. Same as every day."

"Do you know where?"

"Wherever Mr. Belding took her, sir."

He had meant to pass a half-hour or so with Evangeline before returning to pressing business downtown. But he soon had his driver making a frantic search for her. It being just after noon, he directed an itinerary to the better restaurants. His instincts were good. He found them at Tony Pastor's.

By lingering outside he was able to watch Evangeline through the etched-glass of a divider without being seen. She was seated not across the table from Belding, but on a banquette at his side. Her hand was covered by his on the table.

The jealousy that burst upon Victor was more painful for having had no chance to slowly build, to be sensed on approach and braced against. It was there, suffocating him in an instant.

He had taken the first step to confront her when it came to him that there had been no vows between them, and that there could not be. He had taken her against her warning, with full knowledge of his own restraints and of her unhidden reputation. There was nothing but disaster to be had for imagining that the night on the *General Sherman* was anything but a confirmation of her uncaring and reckless way and of his own stupidity for becoming involved with it. The only way to contain the damage and begin to repair it was to return to his office right now and take up the mountain of work that he had thrown almost entirely upon his mother.

But he stayed. For hours he lurked behind the glass and then trailed them through the streets by carriage and on foot.

A stranger observing Evangeline and Belding through the afternoon would have seen nothing but two relaxed and cheerful people enjoying themselves as long-familiar companions. They held hands at times, and when their carriage went through a lonely, shaded stretch, or when they rested on a bench in the park, Belding leaned close as though he might steal an innocent kiss from her. But she always managed to turn away and duck him prettily. If the man was annoyed at her reticence, Victor was too far away to see it.

Still, he knew Belding to be a relentless debaucher, and Evangeline to be given to cataclysmic weakness. Whatever control she was imposing, he suspected, was as loosely attached as the down on a dandelion.

In many ways the loose, apparently pleasurable ease of their innocent day was more damaging to Victor than flagrant passion and outright evidence of debasement. These might have enraged him enough to storm away, leaving his losses. But their day was so like the many gentle ones he himself had known with Evangeline that he felt all the more treacherously displaced.

Only when he had watched them take leave before the dinner hour at her front door did he see how much of a fool he had made of himself and that the driver of his carriage was embarrassed for him. He had no idea of what his future course might be.

For a week, much to Julia's astonishment, Victor made love to his wife every day. He was hoping to find either a licit passion that had been hiding unseen on the adjoining pillow, or a diminishment of sexual tension through total satiation. He found neither, lost what little hope and control he had and turned to eighteen-hour workdays. This did not help him sleep or distract him. Rather, the exhaustion manufactured at his desk undercut the vitality he needed to resist Evangeline's pull.

The absence of any communication from her confirmed his fear that he had simply taken her too far. If he had been unwilling to recognize that he had betrayed Jack Grant's trust as well as Julia's, Evangeline was not. She had seen him for what he was, and, finding no attractions in him sufficient to offset his lack of character, had walked pointedly away. But he lived for the mail delivery and died after it.

It was almost a month later that Jack Grant sought him out at a building site. Victor was deep in a foundation, feeling it emblematic of the state of his spirit, when he recognized the muscular, headlong walk of the man ruining his shoes in the mud.

"So, Victor. If you can't trap the beast in the forest you must go to his lair."

"I've been crushed with work."

"Yes, the time with Evangeline took a great deal from your business."

"Not at all—"

"Please. I don't want you to think that I don't understand all you did for her, and me."

Victor thought that Grant must be able to read the images of the *General Sherman* right out of his eyes. "It was really a pleasure."

"I thought nothing could change her. But, by Jesus, you've done something to her. She's fighting herself. I can feel it."

"Didn't I see her with Belding?"

"She went with him for a while. And Panzer and some of the others. But it was as though she was just trying herself against them again. And she's won. They're gone."

"That's wonderful, Jack," Victor said, not knowing what to feel. "Isn't she lonely? She needs to do more than sit quietly, we both know."

"She's lonely for you, Victor."

"Did she say that?"

"Whenever she pulls herself together to talk, it's about you. You were very wise to leave her when you did. Before there was some attachment that would be dangerous for both of you."

"Yes. She could be irresistible."

Grant's hand on his arm told him that what had happened was not completely hidden. "Goodbye, now, Victor. I just had to tell you how grateful I was. And you must come to see me, even if it's just business. I don't want to lose you again."

It was this parting sentiment by Grant that moved Victor into action.

He would never confess that it was as much to remain in Evangeline's world as to diversify Oakhill Development, but Victor at that moment decided to become part of Jack Grant's Harlem dream. He climbed out of the foundation and walked without looking back, a man who had heard in the waters a siren so compelling that no previous love could resist her.

* * *

Hannah was just as astonished as he thought she would be. "Do you know how much we have committed to what we own, what we have under construction? And everything assured of a solid return if we don't bankrupt ourselves first."

"There'll be a hundred investors scrambling to buy us out of anything we want to sell. We'll be ahead handsomely, and have the cash for an investment that won't grow on just a building plot here and there, but maybe the whole northern part of this island. If we get in on time."

"I've seen what's happening up there, Victor. There's a good chance that you're right. But I thought you wanted to build to the moon."

"We'll keep the best of the skyscrapers, and save the plans for the new ones for another day."

"It will take months to organize such a thing."

"No. It can't take that long. I'll make the banks see what we've got here. They know what I did downtown, and what I can do up north. You watch. We'll be buying land next month, and designing houses the month after that."

"You can't work any harder than you have been."

"I can. But I'm going to have to take a place uptown. I can get back to see the family when I can."

"I didn't think there was a way that you could see them any less, but you've found one."

"Julia will understand."

"I hope so. Mr. Serpa doesn't."

Victor knew he could not openly align himself with Grant Majestic. So the collaboration was a loose one. But it allowed frequent entry to the Grant house.

Although Grant obviously thought it best that there be no more dinners, Victor at least saw Evangeline again. She would come in to greet him when he worked with her father in the study. She was warm enough, rigorously courteous, but she never stayed for longer than that courtesy required and gave not a flicker of recognition to what had been. Any chance that Victor might have had to speak a word to her alone she carefully guarded against, vanishing through doors and up stairways at his approach.

His hope of putting to rest his miserable longing, either by restoring himself to her company or hearing his dismissal positively stated from her own lips, was not realized. In either case, he needed desperately to be forgiven. So he took up the pen.

What he had hoped would be a cool communication of unresolved feelings turned into something else in the writing.

> *My Dearest Evangeline:*
> *The only thing that has caused me greater heartbreak than my unforgivable indiscretion is my inability to approach you to make my most abject apologies plain. Your scorn and dismissal is only what I deserved as one who used a position of trust to tempt and betray. I realize fully that I roused in you just what I pretended to dissuade. That I had fallen in love with you is no alleviation, since that should have made me more, not less, willing to preserve your integrity. I believe I have gained control of my emotions and, seeing the reality of my family position, am ready to resume our friendship with all proper decorum.*
> *I wait eagerly for your permission to address you and obtain your forgiveness and chaste companionship.*
> *Yours in contrition,*
> *Victor*

The servant girl, Ibi, assured him that she had delivered the envelope, but there continued to be no sign of Evangeline having read it. Victor began to wonder if had hallucinated the previous months.

More notes followed, each surrendering a bit more of the control he had promised in the first. Each was ignored in the same way. Finally, he despaired, and more and more began to spend his evenings at home again. It was at home that he finally received a note from Evangeline.

It was a small envelope, almost lost amid the pouch of office mail that Victor had brought with him each evening to prepare for the next day's business. The handwriting was scrawled and jagged. With Julia across the room, it was all he could do to keep from kissing the envelope. The note read:

> *Dear V:*
> *There is to be a ball at the home of Cyril Panzer on the 21st. It is for special friends and there will be no notice in the society pages. Guests are requested to hold their invitations in confidence. In light of our past association, I feel I may be so forward as to request your company as my escort. Please inform me if you will attend, and you will have all details. I do hope to see you soon at the ball. We have left much undone.*
> *Hopefully, E.*

Victor's acceptance was written on the spot, as he informed Julia casually that he would be called out of town on the 21st, perhaps for a day or two. His excitement and happiness rose to a level he had thought lost for good.

Buoyed by his good feelings, he began to dine out again, and it was while strolling home from a business dinner that he met Horace Belding. The man had seen him in the gaslight and crossed the street to step in front of him. Belding was drunk, all signs of the satiny gentleman who had sat with Evangeline vanished. Across the cheek of his blotched, leering face were thick scabs in four long, parallel lines.

"You'll find out all about her, Oakhill. You'll find out soon enough." He tapped his temple, laughed and pushed by. The puzzled Victor watched him go, marking the uncertainty of gait that characterized certain carnally gained diseases. If anyone's mind was deteriorating, it was Belding's own.

The night of the Cyril Panzer ball was one where the city was clouded in river mist. Even though the summer's warmth had returned briefly to haunt the autumn, fires burned in many homes to cut the wet edge off the air.

Evangeline had asked Victor to meet her not at her home, but on the street. Her carriage materialized out of the mist, approaching as from another world. Victor climbed in, feeling wilted in his evening clothes. She, however, seemed charged with her own electric climate and was as fresh and radiant as any woman he had ever seen.

His heart almost stopped as he drew in the remembered fragrance of her, his arms going out reflexively. But she remained in the furthermost corner of the carriage, extending her hand to him. "It was good of you to do this, Victor."

"Nothing could have stopped me."

"Not even good sense, apparently."

"We have so many things to talk about, Evangeline."

"There's been too much talk in my life since I met you."

The Panzer mansion sat on one of the best streets off Fifth Avenue. The family had been a good one, with a hefty fortune gotten out of the lumber forests of Oregon. But there had been a series of scandalous divorces, a suicide and a defection of the better elements to Philadelphia. Cyril Panzer's stewardship of the New York name had not been a good one, and he had slowly fallen from the best guest lists. A small man with pouchy cheeks and a scimitar nose, he had created his own social world. The names were just as resounding, but their owners were likely to be the fallen angels he preferred.

If his parties were shunned by the cream, there were many others who treasured them and the tales to be told afterward. Of course, none would admit to so much as an invitation, much less attendance, at one of Panzer's closed, special parties.

The tradition of the awning, fallen into some disuse, had to be resurrected for this evening. The closed canopy extended from the mansion entryway, down the marble steps, through the front garden and across the sidewalk to the curb. Ostensibly to protect arriving guests from the weather from carriage to entry, it had been used, as now, mostly for excluding the gawking of the public and the attentions of the scandal sheets.

Every room on the main floor had been thrown open for circulation, every chandelier blazed. Behind drapes closed to the outside world, the dancers already whirled to one of two orchestras, and champagne sluiced everywhere. The men in their evening wear and women in their brightest jewelry and most ravishing gowns were not so great in number as Victor might have expected. But in their ceaseless mobility and great animation, the guests made themselves seem a far larger crowd, almost unnaturally loud and merry.

"I suspect you know most of the people here," Evangeline said.

"Actually, I've spent a great deal of effort trying not to know them."

Cyril Panzer came to them. "Evangeline, how we have missed you and the delicious mischief you make. And you have captured the famous Skyscraper Oakhill. You honor us, sir."

"Happy to be here."

"Most probably you are not. But often we can fix that. I must be off."

The rules for such affairs, usually as rigid and changeless as a dance of mating birds, seemed suspended.

There was much fast dancing and hard drinking before the dinner, with distilled spirits more in evidence than wine, although the wine was the finest.

Evangeline seemed little inclined to speak, turning away Victor's attempts at earnest conversation with ambiguous nods or distracted smiles. She would let no serious word be spoken. Yet she clung to him with savage possessiveness, dancing him from room to room.

She was intent on opening herself wider and wider to the music, the laughter and the strong spirits. Men called out to her from everywhere, but she only clung tighter to Victor. Something was swelling and beginning to glow in her.

As they spun on the dance floor, he had a chance to examine his fellow guests more closely. In all of them he now saw some of the suspension of civilizing character that was said to happen at legendary disasters and debauches. He heard words that in the presence of women would ordinarily have called for apologies or fisticuffs in this sort of company. Here they were not resented, but re-echoed and amplified.

Hard though Victor tried to become part of the growing abandon of the party, he could not become comfortable. The drink opened his eyes wider where it should have blurred them. He saw the beginning of tiny lines of wear beneath Evangeline's glittering eyes, and hints of downward cuts of cruelty at the corners of her laughing mouth.

The life in her fed on the sparkling pandemonium, and Victor saw it was a place she was born to be. The aura she sent forth frightened him but also ignited the same irresistibly burning fuel.

Someone organized a dancing of the German, with couples tied together by handkerchiefs dancing between rows of chairs in the ballroom. The stately, playful and completely innocent nature of the old glide was now subverted and mocked, a child's game played by assassins who had murdered the original participants. The mist of the evening outside appeared to penetrate the high ceilings, blurring the chandelier's light.

The magnificent meal was served at long tables whose lines of candles caught the profusion of polished silver and threw glittering pinpoints onto the red-flushed faces. Victor perceived that the servants were not the severely well-bred sons of England and Boston, but too-elegant black men who spoke in the soft, musical tones of New Orleans. They served correctly, even flawlessly, but they touched many of those they served in ways that could not have been accidental.

The music at dinner, which should have been muted, gentle and slow, was quick-paced and insistent, unwilling to let the growing momentum of the evening be lost for a single moment.

Most of the diners were drunk by now, and the niceties of manners thrown to the wolves of disinhibition. Glasses and decanters spilled, their contents running unheeded down priceless table linens and into laps. The beautifully prepared and garnished birds and roasts were torn to bits before they could be properly served, as at some rude medieval manor hall.

Shouting was by now the only possible manner of communication, and Evangeline made herself heard above the others. For all she had drunk, her speech and thoughts appeared clear, and that made it even more disturbing to Victor.

"It seems to me," she called out loudly, "there are people in the room who have not begun to earn an honest night's pay. What's to be done?" Her words cut through the acrid clouds of the cigars that had been lighted during dinner.

"I'll show you right now," bellowed a fat man with his hair glued to his bald head with sweat. He flung back his chair and jerked the tall, buxom, laughing woman at his side to her feet. Then he bent her back her against the table and upended her upon it, her shoulders splattering a plate of gravied potatoes and her hair landing neatly in the center of a spectacular pudding.

To applause, he thrust her blossoming skirts above her head and raised her legs above his shoulders to reveal her innocence of undergarments. "This is the sort of dessert I've always fancied best, Cyril," the fat man said, laughing as he unfastened his clothing. In another instant he had entered her to a ringing cheer and began to grind at her in his oblivious drunkenness.

At this signal, the black servants reappeared and attended to the lighting. Candles were snuffed and chandeliers dimmed. What illumination remained struggled against the smoke and cast the wavering shadows found in paintings of Hades.

On all sides of Victor men's hands went to the women at their sides, and deep, smothering kisses were exchanged. There were no withdrawers from the revelry.

Clothing became loosened and breasts appeared in the gloom, one man coating his companion's bosom from a bowl of glaze and licking at it.

A man appeared from behind Evangeline and passed her a glowing clay pipe from among several he held in his hand. Victor saw that it was Horace Belding, the scratches still livid on his cheeks. He grinned with yellow teeth and continued down the tables, passing out the pipes to those not already too occupied.

Evangeline took a long pull and kept the smoke in her lungs.

"Evangeline, for the love of—"

She pressed the pipe between his lips and blew the sweet-smelling smoke softly into his face. "If you won't go where I go, you can't be with me."

The full shock of what was happening hit Victor with the onset of the wine's effects. There was suddenly no more focus to his thought. He drew the fiery smoke into his lungs and held it as she had as she covered his mouth and nose with her palm.

They lost what was happening around them as they sat face to face at the table, exchanging the pipe. Victor felt himself climbing slowly out of his body, a rising drowsiness not interfering with a new, incredibly heightened knowledge of his every breath and heartbeat. He could hear the blood rushing in his veins, and his mind, while it could not gather thought for speech, reached a plane past paradise.

Evangeline's hand moved into his lap, probing, manipulating. The waves of pleasure that moved up through him froze him in his seat.

"Wait, my sweet," she said. "This will make you live again." She opened a silver snuff box and gathered a white powder on a long, lacquered fingernail. She held this beneath his nostril. "You must draw it up, Victor."

He sniffed strongly and the encroaching drowsiness stiffened and shattered. He might have been one of his mighty buildings, a steel frame soaring to the vault of heaven, proud and alone above the others.

Soon Evangeline stood and helped him to his feet. Her strength and clarity of purpose appeared not only intact but multiplied.

Time had become nonexistent, and he had no idea how much had flown. The candles were burned down, making the room darker than ever. The few people still at the table were long past their first outburst of passion, many entwined and unconscious.

"Come now. Move carefully. I won't let you hurt yourself."

Victor followed the tug of her hand through the dim rooms, past the orchestral instruments scattered on the bandstand, and up the long, marble staircase they had passed when they came in.

Cyril Panzer stood at the head, still fully dressed and almost fresh looking, a punctilious host continuing to look to the welfare of his guests. He offered them a champagne bottle and some glasses from several stacked on a marble table. "You see, Mr. Oakhill. We're not so bad as you thought, are we?"

At the end of a long corridor there was a door at which one of the black servants stood. Smiling, he opened it and showed them through, following them inside. "You'll find everything ready."

They were in one of the main bedrooms. The bed itself was a huge four-poster, canopied and so high that there were small steps on each side to facilitate entry.

The light came only from standing candelabras on each side of the bed, the candles as thick as a man's arm. The servant took up another, smaller candelabra and indicated that he would hold it for their convenience and undressing.

There began to be empty spaces in Victor's consciousness. What was happening was no longer continuous to him, but seen as clearly etched moments, made more vivid and reverberating by their very shortness. And he knew these moments would hang in his mind as long as he had breath.

He would remember the impassive, sweating face of the black man holding the candelabra above them, the hot wax sometimes spilling down to add its burning to what was in him. And he would remember that Evangeline showed him things that were only done by girls who had stayed in special rooms and got double rates at Bill McGlory's Armory Hall.

Staring into her face as she labored convulsively, he sometimes saw the look of a lost child, a genuine terror, as if some alien thing had taken her body and degraded it with unthinkable urges that could never be stopped. But then the alien would gain full sway and Victor would see the bottomless abasement seize her entirely. That same abasement that had so quickly spread to command his own loins.

His final memory of the evening came with her teeth going through his shoulder as he screamed out his pleasure with her. And as the last light of his mind faded, he saw the black man, now shiningly naked, coming down onto the bed with them.

* * *

Victor did not return home for three months, and then only to silently, ashamedly, helplessly gather his belongings before the shrieking Julia and the stone-eyed children. He was grateful that Benedetto Serpa was away, but too far gone to feel fear anymore.

At her home, Hannah could not turn him from what he had done. He could feel the contempt in her every word and look. Whatever he had regained with her with so much pain was wiped away in an instant.

"Can you conceive of the agony in a woman when a man turns on her? The hate, the scorn, even the beating of the cruelest stranger are *nothing* compared to the sudden betrayal of someone you love."

Looking at her and hearing the venom in her words, Victor knew that his mother had once writhed in torments that no one had ever been permitted to see.

"Mother, don't you think I know that? But I can't be with Julia now. It would add lying and deception to what's already unforgivable?"

"Where will you go?"

"I've taken a house for us. Never mind where."

"What about the company?"

His answer was sure and quick. "I'll pull my share and more. Julia and the children will be taken care of handsomely."

"Do you think her father would let her touch your money?"

"That's his business."

"I suppose that your whore was most of the work you had in Harlem. How easily you fooled us, Victor."

"I didn't mean to fool anyone, Mother. I couldn't tell you everything because the woman is Jack Grant's daughter."

"*Evangeline.*" He could not have imagined the impact of his words on Hannah. She hastily poured two brandies, offering him one. "You've been working with Jack? Is that possible?"

"Yes. We're into a tremendous thing. I was honest about that. I was going to bring you into it more when I could."

"Did Jack encourage what happened with Evangeline?"

"Good Lord, no."

"What has Mr. Serpa said to you?"

"Nothing."

"You've got to be careful, Victor."

"He wouldn't hurt your son."

She drained her brandy in one gulp. "He wouldn't hurt someone I loved. But I'm certain he guesses that I've never been able to love you."

The words cut him surprisingly, although they came as no shock at all. "You make me wish more than ever that I'd known my father."

"I'll make you feel better," she snapped, tears in her eyes. "Your father was a filthy peasant who raped me. The man I married was no better." She left the room without looking back at him, and he knew he could never ask her more.

Hannah did not order him out of Oakhill Development or insist that Jack Grant be no part of his dealings. She kept a special eye on Victor's projects and participated to a far greater degree than she had in the skyscrapers, which for her had too little to do with land.

Victor always gave her the chance to avoid Grant, and she always took it. To her son she played the part of a business partner and no more. New employees in the growing firm could hardly believe they were mother and son.

The only time Victor saw her smile, and it was a bleak, bitter smile, was when she learned that Grant had formed an offshoot company to include her son. It was to be called Northern Development. "It has a very cold sound to me," she said. "In fact, it chills me to the bone."

There was not a word from Serpa. Victor, to his great sadness, learned that Julia was humiliated and inconsolable, demanding ever more attention from her father. She refused Victor permission to see George and Jana, which he accepted with some relief. Whatever thin closeness he had won from his cold offspring would have vanished with his rejection of their mother, to whom they at least showed some instinctive warmth.

There was, however, through the first weeks of separation, a stream of letters from Julia. Although he sent them back unopened, knowing they would upset him and that he would have nothing to say in return, he could tell her mood of the moment by the way the envelopes were addressed—*My Lost Sweetness,* or, increasingly, *One Who Sleeps With Pigs.*

Grant did not rage at Victor, but all of his old sadness settled back upon him. "It was my fault more than yours."

"I'll take care of Evangeline with all my strength, Jack."

"I know what you'll be to her. But what will she be to you? Victor, even though you're Evangeline's only hope—and mine—I beg you to go back to your family. This could be the end of all of us."

"If I had one wish, Jack, it would be to ask for the power to put things the way they were. I don't have it."

Things held steady for a time. Evangeline seemed interested in furnishing their impressive new house, which was to the north on the Hudson River, well removed from old companions whom she might run into by chance.

When he returned from the day's work, he had the feeling she had been waiting for him at the door for hours. In front of the shocked servants she would draw him upstairs where, to his increasing discomfort, she reached ever lower to excite him.

"Evangeline, please. You don't have to do that for me."

"I want you to remember always what I am."

Despite his protests he felt the undeniable physical pull of her lovemaking, and images of her body were before him almost every minute of the day.

Victor was watching the first stirrings of the boom in Harlem, and time was short if he was going to be in front of it with Northern Development. The hours of his day began to stretch out as he strove to transfer money from the skyscrapers of Oakhill Towers to the Harlem land. Sometimes Evangeline was barely awake when he arrived home, and she was always sleeping when he left.

Their Sundays, fond memories of their innocent time together, and their occasional restaurant dinners and theater evenings vanished entirely. But there was no slipping away of her ardor. Rather, it fell away all at once.

He returned one night in the middle of the week to find her not only not waiting, but not at home at all. "She must have left some word," he said to the servants.

"There have been telephone calls for Miss Grant from someone named Sturdevant," the butler sniffed, not approving their relationship at all and showing he was not surprised by any further indiscretions.

Victor was a least partly relieved. He did not recognize that name from among her former escorts and she had made no attempt to hide her goings from the servants.

He did not confront her with the name when she returned long after midnight, and she did not bring it up. She told him she had grown tired of waiting for him, although he had been told by a maid that she had left in the early afternoon. She said she had gone to see some long-neglected friends. When he kissed her goodnight she showed none of her customary desire for more.

Several nights later she detected his puzzlement at the change in her habits and said simply, "We should begin to behave more like married people, don't you think?"

After that, at least once a week she was gone when he came home. And very quickly that became twice, three times and sometimes more. She always had a place where she had been and a name or two to go with the place. He recognized those names as women she had known before and some men not of the worst sort. None was above backing whatever story she requested. None of the names, moreover, was Sturdevant.

Victor had not forgotten his madness of jealousy when she had abandoned him after their night on the *General Sherman*. He still felt the humiliation of his skulking and was resolved never to repeat it.

Now he made a strong effort to come home earlier when he could, often with concert tickets and dinner reservations downtown. But even on nights when he had told her of his plans, she was often gone, pleading a boredom that would tolerate no waiting.

His relief at her beginning to be less dependent upon him began to crumble. When he approached her in bed now, she merely lifted her nightgown, asking that they remain beneath the covers against the chill. Unresponsive and often dry, she turned quickly away and slept.

"Are you ill, Evangeline? You're not the same."

"I'm exactly the same."

She began to not come home at all. Her excuses for this were not even as well constructed as those for lost afternoons and evenings. There were a hundred ways he could have checked, but there was a challenging carelessness in her manner, a taunting, a new gathering of cruelty that this told him that was just what she wanted.

"Aren't you curious about my friends, Victor? Don't you ever feel that you'd like to meet them?"

"I'll be ready when you think it's the proper time."

"Yes, let's wait for the proper time," she said, letting the mockery be not quite lost.

A fearful loneliness began to clamp down on Victor. Whatever fervor had been lacking with Julia, she had been a warm loving presence, always willing to chatter away his tension and provide a rocklike base of affection. Even the children had supplied some pleasurable moments when their chilly personalities thawed for some momentarily shared interest.

Most unforeseen was his pain at the loss of his mother's interest in him. He now saw how hard he had worked to occupy a small, lost piece of her heart.

Grant had grown totally still on the subject of Evangeline after his warning to Victor. He apparently knew that forces beyond him had been put in motion, and his caring might now be more intrusive and damaging than his standing aside. Victor guessed that he had made some early efforts to talk to Evangeline, but with no more success than ever.

"I'll divorce Julia," he finally told Evangeline. He had wanted to spare his wife that final shame at least.

For just a moment Evangeline melted and came to him, letting herself be held as before. But almost as quickly she pushed his arms away. "That's sentimental and silly, Victor. It won't do anything for our respectability, you know."

"We could be married."

"Why? Isn't it tedious enough as it is?"

As she withdrew, his memory of her passion began to haunt him. He almost felt that he might have forgiven any wallowing in lust with other men if she had been giving herself as freely to him.

"Do this for me, Evangeline, please. Like before."

"I can't, Victor. It's disgusting when you don't want to."

She moved into a separate room. Night after night he questioned whether he loved her now or ever really had. It could be that what seethed in him was just raw animal need, no different from her own jungle ways. But he would lie listening when she slipped away, and, when she returned, trying to tell if the footfalls were hers alone.

The name Sturdevant began to obsess him, although his role in her life was no more defined than anyone else's.

"Who is this Sturdevant?" he asked her furiously. "This began with him."

Her eyes narrowed. "It did, didn't it? He presented me with something I couldn't turn away from."

"What? *What*, damn it?"

When he finally engaged a detective to have her followed, there were no surprises. There were men, most of them already known to him, including Belding and Panzer, and she spent time with them in their homes or in the best hotels. She was often with them both together, and intoxicated in one form or another. Tantalizingly, there was no Sturdevant.

"Put her out, Victor," Grant begged him at last. "Your kindness, your patience, your love—they mean nothing to her. End your pain. She'll be looked after. You can bet on that."

"The way her mother was, Jack?"

The memory of Marietta's nasty death shook Grant after all the years. "She's not that bad. At least I pray she isn't. Maybe she'll come home to me as she used to."

"I can't leave her."

One icy midnight he heard her fall on the stairs. When he came to her from his room, the pupils of her beautiful eyes were dilated to huge, black pools. She was hardly coherent, but he had never seen her so lovely. He lifted her in his arms and she smiled at him in the old way.

He meant to put her on her bed, remove her coat and send for a maid to finish. But under the coat the buttons at her breast were opened and he caught fire. While she watched, never losing the smile, he undressed her completely, kissing, fondling, whispering his love. He licked her downward, her breast, her belly, the tops of her thighs. And there he met the stale, stinking evidence of the man she had been with.

The frayed cable that had suspended his reason above the pit for so long wore through. He found himself straddling her and hitting her with ringing, open-handed slaps. He saw the blood on her face wavering through his tears and heard himself screaming. "*Bitch.* Dirty *bitch.* Whore, whore, *whore.* I want you out of here. *Tonight.*" The blows filled him with the first satisfaction he had known in months.

The servants who pulled him off her refused his screamed orders to put her out on the street with her belongings. They informed him that they would be leaving his service in the morning, and one of them called a doctor. But after an hour that doctor had still not arrived.

While Victor sat sobbing, he was distantly conscious of Evangeline being taken to her room, dressed and taken from the house by a maid. All the other servants soon followed carrying their bags. After that he went to the study and began to drink his way to oblivion.

He was only half-conscious when he became aware of the doorbell's clang. In abrupt, desperate need to have the company of another human, he forced himself to stumble to the sound.

At the door he found a bent old man in a tall hat, his collar, his face and the fringe around his ears the only splashes of white in a mound of black clothing. Clutched in his hand was a medical bag. "I was summoned to Miss Grant," he said. "I am Doctor Sturdevant."

Victor held himself upright by clinging to the opened door. "Sturdevant? But you're not our physician," he said thickly.

"I have been Miss Grant's for the past three months. Now please let me see her if she has been injured. We must fear for the baby."

"The *baby?*"

"Yes, the fourth month is very critical. Please, may—"

"She's gone, Doctor. I'm sorry. We have to try to find her. Wait."

With all the help gone, and in his drunken muddle, Victor was unable to discover any addresses where she might be. A call to Jack Grant revealed that she had not been heard from there. "Don't worry, Doctor. We'll find her in the morning."

But they didn't. The maid who had taken her to a sister's house reported that Evangeline had made some phone calls, not overheard, and was picked up in a closed carriage. She had been near hysteria, with her face swollen and discolored.

Victor confessed to Jack Grant what he had done. "Hit me, Jack. I'm not as good as the worst filth you ever fought. I beat your daughter like a dog when she was sick in her mind and carrying a child that must be mine."

Grant put his arms around him. "I know what she was like when she hit bottom, Victor. There were times I almost used my fists, too. We can only hope she'll be back when the pendulum swings again."

Weeks passed. There were stories that she was in New Jersey with Panzer and upstate with Belding. But both men appeared and denied having seen her. An acquaintance reported that she had been seen in the Tenderloin with a stockbroker of unsavory reputation, but a search of the area turned up nothing.

Nearly paralyzed with guilt, Victor could not work. He sat at home near the phone, letting his mother and Grant look to his work as best they could. His love for Evangeline had become a weight inside him too heavy to move. But at last there was a letter from her.

No hint of an address showed, and the handwriting had regained a measure of steadiness.

My dearest Victor:

I am better now, in the unlikely event that you still care. We both know that will not last, and that is the reason I do not rush back to you to beg your pardon and feel the comfort of your arms again. I am sure you would take me into your home and heart again in your great kindness, and that makes resisting the urge to return almost unbearable. But I cannot cause you the same agony once more, in a cycle that I know is getting shorter as I descend to a hell that has been waiting for me all along. The same hell that claimed my mother.

I should have told you of your child at once, of course. However, the thought that it must be destroyed was immediately before me. To risk carrying this insanity forward was unthinkable at first. Then I realized it was half your child, and I loved that part too much to lose. So the baby will be born. What we must live with is that it must not bind us together, because I will not be with you or the child as I am. I will send it to you for your tender care and a gentle upbringing.

Please don't search for me any longer. I am with people who rather fancy my fall and look after me well enough. Tell my dear father that I think of him and love him when I am able. As for you, I regret all, and have taken the only action I can.

Love for me is love best forgotten.

Thank you for the only wonderful days of my life.

                                 Eternally,
                                 Evangeline

These words desolated Victor. What little remained of his rage dissolved to be replaced by still more remorse. He considered a thread of hope. There would be some contact when the child came, and he would work his way back to her. There were men who worked with the mind now, who would one day make it as understandable and healable as the body. She would have the best.

With this bit of promise he went back to his work.

Victor found Jack Grant expanding into Harlem so rapidly that he was outstripping his credit even with the enthusiasm of his own banks. The money of Oakhill Development was largely under Hannah's control, and Victor did not know enough of her feelings toward Grant to press the issue of a much greater involvement from her company. Meanwhile, handsome houses began to go up, bringing first lovely new streets and then whole charming neighborhoods into being. A house in Harlem was beginning to be the goal of the upward strivers of the city.

As the excitement of the new Mecca to the north began to mount, Victor felt some happiness returning to him. He clung to this, knowing that as long as he knew Evangeline it would not last.

Victor could hardly be sure it was Evangeline's voice crackling over the telephone. Still groggy with being wakened in the small hours after midnight, he could barely understand her few words: *"Victor . . . Oh, Victor, . . . Come get me . . . I can't think anymore."* She gave the address only once, and she seemed unsure. The call terminated in the middle of a word, as if disconnected by another.

Unable to reach Grant, Victor rigged a carriage himself and sped jolting over the dark cobbles toward the number on Twenty-eighth Street. His dread increased at every instant, the streetlamps becoming the flickering eyes of lines of demons.

The address was a tall brownstone showing lights on only the upper floors. Not knowing what to expect, he took a heavy, brass-headed cane from under the tack box. He vaulted the gate, took the steps by threes and beat the cane against the door. When no one had appeared after a full minute, he broke the glass with a kick and reached in to the lock.

Past the vestibule he found himself in an entry hall. There was a telephone attached to the side of the stairs, its receiver dangling off the hook. A white shawl lay beneath it.

Certain of no friendly welcome, he decided not to call out,

hurrying up the levels of steps to the light he had seen from the street.

Evangeline was in the front bedroom on the top floor, the taut skin of her naked, swollen belly glistening in the light of old gaslamps that flanked the big, brass bed upon which she lay.

One of the men beside her sat up, his sagging abdomen all but covering his genitals. The other, his buttocks white and hairy, continued to suck one of her swelling breasts.

There were empty bottles on the floor and half-eaten plates of food, as if these people, and perhaps others, had been in the room for days.

The sitting man had trouble bringing his eyes into focus. "Is that you, Kail, you sonofabitch? You've had yours." His voice blurred and he fumbled onto a table covered with pharmacy bottles and saucers of powder, feeling for his spectacles.

Evangeline groaned as the man touching her squeezed her breast roughly. Her eyes, wild, desperate, filled with pain, came open. *"Victor. Save our baby."*

Victor first brought the cane down with all his strength on her tormentor's buttocks. When he yowled and sprang to his feet, the whistling spruce caught him perfectly across both knees, and he dropped yapping like a puppy. The second man went across the room quickly, fumbling a clasp knife out of his trousers by the time Victor had circled the bed. The brass head of the cane broke his arm above the wrist, the knife thudding against the floor. The next blow, delivered with an upward sweep of a thick wrist, caught him explosively in the testicles, causing him to faint before he fell.

It was somewhere in the streets during the desperate dash for the hospital, with the whip-driven horse skidding and threatening to go down at every turn, that Evangeline began to scream ceaselessly as the devils in her burst forth to overwhelm what little was left of her reason.

The child was born two days later, a month short of full term. The birth was difficult, with the mother raving and in full restraint. Yet, there was one space when her senses shone through. She saw Victor and her voice dropped to a whisper. "What is it?"

"A boy," he said. "And he's fine."

"Justin," said Evangeline. "Then his name is Justin."

In her next breath she was screaming again.

While Evangeline quieted in the following weeks, it was not the quiet that signaled the return of her mind. With each day she took another step backward into herself. As this happened, the violence in her disappeared, and with it the hard, quick-witted brilliance that had made her such a joy and such a terror. She smiled sometimes, but it was the confused smile of someone who has forgotten something of such importance that she can't believe that it has been lost.

The baby was brought to her when they were sure of its safety, and she held it and cooed to it, but she never at first connected it to herself.

She knew she had met Victor and Jack Grant before, but didn't remember enough of that for it to be of any use to her. So they were reintroduced, and these relationships had to grow, for the most part, as if they were brand new.

Evangeline could read, and did, and carried on conversations that concerned events in the world and the city. But her part in these events, past and future, she was incapable of examining. No interest in eating or drinking was evident, and she would likely have starved to death if not fed by nurses.

A doctor who had come from Austria, where he had studied the labyrinths of the mind, was brought from Atlanta. He spent a week with her before he rendered his opinion, showing his listeners his bald spot as he studied his broad, protuberant belly. "This was never a completely normal personality, I believe. There are still signs of a fatal violence. It is that she flees from. So, in some sense, this collapse is a blessing."

Nervous and much reduced in weight, Victor snapped at him. "You don't know what's been lost. She shined like summer stars."

"She will never glow as brightly as that again, we must expect. But evils will have none of the old strength either."

"There's no way she can get better?"

"She'll get better than she is, but she'll always need care and watching. A sanitarium at first, then perhaps living with someone at home. It's not inconceivable that she could be on the streets by herself sometime, for short outings."

"I don't believe you," Victor said. "She's doing beautifully. If you didn't know what she'd been through, you'd say this was a quiet, gentle woman, perhaps addled by a high fever."

Evangeline, seated just out of earshot, smiled as if she had understood and agreed. Then she took a pen out of its holder and pressed its steel nib into her palm to the barrel.

The sanitarium was far upstate. In the beginning Victor was there three times a week. But she was unreachable by him. Something in her mind shut him out more than the others, not in spite of what their closeness had been, but seemingly because of it. She would chat politely for a short time, blankly resisting all attempts to explore their past. Long before it was time to go, she would tell him she was tired and leave him. Only Grant was able to make any progress at all working her back down the closed passageway. Sometimes he brought the child for her to see, and she appeared pleased.

At length, the caretakers asked that Victor no longer come, they having observed that she became agitated and slid backward after his visits. He reluctantly agreed and went to tell her goodbye.

He bent to kiss her cheek and, as in the earliest days of their childhood, perhaps from dim memory, she turned to meet his lips. He lingered there, and she let him.

"Goodbye, Victor," she said. "You're very nice. It would have been good to have a brother like you."

When he arrived back in the city, the hissing, billowing steam of the locomotive in the bowels of Grand Central Station pictured for him the hell that was his spirit. Night had already lowered and he hid himself in it, stumbling aimlessly through streets whose names and locations ceased to matter. That the way was dangerous to an uncaring man concerned him not at all. Once, on a dark side street, he thought he heard the shuffle of purposeful footsteps, but he did not turn, ready to accept the flash of a knife that would move to terminate his nightmare. But a policeman appeared at the intersection and ended the possibility for the moment.

A shrouded moon rose, drawing his eyes upward. For a second there was a single happy beat of his heart. The hazy light was broken into a towering, boxed geometry by the rising girders of a skyscraper. It was one of his own, already topped out, just a bit of steel waiting to come in tomorrow.

The sight of the one thing in his life that he had been able to love without pain drew him upward. There were some stars and he had a crying need to touch them.

The elevators were not running, and there were sixteen stories to climb, but there were ladders. As he climbed, he wondered if Peter Hanratty was anywhere about.

It had become almost a tradition to have a Hanratty somewhere around an Oakhill project. Hannah had never lost her closeness with the family from the *Dortmund,* and Patrick always had another energetic son or grandson to go to work. Peter, a laughing, voluble copy of his father, had worked his way up from the hods to a supervisor. With the final load of steel coming in before dawn to beat the street traffic, he might be prowling about the site, checking that the derricks were correctly placed and guyed for the lift.

With each higher step, Victor became more of a child again. He half expected to hear the shouts of his mother or Filomena calling him down as he looked for a higher and narrower ledge to run upon.

The years on the skyscrapers had kept him nimble, the power in his thighs undiminished. He lost count of the floors, driving himself harder and harder to lose himself in the effort, so that it was a surprise to find himself at the top.

For him, care always fell away in proportion to distance from the ground, and now was no exception. He let the cool night air wash over and cleanse him, feeling he could touch the moon casting its pale light over the reddish beams of the steel. Through his soles he could sense every drop of sweat, every gasp of effort, every white spark of creative energy that had sent the numberless tons into the clouds.

An enormous beam, unsecured to the structure except by its weight, thrust far out over the edge of what would be the south wall. He imagined that it would be used to rig a temporary hoist for some of tomorrow's work. Without thinking about it, he stepped upon this beam and began to walk out. And then he was standing sixteen stories above the street, arms outspread, balancing himself easily as he looked down on the pinpoints of the gaslamps in the street below. He had not the slightest fear of heights, and he thought how easy, how pleasant it would be to step out into the night. There would be one long, cool rush of air, the feeling of flying that he had always yearned to know, and then instantaneous oblivion and freedom.

Still, if there was a heaven, he didn't want to fall to it, he wanted to build to it.

He drank in one last, glorious breath of the night and carefully turned to walk back on the beam.

But Benedetto Serpa was there.

The moon showed the towering Sicilian braced at the edge of the planks of temporary flooring, stolidly blocking the return. In his huge hand was a ten-foot length of pipe taken from a pile behind him. The fury in his eyes seemed to generate a light of its own. "Your debt is due now."

Victor braced himself against the expected rush of fear, but it didn't come. There was only a leaden sorrow. "I could never tell you how sorry I am for the pain I caused Julia, Mr. Serpa. I'm only surprised you haven't come sooner."

"For the love of your mother I have held back much. Always. But every night I hear my daughter cry as her heart breaks again. She screams out, but you do not listen. That you stain my honor, perhaps I could bear. That you stain hers, I can no longer tolerate."

"I understand that, Mr. Serpa."

"And your mother understands. She doesn't say it, but she knows there is something unclean about you. She will not mourn for long."

"Especially if it's an accident."

"No. For her there is only the truth. It is why I must do it with my own hands even though my people begged for the privilege."

"I'm waiting for you, Mr. Serpa."

The first sudden thrust of the pipe came at Victor's midriff straight and hard. He jackknifed backward, feeling the tip just brush his vest. He moved to the very end of the beam, feeling for the edge with a toe.

Again the pipe shot forward, and this time Victor ducked beneath it, rocking wildly on his heels to regain his balance.

Serpa switched his attack to the legs, calmly and patiently, knowing that he was permitted many small defeats, his opponent none.

Kicking and pirouetting, Victor just avoided the stabs of the pipe. The Sicilian was beginning to time the frantic swaying it took to regain balance, and would soon gauge his lunges to catch him before he could reset himself. This contest would soon end on the sidewalk beneath.

With the close breath of doom, Victor's senses had sharpened preternaturally. He thought he could hear Serpa's heartbeat, see the very breath pouring from his throat. And now, even as another bullfighter-whirl bought another second, Victor saw a figure appear in the shadowy distance on the flooring beyond Serpa. As the huge man thrusted and grunted, the figure came racing forward.

The pipe finally caught Victor directly in the chest. He grasped the end in his hands and pulled, using Serpa's grip to keep him from somersaulting backwards, but losing his footing despite it. He fell flat on the beam, chest first, facing Serpa. Being forced to release his grip in order to grasp the beam with his arms, he had returned control of the pipe to Serpa, who now abandoned his steadying hold on the upright to come forward.

The Sicilian shortened his grip on his weapon, raising it overhead with both hands above the unprotected head of his now immobilized enemy.

Victor looked up to watch his death come whistling down, and saw Peter Hanratty, running onto the narrow beam as if it had been the Great Lawn in Central Park, pile into Serpa from behind. "Hold off, you sonofabitch," the Irishman growled as the pipe flew one way and they, the other.

There was a split-second flurry of windmilling arms and legs followed by two terrifying grunts.

When Victor looked over the edge of the girder, his skin crawled with horror. Peter's hands clung to the edge of the beam. He might have pulled himself up easily, but the huge, struggling weight of Serpa clung to his legs with burly arms.

Pulling himself rapidly forward, Victor positioned himself above Peter and caught his wrists.

"Jesus' eyes, Mr. Oakhill," Peter gasped, "This fella weighs like a safe."

Victor locked his legs on the beam and tugged upward with all his might. His poor leverage and the combined weight of the bodies defeated him completely. "Damn, Peter. I don't have a belt to tie you on."

"It wouldn't hold with all this," the dangling man puffed. "You better turn loose, or we'll pull you down, too. Tell Mom and Pop I was thinkin' about 'em."

Anger tore through Victor. He roared down at Serpa, whose upturned face was an iron mask. "I can't haul you both. He hasn't done anything. Turn him loose."

"For what?" Serpa panted.

Victor's mind sought desperately "For Julia," he shouted. "I'll go back to her. I promise it. I'll be the husband I should have been."

"Swear on your mother who I have loved."

"I swear on Mother's life."

The thick arms opened outward at the last word and Serpa fell away, his face so fierce and devoid of fear that death itself might have thought twice to seize him. The terrible eyes never left Victor's, and they were visible for a dreadfully long time as he dwindled to be swallowed by the shadows underneath.

Using all the stamina left to him, Victor hauled Peter Hanratty to the top of the beam and they crawled slowly to the flooring.

"Mr. Oakhill," Peter said between gagging breaths, "I think you made a helluva deal."

"Yeah," whispered Victor. "One helluva deal."

* * *

Whether Julia would actually ever forgive him, Victor understood, he would never completely know. She shared her father's unshakable hold on the secrets of the heart. But without question some part of the love she had felt for him, the part that existed above all the levels of reason, had survived.

"I welcome you home. I won't speak of what went before. I ask that you do the same. It will be as it was so far as I can make it so."

"I'll spend my life paying back your pain, Julia."

"No life could be that long, Victor." She hugged him. Her arms held no thrills, no terrors and much sweetness.

The death of Benedetto Serpa permitted Mark Northern to live inside Jack Grant once again. The grim pact with Serpa was terminated in the only way it could have been, and the way back to Hannah, he resolved, would be found. And he knew that way lay through Victor.

"Victor, it's very clear. You were entirely correct to go back to your family, and there you must remain. It would be impossibly painful for Julia to raise Justin in your home. So he can remain here in my house, by me, with all the love and presence the two of us can provide. When Evangeline is able to return, she will live with me as well and be with her son."

Victor's gratitude was so complete that Mark felt guilt at having him not know that a great part of his generosity was found in tying Hannah's son to him more closely.

"I'll be here as much as I can, Jack. Justin will know what love is."

Chapter 10

Hannah would not have supposed it possible that her love had remained so entirely intact behind the hard wall her humiliation and disappointment had built. But when Victor brought Jack Grant into her office one shining afternoon, her son having given no word of this intention, she could have flown into Grant's arms in her first confusion.

"Mother," Victor said, pushing the familiar, trim, muscular figure forward, "Tell Jack he was wrong about your throwing him out if he came without an appointment."

She was certain she would have refused him any such appointment if given even a moment to think about it, but she found herself standing and offering her hand. "Mr. Grant usually doesn't stand so much on the niceties, so I won't either."

She forced herself not to squeeze his hand too hard, loathing herself for what she still felt.

He was showing the impenetrable face of business she had seen him put on so many times back in the Cutts day. There was no way to know what was in his mind. "I was hoping it would still be Jack and Hannah," he said.

"All right, Jack. Have a seat. I know this can't be about business, because you once told me, among other things, that you thought very little of my abilities in that regard."

His facade did not crack, but he left her an instant to drink him in before he found his answer. There were things etched in his face now that not even Duplessis' knife could erase, but he was otherwise remarkably unchanged by the years.

"Those stupid words I said that day did terrible damage. Far more to me than to you, if you can believe that."

"I can't, Jack. And I'm very glad you said, if I remember back twenty years or so, that you did not care to be forgiven."

"Then I won't ask it. But I will say that the reasons I spoke are dead and my sorrow will go on always."

"Yesterday's business bores me greatly."

"I'm here about tomorrow's business, Hannah. You know what Victor and I are doing in Harlem, of course," he said.

"Yes. It seems that my son wishes to continue the string of disasters that occur when Oakhills affiliate with Grants."

"Mother," Victor snapped. "That was my weakness and my fault."

"Excuse me, I suppose it was. I'm sorry about Evangeline, Jack. I hope she and the child are well."

"She's better, but not well. Justin is a delight. He does nothing but laugh. You'd love him. And he should know his grandmother."

"If Victor thought that, Justin would be raised in my home instead of yours, I'm sure," she said. She knew that Victor was allowing none of the chill she had shown him as a child to spill onto his own children. He didn't even encourage her presence with the remote George and Jana.

"It's best that he be in the house with his mother, for the times when she's well."

"Yes, certainly," Hannah said. "Now, you were talking about tomorrow's business."

Both men showed relief at the change of subject. They exchanged a glance and Victor began. "I've made a proposition to Jack, Mother. A partnership to exploit what might be the last great boom in undeveloped land that this island will ever know."

Victor was not nearly a good enough liar to fool Hannah about which of them had made the proposition. "I thought you two were partners already."

"Not officially, and not on the scale that will allow us to beat the banks and insurance companies to the cream," Grant said.

"What you want to do is cash in what we've built painfully over thirty years for a speculation," said Hannah.

"The Superior-Pacific was a speculation because the buildings were only on paper and the people were thousands of miles away. This is sure because we have a small island *bursting* with prosperous people who are desperate for a beautiful place to live. They can see what's *there* already. Today. Once we have the land, every house will sell before the first brick is placed, and we'll have more money for more land and more houses. The bidding for parcels will be fast and fierce. But if we commit heavily and as a unit, we can stand with the best of them."

"Oakhill and Grant, Mother. Its more than a financial power. It's the two smartest people in the business, you and Jack, working together again."

"Our last experience working together was not a happy one."

Grant leaned so close, so quickly, that she thought he was going to take her hand and she drew back. "That's not true, Hannah, and you know it. Yes, it ended badly. But those were the happiest days we ever knew. Because it was building something that would change the way a whole people lived. When was the last time you felt that good?"

"Nothing's been that good since," she admitted. "But—"

"Hannah," Grant said, his fists knotted with emotion, "all we're talking here is business. Don't let anything else get in your way. You know what I can do, I know what you can do. If we hadn't met before, if all we had was one another's reputation to go by, we'd have gotten together and made this agreement in a minute."

Yes, Jack, she thought. But if I do this, will it be for business or for another chance for me to be a fool? Will I know the difference?

"Oakhill Development can't break out again without this,

Mother," Victor said. "It's our best chance. Maybe our last one on Manhattan."

He was right, Hannah knew. And she wanted the company to move out of the pack and help her once more find the excitement to fill her now tedious life. She settled on a course. "Very well. The opportunity is there and we should take it quickly. Oakhill and Grant it will be. But I do not wish to consolidate our offices. It makes people closer than they should be . . ."

At the loss of Serpa, Hannah felt a huge part of her past drop away. The memory of the giant body upon her did not easily leave, and for that, and perhaps more, she cried through one long night. But the brooding, emotional presence of the Sicilian had always drained her, and now she felt her strength returning.

Having made her decision to work again with Grant, she put aside any misgivings and immersed herself totally in the project. As was her custom, she began an intense study of the section's history and people. In these examinations she often found unseen problems and opportunities.

She remembered the area from her early days, when she watched Commodore Vanderbilt's fast trotters working out on Harlem Lane. The rich, however, were not so much her concern as the poor, of which the area had its share.

The original squatters and their shacks, polluters of the early beauty, were all but gone, run off by the swallowing of the land. She saw no difficulty there and moved on in her studies. There were Negroes in Harlem. There had always been. The original wagon road between New Amsterdam and Harlem was built by slaves of the Dutch West India Company. They were refined, gentle people still bearing the old Dutch names like Voorhies and Stuyvesant, and they were confined to a few blocks.

Of whites there was a longtime core, including many upper-class German Jews, a shantytown Little Italy and a growing group of tough Irish.

And there was the Canary Island Gang. They inhabited the marshes to the west, degraded descendants, if that were possible, of the riverfront vermin who had plagued the city from the beginning. Roaming the great expanse of the city's garbage that was dumped into their domain, and partially subsisting on it, they were a dangerous wolf pack, sometimes killing Negroes and unthinking intruders.

Of these threats to the coming operations of Oakhill and Grant, the gang in the flats was the most worrisome and hard to contain.

At no small risk, and being careful to keep to the daylight hours, she examined the flats and saw an idea that might work.

"Fill in the flats?" Grant asked, as he tried to wave away a whirring maelstrom of flies with a handkerchief. "Why? The Devil himself wouldn't live here."

"Not with that garbage going halfway to the sky," said Hannah, precariously standing on the seat of the new Dreyfus to survey the grim mounds covered by swirling blankets of feeding gulls. "But the stink and the disease has the whole respectable West Side up in arms. They're screaming for the city to do something. There's a 'Fill In the Flats Committee' already, and the newspapers are taking it up."

"I see. We let the city do our work. As prominent builders we could speed things up pretty well. We've had a bit of experience handling newspaper people, I daresay. The land will be there newly filled and flat. All soft and easy to dig for foundations."

"And cheap."

"We'll work on this together."

"No, Jack. This is yours. I handle the money."

As the century turned, the boom in Harlem went forward, and Oakhill and Grant were first among the leaders. The flats were drained and filled, and their unsavory denizens scattered. Oakhill and Grant bought early and often, and their buildings grew at the western margins while their other properties spurted from the center.

In Harlem's Little Italy, the apprehensive dwellers watched the boom nibble at the edges of their stronghold. The old ramshackle buildings of wood were bought at prices that could not be turned down, and demolished at once for greater things. Prices began to rise beyond the reach of these people as the owners of the old dwellings began to see their value to the madmen from the south. Growth of the Italian community to the north stopped and began to reverse. The same happened elsewhere with the Irish poor.

Even Hannah began to forget her worries. When Frank Chumlin came to her with his wife, the plump, chipper and now middle-age Katie Hanratty, there were no qualms about where they should buy their new home.

"Harlem is the place, Frank. You've worked hard and made quite a success out of yourself with your tack shop. Now you should live where people can see your success."

"It's an awful lot of money compared with downtown," Frank said.

"But in a couple of years it will seem like you stole it. Only the rich will be able to afford to live in Harlem after a while."

"Oh, Frank, let's do it," Katie said. "It's so beautiful up here. The grandchildren can come up to where it's green and safe and enjoy their summers."

Three weeks later they had a lovely brownstone on 127th Street. There was quickly much to reassure them about their choice. Banks sprang up. The new Calvary Methodist Episcopal Church was a magnificent structure that certified a community committed to the teachings of God. There was the Harlem Yacht Club for those who would take their leisure on the broad rivers.

What Greatness Lies in Store for Harlem? headlines asked rhetorically.

During the next three years Oakhill and Grant built steadily on, with all the success anticipated.

Victor could only wonder at the relationship between his mother and Jack Grant. The two old partners pulled together in business as brilliantly as always, but it was perfectly evident that Hannah Oakhill wished nothing to do with Jack Grant outside the work.

For himself, Victor had built a bittersweet life with great happiness and aching sorrow living side by side.

He went to see Evangeline often. She was now comfortably

confined on Long Island. She was no longer raving or dangerous to herself, and his company did not agitate her anymore. Many times, Victor found, intelligent conversations with her were possible. But her mind refused to visit the time between their first meeting and the birth of Justin. He had brought the child to her several times over the months, and she now recognized he was her own, hugging and kissing him, and weeping when it was time for him to be taken away. Victor, though, remained no more than a rediscovered companion of her youth, whose further attachment to her and Justin she could never perceive. When he tried to lead her to what had been, her attention wandered off beyond a high wall where he could not be heard. So, eventually, when she asked after her child, Victor told her that he was growing splendidly and happily in the care of her father. He made no further attempt to place himself in the picture.

"Does he smile very much, Victor?"

"All the time, Evangeline."

"Is that . . . like his daddy?"

"No. Not like his daddy at all . . ."

Justin was one of those children who by nature might more likely have been the offspring of the first couple who came down the street than of his natural parents. He was square, dark-haired and light-eyed, and by the time he was eight gave clear evidence that he would stand only a little above the stocky peasant build of his father. But the greatest difference from his parents shone out of his character.

Justin Oakhill, from his earliest days, showed not the slightest tendency toward the seriousness of Victor or the frightening darknesses that had haunted Evangeline. He was born laughing and never stopped being pleased with who he was, where he was and what he was.

Not unexpectedly, Justin became the riotous center of the gloomy Grant house, and a shining light in the life of his father. In him, Victor found the child to share his heart. His never-ending dismay at the unassailable coldness he had always felt from George and Jana now vanished. While it would not have been fair to say that he felt no fatherly love at all for his children by Julia, he knew it was but a small fraction of what he felt for Justin, although the child sometimes drove him to distraction and put them at early odds.

Away from Justin, for Victor there was only the work and his home. Of these he far preferred his work.

Julia never reproached him. Not by a word or a look did she ever intimate that her terrible heartache during Victor's days with Evangeline had ever happened.

Often he wondered what she knew of her father's death. The police, knowing the thousand shadowy enemies in Serpa's life, had investigated neither long nor hard. Julia's grief had been great nonetheless, and during its height Victor had hoped with all his heart that she would never learn what had happened at the end of that beam high in the night.

He returned to her bed. She slipped beneath him as hotly as in the early days. But when he had rolled away and prepared to sleep, and her lips brushed his throat in a good-night kiss, he often wondered if her eyes were on that throat as well, contemplating dark Sicilian things.

The real trouble began, as is often the case, in the newspapers. There were not enough earthshaking things of national importance to keep their columns occupied, so they began to dwell upon the great Harlem land boom. Each day stories of how this or that plumber or hack driver of a year ago had just salted away his third or fourth million beguiled a dreaming readership. The speculation took on a new, quickly growing cast of players.

It flared up first in the Jewish enclaves downtown. People with a brave, clever, entrepreneurial tradition saw the possibilities of cooperation. A real estate office sprang up in every other tenement. On the Lower East Side the discussions over the sewing machines and the steaming soup were real estate and little else, and the fever began to spread out of control.

Workmen who had expected to spend the remainder of their

days in a factory or storefront shop now suddenly saw themselves as bona fide, big-city realtors, with the rustle of thousand-dollar bills growing ever louder in their ears.

Years of painfully hoarded savings disappeared into lots and homes. Men who had never driven a nail decided they were builders. People who had not exchanged a civil word in years pooled their money to buy these nonbuilders' unbuilt houses.

It was so simple that a fool could understand all that was necessary. You bought property on sixty-day contracts and sold it at exorbitant profits before you had laid out anything like substantial money. Then you repeated the cycle again.

"Avrom, you're a madman. Seventy-five thousand dollars? For a building with five-thousand dollars a year in rents?"

"Why do you women have so much trouble being rich, Esther? You know we're not going to hold it."

"We're holding four buildings that you're not going to hold."

"I want them to run up. Maybe another three thousand each. That's fifteen thousand. You know how many chickens you have to pluck in the shop for that? You know how many people in Lodz own four buildings?"

"The chickens aren't mortgaged, Avrom. And we owned what we had in Lodz."

"Which was a chicken coop. Relax, Esther. Be rich."

By 1904 the Harlem land speculation surpassed anything in the previous history of the city. Now powered by the amazing influx of money from the city's well-off middle class, beautiful, well-built housing finished turning the Harlem Plains into the finest housing outside of the mansion rows downtown. All day long the furniture-piled moving wagons could be seen going north, bringing thousands to homes in which they could live with pride and pass on to their children.

Oakhill and Grant watched its properties increase while values climbed rapidly. Too rapidly.

"I think it's getting dangerous," Victor said to the senior partners.

"No question about it. It can't go on like this," Grant agreed.
"Should we sell enough to cover ourselves and lock in a profit?"
"I don't think that's necessary. But we should stop buying. Now. Let the cash from the rents and the other companies build up to carry us through any lull. Maybe jump in one more time to buy cheap when the people who are stretched too far have to get out."
"You're so sure these values aren't the top for a long, long time?" asked Hannah.
"How can they be? This isn't a lot of speculation junk that's been built. It's the finest design, the best quality in the city. Maybe in the whole country. The market's pretty sure to go soft and back up after a while, but when it comes back, with all the speculation squeezed out, the value will still be there. Harlem will have the fastest-appreciating property in New York for the next fifty years. Unless there's an earthquake or God finds a way to add another twenty miles to Manhattan."

On its incredible enthusiasm, the Harlem boom ran another year. It was not until into 1905 that the market began to break.

It was not as the result of a national financial crisis or the uncovering of a great scandal, as is so often the case. It was just that too much had been built too soon and priced too high too quickly. Many of the people who should have been the tenants and buyers of the splendid residences were their builders instead. The rent rolls lagged far behind the expenses of the heavily mortgaged buildings. The deep well of foolish buyers to make rich the previous wave of foolish buyers dried up. The gray wolves at the banks and insurance companies, at first complacent in the magnificent collateral they held for their loans, began to fear the size of their involvement, and for the size of the market it would take to bring money out of so many foreclosures. They hoped that the desperate speculators would find a way out themselves. Unfortunately, they did.

* * *

After a month of ominous inaction, with it becoming obvious to even the most optimistic that the stagnation was not only not reversing but deepening, cutthroat competition to cut rents and prices began. The trickle of new tenants coming north paid half the rents they expected to for better housing than they had dreamed possible even in wonderful Harlem.

To retain the tenants they had, the other landlords were forced to lower their rents. Enormous numbers of mortgages began to go into arrears.

Having stopped their speculations in time, and having the downtown incomes of Oakhill Development behind them, the Oakhill and Grant properties remained in equilibrium awaiting better times.

"There's panic out there," Hannah said. "I hate to see it. Desperate people find ways to make a bad situation a disaster."

The first "sales" to Negroes were not sales at all, nor were they intended to be. Landlords who saw that their rent rolls could not save them went after money with any weapon they could. With buildings being offered at fire-sale prices all over Harlem, some found one almost surefire way to keep prices up: They sold to Negroes and let associations of white homeowners buy them out to prevent the sale.

"Good Jesus," one distraught owner cried at an association meeting. "We can't meet our own mortgages and we're taking on another one." The answer was the same being given at a dozen other meetings like it.

"If the niggers come in strong we lose everything. Hold 'em outside until the market turns and they can't afford it. It's all we can do."

The scheme of the sellers succeeded. Too well. Landlord after landlord learned that he could get most of his money out intact if he sold to Negroes first. The tactic spread and, of course, there was soon no more money for buying the properties back, and black faces began to appear in some significant force in Harlem.

Oakhill and Grant quickly looked into the threat. If their investment was to be menaced by a substantial black immigration to Harlem, they must be prepared to sell, because nothing destroyed value in the public mind as thoroughly.

Their early investigations were reassuring. "From what I can find out, Hannah," said Grant, "there are maybe sixty-five thousand Negroes in the whole city, including the other boroughs. There are probably fewer than fifty thousand in Manhattan. Really very few when you're talking about a city that will hold millions."

"But if they all decided to move at once—"

"They don't seem to do that. They'd still be in Greenwich Village if the Italians hadn't driven them out. There's nobody pushing them off the Tenderloin or San Juan Hill."

"Suppose they come without being pushed, Jack?"

"That's not really possible. The average Negro earns maybe five or six dollars a week."

"What about the Negroes who are not average? Some are quite prosperous."

"I'd say let's welcome them, Hannah. They're honest and hardworking, and it's about time people found out they make fine neighbors. This could be where the races finally learn to live together."

"And, as you say, there's not really enough of them to make a real presence here."

"Exactly."

"I think we should stay in Harlem, Jack."

But if Oakhill and Grant had hopes that an increasingly affluent black middle class would find acceptance in better parts of the city, the notion would have brought bitter laughter from those who knew better. And if they thought that Negroes would be easily contained in their numbers, they had not been observing the rail stations and river piers.

The steamers of the Old Dominion Line began to arrive with Negroes from the South who, increasingly, did not return after their visits to the grand city. However bad the situation in New

York, it seemed enlightened and laden with opportunity after the repression and slave wages of the unreconstructed parts of the South.

And not all the Negroes were Americans. The poverty-driven natives of the West Indies found that the unused immigration quotas of their mother countries allowed them into the United States through the side door. And they came in droves, speaking French and Spanish and a wonderful, musical English. The number of the newcomers was not yet so great, but the fear of them was.

So, as the forces built, Oakhill and Grant did not know so much of their difficulty as they thought.

Jack Grant was giving a party. Hannah would not have attended, it not being her custom to see her partner socially, but this was very much a business occasion. As the fate of Harlem property teetered, it was vital for the landowners of substance to retain a united front to ride out the sales to blacks. The biggest of the investors had been invited to Grant's house, which now rang with a careless gaiety it had not known in many years. A sprightly orchestra played, the best wines and foods were there in abundance and dancers had an evening to forget the frustrations of the past months.

There were no meetings in separate rooms. Hannah and Grant, as agreed, circulated unceasingly to small groups of worried-looking men and obtained spoken agreements to stand firm in Harlem until the storm passed. Oakhill and Grant would be the main anchor of the indomitable group, Hannah assured them. Victor visited the few investors who were missed by her and Grant.

It was toward morning, while Hannah was whirling in a wide-swinging two-step turn, that a drunken dancer stepped upon the edge of her gown, tearing down the hem. An emergency repair being essential, a maid brought her up a long marble staircase to a sewing room at the end of a corridor, where the work was quickly done.

"Thank you for your fine work," she told the maid. "I'll stay behind here for a few minutes to rest in this chair. You can go now."

It was not until she had been gone for some minutes that Hannah noticed the woman had forgotten a ring of keys that she had removed from a pocket while hunting an errant thimble. No matter, Hannah thought. She would take them back to the maid upon returning downstairs. But she was delayed in that.

Passing a door as she was about to turn into the main corridor after her rest, Hannah became aware of a woman sobbing. The sound was barely audible, but was so filled with wracking heartbreak that it jolted the senses.

A twist of the latch showed the door was locked, and Hannah wondered whom she might call for the swiftest help. A particularly wrenching moan brought her up short and reminded her of the key ring in her hand. Perhaps there was no time to lose. She began to try the keys in the lock in rapid succession. On the fourth key, the lock turned and the door swung open.

The beautiful room was large and furnished more as a complete living quarters than a mere bedroom. In addition to the bed there was a rolltop desk, extensive bookshelves filled with volumes, and a piano. There was also a gramophone and several comfortable lounging chairs. There were two huge windows, but the drapes across them were pinned closed, as if the room's occupant feared the penetration of even a single ray of sunshine. Nowhere was there the faintest sign of clutter, giving the impression that no one had moved inside these walls for a very long time.

Only a single lamp burned, dim and heavily shaded, and the sobbing stuttered in the air.

Hannah eased the door closed behind her and went to a high-backed lounge facing the wall opposite, where she found a slim, small woman, fully dressed, with her knees drawn up and her face buried in the arms that rested upon them.

Something drew Hannah back across the years, to a time when she had heard that same petulant, heartbroken weeping under her own roof. "Evangeline?" she whispered.

The tear-streaked face raised up and turned to her, and she was shaken.

From Victor she knew most of the story of Evangeline and had been able to fill in the rest. She had not laid eyes on the girl since Grant had taken her almost thirty years before, but Hannah did not have to witness all the steps in the degradation to read it in the ravaged loveliness of these features.

Even at her worst Evangeline had radiated an almost supernatural abundance of the forces of life. Physically, much of Evangeline's beauty remained. The damage was not really a matter of lines or fallen flesh. It was more a dreadful vacancy, a stunned misery made all the more terrible by its lack of focus.

"Who is that?" Evangeline said, the tears suddenly stopping.

"It's Hannah, Evangeline. Do you remember me?"

The eyes contemplated vaguely for a while, then snapped into clarity. The dim past was perhaps more obtainable in her mind than the last awful years.

"Hannah, oh, Hannah. Of course, I do. How I cried when Father took me from you and Victor. But at least I've seen Victor since. He comes to see me, you know. And he's been very kind. Tell me about where you've been. They let me know, but it doesn't stay with me."

Hannah had to choke back her tears of pity. "I've done very little, I'm afraid. I didn't know you were home. I'd have come to see you here, even though I couldn't bear to visit you in that awful place where you were."

"I'm not always at home. Sometimes I have to go back. But I've been here for a while now." As Evangeline spoke, the words seemed to be as illuminating to her as they were to Hannah, as though she were contemplating their meaning for the first time herself.

"Do you ever go out?"

"They wanted me to for the longest time. But I never wanted to be in the daylight. Not before Caesar came. I was always afraid I would see people out there I didn't want to see. I didn't even know who they were, but they terrified me. I pin the draperies closed so I won't accidentally see them on the street. Caesar opens them sometimes now, and takes me for walks and rides. He's the only one who understands how it is. He knows how to tell me when I'm being silly. We went to the theater together once, and to two concerts. With him I can walk, or even ride a long way without being frightened."

"Who is Caesar, Evangeline?"

"Father and Victor found him for me when they saw they couldn't help me, not even with all their doctors."

"Then he's not a doctor."

"Oh, no. He's a servant who worked downstairs. When he started to help me, Father took away his other duties and gave him a great deal more money. I don't think of him as a servant at all, Hannah, but as the dearest, strongest man I ever knew."

"What . . . about Victor?"

"He's more like a wonderful big brother now than he ever was. I've forgiven him for those years he stayed away. I swear I don't know why he goes through all the trouble with me that he does, with his family to look after. And I wish he didn't look so awfully miserable all the time."

"What was making you so unhappy when I came in, dearest?"

Evangeline struggled for a moment to remember, and a large tear finally rolled down her cheek. "It's Justin. I only cry for Justin. He's a marvelous little boy who lives here. They say he's mine."

"Do you see Justin very much?"

The tears flowed harder. "No. I don't see him enough at all. And there are always people standing close to take him away just when we're getting to know one another. He cries, too."

"Why would they do such a cruel thing?"

"It's not because they're cruel, Hannah. When they brought him as a baby, I began to get very upset when I tried to think about his father. Once it was so bad that they had to send me to that . . . hospital again for a long time. I think they're afraid it will happen again if we talk too much."

"Will it?"

"No, no, no. That's all over. I'm sure. Can I tell you a secret, Hannah? Caesar brings Justin to me sometimes and leaves us alone. He made Justin promise never to tell and he doesn't."

"How do you get along?"

"We love each other very much. He's fidgety and full of fun, so he doesn't stay long, but he calls me Mother and tells me he wants to be with me all the time. Isn't that sweet? But I feel so terrible when he's gone."

The door latch clicked, then clicked again as someone was surprised to find it already unlocked. When the door swept back, a tall, regal Negro entered pushing a serving cart upon which sat a gleaming silver tea service. He was cocoa-skinned and gray-eyed, with chiseled even features. There was stern disapproval in his look. "May I ask why you are here, Madame?" he said in an uncommonly heavy voice with an accent that was pure New England.

"I'm Hannah Oakhill."

"I know that. I asked not who, but why."

There was no trace of humility in this black man Evangeline had described as a servant. He came closer and seemed larger and more intimidating than ever, his trim uniform emphasizing the great disparity between his grand shoulders and remarkably small waist.

"As an old acquaintance of Mr. Grant, I thought I might have a certain right to look in here. I heard weeping."

He saw the keys that she still held. "That was thoughtful of you, Mrs. Oakhill. But Mr. Grant allows no one to visit without his permission."

"Then I suggest he not be told."

"That would be best."

Hannah found herself beginning to back away from this formidable figure. "Evangeline tells me that you've been a very important friend to her. Caesar, isn't it?"

"I prefer to be called Mr. Stryker, if you don't mind, Mrs. Oakhill. Mr. Grant has consented to that courtesy as well."

"Yes. Yes, of course, Mr. Stryker."

"The sounds from the party have Miss Grant a good deal off her schedule, as you can see. She'll be able to sleep after her tea and some cakes. I think you should leave her now."

"Just as you say." She found she had almost called him "sir."

He swiftly poured the tea and set the cup on a table with the cakes. Then he took Evangeline's hands at the fingertips and spoke to her not as a servant might, but as a visiting gentleman. His manner and voice became incredibly kind and gentle, and the words seemed to momentarily scrub the sad film of confusion from Evangeline's eyes. "Sleep late, my lady. Then we'll walk to the park. Further than last week. And I might take you for a row on the lake."

"I'd like that, Caesar."

Without letting go of Evangeline's hands, the tall Negro turned to stare Hannah out of the room. "Good evening, Mrs. Oakhill."

Hannah hurried down the corridor with Evangeline filling her mind, and she took a wrong turn. She found herself blocked by a large, carved door, before which sat a rolling cart bearing several decanters. On a bottom shelf were three pairs of expensive men's shoes, apparently back from having been shined. This was undoubtedly Grant's bedroom.

She had already turned to go when a surging curiosity, made all the more commanding by its having struck so unexpectedly, began to overcome her.

Thinking about all that had been between her and Grant, and how excruciatingly little she really knew of her business partner after so many years, this room suddenly seemed to represent all the frustrating secrets and shadows.

Hannah found herself blushing guiltily, sweating and dreading discovery. But the intrusion into Evangeline's room had made it a bit easier and she tried the latch with no hesitation. It was open, and in a second she was standing inside.

It was a high, lovely chamber, with four immense windows looking down upon a formal garden at the rear of the house, now bathed in the pale light of the fading moon. The room was not unlike others she had seen in great houses like this, but she found herself deeply moved. Simply because it was his. Why? Why? All her exasperation could not shake the misery produced by the strength of this miserable feeling that would not die.

There were electric lights, but the only glow came from an

ornamental kerosene lamp on the desk. Turning the flame higher, she walked around, her fear of discovery entirely forgotten.

She sat at the edge of the wide bed with the single pillow, trying not to think of how she had once dreamed of a sublime life between its sheets.

At the bed's foot three shirts were laid out, no doubt the ones from which he had made the evening's selection. Taking one up gently, she held it to her cheek and breathed in all she would ever have of him.

To end the sob that had started to come up in her throat, she stood quickly and walked breathlessly around the room, frantic with longing in spite of herself.

It was then that she saw the picture.

The oil painting had been hidden from her by a Japanese screen. It hung above his desk, the only thing other than a mirror that hung upon the walls of the room.

With ringing clarity she remembered sitting for that portrait at Golden Fluss.

The year had been 1866, the height of her melancholy after the birth of Victor. Mark had brought a court painter from Vienna and given him a room for the summer while he worked. Her husband had said that he wanted to remember her as beautiful as she was then in the first years of her marriage. It was also, she had suspected, to help lift her from her gloom.

But hadn't it burned with Golden Fluss? No, she remembered. There had been trouble with the frame. It had been sent away.

Confusion began to overwhelm her. She took the painting from the wall, brought it to the lamp and turned up the light to be certain. It was she. And there was the artist's name and the date —1866.

How could this be? Why would this man, who could not know that this portrait existed, have it?

Her fingertips brushed something behind the frame. Pinned to the backing fabric was a yellowing envelope. It had been sent to this house in care of Jack Grant.

It was addressed to Mark Northern.

She carefully removed the envelope, opened the torn flap with quivering fingers and read a letter on the stationery of a Vienna art dealer who had served the Northern family for decades. It was dated in 1897, eight years before.

> My Dear Mr. Northern:
> I trust this letter finds you well after so many years. I also trust that your interest in this portrait I send remains as high as it was during the period of your long correspondence with my father, the late Hermann Bordeur.
> As it happens many times, your "lost" treasure was quite under our noses all along. My father's searches through the shops, galleries and private collections of Vienna proved a waste. I discovered quite by chance, in some letters I was cleaning out, that the picture had never been shipped here as thought. The upheavals in transportation in 1866 were such that it remained behind in Sadowa. A representative of mine, on other business in the area, looked into the situation, did some advertising and found the portrait in the hands of the very woman who had taken it from a smashed mail wagon.
> The cost of this investigation and acquisition has been not inconsiderable, but I pass it on to you confident in your continuing interest. You will be pleased to know that Monsieur Horace le Var, its painter, went on to establish a fine reputation and the portrait's value is much enhanced.
> Unfortunately, the previous owner placed the portrait for many years in proximity to bad candles, as you can see. Restoration by a specialist is very much desirable. The back of this page holds the name and address of such a man in London. I suggest you preserve it against the day you wish to have this work done.
> I wait your approval of my initiative and your remission confidently, Mr. Northern.
> Your servant,
> Edgar Bordeur

In a dream, Hannah reattached the letter and hung the picture as it was. The face that stared back at her through the years seemed to mock her blindness and stupidity with a steady, rueful gaze.

She let the terrible facts settle into her churning mind.

Mark Northern had returned from the very grave to continue to torment and betray her. If she could not see the body of her treacherous husband in Jack Grant, she could very clearly see his twisted soul. The perversity of this monster was almost beyond her comprehension. To have robbed her and shattered her heart once had not been cruel enough. He had tracked her and found a way to use his torn, deformed flesh to wound and destroy her a second time. And what shameful thefts and humiliations was he plotting in this latest return?

She now saw all the honeyed words and haunting tenderness of Jack Grant as simply manifestations of a malignant genius. The very portrait must be to him a talisman of the kind used by unspeakable West Indian sects to present an image of the victim to the destroyer.

Her first impulse was to run from the house and his evil. But almost at once her shock and trembling agitation began to fade, and the hot steel of her hatred for Mark Northern reappeared to overcome all the other feelings in her. It was with something much like exultation that she felt all the lingering passion she had felt for this brutalizer of her life flow out of her. The void was filled with a need for a great and carefully crafted vengeance, one that violated honor and civilized reason alike.

Even as she left the room and closed the door behind her, she knew the weapons of retribution must be treachery, betrayal—the same barbaric instruments he had used to tear her own soul.

Descending the marble stairway to the glittering party, she was determined that Mark Northern would see nothing of her new knowledge. For it was his continued confidence in her ignorance of his infamy that must form the foundation of her budding plan to destroy him as completely as he had once destroyed her and her father.

The nearness of this long-delayed reprisal began to raise her spirits, and she felt a cold jubilation running through her. She caught Jack Grant—*she would have to begin think of him as Mark Northern now*—at the edge of the dance floor as the orchestra switched from a string of two-steps to a stately waltz. "Come on, Jack," she called to him gaily as she dragged him to the center of the floor. "If we're partners again, it must go right down the line."

He became flustered. "Hannah, you know I wasn't cut out for a dancer."

"A young man once told me I gave wings to his feet. Are you telling me I've lost my enchantment?"

She fitted herself into his arms and began to whirl with him.

It came to her now that his unwillingness to dance with her in these years in America was just some more of his resolution not to show anything that he had been before. Now his first attempts to appear clumsy were worn away by her persistence, her laughing closeness and the irresistible beat of music he had once loved.

In minutes she had him in her power. His feet flashed and spun with all the verve and precision that Hannah remembered. She follow him into the sweeping spins and pivots and felt the years falling away. Mark—he was now Mark in her mind completely—suddenly seemed not afraid to let her see the other man in him. He almost wanted it, she thought. But she permitted not a glint of recognition to flash in her eyes.

But if he could not feel his danger, she could feel hers. Against everything in her, the feel of his body against hers, the memory of the deep-throated laugh that was the golden ghost of the hoarse rasp she now heard, pulled at her heart. She raged at a tear that broke free during one hauntingly beautiful turn, feeling better only because she knew she held more than enough loathing for this man to overcome any amount of sentimental foolishness.

"Hannah," he said. "I feel as though we just met."

"Me, too, Jack," she said sweetly, her thoughts already turning to Harlem, which was the anvil upon which she would break him.

Chapter 11

She accepted that Victor would have to fall with Mark. Her son's loyalty to her partner was as great as it was to her, if not greater. No matter. All Victor's success had sprung from her, and his share of Oakhill Development would establish itself again when her work was over. It would be a lesson of the kind she would have wished to have had earlier herself. In all cases, Oakhill Development would profit to much the same extent that Grant Majestic lost.

Trust would be the implement of Mark's downfall, as it had been for her own. He, like Victor, was extravagantly impatient with the day-to-day details and finance of business. He had been hugely happy to have her assume this work and left her detailed reports largely unread, often unopened. He knew that if anything came up worth his special attention, Hannah would bring it up with him or his bookkeepers. In fact, those bookkeepers, at Hannah's request and to their great dissatisfaction, were now about to be concerned entirely with Grant Majestic, Hannah's financial people handling the affairs of Oakhill and Grant.

Oakhill and Grant, indeed, was not a standard landholding company. At Hannah's wary insistence they had obtained properties in their individual names, not collectively, so each partner would keep autonomy in individual dealings, and dissolution, if needed, would be a simple matter. The value of the association was in the pooling of backup resources. To withstand long sieges such as the one being conducted against them in Harlem, properties outside the partnership anchored their financing. The successful skyscrapers of Oakhill Towers, two-thirds owned by Hannah, represented a disproportionate share of what stood behind the partnership. This was fair enough because Grant Majestic had liquidated more of its holdings to acquire Oakhill and Grant properties in whose profits the partnership would share evenly.

And there, Hannah saw, was Mark Northern's fatal oversight. His stand in Harlem was a good risk so long as Hannah was with him in it. Without her resources the forces of blight could overwhelm his overextended properties, drive the value down beneath what would keep the mortgage-holding banks involved and force foreclosure and ruin.

Two things were needed to obliterate him: First, he must not know that she had pulled out. She must do it slowly and in secret. If he sensed in time what was happening, he would sell with the timid-hearted with sustainable losses. Second, she must strengthen the forces that threatened him, ensuring that Mark would be ground under by events so irresistible that he might not survive even if she had remained behind him.

The initial thing would be simple. The other demanded concentrated thought, and its means of implementation were slow in coming. But come they did, in a wholly unexpected and unrelated event.

Hearing that Jack Grant was on the phone one morning and apparently quite agitated, she took the call in her office. Mark's voice was one long, hoarse snarl of worry and frustration.

"Evangeline's gone, Hannah. She's run off with that Negro—I think he said he met you—Caesar Stryker."

"Run off? What does that mean?"

"I'll read you the letter she left for me:

> Dear Father: Please don't worry about me or come after me. I will be well and happy. You must understand that I couldn't stay in that house anymore, keeping inside that room and going to that awful place when I got sick. You and Victor were awfully kind to me and helped me so much when I couldn't remember things. But I know now that I can only be happy with Caesar. I love him and he loves me. He will take care of me always. With him I feel I will get well. And then maybe we can be together again after a long time. I do love you, Father, and I am so unhappy when I think of all the misery I have caused you. If you love me the same way you will not pursue.
>
> Your sorrowful daughter,
> Evangeline

I found the damned thing on her bed this morning."

"Do you think she's safe, Jack?"

"Physically, yes. He's an intelligent man, and there's not a bit of violence in him. And I know he worships Evangeline. It's why he was so good for her and why I trusted him with her as I trusted no one else. But she's not able to be out there alone. He has no means to give her what she needs, not in care and not in material things. This could destroy whatever little progress has been made. We've got to get her back."

"Are the police involved?"

"My God, no. To them this would be the kidnapping of a white woman by a black man. It would be a bloodbath that she'd never get over. I'll line up my own people. And you can help."

"Just tell me how, Jack."

"You knew people. Serpa's crowd. They're the ones for finding somebody."

Hannah knew that he was right. "I don't know how many are willing to trust me, but I promise I'll try."

She tried hard. Her heart went out to poor Evangeline, and she had liked the strong, independent Stryker. But this was a terrible mistake for both of them.

Once again her old friend Leo was the key. Even with thinning hair, premature false teeth and a respectable bakery business, he retained his old contacts and his love for snooping and sharing. He moved through his downtown acquaintances in what had been the Serpa organization, and they in turn spread through the black Tenderloin using their connections in the numbers business that was so much a part of the Negro community.

Leo's suspicion that Stryker would be hiding Evangeline among blacks proved correct, and he phoned Hannah with an address and an apartment number. "Listen, Signora Oakhill," Leo said, his battle with English still not completely won. "I speak to the woman. She beg me not to tell her father. She want to see you first. Good idea, Signora. They say that the men Signor Grant has hired have made a large prize for the man who kills the nigger who took the white woman."

So she went alone to the address in a miserable block in the Tenderloin, almost against the foul wharves along the Hudson.

The stoop was filled railing to railing with men, their glaring black faces telling Hannah they were not there by accident. No pair of policemen in the city would have tried to force a passage through the hostile mass, but Hannah stepped forward lightly.

"I am Mrs. Oakhill to see Mr. Stryker. I'm expected."

A scholarly looking man in a frayed business suit was standing at the rear of the crush. "Let her through, boys. Caesar said it would be all right, if she was alone."

The men stood and parted grudgingly so she could step between them. They muttered to her as she passed.

"No white boys gonna touch Caesar Stryker while we alive."

"His white lady come on her own."

"Stole his brains."

"He worth a thousand white men."

"Ten thousand."

Her climb to the top floor of the ancient tenement recalled all the horror of her long-ago visit to the Hanrattys in the Five Points. She had thought that terrible places like this had faded except for the worst poor. But of course, she remembered, the Negroes were always among the worst poor so far as housing went. They were pushed from any neighborhood where improvement entered and driven to one where blight ruled supreme.

And for this they paid some of the highest rents in the city.

Books were the overwhelming feature of Caesar Stryker's flat. They were in shelves that lined most walls from floor to ceiling, piled high on desks and tables, and opened and marked on windowsills. Elsewhere the heritage of Africa marked the rooms. Tribal shields, spears, robes and headdresses formed a sharp, colorful geometry that greatly pleased the eye. Much of the furniture was thong-bound wood covered with beautifully carved and stretched animal skins.

Stryker himself was dressed in a loose, ankle-length robe with a bold black and white pattern. He wore a squarish white skullcap. The other black men in the room—there were six of them including Hannah's guide—wore suits and ties. They stood behind Stryker with great dignity, their faces unreadable.

Evangeline stood at Stryker's side, dressed as immaculately as she would have been in the Grant mansion. She was radiant, all the clouds swept out of her eyes. Her hand rested lightly on his arm. "We thank you for coming alone, Hannah." All the fear and confusion were gone from her voice.

"Indeed we do, Mrs. Oakhill. We have much to talk about. May I first introduce my colleagues? Mr. Beekman, Mr. Biesbrouck, Mr. Vance, Mr. Van Glahn, Mr. Deane and Mr. Warmerdam."

Hannah exchanged cool nods with them. "You'll have to deal with Mr. Grant, Mr. Stryker."

"Only if you'll not help us, Mrs. Oakhill."

"It's not in my hands."

"You're very modest. In my stay at Miss Grant's home I observed that you exercise enormous power over Mr. Grant."

"True or not, this isn't my business"

"I would like to think that it is, Mrs. Oakhill. You care about Miss Grant a great deal, I should hope. Going back to when she was with you as a child."

"So much so that I would never permit her to be taken advantage of, Mr. Stryker."

"I thank you for putting it so delicately. May I assure you that Miss Grant has not been abducted or coerced in any way. Her virtue, if that is on your mind, is safer with me than with any man in this city, black or white. And it will be respected until we are man and wife."

Hannah caught her breath. "Such a marriage would not be recognized."

"Because it would be performed by a minister whose face is black, and who shouts 'Hallelujah' too loud, and is too caught up with the spirit of God to stand like a white marble statue while he speaks?"

"I love Caesar," Evangeline said. "I tell you without shame that I would be with him now in every way if he would have me."

"Mr. Stryker," said Hannah, "if it's money you want I'm completely certain that Mr. Grant will include you in his affairs in a way that will make you comfortable for the rest of your days. I myself would contribute happily to that end. And we would assure your safety both inside and outside the law."

Stryker closed his eyes with vast weariness before he spoke again. "I don't want your ransom. I don't want your condescension. What I want is my freedom to provide for the woman I dearly love. Right now I'm a prisoner in this building, in this ghetto, in this skin. Mr. Grant's men would have me before I walked three blocks from here. I want them called off. I want Mr. Grant's neglect, if not his blessing."

The power and dignity she found in this solemn, handsome man impressed Hannah. "I'm sensitive to the injustices, sir," she said, using the last word with intent and respect. "But even if Miss Grant supports you fully, she will be judged—" She hesitated.

"—Not competent? You see her here now. Compare what's before you with the weeping ghost you saw in that room. Mr. Grant and Mr. Oakhill will love her perhaps, but they will not trust her. They'll never accept her potential. With them she'll die in miserable confinement."

"And what will become of her with you? She's accustomed to a life you could never give her."

A dangerous glint danced in Stryker's gray eyes. "You assume, naturally, that I'd soon have any wife of mine taking in washing, scrubbing floors and waiting on tables. Or maybe that I'd send her on the streets while her looks last."

"No, I didn't—"

"Never mind. I'm sure you find tender feeling in a black man quite amazing. Not to mention his pretentious dreams."

Hannah felt the cut in his words, as well as guilty remorse for their accuracy. "I apologize for my manner, Mr. Stryker. And I'd gratefully listen to anything you wish to tell me in your cause."

"The Grant servants are a talky lot and there's little I don't know about Miss Grant's previous life. I am as aware as anyone of what her illness has changed. But I alone know what lost things that change has found in her. There's a sweetness and loyalty, a courage and understanding that can only come from having walked through the flames. If she needs extra care and protection, I'll cheerfully give my life from this moment to make sure that she has it. But it's my thought that she'll become stronger through my love, and find a happiness she never could have known."

He caught Hannah stealing an uncomfortable look at the stately row of black men behind him. "I'm not embarrassed to speak my most personal thoughts before my brothers, Mrs. Oakhill. In that way we're much different from you. We must share everything, stand together in all or we'll be wiped from your earth even more quickly. I promise you that these gentlemen are as horrified at this mixing of races as you are. But I disregard their horror as I disregard yours."

The gray-haired man called Beekman spoke in a thin, cultured voice. "Mrs. Oakhill, the personal life of Mr. Stryker doesn't matter to us except as it concerns his safety. In this fragmented community of ours, our leaders are our only wealth, our only hope. This is no storefront preacher, all thunder and no rain. This isn't a man whose ambition is to open yet another funeral parlor or catering office. He thinks. He dreams. He plans. More than that, he has that thing people follow. If he's been lost in books and serving a white master to advance his learning, it won't be for long."

"We are organizing," Warmerdam said with an upraised fist. "There are schemes, proposals."

"For what?" Hannah asked, hearing the vehemence in the voice and watching some of the others try to quiet him.

"To break our people free of a string of repressions that Pharaoh himself might envy," said Stryker.

"But you're protected by the law."

"The law ends at the tip of a policeman's billy, Mrs. Oakhill. And across that stout wood we have the only real bridge between white flesh and black in this town."

Vance joined in, using the accents of the deepest South. "We must begin to form organizations to match the strength of the white man's. And we don't mean those captive Negro political organizations that deliver our votes for City Hall in return for a few hundred of us getting a chance at some fancy titles and a slab of the corruption money."

"Exactly," said Stryker. "What we put together must be based in economic power. It must be founded on property, on ownership and control of a major piece of the loaf that's been systematically kept from us for so long. There must not be another hundred years where we are jammed into crowded, decaying communities, paying rent to our slavemasters until it suits them to throw us out of our homes and drive us somewhere else. The day must come when a prosperous, educated person of color lives next to a white man of the same station as a respected, fully accepted neighbor."

"How will you begin?"

Some of the dark faces showed nervousness, but Stryker reassured his friends with a wave of his hand. "The men in this room along with several other leading black men in this city will shortly form the Afro–New York Realty Company."

"To what end?"

"To use your panic in Harlem to unlock the Negro community from the fetid prisons of this city's ghettoes forever. To bring the best of our people to take their place beside yours in the best housing in New York."

"How will you capitalize?" asked Hannah, testing him.

"We will issue fifty thousand shares at ten dollars each."

"Five hundred thousand dollars is not enough to buy a really significant number of properties, even in this falling market. And even if Negroes had the money to buy them, Mr. Stryker."

"For now we have no intention of buying. I mean to acquire

five-year leases on white-owned properties and guarantee them a regular annual income. With building sales as they are, owners will jump at the chance, and then I'll lease to well-off Negroes."

"You'll have to charge above-market rents to get your money out."

"My people are paying above-market now to live in stinking hovels."

Slowly Hannah began to see the shape of the way she would bring down Jack Grant. It was emerging full-blown from Caesar Stryker's vision. "To whom will you sell your shares? The real estate interests will keep out the banks and insurance companies."

"That's a problem, Mrs. Oakhill. Our wealth is in the simple businesses that your people didn't want. Our partners are morticians, caterers, cosmeticians specializing in products for black skin and hair. They are wealthy by our standards, but not yours. But they are rich in contacts with the small people. And if I can inflame their imaginations with the possibilities here—"

Warmerdam, highly agitated, couldn't stay still any longer. "For the Lord's sake, Mr. Stryker, be discreet. This woman represents every interest that will stand against us. With this knowledge she'll do us fatal damage."

Evangeline caught his fear. "Please, Hannah. Tell me you would never do that."

Stryker put his arm around her and she grew calmer. "I'm just showing Mrs. Oakhill that we have no fear of her or any of them. They'll fight us with all they have, but we'll prevail. Feel free to do your worst, Mrs. Oakhill."

Hannah took a deep breath and began her move. "Mr. Stryker, not only does the Afro–New York Realty Company have nothing to fear from me, but I would feel honored to become a silent—very silent—supporter of your operation."

"It begins, Caesar," Vance cried. "They're already coming to steal what we're trying to do."

"No," Hannah said firmly. "Let me promise you that I approve your plan with all my heart. All of us must remain dedicated to the second emancipation of the Negro to the exclusion of all else. We must see to it that black ghettoes become just a terrible memory within ten years. I will have it no other way."

"We don't need you," Warmerdam said.

"But you *do*," snapped Hannah in a voice more sharp than his. "I'm sure you're all brilliant men, successful against the heaviest odds. And I can see by your faith in Caesar Stryker that you've found a leader with the fire and energy you've been looking for. But what you are about to attempt is not your business. Not yet. It's *my* business. It has been for over thirty years and I'm *good* at it. Let me sit at Mr. Stryker's side and advise him. Let me help him train the people you'll need. And let me help you with the financing. As simple loans at low rates. I don't want any shares or any control. I don't expect payment until you're in a commanding position. I just want to stand behind your success."

"I must ask why, Mrs. Oakhill," Stryker said.

"Because I've believed in what you're doing since the first time I saw the poor as they were broiling and dying in the tenements."

"Perhaps we will have to believe you. Because I can't see how this will benefit Oakhill and Grant."

"Oakhill and Grant will not be part of this. I speak and act for Oakhill Development only. Since I can't expect the support of Jack Grant or Victor Oakhill in this matter, it will be of critical importance that they know nothing of my involvement."

Stryker turned slowly to his friends. "I think Mrs. Oakhill may have greatly increased the chances of our success."

Almost too low to be heard, one man said, "I smell deception here."

The hard, gray eyes of Stryker rested on Hannah. He seemed to see straight into her teeming mind. "Then let us hope that this deception is not directed against us. What must we do first?"

"You must marry Miss Grant at once. Only in that way can you remain alive and free, and even then it will not be easy. I would like to be the first to congratulate you. Both on your marriage and on something that the Negro race will never forget."

* * *

For Mark the year 1905 was a jumble of desperation and hope.

His annoyance with Hannah for not respecting the great threat represented by the newly formed Afro–New York Realty Company sometimes approached rage. She couldn't see that every additional black face that appeared in white Harlem made the prospect of a resurgence in sales and values more difficult.

He was not insensitive to the striking opportunity this presented for an inhumanly downtrodden people to emerge in dignity. Given a safe way to achieve this end, he thought, he would enter into it with real enthusiasm. But Hannah would have to finally realize that the prevailing fear of a growing Negro invasion of Harlem could ruin what they had achieved over a lifetime.

But the rest of their relationship appeared greatly improved. Since the night of the party at his home, much of the ice had melted out of Hannah's manner toward him. If he still saw a frosty glint in her eye when he looked deeply, he was able to quickly forget it as she laughed with him or accepted his offer to accompany him to a symphony or a ball.

Occasionally she even took dinner with him where they talked with some of the oldtime ease, even though she would allow no approach to what had been between them.

She had apparently seen no connection in his reappearance and the end of Serpa, and it would have appeared a cowardly lie to refer to what had been the terrible truth.

He realized that she held him captivated more than ever. Only Hannah could have made him agree to let stand the marriage of Evangeline to Caesar Stryker. Hannah had convinced him that his daughter's only hope of emotional stability lay in her love of the black man.

But all his attempts to visit with Evangeline had been rebuffed by Stryker, saying that he would not have her with any reminders of the world that had so nearly destroyed her. Not until she was stronger. Only for Justin did he make an exception. The rollicking nine-year-old was allowed to visit his mother whenever she wanted to see him and, to Victor's annoyance, quickly came to prefer life in the raucous streets of the Tenderloin to what he found in the world of his staid schoolmates uptown. Mark saw the beginning of a growing rift between Victor and his son. While there was strong love between them, Justin's uncontrollable ways, his headlong lunges into whatever took his fancy, irritated his father as much as Victor's meticulous calculation bothered the boy.

Any hope of regaining Justin's attention uptown was lost with the birth, late in the year, of a son to Caesar and Evangeline Stryker. The child, named Ford, was a remarkably accurate duplicate of Stryker, though fairer and with somewhat more of Evangeline's delicacy of features. Justin seemed not entirely happy with the appearance of a rival but stayed closely about to protect his place in his mother's affection.

The child's race was not important to Victor, but this evidence of Evangeline lying with another man turned him to ice.

Mark wondered how much of Stryker's steadfast exclusion of the Grant family had to do with the Grant opposition to all the Afro-New York Realty Company was trying to do. Stryker had refused all help with living accommodations, sending back Mark's money-stuffed envelopes unopened. But with the swift success of Afro-New York he had been able to move his family into better quarters in Harlem quickly.

With Stryker, the main point was always his pride. This sudden Messiah of colored might wanted no help, no quarter from his enemies. He stood at the head of a Negro army beginning its first great march to victory, and he wanted the battle lines sharply drawn.

Well, Mark thought, that suited Grant and Oakhill just fine. But Stryker proved far more formidable than ever expected.

Stryker began to turn the promise of Harlem into a Negro crusade. Storefront preachers, stone-church thunderers, politicians and business leaders delivered one message: *Come to Harlem.* Posters, handbills, pamphlets and the Negro newspapers hammered relentlessly and eloquently. There was no other topic in their editorial pages:

> THE DREAM AT LAST IN REACH
> The epic Revolution in France began with a march
> upon a building. The epic Revolution of the Negro
> people of the United States begins with a march on

a thousand buildings. And where the Bastille was a symbol to be overthrown, Harlem is a symbol to be built into our golden dreams.

Our invincible army is the Afro–New York Realty Company, and Caesar Stryker its magnificent general. All people of color must flock to join him.

It stands to reason that when a colored man becomes the agent of a building, and eventually the owner of that building, then there must come an improvement in the conditions of the colored tenants. The cycle of do-nothing, care-nothing, late-everything white ownership is broken and the lot of the Negro at last prospers.

If all in our scattered, downtrodden communities will take that dollar that would have gone for the numbers or a night on the town and put it into the shares of Caesar Stryker's Afro–New York Realty Company, we will at last break free from the bondage of the ghettoes, to the freedom of the first decent accommodations in all of Negro history.

The battle for Harlem was long and grinding. While Afro–New York was by no means the only Negro adversary, Caesar Stryker was unquestionably the leading edge of the dark wedge that entered the community. Time and again Mark believed that he had held the white forces together long enough to run the Negro organization out of funds for further expansion, but each time it held on to grow still more. All Mark's attempts to discover an unknown source of financing came to nothing.

Even when Stryker had leased and rented enough properties to produce a strong cash stream, Mark marveled at the scope of his ambitions.

As the months became years, Stryker broadened Afro–New York's leasing operation into the purchase and sale of buildings.

Mark's knowledge of the business told him that Afro–New York would have been overreaching even in the best of markets.

Stryker dealt harshly with any white interests that might interfere in any way with the freedom of colored men to come to Harlem's bright promise. After a white group bought one of his buildings and made a show of evicting all Negroes, he demonstratively bought two adjoining all-white buildings and evicted every tenant for an all-colored rent roll.

Thereafter he sold no property to whites no matter what the offer and began to give his buildings the names of Negro giants. The Douglass, the Booker T. Washington and the Du Bois, management and tenants, were as completely dark as their titles.

Stryker's legend grew vastly, and he lived up to it. His powerful intelligence and fearless vision made him every inch the pragmatic leader the black population had longed for.

In the early days of his attack on the white citadel, he had been careful—too careful, many thought—to bring the "right class" of Negro to Harlem. His literature emphasized the genteel nature of the new community and its special suitability to the prosperous Negro middle-class. It made many references to the long heritage of the Negro in New York, and how the new quarters were a reward for their long work in the building of their city.

Later, when the new migrants from the South and West Indies began to squeeze in, some landlords let in all who could pay the rent.

Whatever damage the less genteel population of Negroes was doing to Harlem, their swelling numbers greatly increased the difficulties of the besieged property owners. Unable to interest Hannah in the need for a more vigorous defense, Mark took the matter onto himself.

He brought together the toughest and most determined of the property owners and spoke to them after hours in a saloon.

"With 1910 upon us, the news of our long battle is not good," Mark began.

"We slowed them up," someone called.

"Dying slower is all we've achieved. Some might say it's early in the game for more desperate means, but I promise you it isn't."

"Okay, Grant, what's the notion?"

"Some landlords and block associations have found it already. It's up to us to organize it better and speed it up. What we need are Covenant Blocks, supported by an assessment of one half of one percent of the assessed value of all our properties."

"You mean we get whole blocks, whole sections to sign legal agreements not to sell to niggers?"

"Please. I ask that we men of high standing not use that term here. It is not undesirable that honorable men of color live among us in Harlem. We just mean to stabilize the situation."

"We understand the difference between Negroes and niggers, Mr. Grant. No lectures."

"How long do the covenants run, Grant?"

"I think ten or fifteen years will be sufficient. By 1925 Harlem will be a showplace of how the races can prosper together. Now let's get to the details."

Mark's own Harlem Landowners Improvement Association was the most forceful of the many associations that were organized. Certainly it was more high-minded than many of the others, who adapted names such as the Anglo-Saxon Committee, the White Hope Association and the Save-Harlem Order.

With this there was no longer any doubt that a war without bloodshed was raging between the races. The white Harlem newspaper, the *Home Journal*, referred incessantly to "coons," "darkies" and "black hordes." In the pages of this newspaper there was a lively debate about whether to construct twenty-four-foot-high fences (Negroes being held to be formidable climbers and jumpers) between neighborhoods. There was also a discussion of evicting all Negroes in Harlem.

Mark deplored the racist hysteria, and he saw it as the forerunner of panic. He wondered how Hannah could remain so calm.

In fact, Hannah was far from calm. Any thought she had that Caesar Stryker might be tamed to listen to her stolid advice was quickly whisked away. Although he attended carefully to her suggestions, the notions often became the departure point for a scheme that frightened her. "You're promising far too much, Mr. Stryker. And you're not consolidating before you move on. There's a limit to the money in the Negro neighborhoods. And you're taking too much of it for your shares, from people who can't afford to lose it."

"If they knew how important this was, Mrs. Oakhill, they'd be selling the gold in their teeth to buy. It's not just for themselves, but for their people."

"Ardor can't repeal the laws of business."

He let a bit of chill into his voice. "Do I hear a wavering in your promise to support us?"

"There will come a point where I couldn't save a bad situation even if I mortgaged or sold every brick I controlled."

"Come now. You're doing very well selling the properties you control in Oakhill and Grant."

"Money that goes to support Afro-New York for a good part."

"I don't like the people you're selling to, Mrs. Oakhill."

"They're all Negroes."

"The wrong sort."

"The only sort remaining. And certainly no worse than what other Negro interests are bringing in."

"There's a great deal of money left to be gotten," he said.

"Not in the hands of colored men."

"In the very best hands. Will you accompany me to a conference at the St. James Presbyterian Church? The colored brethren I'm calling together there are very conservative and most discreet. They'll feel better seeing I have white support, but they will not speak about it."

The important people of the large Negro churches downtown were a tougher nut for Stryker than his friends in commerce. They were educated, stern, stonily moral and more used to ways of reason than of emotion. They sat quietly, perhaps forty of them, around a polished table and listened to Stryker with unmoving faces.

Stryker adjusted his delivery to the audience, holding his tone low and businesslike. "Our people have found very little in this life, so they have invested the bulk of what they have in the next. That's why the funeral parlors and the churches control such a disproportionate bulk of Negro wealth in New York."

"I hope that's not disrespect we hear."

"Far from it, Reverend. It is by way of pointing out that you gentlemen in this room, through your churches, control the most unified source of Negro capital yet known."

"We are solvent and perhaps prosperous. But our income flows from a poor community, and is not as significant as you think."

"Your wealth is in your land, Reverend, not your collection basket. These churches of ours are squatting on good downtown land by the acre. It wasn't valuable to the white man when you bought it, but now it can hold the new skyscrapers. Every foot is worth a thousand times what it was."

The churchmen exchanged questioning looks. "Do you expect us to sell our churches and give money to your enterprise, Stryker?"

"Only in a way," Stryker said. "Hear me. If we don't support and concentrate our forces now—in Harlem—we'll miss our chance for a hundred years. Your churches, your congregations, belong where Negro culture will be centered. Come up. Land is expensive here, cheap uptown for the moment. It won't last. Take your gains from the white man's pocket and bring it to Harlem in the form of land that will stand with the best. You'll have enough to win control of entire blocks and open them to us. You can build churches that will put what you have now to laughable shame."

"How do you benefit, Mr. Stryker?"

"I move my race further ahead in a couple of short years than anyone has been able to do since the first blackbirders landed slaves. And the war is now in balance. We're losing our momentum. If we can't show the enemy that we've become too strong for his money to outlast us and drive us out again, he'll beat us."

"I'm against this," an old man at the end of the table said. "If we leave where we are we'll just be moving to a new ghetto. One of our own design this time."

"*Ghetto?*" Stryker exploded, momentarily forgetting his

smooth new manners. "Do you think Harlem is one more Niggertown? It's *unique*. There we have a symbol of distinction, not derogation. Broad, clean, tree-lined streets. Spacious homes with the best modern facilities. The finest we've ever had to live in. You gentlemen spend your lives contemplating sin. Well, let me tell you that if you remain sitting down here, you'll have on your souls the greatest sin yet perpetrated against our race."

This outburst broke the rigid masks of the faces around the table. The presiding pastor got to his feet slowly. "We will meet among ourselves, Brother Stryker. You will have our views before the end of tomorrow. Let us thank you for yours."

Suspicious eyes were upon Hannah as she walked out with Stryker, but he made no move to enlighten his colleagues as to who this obviously approving white woman might be. But she had plainly accomplished Stryker's purpose of hinting that his support was broad and important enough to cross the battle lines.

"I think you have them, Mr. Stryker," she whispered. "The black churches are coming to Harlem."

"And they'll be glad of it, Mrs. Oakhill. The churches will be the leading holder of land in Harlem long after Afro-New York is forgotten."

In the next year, just as predicted, entire blocks fell into the hands of churches migrating north. Sometimes the sales were made by subterfuge that employed white intermediaries or exceptionally light-skinned Negroes. But, increasingly, many were made openly to frightened owners who had simply become discouraged by the seeming unstoppability of the black flood.

The cream of the New York Negroes led the way to the prestige of a Harlem address. People of the Tenderloin dreamed of marrying and moving to a home in Harlem as the ultimate goal of life. As churches cleansed their properties of whites, there were all the colored takers they could have asked for.

Brought often to Harlem on business, Hannah sometimes visited Frank Chumlin and the former Katie Hanratty in their fine home there.

Frank wasn't young anymore, and there were business problems that kept him away long hours. He was finding that the new automobiles were to be more than a fad; their popularity was already beginning to make inroads into the business of selling leather goods for horses and carriages. Chumlin's fine stock of whips and bridles was moving sluggishly, and his sons were getting out of the establishment he had worked so hard to build.

It didn't matter, really, he told Hannah. He had taken a nice dollar out of the business over twenty years and possessed all he had ever wanted—a fine home in the best part of the city, a home that he could pass on to subsequent generations of his family.

Katie, as chipper and pretty as she had been as a girl, showed Hannah an airy, bright ten-room house surrounded by trees, shrubs and lovely flowers. Her grandchildren were always visiting, filling the house with delightful noise as they enjoyed a day in the "country" with their still-young grandparents. But lately they had been playing with black children, Hannah noticed. And there were small signs of worry appearing in Katie's face.

"The two new buildin's on the next block were slow rentin', Hannah. Just a few families were in. White. Then that Afro-New York Realty took them over and rented them fast. All Negroes. They didn't toss the whites out, but they left."

"Are the Negroes bad neighbors?"

"Not at all. They're churchgoin', clean and hard-workin' as us. But you know it's not what Frank had in mind. It's not what he was expectin' in a respectable neighborhood. And maybe this batch is okay. But what about the ones in the next buildin' to go? We're afraid of bein' alone with 'em up here."

"The children seem to get on, Katie."

"Yeah. Some of the white moms won't let their kids play with the blacks. Not us. We're pretty good friends with some of 'em. Like the Van Camps. Lewis is a manager for Lenox Caterers. Myra teaches piano. Even has me playin' some. Sometimes I think they're as worried as we are about what we invested in here. We both got all we have sunk into Harlem."

Hannah began to feel the chill wind of doubt about what she was doing.

She eventually met Myra and Lewis Van Camp. They were reserved and, for all the youth of their children, middle aged.

"I'm not reassured by what we see coming in, Mrs. Oakhill," said Myra. "The Old Dominion Line is starting to run a heavier schedule from the Carolinas. Field hands are what they're bringing up. Illiterate field hands. Good people, but they don't belong here."

"They can't afford houses like these," Hannah said. "Not even to rent."

"They're not coming into houses like these. The Italians and Jews who aren't locked into Harlem the way we are—they have other places to go. When they move out of their flats the field hands and West Indians move in."

"I've watched the West Indians. They're natural businessmen. Very industrious. An asset."

Lewis Van Camp grunted his disagreement. "When they get ten cents ahead they open a business, that's for sure. But there's more to it. They're uppity and mean. Too mean to work for anybody but themselves, some say. They will not accept orders from their betters. They don't like us. We don't like them."

"But you're all Negroes."

"Mrs. Oakhill, we're Americans and they're foreigners. They speak French and make a fuss on Bastille Day. Others speak Spanish and others hang pictures of the Danish king on their walls. The ones from St. Vincent celebrate the British holidays and fly the Union Jack instead of the Stars and Stripes."

"Anyway," said Katie grimly, "we've all got to try to hold on."

"Yes," said Myra, her pretty face showing signs of fright, "All of us."

Whites divided, Negroes divided and all of them frightened, thought Hannah. Where had the dream gone so quickly? She began to wonder again if she had helped the beginning of something terrible.

With genuine horror Mark watched the start of the downward slide of the Harlem dream. It drove him half mad because there was still time to reverse the descent. He pleaded desperately for foresight, for a higher morality to preserve what was slipping away. And he poured money against the tide. When Hannah would allow no more Oakhill and Grant funds and obligations to go into Harlem, limiting Victor's participation to his own smaller share of the company, Mark committed Grant Majestic to the limit. His creditors were confident that Hannah Oakhill would not ultimately deny him her still considerable reserves, all anchored in solid, well-financed old buildings and skyscrapers.

It was Mark's very reputation as a bulwark of the white community that undermined him. It became known that he had bought key properties scheduled to be sold to Negroes by faltering signers of the covenants. Many saw him as the means to sell out and still partially salve their consciences. He had arrived back at the problem encountered in the earliest part of the slide.

He might have given up if there had not been islands of hope. There were still blocks where prosperous Negroes and whites lived easily together. The great colored men who had come north to Harlem remained, trying to regain equilibrium for their fragile vision. And although the dark population had soared to over fifty percent in Harlem, they still numbered not much above 50,000, mostly contained between 130th Street to the south and 145th Street north, and running west from Fifth Avenue to Eighth. Many "marooned" white families were trying to hold on, forming a potential nucleus for balance.

Best of all, the Negro professionals had come almost to a man, and they had bought the finest homes and still had considerable capital. They were the foundations of the Negro churches, who had built handsomely and also acquired some magnificent churches from white congregations who were no longer numerous enough to sustain them.

The struggle went on years longer, but in the end there was not a great enough Negro economic base. For all Negroes had bought in Harlem, the community was ultimately owned by white money. "We've got them," Mark finally heard one landlord say. "The niggers can't go back. The ghettoes they left behind them filled up with micks and guineas. It's time for a squeeze."

Rents rose inexorably. Money for other things, always scarce in the Negro community, flowed to the landlords. The economic life of Harlem slowed. The residents who had stretched themselves to buy the enormous houses found they could not sustain them, not alone.

Breaking the beautiful ten and fifteen-room houses and huge flats into smaller apartments did not really start with the landlords, though. The dwellers slowly did it themselves.

The lovely Harlem housing had always been far too big for the small Negro families that took them. Now families of the same blood took the pressure off themselves by doubling up and tripling up in what had been single-family housing.

Soon the magnificent buildings were everywhere gradually broken up with crude walls that turned the spaces into steaming holes. Leases to Negro realty companies were increasingly not renewed so such work could be done. Floors that once took in forty dollars a month were now taking in one hundred and twenty-five dollars for white landlords.

In short years the clipped, hurried accents that had always been heard in the New York Negro community were overwhelmed by the long drawl and idiom of the South. The farm had come to the city, and met trouble.

In full command as the steamers landed more tenants every day, the landlords saw no reason to make even the most rudimentary repairs or make any screenings of applicants. The clean were crushed by the dirty, the pure by the immoral, the honest by the criminal.

Enormous, leaking fissures were opening as the dark flood built behind the dam thrown up by Mark and the more stubborn owners. Prices of the properties had plummeted, and many feared they would go still lower. Some of the less stalwart, afraid of a selling stampede, began to unload and themselves started the rush.

By the time Mark admitted to himself that the downward spiral could be slowed no longer, the banks were beginning to move on both Grant Majestic and Oakhill and Grant. He lamented his heedless stubbornness and thanked heaven for Hannah's prudence.

Hannah could hardly bear to visit Harlem anymore. The tragedy she had begun through Caesar Stryker sickened her. She accepted the responsibility for every lovely building falling to decay, for every ruined white family and for the tens of thousands of Negroes who had seen the brightest opportunity they ever had fade into bitterness and abomination.

The fact that she had slipped her own separately kept holdings out of Oakhill and Grant while prices were still high intensified her guilt.

To quiet her unease, she contrived to heap great quantities of blame on Mark. His evil had driven her to distraction. Made her half mad. She, after all, could not have conceived of where the road would lead.

Over her years with Oakhill and Grant she had been coldly aware of her capacity for cruelty to this man who had so richly earned it. If she could often laugh with him and accompany him on pleasant occasions, she didn't let her enjoying it bother her. She was certain it was no more than an inspired form of acting that would make his fall and ruin all the more unexpected and devastating.

He would come to her soon to cover him. But meanwhile she had to deal with Caesar Stryker.

Hannah's business with Stryker had kept her close to his family through the years. And if she was greatly troubled by what she saw of his business, what she saw in his home heartened her.

Stryker and Evangeline were transformed in one another's presence. The harsh manner he had fallen into in his work dropped away in the company of his wife. He was always smiling and playful with her, forgiving, tender and protective. As for Evangeline, it was as if her ravaged mind found strength and nourishment in his every touch and word. She could go for weeks without a hint of her weakness, and even when seen in withdrawn or erratic behavior it was only at times of extreme stress.

Their flourishing son was the brightest thing in their lives, and Hannah never heard either of them chastise him. Indeed, there was little to chide Ford about.

At ten he was quiet, though not gloomy, and had a mind broken into a thousand compartments. He hardly knew a moment of the confusion expected in a child. When little more than a toddler, his idea of a game had been to take charge of the washed crockery and silver and sort it into the correct piles. As he grew older his room had filled with a dozen collections—jars, insects, autographs, whittled figures—all cataloged into carefully filed copybooks. His room was kept as precisely as a military barracks and his bane was a visit from the cataclysmically untidy Justin. "He's like a bomb on legs," Ford said to Hannah," his voice breaking with annoyance and adolescence. "He's interested in what goes up in the air, not the pieces that come down."

Justin, eight years older than Ford and ready to leave for college, had grown up in two homes, his own and Stryker's. He had never managed to get on with Ford, whom he still saw an interloper, but Evangeline's gentleness and frailty and Caesar's freewheeling ways drew him more than his father's hard-driving precision. He was to enter the architectural program at Yale at Victor's insistence, but showed as little patience with formal education as his father had. Hannah had to speak to him sharply when he talked about running off to England to enlist in the exciting new war against the Hun.

"The nice thing about a war, Grandma, is that nobody's after you to keep things neat."

* * *

Hannah was having difficulties with Stryker. "Mr. Stryker, the integrity of a business is reflected chiefly in the honesty of its prospectus. I believe that yours is approaching the fraudulent. You describe properties of your company that I know you've bought with ninety-day cancellation clauses. And that you've canceled sales and ownership by the time the buyers purchase your shares."

"As a Negro enterprise, Afro-New York has for the moment to answer to a morality higher than the mere business ethic. We can't afford to show our current, temporary weakness to the community that supports us. We would fail, and we can't afford that ever. Afro-New York must be the symbol of the possibility—no, the certainty—of Negro business success. The cornerstone and inspiration of a flourishing, self-sustaining Negro economy. I am no thief, Mrs. Oakhill. You can see that in the way I live."

He had never faltered in his message that an investment in Afro-New York was a moral obligation of the Negro. His protean powers of appeal, based in his toweringly evident sincerity, had pulled huge amounts of money from the wealthiest Negroes and were now reaching down to the poorest. But the shares were now secured by a vastly weakened foundation of properties mortgaged to the last nail, while Stryker continued to extend himself.

"The banks and shareholders will never move against me," Stryker promised. "They know that what I'm trying to do can't be permitted to go under."

For a time he was right. Significant forbearance saved him until it became obvious that he would not stop going forward until he had brought down everyone who trusted him.

There had been stockholder suits earlier, but now they became large and well publicized, and the weakness of the company and the fraudulence of its offerings became widely known. The feared crumbling of community confidence started.

Stryker avoided jail in the civil suit, but the company had to use what little reserves it had to pay damages and refund investments.

Now Stryker wrote desperately to the Negro giants, including Booker T. Washington, asking for the support of their names or for their direct financial involvement. But they had seen the sad, if understandable, deceptions of the company, and they turned him down to a man.

Almost all the mortgages being already well in arrears, the creditors moved in and the Afro–New York Realty Company quickly failed. Its share in Harlem properties had never been overwhelming, and its collapse did not greatly alter the downslide of Harlem as a matter of dollars and cents. But the company had been the beacon to which the movement had steered. And as it was extinguished, the weakened spirit of Harlem flickered out with it.

In the hearts of his people, Caesar Stryker fell from inspired leader to vile betrayer as all who had sent him their hard-won money were swallowed up. He had ravaged the meager capital pool of the Negro community, dissipated the sweated savings of the people who trusted him.

"Some say Jesus was black," a preacher said. "Why not Judas too?"

The proud man was crushed, and Hannah soon learned that his shame would no longer permit her in his home. He never knew that her own shame was no less great.

Even though it was far too late to save his company with any amount of her capital, she guiltily offered him the use of whatever he needed for his personal debts or reestablishment. He never answered any of her messages.

When Hannah visited Katie Hanratty Chumlin for the last time, she was shocked to the roots by what she found on the once-beautiful block.

The spacious single-family buildings had been broken up into tiny burrows that increased the population of the area tenfold. Even the most caring black owners had not been able to hold out against the economic necessities. The neat flower gardens in the front yards were nothing but patches of mud and dirt, overrun by wild children whose parents were away all day trying to get rent and food. The driveways that were to hold fine carriages held decrepit pushcarts. Garbage collections had become spotty because it was well known that these "black animals" preferred to live among their offal. For much the same reason, repairs and maintenance by owners were, as far as Hannah could see, nonexistent.

The Chumlin house was not so much run down as dispirited. The iron gate had been stolen and replaced by the top of a packing crate bound to the gatepost. And though the front yard was swept and clean, what perennial flowers remained were losing the battle to weeds and the lack of replacement for winter losses.

The biggest change was in Katie. The hope and high spirits that had always shone out of her were gone, submerged by harried gloom. "The grandchildren don't come anymore. Or my kids either. The streets are gettin' dangerous if you have white skin. I have a hunch that the white landlords are behind a lot of it. They want houses like this so they can break them up inside for black people. They send their agents all the time to get us to sell. The story is the same. Nothin' can stop the change, they say. It's comin'. Then they tell you a half-dozen names of white people who are goin', whether or not they are. Get what you can now, they say. Before it's worthless."

Hannah wanted to tell her that they were right, to get out now while something could be salvaged, but her shame wouldn't let her. "Maybe things will turn up if enough good people hang on," she said. "What about your black friends, the Van Camps? They're still here, aren't they?"

"You might say so," Katie said with a bitter twist of her mouth. "Lewis came down with some sort of fever a couple of winters back. The house had them so strapped for money that he let one of the herb healers work on him. An intelligent man like that. The herbs didn't work. Or the bleedings. Then he was dead."

"My God, what did Myra do?"

"She'd never worked. She thought the house might support her. So she let some butcher break it up for rent like the others, and he took her for most of what she had left. She wasn't strong enough to do all the work or collect the rent from the meaner ones, so she lost everythin'."

"Where did she go?"

Tears started down Katie's cheeks. "Nowhere. She's still in the big house, livin' in what used to a maid's room with her five children."

"How does she support them?"

Katie had to gather herself to answer. "She sleeps with some of the other renters, and sometimes the agent. Usually she waits until her children are out on the streets, but sometimes the callers are impatient." She wiped her eyes and looked up at the high ceilings and wainscoted walls. "This was the only place we ever wanted to be, Hannah."

Hannah's heart twisted with pain.

While Katie was serving coffee there was a loud, metallic clatter from the front and the raucous voices of young boys. "The kids grab the ash barrels from inside the fence and roll 'em down the hill. Frank'll get 'em later."

Almost immediately there was the thump of the door knocker. When Katie opened the door, Hannah could see a sleek black man in an expensive suit tipping his hat.

"I'm from Gale and Barker Realty, Madame," she heard him say. "Please allow me to leave my card. We are concerned about the situation of people of your race stranded in these unfortunate surroundings. Mrs. Bowland, who sold to us only yesterday, said she hoped her good friend Mrs. Chumlin would soon do the same."

Hannah watched Katie stare numbly at the card in his hand. As she glanced at it and then the smiling black face, a gust of wind sent a storm of garbage and old newspapers whirling down the street behind him.

Now Katie took the card. "I think Mr. Chumlin will call on you," she said suddenly.

After the door had closed she leaned back against it, sobbing. "Dear Jesus," she called. *Punish whoever did this to us.*"

The long-awaited day came for Hannah. Mark was there waiting for her at the offices of Oakhill Development early one morning, looking as though he hadn't slept in a month. There was fury and agitation in his every movement, and he was talking before she had removed her coat.

"The banks have cut us off. I can't believe it. They said we don't have enough behind us anymore."

"Is that important now?" she asked innocently. "You're not thinking of buying any more in Harlem, are you?"

"Of course not. It's over, even I know that. Those values won't come back in our lifetime. But we can save something if we can renovate what we have and go with the mass-rental market. I hate to do it, but that's what would happen anyway if we lost the buildings to the banks. And lose them we will if they don't give us some time and money. Thanks to me we're mortgaged out the window."

"I tried to warn you often enough."

"Indeed you did. Not let's get together with our bookkeepers. We can show those banks pretty fast that we've got more than enough in our other companies to secure our credit."

"What's the condition of Grant Majestic?"

He looked startled. "You know that better than I do, Hannah. It's disappeared into Harlem. Every cent and a ton of debt on top of it."

"Yes, it has disappeared, hasn't it?"

"It's all just liabilities to be balanced against the equity in Oakhill Development and Oakhill Towers."

She didn't let her tone change at all. "You assume that it would be wise to burden prudently run enterprises with the rescue of your speculations."

He turned, bewildered. "Oakhill and Grant was something of a speculation from the beginning, Hannah. We both understood that, didn't we? And while you haven't plunged as deeply as I have, your properties will be rescued as well."

"It happens that my properties have already been rescued, Jack. I sold them steadily as the game went bad. It shows how wise it was to keep ownership in individual names. So the bad judgment couldn't outweigh the good."

By this time Mark looked as though he weren't hearing correctly. "Are you telling me you've been pulling out properties without telling me?"

"It was all there in the books."

"Not in my books."

"We agreed to record our transactions separately. You can't be upset because I was more successful than you. And I covered far more than my share of joint expenses over the past months. I can show you that."

He brightened. "But all this means you sold at good prices. While I was throwing money away, you were saving it behind my back. My God. What a wonderful lesson. We may not *need* the bankers to get out of this."

"For me, there's nothing to get out of."

"What are you *talking* about, Hannah? Oakhill and Grant is a partnership."

"Dissolvable on one month's notice by any of the partners. This is your notice. The legal papers will follow. I'll meet my share of our expenses until then."

She could hardly hear him. "Hannah. I can't believe this. All the years. There was more between us than just business, damn it."

He was struggling in the nightmare she had planned so carefully for him, but her pleasure was somehow eluding her. She had to steel herself to go on. "If you feel there was, I would be happy to meet your share of the expenses for the month, in compensation."

His brow began to knot in the anger that was joining his confusion. "You know what I mean. I had a right to expect trust between us."

There it was.

What she had waited for since she had left Golden Fluss. Now she was on her feet, her face inches from his. "To hear the word 'trust' in the mouth of Mark Northern is a monstrous thing."

No amount of anticipation could have prepared her for the terrible effect of the end of the long deception. No lightning strike could have hit him harder, paralyzed him more completely or brought such instant death of spirit. Only the pain that flamed in his eye told her that there was still a soul alive in him. He could utter no word. She went on until she was spent.

"Nothing I could say to you, nothing I could do to you would ever begin to repay you for your years of treachery and theft. If you find my little punishment a bit elaborate, I can assure you it isn't a patch on what you brought me and my father. I sometimes thought you were a vengeance sent by the Christian God Himself. No injury was enough for you. Our lands weren't enough. You came like a murderous thief for my heart and my soul. And when you got them you spit on them. I had no doubt, when my eyes opened at last, that you had planned more and worse, and I feared what it might be. But I braved it. To ruin you as you did me, and maybe at last get free of this rotting hatred. Now go from here, Mr. Northern. And let me hear nothing from you while this world still spins."

She pulled away his eyepatch, revealing the awful ruin beneath. "How does it feel to have all your hideous truths be seen?"

As great as her fury had been, it did not far surpass Victor's when he came to her hours later. "What are you *doing*, Mother? I don't understand you."

"I'm sure he explained everything."

"He explained *nothing*. . . . He's our partner."

"Not anymore."

"We can't desert Jack."

"I'm running this company, and we have."

"Then I'm out."

"That's a disastrous decision you've made."

"I'm taking Oakhill Towers for me and Jack."

"Not while I own two-thirds of the shares."

"Mother, for the sweet love of God—"

"All right. I'll save your honor with a man who has none himself, since nothing else will do. We'll split the business in half. Take your pick of the properties up to a value of fifty percent. But that's it between us." She heard her voice breaking. "Go to your precious partner and be damned."

When she tried to strike him he caught her hand and held on, completely perplexed. "Why has it always been like this between us? Why haven't I ever been able to reach you, Mother?"

Hannah spat the words. "Because you were conceived a bastard. In the worst kind of shame and pain. Your father was a stupid, peasant beast who raped me. I prayed that you wouldn't be born. You have his eyes, his mouth, his voice. The only thing I have to be grateful for is that there's nothing in you of the man I married, who was worse yet. I've always tried to love you, but, God forgive me, I never could love you enough. Now I want to be free of that face that never lets me forget."

Victor stared at her until she thought the brutal image of Hunzak would leap out of him to strangle her.

She was glad that he backed wide-eyed out of the office then, for in another moment she might have told him that Jack Grant had likely been responsible for the rape of his new partner's mother.

All the things that had festered in her for all the years were now purged. She was triumphant everywhere. But she fell across her desk and wept far into the night, not daring to confront why.

Mark suddenly felt a thousand years old. The vibrant youth that had survived intact in his body and spirit was gone in an instant. He had been finally led to destruction by his shameful lack of courage. After his endless deceptions, she would quite properly hear none of his explanations and protests. The loss of a lifetime's effort meant nothing to him. The loss of Hannah was his finish.

He didn't miss the new anguish in Victor. Was it just his shock at the way Hannah had turned upon them? Or had she told him something terrible, things that tore away the lies about a gentle father fallen in battle? If she had, Mark would never know about it, because other than describing the division of the business, Victor never told him a word of what had been said to him in Hannah's office. And for that Mark was grateful.

Victor did all he could to make up to him for Hannah's cruel defection. Over Mark's protests he made him a full partner in all that was received in the breakup. They would remain Oakhill and Grant.

But for Mark, the fire had lost its heat. The work was empty. His step lost its fighter's spring at last. Something settled into his chest that reduced his already hoarse voice into a husky whisper, and he found himself hoping that the affliction would grow fatally worse.

Hannah missed nothing in her attempts to help the ruined Strykers. But in adversity, Stryker's pride was a dozen times greater than it had been at the peak of his success.

Bankrupt in every way, he would accept not a penny from Hannah or anyone else. He was disgraced in his own community and a figure of derision to the whites.

Soon he was forced to move Evangeline and Ford to a grim tenement. He seemed to accept gladly the menial, backbreaking jobs he took to support his family, as if he were seeking absolution for his failure in the humiliation. He again requested that Hannah stay away, and even Justin, to his heartbroken consternation, was told to spend his time with his own father when not at school.

With Stryker gone so much, Hannah felt it was her responsibility to look in secretly on Evangeline and Ford, and she didn't like what she saw.

The change in Stryker—he was now almost always sullen, tense and distracted—frightened Evangeline even as he tried his best to be kind to her. Her husband's long absences gave her no one to go to, no one to calm her when the demons returned. Her delicate mind began very gradually to unhinge. She spent more hours in a world no one else could reach. Ford tried to look after her, but for all his maturity it was beyond his ability.

Hannah's dilemma was solved by Mark, who found the same things she did and took an obvious remedy. Ford told Hannah about it.

"My mother won't go against what my father wants, Mrs. Oakhill. She won't take anything. But Mr. Grant gives me enough to take care of her without father knowing. I tell her I do jobs after school."

"Do you think she's getting worse?"

"Yes, and she knows it. She asked Mr. Grant to look after me. He doesn't have to. I'm sticking with my family."

"I thought you would."

"I'm proud of my father, Mrs. Oakhill. I think he's the bravest man who ever lived. Nobody ever tried harder to do the right things for us than he did. I hate everybody who's treated him badly."

Hannah had caught the inflection on the word "us," and knew he did not mean only the Stryker family. With Stryker's refined features and his mother's fairness, Ford might have thought of himself as white. But he didn't. His father's heritage would not die in Ford Stryker.

Hannah hugged him, and drops of love were squeezed from her hardened heart. "You must let me see you whenever I can, Ford."

Months later, Stryker saw the damage his pride was doing and permitted some visits from Mark and Hannah, although, of course, never together. He might have let Ford leave the neighborhood school and attend a fine private school at their expense, but Ford would not go.

Victor never went to visit the woman he had loved so. Hannah understood this was mostly in deference to Stryker. But she had a feeling that he also wished to stay away from Ford, so the handsome boy wouldn't remind him that Evangeline had lain with another.

And besides that, Victor had more than sufficient trouble with his own children.

With the twins, George and Jana, in their middle twenties and Justin only a couple of years younger, Victor should have been free of most concerns about his offspring. That was not the case.

Justin was in many ways the most vexing. Although the boy had not a drop of real malice anywhere in him and was unfailingly kind to all the people he loved, he was congenitally unable to get along with anyone who thought differently than he did, including Victor. Now growing to a wide, thickly made young man with an indiscriminately shaped nose and dark hair so dense it could not be made to lie down, he was saved from physical mediocrity by his mother's riveting blue eyes and startling smile. But this smile, lavished elsewhere, was seldom seen by his father.

Justin's rebellious visits to his mother and Stryker had distressed Victor, and the boy's pointed disobedience and willfulness had left a distinct gap between them. "She's my mother," Justin had said, "and if you gave up on her, I didn't."

But there was more to their antipathy than that. From the way they viewed the world, they might have been on two different planets.

Victor took the serious view. Life was not for fun, but for dedication. "Man is on earth to build a better place than he found, setting a carefully considered goal and advancing toward it with sacrifice and precision."

"That belongs on a sampler," was Justin's response.

Justin thought that life was too beautiful and multifarious not to pay attention to each distraction that happened by, provided the distraction had the possibility of great excitement and pleasure. He was no libertine, but he was unable to understand why anyone would engage in anything that didn't fill him almost instantly with delight. Or why a person would not move promptly away from whatever no longer amused. "You put up with something rotten, and pretty soon you get used to it," he said.

His mind was as stalking and wide-ranging as Victor's. In his short time of dabbling at work in the family companies, he had learned as much as many of the old employees had in entire careers.

At Yale his marks had been good in those courses that interested him, and Victor hoped that the architectural studies he had insisted upon would spark him into business.

Out of school he had listened patiently to his father's exhortation to come into Oakhill Development, the need for discipline being mentioned often. Justin, however, could not see the point in piling up mountains of gray stone for the lifetime imprisonment of toilers. He wished to explore the opportunities of the greatest explosion of progress the millennium had known, and he was promptly off to discover the anticipated wonders of the 1920s.

In rapid order he ran through dalliances with automobiles (sales and racing), airplanes (commuting and sightseeing), radio (dealerships and home communication) and, in between, played a skilled first base for a semi-pro team in Yonkers.

At last father and son became afraid to speak with one another for fear of setting off a long, loud and unpleasant debate. Victor mentally wrote Justin out of the future of his business.

As for George and Jana, there was no friction with them. And "them" was the only way he could think about the twins he had produced with Julia. The almost unhealthy attachment they had shown as children had grown stronger if anything, although they now took some pains to cover it. They "dated," as the new term had it, but Victor had no trouble seeing that their interests were only in each other. Still, Victor entertained hopes that time would bring their attentions to others, and that he would have the grandchildren that the butterfly affections of Justin seemed destined to deny him. Then, he hoped, he could like them better.

George and Jana's closeness was so frequently remarked because they could not escape attention. They made an incredibly striking couple, their beauty made more compelling in tandem because of their remarkable resemblance. They radiated a cold symmetry, with elegant, downward-turning noses above full lips that always seemed too moist, too glistening. Their hair was as black, lustrous and straight as an Indian's, and worn long and flowing.

They were both tall, with George running to a tight, refined version of Serpa's physique and Jana to Julia's good, slender, full-breasted body. Both moved like angels, gliding over the ground together and conversing always in their soft, purring voices.

Each had a genius for grooming, their clothing always exquisitely in advance of the mode. They selected just the right motorcar, a handsome Packard Phaeton, and drove it swiftly to unexplained destinations.

"We have more friends than you know, Father."

"We'd bring them home, but they wouldn't come up to your standards anymore than we do."

In their eyes Victor saw too much of the barely contained malevolence of their grandfather, Benedetto Serpa.

Victor was sure Julia had come into a substantial bit of money upon the violent death of her father, although she never mentioned it or made a sign that she would share it with her returned husband. She asked for little from him, and her children always had far more than his allowance to them would have permitted. Which was not to say that they were satisfied.

Unlike Justin, the twins had been frequent visitors to Oakhill Development. They had asked many questions and spent long, patient hours learning how the business worked in product and profit.

Victor should have been gratified, but he saw none of what had shone in his own eyes when he had begun to thrill at the marvel that was a building. Their questions were weighted heavily to the financial maneuvering. In Jana especially he sensed a love of the economic side of the business, the thing that made Hannah such a power.

"Might I study some of these ledgers with one of the bookkeepers someday?" she asked. "That would be more fun than tennis."

For all their hanging about, neither gave any hint of wishing to join the organization. Free from the schooling they had mastered so easily, they appeared content, despite Victor's plainly-voiced annoyance, to live the lives of rich children. Their only contemplation of the future was seen in their plain desire to become far richer when their share of the Oakhill properties fell into their hands.

With the alienation of his children, the split from his mother and the drifting away of Grant in his crushed humiliation, Victor felt the awful clutch of loneliness that was the endless curse of this family. He contemplated what Hannah's life must be now, and shivered for her.

Something terrible was happening to Hannah. Having achieved the relief of revenge, there was nothing left to keep her savagely suppressed love of Mark from growing again like the roots of a cut-down oak. The more she tried to thrust her mind away from him, the more the best days of the past returned to her. And now that she was completely adrift she realized how important he had been to her, even in the years when she was bringing him along to his destruction. Her only respite was in her fevered dreams, when she sometimes felt herself again beneath him, circled by his powerful arms in a long-ago forest in the West.

And there was Victor. Whatever her emotional difficulties with him, he had been the son of her flesh somewhere deep in her, and a reliable, exciting partner whose drive made her work always surprising and interesting. Now the work dragged.

But by this time pain was such a companion that she knew she could live with it and survive if she could but gather her concentration again. Oakhill Development being all she had, she began to dissolve herself in it. Even with what she had given to Victor and lost with Stryker, the business was strong, both in its foundation of properties and the cash it had accumulated in the timely sale of the Harlem holdings. She was resolved that she would put her stamp on the buildings of the 1920s, surpassing anything to be achieved by Oakhill and Grant, now her rivals.

In a furious year of effort, she put her resources to work buying and building in the financial district as she became convinced that the New York Stock Exchange would one day power the world. More speculatively, she sought broad, flat properties outside of Manhattan in Queens County. Commercial air service would explode in importance as surely as the next dawn, and she was going to hold lightly rented acres that would just pay her taxes until the first major airport was built on the land.

She might eventually have fully controlled her memories of

Mark and lived in numbed industriousness for the rest of her life. But on one burning morning in August, she recognized Leo's voice at the other end of the telephone. After some nervous greetings he asked her to meet him at an address that had been at the heart of the Five Points at its murderous peak. Indeed, she knew that the mentioned street had not improved greatly.

"What is it, Leo? Is there trouble?"

"A man is dying, Mrs. Oakhill," Leo said after some hesitation. "It will help his soul if you come to him."

The huge head on the dirty, sweat-soaked pillow had so changed that she might not have recognized the man except that every line of those sunken features, every hair of the fierce, drooping mustache, now almost white, had been burned into her brain in one awful hour in The Ships.

Only the last dregs of evil strength were left in Anthony Rendino. The deeply sunken eyes that turned to her above the caved cheeks spoke of the end of a long and wasting disease. For all his weakness there was a furious urgency in his voice, so she did not have to kneel close to him to hear.

"Signora Oakhill. The new priest will not come to make my last peace. Only Father Alleghiere, rest his soul, understood how it was in those days. But I will make my peace with you."

She tried not to remember the soft clink of the chain in his hand as he had pressed past her to Dennis Lawson. "It's not in my power to forgive your murders," she said.

"It is not that, signora. It was your own life that I was so ready to take. That would have given me great grief, because you were a great lady and the only love of Benedetto Serpa. I thank St. Jude every day that Signor Grant was given to see reason and to let you go without foolish attempts to fight against us. He was not only wise but brave. Even I felt sadness to see how it destroyed his life as it saved yours, signora."

A hot nail of pain drove into him somewhere and he cried out piteously. The sweat ran from him in streams. His eyes closed from the agony, so he did not see that his own pain was as nothing compared to hers. He groped out with his hand, his words trembling with fear and effort. "It is close. *Please*, signora. Take my hand to tell me you forgive what we have done. Take a moment off the time I will burn in hell."

"No, Mr. Rendino," she said, hardly able to find breath. "That I will not do."

His last, quavering wail faded behind her as she ran for the sagging door.

Mark was not at home. After her headlong dash across town, a servant told her that he had gone out early in the morning. The cook had prepared a picnic basket for several, and Mr. Grant had taken it with him. He had left no destination.

It being Sunday she could think of no other place to try but Victor's, and she directed her driver to speed to his house. The streets had never adapted to the mixed tangle of horse-drawn vehicles and the automobiles that were supplanting them, and the trip was impossibly slow. But at least Victor was there.

She had completely forgotten their bitter parting and showed herself completely undone. "Victor. I've got to find Jack. Now. Please. Where is he? Do you know?"

He tried to take her inside, but she pulled away. "What's wrong, Mother? You look sick."

"Tell me where he is, damn you—"

"He's on the river. With the Strykers. They're having a terrible time of it. Jack got Stryker to let him take them all on an excursion up the Hudson. On the *General Sherman*. They're not due back for two hours."

"I've got to be there. Will you help me, Victor?"

Although they had all the time in the world, she abandoned her own staid driver and urged Victor to take desperate chances in the clattering automobile. And at last, at long last, the full story poured out of her. At each revelation, from Golden Fluss to Serpa to Harlem, she saw another piece fall into place for Victor, and she hated herself for having let what festered inside her keep them so separate for so long.

She finished as they reached the long, ornate pier of the Hudson River Steam Line, and he kissed her cheek with wordless intensity as he helped her out of the automobile, and she felt her love returned, and gloried in it.

In a few minutes she had shown amazing agility for a woman past seventy, hauling her son to the pier's upper gallery, where she locked her eyes steadfastly up the river. From the water the heat sent up a glaring haze.

"Hurry up, darling," she whispered. *"Hurry."*

Mark, standing on the upper deck near the big, square pilothouse to make the most of the breeze generated by the ship's motion, sadly observed the deterioration visited by time on this ancient vessel since he had last seen her in her prime.

Even so, days like this brought back the tradition of excursion cruising. On the fifth day of this heat wave, and the first Sunday, the ship had been sold out by eight in the morning.

By its meager freeboard and sluggish maneuvering, there was little question that the *General Sherman* was substantially overloaded. Each deck was so packed with people escaping the burning streets that movement was difficult or impossible. The band on the second deck had hardly room to handle its instruments, and the tiny dance area only existed because of the enthusiastic elbow-swinging of the dancers.

Mark was not fully able to put away the pain of his life, wasted in a series of lies while everything that would have saved him stood tormentingly at his side, but this was as close as he could come. From where he stood on the top deck he could look below to the second, which extended forward. There, at the front, beautifully situated for the cool air, sat the Strykers on the front bench. Evangeline waved to him, the outing having cleared the clouds from her mind for the moment. Stryker waved his hat and gave a rare, unrestrained grin. His other arm was around Evangeline, and Ford sat alongside him, his hand resting fondly on his father's knee. Justin was behind them talking nonstop, undoubtedly making some point about his latest fleeting interest.

Mark grinned and wig-wagged back. The day had been a miraculous success in momentarily easing the grim present for all of them.

Soon Mark noticed that a second excursion steamer of the same line and vintage, the *General Hooker*, had pulled up out of the heat haze from behind and was now running almost bow and bow with them. From the far greater volume of smoke belching from its towering side-by-side funnels, and the infinitely more rapid rocking of its walking beam, it was clear that the second craft, every bit as loaded, carried much more steam. This did not please the captain of the *General Sherman*.

"Shit," Mark heard him snarl to the man at the helm. "If he beats us in we'll be boiling on the river for an hour waiting for him to get that load off. The bottom of that thing hasn't been scraped in three years. We can beat him, Wilson."

"Full steam, Captain?"

"Yeah. The boiler room'll be howling that we're cooking 'em, but to hell with 'em."

There was a clanging of engine telegraphs, and a short time later Mark could feel an increase in the tempo of the *General Sherman*'s engines. The paddle wheels on each side of the old ship creaked and ground as the extra steam drove them harder through the water. The bow wave turned from a white feather to a heavy bone and they began closing the gap on the *Hooker*.

It quickly became a furious race for the first berth at the pier. When the *General Sherman* was almost abreast, a shower of sparks from its rival's stacks told of frantic stoking below.

"We'll show that sonofabitch," Mark heard the captain bawl from above. "Get one of the kids to run down and wire the safeties."

"Jesus, Cap', them boilers is older 'n we are."

"They don't build 'em that way anymore. Get it done."

Before long the *General Sherman*, shuddering in every frame, blackening the sky with it streaming smoke, had pulled ahead, and the passengers of both ships realized that they were in a race. They set up a mad cheering, and their press for the rails on the opponent's side gave each surging ship a pronounced inward list.

Mark looked into the wheelhouse and saw that the captain had taken the wheel, laughing and swearing, a bottle set on the ledge before him.

Something started to tingle in Mark, and he used what remained of his athlete's strength to fight his way down to the second deck and then forward to where the Strykers and Justin were cheering the action.

The pier with all its welcoming flags was visible in the setting sun when the starboard boiler blew. The people above it at the center of the ship had no chance. A red geyser of steam and flame shot skyward in a volcanic thunder of steel and wooden splinters.

The maimed had hardly begun screaming when the screeching steam blossomed out and hideously scalded hundreds more.

Dozens who could not swim, or who were too badly injured to do so, leaped unthinkingly into the boiling current of the river, now intensified by the outracing tide. They quickly drowned.

Somehow one paddle still churned, powered by the second boiler. The ship slewed wildly, the captain trying to control the disproportionate thrust with the rudder.

In the instant before the howls of pain drowned out all else, Mark heard the second man in the pilothouse crying out. *"Beach her. Beach her. Now."*

Although the ship had been unbalanced by the crowds, it now began to straighten as it fought drunkenly toward the shore, wildly blasting its distress from the whistle on the one stack that had not fallen. Mark knew that the countervailing ballast was inrushing water on the holed side, and it must soon reach the second boiler.

The hell had only begun. *"Fire . . . Fire . . ."* The flames that had begun small on the starboard side ate hungrily at the kindling of the explosion and tore into the ancient wood. What windows remained in the lower decks blew out in the heat that began to build. Flames shot skyward as though under draft, and a devilish breeze rose to fan them further.

The maimed, torn and catastrophicaly burned, were ground to bits in the insane, tearing stampede from the blazing center of the careening ship.

More went into the water, some in the path of the still-flailing paddle wheel, which hammered them to bits.

Mark's group, at the front of the second deck, was in the safest spot on the ship. The forward motion kept the flames streaming aft, and the senseless rush down to the first deck bypassed them.

Oddly, Mark noticed, none of those with him showed the slightest sign of fear. It was as if what they had seen of the world up to now precluded all lesser terrors.

Stryker held Evangeline and Ford close to him. Justin held his coat in front of them to hold off what sparks exploded forward.

"Justin," Stryker cried. "Find something that floats and get overboard with Ford. Mr. Grant and I will stay with Mrs. Stryker until we get ashore."

Both boys were aware that the ship would sink, blow up or burn to the waterline long before then.

"I won't leave, Father. You can't make me, and Justin can't."

"Good boy, Ford. I'm with you," Justin said.

"There are boats coming," said Evangeline, calmest of all.

"They may be too far away," Mark said. He found that in the last moments of his life he had only Hannah on his mind. Through eternity he would carry the impossible weight of the unsaid and undone.

Hannah had screamed the loudest of all the onlookers on the pier as she heard the shattering roar and watched the rolling curtain of steam and flame rise to the sky, billowing smoke that took the blood-red color of the setting sun.

She had not permitted herself to be shaken off by Victor in his dash to the big launch that was being prepared by cursing rescuers at the tip of the pier. Now she sat in it with him as it struggled to overtake the still-speeding pyre that was the *General Sherman*.

The ship was down by the head, and the increasing list was now to starboard. The rear of the ship, aft of the explosion, was a trailing sheet of flame and the sound from the people still aboard made a long, piteous wail drifting across the water.

"My God, can't you make this thing get there?" Hannah shouted.

"Wide open, now, ma'am," said the white-faced man at the tiller.

The people who continued to jump from the deck were swept quickly downstream, eluding most of the rescue craft headed for the ship. The tillerman managed to swing wide enough for Victor and the other crewmen to pull some of them aboard. They were in dreadful condition, burnt skin hanging in rags, and muscle exposed by gaping wounds. Hannah tore her dress to pieces making bandages and tourniquets.

The launch pulled closer as the *General Sherman* began to lose weigh, and soon the flaming paddle-wheeler was towering above them. Other small boats were appearing and found themselves being bypassed by the moving ship.

"Stop engines, damn you," Victor roared.

Hannah had just spotted Mark among the others at the front of the second deck when the cold water set off the second boiler. She was deafened and cut in the cheek and arms by debris, but the launch was standing off just far enough to avoid destruction.

The havoc and tumult aboard could grow no worse. The *General Sherman* drifted to a stop slowly, her sinking bow just beginning to slip the main deck beneath the surface of the churning river. The ship's list, which had been increasing gradually, began to take on visible momentum. The rest of the bottom amidships had been blown out. The towering decks began to tilt slowly toward the launch.

"Christ, back off," one of the launch men yelled. "She'll come over on us."

"Stay where you are," Victor barked at the helmsman. "We're no good back there."

The freshening evening breeze pushed at the heat, and the swirling smoke and steam cleared over the bow. The forward structure of the upper decks had partially collapsed, the wheelhouse tilting crazily. Hannah's eyes sought wildly before she saw Mark again, this time with Justin and the Strykers. They were at the downward-tilting rail. Even at this distance she could see raw evidence of terrible burns. Evangeline lay inert in Stryker's arms. Justin held Ford. They seemed stunned, weary, unwilling or unable to move.

Victor bellowed to the tillerman, "Get to the side, I'm going aboard."

"The hell I will—"

Victor was on him in one bound, his look saying all that needed to be said, his hand on the man's neck. The boat eased to the ship's bow, now awash, and Victor slid onto the rail, balancing along it until he made the ladder to the second deck. When he was away and could no longer stop her, Hannah followed him, calling upon strength she thought she no longer possessed.

Justin met her above, tears on his pale cheeks. "Grandfather and Caesar threw themselves over us when the steam spread out. They're terribly burned. Mother is dead."

Mark and Stryker had been propped sitting against the rail, only their eyes still alive above the blistered faces. Evangeline lay in Ford's arms, a foot-long splinter of white-painted wood driven through her chest. The searing clouds had not reached her and the sweet release of death had let the old, wild beauty steal back into her face.

Hannah looked at Victor and saw that his heart had cracked. She scrambled to Mark.

"Mark . . . Mark, my sweet. My own love." She knelt before him afraid to touch him because of the fearful burns, terrified that his scattered consciousness could not recognize her. But with the strength she had known in those arms so long ago, he reached and drew her to his torn lips, and kissed her against the pain to draw away the greater agonies of a lifetime. Whatever torment he felt seemed as sweet to him as heavenly glory. She felt in their fading bodies a fire greater than the one that consumed the decks around them.

"Tell me you love me still," she sobbed desperately. "Say you forgive me for all my blind, stupid hating."

For just a moment, somehow, the hoarseness lifted from his voice. "I love you and I have never stopped loving you, Hannah. You were all the life I ever had."

"I'm sorry, Mark. I'm so sorry."

He smiled, an incredibly beautiful smile in spite of all that had been put upon that ravaged face. She was kissing him when there was a great lurch under her feet. With a hissing sigh and one last, rising lament from its doomed passengers, the *General Sherman* rolled onto its side, and the blazing world became a cold, strangling smother of twisting water.

Hannah never lost hold of Mark, and there was nothing but happiness in her as she bumped and tumbled and was at last snatched up by unknown hand. She just kept repeating, "*Mark . . . Mark . . . Mark . . .*"

Victor brought all the children to be with her at the last.

Ford stood with Justin, George stood with Jana on the opposite side of the bed, the twins appearing annoyed by the antiseptic smell of the hospital room.

Hannah was awake. She had not been badly hurt when Victor had pulled her free of the overhanging deck and towed her to the launch, which had just managed to back clear of the capsize. She hadn't even fully lost consciousness. But the weeks since the sinking had been one of continuous physical slide for her, as all the tiredness of her years dragged her downward without resistance.

She knew of the death of Grant and Stryker, and how Victor and Justin had swum back into the maelstrom of struggling people to find only the bodies. The river had mercifully released them from a more lingering death by burns.

Well content to be joining the world where Mark had gone, she had wept no more but enlisted Victor's help in putting her world in order.

Now, feeling the last hours running out of her, she spoke to them in the old tone, although the volume was much faded.

"Victor, you will have all of Oakhill Development to add to what you have. Don't let it become just another machine to grub money. Make it *build*. Exciting things. *Risk* it. Change lives with it."

"I will, Mother," he said, not letting her see how empty he had become, how little inclined to challenge himself anymore.

"There is one thing I expect you to do. It will be good for that dead heart of yours. Keep Ford with you. Raise him as you do Justin. He's a fine boy and has nothing to do with your bitter memories."

"Just as you say, Mother." Ford met his eyes with a level gaze that revealed nothing of his feelings.

Hannah looked around at the children. "I hope some of you will want to build," she said, "but don't give up your lives for it. I'm afraid that I loved the things I built on the land better than the *people* I should have been loving."

Ford came up and took her hand. "I think my father would like me to do the things you would."

Justin went to her her and kissed her, his eyes full. "I'll have to see how it works out, Grandmother."

Difficult to the end, Victor thought.

The twins stood where they were. "I expect we will remain interested in the business," Jana said.

"Very interested," said George.

Victor saw that their eyes rested not upon their grandmother, but on the sad faces of Justin and Ford.

Hannah held on until nearly midnight, by which time the children had left. She woke from what had seemed to be the final sleep for just one moment. She signaled Victor to hold her and breathed these words into his ear: "Tell them all to be careful, Victor. Love drinks your happiness like blood. And even when you're dry, it's still thirsty."

CHAPTER 12

It was Julia's death that brought Victor and Justin to Florida together.

She went quickly, and as quietly as she had lived, a victim of pneumonia contracted from walking five miles in freezing streets clogged with slushy snow that had stopped all transit. The intensity of his pain at her loss was somewhat surprising to Victor. She had not been one of those women who made herself unforgettable with firework displays of wit or temperament, but she had always been there with a gentle understanding and a loyalty that burned unflickering. He now realized that her quiet acceptance of his disastrous lapse was an act of devotion almost unimaginable in a woman so fierce and jealous by nature. And she had been a formidable wife in more than affectionate forgiveness. In the bed she had never lost the straightforward, deeply physical passion she had shown in the first days, and she had brought him back to his body after his ordeal. He now found that he missed her deeply, and the bleeding guilt that he had half-forgotten came back to sit heavily upon him.

While Hannah's death had fully restored his fortunes, and the bustling economy had sent the worth of the Oakhill holdings climbing, there was nothing of great interest to him on the horizon. Brooding, he sat at home for days at a time, as gray, icy weather persisted for weeks.

When he saw at last that he must do something to break the deepening hold of depression, he determined to go south for the cheer of sun and warmth. Half mad with loneliness, he found himself pleased when Justin, between short-lived projects and terribly restless, decided to come with him.

"With nothing to fight over but the suntan oil, we might actually get along for a while," Justin said.

And so Victor put Oakhill Development into the hands of associates, gave instructions that Ford should be welcomed in anything he wanted to do in the office after school and prepared to take his first substantial vacation ever.

"If I build so much as a sand castle, break my fingers."

They were to be gone for a month, their destination The Waves, one of the magnificent Harley Ellison Ragland hotels in Saint Augustine. Their spirits improved as the train ran out from beneath the snow clouds somewhere in the Carolinas and the sun began to shine warmly through the windows.

Just as they had always heard, The Waves made every other hotel they had ever seen, including the best in New York, seem as plain as a red barn. In the Ragland tradition, every stone, turn, angle and color were a breathtaking surprise, all of this on a scale that would have been dazzling all by itself. It was enormous, rambling, endless, with 475 suites and rooms furnished in unparalleled luxury. In keeping with the surrounding nature, the building was faced with coquina, the beautiful white rock formed of marine shell and coral. The carved arches of the main gate would have suitably welcomed and engulfed a returning Roman legion.

Verandahs covered in exotic flowering vines ran everywhere, and the interior court had a many-hued fountain fronting an entrance rotunda supported by massive pillars and resplendent with mosaic. The dining room seated 800 between awesome stained-glass windows.

This building had been the single thing that had begun the

stupefying change of Florida's east coast from malarial swamp thirty years before to an apex of the nation's high society.

Victor could hardly believe how quickly Justin was swept away and captivated. It was as if all the drifting confusion of his youth had suddenly focused into a crystal-clear vision of what his perfect world must be.

The days of warm, endless sunshine; the rich, laughing people always on their way to some new pleasure; the lushly flowering vegetation and brilliant birds—all were the stuff of the dreams of which he thought life should be made. But it was the hotel, that incredible hotel, that exploded in his imagination. "How could anyone be in a place like this and be sad or mean? It's like a beautiful woman," said Justin, who by this time knew quite a little about beautiful women. "Every inch makes you tingle and want to do greater things than you've ever done before. I could look at it forever."

An elevated dreaminess settled over him. And when they fell into conversation one morning with a South American fruit baron who asked Justin what he did, the answer came instantly. Victor heard him say, "I'm an architect."

Such a glimmering of ambition toward the family heritage could not be ignored. Victor got busy on the telephone, and after three days was able to approach Justin with high anticipation. "Find yourself some dinner clothes. We're due for an evening you'll tell your grandchildren about. I guess all those skyscrapers got me at least a little attention. I've wangled us an invitation to dine with the ancient and honorable Harley Ellison Ragland himself at Ocean Hall. You'll get to meet the man who made Florida, invented Palm Beach and Miami, and built hotels like this as though they were bathhouses. He's way up in his eighties and deaf as a post, they say. But we're going to listen, not to talk."

If The Waves had astonished Justin, Ocean Hall hypnotized him. Ragland's wedding gift to his wife had, among other wonders, seventeen guest suites, each one decorated to present a separate period of history. There was also a Louis XIV ballroom, a music room with a pipe organ worthy of an Italian cathedral and a hall 115 feet long and 45 feet wide, all of it in eight different shades of marble.

The dining room in which the Oakhills sat could hold sixty, and the three diners, surrounded by Aubusson tapestries and a table service of solid gold, made a lonely archipelago on the great white sea of the tablecloth.

Victor was not unaware that the spot at which he was seated was the one most valued by those on the Eastern Seaboard who reckoned their worth in tens of millions. It was the diamond at the end of the society rainbow. And so he was proud to accept the unabashed admiration of the old master builder and overjoyed that Justin could sit in his spell for a moment.

Ragland sat in a wheelchair, having broken his hip a year before. The pain was never completely out of his face, and it was evident his time was short. But the vigor of his pronouncements was not diminished. Now, as white as the wraith he must soon become, his suit, his skin, his hair, his mustache making a radiating brightness, he held forth as one who expects no interruptions.

"I liked what you did in New York, Oakhill. Opened up the skies before there were a lot damned fool laws and idiot organizations to tie you up. But that kind of building is constipating to a man's soul. There's not enough land to play with and too many so-called leaders. That's why I came down here.

"Fever swamp was what Florida was. Heat. Mosquitos. Ignorance. No highways. No railroads worth a spit. Bought out the tin can line they had, changed the gauge and got a land grant to build south. Started in Saint Augustine because there was some civilization there, and because it was the prettiest damned place I ever saw.

"Hotels were the answer. I saw that from the first. What rich people need more than anything else are new places to go, a new climate and somewhere to stay where they can show themselves to as many of one another as possible. They were all up in Newport then in their goddamned ninety-five room cottages, having to give another party for three hundred every night or having to go to one. The shit climate meant that the season was two months long, and it was the same stuff they got every day in New York across the Sound. Not a damned thing exclusive about it. And worst of all, the society was set in rock for the last thirty years.

You couldn't break in, you couldn't go up. Everything had to trickle down from the Astors and Vanderbilts, you see.

"Well, sir, I made the opening of The Waves the event of the decade. I had those snobs met at the railway station by a coach pulled by eight white horses. It made Trooping the Colours look like a Boy Scout ceremony. They sucked it up. I was sold out from the first night and had the pleasure of turning the latecomers away in droves." Ellison chuckled long and happily at the memory and went on.

"I broke all the molds. Up to then these people thought a vacation was to sit around on their asses taking tea, smoking cigars and clearing their throats. I put in some fun. Casinos. Shocked 'em all, inviting the ladies. Swimming pools, hot health baths, golf courses, tennis. The works. All of a sudden your backhand was as important as your grandfather. My wife became a queen like they didn't know since the real Mrs. Astor. But the social season didn't really move down here until I got to Palm Beach.

"You see, I had figured out that if one hotel pulled a crowd waiting to be seen, another hotel would increase the ogling geometrically. And all the other development in the land surrounding would radiate out from the hotels. Now tell me I'm not smart."

"It wasn't just hotels, sir," said Justin. "It was the kind of fairytale hotels they were."

Ellison went on as though he hadn't been interrupted. "I saw the whole coast as mine, right down to the Keys, and Palm Beach was the plum. Just a handful of houses between the Ocean and Lake Worth it was. I pushed the railroad down there there, bought an old estate for seventy-five thousand and put up the Royal Palm. The land all around it went up a thousand an acre and I had gobs of it. It was off to the races. Spread new hotels like a skin rash. Almost missed Miami. Would have, except for a woman who got me to branch the railroad in there to increase the value of her property. Gave me land for a terminal. Don't like the city much. It'll always be a low-end town giving people trouble. They sued me every time I farted.

"But I had a bigger dream after the Spanish War, and you'll live to see it even if I won't."

"You're talking about your railroad to the Keys," Victor said.

The old man chose to hear this and nodded proudly. "That's what they'll remember me for. There's Cuba, best soil there is, free of Spain now, ninety miles from Key West. The Atlantic Seacoast Railroad I built down there will be this country's most fabulous trade link one day, I promise you." His eyes grew distant as he dreamed old victories. "The engineers said it couldn't happen. The contractors wouldn't even bid on the job. But I pushed those tracks a hundred and fifty-six miles, Miami to Key West, half it across open water, by God. Wind, waves, three hurricanes. Equipment lost, men lost, ships lost. Twenty million dollars. But those viaducts went up. And that Cuba trade will come to make Florida the richest state in this union. Key West will be America's greatest port."

Second only to Duluth, Victor thought to himself.

Ragland paused so long in contemplation of his disappointed expectations of the Cuban trade bonanza that the Oakhills thought he had forgotten them.

"What you've done already could bring those riches to Florida, sir," Victor said.

The old man roused himself to scoff. "A state can't find its destiny on the backs of a bunch of swells, no matter how rich. There's more land here than in England and Wales combined. Did you know that? The people—the common people, the productive people—have to come in millions or we'll just be a resort state selling one another oranges. I tried to promote immigration from the North, but I might have been describing the far side of Mars. This is still a swamp in the country's mind."

"I'd give everything I'll ever own to have been here with you when there was still pioneering to do in those early days," Justin blurted.

Ragland's white eyebrows rose. "Don't you have eyes, son? Nothing's happened here yet. I've only set the first brick compared to what's left to do. I'd give all *I* ever won to have *your* opportunity to build this state. The powder is here. Find the match, damn it."

Justin swallowed sheepishly. "Actually, building down here is what I have in mind, sir."

This was remarkable news to Victor.

"What kind of building?" Ragland asked.

"I thought I'd start with some important homes," Justin said in the manner of one plucking a fly out of the air. "Something in the wonderful feeling, the magnificent boldness of your hotels."

"Some of them were designed by men who built the New York Public Library and the Metropolitan Opera House."

Justin appeared not a bit impressed. "I wouldn't want to be stuck with their ideas. I expect I'll have some better ones of my own."

A laugh escaped Ragland. "I see. Got any commissions?"

"Not precisely yet."

"Tell you what. Ezra Allen Draper is down here. Every time somebody in the word buys a sewing machine he makes twelve dollars. He's looking to build a house for his fifth wife and he's going through architects like a shark goes through a goldfish pond. We're old friends. I'll call him for you."

Justin beamed. "Wonderful, sir. I've got a lot of things to show him. And if anything comes of it, rest assured a little something will come your way."

Fortunately, Ezra Allen Draper did not call for three weeks. Justin had been able to obtain his old books for refreshment, race around the coast for inspiration, buy a thousand dollars' worth of architect's supplies and fill a separately rented room at The Waves with sketches. He even found time to squabble steadily with Victor during the work.

"Justin, you didn't finish any of your courses. You don't have any certificates."

"The people who built the pyramids and Saint Peter's didn't have any certificates. I'm having Zeb Carson come from New York. Hope you don't mind. He's a solid architect even though he has the imagination of a salamander. The sunshine is a little bonus for him, and he has plenty of certificates and a lot of pencils to sign things off."

Victor studied some of the elevations for the house. He found himself nodding admiringly at the quality of the sketches and the untrammeled breadth of imagination. "These don't look like any house I've ever seen. They look like illustrations for a book of fairytales."

"Father, they're supposed to. We're stuck in bodies that haven't changed in a thousand years. Why should we be stuck in gray, square, boring houses? Haven't we all wanted to live in a castle with turrets and swirling passages and vaulted rooms?"

"Only when we were six. Where's the stairway to the third floor? How is the plumbing going to go through that fireplace?"

Justin grabbed the plan and studied it. "Well, that's just the boring sort of thing I'm bringing in Carson to catch."

"I hope Draper is old and feeble. I wouldn't want you to be killed when he throws you out."

An undersized man with an undershot jaw and a perpetually spectacular scowl, Draper scanned Justin's plan. They were standing on the twelfth green of a golf course, Draper in cap and plus fours, Justin in a business suit soaked with sweat by the hike across the fairways ordered by the man's secretary. The others in the foursome stood quietly with the caddies near the flag, toying with their putters.

"I like the electric drawbridge," Draper finally growled, dropping sketches to the green as he finished with them. "And I like the elevated walkway between the wings, with all those windows. I like to see that lady of mine coming."

"I don't think there's anything else like it here, sir. It's an old Moorish idea—"

"Nothing else like it here. At last somebody's got the idea. What's it going to cost?"

Not having the remotest idea, Justin said, "About a million and a half."

"Make it two and a half. I don't want to chintz anything. I'm going to be the kingpin around here, and I want my house to look it."

"It will be pure kingpin, sir."

"My parties are the best place to reach me. Can you come to all of them?"

"A pleasure, sir."

"Putnam," he said to one of the waiting golfers, "you look hot. Give this guy your clubs and hike in for a drink. He and I have things to talk about."

The parties discovered a Justin Oakhill that had never before existed. The fame of Ezra Allen Draper's unbelievable new house brushfired through the community. The young architect became a central figure at endless glittering galas given by his patron.

Justin found himself invested with unlimited stores of wit and charm, waiting only for the delightful rich to water it to flourishing life with their generous attention.

"I say, Justin, what is this pleasure dome of Draper's costing?"

"An architect is like a physician, Mr. Mears. That is privileged information. But I can tell you," he said, his ability to lie growing like Pinocchio's nose, "that at least two of the distinguished gentlemen present here have approached me about commissions that would exceed Mr. Draper's in cost. Subject to my availability, of course."

"Did you commit?"

"Not really. Not yet."

"Don't until you speak with me. Some of these people who think they can buy anything have a surprise coming."

"I know what you mean, sir. Someone's got to put them in their place at last."

Inevitably there were young ladies who found him as fascinating as he found himself. If he had let his bedroom schedule fill as they wanted, his career as an architect would have been over at once.

Suddenly the fascination of building in paradise was all there was for Justin. He found himself wanting to bring all the frozen victims of the North to this empty, beautiful state and house them in a tropical opulence that would virtually end unhappiness.

To Justin's boundless delight, his father caught his enthusiasm. The black clouds that had smothered him since the deaths of Evangeline and Julia began to burn away in the lush, moist heat as he caught some of Justin's wildness. They both extended their stay indefinitely.

"Ragland was right, Justin. They've hardly scratched the sand down here."

"I've got to be in on it, Father."

"You're already in. I need something new for Oakhill Development."

While his son became an architectural icon of Palm Beach, Victor traveled tirelessly along the coast, looking for the opportunities that someone else had missed. Hannah and Grant had taught him that this was the difference between people who created buildings and people who created history.

For many days his quest turned up nothing. There was much coastline available, but it was unstable, located away from the mainstream or inaccessible by standard transportation. If he had not found himself stuck overnight in Miami in a considerably less than first-class hotel because of a confusion in reservations, he might soon have returned to New York.

Reading his newspaper in the seedy lobby after a bad dinner, Victor found himself verbally accosted by the man in the next chair. His new companion was probably in his seventies and showing every possible sign of it, from a huge drunkard's nose to a uniquely pendulous gut. He had taken in too many spirits at his own dinner.

"I observe, friend, that you are making the mistake of reading the real estate section. I must warn you against that. Real estate kills more unsuspecting Floridians than this atrocious climate."

The man's apparent bitterness was alleviated by a natural good cheer. Victor put the paper aside. "You've had a bad experience?"

"Job himself sent me his condolences. My name, by the way, is Lloyd Howland."

"Victor Oakhill." The man showed no signs of recognizing the name. "Are you a real estate man, Mr. Howland?"

"I would sooner be a molester of children. No, I am a horticulturist. As such, I conceived the idea of that magnificent bridge to nowhere you might have seen out there."

"Yes, the . . . let's see . . . the Howland Bridge. Good heavens, is that named after you?"

"Yes. Part of the curse. You see, back before the war, what they had the nerve to call Miami Beach, out there across Biscayne Bay, was essentially a mangrove swamp. I figured if you filled up the swamp you'd have the best avocado and grapefruit country God ever made. I had some money then, and I went everywhere to get support for a bridge from here to there so I could start developing. Put in a bunch of my own cash, I did, but ran dry before it was anywhere near done. Finally I found a guy named Joe Taylor who had made a pile inventing something that made auto headlights work. He was hot to go and pretty soon he had the thing done."

"You were partners?"

"I thought so, but the partner who had the money seemed to have a lot more to say than the broke partner. And pretty soon I saw he didn't care a hoot in hell about farming. He figured to build a lot of junk there."

"Houses?"

"And hotels and anything else he could think of. I'll give him this. He poured that headlight money into that swamp like he had a printing machine. Seems like it was a lot bigger job than I figured. But when he was done the mosquitoes and rats were gone, and he had a nice beach with plenty of trees and shrubs to keep it from blowing back into the ocean."

"So what happened?"

"Take a ride out there and see, Oakhill. What happened was nothing. Absolutely nothing. The war came and the people didn't. Not even when he offered free land to anybody who promised to build a two-hundred-thousand-dollar hotel. No takers."

"And you got nothing."

"A few dimes. Lucky the climate kills so many people down here. I grow flowers for the funerals. Gives me the money I need to pay for the safe deposit box where I keep all those worthless partnership papers."

Victor pulled out a checkbook. "Mr. Howland, you might be wanting to call for reservations at a better hotel. I would like to buy your share of the holdings on Miami Beach."

Howland almost giggled. "Don't you want to see it first?"

"No, all sand looks the same."

After a short negotiation, Victor obtained land on Miami Beach to the value of Howland's partnership, and soon a great deal more from Joe Taylor. Then he made his own plans.

Those plans did not at first include Justin. His son had several times declined to enter Oakhill Development; besides which, he was deeply involved in becoming the architectural lion of the winter-season rich. Beyond that, Victor had the gravest doubts about Justin's depth of knowledge of the business, despite much schooling and the heavy efforts of himself and Hannah. It was fairly certain that without the help of the experts from the North —even allowing for his uniquely flamboyant imagination—Justin's houses might be built upside down.

But on the first day that Justin walked the empty sands of Miami Beach with his father, he overrode Victor's doubts with a cavalry charge of pleas, laments, vows, threats and allegedly-foolproof schemes. By the time they were back putting on their shoes and socks, Justin had entered Oakhill Development, vowed to surpass his father and grandmother in every way and had become director of something he had decided to call Florida Coast Oakhill.

"We're going to build a new state, Dad."

"I don't like to be called Dad."

"Father is too formal for partners."

"I'll take you through my thinking tomorrow."

"No, Dad. Today."

And so ended the first completely delightful conversation Victor had ever had with Justin. Victor wondered if he was to old to turn a cartwheel in the sand.

* * *

Victor was at war with his unexpected partner very quickly. The total divergence of their natures made their agreement on almost anything impossible. As the senior partner, Victor made the decisions and ignored Justin's continual threats to storm away with "my share."

Essentially, Victor wanted to deal in patience, value and certainty, and Justin favored reckless attack, dreams above substance and adventuresome bounds into the unknown.

"I'm the ship," Justin lamented aloud. "My father is the anchor."

For a time Victor was in firm command, Justin taking out his frustration with increasingly fanciful additions to the Draper home, which brought him a shower of commissions but not the satisfaction of performing on a greater stage.

"Why don't you spend more time at the Draper site, Justin?"

"To make sure everybody doesn't go Rip Van Winkle down here," Justin said, referring to the staff of the southern office Victor had assembled in Miami.

"Carson said you changed two of his chimneys to turrets."

"So what, unless you use the fireplaces."

Their squabbling was beginning to have a more pleasant undertone now, as Victor began to see his own young self. He already knew he would be doing a lot of giving in to his son.

Victor's hope for Miami beach was based principally on observation. The end of World War I had brought an explosion of automobiles and a blossoming network of roads to serve them. The railroads were no longer the tools that opened the country, with development limited to where they went. The most dynamically growing young states, Florida and California, would grow with the speed and flexibility of the automotive revolution.

A year passed. The automobiles came. They raced on the sands of Miami Beach. Then, unfortunately, they raced back to Miami, Palm Beach and St. Augustine. The prospects of Oakhill Development in the South were miniscule. As Justin's fame in the state grew, his father's dwindled and it made him fume.

"I think it's about time I sold out of this damned place. They need me in New York and I'm starting to look like an old leather valise, from sitting around in the sun."

That was all Justin had been waiting for. "Bon voyage, Dad. Sell nothing. Your interests are now in the hands of Florida Coast Oakhill. I'll need a healthy credit line."

"Okay. But for what? We've got all the sand we need."

"You really should have talked to Grandmother more, Dad. You might remember a little more of what she did with Mr. Grant and a man named Jay Cutts."

Irresponsibility became Justin. One of the criteria for any of his moves was how furious it would make his father, now shivering in New York.

"You're not going to build anything, are you?" Victor would bark into the phone.

"Of course, I am."

"You can't out-Ragland Ragland with fancy hotels. Especially with nobody in them."

"I just want some modest starters, Dad. Just enough of a hotel —maybe *two* hotels, but nothing flashy—maybe a golf course or so. To make a *center* for what's going to bring the real money down."

"What's *that* going to be? . . . Hello . . . *Hello* . . . *Justin* . . ."

Justin knew Victor would be able to follow his exploits very well in the northern newspapers.

Sex was never a bad place to start. With the beginning of the twenties the clothing had begun to fall from women's bodies as quickly as the styles could change. Skirts shot from the ankles to above the knees in a dizzying rush. Bathing suits shrank with such speed that hard-eyed inspectors roamed the more staid beaches with rulers to be certain hems had not strayed too far north. The bluenoses were overwhelmed, deploring the bathtub gin and wailing saxophones that seemed to be sending young people into fits of licentiousness hitherto unknown.

Justin Oakhill, early into the breach, invented the Miami Beach

Bathing Beauty. He hired two publicity agencies to compete in brassiness and had them scour the beaches for the loveliest young creatures who could be persuaded to pose in the most daring of the new swim attire. Then unscrupulous photographers pushed down straps and stockings until the churches began to howl.

The photos of these voluptuous nymphs began to flood front pages wherever a snowflake flew. They competed in contests judged by movie stars. They frolicked in surf that had apparently disarranged their beachwear provocatively, and slept in the sun in remarkable poses. They swam, sailed, golfed and fled coquettishly from pursuing dandies. The pictures of all this, of course, ran thickest immediately after the great blizzards.

In a short time it appeared to the blue-lipped North that all the fun and sensuality left in the nation were concentrated on a little strip of sand called Miami Beach. Not surprisingly, many left their long underwear behind and headed south into Justin's hands. And when they arrived in the great, startling, wooden palaces of hotels he had waiting for them, they found even more good times than they had dreamed.

The big-name bands were there. Paul Whiteman's jazzy arrangements floated out on the warm air each night and made the fairyland of light seem even brighter.

There were shows. Not the painful third-raters of the New York State mountain resorts, but productions nearly intact from Broadway, with Follies stars doing their astonishing turns. And during the day one could sit about in one's turned-down bathing suit and sip drinks and crack jokes with the great entertainers.

Justin became a central figure for the stars, both for his charming sense of outrage and because Justin Oakhill's Miami Beach was becoming more than just a place to make money for them. "The Beach" was *the* place to be seen doing your act. Gilda Gray, Ruby Keeler, Helen Morgan, they all came.

Nobody, except Victor, much noticed that Justin had been steadily buying more land all around him, and that it was appreciating with alacrity.

Will Rogers became a special friend of Justin's and jokingly accused him of "selling sand at a thousand dollars a pail so the rest of us could sell it to one another at a thousand dollars a grain."

Justin's stodgy father, funding all this, was quite forgotten by both the crowds and his son. But he had now seen to what ends the madness progressed.

Unintentionally at first, Justin became a style setter. Dashing about in the southern heat, he dispensed with ties, hats and jackets, and raced about with his shirttail trailing behind him. Soon shirttails were cut away by custom tailors and the square-bottomed sports shirt was born to plague a nation. To Victor's horror those shirts were sometimes called "Oakhills."

Very occasionally Justin caught up with his father. "It's coming, Dad. Let's get all the land we can before the others do. We can start developments along this coast as fast as we can name them. Let's keep the best ground for ourselves and sell the rest to the other developers to cover the original costs. Then we're profitable right off the bat."

Victor couldn't believe he was talking to the same boy who had once sought a dealership in battery-heated underwear. He could hardly hide his joy at the totally unexpected emergence of the inbred ability to spot the daring future. But hide it he did. "Justin, I don't care how well this is going, you're turning it into a cheap carnival."

Sensitive—for him—to the criticism, Justin suspected Victor might be right and branched out to the classic. Ignace Paderewski, the great pianist, arrived to play at new Oakhill hotels, and then came Boris Chaliapin and Madame Alda, the magnificent opera artists. Justin enjoyed the way the newspapers played up the purported friendship between Paderewski and Gene Tunney, the boxer whom he had brought down to fight an exhibition. Not just building worlds, but uniting them, Justin thought righteously. His clientele held that their prestige had vastly improved, and sent for their friends.

Victor was caught in a whirlpool a thousand times stronger than the one into which he had dipped his toe just months ago. He could have stopped his son in an instant, Justin knew. But wrongheaded, overblown, crass and headlong as Victor thought

Justin's schemes were, they had that scope, that imaginative flame, and Victor found himself pulled in by it all in spite of himself. So Justin made the great plans and it was up to Victor to make technical and monetary sense out of them.

"One more idea will finish us," Victor moaned.

As the developments along the coast sprang up, Victor recognized the way the new phenomenon of radio could help build Florida mania. He called together a half-dozen of the best and fastest songwriters he could buy, bringing them down for a wild, expenses-paid month at The Beach. He was rewarded when the airwaves to the North were soon saturated with songs like "On Miami Shores," and "When the Moon Shines on Coral Gables," not to mention "So Mister Engineer Open Up the Throttle, I'm Gonna Throw Away My Hot Water Bottle, We'll All Be in Miami in the Morning."

Meanwhile, salesmen went north with trunks filled with fanciful literature for farmers, homesteaders and retirees, and in Detroit, Chicago and New York, people were beginning to pack bathing suits.

Also attracted were thieves, pimps and hustlers.

Sporadically concerned with the moral fiber of his work, Justin got together with some fellow promoters, and William Jennings Bryant was soon conducting "The Largest Outdoor Bible Class in the World." Bryant must have been impressed with Palm Beach because he proclaimed it the only city in the world "where you can tell a lie at breakfast that will come true by evening."

When Justin tempted President Harding down for a much-photographed game of golf, the other developers recognized his preeminence and made him the head of a promotional consortium that committed new excesses of publicity every day.

Justin observed to Victor that he was becoming very rich, and that Florida Coast Oakhill was on its way to beggaring all that Oakhill Development had earned since its inception.

"Dump everything up north, Dad. Bring the cash down. New York's day is over. Florida's is here."

"Sure," Victor said. "We can store all the discarded overcoats in the country in Central Park."

* * *

Justin had thought that he would finish the Draper house and one or two more and then move on to his development interests. But he had become completely infected with home-building, to the joy of the high society to whom he had become a central treasure. They literally would not permit him to slacken his architectural efforts, and the more bizarre, the more they wanted them.

He had taken Moorish as his keynote style. It went back to the Spanish traditions of Florida, yet allowed Islamic fancies and utility. The lovely open-air designs had much deep, cool shade, and lovely fountains took away heat as they added tranquility.

The architectural critics, seething with indignation and jealousy, were appalled. For his designs were neither truly Moorish nor Spanish, but rather his peculiar notion of what they would be if they had evolved in the state he now considered his own.

His mind fulminated with stunning facades, interiors flowing with flabbergasting busy-ness, and a treasure of theatrical spectacle. He became fanatically involved in his main designs and in superb finish detail. European woodcarvers of the first rank found they could have all the work they wanted on the Florida phantasmagoria of Justin Oakhill. Their wages were handsome because money had meaning to neither client nor builder.

Starting wars between the grand names of society became Justin's specialty, with his homes the chosen weapon.

"Of course I'm giving your house my best effort, Mrs. Epps. But Mrs. Sanborn has asked for something reminiscent of a medieval city. You certainly couldn't expect your little million-and-a-half-dollar bungalow to equal that in audacity. It wouldn't be fair to the poor woman."

"What *could* equal it, Mr. Oakhill?"

"Please, Mrs. Epps, you're getting overheated. Well, for perhaps a million more we could nicely embellish your Spanish-Moorish. A Romanesque tower here, Gothic arches for the doors and windows there, Renaissance-style battlements connecting a wing that suggests the best of Versailles—"

"Might I see the plans?"

"Plans are the death of inspiration, Mrs. Epps."

Strangely enough, as even his most adamant critics admitted in private, he had an innate architectural touch that not only saved his most extreme creations from appearing ludicrous, but gave them a lush, sensual, dreamlike beauty that captivated far more often than it repelled. It fit with the melodramatic flora and colors of the tropical climate, and a house by Justin soon became the entry requirement into Florida society.

All in all, Justin was the trumpet that woke the steaming giant. The Florida season stretched out from early fall to late spring. Every new frescoed portico, Byzantine loggia and colonnaded orangerie added to Justin's fame and the general feeling of an opium dreamworld.

"Money is arriving in barrels," Victor said to Justin. "Madness will not be far behind."

Jana Oakhill arrived unannounced and, almost for the first time in Victor's memory, without her twin brother. George had chosen, she said, to remain behind in New York, although she hinted that her business involved both of them.

The mountain of luggage she had brought indicated a lengthy stay, and she confirmed that by taking a house for the season.

Approaching thirty, Jana was no conventional beauty, but a beauty she was. Her face was Serpa's in the black, hooded eyes and full lips, Julia's in the perfect skin and the nose out of a Roman fresco. But all of it had been refined to haughty proportion by an artist's hand. Of Victor there was only a broad-shouldered grace of movement and cleanness of limb, but that was breathtaking in the high skirts and bareback styles of the moment. Her thick curling hair had been bobbed short now and suited her superbly. And while her voice was low and feminine, there was sometimes a hint of Serpa's rasp that made it quite special.

Less than a week after she arrived, she was seated in the cockpit of a forty-four-foot sloop that Victor—back for Victor's carnival—had rented more as a breezy, comfortable office than as a pleasure boat. It was time for Victor to find out what she had on her mind, and she told him.

"Father, I'm sure you're going to suspect us of envy. Not that we wouldn't be entitled to that. We've had to sit in frosty New York reading every day about the successes of our brother and the wonderful excitement of his life down here."

"You didn't have to sit anyplace you didn't want to. You were free to join us at any time, as you now have. George should have come too, I suppose."

"I asked him not to, actually. George is so protective of me that he sometimes gets in my way."

"He should be married by now, and so should you, Jana."

"We have our admirers, father. But to hold to the point. We feel that Justin has been given opportunities denied to us."

In her words Victor heard the dark coldness that had always been part of the twins.

"Justin has not been 'given' anything. He's won what he has with considerable effort. And talent, I might add. What is it you think you're missing? Money? Your grandfather, I know, didn't forget your mother. And I've been as generous as any father could be."

She detected the irritation in him but was not ruffled. "Grandfather's friends managed to shrink considerably whatever fortune he had, before it was passed to Mother and then to us. And your allowance is just that. An allowance. We live well, but not as our station asks."

"Someday you'll share with Justin what I have."

"And Ford, Father. And Ford, I believe," she said coolly.

"Yes, Ford. I sometimes forget. What do you expect of me?"

"We wish to be part of Oakhill Development now. To share in its opportunities as Justin does."

Victor's annoyance grew. "I expected the trainloads of speculators at any moment. I didn't think my own children would be among the leaders. Well, I don't think either of you are equipped to be part of this. And in any case it's another overextended situation that I wish to carry no further. If I'm successful in what's been done so far, you'll have it when I'm dead. In the meantime I'll increase your allowance so you won't have to suffer in your present poverty of Packards and hundred-dollar hotel rooms in Nice." Once again he found himself torn between annoyance at their lack of real commitment to anything he cared about and a definite satisfaction at not having to have them around him.

"I see I've made you angry somehow, Father. This is probably the wrong time to insist that I've paid more attention to our business than you think. So, if you'll excuse me, I'll simply enjoy my stay and renew my acquaintance with your talented son."

"Your brother, Jana."

"My half-brother. As I've reminded you before. My half-brother."

By the time Justin was able to break away from his business down the coast, he had already heard a great deal about the effect Jana was having on Palm Beach. Even outside the notoriety that would have been her due as one of the powerful Oakhills, she was causing something of an earthquake in the community of males.

A friend told him that she had received three proposals in a single week, and Justin could not imagine why. He had not seen Jana in many years, and all his memories of her before that were unpleasant. As the son of Victor's indiscretion with Evangeline, he could not, of course, have been openly exposed to Julia's children. He had quickly come to understand that. Living with Mark, he had met the twins only occasionally as a child, when Victor had tried to bring them together on outings and shopping trips for toys.

Justin, slightly younger, openhearted and lonely as a child, had been almost pathetically eager to be friendly. But whether from things they heard from Julia or from their own cold hearts, he had from the twins only a scornful and often elaborate cruelty. Jana, he remembered, was a dark child, all glares and angles, who pinched him without mercy when Victor's back was turned. She had been remarkably articulate in her vituperation.

Victor had mercifully terminated these get-togethers, and the twins did not reappear in Justin's life to any extent until their college years, when they made periodic visits to the offices of Oakhill Development and Mark's home to inquire after what they frequently referred to as "our future interests." By this time George had acquired his fine handsomeness, which some likened to a younger version of the movie player Valentino. But Jana had not yet matched him in looks. To Justin she was too tall for a woman, too wide-shouldered. Although she carried herself superbly, there was still not flesh enough in her face for her bold features or on her body for her robust frame, and all her fine clothes could not hide it. She and George had grown more correctly polite and talked with Justin just enough to evade rudeness. But the words only seemed to be a military probing of an enemy whose strong position temporarily defied annihilating assault. Justin had never felt guilty about his thorough dislike of Jana.

But now he saw her in the sunshine of Palm Beach, coming toward him across the newly sodded lawn of the Draper "cottage." Her new voluptuousness was barely contained in a thin, white dress that showed the tops of her stockings and eight inches of firm, white thigh. He saw what the fuss was about very quickly, already liking her better.

Her face was shaded by a jaunty, wide-brimmed straw hat that fitted her features exquisitely. He was amazed to see a smile of utter delight and friendliness.

With a demeanor as thoroughly new to him as the rest of her, Jana embraced Justin and kissed him with such disregard of her generously applied lipstick that she was forced to scrub at his lips with a deliciously perfumed handkerchief. "Goodness. My little brother—turned into an idol of fashion as well as a genius."

Justin, dressed in a bizarrely patterned sport shirt, saw all the spectacular things that Victor had, but with the eyes and heart of a man twenty-five years younger and without the emotional perspective of a father. He brought some primitive emotions up short and hugged her back hesitantly. "Jana, may I say that you've improved in many surprising ways."

"I'm coming out from under my wet rock. I discovered men some years back, and nice places and good times. And I think Florida has more of all those things than any place I ever saw. This is *gorgeous*." She was captivated by the house.

"I have almost twenty of these, either finishing up or in planning. If you have time, I'll show you some."

"I expect I'll be here for quite a while."

"Any particular reason?"

"Not anymore, in case you haven't spoken to Father. I wanted George and me to be part of this. Getting our hands dirty, so to speak, although yours don't look dirty at all," she said, turning them in hers. "It's all so exciting and fascinating, Justin. But your daddy feels that all the family talent ends with you, apparently. He said I could watch, but not touch."

"You're giving in too fast. He tried that with me. Now I've made him sort of my bookkeeper."

"Bookkeeper is a very important job in this company, unfortunately."

"I know what you mean. I could be doing even more if he'd give me my head."

"You're a better fighter than I am. But would you mind awfully if I tagged along and asked you a lot of things that I hope won't be too silly? I'm done wasting time. I have to start looking after—"

"—your future interests?" Justin finished, just managing to stifle the old sarcasm.

She laughed. "Exactly. I know I'll be a lot of bother, but I promise to make it up to you by making sure you have a lot more fun than you do."

"Who says I don't have enough fun?"

"Ah, yes. Those lovely things I hear you spend so many evenings with. I'll have to try very hard to be more amusing than them, won't I?"

"I'll take you anywhere and show you anything, Jana. It's great to see you interested at last."

"And let's be certain that includes beautiful beaches, wonderful parties and fabulous restaurants. Aren't we tourists terrible?"

"Not at all. You're probably keeping one of those flea-brained debs from branding me on the haunch."

"We must look after that lovely haunch," she said, giving him a hint of what she was turning on the local men.

"Are you missing George?"

"We mustn't think about that. We've all got to pursue our own game."

"Game? As in Parchesi or as in rabbit?"

"You'll find out. Now show me Mr. Draper's house and, if possible, Mr. Draper."

If Justin had expected that Jana's expressed intentions were just chatter, he was proved very wrong. Beginning the following morning, she began to move in, staying almost as close to him as she had to George.

Her interest in him and his work persisted remarkably. He went from being surprised, to being flattered, to being happy in her presence. He believed in taking good things as they came, and did not pursue any slight apprehensions he might have felt about her being there.

Jana was scintillating company, with a mind that was both deep and fast. What he had not bothered to absorb in his desultory schooling, she had taken in utterly. In the company of glittering men who fancied themselves great wits, she carelessly held her own, sometimes with half-hidden flashes of the cruelty he remembered.

"You have creamy, beautiful hands, Mr. Thomas," she said to the man next to her at one gathering.

"Thank you," he said holding up a palm for admiration.

"Touching them is like touching a woman's breast. You should wear gloves when you're dancing."

There were times when the toplofty conversations made Justin feel like a fool. "We really have to find you an escort more at your level," he said, not quite keeping the huffiness out of his tone. He found he was hoping she would reassure him.

She wound his arm through hers. "Oh, they'll find me, darling. They'll find me."

As all teachers do when they find a truly willing and exceptionally able student, Justin began to enjoy instructing Jana in the builder's arcanities. He was startled to see that her grasp of the business side, gained over the years in the separated but intense sessions with Victor at the office, in some ways exceeded his own, especially where work with numbers was involved. But from Justin she learned the temper and direction of the Florida market, its tastes, its possibilities.

It wasn't long before they were talking almost as equals in many areas of the business. To him she seemed incapable of saying a boring word.

Victor began to see advantages in her being there. His son had been pushing himself too hard. And those women he ran with were a dangerous and enervating influence. He welcomed Jana's intercession, however brief he thought it might be.

Justin's many lady friends were not equally pleased. Spread thin by his obligations to begin with, he was no longer even remotely a dependable amusement, and they complained to him. "Granted that your sister is a charmer, Justin. But she can't do all the things for you that I can."

"I imagine that all the guys who have an eye for her are saying the same about me."

"Don't you think, for everybody's sake, you should give some of them a crack at her?"

Justin was surprised and a little embarrassed to discover that he didn't think so at all.

There was nothing insistent in Jana's presence. She presented herself to Justin each day in a way that made it easy and graceful for him to beg off. And she never gave any inkling of a pout when he did, assuring him that she had many attractive alternative things to occupy her. Indeed, one evening when he had taken a lovely Raleigh debutante to the beautiful Alligator Club for gambling, his car had passed an open Studebaker touring car. It held a blond young man in evening clothes and Jana, crushed close together and laughing. He had waved to her as she passed, but apparently she had not seen him.

He was not as pleased as he should have been that his date had not inconvenienced her.

Jana demanded all the relaxation from Justin that she had promised, and she got it. With her at his side, he did some things he had never done in his years in the state. They went out for sailfish, played tennis, rowed down streams whose banks swarmed with alligators, played elaborate systems at the casinos and swam for miles beyond the breaking surf.

Justin first felt the tidal pull of her sensuality at a lonely beach, when Jana's body was glistening wet and tawny against the bone-white sand. Desire didn't steal upon him, but broke abruptly through a wall whose strength he had never questioned. He blushed and sweated and found himself completely helpless. He was lying at her side, and he thanked heaven that she dozed for the moment so he could drink her in insatiably, unable to pull his gaze away or even blink. He wanted to scream for joy and kiss her, even as he was realizing that that such things could never happen. And it was at this instant that her eyes opened and she saw what had happened. For one delicious second he had a fantasy in which she slid her silky arms around his neck and told him that she felt the same forbidden tug.

She rested the lazy smile of a purring cat on him, then rolled slowly to her feet and glided for the water.

"This sun can make you crazy," she called over her shoulder, running into the surf on long, powerful legs.

Driving home in the open car she sang softly, apparently oblivious to him, and he was silent. If he did not get hold of himself at once, he knew he was lost. A word or a look might set him off irretrievably. He was afraid to draw in the scent of her salty skin. He did the only thing he could.

"I won't be able to see you for a while, Jana. I've got a very big thing to do that I've put off too long."

"All right," she said easily. After she got out of the car she reached back and patted his cheek. It was all Justin could do not to chase her into her house.

Justin's project, into which he threw himself with a desperation that no one understood, had been emerging into a series of sketches for months. Everyone with whom he had discussed it had declared it an impossibility for one so busy with his Moorish cottages and the developments along the coast. Victor had warned that there was a limit to what even Justin Oakhill could get from the very rich. And that even if Oakhill Development were foolish enough to back the project, it would pull them too thin everywhere. So Justin tried to do it with Florida Coast Oakhill alone, insisting on commitment from lenders with a zeal bordering on insanity. Someone remarked that he seemed terrified of finding an idle moment in his days.

To all who would listen, he argued vehemently that none of the communities draped down the coastline were enough to storm the imagination, to go the last step in making Florida the ultimate destination of the world's discriminating wealthy. With or without support, he announced, he would build the maximum retreat —Loco Noches.

His imagination fevered by the frustration of his impossible passion for Jana, he added new wildnesses to his already grandiose plan. Under the aegis of Florida Coast Oakhill he would create a wonderland city, with every man a millionaire. Other developers were content to create their communities around a single major feature, perhaps a hotel, setting the style and tone of future buildings around which others would create the community. Justin saw the entire Oz rising full-blown out of himself.

He projected nothing less than a Ritz-Carlton Hotel, an airport for both airplanes and Zeppelins, a yacht harbor patterned after the one at Monte Carlo, a polo grounds complete with stables and training facilities, and two hundred custom homes, each of his own design. It would have filled the lives of ten men, but Justin was determined to design his city virtually alone. And he kept adding to the concept.

"A city like this," he told the men from the newspapers, "not only must have a unifying spine like no other, it must be conceived to extend itself as it grows. Loco Noches will have as its center the most magnificent road ever to spring from the mind of man—El Camino Grande. It will march twenty lanes wide—two hundred and twenty-eight feet—the widest road in the world. And bowing to the genius of the ancient builders of Europe, down the center of El Camino Grande will run a precise duplicate of the Grand Canal of Venice—ornamental buildings, rialtos, and filled with electrically-propelled gondolas."

"Mr. Oakhill, can you mix Italian with Spanish and Moorish that way?"

"It's all Mediterranean. What those nations mixed with sword and blood over centuries, we will mix with blueprints and money in a single year. Or two, or three."

Exercising executive instincts that his father never knew he could posess, he began by organizing a board of directors that read like a celebrity register. From the nation's greatest songwriter, to its cosmetics queen, to its movie giants and its literary goliaths, he soon established an awesome publicity machine. Every time one of the great personages spoke, another hundred pages of ink spoke about Loco Noches.

Before Justin could solicit a single sale, fourteen million dollars' worth of lots was sold to buyers who would simply not be turned away. And things went straight upward from there.

The foundations for the Ritz-Carlton went down.

Fueled by gallons of coffee and health-shattering stimulants, Justin ran from long before dawn to long after midnight. It was still not enough to pull his mind away from Jana.

At last, in spite of himself, he called her to try to reestablish some contact, to at least partially assuage his hunger for a look, a touch, a word with her. He had to hope it would not overwhelm him. But now she was not available.

A man named Deak Davis had come into her life.

"Deak is nothing pretty," she told Justin airily on the phone. "He looks like a grizzly bear in English clothes, with manners and speech to match. If he didn't own all those mines in Colorado they'd lock him into a cage. He's actually frightened away my other beaus."

"Why don't you tell him to slouch back to Denver?"

"Gee, I'm a little afraid of him myself. Do you know he actually tore my gown trying to get me to go to bed with him? I had to bite him on the wrist."

Justin's heart almost stopped. "Call the police. I'll send bodyguards. He'll never—"

"Oh, no, Justin. Then he'd leave. And you don't know how thrilling a man like that can be. I really must go now, Justin. Deak is taking me to the lovely beach you and I found. Think of me." The phone clicked off.

He plunged into desolation. She had every right to be with whom she wanted. But he had to do something. A desperate idea occurred to him, and he called New York.

"George," Justin said, trying to sound only sensibly concerned, "I'm worried about Jana down here. She's fallen in with a pretty dangerous man, they tell me. It's none of my business, naturally, but she is partly my sister. Neither Father nor I was ever as close to her as you. I thought you might talk—"

Justin had never before heard George lose his chill demeanor, but now, abruptly, he was raging. "I told her I should be there. I should have gone no matter what she said. She's been almost out of my control for the last five years, and getting worse. You can't leave her with a man. Not for a moment anymore." George caught himself and tried to restore a measure of calm. "I'm concerned, Justin, because, appearances to the contrary, Jana is not at all worldly. And she'll come into a substantial fortune someday. There are men who would deceive her in any way to have it."

"What will you do, George?" said Justin, hoping.

"I'll be down, of course. Immediately. Tell me something, Justin," George said, suddenly gone quiet. "Has she . . . do you think she's . . . been with anybody?"

"I think not," Justin said. "But please hurry. It only brushed at Justin's mind that he might have invited something worse than Davis.

When Justin arrived home at nearly three o'clock in the morning, soaking with the steaminess of the torrid day only now beginning to surrender its heat to the evening air, Jana was in his bed.

There were no lights on in the huge bedroom, but the full moon poured its brightness through the tall, glassed doors that stood open to the terrace. A lovely wraith lying naked on the enormous four-poster, she watched him without moving. His breathing stopped.

Somehow he was able to will himself not to go to her, even as his throat dried and he felt the compulsive tightening in his loins. "How did you get in here, Jana?"

"Deak brought me," she said matter-of-factly. "And I came through those windows."

"Jana—"

"A proposal of marriage from a man of such substance is not something to be taken lightly. I had to come here to discuss it with my brother, hadn't I?"

"George called you, didn't he?"

"You must have known he would. It was your way of telling me what you wanted, wasn't it, Justin?"

". . . Perhaps . . . Yes . . . it was. But . . . we can't—"

"We can. The blood we share makes us alike in ways no ordinary lovers could ever know. Maybe those things are permitted only to us, because it's a honey too sweet to trust to ordinary people."

"I love you, Jana. But we can't do this."

"I must have it this way. Otherwise it would be unbearable. And I would have to move on. With Deak."

He thought of Davis waiting. The jealousy was impossible.

She left the bed and glided to him. The breath of the scented oil that glistened on her body floated in the air. She opened his shirt and with hard nipples brushed his chest. "Should I go?" she asked.

He didn't move, except for his trembling. Now she undid his belt and then his trousers.

Her hands ran down his hardness, the skin of her hands silky. His testicles rolled into her palm. "Heavy," she said. "Lighten them in me, Justin."

His fingers slid up her thighs, found wetness before they arrived in her. She tightened around his hand. "Should I go?"

They were sweating, rutting animals until first light. Then they slept briefly and continued through the day and into the next evening.

Justin's revulsion rose as swiftly as his desire. "What if Father knew? What if George knew?"

"George will know," she said sleepily. "I'll deny it, but he'll know. Don't worry, darling. I know all the ways to handle George."

When George arrived two days later, she sent him to Deak Davis to terminate her relationship. He had been furious enough to do violence, George reported grimly, but George had told him that violence was something he himself would relish in the case of a man who was forcing himself upon his sister.

"She'll hear from me," Davis had said.

"Then you'll hear from me," said George.

That George might know what was happening with them, Justin could not verify. George said nothing, though, and tried to move himself into rooms in Jana's house. But Jana said that she had told him that he must learn to be by himself more, and, very grudgingly, he had gone elsewhere.

Justin found himself unable to worry about what George, Victor or anyone else would think. He met Jana secretly whenever he could for feverish love, his need for her growing with every satisfaction, his shame never quite enough to stop him. It was she, after some weeks, who finally showed concern.

"You must have a lover to be seen with, darling. It's simply too dangerous for both of us, otherwise."

"I couldn't be with anyone else," he snapped angrily.

"There's a friend of mine. Completely beautiful. She likes women. So you both have something to cover."

"What about you?"

"Deak understands we can only be friends now. He's calmed down completely. We can go out."

"I don't want you with him, damn it. Neither does George."

"Then neither you, nor George nor Deak will be completely happy. But it will suit all of us. And there's something we can do for George."

"I'm dying to know."

"Father has shut us out. It's not fair. And George and I could give you some of the help you need with your work. For a share. Just tell us what to do."

"There's nothing available for you. It's all going to Loco Noches."

"Bring us in any way you can. No money. All we want is your name behind us."

"I thought our names were the same." Some of the doubts he should have had earlier tried to return, but he was too far gone.

The tales of overnight wealth in Florida did their work. Into the midst of the big land sharks taking their fill, an unbelievably large school of minnows swam south.

The streets filled with milling thousands becoming rich by selling lots to one another. Buses roared into the boom towns bearing potential millionaires with cardboard suitcases and five dollars in their pockets. When the same vehicles had discharged a load, they filled up again at the next corner with brass-voiced hunters who barreled down rural roads in clouds of coral dust to seek new El Dorados in every swamp.

The costume of business was whatever the new entrepreneur happened to be wearing when a deal heaved into sight. So the sidewalks and cafe tables were stacked with people in bathing suits, bathrobes and uniforms of jobs left precipitously behind, all bellowing staggering figures of money into one another's ears.

Never had the money come in so fast, even in the salad days of Harlem. And never was Victor so apprehensive. Justin had gotten away from him almost completely, and a good part of his day was taken up denying that Oakhill Development stood behind any subsequent excesses of Florida Coast Oakhill. Half in admiration, half in fear, he had given responsibility of Florida Coast over to Justin. He remembered how Hannah had originally trusted him with the skyscrapers and thought he could do no less for his own son. But his earlier appraisal of Justin's newly found judgment might have been too hasty. Victor would now hold himself clear.

* * *

Victor was trying to keep his own more sensible investments moving late one afternoon, when he looked up from his desk in Miami Beach to see a smiling, snub-nosed young man standing before him with his hand stuck out. He wore the pinstripe trousers of an old suit cut off at the knees, a shirt worn bloused-out, a leather bowtie and a taxicab driver's hat.

"Hi, Mr. Oakhill. Maybe you don't remember me. Dennis Hanratty. I used to hang around Katie's house in Harlem. She's my great-aunt."

"Well, my God, sure. You were wearing knickers and you were a long way from that fancy pencil moustache. How are Katie and Frank?"

The speech was pure New York. "Frank's gone, Mr. Oakhill. Opened the gas about five years back. He never got over losin' the place."

"Damn it, I hate to hear that."

"Katie's still creakin' along even though she can't hear anythin' much under a foghorn. She knew you was down here. When I called to tell the family where I was goin' she made me swear I'd look you up and say hello."

"What are you doing?"

"Up until three months ago I was drivin' a cab. I was cruisin' by Times Square in the middle o' the night when three swells wearin' soup 'n fishes and a dame wrapped up in a fur jumped in and said, 'Palm Beach, cabbie.' They hauled out this big roll o' Jacksons to show me they had what it took to make it worth my time. 'We're goin' down to get a lot more o' this,' they say, and all the way down—five days with hotels and eats—they're tellin' me the real estate is makin' people rich down here faster'n a 'gator can bite your ass."

"And you believed it?"

"You betcha, and lucky I did. They gimme a hundred and fifty for the trip and a fifty-dollar tip too. Then I sold the cab for four hundred dollars more and I had my stake."

Trying not to feel sick about poor Frank Chumlin, Victor questioned the boy. "What did you do with your money, Dennis?"

Dennis lit an expensive cigar, flopped into a chair and hoisted his feet onto the edge of Victor's desk. "It took me three, four days to pull my head out of my keester and figure out what was goin' on. Y'see, five percent closes most deals. Sure, the next payment is maybe twenty-five percent of the whole price, but you don't have to come up with it 'til the title clears. Now with all these sales those clearances take four weeks, maybe six. That's operatin' time."

"For what?"

"That first weekend I put my whole six hundred-dollar boodle down as a binder on a nifty parcel. Must've been a good six inches above sea level. Then I just scrambled around to find somebody to buy my binder at a better price."

"That's a dangerous way to operate, Dennis."

"Oh, I dunno. It took me all o' two hours to turn my six hundred into seventeen hundred ironmen."

Victor had to laugh in spite of his being appalled. "Superb. You can go home with your money tripled in one day."

"Home?" Dennis said, as though Victor had mouthed an unspeakable obscenity. "*This* is home now, Mr. Oakhill. I had that seventeen hundred down on another binder by the next day."

"And?"

"Not so good that time. Only doubled it in an hour. But things picked up and I made eleven thousand the first week. And by that time I really knew how to operate."

In spite of himself, Victor was fascinated. "Tell me more."

"It slows you up tryin' to find buyers at prices you want. So you use binder boys."

"Binder boys?"

"Street kids. It didn't take 'em long to learn the ropes. You give a bunch of them ten bucks each, tell them what you want and fan them out in all directions. They steer the buyers to you. I guess you could send them to find sellers, too, but what the hell does a twelve-year-old kid know about real estate?"

Now Victor knew the end could not be far away. But he also knew it was not in his power to deflate this intrepid and hopeful young man. "It's wonderful to see you, Dennis. Is there any way I can help?"

Dennis chuckled as he stood. "A guy who's piled up eighty-seven thousand in three months don't need much help, Mr. Oakhill. Thanks anyway, though. Maybe in another five, six months I can help *you* out with somethin'. I never thought that Harlem thing was the Oakhills' fault the way Uncle Frank did."

Justin learned that Jana had plunged into her own version of the game with a cold courage possessed by few of the plungers he knew.

Using his name as a reference, she had acquired parcels south of Miami Beach for a staggering nine million dollars, for which she offered to pay four million down. Within a week, during which she carefully avoided his phone calls, she had sold them for five million down to a buyer she had lined up previously. A million dollars of profit in one week.

She had not asked Justin for any money, which he could not have raised at the moment in any case, and he knew of no place where she could possibly have raised the four million dollars she would have needed. And why had his own backing not been checked and found wanting? He was utterly baffled.

A pale, tight-lipped George gave him the answer over cocktails at The Waves. "Jana knew the check wouldn't be cleared until the deal was complete, dearest boy."

"How could she be sure of that?"

"By sleeping very skillfully with the president of the right bank." The bitter set of his face broke into a grim smile as he observed the effect this had on Justin.

"There's no way you could know that," Justin said, trying vainly to smother his despair.

"There certainly is, Justin. She told me, just as she tells me everything. I might add that she was unnecessarily graphic about it. Our sister can be quite a whore, you know, when it suits her purpose."

Justin restrained himself from smashing George's jaw. "How could she tell such foul things to her own brother?"

"Because we trust one another as other people could never

understand. Do you know she's given me the million dollars to protect it? Oh, yes. We share everything." His eyes burned on Justin. "No matter what rage it might cause."

Jana had Justin in bed ten minutes after he confronted her with his unrestrained fury. When she had drained him imaginatively of both rage and ardor, she spoke to him.

"It's nineteen twenty-four, darling. A woman's body is her own now, just as a man's has always been. I hope you'll believe that my potbellied friend at the bank was as much a tool to me as a contractor is to you, and I used it with no more passion."

"Might I be a tool, too?"

"Why, of course you might. Doesn't that make it more interesting?" she asked teasingly as she rolled on top of him and began very expertly to bring him up again.

Months went by. The work went forward. The boom heightened.

Miami issued 7,500 real estate licenses in a single year. Five-hundred-acre tracts of swampland sold out in two hours. The fantastic buildings and Grand Canal of Loco Noches began to take shape. Every nickel in the state was being used to invest further, in hope of the return of a quarter.

There was a story of a sign painter who had executed a sign reading, *A Million Dollar Hotel Will Be Erected Here,* and who was then unable to collect the twenty dollars due him from the builders.

Justin's life reached a fearful equilibrium, with his forbidden time with Jana balancing the nights against the exhausting days of building on impossible schedules. The only thing that relieved his despair that they could not go on together indefinitely was knowing he would soon have her under him.

Then Jana disappeared.

When Justin arrived one night at the clandestine villa they had taken at the outskirts of Palm Beach, she simply never came. No call. No note.

He waited a day to ask George if she had been at her house, and learned that her brother had been about to make the same sort of call. They waited together, talking little, growing more restive and beginning to speak of the police.

Jana appeared at Justin's house on the third day, cooler and more beautiful than ever, a fabulous diamond on her finger. "Come kiss Mrs. Deak Davis," she said to Justin at the door of the villa. "He'll make a fine divorce, and I do need him for a while to front me the kind of money that you can't."

"Almighty God, Jana," Justin cried, "look what you've done *without* money."

"They're getting onto that one, darling. People talked."

He was destroyed. "Come on in, damn it."

"No, I just came by to get some things. Deak is all over me all day."

"You're not going to stay with him!" Justin shouted.

"How can a wife not stay with her husband, Justin? Naturally, my frail health will make it increasingly impossible for me to sleep with him."

"When . . . when will we be together again?"

"I can't think about that until we come to some understanding about how George and I are going to become full partners in what this company will be earning. When you're out from under the debts."

"That's for Father to say, not me."

"Nonsense, Justin. You've all but taken the business away from him already. Virtually everything that's happening down here is because of you. He's becoming a tired old man. What more could he want that he doesn't already have?"

"He'll turn us down." This was the Jana he had known.

"He doesn't have to know how we share. And he won't live forever, will he?"

"I hate you this way," he said, trying to stop his passion with what he was beginning to see in her.

She stepped inside. "It's been a tiring week. I think I'd like to lie down a while. Will you join me?"

* * *

Soon Justin was watching his schemes beginning to disintegrate on several fronts.

For one thing, Davis kept Jana away from any substantial share of his money and also made sure that his gifts to her were not too saleable. This made her mercenary approaches to Justin all the more savage.

And then there was Loco Noches. It was devouring cash at an even greater rate than strong preliminary sales could bring in. He diverted every cent he could from his other projects. This capital starvation might have been soon fixable in the flushest days, but the Florida real estate phenomenon was beginning to vaporize.

The National Credit Association, powered by men unhappy with the amount of money being siphoned to Florida, launched a major campaign to describe the perils of what was happening in the state.

Some of the Better Business Bureaus did likewise. The Florida Credit Association returned salvo for salvo in defense of the boom, but it was not fully effective.

Victor, with the grim lessons of the Harlem debacle well learned, began to divest himself of his more speculative holdings, keeping what was solidly financed and would appreciate in the long run. He thought wryly of how he was now duplicating the role of Hannah in Harlem, if with more honesty. The roles of youth and age were never reversed, it seemed.

His long-range faith in the state was undiminished however. "Get out from under Loco Noches while you can, Justin. There are still enough buyers to pay your debts and let you come out even or better. Buy away from the boom areas. I'm going to begin looking in the Keys. Come down with me and help. You can still be all right down here for the future."

Justin knew that Jana was not interested in the far future of anything. "No. It will hold long enough to let me make my kill. And Loco Noches is the kind of development that can keep it all going. To begin backing off now could start the real tumble."

"Then I won't rescue you."

"Understood. But it would take something like an earthquake to stop this so suddenly I couldn't get out."

* * *

Deak Davis proved a much larger problem than anticipated. The mining magnate, hulking, sullen, bewhiskered in an age when beards had all but vanished, hovered about Jana day and night, paying no attention to her exasperated rages. He was a man of few words and short ones, speaking at length only when he meant to be understood unmistakably.

"Stop bothering my wife on the phone," he said to Justin. "Between you and that goddamn George she doesn't have time to say ten words a day to me."

And so Justin was all but cut off from the woman who obsessed him.

When everything else had failed, Jana complained of exhaustion and began to take "rest trips" away from Davis, having to slip from him to do so. Davis' possessive fury was not helped when he found that she was joining her brother George. Wherever it was that they went, Justin was not invited anymore than Davis was.

Less than three months after her marriage, having not received the backing of Davis or his banks for the five million dollars of loans she wanted, she left him. Now seeing how he had been used, Davis alternately thundered and pleaded for her return. He would not relent on the money because he wanted to be loved for his unpleasant self.

"Deak," she said to him, "only a syphilitic hog in heat would tolerate your attentions."

Whatever hopes Justin had for her return to his own life were dashed. She spent almost all her time with George, who worked mightily to shield her from the tireless harassments of Davis. Soon her husband began to hint of physical retaliation as his efforts at reconciliation went unheeded.

George wanted to take her from Florida, but she guessed Davis would follow her anywhere. Beside which she had grown possessed with the idea that Loco Noches would be both the salvation of Florida Coast Oakhill and the path to sharing the Oakhill wealth.

The only times she called Justin was to ask for progress reports on sales and building and to urge him forward in the work.

In only one respect was Justin's lot better than Davis'. As the holder of something she wanted, his desperate pleading for her was sometimes answered with words that just might hold out some hope for her return. "Darling, maybe when the weight of this thing is off both our minds it can be the way it was. George and I have your success as our greatest wish."

He didn't tell her that he had already despaired of the half-built fantasyland that was to endure as his monument, but he went forward more recklessly than ever, heedless of Victor's ferocious warnings.

The boyish King of Palm Beach had in months become a haggard, driven ghost, his every day a misery of longing and mind-numbing labor. If he believed in a Devil, he would have prayed to him for the continuation of his sin.

The end began three hundred and fifty miles to the southeast, as a malevolent swirl of heated air gathered itself sullenly and began to take on juggernaut force as it drifted toward the Florida Coast.

Its approach was not entirely a surprise. Wireless reports from ships at sea told that something ominous was building. The Weather Service began to track it. Some islands caught the fringe of what were certainly hurricane winds, and their damage was brutal. But things like this formed again and again in September, and most of them blew over before they struck Florida. Life went on heedlessly for most.

Before he had boarded the train for the Keys with George and Jana, Victor knew that some of the oldtimers were beginning to batten down and move inland. But what was prudent in the case of a beach bungalow, he thought, had nothing to do with one of H. E. Ragland's giant locomotives tugging a tender, five gondolas of crushed rock, the palace car *Delia Ragland* and a sturdy caboose. Even on this slender causeway across the sea, the tracks skimming the water as they reached for the Keys lying far below the distant horizon, they were safe. As the train flew forward, Victor reminded himself that these viaducts were designed by many of the same brilliant men who had built the Panama Canal. Over the years these tracks had proved they could withstand any unexpected onslaught of wind and water. Yet his nerves tightened alarmingly.

Blotched with the sweat that had soaked through his shirt, George pried open a window further.

"The soot from the engine will ruin my dress," Jana said.

"The air is like lead," said George. "We'll die if we can't get some moving air." But he lowered the window and returned to sit close to her.

"I think it was silly of you to make us come with you, Father," George said.

"Hardly. That fire in Jana's house started too quickly and spread too fast for it to be accidental. If that rainstorm hadn't come just then to hold it down, she'd be dead. And that automobile that sent you diving into a ditch to save yourself? Davis' work, or his men's. I'll deal with him when I'm back. I'd have done it right away, but I've been waiting to get this tract in the Keys for a year, and it won't be available long. I feel better that you're both out of his way here. Besides, it might be interesting for you to sit in on a tough negotiation."

"It had better be more interesting than this trip. Thank God Ragland had the courtesy to lend you this marvelous car of his. Those sleeping compartments must have cost a hundred thousand each to furnish. You really have to learn to live like this, Father."

"Where are the birds?" asked Jana, searching the empty expanse of leaden sky on both sides of the train. "They're usually swooping by in clouds."

"They're probably waiting for us in Key West. We'll be there in less than two hours."

"This heat is exhausting. I'm going to my compartment to lie down."

She left, and George began to read a newspaper. Victor tried to light a cigar, but he couldn't get a match to spark in the sodden air. He loosened his tie and collar and was powerless to keep his eyes from closing.

He dreamed that Evangeline had returned and was in the coach as a demon. She hovered above him and demanded that he do terrible and unclean things with her. When her hands touched his body they were icy, but they woke fantasies of the flesh. Her lips, pale now but still beautiful, came close to his, and he just too late saw they were the sharp, tearing canines of another creature hiding in her body. He groaned and flung up his hand to shove her away, and she dissolved in flame with long shrieks of rage that shook the earth, and guttural roars that assaulted his ears with massive concussion.

Victor awakened, pouring sweat in streams, but whatever monster was howling did not relent.

The train had stopped, he realized at once, but the private coach shuddered more frantically than it had at full speed. His question to George died as he realized he was alone in the salon, and when he swung his legs off the lounge on which he had slept, he found his feet submerged. Before he had a chance to look up, a wall of water slammed through the opened windows to the east and sent light furniture across the car. Victor tasted salt water. Then the windows were admitting blowing sheets of rain, and the air pressure in the car built until he thought the walls would blow out. It was all he could do to fight his way to the windows against the shrieking wind, and it took all the force of his arms and shoulders to fight them closed. What he saw through the panes strained his courage to the breaking point.

He was no longer on a train, but rather a gale-tossed ship. The gray water that had lain peaceably below the tracks had risen sickeningly, and giant, gray-bearded waves, building every moment, were rolling down in undulating mountains to break against the undercarriage of the halted train.

No earthly power could save them if they remained stopped at this place, he saw. He had to get to the locomotive to see what was wrong and how they could get away.

"*George . . . Jana . . .*," he cried, but the shattering uproar made the cry inaudible. No matter for now. If they couldn't get away from here they would die on the train no matter where they were.

Victor made his way forward in the coach, jerking open the door at the forward end. Even as he did so, a wave burst across the opening and swept him backward as it gushed sideways. Struggling to his his feet, he caught sight of the ladder to the top of the gondola car opposite and staggered for it. He was across the treacherous, greasy coupling and onto the rungs as the next wave was sweeping down. Up, up the slippery rungs he went, the wind trying to tear him away.

He tumbled over the edge of the gondola car, falling downward into the cargo of crushed rock, sharp edges tearing his flesh.

Gripping the brake wheel, he forced himself erect and looked forward.

The train was broadside to the hurricane, the slender trestle being the only interruption to immense seas rolling to the west. Spray leaped a hundred feet into the iron gray of the torn sky. The wind ripped the tops off the mountains, turning them into stinging spray and leaving white stumps behind in the ocean. The combined roar of sea and wind was mind-numbing.

At the train's head, the locomotive was a mortally wounded dragon, steam pouring out into the wind from the stack and cab.

Victor had hardly started forward, crawling across the drenched, tearing rock, when he saw with a start that there was another figure crawling from the forward end. It was not until the man was three feet from his face that he saw it was Deak Davis, and that his big hand held a heavy automatic pistol.

Words were not possible, but a menacing wave of the gun barrel told Victor he was to return to the coach.

With agility greatly surpassing Victor's, Davis covered him as they negotiated the wave-battered passage between the gondola and the coach. They returned to the palace car, both of them breathless and exhausted.

There were no lights, only the dull glimmer from the water-lashed windows revealing the soaked, shuddering interior.

Keeping Victor in close range, Davis searched quickly around him, not finding what he wanted.

"They're not here, Davis."

Davis was dressed in the torn, soaked ruin of what had been an elegant suit. A thousand gallons of water had not been enough to wash the rock dust off him. "That's funny, because I saw her and that slimy shadow of hers come aboard."

"Where were you?"

"On the locomotive. For two hundred dollars the engineer was willing to allow an eccentric rich man his dream of being at the throttle of a locomotive crossing open sea to the Keys."

"So it was you who stopped the train?"

"Oh, no. The waves did that. Drowned the fires. I was willing to wait until the Keys where nobody would be looking out for me."

"Get hold of yourself, Davis. You're not the first man who was left by a woman."

"Did you know she left me for another man?"

"You're wrong. She couldn't hide that from me and Justin."

Davis quaked with soundless laughter. "You and Justin, huh? Well, maybe you weren't looking too hard. But she had a Cuban maid who had a boyfriend who liked to peek. He drilled some holes into the bedroom and saw interesting things. Interesting enough to sell to her husband."

The car jolted and the sea broke through two windows, pouring in water. The wind, admitted again, filled the interior with blowing newspapers. After a second shock that followed almost instantly, the car gave a new sort of twist, and there was an agonizing rending of wood and steel beneath them. It seemed to bring cold amusement to Davis. "I've shipped enough ore over this trestle to know what it can stand. Those five cars of rock and those waves are too much for it. It's all going down, and so are we."

"My God. Couldn't we leave the train? Make our way to the next span?"

"Maybe. If the waves didn't get us. It's what the train people are trying. They're gone. But I've decided to stay here with you and your children. Seeing their faces as we go under will repay me just a bit for what she did with my love."

"I won't let you hurt them."

He shot forward, but Davis caught him a short chop with the barrel of the automatic. Victor didn't lose consciousness, but fell to his knees as the strength left him. There was blood in his eyes as Davis hauled him to his feet by the arm.

Above the roar of the hurricane, Victor could hear Davis snarling into his ear as he dragged him to the sleeping-compartments. "Let's find George and Jana, shall we?"

The blow had left Victor stumbling and all but helpless for the moment, and he could not twist away from the mad grip of the younger and more powerful man.

A terror such as he had never known clutched at Victor, and it had nothing to do with the annihilating dangers around them.

The first compartment, his, and the second, George's, were empty. At the last door, Davis's lips drew back over his teeth like those of a hunting wolf and he swung a hip at the flimsy latch just as the wind rose to a horrendous screech.

The writhing, naked creatures on the bed might not have heard the crack of doom. As though the madness trapped in their bodies were part of the storm itself, and now fully unleashed by the moment of the wind's highest fury, they knew nothing but one another.

Jana, eyes screwed shut, knees drawn impossibly backward, nails tearing at George's sweating back, yowled now like a rutting cat. Arched above her on straightened arms, muscles coiling and twisting, George drove his flanks with culminating power.

Even above the din Victor heard Davis's sob of torment rise with his own. The crushing grip on his arm came loose. Davis took two steps forward, his trembling hand raising the huge pistol level with George's temple. If George glimpsed the approaching nuzzle or heard anything above his fevered breathing, he gave no sign.

Victor's mind, with all the igniting instincts of a father, urged his body forward to save his children, but his battered flesh produced only a stumble forward that missed its mark, bringing him to his hands and knees beside the bed inches from Jana's face. From there, with the expanding and paralyzed time of a dream, he saw all that happened.

In the heartbeat it took for Davis's finger to drag back the trigger, Jana's eyes, responding to a primordial alarm, flashed open. As quickly, her hand shot up and pulled downward on the barrel of the gun.

The booming explosion tore at the walls of the paneled compartment, the shock to the eardrums momentarily cutting short the sound of the wet, gray beast tearing at the window behind the berth. The ejected shell case, stinging hot, skipped across Victor's cheek. A blue-rimmed hole appeared just above the nipple of Jana's right breast. After a moment, with the universe seeming frozen, a great red bubble appeared around the wound, swelled and burst. Powder burned at Victor's eyes, mixing with his tears.

George sprang upon Davis, an uncoiling panther. Their bodies careened crushingly in the narrow compartment for only a few moments before Davis's bulky automatic appeared in George's hand. George was too far gone to use the weapon as other than a club. He held the barrel and smashed thunderbolt blows against Davis's forehead until the giant fell wedged into a corner. There, one last downward drive split the scalp and thick bone bloodily and ended his breathing in mid-gasp.

Jana was not yet dead when George and Victor got to her. Her eyes were huge and surprised, without fear or anger, the look of a wiped-out gambler who has enjoyed the game. She licked at the blood on her lips, tasting the escaping sweetness of life, and tried to touch George's face. The murderous battler of moments ago had become a pathetic wreck, swaying with shock. He said her name over and over, kissing her hand and holding it to his cheek.

Her lips moved painfully, her voice bubbling and broken. *"It's ours,"* she said to George, putting everything that was left of her life into the words. *"Get it. It's ours."*

As if the breaking away of her fierce soul had wrenched at the earth, the car gave a huge, swaying lurch. There was a creaking, then a series of cannonshot cracks far below them.

Victor shook his head clear and willed the return of his strength. He grasped George by the shoulder and yelled to him above his wails and the roar of the storm. "The trestle under us is failing. This train will go into the sea. We've got to climb off and go for the next span."

"We can't leave her," wept George, clutching Jana to him more desperately.

Mingled with his grief, Victor felt an overpowering need to be away from the defiled body of his daughter. "She's gone, George. Come with me."

George turned on him, the old calm, coolness suddenly descending. "No. She's not gone. She'll never be gone."

The groaning of the span of tracks was now steady under the succession of watery blows from beneath, and the sickening oscillation would clearly destroy then in only minutes.

"You'll be throwing yourself away," Victor said, a part of him not caring.

George appeared to hear not his father, but another voice. Then he kissed Jana's brow and relinquished her, prepared to follow Victor out.

Once on the tracks, it was a matter of timing the waves between short sprints along the wet and slippery ties. The distance between the men and the doomed train opened with tormenting slowness, and they had no way of knowing if they had reached the end of the threatened span.

As each wave thundered down, the two dropped to the trackbed and entwined their arms and legs about the ties. There they braced against the rails to keep the gale-whipped sea from sweeping them away on its shoulders.

Victor's grasp was almost broken when a demon's hand grasped train and track and gave one last, exasperated twist.

The sound of a thousand rending timbers and screeching, separating steel trusses joined the deafening wind. Victor turned to see the train writhing on the disintegrating snake of track beneath it and then begin to droop sideways. Beneath him, the span was pulled irresistibly by the tons of stone in the gondola cars.

The locomotive spilled first, balancing precariously on one set of wheels, then tipping into the white churn of sea. Its weight pulled the other cars behind it in succession, the falling chain carrying the springing rails downward.

As the stone dumped tumultuously into the sea from the overturning gondolas, there was one last, chilling rip. A dozen feet behind Victor, twisting rails sprang into the air as they separated from the falling trestle.

Train and span showed their belly in the white water, appearing for a brief instant to try to float upward to life before they vanished under the foam.

Freed of its attachments and the crippling weight, the remaining trestle surged upward on its deformed trusses, almost hurling Victor and George loose at the moment of their salvation.

There was no more strength for crawling, even if there had been a purpose to it. Only half conscious, they clung there through the storm, and as it passed they lived to see the sky fill with stars.

A work train found them in the the morning, no longer the men they had been.

The great hurricane finished what was left of the Florida land boom. More than a hundred people were dead in Dade County. In Miami, two thousand homes were destroyed and twice as many damaged. Destruction up and down the coast was severe. Suddenly Florida seemed as vulnerable to death, desolation and calamity as anywhere else. The vision of a paradise of eternal sunshine and balmy breezes was blown out to sea and lost.

Speculators waiting for the greater fool to appear now waited in vain. The torrent of people and money from the North slowed to a trickle and dried up. Prices collapsed and the birds of passage flew back to the blizzards.

Only the natives and a few tenacious people of vision retained what they could and held on for the long stay, still expecting that one day the golden peninsula would again have its hour.

Meanwhile the sprawling developments froze as they were, half-built. Wheelbarrows of cement stood at the edge of forms, shovels imprisoned in their hardened loads where workers, no longer paid, had walked away. The skeletal frames of unfinished second floors loomed above first floors occupied by stranded squatters, or sometimes by the destitute builders themselves.

The unfinished masterpiece of Loco Noches stood pathetically incomplete, its Grand Canal filling with silt before the first electric gondola could appear, its Moorish battlements looking upon a spectral city emptied by a nameless plague. Its twenty-two lane highway, El Camino Grande, once destined to open the entire coast, ended in tangled jungle a half-mile from where it had begun.

Months passed before the bodies in the train were retrieved, by which time the underwater creatures had erased all evidence of violent ends.

Jana was buried with her husband in a family plot near Leadville, Colorado. Victor attended with George and Justin. What other mourners there were shrank back from the three men, whose faces bore something far more terrible than grief.

Before they left the cemetery, Victor spoke privately to George. "You are no longer a member of any family of mine. If Justin was too mesmerized to see what you were trying to do, I wasn't. You'll have nothing of the Oakhill estate. Not now. Not ever."

George, already death-white, showed no change at the words. "Jana made me reinvest what we had, in Florida. It's gone, along with most of what we had from Grandfather."

"Oakhill Development was no part of that."

"You can't hold us away. *It's ours.*"

"There is no more *us*. Remember? She's dead. You must make your own life now. I pray that all the corruption was from her, and you'll find your way."

"Do you think your pristine little Justin was any better than me? You know all the time they spent together? Why don't you ask him whether he—"

At the age of sixty Victor might have lost a moment of reaction time, but George was not able to see the punch coming. As Jack

Grant had taught him so long ago, he lashed out with the full turning force of his body behind the blow. George hit the ground hard. "You won't take *everything* away from me, George," he said as he strode away.

"We'll see," he thought he heard George say.

Waiting in the funeral car, Justin saw George fall. He had never before seen Victor angry beyond control. The words he had with George could only have been about Jana, and Victor could only guess what they had been. One thing he knew was that he would never ask. Then at least, the damage she had done would end for him at the grave. After that there would be only the waiting for the obsession to die. He guessed that would be a slow death.

Finishing up in Florida before returning to New York with Justin, Victor almost lost his toes to a taxicab that screeched to a stop in front of him.

At the wheel, his taxi hat and smile intact, was Dennis Hanratty. "Thought I'd drive over and say bye-bye, Mr. Oakhill. The guy I sold this to had some hard luck on a tract that the alligators wouldn't move off of because it was underwater at high tide. I got the thing back for fifty bucks. I'll send him the thirty I owe him when I'm drivin' on Broadway again."

"I don't suppose you have a fare, Dennis."

"You kiddin'?"

"Not at all. I have a lot to think about, and I need some time. Give me a couple of hours to pack."

"Make it snappy, will you? This place is a tomb, and I want to get out of it."

"Yes," Victor said, looking up and down the desolate streets. "It's a tomb. But it's a pretty one."

Chapter 13

FORD STRYKER had been raised as an Oakhill since the burning of the *General Sherman*, but knew that in Victor's eyes he was not. Twelve years old then, he had also been raised as a white man but knew, proudly, that he was not.

Victor had been as true to the promise Hannah had exacted from him as he could. From him, Ford had never known anything but politeness, privilege and kindness. But the thought that his Evangeline had been with Caesar could never be erased.

Ford's almost-hidden blackness had never mattered much to Victor, it seemed. But there was no question that he felt that knowledge of his ward's black blood would do the boy no good. He had always appeared glad that Caesar's light eyes and skin had been passed along, and that Ford's features, while every bit as striking, were somewhat more in the white mold. For as long as he could, Victor had specified haircuts that showed Ford's hair in handsome waves rather than tighter curls, and saw to it that broad-brimmed hats were worn where the sun was strong and likely to darken the skin.

Measures like these might have succeeded if Ford had cooperated. But Caesar Stryker had spent too many loving hours talking to his son. "Ford, the men who wear this skin of ours must never deny it. The way people hate us can be beaten if they can't make us hate ourselves."

The way his father had conducted himself through his awful trials had never been lost. Ford remembered that he had never seen his father hold back what he thought, or seen him back down, even when the cost was catastrophic. He had not bent to the flattering or quailed at the eventual attacks. If he had cut sharp deals in those last days in Harlem, it was because he believed that anything was justified to preserve the golden promise —that once it was lost, the black race might languish in American slums for a hundred years more. Besides, he later knew, the hand of Hannah Oakhill had been behind the worst of it. If Caesar had led badly, he had at least led bravely—in the open, with dignity, inviting all fire. The white woman had skulked, betraying her own as she had ultimately betrayed Caesar and his people. He often wondered how much of Hannah's guilt had to do with the promise she had gotten from Victor.

Anyway, Ford had never taken long at his snobbish schools to tell the sons of privilege just who and what he was. He accepted the inevitable sneers and snubs, but seldom the taunts and never the blows. Fists would swing and then he was glad to have the blood of Gentleman Jack in his sinew. Many of the older boys became more than content to insult "the darky" from a safe distance behind his back after a bloody half-hour behind a dormitory with Ford Stryker.

Although it was hard to get close to Victor, Ford liked him and respected him well enough, and whatever relationship they had was cordial. It was his relationship with Justin that was not.

The two boys were eight years apart, with Justin the older. Justin's fierce loyalty to his exiled mother had brought him to the Stryker home for many hours a week as soon as he was able to take to the streets alone. There the half-brothers competed shamelessly for Evangeline's love, although she had more than enough for both.

The great difference in ages leveled out quickly. Ford's efficient, thorough and preternaturally mature ways quickly made him more than a match for the impulsive, disorganized and perpetually childlike Justin.

"Good God, Ford. Nobody alive ever saved their homework in binders from the first grade."

"And no other eighteen-year-old I know is still rigging string to knock off people's hats."

If there was a racial undertone, it was on Ford's side. Justin adored Caesar once he knew him and never seemed to resent his "new father." But Ford saw the pure whiteness of Justin's blood as some lurking menace that might one day tip his mother's love more to his brother.

As they grew older, the strained feelings between them began to revolve about a natural and irreconcilable difference about what—and where—a man's life should be.

Ford loathed the city. Roaming the streets of Harlem as it turned black, he had found a cheerless, filthy concrete desert that was a pitiless sinkhole for the spirit. Even when he lived comfortably during the best days, the walls of his room were covered with an ever-changing series of outdoor pictures. Beautiful forests, lush green plains, rushing rivers and mountain lakes let his young soul breathe. He kept scrapbooks of ideal places in the countryside, where a single uncrowded family might live in its own house with its own grass and trees.

Central Park became his haunt. Going into the trees as far from the roaring crowds and traffic as he could, he would find a place where no city buildings showed and pretend he was a thousand miles from where fifty families might huddle together in a single stifling concrete trap.

Something in his early instincts told him that people had never been meant by God to live away from outdoor spaces of their own. The steaming, crowded sidewalks without a tree, the streets choked with automobiles, the fumes and stinks, the subway cars so crowded you couldn't fall if you fainted—all made him physically ill.

As he grew, Ford saw it even clearer.

The landlord was the new feudal baron. He was motivated to provide the meanest quarters he could for the most money. He could beggar, demean, evict. The tenant had no more rights than a serf, and if he missed paying his rent after twenty faithful years, he would be gone without a splinter to show for all those years of departed treasure.

With nothing they could ever hope to own, there was no dream, no family stability for the likes of the renters who came to blasted places like latter-day Harlem. Away from the open fields and streams that had given some natural nobility to their poorest forefathers, people shriveled and became husks in burrows on streets where nothing could grow.

Justin, to Ford's disgust, loathed anything that was *not* a city. A countryside was an empty, boring tangle of obstacles to speedy progress. The sun baked you, rain fell far from sheltering shops and doorways. Snow sat uncollected in the winter and insects gnawed in droves in the summer. He found the people who occupied this green hell, observed firsthand in upstate vacations, a mass of stunned oxen, little removed from the animals who had recently occupied the same ground. Without newsstands, movies and popular records, their minds were geared only to the cycles of night and day, hunger and thirst, copulate and populate.

To Justin, who had taken many of his ideas from Victor, the city was the marketplace of genius, where visions were bought, sold and traded to power the world.

In later years, after his ordeal in Florida, Justin had told Ford that he had been only momentarily pleased with his opportunity to fill the Florida wilderness with his homes. Even if Loco Noches had been able to multiply itself dozens of times as El Camino Grande marched down the coast, it would have taken fifty years to concentrate people at the rate he wished, and to push them into the sky in real buildings.

Ford had observed the sad new heaviness in Justin since the death of his sister in the Florida tragedy. Neither he nor Victor had returned with the same verve, the same certainty that the world was theirs to control. Apparently Jana had occupied places in their hearts he had not suspected. But they had both tried to press on.

Justin had after a time regained his impatience to begin grand works and tried to make himself the adventuresome component in Oakhill Development despite his Florida chastening. But they all had soon found that their dreams had to wait.

The crash of 1929 had pulverized not only the hopes of renewed prosperity in Florida, but in the nation.

Justin and Ford watched the Depression rob them of any opportunities for significant ventures.

There was never the faintest suggestion by either of them that they might work together on something for Victor, since it was clear to both that their wildly differing temperaments would not mesh. Indeed, even with nothing to do they found it increasingly difficult to have discussions of any sort without flying at one another after a short time, so that one of them would storm away thinking the other the worst kind of fool.

"Ford, show me somebody with deershit on his shoes and I'll show you somebody with horseshit in his head."

"People who live in cement end up with cement hearts."

In this mired economy, Ford saw that Justin, the son of Victor's blood, was destined to have an easier time of it. It wasn't as if Victor had not saved a substantial enough portion of Oakhill Development to keep them all in reasonable comfort while he waited for his solid holdings to regain value; they would probably survive. But building, the soul of Oakhill Development, had halted utterly. Rents were falling and often in arrears. Vacancies, commercial and residential, multiplied as businesses failed and evictions took their toll. Even with the staff cut to a skeleton and the offices an echoing wasteland of empty desks and cubicles, there was not enough to keep Victor and Justin occupied. They did not need another junior partner. Any plans Ford might have had to enter business under the Oakhill flag now seemed impossible.

It was plain to Ford that Victor was using the slow years to fill the ever-chafing Justin with the arcanities of big-city building and financing, the groundwork that he had plunged past in the headlong years in Florida.

Ford supposed that Victor would have been glad enough to do the same for him. But for him, the world of city buildings held no special interest. If Victor's business had been banking or apparel or heavy machinery, it would not have mattered to Ford. And if the economy had been functioning enough to present sufficient choice, he might have gone a separate way.

Instead, he searched the Oakhill operation for his own corner.

What he finally suggested to Victor asked nothing of the company for start-up costs, and therefore relieved him of the never-absent feeling that his call on the family and its holdings were based on nothing more than the old promise to Hannah. His idea would let him use the marvelous organizing powers that had been his since he had collected bottles as a child. And it would also give him a piece of the business for himself—valueless at the moment—to which he could attach his father's name.

"Stryker and Oakhill is what I'd like to call my unit," he said to Victor after he had outlined the basics of his plan.

"Fine. Set it up any way you want, Ford. But you're not going to make a nickel. Nobody could."

"Indulge me, Victor. So that my 'allowance,' which you've been kind enough to call a salary, might buy you something someday. I'm as sure as I can be that there are enough people like you, holding and planning for when this mess ends, to give me the nucleus of a good business. I'll use a part of the office, if it's all right."

"Good. It'll keep the cobwebs down. Make it far away from Justin. He's like a wounded bear. Take whatever help you need out of the staff part-time. There's slack enough. If you ever generate enough income and work—which I doubt—we'll transfer them to your own payroll."

"Thanks, Victor. That's generous."

"Who knows? You might get interested in the building business. He smiled at the thought.

And so Ford set to work.

He had seen his opportunity in the brokerage side of the operation. So far as he had been able to see, the city's commercial real estate brokers, the firms that filled the space in the buildings, had carried the habits of the flush twenties into the collapsed thirties with catastrophic results. They had sat quietly by their phones waiting for a needful buyer or seller to call for a matchup, after which they hoped to negotiate the deal and take a commission. But with the phones not ringing at all, the brokerages had disappeared by the hundreds.

Ford, confident only in his basic idea and dreadfully afraid of all he did not yet know, got hold of old commission lists from the failed companies and contacted the top one or two brokers from each. They were skeptical, but men with no jobs listen harder than others.

"Look, Stryker. I think it's nifty you're offering me commissions fifty percent higher than I was getting before. But fifty percent of nothing makes thin soup when there's no base pay."

"Listen, good real estate deals are too complicated to happen by themselves in markets like this. We've got to be matchmakers and then midwives. It's got to be *us* that find and create the great deals. Then the money will come."

"What great deals? There's not a thing happening."

"The deadness is the opportunity. Companies can pick up whole buildings now for only a little more than they're paying for rent in a lot of scattered, inconvenient locations. Today's thousand-dollar parking lots are the heart of tomorrow's million-dollar assemblages. The big payoff will come when the hard times end and the value of what they pick up now explodes."

"I can't sell tomorrow's meal today, mister."

"Then you're not the salesman I thought you were and not the man for Stryker and Oakhill. Go wait by the phone for another five years."

Led by Ford, a core of ten men who saw glints of the opportunities made the calls.

Ford himself did most of the scouting, looking for tiny nuggets in the seemingly barren fields of Manhattan. Revealing his lack of knowledge shamelessly to Victor, he questioned him a dozen times a day about his ideas, listening and learning always, but often going his own way against advice. Then he would lay down the selling strategy to his hungry staff and send them out.

For almost two months nothing came in but higher phone and subway bills for Oakhill Development. Ford dug into his allowance to keep his salesmen going.

Even with no money returning, Ford saw Victor's indulgent patience turning to surprised respect at the scope and organization of the effort. He offered Ford more of the cash resources of Oakhill Development to carry him along, but Ford refused until his guardian agreed on a formal division of the nonexistent profits. Papers were drawn and Ford went from something of a mascot to a legal division of the parent company.

In the third month, the first small deals were made, five of them, and Ford took his salesmen to a disproportionately enormous celebration dinner.

Soon they came to know which were the companies with patience, and where in them were the men with foresight. They learned quickly and sharpened their techniques both in selling and in their methods of research.

The salesmen were on good base salaries long before the end of the year, but the oversized commissions that they were now collecting with increasing regularity made that unimportant except in the case of the several new men they took on.

The corner of Oakhill Development taken by Stryker and Oakhill became a noisy and crowded oasis in what had shortly before been a desert of empty desks.

Justin would admit no interest in the new commotion. "Selling any barns to the farmers?" he would call scornfully to Ford when he passed unavoidably.

Victor, though, did not conceal his pleasure or surprise that his charitable gesture to Evangeline's son had so prospered. Examining the S & O books, Victor said, "If I'd known you were going to do this well I'd have asked for more than fifteen percent."

Ford was on him in a moment. "Then let's make it twenty-five percent. And I stay in your space without rent until I get big enough for my own place."

"That's not a very good deal for you."

"It might get better, Victor. When I ask your backing for some things in the future and you have more to gain by giving them to me."

"The future could be a long way off. What kinds of things?"

"I'm not sure. But outside the city. The sort of stuff Justin laughs at."

Later on Ford overheard Justin laughing at his father. "Chicken coops," he said. "You just got twenty-five percent of a bunch of chicken coops out in the weeds. Put that together with your share of the commissions on the empty parking lots, collapsed piers and bankrupt warehouses he's pushing and you can buy us a new electric fan someday."

There was animosity there, Ford thought. Justin and Victor had always been somewhat at odds, but it had grown worse since Florida, even as they worked together more closely. There were times now when Victor was closer to Ford than Justin, his flesh and blood.

As the nation struggled to rise, the commercial brokers trying to return to the field found Ford had made S & O dominant. He had turned the business from one of reactors to one of initiators. And he added something new:

Stryker and Oakhill did not disappear when the initial deal was done. Ford used his inside position with his building clients to sell them service grids.

"Look," he would tell them, "it's not in the interest of either efficiency or economy to have to deal with a dozen different organizations for your building's services—sales, leasing, management, insurance, interior construction, office cleaning and all the rest of it. S & O can give you one organization that does it all. It will be so streamlined that we can charge you less than you're paying for all of it now."

The service grid quickly became an industry standard. The profits were not huge, but the grid tied the client to S & O and brought in the more lucrative brokerage deals.

Important clients began to see what kind of man Ford Stryker was. His genius for organization was transferable to any business, and they made him substantial offers to come to them in positions that promised greater power and money than he knew now in a struggling industry.

When he had begun S & O, he thought that it might be a stepping stone to just such things as they now put before him. He could now sell his part of the business back to Victor, complete with the building that now housed it, for important money. He could go on to his own conquests free of the family and the business that had destroyed his father. But as the opportunities came, he remembered Hannah's wish for the children to carry on the work, and how he had thought Caesar might have wanted that, too. He stayed.

Ford plowed ahead for several years, building S & O more rapidly as defense spending pumped more money into the business economy in the early forties, but he began to see there wasn't enough in his company to challenge him anymore. He had to do more he felt, but didn't see clearly what it was.

Early one Sunday morning he left his home in the woodlands of Long Island to talk to Victor about it.

As the car rolled past the long, flat potato fields of Nassau County, he thought how Victor had slowly become almost as much a father as Caesar had been. As the unexplained void had widened between Justin and his father, Ford had begun to fill it for the old man. Victor was the only person in the world to whom he felt close enough to ask for guidance.

The streets were strangely, almost ominously empty as he drove through the sparse Sunday traffic to Victor's apartment.

No one answered the door, which Ford found open. He went in and followed the sound of a radio in the living room.

Victor, in his pajamas, was sitting cross-legged on the floor in front of a console radio. He look suddenly far gone in his seventy-six years, and Ford had to call him twice to get his attention.

"The goddamn Japanese just nailed us at Pearl Harbor, Ford. The fleet is burning."

Ford crossed the room furiously and turned up the volume. "We'll slaughter the little yellow bastards."

"Not so easily," Victor said. "I've dealt with them in scrap disposal. They are more clever than you can ever imagine. They can be very dangerous because they move in coordination to a central idea. You can only beat them by poisoning that idea."

"I think that bombs and bullets might do something."

"Not with you behind them. People in our business make poor destroyers. Whatever you do for soldiers, it won't be with a gun, even if you were young enough to use one."

And that was the way it turned out for Ford. A bout with scarlet fever as a child in Harlem had left a murmur in his heart that helped thwart his attempt to get into the army as a volunteer in his late thirties.

Justin, even older, and impossibly bored with his career throughout the Depression, wangled his way into the Navy in the war's first week and became an over-age and overbearing ensign within months.

Victor ceased his yearly promises of retirement and took up the management of Oakhill Development with new verve as wartime construction began to accelerate.

With the work of Stryker and Oakhill contributing nothing to the war effort, Ford was feeling more useless and frustrated than ever when the call that changed his life arrived.

It came from James Tuthill, a client of Ford's for seven years. He had gone to Washington to join the shock troops of mobilization and found the problems monstrous. "Everybody's running around like somebody pissed on an anthill. Ten thousand policymakers and not one of 'em knows how to get it off the papers. That famous American knowhow hasn't got the first idea about getting out of its own way. I need you worse than I need my ass."

"Planes and tanks aren't my talent, Jim."

"Yeah, but construction is."

"Wrong. I don't know a shingle from an I-beam."

"Shut up and listen, Ford. You're the best organizer I ever worked with. You've got more ideas about streamlining complexity and making it fly than anybody I ever saw. And don't tell me that a man who's worked with Victor Oakhill all these years doesn't know more about the building business by osmosis than the first ten experts I'll meet in Washington."

"What do you need?"

"I have a title a half-yard long that puts me in charge of hurry-up housing for the Navy. From a few hundred-thousand men under arms we're headed for millions, and damned fast. If we use the methods they've been building with up to now, Yamamoto will be sailing up the Potomac before we get an outhouse built. I need a man to handle all the housing construction we can throw at him, and make it happen ten times faster and cheaper than it's ever been done before. Around every key naval installation in the country."

"That will take an awful lot of power, Jim. I'm not up to being swamped by a fleet of bureaucrats."

"I'll keep you clear of all the LMD commanders."

"What's an LMD?"

"A large metal desk," Tuthill laughed. "Power is what I'll give you. All the titles you can write on a piece of paper in twenty minutes. When you walk in at a Washington or New York cocktail party, people are going to rush up and salute. The men will kiss your ass and the girls more interesting things."

Ford turned his work over to Victor and was sitting in a barn-sized Washington office in a week, with a staff of fifty.

At a time when men who could cut through the morass were worth a deskful of diamonds, Ford's abilities were soon the talk of the city, and the new undersecretary for Naval Housing became something of a star.

He had hardly begun when he knew he had found what he had been born to do. If he had no desire to draw a blueprint and no talent to so much as drive a nail, his satisfaction at taking the shortest, fastest route to gratifying the primal need for shelter was nothing short of intoxicating.

His lack of specific building knowledge was not only no handicap, it was an asset. It enabled him to see that housing construction methods had remained positively feudal. The efficiency that had evolved in commercial construction in cities had never been handed down to builders of housing. The construction people recruited from the civilian workforce were quite prepared to bring all their slow, miserable inadequacies of method with them, and institutionalize them with their unions. It was Ford's prevention of this that quickly had his picture in every major newspaper and picture magazine.

Month by month, year by year, he improvised machine-line methods and economies of scale to create a model department that eventually began to almost run itself.

By late 1944, Ford Stryker was actually finding the time to pursue some of the enjoyment he had let elude him since he had formed Stryker and Oakhill. Part of that enjoyment was Anne Bennington.

"There's something deliciously illicit about them," one Washington hostess was fond of saying after they had been identified as a steady pair.

Ford had no consuming interest in Anne Bennington, other than in her being a still considerable beauty, and in the mild sensation they created together. Certainly he had no interest in becoming entangled.

He had been aware from early boyhood that women could be a source of excruciating unhappiness. He had pieced together the tragedies of both his father and the man he had known as Jack Grant. He knew that their great love for his mother had cost them as much torment as joy. So, made wary, he had taken his women for his needs, offering brief friendship, straightforward passion and early departure. What had been a reasonably lively sensual life before the war was now something of a cornucopia of wartime dalliances.

Ford moved exclusively in the upper layers of Washington, and at the countless parties might have had his choice of most of the lonely wives and breathless name seekers. He had some wonderful things going for him. He was a strikingly good-looking man in his early forties, a darling of the administration, and knew everyone up to Mr. Roosevelt. What's more, he was wired into the

Oakhills, who had built a good part of New York and who were doing very well in the war. And, oh, yes, he was said to have just the right amount of hot black blood.

"Not enough for the southern senators to keep him out of their parties, but enough to make the pure-white boys look like they were wounded in the war down below," simpered one deb who pretended to know.

Ford especially enjoyed the disapprobation of parents and rivals, making it a point to sprawl in the sun for an hour in front of the Department of the Navy to let his skin darken scandalously. The fairer the girls, the madder people got. And Anne Bennington was one of the fairest.

She was in her late twenties, a wonderfully-rounded golden peach of a girl, with eyes so pale they were hardly blue and hair that held the sunshine at any hour. Her body was sleekly hardened by riding, and she made it a joy to watch her move. Shining star that he was, Ford still might never have gotten close to her except for her father, Little Tim Bennington.

Little Tim had been handed great agricultural lands in Georgia after the death of his father, of course called Big Tim. The family name was terribly old and its aristocracy had through marriage penetrated the peripheries of both the Vanderbilts and the Sands. Anne had narrowly missed being Deb of the Year in a year with a very strong field. Little Tim would not, Ford suspected, have ordinarily allowed any touch of suspect blood near his daughter. He also suspected that Anne would ordinarily share her father's feelings. But things had happened to make a relationship possible.

To begin with, Little Tim's finances had taken some crushing reverses in the late depression. He had mortgaged and sold choice, productive land continuously in the thirties at ruinously low prices, and attempted to recoup in a market that always seemed to be running away from him. A name alone could keep one afloat for a good length of time in the South, but that time had run out. And Tim's stay in Washington had not turned up the financial backing he needed to buy into a piece of the war-production pie.

His land being almost all gone, his last viable piece of trading goods was Anne. But, still short of thirty and lovely as she was, she had become badly damaged merchandise.

"Hear you're seeing Annie Bennington, Ford," a friend said, keeping his face straight. "Mind paying me the forty you owe from Friday's poker? In case she asks you to take her canoeing and you don't come back."

Ford knew the details, along with the rest of the East Coast. Annie had been married. She had been one of the most desirable debutantes, but had chosen to ignore the most impressive proposals for the dubious charms of one Evans (Sailor) Boatwright. Sailor, a lively ornament of café society, held a name that ranked not far beneath the Whitneys, but had not found anyone tough enough to share it with him for long. His three wives prior to Anne had succumbed to his strings of mistresses, racing cars and swiftly delivered right hooks. But Anne had outlasted him, and the way she had done it made headlines for more than a year just before the war.

Sailor had been found shot to death on a yawl in the middle of Long Island Sound, Anne having been the only other passenger. Her coolly told story of having been boarded during the night by thieves in a powerboat was thin and rigorously questioned by the Boatwrights and the police. But she could not be shaken in her tale. And the services of an entire firm of brilliant lawyers, aided by the desire of potential testifiers to not fly the dirty laundry of an entire class from the masthead of Sailor's yawl, got her off.

But she had been finished as a first-class marriage. The fading of her father's fortune was known, and Sailor's ironclad marriage contract could never be broken. She got little more than the yawl, although it was very beautiful.

It was whispered that "One cannot be forgiven for shooting one of the too-few great names."

Ford knew that his meeting Anne was no accident. James Tuthill had confided to him that Little Tim had been after him for days to arrange it. So Ford was under no illusions about Anne's intentions, and was at a great advantage when they were introduced at the home of an English correspondent.

She had offered her hand and said, "What a pleasure to meet one of the famous Oakhills."

Looking behind him as though seeking someone not present, Ford had quickly speared her. "Actually I'm one of the not-so-famous Strykers."

She blushed to her considerable cleavage. "Excuse me, Mr. Stryker," she said, hiding her fury with herself. "You're so closely connected—"

"That's all right. Say the name with the money and you're almost always better off."

"You're certainly one of the family—"

"There's a blood connection, somewhere," he said. "But then there's another connection that puts the first in the shade, you might say." He might have said *I'm a nigger* from the way she looked when he spoke the reminding words. It was evident that she found them unforgivable.

"Oh, dear," Anne said, her temper rising at his smooth taunting, "I'm afraid we're not going to get along."

He found her distaste for having to be with him even more interesting than her wonderful looks. "We'll get along fine. Call me Ford so there won't be any mistakes." He had already decided to take her to bed for a while.

"That will be nice. You can call me Miss Bennington."

"I'm glad you said that. I might have called you Mrs. Boatwright."

The tone of their relationship had been set right there. They did not like one another and obviously never would. She was humiliated with everyone knowing why she approached him, and what was in his veins plainly filled her with distaste. She could snub him now and still win, he knew, or he could do the same. But in each of them he felt an urge for the combat to continue. It was the thing sometimes found in pit bulls who went instinctively for the most dangerous opponent.

"Lunch tomorrow?" she had asked later on.

"Yes," he said, deciding to go for everything or nothing, all at once. "Right after we fuck."

She did not blink. "No, no. Right before. Or my stomach growls."

* * *

Ford's intention of humbling Anne sexually and moving on did not succeed. In bed she accepted his most outrageous demands. But the only sign of pleasure she would let him glimpse in her was something gently suggesting that he was after all the genetically degraded animal she had suspected.

This nettled him more than he could ever have anticipated. He would finish her off.

Once he discharged into her throat without removing his clothing, and at other times made penetrations in grossly undignified positions. The force of her scorn redoubled, but she did not break. Ford did. He swore at himself for needing the sexual approval of a supercilious blonde witch.

"Justin is the one you should be sleeping with," he would snap. "He's the direct heir. And as white as a summer cloud."

"He's also in New Guinea somewhere. Can you get me a navy pass?"

No longer able to endure her silent contempt, he also found himself postponing leaving her. In fact, he began to have fears that she might leave him, a feeling whose motivation he chose not to closely examine.

Now he began to make love to her more tenderly, starting to cater to her needs in detail. The first time he pressed his lips between her legs, she gave the first wholehearted laugh he had ever heard from her, and her thighs closed tightly and quickly around his head, a sprung trap with silky teeth.

Anne understood his joy at shocking the local Southern society and helped him play to it. She showed up on the arm of the part-black son of his guardian's mistress wherever he wanted to be seen.

But even this dubious pleasure she turned against him. As part of a delicious, ongoing scandal she retained access to the best homes in Georgetown, Newport and Sands Point. She brought Ford with her to regattas, polo matches and lawn parties, and was always careful to see that he met the people who would let him know with a look that he could never, never belong in a grand home or in the body of an Anne Bennington.

Against all reason, he wanted to show them that he did. The more it became obvious that his proper move would be to walk away, the more their relationship took on the air of a rough courtship.

Out of the bedroom he found that she was full of the accomplishments of the old-family rich. She had been trained to the graces of presiding over huge wealth, which unfortunately no longer existed. There was little in the fine arts that she had not mastered so she would be prepared to stock and endow a wing in a great museum. At the piano she could play the classics well enough to coax sincere applause out of a grand maestro brought to grace a special party. Her taste for the best clothes, the best houses, the best dishes brought invitations to do guest columns in national magazines, and she acceded in a spirited and remarkably articulate flow of prose.

Once Ford had grown too close to her for them to fight interestingly, she would speak to him of these interests in detail, knowing it was all beyond him and would make him feel a bit more inferior to her. She had no interest in his work, and his first words on the subject triggered practiced yawns.

Her first weapon remained her best—the faint air of shrinking back inside as he made love to her, as though he were covered with a layer of offensive dirt that could never be properly scrubbed away. It should have destroyed his ardor, but, as sometimes happens in the quest for the unattainable, his excitement for her only increased.

Their sessions of lovemaking lengthened as he became more giving and inventive. He looked for some building in her response, but it never came. At times he believed that she had preferred his uncaring roughness.

Then, very unexpectedly one evening, when he had been working unusually hard at her loins, she shrieked and squirmed in her first orgasm with him, and an uproarious one it was. So pleased were they both that they sat in the bed hugging and laughing like children, as though this one delightful instant—repeated without remark in ten million other American bedrooms in the same hour—erased forever the thousand things that were impossible between them.

Ford Stryker kissed Anne Bennington as he had never kissed another, and proposed to her. With a smile that in a soldier would have bespoken the end of a long, dirty campaign, she accepted. "Thank you, Ford. Now we can get on to other things."

Little Tim Bennington, bluff, broken-faced and looking like the Southern-college football player he had been, insisted on a tremendous wedding at St. Thomas' in New York, and a notable reception at the Pierre drew every society-gawker and gossip columnist north of Tierra del Fuego. He would not accept Ford's offer to help with the considerable expense, and rumor had it that it sent him well into debt.

Victor shook the creaks out of his seventy-nine-year-old bones and did much dancing with many glittering widows who entertained hopes. So it was reasonably late in the evening before Little Tim could corner him and Ford at a quiet corner table. Tim was not the least bit drunk, his quarry were quick to notice, and he disposed of the what-a-great-day platitudes quickly before he began in the reedy baritone of the southern plains.

"Helluva place to bring up business, boys, but informal's the way we like to do it back home. That's why nobody's talked about Anne's paper up 'til now."

"What paper?" asked Ford, watching Anne dancing across the immense room, seeming to have forgotten why she was here.

"The one that spells out legally what Anne's interests will be in the Oakhill enterprises."

"Excuse me?"

"Where we come from, family ties by marriage—the right kind of marriage, of course—are as important as blood ties. Time was when the boys in business down there would take it as gospel that the Bennington interests would now be linked with the Oakhill's. And any loans from me to you, or you to me, would have backing from the other family to a powerful degree. But these days, it seems, a man's word's not quite good enough. They want to see what you've got behind you on a paper signed by ten Memphis lawyers."

"Damned shame," Victor said, exchanging a look with Ford, who had busied himself cutting a cigar.

"Sure is," Little Tim said. "Now if you want you can stipulate that I have to be in your offices up here in New York three, four days a month. We can work out the furnishings later. Something in the corner with a room for a pool table and a big soft leather couch." He winked at them. "Since the divorce from the second Mrs. Bennington I gotta be ready to get lucky."

"I'm sure," Ford said.

"I'd appreciate a little rundown on your principal bankers. Preferences, weaknesses, that kind of thing. Then I'd like a few words with them at lunch or on the phone. I'll do my own negotiating, of course, once I have the paper and I know what's in back of Annie and me. And naturally I'll give you the same courtesy with my financial people."

"Exactly what would you be negotiating, Mr. Bennington?"

"Tim, for God's sake, Victor. Tim. Well, whatever comes up. Loans. Deals. You don't know the kind of contacts our crowd has. Past anything you European people can understand."

"Not to say us African people," Ford muttered so low that Tim could pretend not to hear.

"Soon as I get some of our debts squared up, Vic, we're going to be doing big things together. Wait'll you hear some of my ideas."

"I expect they'll be fascinating."

Little Tim pulled out a business card and put it on the table. "These are my attorneys. May I know yours?"

Victor placed the card back in Tim's breast pocket. "No, you may not. My attorneys are far more European, as you say, than I. They are three grandsons of Polish Hebrew bankers who would not be persuaded to trade a paper giving up equity in a going business or collateral on an established fortune for a deed to the Indies."

A cloud began to form on Tim's face. "Jew lawyers are always a mistake."

"They say the same thing about Jew father-in-laws," Victor said. "I hope they're wrong for your sake. I've got a bit of the people of Moses in me, too, you know. I've been afraid to tell Anne. Will you do it for me?"

Tim started to look as if he had been poisoned. "Hey, Vic, hold the needle. The Benningtons are people you want to keep friendly."

"Sorry," Ford said. "I can't marry all of them." He gave Victor his arm and they left Tim holding out his card again.

"Take it, damn you."

"Good night, Tim."

"We used to take people like you out behind the fieldhouse, Stryker."

"I'm still available for that."

Tim grabbed someone's unfinished drink off the table and finished it with a gulp. "Anne will cut your black balls off. You don't know her."

"Oh, yes I do, Little Tim."

Shortly thereafter Victor said his goodbyes and went to pick up his coat. A tall, immaculately dressed man, gray just beginning to show in his sleek black hair, stood up from the wingback chair in which he had been waiting. As he walked to Victor, the eyes of every passing woman turned.

"Hello, George," Victor said, nothing in his voice indicating that this was the first time he had seen his son since after the great hurricane almost twenty years ago. Neither of them offered a hand. "What are you doing here?"

"I hoped that the bad feelings had gone on long enough, Father."

"They have not."

"I supposed that when I got no invitation, which I'm sure was your doing. Ford and I had no real problems. I thought I could come by on this very important day and wish him well. I have an interesting diamond stickpin from Grandfather Serpa for him."

"Possibly taken from someone he strangled. Why was it necessary to wait for me? What do you need?"

George, who had at first struggled toward cordiality, resumed his standard manner. "Considering the way you treated me, you should know very well, Father."

"You look prosperous enough."

"This suit? I've been working for the very best custom-suiter in Chicago," he said, mocking himself. "I'm a very good salesman, it seems. Their best. So in addition to my commissions I get my suits at cost. Some of the customers let me style and order for them. I made eleven thousand dollars last year. What Ford spends for tips in restaurants."

"Perhaps you can ask him if he needs a suit."

"I'm afraid I've left Chicago. I'm going to establish in the East."

"Not New York, I hope."

"Maybe Washington first. It might be nice to be close to Ford and his lovely wife. A man begins to miss his family, you know."

"I promise you that the man's family has not begun to miss *him*. I'll say goodbye to you, George."

"Goodbye, Father."

On the day that the final atomic bomb of the war fell on Nagasaki, a son, Ronald, was born to Anne Bennington Stryker. Her father did not come to see the child for many days, and Anne held him for only short periods, as if she were not going to ever completely forget what she had let into the blood of a child of the Benningtons.

She was not without natural love for Ronald, Ford saw. But some of it was for the way the robust infant cemented her claim to the fortunes of his father, for whom she now had no discernible affection.

With the end of the war came the end of Ford's years in Washington. Overnight the smoothly-humming housing machine he had perfected shuddered to a halt. The problem of how to construct more quickly and effectively became one of how to dispose of what had been thrown up in such quantity for millions of servicemen, but that was not to be any concern of his.

By the time he had moved his family back to New York, the first troopships were returning. He, with tens of thousands of fascinated New Yorkers, watched the towering converted ocean liners come down The Narrows to a riot of steamship whistles and rising white plumes of skyward-flying spray from accompanying fireboats.

Along the huge gray hulls, deck upon deck, a happy, waving anthill of khaki surged, pathetically eager to be on with their lives.

Seeing them pour ashore month after month, swamping the streets, stores and ballparks, Ford began to realize that few of these returning millions would be going back to live in the homes they had left four years ago. Vast numbers had married and as many more intended to as soon as they could get their uniforms off. The others had seen exciting new worlds beyond their hometowns, and the boys that had become men would go to places not explored as boys.

Where were they to be put? Ford wondered. The Depression had shut down new housing since the early 1930s. The war had shut it down past the middle of the 1940s. The builders of America had a challenge of unimaginable dimensions. He found himself bitterly regretting that he was caught up in the largely urban and commercial business that was the Oakhill heritage.

His share of the organization, Stryker and Oakhill, with its brokerage work, proved more tedious to him than ever after the years in Washington. The cement canyons choked down on him worse than before. But he could not look far afield. Victor was wearing out now. The son of Hannah Oakhill had paid the price of stubbornly carrying his own workload along with that of Justin and Ford in their absence. He was slipping slowly into heart failure, his ankles often swelling when he neglected his pills, his lungs filling with the fluids his circulation could no longer fully remove. Against all advice he struggled to the office for a few hours a couple of days a week, and still occasionally spoke at universities and professional societies about the pioneer days when Skyscraper Oakhill knew his golden days. But the end was coming and he would be passing the work on.

Justin had returned a lieutenant commander, having performed prodigious feats with the Seabees in the South Pacific campaigns. Ford suspected that the old man would turn over enough of the business to his old mistress's son to honor Hannah's wishes for him, but never doubted that Justin would take the overwhelming share.

In this he found he was wrong.

Victor had himself driven to Ford's home in the rolling hills of the North Shore one Saturday afternoon, arriving unannounced. He had a toy automobile for Ronald, who bubbled and showed him his new pony. After a few formal pleasantries with Anne, whom he regarded less as Ford's wife than as Little Tim Bennington's daughter, he indicated he wished to talk with his son alone in the study.

"I'm going to make it an even split," Victor said, his breath laboring heavily. "Justin has it in his abilities to make Oakhill Development the most exciting builder in the country—maybe the world. He also has it well in his power to destroy everything that's been accomplished."

"That would be hard to do."

"Not so hard as you'd think, Ford. I came pretty close to doing it myself a couple of times. Once in Harlem and once in Florida."

"It was eventually you who got Justin out of that with his hide."

"Maybe I did. And maybe it humiliated him. He sees himself as a man approaching middle age with one great failure and a business lifetime spent under a father who lived too long and never gave him his chance."

"There might be something to that, Victor."

"Yes. And he's still so breakneck in everything he does that he's liable to begin going for the stars to make up the time. Without considering any of the risks."

"What makes you think *I* won't?"

"You've got all the imagination he does. Every bit of it. But he thinks of building as architecture, steel, concrete and money. You think of it as people. That's why you were so good in Washington. You always remembered that buildings ultimately contain lives. And change them, nurture them and sometimes destroy them. My mother passed that on to me. You picked it up for yourself."

"No, my father helped," Ford said, and was immediately sorry as he saw pain cross the lined face even now.

"Of course he did, Ford."

"Justin won't like this. We don't get on well. A division will be difficult."

"I hope I'll hang on long enough to do that myself. Go on as you are. I'll ask both of you to consider what you might want."

Ford already had the first inkling of what that might be.

As it had after the First World War, the American construction industry failed dismally in its opportunity and responsibility. Its principal response to the overwhelming need for houses for millions of returned veterans was to raise prices steeply in the face of the ravenous demand.

The frustrated veterans found themselves fighting one another for living spaces often little better than those of the bombed-out societies they had conquered. They fought for space, not just in cramped, cruelly dilapidated houses that were almost antique, but in outbuildings. New families found their first homes in garages, tool sheds, granaries, even hen coops. Almost worst of all was having to endure the tensions of sharing cramped houses and apartments with often-reluctant parents and in-laws. There appeared to be no hope for any of them.

Ford slowly became aware that his idea had been cooking slowly at the back of his mind for the better part of two years. He had been unconsciously pursuing it as he served on countless government advisory groups, important congressional committee chairmen. His continuous fervent championing of legislation to grant mortgages guaranteed by the government had been, after all, more than a desire to reward returning GIs. It was part of the dream that had glowed in his head. The dream to create new, better centers of civilization as part of a green, fresh countryside. Where families flourished not in jammed, degrading stacks of bland masonry, but in charming, individual homes of their own.

As his excitement grew, he became overwhelmed by what he was about to begin. It was one thing to implement construction ideas with the almost limitless resources of the United States government, and quite another to plunge unblooded into cutthroat battle in an untried marketplace. He badly needed to share his spinning thoughts.

A bit at a time, he began to explore his plans with Victor, whose blessing he would need in any event.

"Let's look at what's against us first," said Ford.

"Essential," Victor coughed.

"It's been said that if Jesus were to return to earth, the only thing he would recognize is the homebuilding industry, and I couldn't agree more."

"Nor I, Ford."

"Did you know that sixty percent of the homebuilders have never built more than one house? And that eighty percent haven't done more than two?"

"Shocking. Medieval."

"Not so surprising though, when you think about what the mortgage situation has been, Victor."

"I know. Before the war, loans of as much as sixty to seventy percent of the purchase price were as rare as guano in a cuckoo clock. And the terms were often for five years or less."

"But with the government ready to guarantee at four and a half percent and thirty years, I think we're ready to start talking about what I see on our side."

"*Damn.* What a time to be so old," fumed Victor, color beginning to come back to his cheeks.

"There's the National Defense Highway Act of '41. The government paid the costs to build highways that could shuttle troops and supplies in a war. So what we have are wide, gorgeous roads, connecting places nobody particularly wanted to connect before. 'Highways through nowhere to who-cares,' they call them. Well, I want to start turning all those big empty nowheres into somewheres—the places where the best of America will be living in twenty years."

"Who will sell you the land?"

"The agricultural land around the cities hasn't been farmed since the thirties. It's lying there as scrub pines, weeds and tired potato fields. The owners, those who remember the ground is still theirs, will be tickled to get back money they thought they'd never see again."

Victor lit a forbidden cigar and walked in tight, rapid circles around the wheelchair he was supposed to use. "A lot of the cities have rail systems that could be extended. The work of the metropolitan area would still be there for the people in the country."

"Commuter trains would help, but people won't be going into the cities for long. I mean, eventually, to make complete, self-contained communities. Everything there, including the jobs. And noisy, crowded, uncomfortable cattle cars will be out of people's lives. Happiness will be built around automobiles. Not city automobiles with stoplights, traffic jams and clogged curbs. But suburban automobiles, cruising on limited-access, three- and four-lane superhighways at speeds of eighty miles an hour. Going to and from work will be a joy instead of an agony. Rather than hating one another, drivers will exchange a friendly wave when they pass."

The old man almost laughed. "Ford, sometimes you sound uncomfortably like Justin."

"It's the time, Victor. I know it. Even the electric utilities are getting into it. They're so anxious to get more users that they're making loans to builders. And why not? Yearly average utility costs have crept up to a hundred and forty-five dollars."

"Good business for them. And maybe us, too."

"I don't have to tell you that this is the business I want to run.

I'll retain the name Stryker and Oakhill. Justin can take the brokerage or not, as he wants."

"It's too tame for Justin. Keep it for cash flow."

"Are you behind this idea, Victor?"

"I am. But I don't want war between you and Justin."

"No way to avoid it. He wants to keep the Oakhill money in the city. All of it."

"Whatever he wants, he's either got to learn some discipline or wait until I'm dead. Meanwhile, I want to be in on one more big one. Tell me what you need, Ford. Then get those people out of the woodsheds."

Ford called his projected instant city Strykertown.

Over Justin's protests, Victor put Oakhill Development behind $7-million worth of bank loans. The potato farmers of Long Island were eager to unload their drab fields for ten times the $300-an-acre prices they had paid before the war. There were quickly one thousand acres ready to go in a single parcel. More land just like it was optioned in Pennsylvania so that no momentum would be lost when it became time for the next Strykertown —if the first ever came to pass.

The Oakhill architects, their imaginations awakened by the challenge, came to Ford with their first ideas. "Prefabrication is the way, Ford. A lot of damned good theoretical work's been done and we've studied it. They're already beginning to set up factories to build houses in sections. We'll set up assembly lines the way Detroit did."

"That's not the way I see it," Ford said. "For a lot of reasons. The first thing is, we don't want overly big subcontractors taking too healthy a bite out of us and production control out of our hands. Second, we don't want to be wasting money shipping a lot of air, which is what you do when you assemble off the site."

"Then you lose assembly-line economy. We can't get the pieces to move past the workers."

"Maybe not. But we can sure as hell get the workers to move past the pieces."

One lazy day shortly thereafter, the vast, dusty potato fields of Long Island were baking peacefully in the sun as they had for centuries, silent except for buzz-sawing cicadas, and empty except for some boy's hitting fly balls against the blue sky. Then, on the horizon, there appeared an advancing army.

Trucks cut through the fields, trailing boiling clouds of dust, pausing with eerie precision to discharge columns of infantry in overalls, their weapons and their ammunition. Bulldozers led the attack and lumbering concrete trucks moved in behind to consolidate the gains. Everything in the operation made it plain that the assault was to be a blitzkrieg, and the timetable unyielding.

Other builders came to gawk and recognized almost nothing from their hallowed one-house-at-a-time experiences. In fact, the first days of careening bulldozers had nothing to do with houses, but with streets. The roaring monsters were cutting them out of the field not by the yard, but by the mile. And there was no trace of the old gridiron street pattern.

"Why ya makin' life hard for yourselves?" a confused builder asked a young architect.

"Curved streets are safer. Fewer four-way intersections, and the streets don't get to be raceways. That's important with all the kids that are going to be here. Looks better, as well. When the houses are going to be a lot alike, you don't want to make it worse by lining 'em up in rows. They'll be set back different distances from the street, too."

"Jeez. How many houses there gonna be? A hundred? A *thousand?*"

"Dunno. But there's room here for about seventeen thousand."

The builder spat out his toothpick. "Yeah. Should be done about November, nineteen ninety-eight."

If Ford Stryker was going to build a small section each year, his crews didn't seem to know it. Because as the streets were being set, the storm drains, the sewers and the underground utilities were being trenched out over the whole thousand acres. A bulldozer operator tried to explain to his wife what he was doing all day. "Hon, it's like we're laying down a zillion sockets that they're going to plug houses into." That was exactly what Ford had in mind.

Every day satisfied another curiosity for the watchers, who began to make awed pilgrimages to the site. Victor, who had himself brought out by limousine every week, remembered the crowds at the Triangle Building and got a good feeling.

It became apparent to the onlookers that the basic plot was to be fifty feet by one hundred—a sprawling estate to most. And the houses were to measure thirty-two feet by twenty-five feet. This could be gauged precisely because that was the size of the narrow four-foot-deep trench that the machines dug out for a foundation in just thirteen minutes each.

Those who observed sharply as four inches of cement were poured into the center of the foundation's rectangle, realized a couple of shocking things. Heating tubes were going right into the concrete slabs. No radiators. And there was going to be no basement.

"What kind of cheap crap are you putting up here, Ford?" Justin wanted to know on a rare, grudging visit.

"Cheap, yes. Crap, no. To bring these in at a price where anybody with a job can afford one, I cut the traditional frills. So you've got concrete slabs instead of cellars, which saves me digging and dirt-hauling. You've got rockboard instead of plaster, which saves me thousands of hours of plasterer's wages and makes the interior easier to change later on. And you've got asphalt tiles on the floor instead of hardwood lumber that takes a lot of carpenter's time and gets covered with carpet anyway."

"People wouldn't put their dogs in those things," grunted Justin. "Even if you could find somebody dopey enough to come out to the sticks."

"Let's wait until they hear the prices."

Those prices made history and put Strykertown on the national map before the first house was completed.

Ford put it to the press simply. "A veteran can buy a home of his own with green lawns and a backyard for seven-thousand seven-hundred and ninety dollars, or rent it for sixty-five dollars a month. There's no down payment and he has a thirty-year mortgage at a government-guaranteed four and a half percent.

"For this he gets a living room with a working fireplace, a kitchen, two bedrooms and a bath. But any man who can swing a hammer will see that one closet is beautifully situated to take a stairway, and there's a generous attic under the roofpeak that will easily take dormers to make two more big rooms upstairs."

"Sound pretty minimal, Mr. Stryker."

"The most important thing anybody ever gave out in this country was a start."

Interest grew so quickly that the back-office men at Oakhill Development expected to lose two-thirds of their sales to other builders because Strykertown homes would not be available in time in the needed numbers.

"Bullshit," said Ford. "I want to get to where we finish a house every fifteen minutes."

"And I want to flap my arms and fly to Canarsie," a foreman muttered under his breath.

Ford's assembly line began, picking up momentum every day.

Trucks rumbled down the emerging streets, stopping every fifty feet to drop off identical bundles at every homesite. In these neat stacks, one from each truck, were lumber, bricks, pipe, shingles, sheathing, siding, bricks, nails—all the dozens of things needed, and in the precise quantities required to throw up one house. The door and window frames were preassembled, and the rafters, joists, studs, stringers, sleepers, headers and all the rest were precut. Ford did not need master carpenters because there was almost no precision measuring or sawing needed. Journeyman hammer-swingers, directed by a few skilled foreman, framed a house in a day.

Orders were pouring in. The banks rubbed their hands in gleeful surprise, and Ford took full advantage of their early enthusiasm.

"Everything we're doing in Strykertown depends on scale. The bigger we operate, the more we save and the more we earn and the more we build and the more we sell."

"It looks like you've got some notions, Mr. Stryker. Share them, please."

"I want to buy our own timberlands out West, before prices take off, and I want a sawmill to go with it. We'll not only guarantee our lumber supply against shortages and price hikes, but we can cut everything to size before we ship it so a third of every car isn't loaded with waste ends. And we can ship straight to the site without stopping at lumberyards. I guarantee we can save thirty percent on our wood."

"Have you found what you want, Mr. Stryker?"

"I have."

"Then buy it."

"I have."

Ford handled the unions. He had no problem with their wages and benefits, but found their outmoded work rules, unexpected stoppages and complete unwillingness to cross craft lines intolerable to his schedule. So he brought in nonunion labor and accepted picket lines and confrontations. The union efforts faded when Ford offered a guaranteed income and paid prevailing rates.

A frustrated union chief fretted, "When a guy builds that much he can offer work as steady as most office jobs. That's never happened in homebuilding before. He gets all the guys he wants, including our own men."

Thereafter, the paint sprayers and automatic trowels that union people wouldn't handle were standard tools in Strykertown.

"Now we've got to set up a bidding system for the subcontractors," Victor said.

"That would be wrong," Ford said with a vehement shake of the head. "Two contractors add up to one crook. Ten contractors add up to a robber band. We can't let them rig bids. We pick one and negotiate the ass off him. With what we have to give out, he'll cave in every time."

With the subs and the unions under control, the houses went up at the rate of sixty a week, and the other builders were incredulous. Then the rate climbed to a hundred and they were speechless. Whereupon Ford began to complete one hundred and fifty new houses between sunup and sunset.

The houses, from foundation to final nail, were completed in twenty-six exquisitely organized operations. What seemed like swarming, milling gangs were actually several crews of two or three, each doing its specialty at a speed that approached maniacal. Nailing studs, lathing, sheathing, painting, shingling, laying bricks, the wizards of Strykertown made the houses grow faster than the springing dandelions on the newly seeded lawns.

The model homes were so chaotically submerged by crowds that some of the more enterprising salesmen took to showing sold but still-unoccupied homes by appointment, making it some sort of privilege. It was on a list of these naive viewers that Victor, poking his nose happily wherever he could, spotted the name Dennis Hanratty, Junior. The appointment being only a half-hour away, he waited on the off chance that this was more than a coincidence.

Happily, it was not. He knew it when he saw that face, not appreciably changed since Patrick had brought it to these shores on the *Dortmund*.

"The last time I saw your dad he drove me from Miami to New York in a taxicab that looked like it wouldn't make Jacksonville," Victor said after he had introduced himself and confirmed his suspicion.

Denny Hanratty had heard plenty of tales about there being at least one of the family on the Oakhill payroll for the best part of seventy-five years, and was delighted to meet one of the old legends. "He'll probably pass out when he finds out you're still —uh—"

"—that I haven't kicked off. I was thinking about it, but I started having too much fun with all this. Isn't it the goddamnedest thing?"

The exhaustion that had shown itself on Denny's face as he had led his pregnant wife, Rhoda, and their little girl out of the battered prewar Plymouth seemed to lift as he looked at the marvels around him. Rhoda, plump, plain and pleasant, hugged him around a waist so slim that six inches of belt dangled past where the buckle closed. She couldn't seem to get the smile off her face. "We found it, honey. This is it. We're *home*. Don't you *feel* it?"

Victor sent the salesman away and took them around himself, not even using his cane. He heard their story and understood their awe at what they had found.

"I was the last kid out of the army, Mr. Oakhill. So Pop was out of room and out of money when I got home. We ended up in an old aunt's spare bedroom in the Bronx. Twelve by eleven it is, on an airshaft. One window, and it's stuck closed. Aunt Jo said we could use the kitchen and the living room when she wasn't there, but we didn't know she ain't been outta the house since Pearl Harbor. The only company we can have is the mice, who are welcome 'cause they eat the roaches. It was a hundred and two in the room by noon today, and the kid had a heat rash that was startin' to look like leprosy. The drive out here through the Sunday traffic took three hours and the old lump overheated twice, but it was a cruise to Bermuda next to bein' home. Excuse me if we mistake this house for Buckin'ham Palace, but that's the way it looks to us."

"Look at how clean the streets are, sweetie," Rhoda whispered. "Smell how clean the air is."

"I can see *far*, Daddy," the little girl chirped.

As they approached the model, an image stirred that Victor had not realized was still in his memory. He again saw an open space under a raw, gray sky. And there were people, rudely dressed in the clothes of another century, with this same awed look as they moved to enter a house on a hillside, a house not much different than this one in some ways. He had been holding Jack Grant's hand, and people were whispering all around them in a language he did not understand. He wondered if these Americans would find their dream as completely as those long-ago Swedes had found theirs.

Victor took them up the new cement of the walk crossing the newly-seeded lawn.

Rhoda might have been a pilgrim approaching a cathedral. "There are bushes, Denny. And trees." She pointed to shoulder-high saplings that had been staked out in front of every house.

"Six evergreens, two maples or two fruit trees. Fast-growing rye grass already seeded. You'll need a lawnmower and pruning shears before you know it," said Victor, proud of what was here.

"Hey, they ain't all exactly alike," Denny noticed.

"You get your choice of five different exteriors. Pick a color, pick a shingle and pick a design pattern."

When Victor had swung the red-painted front door back, Denny swept his laughing, great-bellied wife into his arms and rushed her across the threshold of heaven. She was furnishing the room with her eyes before her feet were back on the floor. "The kitchen is in the front, Denny. And the living room in the back. I never saw a house like that."

"Think about the sense it makes," Victor said. "The room you use most should be near the front door, where you come in with the groceries and where the kids won't have to cross the living room for a glass of milk. And the woman in the kitchen doesn't get shut off from the world at the back of the house. She can look out on the street. She's right there when somebody comes to the front door. The living room? That belongs at the back where it's quiet, and next to the back yard so you can get what they call a patio opening out there." The last building he had pushed this hard was selling for eight million, not eight thousand, but he was enjoying this much more.

Rhoda was by now twirling starry-eyed in the kitchen. "What beautiful appliances." Postwar production bottlenecks were making every new appliance beautiful. And expensive. "Can we save up and buy exactly what's here?"

"You can't buy 'em," grinned Victor. "They come with the house. Stove, refrigerator, washer. That sink and the steel cabinets, too."

The couple almost dissolved in rapture. "Jesus, Mr. Oakhill, how the hell does Stryker do it?"

"Other builders go to the appliance wholesalers. With our kind of volume, why not be our own wholesalers? We get these straight out of the factory. We furnish a whole kitchen for not much more than the price of a good stove at retail."

"It's a dream."

"That's what we're selling, Denny. The house you used to dream about in the barracks, complete in every detail."

"What's that in the corner under the blanket?"

"Something we'll be including next year with every house. When I saw we might be getting a Hanratty, I rushed things a bit. Take a look."

Rhoda Hanratty tremulously pulled away the blanket and saw an unspeakably beautiful Dumont television set, its giant twelve-inch screen peeping through the polished, sweet-smelling wood and promising a lifetime of pleasures past imagining.

All Denny could do was wring Victor's hand while tears of joy kept Rhoda from seeing her thrilling new home as clearly as she wanted to.

Not even in the old farm towns of the Midwest had there ever come together such an astoundingly like society.

Almost to a man the buyers were veterans between twenty-five and thirty, going into homes for the first time in their lives. They were married less than five years and had between one and three children averaging four years of age. An astonishing number of the wives were pregnant or would become so within weeks after the "master" bedroom was furnished. The family income on any one street probably did not vary from home to home by as much as a thousand dollars.

Uniformly experiencing the greatest, happiest adventure of their lives, the swelling masses of Strykertowners became one big club whose members held a harmony of views, ages, background and incomes that would never come together in one community again.

Lifelong friendships were formed, based in back-yard barbecues, common employers, Stitch 'n Chatter societies and schools that had nearly empty classrooms above the fifth grade and notorious crowding beneath it. The noise of tricycle bells and happily shouting children became the universal sound of Strykertown and would be remembered joyfully by parents as marking the happiest hours of their lives, no matter how high they climbed.

Ford put four-thousand houses into Strykertown in the first year, and had eleven thousand in three.

Realizing he had formed for himself a political steamroller that no local government could withstand, he went to work on every outmoded building code, every hamstringing ordinance, every avenue of financial advantage he could, to get more people into more homes. Rules for the curing time of concrete slabs eased from a five-week period to one. No piece of veterans' homeowning legislation began or ended without a massive input from the telephoners and letter-writers of Strykertown after they had been organized by Ford.

"Get the VFW to get five thousand written bombs to the Senate by Thursday, Eddie. I've got three-hundred appointments set up at the local banks, presuming that bill is going through."

The construction epic that was Strykertown gave rise to a sub-industry of its own—in books, in newspaper columns, in learned articles, in broadcast panels there rose a fixation with the "virus" of a wildly spreading suburbia.

By the time Strykertown approached its full development, there was no longer a question that the "Stryker Disease" was going to spread across the country like a billion gallons of machine oil. The early argument as to whether Ford Stryker was a curse or a blessing devolved into a strident examination of just how much sociological damage he would do.

Ford watched Justin seethe for three years at the success of the project so opposed to all he believed was right. Then he exploded against it. Justin appeared on a Sunday press panel and gave his views.

"There's something obscene in these cookie-cutter towns that seem to drop out of the sky like an alien space ship. There are more than seventeen-thousand houses in Strykertown now. More than seventy-five thousand people. Do you know it took Stamford, Connecticut more than three hundred years to get that big? What hope is there for an instant city like this to develop the cross-section of classes and ages and experiences that build a worthwhile civilization? We'll become a nation of people insulated from the nurturing influences of the great cities, and without even the dignity of farm families taking mental nourishment from their individualism. The Strykertown zombies will be numbed duplicates of one another, looking out of the seventeen-thousand picture windows into the picture windows across the street. What can you learn from a mirror, gentlemen? What we are building here are the slums of the future."

Justin turned aside the angry objections of Victor and Ford. "I might as well be speaking against malaria for all that words can slow it down. I was always proud of what this family built, whether it succeeded or not. I'm ashamed of Strykertown and terrified of what it's begun. And I tell you I'll fight against your carrying this poisonous idea any further, Ford."

"The plans for the next Strykertown are already drafted, Justin," said Ford. "The mistakes I've made are fixed. I'm going to throw up whole cities. Build the schools, the churches, the shopping centers and the recreation grounds right along with the houses."

"Throw up is the right word."

"The Strykertown in Pennsylvania will be five thousand acres. It will be America's first perfect city because my planners will break it up into ideal neighborhoods, each with everything it needs."

"Don't you understand, Ford, you miserable ass, that neighborhoods are different kinds of people, not different churches and swimming pools?"

"I'll take it as a hostile act if you try to get in the way of what I'm doing anymore, Justin."

"Then take it and be damned."

Even with the first Strykertown an already completed and successful reality, Justin campaigned against it. He became a familiar figure in the legislative circles of New York City.

"Those people out there in the potato fields of Long Island are using our roads and bridges to suck payroll money out of our city. They make it here, spend it there. Yet they're protected by our Fire Department, our Police Department and our hospital facilities. They plunder the fruits of culture in buildings paid for by the tax dollars of our citizens and pay not a cent of tax to us. Let's stop that free ride. A commuter tax—a good, stiff one—would be a first step. It would make people think twice before they left us. If we don't act, our middle-class taxpayers will hemorrhage away to leave us with dregs."

There began what would be a long, nasty guerilla war between the city and its suburban towns. With the preponderance of the State Legislatures representing rural and suburban constituencies, the taxation could only succeed to the smallest degree. But the bad feelings blossomed.

Justin and Ford barely spoke to one another. But they spoke mightily to others, so that their bitter battle continued in print and on the airwaves.

"The death of thought," Justin would say. "The death of individualism. The death of the American dream of the great melting pot."

Ford would fire back ferociously. "Strykertown isn't the death of a dream, but the return to one. When this nation began it was every man's dream to have land and a house of his own for his family. We've made it possible again, and no American now needs to be satisfied with less."

The doubters increased as fast as the buyers. One wealthy woman motored down from Manhasset to Strykertown in her limousine to show friends "the wonderful thing Mr. Stryker has done for the poor."

But they were not the poor, Ford knew. They had a king's ransom of energy and ambition to spend and they were to be the heart of the country's wealth. There were blue-collar workers putting the first generation of their families into houses. And living next door were fresh-from-college junior executives starting out in homes years sooner than was possible any other way. The friendships formed here between classes would endure through the lives of the early dwellers and expose them and their children to the vast and deep strata of American possibilities.

Those who deplored the conformity of Strykertown had not considered the deep traditions of the American handyman, his mighty hammer and his wildly divergent tastes. The paint was hardly dry on the new homes before the ring of those hammers and the rasp of saws began to be heard over the roar of the new power lawnmowers.

Houses began to sprout dormers, extensions, porticos and patios. Garages, breezeways, carports and new rooflines appeared so rapidly that families strolled and bicycled through the streets every weekend to mark the progress of their neighbors' improvements while plotting their own.

Local nurseries could scarcely keep up with the ravenous demand for trees and shrubs, and one departed potato farmer who walked through his old field one Saturday morning said to his wife, "I never did that much plantin' in thirty years in the furrows. In thirty more this here's gonna be a goddamned *forest.*"

Very quickly the cookie-cutter look began to go, and the old joke about the Strykertowner walking into the wrong house and kissing the wrong wife and children faded.

As the streets filled with the offspring of a vast baby boom, they still called Ford's instant community "a womb with a view," but whatever rancor remained about the new community, no one doubted it had changed forever the way a nation lived.

Victor battled his precarious health far into his nineties before he started to subside in earnest. It was no wasting disease or dramatic failure of his tired heart, but a roaring fire suddenly coming to the last of its fuel.

530

He would accept no hospital or nursing home, nor would he remain housebound. Instead he settled grudgingly into his wheelchair and accepted the services of a large, good-natured nurse to push it and see to his medication.

Dismayed that there would be building that would continue unseen and without his participation, he had his limousine bring him on his good days to one of the Oakhill or Stryker sites, and he would take it in voraciously with an eye almost undimmed with age.

With Justin he never discussed Ford, with Ford he never discussed Justin. They would have his legacy, but he was now resigned to its being carried forward separately.

Memories of Hannah and Grant and the early days now took up many of his hours, and he saw them all again on the streets of early New York, impatient to make it grow.

It was near evening on a golden day in May, with the visibility unlimited and the wind gusting merrily, that Ford bowed to Victor's obdurate demand to be allowed to accompany him on an aerial viewing of the completed Strykertown.

The small airplane was warm and comfortable, and the pilot strapped the frail frame into the seat beside him, with Ford in the rear.

As they roared into the air, Victor grinned delightedly, remembering how he had raced high up the cables of the rising Brooklyn Bridge, wishing he could keep going straight up to the sky. Now he was there, and the happiness of it made his chest tighten.

Beneath the dipping wing they saw a sprawl of streets, and long, sinuous curves of roofs, the four choices of shingle obvious. The pilot spiraled lower, and the cars, hurrying in thousands among the houses, became visible, and then the back yards and sidewalks alive with playing children. The rich green of springtime had come out of the ground already, and the community floated on emerald lawns among new trees, with the pale, dusty fields still spreading for miles around it.

Under those roofs people were making love, making children,

planning, dreaming, cooking, carrying the world forward in that unique yeast called a community. Millions of lives would eventually go forth from these fields that had once brought forth only potatoes, and he had been part of it.

When the airplane settled again to the ground, Ford found that the soul of Victor Oakhill had remained behind, high up in the great clouds that the setting sun was now edging with molten gold.

His gaze drifted to the horizon. Miles away to the west, showing clearly at the end of Long Island and across the bridge at whose end once lay the Golden River, he saw the city he had led into the sky. His practiced eye picked out the towers that were his, and knew that they would continue to speak his name.

The faintest whiff of a long-forgotten perfume brushed him. "Look, Mother," he whispered under the roar of the engine. "Look at what we did."

When the airplane settled again to the ground, Ford found that the soul of Victor Oakhill had remained behind, above in the great clouds that were now beginning to build high up where the setting sun could paint their margins with molten gold.

It had always been George Oakhill's talent to sniff out a sordid weakness, even when it was as elaborately hidden as Anne Bennington Stryker's. And at turning such a weakness to his own uses he was a genius.

He had left Anne Bennington Stryker tied and gagged. The silk ropes that bound her spread-eagled to the big brass bed would not break the skin at her wrists and ankles, but they were pulled tight, and he knew the pain of the interrupted circulation must be considerable. Just the way she liked it.

He guessed that she had never admitted to herself that she enjoyed being hurt. So it had been up to him to teach her what she really was.

As naked as Anne, he pulled up an easy chair, propped his feet on the side of the bed and lighted a cigarette. Lounging there he could contemplate her, lipstick smeared across her cheeks under the gag, his fluids smeared across her belly, the light red stripes where he had hit her with a knotted silken rope now beginning to fade. She would have liked to be hit harder, but he was always careful not to send her home to her husband with things that could not be explained.

Not that Ford was likely to see her naked. If she was to be believed, they made love perhaps once a month now, just ten years after their marriage. It might have been less than that if the allure of being taken by a man with black blood did not still occasionally appeal to some uniquely Southern sense of degradation.

"Maybe I'll bring in a nigger to work on you next time. One that hates your kind enough to do anything. If you're good."

She was still a lithe and beautiful woman, George saw. But while that helped his physical performance, she was of no more interest to him as a sexual object than she was as a person. His last act of genuine passion with a woman had taken place many years before in a hurricane-lashed railway car.

He was glad there had been no need to pretend love or courtesy to Anne after the first few times he had lain with her. In fact, it was the scorn and cruelty that bound her to him in a passion that often approached distraction. She would endure anything from him except his attention to another woman, and that he was never even remotely tempted to do. After Jana, women were no more than steps to him, and he climbed them well.

Anne, through the gaudy allowance she extracted from Ford, kept this impressive apartment in the Pierre for him and had paid for his sleek red Packard. He also had the use of her forty-foot yawl. Ford's massive inattention to all except his work made it so easy.

He saw by Anne's knitted brows that she appeared ready to be set loose, but he wished to make his plans uninterrupted for a while. "All women should be bound and muffled during and after lovemaking, I think. None of that ridiculous moaning and posturing, no flying knees and elbows, no prattle later on."

He walked to a bowl of fruit on a sideboard and observed his tightly muscled frame in the mirror. Whatever scorn he felt for his Oakhill blood, he appreciated its remarkable resistance to the imprints of time. Well into their fifties, both he and Justin would easily have passed for a dozen years younger.

Selecting an apple from the bowl, he rummaged in Anne's purse lying alongside until he found a handsome silver pocketknife. He knew it would be there because he had given it to her and she carried it always. It was large for the needs of a woman, but just right for his own eventual needs. The handle was customtooled, and the initials *A. B. S.*, prominent. The knife's long, thin blade made short work of the apple peeling. "I'm glad you keep this sharp. A sharp knife can make your life a good deal easier."

He returned to his chair and began to eat slices of the fruit, addressing Anne although she was unable to answer. "Things are going to be different now that Victor is dead. I'm going to be seeing a lot more of your husband. You're going to help me in that. Whatever reason my father had to deny me a part of what was his during his life may never be known, and I'm sure the terms of his will won't give me any help. My lawyers could never stand up against theirs, so I'll have to have what's mine in other ways."

She was squirming to be free, but he ignored that. "In a way, it's good that Father shut me out and lived so damned long. I could never have run up the fortune so well as my brothers. Even that rattle-brained Justin turned out to have the family touch for turning holes in the ground into money, that mess he made in Florida notwithstanding. Christ, he's even made *me* a little famous by making me a movie princess's brother-in-law, thank you very much. People actually ask me if I can get them Liza Hayborn's autograph, and whether she sleeps in the nude."

He chuckled and took a pull from a half-empty vodka bottle that stood open on the floor beside the bed. "I don't bother to tell them that Justin and his fabulous wife accept my visits as willingly as those of a cockroach. Or that Ford pays less attention to me than to one of the shingles on those shanties of his. Of course that means he doesn't mind my visits to my least glamorous sister-in-law and his son and heir."

She was now making angry sounds behind the gag, to which he

continued to pay no heed. "Did I ever tell you what a perfect little shit you've turned darling Ronald into? Even though he's had only nine years for you to make him obnoxious, I dislike him almost as much as you do, Anne. Did you really think sending him to all those fancy schools and telling him that he's better than anybody else on earth, would make you, him, or anyone else forget that he's part coon? It didn't work for Ford and it won't work for him, not even with that fair hair. His lips are a bit full, don't you think? And don't pull on the ropes so. You'll bruise yourself, after all the care I've taken."

"*Um . . . ummmmmm . . .*"

He thumped her roughly in the ribs with his bare foot. "Here's something he told me, that you'll love. Some of the kids at school were ragging him about his darky background, and it got him down. And what do you think? Ford sat him down and told him all about his grandfather. All about *Caesar*, for Christ's sake. Showed him pictures and everything. With all kinds of purple bullshit about what a great man he was, and how proud li'l Ronnie should be to own a piece of him. Know what? The boy bought it. He'll be putting shoe-black on his face and curling his hair pretty soon." The brass bed rattled against the wall behind it as she tugged and grunted. He took another deep pull from the bottle.

"I shouldn't be talking that way about the kid who's going to be my own sweet sonny-boy after we're married." Her struggles stopped when he said that, and her expression softened. God, did she really think he'd take Ford's tortures upon himself? "The trouble is, Annie, that he's not giving us a case for the divorce. I've had him stumble over some women who made you look like a bag of meal. They're very good at what they do, and I paid them awfully well. But old Ford won't bite. Seems like he'd rather hump you or one of his houses. And he's so healthy. He could live longer than Victor, who almost outlived the rest of the world. But I want my money. Excuse me, Anne. I *do* mean *our* money. I'm really going to have to try much harder."

He hoisted himself from the chair and slid next to her on the bed with the bottle and her knife. "I miss the sweetness of your voice telling me how much you love me. How you want to suck my jumbo." A flick of the knife cut the gag way.

Before she could say a word, he thrust the bottle into her mouth and began to force the fiery liquor into her, making her choke and splatter. "We really should go out for drinks more."

The bottle was empty by the time he cut her loose. Whatever anger that had risen in her was gone and she rolled joyfully into his arms. He let her kiss him as much and as long as she wanted so she would remember that she could not live without him.

"We don't need Ford's filthy money," she purred.

He grabbed her hard enough behind the neck to make her cry with pain. "You've said a nasty thing, and we have to punish you for it," he growled, and thrust her head down into his groin until he felt her lips where he wanted them.

Even with the oilskins snugged as tight as he could make them, Ford felt wet to the skin. The sea boots, which he supposed were what George wore when Anne took him sailing with her, were too big and he wobbled in them uncertainly as he held to a line near the vibrating mast.

For the first time that he could remember, Ford wished that George were along. Cold, chronically disinterested fish that he was, George had made himself a splendid seaman on Anne's yawl, far better than Ford, despite all the lessons at Victor's schools. George and Anne handled the big yacht as easily as a catboat when they had previously taken him along.

Ford had not been surprised at Anne's return to the water on the treasured, but little-used yacht. After all, she had sailed thousands of miles with Sailor Boatwright prior to her first husband's notorious final voyage. What did surprise him was Anne's apparently strong attachment to her brother-in-law. As nearly as Ford could figure it, George was the only person she knew who shared any interests with her—he liked polo and the opera as well as sailing—and one she could be with without causing too much talk. It was all fine with Ford.

George's reentry into the family, such as it was, might have been simply the act of a man who did not make friends easily becoming lonely at last. He was extremely attentive to his young nephew, although Ronald did not respond to him nearly as warmly as George would have liked.

Ford couldn't find it in himself to discourage George's visits, the way he heard Justin did, and was more than happy that they filled up so much of Anne's time.

Anne had probably not missed his presence much after the first year. Any chances he might have had to solidify her suspect love by close attention were lost in his absences, and it nagged at him. So he had found himself somewhat pleased to come along when she had invited him for a series of cruises with George that had lasted through the summer and deep into the fall.

Too deep into the fall, he thought, as eight-foot waves running white at the tips swept down on the sleek hull. And too deep into the evening.

Anne sat at the helm, tense and elated as she always was in hard weather, and completely fearless. She had laughed at him when he had fished two lifebelts from under the seats for them, but had put one on as a favor to her nervous husband.

He was glad he had the jacket on now, even though it was one of the old prewar designs that circled the body with clumsy cork floats. The new kapok vests were far more comfortable.

George would be glad he had been stuck with a lawyer at the last minute on an apartment lease. Anne had so set herself on going that there was no turning her back even after George's cancellation, so here they were, alone in the blow in the middle of Long Island Sound.

Hungry, beginning to shiver, and with whatever spirit of adventure with which he had started the day beginning to fade, Ford waited for Anne to begin the run for home. When she merely turned on the running lights after he could barely make out her silhouette on the stern, he made his way back to her, timing their porpoising through the waves and progressing hand by hand through the rigging.

"This is getting crazy, Anne," he shouted when he arrived

above the cockpit. "Let's get the hell out of here. Enough is enough."

Her face was only a smear below the brim of her sou'wester. "Yes," she said, "maybe it's time to go now. Go get the jib." She reached down to start the diesel.

They had been running back into the narrow end of the Sound toward Cold Spring Harbor. It would only take a turn south and a twenty-five-minute run to bring them in, he estimated as he fought his way to the bow.

He felt the wind shift as Anne steered to take the pressure off the sail. He uncleated the jib halyard and brought the stiff, wet canvas down, the waves coming over the bow as the *Queen Anne* plunged ahead under bare poles.

As he dropped to his knees to bring the soaking heap of canvas under control in the wind, he heard a sharp bang of wood upon wood behind him. Mindful of the damage that unsecured gear might wreak in this sort of blow, he turned quickly to catch an astounding sight.

A lithe figure, dressed all in black, was scrambling nimbly out of the thrown-back ventilating hatch that led from the V-berth cabin below the forepeak. The figure wore no sea clothing and no hat. Looming above Ford, the face was visible.

"George," Ford had time to gasp before his half-brother was upon him. One powerful hand reached down to clutch him by the throat and the other flashed lower. Ford felt something thud into his chest so hard that it knocked him onto his back against the piled jib, one shoulder sliding outward over the sea. A white-hot slash of pain slid along a rib, found softer flesh and moved deeper into him. The flash of agony sent a great awakening jolt through Ford, and he reached up to catch George by the turtleneck of his dark sweater and drive an arm upward with all the power that terror could raise.

With no purchase on the streaming deck, George's feet went out from under him. He rolled up into a flailing ball that tumbled straight over the side. He missed a frantic grab at the lifeline as he went over. Ford saw only a quick swirl of white where a trough swallowed him.

After an endless instant, Ford thought he heard a despairing wail above the roaring wind and dashing waves. *"Jannnaaaaaa—"*

There was no line, no raft, no float, within Ford's reach. He grabbed the jibstay and reached a hand far over the side, as if the lost man, propelled by fear alone, might break free of the grip of the waves and outfly the pounding diesel to regain a grip on life.

Utterly unable to sort out what had happened, Ford scrambled on his hands and knees for the stern. He screamed for Anne to come about, knowing that she could no more make out his cries above the wind than she could hear those of George in the dark sea.

Whatever chance he had to move quickly vanished as new streaks of pain ran down the side where he had been hit. When he pulled himself at last back into the cockpit, Anne was holding the *Queen Anne* steady on course. The life ring behind her was still secured to the rail.

"It was George," Ford said wonderingly. ". . . He was on board . . . down in the V-berth. I don't know . . . He went over the side—"

She screamed and swung the boat so sharply into a broaching sea that they almost went over. For another two hours she pushed the *Queen Anne* through deep darkness and growing waves as both she and Ford howled themselves hoarse, searching into the night while they played an electric lantern on the wild, empty waters.

By the time they gave up, Anne had grown deadly calm and quiet. Her expression did not change after they motored into Cold Spring Harbor and Ford brought her down into the light of the forward cabin to show her what he had discovered while they searched.

"Recognize that?" he asked her drily.

The lifebelt he held in his hand had one of its cork squares skewered by a silver-handled knife. A bloody inch of its tip emerged from the far side of the thick square, and a bright trickle of red ran down his yellow oilskins.

"I . . . thought it was in my bag." She seemed genuinely shocked. If she had been part of it, something had at least surprised her.

"It would have been very interesting for you, Anne, when they fished me out of the Sound with your initials sticking out of my gizzard. Considering your previous bad luck in this situation, I mean. I guess they might have been heating up the chair for you."

Her eyes widened and he thought he saw her shudder.

"You'd think he'd have just shoved me overboard, wouldn't you?" Ford said pointedly. "Or picked anyplace except this boat."

"What will you do?" she asked, her face frozen again.

"Well, since that lifejacket kept the point out of my lung, I'm just fine, thank you. So we'll report this awful accident, cry a bit, and I'll have my doctor handle this little cut I got falling against a lock hasp in the blow. Here. You can have this sticker to remind you of your brother-in-law. Not the man we'd have wanted as guardian for Ronald and the estate, I'd say."

Her face broke and she was taken by wrenching, strangling sobs. She fell into his arms and buried her face in his chest. "Oh, my sweet," she said, her voice somehow still hard. "I might have lost you."

Anne's arms slid around his back and she stood on tiptoe to kiss him. He caught just a glimpse of her eyes before they closed, and, as she clung to his lips, he half expected to feel the bite of the silver-handled knife making good on its earlier failure.

Was that the heat of a low, smouldering hatred he felt in her chilled body? And was it just that heat that held him to her? There would be no questions.

CHAPTER
14

It was unseemly, even for 1964.

Justin Oakhill, holding back nothing as usual, right in the middle of the Madison Avenue sidewalk halfway between his twenty-four-foot limousine and the towering glass facade of the three-story lobby fronting Oakhill Development, screamed at the most famous beauty in the world.

The most famous beauty in the world, as was her custom, screamed right back.

They knew they had to hurry their vituperation before the inevitable army of camera-clickers and scribblers appeared.

"I heard you balled every one of the Beatles, including that drummer they tossed out," roared Justin.

"On the sidewalk in front of Buckingham Palace. With Prince Philip and the Horse Guards lined up to go next," shrilled Liza Hayborn.

"Then you could have had a rip at the ponies, too." Justin knew this was good enough to tempt her to one of her wonderful, open-throated laughs, but she was having too good a time with the fight.

"I'd screw whatever I could catch. Trouble is everybody knows

I've been screwing you. And they're afraid that middle age, ugliness and boring professions are catching."

She knows right where to put in the zinger, Justin thought. Three sore spots in one sentence. The ravishing little streetfighter from Liverpool used her rattlesnake tongue with the wonderfully cultured voice and accent given to her by the studio's voice coaches, but the stevedore's vituperation was all her own.

"You are a *twat*, Liza. That mink muff you're carrying is half the size of the one between your legs."

"You should know. You've got your face in it enough."

God, she's beautiful, he thought. He could have watched those violet eyes snapping and those deliciously curling lips all day. "Liza, doesn't it make you feel cheap to talk about our bedroom with your daughter standing right here?"

Ah, hah! Good shot, he thought, chortling inwardly. Liza knew her husband was a helluva lot better parent to Fiona than either she or that whacked-out swashbuckler who was the natural daddy.

"Our *bedroom*," sputtered Liza. "When did you ever make love to me in a bedroom? Pool tables, elevators, beach cabanas, desks, *yes*. Bedrooms? *Hah!*"

How the hell did Fiona ever grow up to be such a lady with the likes of them raising her? Justin wondered.

"Mom . . . Justin. That man running across 53rd Street is a photographer from the *Daily News*. Can we get in the car?"

"I'd sooner get in a shower with ten Himmlers," said Liza.

"Get in that back seat, Mattress Back," said Justin.

"Not for five million dollars, you neckless asshole."

"You mean *another* five million, don't you?"

"I can buy you and sell you, you frigging *landlord*."

"Better check the box office on your last picture, Movie Queen. It's drawing flies and vultures."

"You're . . . you're . . . *stocky*, Justin. Women can stand any kind of man. Unless they're *stocky*. And that's what you are." She slammed him across the face as hard as she could with her mink hat, inflicting little damage, and went clicking away down the avenue, her superb legs flashing beneath her short skirt and her marvelous hips rolling magnificently.

"Damn," said Fiona. "I've got genes from the two best-looking people in the world. How can I look like this instead of like that?"

Her attempt to distract Justin didn't work. He started after his wife. "Liza," he yelled after her. "I haven't seen you in two goddamned months—"

She turned and yelled back from the corner, beginning to draw a crowd as soon as she stopped. "And you won't see me for another two, you stocky boor."

Sensing a camera aimed at her, she turned instinctively to deliver a devastating smile and smart pose for the readers of the *Daily News*. Then she was gone in the crowds.

Fiona, half a head taller than Justin and with the strength of a twenty-four-year-old who played a lot of hard tennis, managed to wrestle him to a stop. "Give it up, Jus. It always just gets worse. Come on. We've got to talk to the people at Chase Manhattan, and we're behind."

A blanket of depression settled over Justin. His body, every bit as square as Liza had claimed, sagged beneath its sheath of muscle, and his broad, pleasant face took on a scowl that usually only appeared when two things crossed his mind: his brother, Ford, or The Hole.

"Yeah. The Hole. We've got to work on The Hole. And maybe those bank geeks can finally explain to me how a man who owns half the Manhattan skyline happens to be going bankrupt. Climb in."

Watching his stepdaughter slide her tall and tidy body into the limousine with beguiling nimbleness, it occurred to him that she had little to apologize for in the way of looks. True, she was no match for Liza. But who the hell was, even if Liza had passed forty a while back.

Fiona was special. For one thing it was sheer pleasure to watch her move, even though a purist might say she carried a bit too much flat muscle for a woman. Like a ballerina. She came by all of that honestly. Hell, wasn't she the daughter of Derrol Keefe, who could laugh and jest as he swung through a ship's rigging or a castle's tapestries while skewering Basil Rathbone on the end of a flashing rapier. She had Derrol's features rather than Liza's, which wasn't half bad, and his smile, which was dazzling. Her eyes had the Keefe downward tilt and not the spectacular Hayborn size. But they did have her mother's coloring precisely. Violet eyes touched with gold, and the irises ringed with sable blackness.

How could today's assured and quite delicious woman have been such an introverted, unsure mess at the time he had begun to sleep with her mother eighteen years ago? Even as a beanbag in an epic custody fight in which she had been caught between two rock-crusher personalities from the age of five, you would have expected Fiona to take on some of the thunder of her high-pitched parents. Instead she had retreated into a shell of sweet dreaminess, creating worlds in her imagination. She loved much, spoke of it little and learned to greatly fear how much people could hurt one another. What attempts Keefe and Liza had made to reach her were ruinously strident. All the work, love and patience of bringing her out of herself had flowed from her doting stepfather. He was as proud of what he had done for Fiona as anything he had ever created, and he had created much.

"Do you want to go over the papers again while we're headed downtown?" she asked him as the limousine headed into the traffic.

"I'm sick of papers. You handle it. I'll grunt in the right places . . ."

"I don't think Mr. Rockefeller likes to deal with girls two years out of college—"

"I've dealt with Rockefellers before. Made damned heroes out of them with that United Nations thing," he said with a chuckle. "And you didn't just graduate from Stanford, you graduated from Oakhill. We teach our own and we teach them right, and the bankers know it by now. If I haven't shown you enough tricks about our business in sixteen years to stand up to anybody we know, I'll hang up my supporter and everything in it."

She slid next to him on the wide seat and squeezed his hand. "You look bad, Justin. It's getting worse with Mom, isn't it?"

He shrugged. "I don't really know. That's the whole trouble. The yelling doesn't mean much. We did that from the first day. But the separations are getting longer. She's getting more and more bored every year. 'Come along,' she says, knowing I've got ten years of work to finish first."

"You think she's fooling with the studs, I take it from that little conversation on the sidewalk."

"Who the hell can tell?"

"Yeah. She had so many pals before you that she might sleep with a rhinoceros and not remember it."

They laughed at the exaggeration, but there was hurt in Justin. "I knew the number one lady box-office draw of the last fifteen years wasn't going to be a hermit. But it's kinda tough to pick up a paper or some sleaze magazine and see her sitting in Zamboanga with some racing-car greaser or multi-penis cowboy star who's trying to demolish her drawers."

"That thing about her and the Beatles got to you, huh?"

"My mind tells me it's just one more whacky news story. But still . . . What to you think, Fi? Are guys getting to her?"

Fiona twisted her fingers in his. "I don't know. I . . . can't say for sure."

"Shit. That's not what you've been saying all along."

"Sorry. Maybe you should stop asking."

He grew silent, contemplating how he could have come so far since he returned from the Navy less than twenty years ago, and still gotten into so much trouble.

Remembering back to the forties, he had been suitably furious at Victor's decision to split responsibility at Oakhill Development, with he himself being kept on a short leash while Ford was turned loose to proliferate his suburban cigar boxes. Luckily, it hadn't taken long to find an opportunity with which to intrigue his father in spite of Victor's doubts. And Justin was to this day not one bit sorry that Oakhill Development finished by making almost nothing on the deal. Because he had used it to land Liza.

He had been deeply, irretrievably in love with Liza Hayborn ever since he had seen her a dozen times in a movie in which she played a hauntingly beautiful fifteen-year-old riding her grandfather's horse to victory in the Kentucky Derby. It had been an early color movie, with the hues something less than wonderful. But those violet eyes had overpowered the limitations of the emulsion and scorched forever into his heart. He had kept the innocent passion of a thirty-eight-year-old businessman for a movie moppet to himself as he cut a swath worthy of the holder of a proud, wealth-bearing name through New York's lovelies. But even in New Guinea during the war, when he had dallied with some military beauties and aborigines, he had kept track of Liza Hayborn. On one stormy night he had walked eighteen miles through pestilential swamps to watch her win the Derby again at an Army screening in Port Morseby.

Not all the news of her had been good. After an uncomfortable succession of whirls with adolescent actors and then heavier leading men, she had shocked him by marrying Mickey Brandon, son of the restaurant king. His relief at this liaison's lasting only four months dissolved when she had married Derrol Keefe, the luminous swashbuckler. It wounded Justin terribly to get magazines showing them together at the beach or at some glittering premiere, apparently moments away from slipping under a blanket or theater seat to indulge Derrol's beastly appetites. ("Beef Like Keefe" was a contemporary description of fine male genitalia.)

However, those very appetites had come to Justin's rescue near the end of the war, after Fiona was born, when Keefe was found by Liza to be supplementing his sensual fare with sub-teens of various lands.

By the time Justin had been discharged, she was again at liberty. Now playing grown-up women, and with her stupefying beauty at full flower, she had turned into a surprisingly powerful dramatic actress and gained magnificent parts opposite the biggest names. Her movies coined money and those big names resumed the assault upon her fabled pelvis.

Announcing that she was through with marriage, she made some successful defenses of her availability, but Justin had despaired for the long run as he was entering his first major deal for Oakhill Development.

He had sniffed out—both literally and figuratively—the old slaughterhouse district on the east side of Manhattan. It ran between First Avenue and the East River, between 42th and 49th Streets, a stinking anachronism in a modern city, considering that meat could now be shipped conveniently from anywhere. But the Rush family, the great meat-packing dynasty, had acquired the acreage for so little in the dim past that their expenses for slaughtering there were next to nothing. Although the land, and that around it, was valued among the cheapest in the city because of the dirt, noise and unbearable stench, the Rushes were asking an outrageous seventeen dollars per square foot for their property. The going rate in the area was less than five dollars.

To the Rushes' amazement and Victor's dismay, Justin agreed to their price. Victor, unconsulted, had hardly started raging when Justin told him they should also buy up more land around the site.

"Look, Dad, the slaughterhouses are the damned *reason* values are so low around there. Who cares if I'm—we're—paying three and four times the so-called going rate? What's seventeen dollars when that property's going to be selling for fifty dollars a foot when I get that garbage torn down?"

It had all been going exactly as he planned when Justin attended a charity premiere of Liza Hayborn's smash hit, *An American Dream*. He met her at a reception backstage before the performance. In the moment she held his hand and put those violet eyes into his heart forever, he was lost and so was the Oakhill project.

He never saw a frame of the movie. Seated behind her, he feasted his soul on her neck and shoulders, glaring thunderbolts at her date, a willowy modern god with whom she had just returned from Monte Carlo. Justin's only consolation was that the man was even older than he was, and a helluva lot grayer.

Straining to take in the voluptuously delicate scent of her, his mind had begun to move in the Byzantine intricacies that were to become his hallmark. Before she had turned, smiling like paradise itself, to receive the audience's applause, the first of his hundred grandiose schemes was in place in every detail.

"I'll be seeing you," she had said absently as she eased away.

"You bet your famous fanny, you will," he had replied with a passion that caused her to look back after him.

Having for years read every word printed about Liza Hayborn, he had remembered an interview given only a year before. He knew that much of what movie people gave out was the work of press agents, but this was too ridiculous to be that. When he found the piece in the library, it read, in part:

> ... But Liza has it in her wish book to be remembered for more than whatever mark she may leave upon the silver screen. She told this reporter, "A hundred years from today, I'd like some little girl, just like the one I was, to come across my name in a historical document. And when anyone asks her who Liza Hayborn was, I dream of her saying, 'She did something wonderful to insure the peace of the world back in the twentieth century.' Who would be satisfied leaving their name on movie history when they could leave it on world history?"

Before Justin left the library he did some more research to confirm something he already pretty well knew. The fledgling world peace organization to be known as the United Nations had been having the devil's time finding a satisfactory spot for its world headquarters. New York would have been the natural place for it, but there was nothing suitable in size or setting on the crowded island, so Philadelphia seemed ready to get the official nod.

He had vowed that this would never happen. The United Nations would be built on a magnificent site right on New York's East River. Where it would always stand as his wedding present to his fairytale bride.

Thereafter, every time Liza Hayborn looked up, the broad, grinning face of Justin Oakhill was there. At backers' parties, at movie industry dinners, at awards ceremonies, he appeared ten times an evening for as many words as he could squeeze in before she was whisked away. What he said to her was of little importance, his message being plain in his voice and eyes.

He had been aware that his squat fullback's body and bristling haystack of unmanageable hair made him a toad among his elegant competition, and that none of them were twenty-three years older than she was, as was the case with him. But he had the faith of a Biblical outcast.

Her years of fame having given her a healthy dislike of obsessed pursuers nearing fifty, she began to take some pains to avoid him. To partially counter this, he intimated that the Oakhill organization was becoming interested in backing worthwhile film ventures, such as Miss Hayborn's, and he was invited to many get-togethers of potential investors where she was forced to appear nice to him.

"Hey, Liza," he had finally said to her after a screening of a famous director's latest turgid work, "you can treat me any way you want. I'm not putting any money into this turkey anyway."

"Good," she said, her actress's standard smile quickly replaced by one decidedly more wicked. "Then spread those thick thighs a little so I can get a good shot at your balls without getting my shoe stuck."

He laughed so hard he almost knocked over a buffet table, and she joined him after a moment in her great, rolling guffaw.

"Gee," said Liza. "The old gutter-talk dismissal usually works a lot better than that."

"Liza, can we have one real, live, alone date where I can talk to you?"

"Look, Justin. I know you're probably going to tell me that you fell in love with me in *Katie of Kentucky*. God, my tits must have been just right for that one. Half the guys your age in the country still write to me."

"I didn't even see it," Justin said, outraged at the presumptuousness of his unknown rivals and her unkind allusion to his age.

"Maybe you can build me a house sometime. I stayed in one of those outrages you built in Palm Beach. I *loved* it. It was fun and made me feel good all the time."

"We start tomorrow."

"What?"

"The house."

"I don't need another house."

"Lassie wouldn't live in that mess you have now."

"I don't have any land."

"Yes, you do. I'll swap a corner at Broadway and 92nd for a spot over Malibu."

"My money's all tied up."

"This is a present."

"Can't impress me that way, Justin. This is my last present." She showed him a ring of staggering proportions.

Justin squinted at it closely. "Aw, shit, you couldn't get more than two rooms and a small pool in that thing."

Laughing, she had choked on her drink, and he had to pound her on her back and then rub it reassuringly for a while. And they were off.

He had the foundations in before she showed up for the first time, and then she came almost every day. They fought like gamecocks over every detail and afterward indulged a shared mania for Japanese food.

On the day that the tall, octagonal tower room overlooking the sea was finished, Justin had lowered her to the unfinished, sweet-smelling oak floor and entered her in every way he could think of. And one that was her idea. She had gathered some splinters in her classic behind, but Justin was pleased to remove them over the next several weeks.

"I adore it," she crowed when the house was completed.

"Too bad. You'll miss it when you're living in New York."

"I only go to New York to buy galoshes."

"My wife's got to live in New York."

"I wouldn't marry you if your honk was gold and had a better circumcision."

"Not even for another neat present?"

"Not even for the Eiffel Tower."

"We'll see. Be faithful while I'm back in Gotham."

"Until you're over Denver. Make that San Jose."

"Cunt."

"Prick."

"Talking dirty inflames me. C'mere."

* * *

Since it didn't make any sense to make a grand gesture with a piece of property nobody in the street had ever heard about, he had made his East Side parcel instantly famous. He announced that on the site would rise something called Twenty-First Century. It would be the avatar of a master plan to save the city from strangling on its traffic. The entire complex would sit on forty-foot stilts through which traffic could speed unimpeded. There would be parking underground for six thousand cars. Above would be office buildings, one of sixty stories and four of forty stories, not to mention three thirty-story apartment houses, a seven-thousand-room hotel, a seven-thousand-seat convention hall, an opera house, a yacht basin and helicopter landing pads. He budgeted the project at sixty million dollars.

After the plans had been hastily drawn for the site, they were immediately released to the press, and the publicity came pouring in just as expected. Every real estate page and architectural magazine featured articles on the coming wonder. Justin had to reassure Ford continually that it would never be built.

At the moment of peak interest, Justin had called the mayor. "Bill, our city can't let the United Nations get away. Damn it, I love this place, and I'd give up a couple of hundred million to bring the honor here. Say the word and you've got seventeen acres on the East River and the UN can name its own price."

Knowing that the mayor would be calling the site committee with the astonishing offer, he beat them to it, calling a member with whom the Oakhills had some high connections. "Nelson, this is the kind of thing the Rockefellers should have their name on. Speak to your people. I've made the price controllable. Buy the parcel and donate it."

"You know what that land could be worth?"

"All I want is some credit for me, Dad and some of my colleagues who made it possible."

The patrician voice rose with excitement. "Just send me the names, Justin."

"I see them on a silver plaque—not gaudy, but enduring—with a nice dedication from a grateful world. There should be a spot for it someplace in a plaza."

"I'll tack it up myself, my friend."

The news had made every front page in the country, with Justin's sacrifice of his life's dream of Twenty-First Century prominently lamented. Nowhere in the descriptions of his epic offering did it mention that he had actually come out three million dollars ahead on the negotiated price and the disposal of other parts of the parcel.

It had been the middle of the night when he arrived in California with the silver plaque and a bottle of champagne under his arm. He let himself into Liza's house and was pleased to find her in bed alone. "Rise and meet destiny," he boomed, flooding the room with light.

She struggled up on one elbow, the only woman in America who could look so beautiful after being torn from a sound sleep. She grumped and swore but showed signs of being glad to see him. "You've got some balls. Suppose I was knocking one off with a goat?"

"You wouldn't do that unless he promised you a good part."

"I hope that's a pizza you're carrying to go with that champagne." She tossed back the covers to reveal that she wore only bikini briefs. Her nipples had hardened.

He swiftly unwrapped the plaque and propped it in her lap. The incredible eyes widened luminously.

"Oh, *Justin* . . . Oh, my *God.*"

"Should the firm be God and Oakhill, or Oakhill and God?"

Beneath a flowery dedication in blank verse by an incredibly aged New England Nobel winner, there were several names of those who had made this ageless contribution to "peace on earth." The last two, right beneath the appropriate list of Rockefellers, read:

Justin P. Oakhill
Elizabeth Hayborn Oakhill

"Is that Oakhill chick *me?*"

"Only if you marry me. Can't have us biggies bringing casual humps onto the UN Plaza."

"But I didn't do anything to deserve this honor, goddamn it."

"The hell, you didn't. If I wasn't trying to impress you I might have let it all stay a pile of dead cows."

"I don't believe it. You gave me the whole United Nations."

"Liza, I love you so much I can't see straight. Will you marry me?"

She had slipped off the bikini briefs. "Only if we can start the honeymoon now and I can read my plaque while I'm coming."

The spectacular marriage, never far from the newspaper columns, had not notably improved their relationship, but it freed Justin's mind to the point where he could plunge into the pursuit of Ford's galling success almost full-time. The publicity splash of the UN had given him fame and credibility. It still had not given him a free hand with the Oakhill cash, but fortunately he found a money tree of his own.

Already fabled as a man who preferred a complicated deal to a simple one, he had used this predilection to discover that the parts of a building were worth far more separately than the structure as a whole. Reckoning land, mortgage interest, retail space and leasing possibilities, he was able to buy for what seemed high prices and then dispose of pieces that made the price a steal. All while retaining control through leasebacks. Victor had been growing forgetful in his great years, but it was doubtful he could have followed Justin around these turns even at the height of his powers.

"It's really as simple as hell, Dad. Take our building at Lex and Thirty-eighth. I paid ten million. Kind of high. I could only sell it for nine and a half. But it's producing a million a year, and a good manager could get that up to two. So I sell an operating lease for five million to somebody who wants a shot at the rents. They give me a million and a half and a mortgage for the rest. We get six hundred thousand from them, and they collect the rents. So they get a four-hundred-thousand-dollar profit from the million-and-a-half they put out, minus the interest on my mortgage. Good deal for them. But look at what we get. I mortgage the whole shebang, six million seven on a first and, say, another two and a quarter on a second. We get fourteen million dollars in cash and mortgages for something we might have sold for nine million. The six-hundred-thousand-dollars of the operating lease more than pays the interest on both the mortgages."

"I didn't understand a word you said, Justin."

"Well, understand this, Dad. We're going to use the cash and the leaseholder's mortgages as collateral for a *really* big mortgage from Vesuvius Life Assurance. And with that, allowing me some time, I'm going to go for a majority in both the Graybar and the Empire State. I always liked the Chrysler Building, too."

He had gotten most of what he wanted and went on from there. Unfortunately, Victor had remained alive only long enough to see the promising beginning. Or he might have seen that his son was using his split-up technique not as the first safe and sane operation of his life, but as the means of gathering finances for increasingly overwrought schemes of a scale bordering the suicidal. And he might have introduced some much-needed caution.

Still, Justin had shown remarkable patience—for him—in assembling bread-and-butter operations not only in New York, but in Canada and the West. And he had been the builder who had seen that the government's Title I Program of the National Housing Act could be good business as well as a help for his beloved city. The program was ultimately termed the "Oakhill Relief Bill," but by 1960 he was developing more public housing than any other developer in the world.

The city filled with his work. The roll of first-class residential projects and blue-ribbon hotels was a roll of the Oakhill holdings.

One of his favorite coups had been Coolidge Field. The old airfield on Long Island was no longer in use, and he had heard that Ford was preparing to acquire it for one more of his damnable instant slums. But this time he had beaten his half-brother to the deal. The 370-acre shopping center he had erected, the world's largest, was not what he enjoyed building, but it made him a great deal of money and had the most important of the desired effects: It spawned industrial renters who sprawled out into the acres outside the holding and created a small, closely packed city out of what Ford would have turned into another of his dollhouse towns.

Ford had called Justin. Usually the least volatile of men, his voice had shaken with fury. "Someday, Justin, you'll need something to save you. Reckless people always do. Then I hope you'll come to me after everybody else has spit on you. Your father was right. You're out of control, and all you'll ever be able to see is yourself and your own needs."

The rebuke had stung, because Justin had a sudden fear that it had a terrible merit. He had been increasingly unable to control the scope of his plans. Things that started out with containable goals grew like beserk yeast. He had a taste for the wild and gigantic that he could not contain.

In addition to his Twenty-First Century Plan, which he now saw as a real possibility, he had the organization working on plans for the Clouds Project—the world's tallest building, looming several hundred feet above the Empire State and standing on columns that enclosed Grand Central Terminal. The outside of the tower would contain open intervals in the facade through which glass elevators would carry entranced passengers. For thousand of tenants, the daily trip to the office would be a fabulous adventure, he dreamed.

But the best of his visions was his projected Palace of Tomorrow. It had begun as part of another labyrinthine deal, one of his favorites.

The Central Pennsylvania Railroad, bankrupt, owned the Grand Admiral Hotel, once magnificent but now decaying and leaking millions. The hotel owed six million dollars in back taxes. Sensing the railroad's desperation, Justin had laid down strong terms for the Grand Admiral's purchase. A price of ten-million dollars would include gigantic riverfront railyards, now little used by the crippled carrier.

In the meantime he had negotiated with the chronically financially-strapped city. He would not make the Grand Admiral deal and hand them their otherwise unrecoverable six million dollars unless they granted him forty years of a huge tax break. The difference between getting something and getting nothing being vast, the city had agreed to the break.

But Justin was not done dealing. He turned to the Wyatt Hotel Chain, which had been looking for a fast entry into New York, and ended with a partnership deal in the hotel. With Wyatt's expertise, the Grand Admiral had been quickly renovated and—freed from its tax burden—turned to handsome profit. Justin had then refinanced to recoup all the money he had put up, and continued to enjoy the cash flow of the hotel.

When the city had begun to realize it had given away four hundred million in taxes over the forty-year life of the deal, he had coolly applied for—and received—a further abatement under an old law covering improvements on underutilized land.

However, all of that was incidental to the real prize: the railyards upon which the Palace of Tomorrow would rise. This was to be a single office building with twice the cubic footage of the Pentagon. It would feature a theme park (Gaslight New York), a permanent World's Fair, a merchandise mart and—his neverending quest—the inevitable rooftop airport. The problem of air-traffic control would not be serious, he always explained, because he would wangle an FAA control tower to handle the helicopters and vertical take-off jets.

His attempts to get these leviathan projects moving drained enormous resources from his company even as he gained shocked admiration from his fellow builders. There was simply no one else with his courage, vision and organizational daring; his ideas were simply too marvelous for his means.

The financial and building trade-publications, for years in awe of his daring machinations, began to question him publicly.

The most prominent of the business magazines wrote:

> If magnificent schemes initiated were the measure of a great organization, Oakhill Development would go down as the wonder of the ages. Unfortunately, there is the little matter of completions, that magic moment that allows a corporation to recoup and increase its investment. Oakhill has precious few of those lately.
>
> Justin Oakhill announces $200,000,000 and $500,000,000 projects as casually as others announce plans for a dozen new bus shelters. But the giant schemes, any one of which would tax to the limit any organization known, have overwhelmed the ability of the solid—often

brilliant—smaller schemes that must pay for them.

Oakhill's cash position is laughably low for a company of such magnitude—probably less than $5,000,000. Stock can't help, because there are already 21,000,000 shares of common outstanding, on which he has never paid a dividend. There are also debentures, and the company's building leases and other holdings are pledged to its mortgages.

Mr. Oakhill had better pull in his ingenious horns, even though it would make the New York real estate scene a much duller place. If he does not restore equilibrium to his vast operation, there will be a fire sale of fabulous properties that is past our imagining.

Justin had taken the criticism to heart and responded—with an immense new project, which only he regarded as modest and level-headed.

"If it's a major completion they want, I'll give it to them" he had stormed to the uncomprehending Liza. "Something solid that they can all understand, even with their little chick-pea brains."

"Let me guess. A two hundred and twenty–story newsstand."

"Nothing so interesting. A hotel. The Grand Oakhill."

"You? Building a little old hotel?"

"Actually, not so little. Think of this. There hasn't been a major hotel put up in New York since thirty-one. Almost thirty-five years ago. People brag about staying in the Plaza Athenée or the Ritz in Paris, or the Connaught in London. All New York has are a few tired old-timers. I want the Grand Oakhill to be quite simply the greatest hotel on earth for the next fifty years."

"Oh, dear."

"Fifty stories. A skyscraper that's a hotel. Ten banquet halls, every one of them more magnificent than any existing, and all decorated to a different theme. Foreign corporations will fly their staffs here just for the prestige of a banquet at the Grand Oakhill. And they can do it for ten years without repeating the hall. For their meetings I'll have twenty private dining rooms served by the great chefs of the world, who will fight to get into the kitchens. I'll put in twenty thousand palatial rooms. Not little cheese boxes, but ones where you can fuck on another major antique every day for a month."

"So you'll be needing an antique factory."

He ignored her. "The shops and offices in the promenades on the lower levels are going to make the ones in Rockefeller Center —right next door—look like stalls in a leper's bazaar in Marrakech."

Even Liza, understanding little of what he did, had begun to look worried. "That sounds like you picked a site already."

"Yep. The low Fifties along Sixth Avenue. Nothing but beat-up brownstones with some dying nightclubs and some restaurants."

"Have you thought this through complete—"

"A great—truly great—hotel is a magnet for the elite of an entire world. The center of the city, I tell you, Liza. The crown jewel... *Until*... I take the money out and turn it into the Palace of Tomorrow over the old railyards. *That's* the one I'm living for. The one that will make Ford shit. *That's* the—"

"The hotel, Jus. You're forgetting the hotel already."

"Ah, yes. The Grand Oakhill."

And thus had been born The Hole.

It had become symbolic of all that plagued him. It was 450 feet long, 300 feet wide and sixty feet deep, a Grand Canyon gouged into the heart of the world's most expensive real estate. And it did not progress to a structure. Instead, it sat there while millions upon millions poured into it with no effect.

His difficulties had been numerous and cumulative.

News of the assemblage had leaked, and the landowners, knowing the scale of Justin's operations, stung him dearly. But at least they sold. All but one. He, Boops Day, old-time owner of a speakeasy that had become a popular restaurant hangout for sports celebrities, refused offer after offer.

"Dese rich bastids t'ink dey can buy anyt'in. Havin' a joint to hoist one wit' Hornung or Joe D. on a slow day is wort' ten million to me."

Boops' brownstone was at an awkward spot, spoiling the projected facade of the hotel. The builders negotiated desperately since the architects were unable to deal satisfactorily with the obstacle. It was going to be expensive whatever happened, but the real cost was a loss of investor enthusiasm. On Justin's promise to the Chase Manhattan Bank to concentrate on the Grand Oakhill, he had been able to borrow twenty million dollars to pay for the land and its leases. Vesuvius Life Insurance was to come up with another thirty million, but only if he demonstrated that he could raise the rest of what he needed from other backers. And now those other backers had begun to get nervous at the delays and increased costs, and they sat on their hands. The thin cohesion of the deal was beginning to loosen, and The Hole yawned like the mouth of a devouring alligator.

Fiona Keefe knew perfectly well that she was not the first young woman who had fallen in love with her stepfather. She had realized that when hardly into her teens. And she had been wise enough to expect to grow out of her crush the way other young girls did when they were no longer overawed by their guardians. But it hadn't happened that way.

Her secret love turned to her in the back of the returning limousine.

"You did fine with the bank goons, Fi. You had them licking your hand."

"My paw, you mean, the way I was sitting up and begging."

"Yeah. Kind of cowardly of me. Making you do all the groveling for us."

"That's okay, Justin. You stink at it."

He slumped into a corner of the seat. "Those guys affect me like nerve gas. Wake me up when we're back at the office."

"You can't do all your sleeping in cars between meetings."

"Why else would I need the car?" Before the next stoplight, he was deeply asleep.

Tenderness welled up in her. She wanted to nestle up to him and rest her head on his lap the way she had when she was a little girl, and stroke his big, square hands. He always made jokes about what a squat old ape he was, but to her he was as beautiful as any movie god her mother had ever dragged home. Sleep didn't soften the strength and courage in his face, but now there was a sweet vulnerability that others didn't see.

Fiona remembered the first day she had met Justin Oakhill, when she was seven years old. He and her mother had just been married. Liza had never permitted her to meet any of her men after she had left her husband, because she didn't want Fiona forming attachments with people not famed for high-minded morality. Especially when those attachments were likely to be fleeting. Actually Fiona would have loved to have attention from anyone. Liza's divorce from Derrol Keefe had been long and bloody, with her daughter's custody in the balance for many terrible months. Each parent had tearfully begged Fiona to declare herself for him or her. It shredded what little tranquility remained in her life after years as pawn in a marriage that had been more like a barroom fight in a John Wayne movie.

Wanting to protect Fiona from the ravenous attention of the world during the great court battles, they had cut her off from any meaningful tenderness from outside. In distant apartments in Palm Springs and Carmel, she knew only the attention of governesses.

Another child might have shrugged it off, but being caught all those years between the rock-crusher personalities of Derrol Keefe and Liza Hayborn, she had grown sensitive, introverted and unsure. Her physical assets had not helped either.

The devastating beauty that the press and movie colony had expected from the daughter of Hayborn and Keefe had not materialized. The society that worshipped looks had not been good at hiding its disappointment. "Holy shit," she had heard one lovable old character icon say at a pool party, "the kid must belong to Eddie Cantor and Martha Raye. She's all mouth and eyes."

It had not helped a bit to find that she was much better at running and tumbling and swinging rackets than she was at learning how to dress and behave like a little lady.

Her body had not cooperated either. There was not the least promise of the round, seductive curving that made her mother so breathtaking. A national magazine showed pictures of them side by side at the same age, and it was the difference between a stunning, immature movie queen and a tough, lank-haired, flat-shanked little boy, complete with scabbed knees and a black eye acquired during an all-out tennis lesson.

Justin had appeared while she was paddling in the middle of a Palm Springs swimming pool. Walking across the patio with her mother, tanned, grinning, he had looked like he was on the way to take on the universe in his white flannel slacks and blue blazer. She had instantly adored him and hoped he was the one her mother had chosen. And then he had not stopped. He strode straight to the side of the pool, waving to her as he came, and with a vibrant whoop had dived in, clothes, watch, shoes and all. With beautiful grace he had swum to her and planted a resounding kiss on her forehead. "I'm Justin, Fiona. Sorry, but I couldn't wait to meet you."

Fiona had laughed as she hadn't for three years, and throwing her arms around the new miracle, she half-drowned kissing him back.

Later on, she sometimes wondered if he would have become so close to her if her mother had remained around him more. But it was idle to speculate, because Liza was quickly away into a world that could never be his. And Fiona had often thought, hadn't it been a perfect thing for both her mother and Derrol to have Justin to care for her.

Justin might have guessed that nothing under heaven could have made Liza Hayborn give up her fairytale life to sit at home waiting for a man who went to meetings and played with cement on the other side of the country. But then he had not been in a position to understand that big movies were no longer shot in

Hollywood studios in three weeks. They were made in Rome and London and Paris and Belgrade and went on for months and months.

Also, he had no way of comprehending how a woman, one who was so unabashedly wild in loving him in those times when she returned, could allow herself to be linked so incessantly with an army of romantic pursuers who approached the Golden Horde in numbers.

"Didn't our marriage make the papers?" Justin asked dazedly.

There were screen Adonises, Shakespearean thunderers, lyric tenors, legendary symphony conductors, rock-and-roll vandals, silver-haired Italian auto magnates, ocean racers, White House whizbangs and a famous center fielder.

That Liza was under such furious siege didn't mean that she capitulated, but Fiona knew it made him furious that some wispy Welsh poet was breathing things in his wife's ear that might be more interesting than anything a builder in a 46-regular sport jacket might ever say.

As vexing as Liza's long absences and hectic preproduction schedules might have been to Justin, they had been a godsend to Fiona. Her stepfather had time to sense her loneliness and set out to correct it. He arranged her schooling so she could be on either coast anytime. And he let her be at his side all she wanted, which had turned out to be almost all the time she was not in school or he was not asleep.

Far from being burdened by her wide-eyed presence, Justin had been as jubilant to have her company as she was to have his.

There was a part of him that would never grow up—the part that had created the throttle-to-the-floor deals and fantasies of Florida—and he was as pleased as he could be to have a like-minded little accomplice.

Behind Liza's busy back, he instilled the sense of play and adventure that Fiona had never learned. He turned her tennis playing into fun instead of a grim pursuit of perfection, shouting with laughter when the little girl defeated him, but never intentionally losing a point, so she would not feel demeaned.

The man who could steamroller a conference room full of

hostile planners would emerge to giggle and gossip with his stepdaughter as though forty years had just dropped off his age.

And as she had grown, it was his genius to be always at just the necessary level for them to be perfect friends.

To be sure, he hadn't tried to keep her all to himself. Knowing that she had to come out of her private little world, he had gone to great efforts to establish her in a circle of companions her own age. He gave the best parties for young people on either coast, hand-picking the guests—boys and girls—to be the kind she would like. It became known that friends of Fiona Keefe got flown to the Caribbean, ski lodges and mountain lakes, and her once-empty world speedily filled. She became as comfortable with people and as popular as any young girl could be. But she continued to prefer Justin's company to that of any of the others.

His colleagues, all aware of his eccentrically youthful way, became used to the young Fiona coming to meetings and sitting quietly until her stepfather was done. They understood her presence less well when she became older and began to sit at his side, apparently taking an interest in the impossibly arcane proceedings.

Thinking back, Fiona recalled that Justin had for a time attempted to discourage her interest in his business.

"Listen, Fiona," he had said to her in her mid-teens, "I don't want to be like my damned brother Ford. He's been raising that stuck-up twerp of his to take over the business since the little sonofabitch could say 'goo.'" Justin had seen early on that you didn't have to watch your language around a daughter of Liza Hayborn and Derrol Keefe. "The kid's going to grow up with I-beams for bones and cement for a soul. This business has screwed up every one of us who's ever touched it, and you deserve better."

"Justin," she had replied, her eyes growing older for a moment, "I watched Mom and Derrol crash and burn trying to make believe that little squares of film were important. I want to live with something *solid*. The way you did, and your father did and your grandmother did."

"How do you know what my grandmother did?"

"I've got a library card. She was a piss-whistler, wasn't she?"

Justin had whooped and jammed her tennis hat over her eyes. "Yeah. Just like you. Okay. You asked for it, dummy."

After that he had included her in all his plans. He suggested courses and sent her to spend time with the builders and architects he respected most, telling her of how Hannah had let Victor go to Chicago to learn when he was no older than she was now. They had decided together that she would train at Stanford, and he kept her close to him to get her ready. It was during these days that she had realized, with consternation and ever-growing shame, that her love for Justin was more than that of a stepdaughter. Derrol Keefe had always been her father. Justin Oakhill had always been something else.

Each morning that they were together in California or New York, whether or not Liza was there, Justin and Fiona had met for a long and grueling swim. In the big pool at the Hollywood Hills house or the one at the Henry Hudson Hotel in New York, they churned out energetic laps for almost an hour, talking almost nonstop while half-submerged. It was at one of these sessions, at the age of seventeen, that she had found herself admiring the powerful slope of his shoulders and the glistening wedges of muscle in his chest and belly. She enjoyed toweling the broad sweep of his back and lingered, rubbing after the last drops had disappeared. Her eyes wandered continually to where the stripe of dark hair ran down the division of his abdominals and vanished down the top of his low-riding trunks. She had become terrified that he would see how often her eyes brushed at the bold prow of him, but it never caught his otherwise omnivorous attention.

At this time she had tried bravely to settle on one of her dates as a proper object of affection. He was the son of a studio head, serious, attentive and loaded with Levantine good looks. He was the first boy to take her to bed, and was tender, patient and expert. Soon he had begun to proclaim his love, and gossip columns sensed a newsworthy romance.

It should have been a perfect and painless way out for her, but after Justin's company her schoolboy lover seemed a ridiculous infant.

When Justin had met the young man, he had liked him and told Fiona that she had made a helluva fine choice. Furious, Fiona broke off with the boy the next day. There were other boys for shorter times, and then some men, but with no more satisfaction.

The separation brought about by college in California had come too late to be divisive. She missed Justin horrendously, and now had the knowledge of the joyous possibilities of physical love to bedevil her further. Once, to her burning shame, she had been compelled to relieve her sexual tension while he was on the phone to her.

She had sometimes thought she might do some serious sleeping around in college with the students who came on to her. But she couldn't bring herself to betray the man who didn't know she thought of him as anything but a father.

One of the campus pursuers she had turned away was Ronald Stryker. That had been exceptionally easy.

Even at a school so loaded with spoiled children of wealth, Ford's son had been considered excessively arrogant. He drove a red Lamborghini, and tales of his insolence were everywhere. He was said to be too uppity to retain any close male friends, and he approached girls directly and crudely, practically daring them to turn him down.

In Fiona's case, her annoyance was compounded by her—a senior—being approached by a mere sophomore. Ronald, tall and then wearing a magnificent beard, did look older than most graduate students. But the fact remained that he was three years younger than she was. And besides that he was the son of Ford Stryker, which alone made him enemy enough.

He had plunked down next to her in the library and spoken like a salesman working his way through a long, onerous list of cold calls. "I hear we're related."

"Same thing I hear," she said, opening a book and beginning to search through it. "It doesn't really make my day." He never carried any books of his own, although she had seen his name on the Dean's Honor List.

"Don't you think it's weird we never met?"

"No. Justin worked pretty hard at it."

"Yeah. I guess my dad did, too."

"Then suppose we defer to the wisdom of our elders."

"I want to take you out. I like the way you look, and we're not related by blood, you know."

"So the news isn't all bad. Tell me, Ronald. How'd you ever get such a smooth line?"

"I get it." He was scowling more than ever. "You heard I had some tar in me."

"No, I heard you were obnoxious. Thank you for removing all doubt."

He finally blushed. "Does that mean no?"

"It means more like not in ten thousand years."

He had left her, appearing more uneasy than angry. From across the room, where his voice carried to everyone, he turned and spoke to her before he went through the door. "I watched you in the Vietnam debate. I really liked you. Besides the way you looked. You've got some mouth."

A chorus of shushes had driven him out.

But there was something about him that struck a chord of recognition in her that she couldn't quite pin down. She had shrugged after a while and went back to reading. And to missing Justin.

She had been so wound up around her mother's house that Liza had said, "Go find yourself a guy to love. There's probably one waiting right under your nose."

But finally she had graduated and gone to join Justin at Oakhill Development.

She had trouble waking Justin when the limousine got to the office. When he finally roused, his breath was rapid and shallow and he was slow to gather his wits.

"Hey, big chief, if you don't knock off for a while, they're going to bury you in The Hole."

"I can't sleep for two days after I take that night plane from Paris. Not in bed, anyway. Let's get upstairs."

"Right. But not to the twentieth floor. You're going to twenty-one." He kept a suite of rooms there.

"Okay. Maybe for a while. You come up, too, and hit the couch for a while. You haven't been down since you met me at the airport in the middle of the night."

"Sold."

Upstairs, he waved, shot her a tired smile and disappeared into the bedroom. When the door had closed, she kicked off her shoes, threw her jacket aside and fell onto the enormous leather sofa.

"Damn it, Jus," she said under her breath. "All I want to do is lie next to you and hold you." But she knew she wanted a lot more than that. "Sorry, Mom," she murmured. "Can't help it."

Not a drinker, she nonetheless finished almost a third of a bottle of Wild Turkey before she dropped off.

It was so deep into the evening when she woke that the buildings outside the windows sparkled with only a few lights. A blanket had been thrown over her, so he she knew that Justin was up. But she didn't see him when she looked around the darkened room. He didn't answer her weak call.

She was no longer drunk, but she had never held her whiskey well and her head felt filled with a dizzying gas. Her usually steady nerves seemed slack and suddenly unable to bear the weight of her years of hopeless love.

The bedroom door was closed. There was no answer to her knock. When she eased the door back she saw the empty, rumpled bed with his clothes strewn across it as though he had decided to get out of them quickly.

No lamps were on in the room, but a rectangle of light shined from the opposite wall. It was the window to the sauna he had installed to relieve tension. Steam boiled thickly against the glass, showing he was in there. Good, she thought. It would keep him relaxing for a while.

She went to the door of the steam room, fully intending to knock and call her good-night to him. But when she got there she stayed her fist and peered through the glass. Inside the small room the steam swirled. Perhaps eight feet away he sat asleep on a bench facing her. He was leaning back against the wall, a towel, a decanter of scotch and a glass beside him. Perspiration gleamed on his wide, tight body. His powerful legs were spread carelessly, and she looked upon the great sledgehammer of him resting on a bull's testicles.

Something in her stretched and broke.

Inside the sauna, Justin had maintained exactly the degree of drunkenness he wanted, and he was just skimming a drowse as he let the steam work the clutch out of his muscles. He hadn't felt this good since The Hole had appeared. He was actually contemplating taking the morning off when he felt the hand on his cheek.

His eyes shot open. A foot from his face were the naked breasts of Fiona, perfect pink-nippled duplicates of Liza's, but with the delicious tilt of youth. Involuntarily his eyes moved downward to where she was neatly cropped to accommodate the bikini she wore to their morning swims. The droplets were already running down into the dark bristles between her tennis-hard legs.

When he looked up again to her face, which moved slowly down to his, he finally saw the longing that must have been there for years.

His whiskey-fuddled mind tried to stagger to his aid, but tilted and fell. The violet eyes that should have belonged to Liza were coming at him in another body and he froze with confusion. The wide, full mouth covered his, and a sweet tongue brushed his lips.

As she kissed him, the hands that had been touching his cheek slid away. A dazzling and reverberating knot grew at the base of his suddenly tensing belly. He looked down to find his violently swelling flesh in her cradling hands.

"*Fi, what the hell—*"

His words turned to a strangled gasp as she moved her legs around him and prepared to sit and ingest him.

"*No,* damn it—"

His first spurt leaped up between them, and he continued to pump thickly as he grabbed her waist in his big hands and lifted her away while the jolts of release shot through him.

She raised her dripping hands to her face and began to cry.

"Oh, Justin. I screwed it up. I screwed everything up completely. You'll never talk to me again. Mom will cut my throat and I'll deserve it."

Now she was trying to cover herself with her hands.

Justin grabbed up the towel and wrapped it around her. There was nothing to cover himself, but he knew he had to hold her and talk to her right then, or she would snap back into the inner world from which he had worked so long and lovingly to bring her.

His unwanted physical spasm passing rapidly, he embraced her in the billowing clouds of steam. "Fiona, we just can't do what you want. It would be hypocritical now to say that I could only love you like a daughter when you're standing here with my juice all over your hands. The truth is that if we stand here like this another two minutes, I'm going to want you, too. It's the worst kind of forbidden dream."

"I *want* you to have me, Jus. I want to make love with you. Now."

"No. I'm scared that—"

"Bullshit. You've never been scared of anything in your life. What is it? Mother? She's ignored both of us so much that we don't owe her a thing anymore. Afraid she'd be devastated? Or lonesome? She's probably in Yokohama right now enjoying three geisha boys."

"I don't believe that, Fi. I never really did, even when I worried about it. Liza's got a furnace in her, God knows. But she's strong and loyal. And too damned straight for her own good. I think that when the last flashbulb goes off, she sends all those swinging cocks away."

"Yeah. After she sucks them. You're dreaming, Justin."

"Maybe. But I love her. And she trusted me with you. I won't let her down. I won't."

"You didn't seduce me. God, I would have kicked that door down if it'd been locked."

"Don't make it harder, Fi. I want you to do what I'm asking now. It would wipe me out to lose you. You'll never, never know how important you are to every part of my life. When Liza told me after we were married that she'd been sterilized, I knew you were the only little girl I'd ever have. And you've been the morning star to me ever since. But I'll have to send you away if you don't swear with your hand on my heart that you'll never come to me like this again, and that you'll never mention this night or any of the things it might have meant."

She rested in his arms, her face hidden in his chest for so long that he began to fear that his passion would reawaken. But then she lifted her face to his, and there was a little smile on the wonderful lips. "Just as you say, big chief. Not another grope. Not another romantic word. We go on just as before, working three inches apart for days at a time. You'll be safe from that part of me, and I love you so much that I probably won't mind so long as you're around. But hear this. I'll be there any time you want me. Never forget that. Say one word and you can be in bed with me, having all I've got. If you're strong enough to know that every day, and to walk away from it, you'll be safe forever."

"I'm strong enough." He dropped his arms from her so she could go.

She let the towel fall from her and brushed her fingertip down his penis as she turned.

He watched the sweat roll down her back and slide into the cleft of her hard, lovely buttocks as she vanished through the steam and out the door.

The perspiration that streamed off him had very little to do with the steam.

Justin was on the phone to Japan three times the next day, growing more desperate each time he spoke with Liza. "I miss you, sweetheart. Screw the picture. Come on home. I miss you so goddamned much. I'll hump you four hours at a time. I swear."

"Honey, I keep telling you that they've got thirty-one million bucks tied up in this bowl of rice. *Lotus Fire* is going to be the hot release next year."

"If I had you under me right now, I'd show you a hot release."

"This is a shot at the little naked statue with the gold cock."

"I'll show you a gold—"

"Justin, come on. They've got too much of me in the can to turn back."

"I'll get something in your ca—"

"They're behind on principal photography, so I can't get any time off. Come over if you miss me so much."

He groaned. "I can't with that motherless Hole eating me alive."

"Then stop making me nuts. Besides, you're liable to need the two million I'm getting for this kimono flapper."

"Two million wouldn't buy enough pens to sign all my foreclosures. Come home. Please. Please. Please—"

She laughed at him. "We'll have two weeks between the end of this and *Alpine Serenade*. We can catch up on the dinner parties in the first week and have the second one to ourselves. Maybe fly to Zurich and tramp the hills and screw Heidi and her goats. We've got some preproduction there anyway."

His heart dropped. "I'll wear an Edelweiss so you recognize me."

"I'll call Fiona and tell her to drag you around for a good time. Oops, there's my call for the chopper. It's out on the lawn. I've got a nipple shot on top of Fuji. Hope they don't drop off in the cold. Love you, dongmaster. You're so tender. 'Bye now."

With huge relief, Justin found Fiona true to her word. She remained as cheerful and loving as ever, pretending not to notice that he tensed whenever she touched him unexpectedly or kissed his cheek. She allowed no hint of a change in their former innocent relationship to show.

But he expected that she knew that the long hours of exhausting days weakened him for the lonely, dreadful nights. He began to believe that she might even be manipulating his longing for Liza by playing up what physical similarities she shared with her mother. She did her hair and her eyes in just the same way and let the Hayborn silkiness creep into her voice.

For all his iron resolution, there were times when Justin had to get away from her quickly so that he would not risk a fatal mistake.

57[1]

If it did not so thoroughly bode to destroy him, he would have been grateful for the grim distractions of The Hole.

Time and again he would announce that he was ready to begin the final push to completion, appearing in his hard hat in newspaper photographs as a few hundred yards of concrete were poured or several beams were bolted together in a feeble poke at the sky. But people had gotten harder to fool and easier to disappoint since he had announced the first of his series of ephemeral giants. The publicity pushes didn't work to bring in the money anymore.

As two more agonizing years slid by, it became obvious that the Grand Oakhill was his last chance and it was slipping ignominiously away.

Fiona was surprised to be summoned to the Chase Manhattan Bank alone. The gray, somber men in the thousand-dollar suits had always just barely subdued their outrage when Justin had appeared with his lovely protégée at his side to examine lofty matters. Even when she had finally seen involuntary respect appearing in their faces after she had made an important contribution, she was sure that they felt her relationship with Justin was as carnal as she indeed wanted it to be.

The worst of those who had sniffed at her presence was Enos Coleman, heir of a family of merchant princes and second in command at the bank. She half-expected that he had called her to ask her to for God's sake leave the old boy alone so he could concentrate on getting together all the money he owed them. Instead, he couldn't have been more courteous and glad to see her. He ushered her into the most sacrosanct of the executive dining rooms, where a sumptuous table had been set before windows that looked almost a quarter mile straight down across the tip of Manhattan, revealing the entirety of the vast bay swarming with ships and drenched in sun.

"Nice view," she said. "Who does your harbors?"

Coleman managed a laugh and pulled out her chair. With his silver hair and striking profile, he would have been very handsome if his eyes had not been set so close together. "God did it,

Miss Keefe. But unless He can find a way to budge Justin Oakhill, we will reserve being impressed. Shall we begin?

"With the business, not the lunch, Mr. Coleman. I hate suspense."

"Just as you wish." He picked at the salad as he chose his words. "We do not . . . wish to see Mr. Oakhill go under."

"Then loan him what he needs."

"That's what we've been doing for years. And all he ever does is stop working on what we gave him the money for and start something bigger, agreements notwithstanding."

"You never gave him enough."

"You're probably right. There's never been a builder that thought as big as he does. Or organized people for an enormous deal so well. Perhaps we were just too timid for him. But it's too late now. He's into us too deeply. And he can't even get a comparatively small—for him—hotel into that hole of his. If it breaks him, he'll go under for good and we and our sister institutions will be stuck with liquidating so much of his real estate that we'll flood our own market. We'll take an awfully big bath."

"Did you invite me to lunch so I could watch your mascara run? Or just to tell me you're going to gang up and foreclose on him?"

"Don't be upset, Miss Keefe. Many of us still have the greatest faith in Mr. Oakhill. If he can get the rest of that backing he promised us, we'd certainly consider increasing our stake in the Grand Oakhill."

"I suppose I could slip one of my stockings over my head and hold up your bank."

"Spare me your bitter patter. You know perfectly well where he can raise that money. Quickly and easily. From his brother."

"Ford is his half-brother, as you must know. And Justin could get money easier out of hell. They loathe one another."

"That's not the way I hear it. Justin's the one who keeps antagonizing Ford. Crosses him up every way he can. Shoots his mouth off on political committees and in the newspapers. It's time to leave off. Patch things up. It's ridiculous that Oakhill Development and Stryker and Oakhill are separate companies now. Christ, they even share a name."

"The men are too different. Ford dreams of ten-thousand-dollar houses and grass and trees, and plans down to the last nail—"

"Yes, and Justin dreams of ten-billion-dollar cities and concrete and girders, and forgets somebody has to pay for them."

Fiona reached for her purse. "He wouldn't go groveling to Ford if you burned his eyes with hot irons."

"I know that. That's why I made the suggestion to you, not him. You've got . . . *power* over him, if my observations are accurate." *You're balling him,* was what the tone said. "You can sway him, I believe, the way no one else could."

"You're dreaming. Ford would have to come to him. I guarantee it."

He smiled glacially. "Then *you* go to Mr. Stryker. You're family by marriage, after all. And a most charming persuasive young lady when you're after something, as you have often demonstrated here. He'd give you a hearing. And you could point out what a fine piece of business the Grand Oakhill would be for him, no matter how intense the mutual dislike. I think you agree with that yourself."

"Yes, maybe I do. Trouble is, if you can believe it, I've never met Ford Stryker. You and I are old buddies compared to him and me."

"You must know someone in his family whom you could get to. And for more than an introduction, perhaps. Somebody you can tell our story to, so he can be convinced and intercede for us."

"I don't know anybody on the Stryker side at all."

"Think hard, Miss Keefe. A name will come to you."

Ronald Stryker had spotted Fiona as soon as she had come into the crowded meeting room. He re-experienced both the embarrassment he had endured after his clumsy approach three years ago at Stanford and the pleasure he had always felt when he had seen her crossing the campus during those years at school. He wondered if he would have had the nerve to approach her again if he had not been pinned at the head of this meeting table by the fund-raising committee of the Museum of Impressionist Art.

The committee's chairman, a man with no chin and beautiful red curls, was droning on. "It's just disgraceful that we have to do this periodic begging. Here we are, the premier institute of modern art on earth, and we're about to be thrown out on the street because we can't meet expenses. In every other civilized nation the government supports the arts. Or the city helps, or the state. Here we must come on our knees to the city's exploiters. Well, we would like to say, Mr. Stryker, that the people of New York are anything but satisfied by the funding performance of you and many of the members of the power structure in this room. We in this town see major participation in vital civic projects like this as your duty as well as your privilege. And, if I may say so, on behalf of all the working people of New York City, we take it as one of our basic rights to have the massive support of those who have taken their millions out of—excuse me, I've got to say it—out of our sweating hides. Thank you."

The speaker, an executive vice-president at an advertising agency, had sold the committee a strategy of shaming and bullying the deep pockets into solving the museum's never-ending financial problems. He had chosen his words for their headline-grabbing ability, keeping one eye on a notion to edge into city politics after he had cashed in his company stock and profit-sharing. Those who expected to be on his campaign committee, and to perhaps gather in a spot on the Taxi Commission, applauded and yelled *Right on!* a lot.

Ronald stood and spoke with a harsh, decisive force that they had not remotely expected from this elegant young man, who they believed was sharing the running of a great corporation only because his father had put him there. He wondered if any of them could have guessed how hard he had worked and fought to win that spot from the careful, conservative Ford.

"Ladies and gentlemen of the committee," he began, and then looking to Fiona added, ". . . and guests. I'd like to answer Mr. Picalora's silly attempt at a holdup by walking out of here and leaving my fellow exploiters to stand and deliver. But then the marshalls of this heartless city government would be along in a couple of months to put your paintings out in the street, where, as far as I'm concerned, a little rain might do some of them some good. But I won't indulge myself. Nor will I offer you a donation to only postpone the inevitable. Instead, if you can tolerate my polluting presence for another couple of minutes, I'll tell you not only how to save your smudge factory, but how to make it the most solidly financed museum in the world. Permanently."

"What? Sell it to you?" Picalora squeaked. "So you can give parties here and allow a branch of Bloomingdale's in the Sculpture Garden?"

"For heaven's sake, Jed, don't start running for councilman here," said a tough old mummy of a woman. "Let the man speak."

Ronald's baleful glare finished the job of sitting down the sullen Picalora.

Now Ronald took control of the room with a force that startled people who presumed to read his character from a face that might have been more at home grinning out of the New York *Times* Fall Fashion Supplement above the new Armani tweeds. "You've got all the money you'll ever need right here under your shoes. I'll show you how to unlock it. With air rights." He pointed upward. "The space above this museum, on a block in the Fifties, three hundred feet from Fifth Avenue, is priceless. You control it. Put it into the market."

An uproar erupted instantly.

"So we become a basement store for some skyscraper."

"The world's greatest modern art museum turns into a singles bar for secretaries and junior account executives on their lunch hour."

"They'd overwhelm us with their noise and delivery trucks."

"And their architecture."

"They'd have the power to do anything they wanted with us before long."

Ronald stared them quiet. "Those are all the dangers. Here's how you avoid them. First thing, it's got to be a residence, not an office building."

"You mean an apartment house?" someone called.

"No, a condominium. This might sound wacky to you now, but inside of twenty years, wealthy people are going to be happy to pay two hundred thousand a room, even three hundred thousand, to live in spaces like this one. What they'd pay for this kind of prestige address right now would knock you over backward. Let's lead the way."

"What kind of prestige?"

"How big would the building be?"

"You go maybe forty stories high. And tie the name and the architecture right into the museum. Tower of the Arts, you call it. And make it a stipulation that the design not only doesn't overwhelm the building we have, but *adds* to it. The spire becomes your signature, something you can see from miles away. Also, have it part of the deal that the builder makes improvements that you've been dreaming about for twenty-five years. More space upward. Skylights a half-block long. Turn this homely box you're so proud of into the best design in the city. Something so exciting the world will come to see the building as much as the pictures."

"What price could we get?"

"The price could be enormous, but that would be just the beginning. It would be in the terms of purchase that a portion of the sale price and the maintenance payments of every apartment would go to the upkeep of the Museum of Impressionist Art. And any lawyer who can't turn that into a nice tax deduction should be disbarred."

There was some silence, then a woman asked, "Will we get first shot at the rooms?"

The scales had tipped irreversibly. Ronald already heard approval in the excited buzzing that rose all around him.

Picalora looked as though he were building to a cardiac accident. "And, of course, Stryker and Oakhill will handle it all and make a very pretty bundle at the end."

"That would make the most sense, because we'd do the best job and nobody's going to do it for nothing. But since people like you would make our company's participation impossible, I withdraw us from all monetary participation."

A woman stood. "I like Mr. Stryker's idea. I move we vote on it and begin to organize a committee to supervise the details. I also move that we fall down on our hands and knees and beg Mr. Stryker to chair that committee after all the difficulties—let me amend that—all the crap that we've given him."

There was applause and laughter.

"I won't say I'll be happy to accept that invitation, because I won't be," said Ronald. "But I'll do it because nobody else here will. I'll need help. And before you volunteer let me tell you that I'm pure poison to work with. *I* get things my way, and all *you* do is ask, 'How fast, sir?' If any of you are thinking all this job will be is another line in your college reunion bulletin and a chance to meet the mayor every Wednesday, throw yourself out on your can right now and save me the trouble later. I'll be at that table at the back after this confab adjourns. Thanks."

The prospect of hard work, responsibility and abuse being no more attractive to the rich than to the poor, Ronald later on found himself the recipient of many heartfelt handshakes and 'Attaboys,' but without volunteers. When the crowd around him had passed by, there was nobody lingering at his table but Fiona.

"My, my," she said. "Your charm just seems to build upon itself."

In all the times he had seen her on the Stanford campus, he had never seen her like this. Her jeans, baggy sweaters and haystack hairdos had disappeared long ago in a hundred trips through Bergdorf's. Those amazing eyes, now made up to their full, explosive splendor, were the centerpiece of a remarkable-looking woman.

"You gave me a lot of good lessons the last time we chatted, Miss Keefe."

"Actually, the last time we chatted is why I'm here. You said I had quite a mouth on me. I've been wondering ever since whether that was a sensual or pejorative observation."

"Pejorative then. Sensual now. What's a snappy-looking chick like you doing in a dump like this?"

"Volunteering. I'm your man, in a manner of speaking."

"This is some cruel joke, right?"

"Don't you think I can do it?"

"Shit, yes. I hear Justin's forged you into quite a tool. But he'll give your head two full turns when he finds out you're working with one of the dread Strykers."

"His name is Oakhill, not mine."

"And you're just a patron of the splatter-paint arts?"

"No more than you. But a builder can pick up an awful lot of IOUs on a thing like this. Why should Stryker and Oakhill get 'em all?"

"That deserves a detailed answer. Maybe I can think of one over dinner at the Four Seasons. Will you come? We can handle two seasons each."

And so Fiona began. She went into her life with Ronald Stryker as a not-very-honorable chore, hoping that the young man's fabled arrogance wouldn't drive her mad before she had enticed him close enough to help her approach his father. But, as she could not have learned from his performance at the museum, it was to be no problem.

Beneath his golden-boy exterior and insolent way was a voracious intellect that missed nothing and grew hungrier every day. Fiona was proud of what she had learned about the business of land and building since she had met Justin, but Ronald, three years younger, had passed her in every way.

Her plan to toy with him as a mature woman with a little boy had no chance of working. It was as though he had acquired three years of confidence and experience for every one of hers since they had left school. It was fortunate for her plans that he had taken a long-ago liking to her, because her attempts to captivate proved unnecessary.

Damned lucky I'm Liza Hayborn's daughter, she thought. Knocking me over would make a great story for the guys in the drafting room. Well, if I can hold him off for a couple of months and get him panting hard, I'll get what I want. And he won't.

But he made no sexual moves on her. They dated once a week at first, then twice, and then he was calling her or seeing her almost every day. When she realized he couldn't be seeing anyone else and was conducting something of an all-out campaign in her direction, she became confused and edgy. What did he want from her if not her bedsheet acrobatics? Was he so puffed up with himself that she had to do the asking? Was he injured or incompetent in some way? Surely he wasn't intimidated by her looks. She was more than good-looking, even extraordinary in the right makeup and rig. But she had seen pictures of Ronald with French and English models that made her look like homemade horse manure.

The places he took her were a surprise, too. She would have thought he'd have her where the photographers were thickest—the clubs, the openings, the major parties. Instead, they went to places that were almost a secret. He liked little bars on the unfashionable West Side, tiny restaurants in New Jersey with exquisite food, and places on the Palisades where they could sit in the sun and watch the majestic Hudson bending around West Point.

She was never invited to set a Topsider on the deck of his sixty-foot cabin cruiser or to take a quick flight to the Cape in his Beechcraft Bonanza. She didn't once get invited to the Stryker hunting and fishing lodge in the Thousand Islands. If she hadn't read about these possessions in celebrity magazines she wouldn't even have known that he had them. Could he be *ashamed* of her, she wondered? Then why all the attention?

Any idea she had about his being interested in a crack at the daughter of Liza Hayborn and Derrol Keefe evaporated when she realized that he had never had the faintest interest in films or the people who acted in them. He confused Tyrone Power with James Stewart and referred to "Marlo Brandon."

She should have continued to be delighted and relieved that he made no physical attempts on her. But after the first five weeks the relief turned to annoyance. Damn it, a girl liked to be asked or groped at once in a while, so she could say bugger-off after she knew her charms were moving the right hormones. Still, it would have been more vexing than it was if she didn't enjoy talking to him so much.

Once they had gotten done with the inevitable fencing and life stories on early dates, where he had seemed much too stiff to justify his reputation for infuriating self-assurance, he began to open up to her in a way that startled her. He became not more obnoxious and aggressive with familiarity, but steadily less so. It was as though a rough warrior, feeling safe and at home, had begun to peel off layer after layer of his armor and to lower his voice from the bellows of battle. And he only did it for her.

"How come you're nice to me, but still a dick to everybody else?"

"My dickiness has been perfected. It's my niceness that needs work."

Each evening they arrived at the office the museum had established for them to begin assembling operatives for the Tower of the Arts. Here again he was the buzz-saw she had seen before, slicing bloodily through egos and opposition to get the plan moving. The only deference he showed her at this work was to give her some of the knottiest logjams to get solved on her own, which pleased her wonderfully. Because she suddenly found herself wanting his respect.

After two months with Ronald, Fiona took stock of her situation. In one way her little intrigue was a success beyond her hopes. She had found a way to put herself at his side every day and had won his friendship and trust to a remarkable degree. But those were the problems, too.

Her hopes of catching the romantic fancy of a callow and silly young man and keeping his head turned just long enough to have what she wanted from him had come to grief completely. His trust had begun to bother her. The trust of a growing sentimental attachment seemed somehow more sacred than the more wary trust she gave to business attachments.

Justin's lenders were becoming restive. There had been calls from Coleman already. She could make her move on Ford now. Or she could make her success more certain. By moving harder on Ronald.

At high noon Fiona and Ronald sat with their backs against a tree, looking out on the sunshine bathing the Great Lawn in Central Park.

Ronald, tie loosened and suit jacket removed, bagged the remains of their lunch and shot it neatly into a wastebasket. Fiona saw some passing secretaries look him over hungrily and exchange low, giggling observations. When he was relaxed and rumpled, as he was now, he was hard to pass by unappreciated.

"I think the museum is going to be picketed," she said.

"Huh? By whom?"

"By the Beauties Union. The job's been keeping you out of circulation as a hot date."

"Don't be modest, little partner. You know who's been doing that."

"I guess I was hoping that's what you'd say. But now I've got to ask why. To put it petulantly, you might as well be running around with Justin."

"Not exactly. Does he know I'm sweet on the enemy?"

"How could he? I didn't know it myself."

"Because I haven't been trying to roll down your pantyhose?"

"Among other things."

"I wanted everything to be different with you, Fi."

"Just my goddamned luck. Why?"

"I wanted us to be more than a quick flop. Ever since you sent me skulking at Stanford."

She found herself flustered. "I should have told you about that new mouthwash made especially for men—"

"Hey, be serious a second, lady. This is tough to get out."

"Oops. Sorry, Ron. Around men I'm still about as graceful as an elephant wearing snowshoes."

"That's what got me. I could see how you were when people tried to get close."

"How was that?"

"Just like me. I could see you got chopped up in the home wars the same way."

"Maybe so. Living with Derrol and Liza would have scared Patton. I really thought men and women were supposed to start the day by calling each other cocksuckers and throwing coffee with the pot attached."

Ronald winced with memories. "Ford and Anne could give them lessons. Except what they threw around was coldness. Anne could freeze an Acapulco swimming pool solid with a look."

"Made it kind of hard to learn affection for your fellow man, didn't it?"

"And fellow woman," Ron said, looking at her.

"Funny. I read you got balled more than Derrol."

"What's getting balled got to do with affection, Fiona?"

"Not much is what I found out. I spent most of my sixteenth and seventeenth years trying to catch some love between my thighs before I gave it up."

"You had the look of somebody who was going to kill the next guy who came on to her."

"So what was that stuff in the library that day?"

"For me, that was Charles Boyer."

She laughed awkwardly, not knowing what to do next. She was surprised and touched. Worse, she was pleased and excited. But that wasn't going to help Justin. *He's biting, you jerk. Set the hook,* her reason shouted. "I can't figure out if we just decided to run like hell away from one another or to fall in love," she finally said.

Incredibly, he seemed almost timid. "I was just so damned scared of chasing you away."

"I wanted to be caught," she said, realizing with distaste that it was almost the first honest thing she had ever said to him. She now found herself at a pivot point. With little doubt she could now set the pace of the involvement she wanted, holding him at any length she desired until she had her shot at Ford.

Adoring Justin as she did, she never had the vaguest intention of following Ronald to his bed, much less trying to lead him there. She would at any time have abandoned the operation if that were the only way to carry it through. But now she found herself feeling for reasons to make it happen. *It will speed things up,* she told herself. *It's not as though I'm a sweet virgin saving myself for Lochinvar. Or that it will really mean anything to me. And what is it compared to coming on to your mother's husband, for God's sake?*

"Fiona, I—"

"Maybe we should be getting back to the office."

He lost his hard-won momentum. "Yeah . . . I guess so."

"I've had my eye on that big chrome-and-leather Eames chair behind your desk."

"We can't—"

"I've never made love in a museum before, much less on one of its classics."

He pushed her down on the grass and kissed her until even the lunchtime strollers of New York began to take notice. But when he decided to go, he did it quickly and with such distraction that he left behind the jacket to a six-hundred-dollar suit.

Fiona, having made one fatal mistake, compounded it with another. Where one additional week might have sufficed to put Ronald thoroughly where she wanted him, she asked Coleman for two. This allowed the happening of several unfortunate things that fed upon one another. The most important was her having time to finish falling in love with Ronald Stryker, although she refused to confess it completely either to herself or to him. She was devoted to Justin for his years of tender devotion, and she wasn't going to be turned away from him by the first young and pretty rich boy to tell her that all the cars and swimming pools weren't enough.

"I know it only gets said in bad movies anymore," Ronald said as he soaped Fiona's back in the shower, "but 'I love you' is still a nice thing to say. I estimate that I have said it to you fifty times. And that gives me a lead of fifty over you."

She turned around, but he kept soaping what was before him. "Would I let you wash those if you weren't special? *Eeek.* Or that?"

"A dog who plays 'Chopsticks' on the piano with his forepaws is special."

"Hmmmm, I must say that I am very intrigued with that forepaw of yours. Can I be the piano?"

"Come on. Be straight."

"That's the man's job. Which you are fulfilling beautifully."

"Fiona . . . *Fiona* . . . You'll get soap in your mouth."

"Can we finish this talk another time?"

"No—"

But by this time she was unable to. As she knelt with the delicious sweetness of the hot water running down her back and the hefty weight of him on her tongue, she told herself that she simply had been too long away from men and that this one just happened to be a dozen-times-better lover than the others. But she knew that she had better get done with him soon or nothing would pry her away.

When she was done she stood up and pulled his hips close to her. "You were very brave not to collapse," she said. "Now wasn't that better than talking a lot of mush?"

"I love you," he said. "That's fifty-one to nothing."

"How about a nice salty kiss?"

He came to her. Yes, she had to leave him soon. But not too soon.

Justin might have been able to stay away from his stepdaughter, as was his steadfast intention, if Liza had not returned from a location shooting in Australia just long enough to provoke him into a battle with her that Derrol Keefe himself might have envied.

"Right there for four million depraved readers to stroke themselves over. In perfect focus. His hand, all six, greasy Italian pounds of it, lying right there on your tit—all sun-oiled twenty pounds of it—"

"We weren't *humping*, were we? You *know* how actors are, especially the wops. Touchy, touchy. He was buggering the bellboy the whole time we were there."

"Then why didn't he have his hand on the *bellboy's* tit?"

"Because the bellboy wasn't discussing the script with him while taking an *innocent* sunbath."

"Did you think that guy with the camera was going to be interested in your innocence?"

"He must have used a ten-thousand-millimeter lens. There was no way he could've been closer than five miles away."

"Does it occur to you that I'm trying to raise money to save my professional life and that you're making me look like the keeper of a girl-and-monkey act in Port Said?"

"I'd replace you with a monkey if I could find one as short and ugly. And who gives a shit about what you see in some rag you read on the checkout line?"

"Your husband does."

"I have no husband. I have a guy who plays in a hole in Manhattan when he should be with me, putting *his* hand on my knocker."

"Did he ream you?"

"*No.*"

"Like shit, he didn't. And he probably brought that bellboy to work what he couldn't reach."

Her accent returned to the streets of Liverpool. She began to tear the buttons off the front of his suit jacket. "*Bloody bastard. With all the beautiful blokes in the world, I had to marry something shaped like a flaming desk, who'd rather pork a hole made of dirt.*"

"You have a dreadful tongue."

"That's not what my wop says," she said, going for the vitals.

"He should know."

"You bet he should. He's very inventive. You know what it says on his card? *Eye, ear, nose and throat.*"

"You're staying home, Liza. Starting *now.*"

"No, I'm *leaving* home, starting now."

"Liza—"

"Read about me on the checkout line."

She left the house, pausing only to put the fireplace poker through their wedding picture.

* * *

The separation of Justin Oakhill and Liza Hayborn filled the newspapers for a solid week, only the *Times* not managing to run some portion of the offending photograph.

Justin fell into a black gloom. Standing at the bottom of The Hole one day, his hard hat a mockery where not a man or a machine moved in the puddled rubble, he felt that the scene pictured perfectly the growing disaster of his life. He threw back his head and gave a great howl of loneliness and despair. The sound never even got out of The Hole above the roar of the traffic above, and not a single New Yorker learned his pain.

Again he called to the sky. *"Li-i-i-za-a-a-a."* And then soon, *"Fi-o-o-o-n-a-a-a-a-a."*

Fiona's days were like tirelessly attacking animals clawing the strength out of her. With Justin she carried forth the daily round of hopeless assaults on the money centers of the world, flying overseas at least once a week. With Ronald she did the work of the Museum, trying to marshal the hordes of municipal bumblers and backbiting amateurs into a matrix of professionals who would make the building rise. But none of her work was as draining as the tensions of her high-wire act between Justin and Ronald.

Justin had seemed glad enough of her interesting herself in something outside the heart-numbing battering of The Hole. He took it as a service to his beloved city and often said that he wished he had more time to help such projects himself. But he had no idea of how far she had gone with Ronald into the enemy lines.

Bitter and sweet were her days with Ronald. Every kiss, every laugh, every tumble into his bed pulled her two ways she did not want to go. The more she was drawn to him, the greater her duplicity loomed. And the more she tried to draw her emotions away from her new lover, the more she felt her hours in his arms mocking her secret vows to Justin. She worried that these were inexorably weakening.

For all her evasion, she knew Ronald would soon demand a

commitment. With her eye on this danger, she was in no way prepared when the demand came from Justin.

It was after midnight in Justin's Sutton Place penthouse. Fiona was operating on nothing but coffee and nerves. She had come from Ronald's bed a half-hour before, where she had expected to spend the night. But her answering machine had beeped back to her a message from Justin. *"Fiona, it's me."* The voice was husky, unsteady. *"Whatever time you get this message, come straight to my apartment, please. Or call and I'll come to you."*

Unwilling to speak to him from Ronald's phone, she had dressed and hurried to him across town.

She found him dressed only in robe and slippers, the glass in his hand showing a faint tremor. Every light in the vast apartment blazed as if a child left alone had done all he could to dispel his fear of the dark. As usual, the dining-room table was a foot deep with blueprints, renderings and the ten thousand papers of a thousand projected deals. Fiona saw that the lights that had once focused on a huge oil portrait of her mother now illuminated an empty wall above the fireplace.

Justin followed her gaze. "Everything about her is gone from here. The pictures, the gowns, the awards, the five hundred pounds of makeup. All of it. I'm not going to live with any part of that mistake anymore."

"Sweet God, Jus, you look like you're going to collapse. What is it? Big trouble? I came as soon as I got the message." She threw off her coat and went to him, kissing him on the cheek. His skin was hot and moist.

His mouth worked, groping for words that didn't come until his eyes fell on the paper-strewn table. "It's . . . the Lambert Frères meeting in Paris the day after tomorrow. I'm not easy with the repayment section. I'd like us to go over it and talk about it some more."

Alarm bells went off inside Fiona. The Lambert meeting was one of farfetched desperation. Justin had only been given time with them as a courtesy to a fallen friend who had once given them much business. The negotiation of the repayment schedule was so subordinate in importance to the granting of the loan as to be ludicrous. He had not called her here for that, but she would have to bear with him.

He poured drinks and routed out papers so buried that they could not possibly have been on his mind for weeks. He pulled up a chair next to hers. "Read. Go ahead," he said nervously.

With burning, tired eyes she read down the pages of figures, making notes in the margins. In her peripheral vision she saw that his own pages did not turn and that his gaze had settled upon her resolutely. She tried to concentrate for a while, then turned to him, dropping the papers.

"Justin, this is me. Fiona. Whatever it is, you can say it. Even if you can't say it to anybody else in the world."

A huge sigh of relief and resolution poured out of him. Energy that had been missing since Liza left burst out of him suddenly. "I've been such a blind asshole, Fi. Looking across oceans for a love that remembered me about as far as the next defecting ballet stud." He sprang out of his chair and pulled her to her feet and then up into his strong, thick arms. "And all the while you've been here waiting for me. Forgive me, sweetheart. Now I know what I've got."

"Justin, I hav—"

As his fierce kiss cut her short, she was aware that she was being carried on the long trip to his bedroom.

Pinned to his lips, she tried to remember that this was the moment she had dreamed of for years. She tried to open herself to Justin, calling on the great love she had always felt. It was there, tender and full of loyalty and good memories. But it had changed for her somewhere in the space that she had known Ronald. This beloved man who had so restored her and so dazzled her with his Promethean powers and reckless brilliance, with his endless warmth and rugged manhood . . . had become her mother's husband . . . her *father*. By the time he released her lips, it was far too late to say anything.

The bedroom had been prepared. The covers on the huge bed overlooking the skyline had been turned back on the satin sheets. The cunningly designed lighting filled the room with romance.

Fifty thousand dollars' worth of high-fidelity advances brought music rich in violins to swirl in the air with the haunting scent of beautiful, freshly cut flowers.

"Justin—"

Hurricane that he was, there was no standing up to him.

"I'll build a whole new world just for you, little love," he said as he undressed her at the center of the sprawling bed.

She was so glad to see his happiness momentarily returned that she could not bear to hurt him by trying to move away. That would have to come another day, when she could be gradual, persuasive and filled with the sweet kindness he deserved.

The last of her clothing disappeared over the edge of the bed. She lay back to receive what must be.

His face suffused with joy, he was beautiful in the marvelous lighting. His robe fell away, and his massive shoulders framed the ridges of muscle across the broad chest.

Trying not to think, only to feel what was harmless and good, she let her gaze travel along his strong torso. She caught her breath.

"Oh, goddamn. *Goddamn,*" Justin said plaintively. He lifted his eyes and hands to the great beyond. "Let me *go*, Liza. Let me *go, damn you.*"

He was simply not prepared to go further. And no amount of coaxing, raging, cajoling or apologizing could do anymore than send the robust center of him into further retreat.

As soon as she could do so without shaming him, Fiona slipped from beneath and let him collapse face downward, too dispirited and humiliated to speak.

She straddled him, rubbing his back and reassuring him for the minimum time commensurate with good bedroom manners, and then hopped away to dress quickly.

"I'm sorry, Fi. I'll get over this. I promise."

"Of course, you will. Put it out of your mind. I understand."

"I think it's better you don't stay this time," he said into the mattress.

His words reached her as she was on her way out of the bedroom door, carrying her shoes and stockings. "If you think so,

Justin." It was hard to keep the relief out of her voice. "I'll see you at the office."

"Next time I won't let you down."

Wriggling into her pantyhose in the cab, to the chuckling bemusement of the driver, she saw how out of time she was. She returned home rather than to Ronald, who had a morning flight to Mexico. At the stroke of nine she made two telephone calls.

The first was to Enos Coleman at the bank, promising that she would have his answer on the possible participation of Stryker and Oakhill before the end of the week. The second was to Ford Stryker's secretary, to check the managing partner's availability for the next few days. The woman told her that the elder Stryker now conducted most of his business from his country estate on Long Island, but that she would be glad to call him there. Was there any message?

"No," Fiona said. "There's someone else who can get me through." That person she hoped, was Ronald.

Late the next day, back from Veracruz and tired, Ronald went to the Metropolitan Club for a fast drink with some old friends from London. There was a family tradition of membership in the old club, and he liked it as a respite from noisy bars and restaurants.

His guests had a plane to catch and stayed for barely an hour, which was fine with Ronald, who had in front of him a whole evening of work on a proposed French Strykertown. He had been unable to reach Fiona.

On his way to the cloakroom he encountered the sleek and silvery Enos Coleman.

"Ah, Ronald. It's been a while."

"Good evening, Enos. Let's grab a bourbon sometime."

"Now might be a good time, considering that we might be together on quite an important project soon."

Ronald stopped and turned. "Has Father been talking to you? Or has this project just slipped my fading mind?"

Coleman smiled quizzically. "I hardly think that The Hole can have slipped anyone's mind."

"We'll have that drink right now," Ronald said, guiding him by an expensively tailored elbow and starting to feel a slight, unpleasant chill.

As an early dusk came down on the city, Fiona turned into the entrance of the Museum of Impressionist Art and found a different Ronald waiting for her. Or rather he was the same, the way he had been back at school and before they had become comfortable together. She knew something had fallen out of bed, and suspected it was she. "Hey, I thought I wouldn't see you until tomorrow, Ron."

"I couldn't wait."

"That look tells me you've got some pretty urgent and ugly business."

"Actually, Fiona, I don't. But I think that you might. I just had a drink with Coleman. Then a couple of more on my own. Let's walk over to the St. Regis and talk about it."

They didn't say a word all the way over, and Fiona had time to run through several lines of defense. One seemed phonier and flatter-sounding than the next, and none addressed the cold calculation by which she had come to him. By the time they sat down at a quiet corner table, she had decided that she didn't have the strength or heart for anything but the truth.

"The answer you must be looking for, Ronald, is yes. Absolutely. I came to you to make Brownie points for a swipe at getting Stryker and Oakhill to help save The Hole."

His expression grew even harder than it had been. "Well, you sure made those points, Fiona. In a little while I would have hocked my balls and jumped into that Hole with a shovel if it was what you wanted. Why didn't you go straight to my father? The last word had to be his."

"He'd have thrown me right through the window. You were the only way in."

"You were right both times. Smart. Treacherous, but smart. Thanks for being straight at last."

She was trying not to be sick with her shame. "I've been straight about . . . the other thing. Honest to God, Ron."

"Yes. You were good about that. I never once got you to say you loved me, even though it would have made the job a helluva lot quicker and easier."

What can I say? she thought. *I couldn't because I was trying to jump my stepfather? Or that I think I love you, but I might end up balling Justin?* "I'm sorry, Ronald. Nothing I could tell you would help."

"Try me. I love you so damned much I might settle for a really good lie."

"What would you like to hear?"

"That you might've gotten to care something about me."

"I can do better than that. But I have to clear up something first."

"Keep talking," he said, waving away a waiter.

"Nobody was trying to steal anything from S & O. The Grand Oakhill is one helluva deal. It's on a scope that only Justin could handle. Maybe more imagination than any bank or bungalow builder could handle." She hadn't intended to sound so sharp.

"You can always tell us bungalow builders by our tiny imaginations." He was stung, she could see.

"The roadblocks are all gone, including Boops Day. The World's Fair showed up the city's hotel stock for the hopeless, outdated pile of junk it is. We've become the wealthiest international city in the world, but with no modern, exciting world-class hotel to soak up the money. Whoever brings it off first is going to be off in front and make Mr. Hilton run fast to catch up."

"That's a reasonable argument."

"You bet your eyes it is. If they weren't always at war, Ford and Justin would have both parts of the old Oakhill outfit together on this in five minutes. And they'd make a diamond mine out of it. Then Ford could have Strykertowns from Tokyo to Kiev and Justin could have his Palace of Tomorrow dream over the railyards."

"Care to tell all that to Ford?"

He had shocked her, as intended. "What?"

"We'll go over the details fast tomorrow. Fill me in on everything. If it's as good as it sounds here, I'll set up a meeting and get behind it."

"Lord . . . That would be incredible . . . But why? After I—"

"At worst this is pure business. I find a good investment and put it to my management, who happens to be my father. No emotion involved. At best it gets the deal out of the way, one way or the other, and afterward lets us look at one another straight. What do you think?"

She felt tears spring to the edges of her eyes. "I think that's a pretty good deal for a girl who deserved to have her nose flattened instead."

"Maybe if it wasn't such a nifty nose. Does Justin know? Really, now."

"Oh, *shit*, no. I swear it. If he knew—"

"Okay, okay. Dopey question, knowing how they feel about each other."

"When?"

"Day after tomorrow, I think. Out at his place. But you must know it won't be easy, Fiona. Impossible is more like it."

"He'll listen to *you*, at least. You can help it happen."

Ronald shook his head. "My day is coming, but it's not here yet. I'm not a partner, but the world's most overpaid apprentice as far as he's concerned. I don't control a thousand dollars of the company money until he lets me into the cockpit. Could be I'm not enough of a bungalow builder."

"I'm so sorry I said that." Impulsively, she leaned over to kiss him in contrition before she caught herself, remembering that things were changed. And she didn't want them to be changed. "I guess I have to earn that all over again. Later, I mean."

"Suppose it goes against you, Fi?"

"I'll let you see that for yourself," she said, wanting it to be over either way so she could show him what she wanted to without shadows.

"Call me tomorrow," he said. Color had crept back into his face.

* * *

594

Ford Stryker had received Ronald and Fiona on the spectacular bluff that marked the end of his estate where it looked over Long Island Sound. The sun was warm for late autumn, and he sat in a cap and heavy sweater on a concrete bench that was part of a replica of an ancient Roman garden. He had more comfortable seats set around a table upon which coffee and a delightful lunch were spread. Behind him, the Sound was a blue expanse as calm as a lake, with the white wings of gliding sailboats visible as far off as the Connecticut shore opposite.

He had been impressed with Fiona Keefe from almost the moment he met her, chatting her up happily and marveling that such a likable and sensible woman could have sprung from such explosive forebears. The fact that she had no Oakhill blood let his guard down somewhat.

As a man so aggrieved by women, it was often hard for him to be civil to even the best of them.

Anne had clung to him. She was a warped but considerable genius at gauging just how much of her malice he could take before she must intrigue him back with elegant and apologetic attentions and—even now—with her sex. Sparsely given but exquisitely administered when it was, her body presented a mixture of heat and cold that he could not quite do without. Without these powerful moments he would have long ago surrendered to his suspicions of the circumstances surrounding the loss of George and sent her and her expertly hidden hatred away. As it was, he had secretly and utterly cut her from his estate.

Ronald could keep his mother comfortably enough. But she would not squander the Stryker legacy on things that were not buildings. Ford had great hopes for Ronald carrying on, once he had learned some lessons. One of which, he suspected, might take place right now.

"Hold out your cup, Miss Keefe. Hot coffee in big mugs is absolutely essential to long meetings. You may begin, either of you, right after we finish our sandwiches. It's rare roast beef, because that makes business people suitably mean."

For the next hour he listened with total interest and elaborate patience, questioning frequently and being certain he had heard the best of their arguments.

By the way Ronald supported her case, with emotional vehemence that undercut his great desire to appear utterly businesslike, he guessed that their work together at the Museum had produced more than mutually respectful colleagues. Except for her being trapped in the Oakhill family, he didn't mind.

Fiona summed up their position at the end. "Outside of the solid economics of this venture, it will represent a de facto reunion of the old Oakhill empire, with combined strengths that would establish you again as the dominant force in building. Whatever divisions there have been can be reconciled and forgotten for a move into the future that will make history in the industry. It's too important an opportunity to pass by, both as a business decision for today and as a chance to command our field for the rest of the century."

Ford gently applauded. "Wonderfully presented. Both of you. Fiona, you're certainly a worthy disciple of Justin. I might have been listening to him. Big thoughts. Powerful selling. Impressive."

"Thank you, Mr. Stryker. I hope I can have an answer very soon. The banks are pressing hard."

"There's no need to wait a single moment for that answer. It's no." He said the word gently, but his tone roared finality.

"Father—," Ronald began angrily.

"Don't beg him, Ronald," Fiona said, obviously surprised at the suddenness of the answer. "He had his mind set before we said a word."

"That's not true," Ford said. "It was listening to Justin through you that decided me."

Ronald was deeply upset. "You're letting your dislike of a man twist your judgment."

"And that is proper," Ford said. "To me, what gets built on the land is the most direct personification of the man who does the building. And I see that your Grand Oakhill Hotel is every bit as arrogant, overbearing and beyond any decent human scale as Justin himself. If he were in a business less important to the way people live and the way our world evolves, I might forgive him the hundred calculated hurts he's done to me. But I will not have his colossal brutalities distorting lives and landscapes for a hundred years. And all this is not including the fact that he's a stubborn and reckless man who has it in his power to bankrupt any backer. I regret his failure for your sake, Fiona. But I believe people will thank me for forcing it."

Frostily, Fiona stood and regarded him. "And it might be a lesser pain for him than accepting help from you. Good afternoon, Mr. Stryker."

Ronald drove Fiona back to New York. For a long time she was too let down to speak. Then she felt him take her hand.

"Sorry, Fi. Truly."

"Don't be. There was no chance. You were terrific and I'll never forget it. But it was all just a big, painful waste of time."

"Not all of it, I hope. Can we start putting things together again now?"

She was still boiling. "After I get done helping pick up the pieces of a couple of hundred million dollars' worth of real estate that's about to go into the fan."

"But I can count on you?"

"As soon as I get some things straightened out with Justin."

On the horizon, the black, rolling billows of a fast-moving storm were closing on the towers of Manhattan. As when she was a little girl, Fiona found herself wanting to run from it.

Coleman had the bad news by the following morning, and the thunderous collapse of Oakhill Development began. The other lenders, fearing to be left out of their full share of what was to be the greatest forced liquidation of real estate in all history, moved in on Justin from every front. The bold, high-interest, high-leverage techniques that had made him powerful now turned viciously against him.

"I used to say better to be in business at twenty-five percent than broke at the prime," he said ruefully to Fiona. "Now I can see it happens a lot slower at the prime."

Piece by piece everything went—the skyscrapers, the chain of hotels, the vast rental projects and, most painful of all, the sites for the great dreams. "They can't have my railyards," he continued to insist.

He pleaded desperately for some deal that would allow him to hold on to the yards over which would rise his fabulous Palace of Tomorrow. But the powerful people who had for so long been trampled and overshadowed by his gargantuan progress were not the ones to get in the way of the most dramatic business tragedy in decades. The downfall of the mighty Justin Oakhill spawned newspaper and business-magazine main features like snowflakes in a howling blizzard. Publishing houses commissioned Oakhill books at every literary-elite restaurant in the city.

To the very end—and a prolonged and nasty end it was—Justin did not admit defeat. Daily he proclaimed new backers just a phone call away, and hinted at projects whose magnitude and success would beggar all that he had previously proposed. He swaggered more, appeared at more restaurants and parties, and smiled as if he knew the gloating world would soon be astonished by his imminent escape and resurrection.

"I have here in my pocket a sketch of what the skyline of this city will be in five years, after I get through with it. Its beauty would make you weep."

Only Fiona knew that a huge, bleeding piece of him was torn away as each lovingly acquired jewel was sold to pay the bankers. Far into the night she labored with the lawyers at his apartment to work out the onerous details of disposal that he could not bear to prepare before his office staff. Her heart broke for him, and his wonderful bravado with nothing behind him made her more proud of her old friend than she had ever been.

If there were any advantage to Fiona in the deepening disaster, it was that the exhausted Justin had no strength to press his pursuit of her with his usual unstoppable dedication. But by the way he smiled and rested his weary eyes upon her in the long, frantic days, she knew that she was the only emotional support he had left and that when the desperation slackened he would be back. She prayed that by then the worst would be over for him and she could tell him about Ronald gently. Then they could remain the friends they had always been.

That prayer was not answered.

Toward the finish of the ordeal, when cracks had at last begun to appear even in Justin's brave spirit, he was pulled down by the final and supreme insult.

After Justin had not answered his phone or appeared at the office all day, Fiona rushed to his apartment. When he failed to answer the door, she had the superintendent unlock it and slipped inside. Fearfully she went through the empty rooms. His bed was unmade. There was a litter of glasses and bottles in the living room, and a cigar had burned through the arm of a twenty-five-thousand-dollar glove-leather couch.

She found him slumped on a chair on the terrace. Although the air was deeply chilled as evening drew down and a light rain fell, he sat in his pajamas. A thick, graying stubble covered his jaw. His puffed eyes were locked on the horizon to the southwest.

"Justin. What is it, Justin? God, you're soaked. Come inside. Come *on*, damn it."

He looked at her bleakly. The big shoulders shivered beneath the pajamas the rain had glued to them.

Fiona saw that not all the droplets running down his cheeks were from the rain. He was one huge wound. "They took it," he whispered. "Those fucking Strykers took it away from me, Fi."

"Inside, Justin. You tell me inside."

She took his hands and pulled, urging him to his feet. Slowly he stood, his breath heavy with brandy.

As if the act of rising had sent a huge draft of air to replenish the fire smoldering inside him, he burst into an ungovernable fury, shouting out over the city. "They got my railyards. Those Stryker bastards came in and got them for sixty cents on the dollar. I still might have gotten a deal hammered out to hang on. They came in and cut the legs off me. Why? Why? I'll tell you. Because they didn't want to see my Palace of Tomorrow there, mocking those huts they build in the swamps."

"When did this happen? I didn't know—"

He turned on her. "Coleman called me last night. They must've been setting this up for weeks, without a word to me."

"But *somebody* would have probably gotten it—"

"It wasn't *somebody*. It was the *Strykers*. You were cozy with that little sonofabitch Ronald at the Museum. Did you talk to him about what the Palace of Tomorrow meant to me? Did you?"

"Yes. Yes, I might have. But that doesn't mean—"

"It means you showed them the way to cut my heart out, Fiona."

"Please, Justin. Don't do this to yourself. Or to me."

Fury shook him to his toes. "I've had my differences with the Strykers, and I never liked what they did. I didn't try to hide it. But I never really hated them. Not until now." He shook his fist out into the blowing rain. "I'll pray to God or the Devil, whichever one will strike those backstabbing pigfuckers dead. And extra prayers if it's slow and painful. Or maybe I'll do it myself—"

Fiona hit him in the face with all her strength, first with her open hand, then with her fist, finally pulling him into her arms. But it was many minutes before his rage completely collapsed.

And then, a hunted, bleeding animal looking for a lifesaving moment of respite from his deadly pursuers, he tilted up her face and kissed her hungrily as the rain soaked into her and brought down her hair.

"Fiona," he said with a voice that hung at the edge of a sob, "you're the only thing I have left in my life. I couldn't believe the first time you told me you loved me. Can you tell me again?"

She read the torture in his eyes and knew she would do anything on earth to take it away and give him peace. "I do love you, my darling. And I'll be here for you as long as you need me. I swear that to you."

She let him kiss her, and then slipped gently out of his arms and pushed him inside. "Get out of those dripping clothes." She found him a robe and was careful to throw it to him from where he could not quite reach her. "Now jump in that bed and stay there."

"This will be my first night's sleep in a week."

"That's why you should sleep alone."

"Fi—"

"I'm with you now, Justin. Keep thinking of that."
"I need you, Fiona."

To keep the pain short, she disposed of Ronald as quickly as she could. She used the telephone, where she could cut him off without him seeing her face. Her acting would not have held up otherwise.

"I just heard about the Central Penn railyards. You knew what they meant to Justin."

"Sure, Fiona, but he couldn't hold them anyway."

"Not after you bid them up."

"That's prime property. Everybody—"

"You went for it because you knew it would kill him."

"Of course not—"

"You mean you couldn't guess that it would seem like Ford was picking his bones."

"It wasn't Ford's idea. It was mine, Fiona. Because—"

"Jesus. You were putting this together all the time after Ford thumbed us down. Without a word to me—"

"You'd have told Justin. It was a delicate negotiation. I couldn't have him throwing his weight around."

"And I was just a spy of his, I suppose."

"Fi, you and Justin are like father and daughter. You'd *have* to let him know, even if it couldn't help him."

"You know, the Strykers are every bit the devious sons of bitches that Justin said they were."

"Hey, hold on, pal," Ronald said, the phone not hiding his bewilderment. "We've got to sit down where I can show you—"

She put everything she had into hardening her voice. "I'm not your pal, much less anything else it might have pleased your disgusting ego to imagine. And you're the last bastard on earth I'd like to sit with, because seeing you would remind me what a sap I was to let you into my shorts."

"Where are you, goddamn it? I'm coming over."

"You ever show up in any part of my life again and I'll have the cops on you."

"You can't *do* this."

"Look, Ronald. Justin needed something and you were the only way I could get at it. You smelled that out and it's not my fault you were too stupid to believe what was true. You were as dumb to give me a shot at Ford as I was to believe there was any chance of getting somewhere. Let's call it even. I screwed you once, and you screwed me once. Not counting what happened in bed."

"*Fiona.*"

She was beginning to strangle in the tears. "Goodbye, Ronald. Enjoy what you stole. I hope I won't be seeing you around." Fiona hung up before his answer and barely before the first sob. She implored the heavens for the phone not to ring again, because at the sound of his voice she might have told him how much she had grown to love him.

The phone stayed quiet.

After Ronald had dragged himself around in depressed shock for two weeks, Ford estimated that he was ready to listen to some reason. He met him for lunch at '21.'

"Don't be so down, Ron. Damn it, she even had me fooled. And I know better than anybody breathing what women can do to you, especially when they get tangled with Oakhills. Write the damned thing off like a bad property."

"I'm afraid I paid too much for that property. And so did you."

"Yes, the Central Penn yards. Actually I was kind of touched by what you did there. That's why I let you talk me into picking them up. I knew what was in your head all the time."

"God, what an ass. I actually saw myself going to her someday and telling her like Galahad that I was only holding them until Justin got back on his feet."

"He'll never get on his feet again. Too old. Too tired. Out of credibility. But it's the thought that counts, huh? And the terms weren't too bad."

"Will you resell?"

"Not now. The boom's running out of steam. The taxes aren't

that bad and we can build a few two-story rentpayers to hold us even. In ten, fifteen years, after I'm gone and the city's strangling on its traffic, some other railroad, probably owned by the government, might pay you three, four times over to have those tracks and that space back."

"We could build on it."

"Not me. You, Ron."

"What does that mean?"

"This old man's crossing seventy. History's caught up with the Strykertowns now. It's not pioneering anymore. It's just building."

"You got to change the way a whole country lived. But look at me."

"I have been looking at you. I like what I'm starting to see. And it's time for me to get off your back. All the way off. There's no more to learn. I'm going to start phasing out now, so I can stay out of the city. Congratulations."

They shook hands. Ford was surprised to see how moved his unemotional son appeared.

"Thank you . . . Thank you, Father. But you know the center of the business isn't out where the grass grows now."

"It's where you decide it is. I did what I wanted. And I want you to be as proud of what you do as I am of what I did."

"When can I make plans?"

"Start now, Ron. It will take your mind off things."

The last of Oakhill Development toppled. The sharks at the banks swam away, sated by a meal they would be talking about for many years.

The last holder of the Oakhill name was as landless as Hannah when she stepped off the *Dortmund* all those years ago. Justin quietly sold his magnificent duplex and moved into a two-bedroom apartment on the far west side where his neighbors were stenographers and accountants, not investment-house presidents and expatriate baronesses.

There was no more office, so there was no place where Fiona

would see him automatically every day. She was glad of this at first because it made it easy for her to control where she was with him, and so his romantic attentions could be checked. But soon she saw there was a greater and more immediate problem, and it desperately demanded her presence with him.

She had overestimated what a proud man, even one with Justin's overflowing resources of optimism, could absorb. He seemed suddenly to crumble before her eyes. For the first time she noticed his age, which struck suddenly like some disease long in miraculous remission. But worse that that was his diminishment in his own eyes. He no longer felt worthy of her and now carefully kept his distance.

As so often happens, as soon as the dreaded business warrior lost his sword and shield, the people who had once feared and hated him transformed him into an honored relic. They invited him to parties in the confraternity, where they told classic stories about his former prowess, roaring with every legend but never really glancing his way, as though he were already dead. Then they would gather with cigars and hotly discuss the business of which he was now no longer a part.

He was asked onto a great number of civic and charitable committees, where his contributions, all necessarily intellectual, were considered commensurate with his nonexistent power.

Justin grew ever quieter and stayed home more and more. Fiona no longer feared to visit him: He looked at her with the same frightful longing as he had before, but he would not approach her as a figure of pity.

If there was to be any move to bring them together, it was plainly going to have to come from her. Agonized as she watched his disintegration over the months, she began to prepare herself to go to him. "Listen, darling. Let's make it a special night on Friday. I'll cook us a nice dinner here. Even I can't muck up a two-inch steak and a bottle of good wine. And . . . I'll bring my pajamas and toothbrush, if you don't mind."

The look of gratitude on his face melted her away, and she knew she was doing exactly the right thing.

Ronald was no longer anyone to agonize over. Less than a

month after she had slammed down the phone on him he had been sailing in the Mediterranean with one Snugge Gustafsen. Snugge had come out of a small town in Norway to model for Chanel and had soon become the international model of models. Her mile-long legs, curls of golden flax and cerulean eyes had quickly hammered a breathless succession of notable males into the feathers, even stealing a Basque tenor from Liza Hayborn who was cutting her own trail across the French littoral.

According to the New York *Daily News,* which was giving the story a half page every day, Snugge had at last found that one man for whom she had been so restlessly and unhappily questing. In all the photos, Ronald's smile was almost as dazzling as Snugge's bosom.

The relationship lasted and the model came back to the United States to live with Ronald in a new apartment that was featured in *Architectural Record.* In the enlightened days of the early seventies nobody cared the least about the sins of Fiona Keefe, who was nothing at all to him.

The appointed Friday arrived. But Fiona did not carry her pajamas to Justin in his apartment, but in St. Luke's Hospital.

Sometime in the afternoon, while running across Fifth Avenue with an armload of flowers as two maddened cab drivers bore down on him, Justin had frozen, gasped and collapsed face forward. One of the first people to come to his aid had stolen his wallet, so he lay in the hospital unknown and unconscious for hours until a nurse had seen his name in his Burberry raincoat.

The doctor shook his head in wonderment as he talked to Fiona in the corridor. "When somebody goes down like that, I'm ready to bet my socks that it's a heart- or head-artery blowout and the next step is the churchyard. But this is just the most complete collapse from exhaustion I've seen since I worked the Boston Marathon. The reporters that got here before did get a look at him before he came around, and the emergency room interns went off a little half-cocked. I can't really blame them. The papers will have him dying. But he'll be okay in a couple of weeks because he's got the constitution of a water buffalo. And chances are this was as much emotional as physical. Get somebody to keep him happy with a lot of tender loving."

"That's my job, Doctor Weiss. Can I go in?"

"Yeah. We gave him something to perk him up. Don't stay long."

Justin was lying, as white as the walls, in a circle of light cast by a gooseneck lamp. His eyes were half-closed. "Sorry I fell apart on us, Fi. Can't get anything right anymore."

She kissed him on the cheek and then on the lips. "Ah, the longer you waits, the better it feels, they tell me."

"Open your handbag for me."

"Sir. There are certain intimacies that even depraved women do not permit."

"Please."

He rummaged weakly inside and brought out a holder containing a toothbrush. "Well, I'll be damned. I thought you were going to dance away from me forever."

"Sorry. I just wanted you to be sure," she said.

"What about you?"

"Just wait. They're going to have you back in here for the same complaint, but more gleefully acquired." Fiona managed to keep all the sadness out of her face. He was reaching for her, when there was a great and growing clamor down the corridor, as if a gypsy wagon were being towed by an express train.

A knifing, wonderful voice was heard, distant but distinct. "Get that rolling cafeteria out of my way, you white sack of meal."

The sounds progressed until they were outside the room, and then a bedraggled but very beautiful ball of furs and international finery shot through the door and hurled itself upon Justin. The shock might have killed many a completely healthy man. "Justin, Justin. Oh, Christ, I'm sorry, Jus," bawled Liza Hayborn Oakhill, her tears streaking her mascara. "The plane was laying over at Kennedy when I heard. A customs guy tried to hold me back and he's looking for a place to get his balls reinflated." She crawled up on the bed next to him and kissed every inch of his face and neck. "God, I thought I was going to find you propping up a lily, you crazy sonofabitch. I almost threw that doctor a hump when he caught me coming in and told me you were swell. Hi, Fiona."

A sunbeam awakened somewhere inside Justin. A color that Fiona hadn't seen in months flew back into his cheeks as he grabbed his lost wife and kissed her as though he could pull back all the lost things in his life. "I've been reading all about you, you twat," he said between kisses. "I hope you didn't break off some director's dibber inside you rushing here like this."

"I've been reading about you, too. I hear they took away all your Tinkertoys. Now you've got nothing to play with except me."

"Liza. I take the subway. I live in a broom closet."

"That's okay, Jus. I just did a roaring king movie with Sir Larry and they gave me enough to buy—let's see—five million subway tokens. And we can store my old bras in your apartment."

"I don't like living with bras. I feel like I'm being stalked."

"Then you'll have to move in with me. I've got a shot at nine rooms on Central Park South from one of the Rolling Stones. There's enough joint smoke in the walls to keep us giggling all the time. And speaking of joints, dongmaster, let's see if inexpert attention has done any permanent damage." She jerked back the covers and was beginning to lift Justin's hospital gown when she remembered her daughter was present. "Uh, hey, Fi. You better go. There are things we big guys do that you kids shouldn't know about."

"Mom, for God's sake, he almost *died.*"

"Yeah, maybe I'll let him just lie there and drink in my great beauty. But toddle along anyway, okay? Jus and I have to talk before we sleep."

Justin, who had forgotten Fiona from the moment Liza came into the room, turned red and looked stricken.

"Fi . . . uh . . . I—"

Fiona tried to strike just the right balance of looking crushed yet brave and completely resigned. She hugged him and planted a loud smack on his ear. "It's okay. I've seen enough of Mom's flicks to know she always gets the hero. Good night, Mom," she said, embracing Liza fiercely. "Good night . . . Dad." Then she was out the door feeling as though the Chrysler Building had just been lifted off her back.

She might have remained happy all the way home, except that she saw a *Daily News* on a stand, and there were Snugge Gustafsen and Ronald Stryker in the Caribbean coming as close to fornicating on water skies as possible.

Fiona did not quite cry, and said a terrible word. She had to find somebody and forget Ronald before she lost her reason.

Chapter 15

IN THE NEXT YEARS, Ronald seldom made love to the spectacular Snugge without thinking painfully of Fiona. He found it no use to tell himself what a fool he was to long for a vicious and deceitful woman allied with the Oakhills. He remembered instead the effortless joy he had found in being with her, something he had not experienced before or since.

He didn't confess it to himself, but he more than once suspected that he turned aside Snugge's occasional invitations to marriage because he still held some insane hope.

That hope should have ended when Fiona had married a tough-looking and handsome Marine captain she had met on a Shelter Island weekend.

His name was Craig Stubbs, and he would have had a fine career in his father's expensive boatyard in Connecticut when he returned from the war.

But a North Vietnamese gunner found Captain Stubbs' troop helicopter hovering low and vulnerable above a landing zone. He had not returned.

Ronald seldom saw her about town, but he saw her work in the business she had started with Justin Oakhill.

Justin, seen at industry get-togethers now and again—at which he would knock over tables to avoid Ford and Ronald—seemed at least partially happy and fully functional again. His restored love affair with his wife was a favorite topic in the celebrity publications, and the scandal sheets appeared for once to have it right. The great Hollywood Queen of Hearts had at last found what she really wanted. Not a handsome, all-powerful god who needed no more than a stroked ego, but a torn, broken, unpretty man who loved her until he ached. She defended him against defamation like a tigress and committed what she could of her movie riches to his mountainous personal obligations.

Liza had also bankrolled his reentry into the business, necessarily modest after the sources of major capital were closed permanently to him. Ronald understood that the basic idea had been Fiona's, although Justin had plunged in with a storm of good ideas once he had seen he would go insane in total exile.

The plan had been good, original and exactly right for the times, and Ronald admired Fiona's quick accurate appraisal of the opportunity.

The city was becoming aggressive in its granting of bonus stories on buildings in exchange for inclusion of promenades and atriums on the lower levels, the idea being to prevent the disappearance of shops and stores as high-rise construction replaced retail rows.

The builders had begun to respond eagerly to the incentive, but they never regarded the stores as anything except pestiferous but necessary intrusions on their structures. The results of this attitude were almost universally deplorable. The stores were shunted out of the way, lost in labyrinths. Even when they did face the sidewalks, they were stuffed with whatever sleazy establishments that could be corralled by a disinterested part-time sales staff. These merchants, at their will, plastered their storefronts with garish neon, hand-lettered signs and painfully ugly displays. When the individual store happened to be tastefully done, no attempt was made to coordinate its decor with other stores in the line.

The consequence was that an otherwise stunningly designed

building had a row of running sores at street level, draining away its beauty, its prestige and the overall value of rentals.

Into this morass had stepped Justin and Fiona with their brand new operation, Oakhill and Keefe. And the offices of building managements all over the city had begun to reverberate with the kind of selling assault that only Justin could mount.

"Excuse me, Mr. Elbaum, but I must respectfully tell you that your retail tenants have your buildings looking like a skunk's ass in flytime. It's costing you big money. Let me sketch out how Oakhill and Keefe will take over your store operation and give you back the hundreds of thousands—maybe millions—of dollars that you're losing.

"First, we take over the design function of the store placements before the building goes up. Instead of making concourses just places to hide from the rain, we place them so that at least seventy-five percent of the traffic has to pass by the stores. We also design the storefronts themselves for beauty and unity. The renters aren't allowed to touch them. And we extend our control inside the store so nobody can put up a lot of crappy lights and displays. Carpeting, color schemes, lighting fixtures become all ours to dictate.

"Most important, our full-time sales staff selects and solicits prime tenants. No two-dollar-a-yard rug merchants and plastic-spoon restaurants. Elegance. Opulence. Restraint. Taste. Create a place where the better stores will compete to be. Pretty soon the space you were getting forty dollars a foot for is going for eighty dollars. And the big corporations want to be upstairs in such a stylish building. One prestige corporation attracts another. Again the rents go up. I don't think you can say no, Mr. Elbaum."

Increasingly they said yes, and Oakhill and Keefe prospered and moved to command a lucrative, fast-growing market. For most it would have been the triumph of a lifetime. For Justin, Ronald saw, it was the palest shadow of what he had known. A man who had once built mighty ocean liners now tinkered with ships in bottles.

As for Fiona, so far as Ronald could tell, she devoted herself to keeping Justin interested, and to doing much unpaid work in city housing commissions. She dated, he knew, sometimes seriously, but she didn't marry again. Not yet.

He fretted over her every day, until some greedy Arabs and a vicious little war distracted him, along with the rest of the nation.

With the coming of the oil embargo and OPEC, the building business suffered wrenching and unnerving changes. And here Ronald at last emerged into his own.

As a frightening inflation flooded in, he became convinced that interest rates were streaking for twenty percent. He went quickly to Ford. His father had stuck to his promise of surrendering control of Stryker and Oakhill to his son, but reserved the right to hear, be appalled by and rage against the important decisions.

"Look, Dad. With these interest rates, the old builders' trick of using expensive short-term construction loans and retiring them with low-interest long-term loans isn't going to cut it anymore. Building—all kinds—is going to stop dead unless someone thinks his way around the Federal Reserve."

"And you've nominated yourself?"

"Since nobody else has."

"Okay. Don't spare me, Ronald."

"Joint-venturing is the way. On a scale like it's never been done."

"You'd need huge partners."

"I've gone to Vesuvius Life Insurance."

"A very tough company. They make a merciless deal."

Ronald took a deep breath. "Very merciless. Here it is. I mortgage myself—"

"*We* mortgage *our*selves—"

"—ourselves to the hilt to get the new General Telegraph Building up. Vesuvius agrees beforehand to purchase the building outright at the end of two years. As the lender they get the mortgage rate, plus amortization, a piece of the building's earnings and future tax goodies. And they're factoring in the inflation."

"Hold it, Ronald," said an alarmed Ford. "How can you negotiate a safe price?"

"Ah. There, Dad, is the potentially fatal catch. The price will be based on the building's income performance—its rents—*at the date of closing.* We, the builders, will receive no fees, no bonuses, no salaries."

"You risk everything on a project that starts up to its neck in red ink and might stay that way?"

"Hey, what happened to 'we,' Dad? Yeah, that's it. If the rental market goes flat or—and here's the real killer—there are any substantial delays in construction time—".

"—then Vesuvius' payments to you could be twenty-five or thirty million dollars less than your constructions costs. A wipeout of classical proportions."

"Dad, for what an old friend of mine called a bungalow builder, you have an impressive grasp of the big picture."

"In this case I'd feel better if I didn't have the slightest notion of what the hell you were talking about."

"You're nervous already, huh?"

"Very."

"Then maybe you don't want to hear about a little something called fast-tracking."

"Fast-tracking?"

"Right. The general idea is to activate planning and building more or less simultaneously. We're pouring foundations while we're still designing the first floor. Nothing goes to the drawing boards until the step before it is getting hung."

"*Preposterous,*" Ford snapped. "You destroy your flexibility. The mistakes you make below will lock in what you can do above."

"That's why we have to be bloody careful about mistakes."

"What's the goddamned *point?*"

"Savings. Breathing room for the agreed-on price. Vesuvius gives us a whopping bonus for every month we knock off the completion schedule. That's a bargain for everybody. Because it's pin money compared to the cost of tying up their money in construction. With a hundred million laid out, every month saved probably puts an extra million in their pocket."

"How many months do you figure to save?"

"Maybe seven. Maybe nine."

Ford's gray eyebrows shot up. "Not possible."

"With the kind of overtime I'm going to load on it is, Dad."

"You know what that will cost?"

"Nothing like what we'll save."

"One strike could chew up all the time you gained and leave you with all that overtime wasted."

"True. But I've been sleeping too good anyway."

"This building's going to kill me. And I hate what it is and where it is. Call me in the country if it falls down or you forget to put in the ground floor with all that hurrying."

As Ronald hurriedly designed the principles of fast-tracking, he saw that the key element was a special breed of ramrod—a construction manager who had the stomach, brains and iron will to give up everything else in his life to organize the massive project and hold it to a heartbreaking schedule. He knew who the man had to be.

Laird Hanratty was disposing of his third boilermaker in a Tenth Avenue bar favored by the high-iron unions when he saw Ronald Stryker hurrying in for their meeting. Ronald was distinctly out of place with his cashmere overcoat and forty-dollar haircut. But much less so than Laird would have been if he had met Ronald in Stryker's uptown offices.

As his potential employer made his way through the unimpressed scowls showing beneath a grimy sea of hardhats, Laird folded forearms like tree-trunks across his vast chest. Above a black, foot-long pirate's beard, his snub-nosed face might have appeared almost jolly except for an indifferently repaired cheekbone and too-wide blue eyes that appeared hammered out of iron. He had never met this Stryker, but knew from the Hanratty family storytellers that his forebears had connected early with the great building Oakhills. And the Oakhills and Hanrattys had shared a strange, almost fated relationship over the generations, of a sort that only a good Irish mystic could properly appreciate.

Although Laird still sat on a good remaining chunk of the forty-five-thousand-dollar bonus he had taken out of his last successful ramrodding and was not particularly eager to cut short his vacation—a good deal of which was enjoyed in this very chair— he scarcely doubted that the longtime forces would put him and Ronald together. He waved him over.

Ronald sat and poured the contents of a briefcase over the table. "A pleasure, Mr. Hanratty," he said as he offered a pretty good grip for a desk commander.

"My granddaddy used to talk about your grandmother and old Caesar and Victor. We rushed a lot of bolts together, your people and mine. And I grew up in Strykertown—my old man was a charter buyer. So I guess you can make it Laird. Okay, Ron?"

"Our first agreement, Laird."

"Let's see if there are going to be any more. What's the bonus?"

"Eighty thousand above salary if you hang floors as fast as I want you to."

Laird whistled between widely spaced teeth. "I'll sky with the boys myself to make that happen."

"Like hell you will. Let the foremen run the six-inch highway and then go home and lay pipe with the old lady. Sign on and you're in the ground war. Your ass is mine. You live under the steel for the duration. Interested?"

"How can I resist soft soap like that?" He pointed at the papers. "Spread 'em."

They closed the bar that night, and before they left Laird had joined Ronald in the ancestral weakness—a crazed lust to build the impossible. As they walked out they passed an elegant cigarette poster modeled by Snugge Gustafsen, who liked to keep her hand in.

Laird looked at her and laughed. "Ron, do you realize that I'm now more important to you than she is?"

"You certainly will have a lot more chances to fuck me."

In an incredibly short time, the mighty General Telegraph building began to punch its way skyward, and Laird Hanratty showed why he commanded the prices and fame that he did.

As construction manager, he was the field general for the job. More than just a glorified foreman promoted from the high-iron ranks, he held an M.B.A. from Columbia and was as much a sophisticated business executive as a hardcase hardhat. He could cook the operational numbers as well as Ronald could handle the ones in high finance.

Laird needed all his mules's stamina, because he had enlisted for sixteen-hour days that rasped away at everything in him, both mental and physical. His only home in the world until the building was ready for leasing was around a gouged Goodwill Industries desk in a cobbled-together tarpaper shack at the center of the vast foundation. His only warmth came from a kerosene heater and occasional late-night visits from his wife, who traveled up from Brooklyn. She often found him unshakably asleep.

All components of the job, including legal, engineering, mechanical and accounting, reported to him. Laird controlled all the materials and workmanship that went into the huge project. He had near-absolute power of the developer's people and something more than that over the subcontractors. He went to these independent sources to buy virtually everything that went into the building, from topsoil to steel, from glass to ceramic tiles and wiring. And it was the leverage he exerted against these suppliers that was his only hope of raising the building by his deadline and making his hefty bonus. For even as they depended on his whim for a nod that could make them anywhere from hundreds of thousands to millions of dollars, he depended on them to deliver everything he needed in precise quantities and in split-second time to fit into the evolving jigsaw of fast-track blueprinting.

Each component was assigned an exact start and completion date, and failure to deliver at the specified moment—too early could be as bad as too late—meant loss of hours as valuable as rubies. The subs who failed would never earn money on the construction manager's multimillion-dollar projects again.

Which did not guarantee that they would not try to get away with all they could.

Each sub might be supplying a dozen other jobs, each with its own manager demanding miracles of precision. When there were conflicts, they had to find a manager who was less tough, less demanding than the rest, and let him take up the slack in their scheduling.

The more experienced subs knew that to interfere with the synchronization of a logistical grid run by Laird Hanratty could be physically as well as economically dangerous. But one new man decided that Hanratty's steel could be delivered a day late. He called Laird two days before the scheduled delivery and told him that sabotaging unionists had slashed so many tires on his trucks that he could not be rolling until the day after tomorrow.

Within two hours Laird had a man at the sub's out-of-state terminal, who determined that the trucks were being readied to roll on perfect tires with someone else's beams. So when the drivers and loaders of the trucks being prepared returned from their lunch break, they found that the lie had come true. Somebody had gone through a great many tires with a lustily swung pickax.

The sweating sub had barely time to fly into a despairing rage before he was told that a Mr. Hanratty was on the phone for him.

"Sorry about those flats you called about, Barney. I hear those union geeks are just everyplace around your terminal, and they'll just keep fucking you up until they get a settlement. Tell you what, though. I got friends at the International. Bet if I told 'em that I had to have those beams tomorrow he'd call off the problem and save you a lot of time and Bridgestones. What do you think?"

"That . . . would be great."

"Swell. There's a couple other pals of mine hanging around in a jeep out in front of your place. If you need any help supervising our loading, they'll help."

"You're a real prick, Hanratty."

"Guaranteed, you snake-humping pissdrinker. Eleven o'clock, Barney. We intend to top out right on time. And if we don't because of you, it's not going to be an American flag waving from the top. It's going to be your nuts. Have a safe trip."

Steel deliveries were subsequently not a problem.

Again and again in the frantic months following, Hanratty muscled, improvised, bullied, bluffed and cajoled to defeat every failure of his treacherous suppliers. Every week brought its desperate saves, and sixty floors began to head for the sun at a rate not possible before.

But the miracles of Hanratty and fast-tracking brought Ronald another ghastly problem. The specter of finishing *too early*. The pace of the General Telegraph Building put it far ahead of the leasing agents. They were behind in assigning staff, commissioning artwork, printing brochures, writing copy and making their calls. A complete building devoid of tenants could wipe out all the savings of time bought by putting the trades on sixty-hour weeks.

Ronald moved in with the brokerage arm of Stryker and Oakhill and turned up the pressure. He flew to every important city in the United States and overseas, turning over rocks to find big companies who had windfalls or reverses that might sweep them to New York City and his rapidly growing empty building. He established a network of bounty-hunting informers who penetrated government networks, like espionage agents, to get secret information that might bear on moves and leases.

His efforts caught up the pace of leasing to Laird's rocketing pace of building.

With almost every snag there was a phone call from Sands Point, and Ford would predict doom before Ronald or Laird got things straightened out. It became one of the few light moments in the week, with Ronald putting the calls on the speakerphone so all in the shack could have a laugh at the old man's worries.

Then, one day, it was no laughing matter.

"A cement strike, huh?" Ford's voice crackled over the speaker.

"Well, that's it for a month. I've been around those bastards enough to know there's no such thing as a short walkout. Especially in the winter. They can't pour every day anyway, and the members like to get down to Florida for a suntan."

"Maybe it won't be so long, Dad."

"It doesn't have to be long to murder you. After fifteen stories of steel you have to pour concrete floors to make your diaphragm. Otherwise the whole beam structure will wobble and destabilize. It will all end up in the street if you keep going up. So your whole pinpoint delivery schedule goes into the dumper."

"Sounds like you've been reading," Ronald said glumly.

"Sure as hell I have, with the money from fifty thousand beautiful little houses teetering on the whim of some truck driver with a room-temperature IQ. What are you going to do?"

"I've already decided what to do."

"What? What, what?"

"I'm going to ask Laird to think real hard about it. Call you later, Dad."

Laird had already done that. "Only one thing I see to try, Ron. A guy in Australia got away with this, although he wasn't up nearly as high as we are. What he did, I understand, is work out a whole bracing system using steel cables the way they used wire struts on the wings of rickety old biplanes. He pulled the whole thing taut with winches and kept going up until he could get the floors poured behind him. No time to wire for more information. I'll have to design the rig myself."

"Dangerous, Laird?"

"Dangerous enough to want to keep what we're doing in low profile. There's so much building going on we can sneak it by."

"We can't go all the way to the top that way, if the strike keeps going. And after it's over we have to sit on our hands anyway until the concrete catches up."

"I doped something together for that last part. As we brace and the floors go up, we get the forms for the concrete all in place. Not only that, we put in ramps for the cement trucks. Drive 'em right on up for a direct pour. We can cut the floor-pouring time by two-thirds. Maybe more."

"Do you know what one of those trucks weighs when it's loaded?"

"Sure, but I'm trying not to think about it."

"What happens if a cable lets go under that kind of strain?"

"You'd get a helluva rebound and, if the other bracing held, a sudden, whipping imbalance. If you had one of those loaded trucks in the wrong place to accentuate the sway, we could go south awfully fast. So what do you say?"

"I'd say it's the worst idea I ever heard. Order the cable and winches, Laird. And a case of Pepto-Bismol."

The building grapevine got wind of what was happening on the General Telegraph Building, and soon observers were dropping by from all over the city. They saw the critical sixteen-story level surpassed by the rising steel. The painfully designed web of cable was applied and pulled to just the right tensions by winches the size of automobiles, anchored to the framework and creaking with the huge stresses. Crisscrossing the temporary wood of the flooring were the truck ramps, more sharply angled than Laird liked even though they ran between the outermost edges of the floors.

"Make sure those truck brakes get checked a dozen times each, Laird. If one of those big bastards rolled down backward, there'd be a low-flying Mack over Broadway."

"Don't worry so much about the brakes. The gears will do the real holding."

Every day, every hour, carefully watched instruments verified the stability of Laird's jury rig. Twenty-nine unpoured floors went up before the strike ended.

Even the truck drivers whose union power was undermined by the effort were impressed. And they enjoyed the new thrill of pushing their gargantuan ready-mixers, drums ponderously revolving, up the ramps and far into the sky.

"Got an altimeter on that thing?" was a common jest roared across the iron.

Ronald couldn't relax. Rolling around the clock, the trucks, shuttling on the ramps to opposite corners of the building, could not be kept synchronized well enough to distribute their weight as they climbed through the framework. The drivers would not believe this distribution was important, and the other work presented often insurmountable obstacles to the balance. At times the instruments showed the stability of the braced structure as no more than marginal.

Now Ronald deserted his offices completely, loaded up on Arctic clothing and stayed up in the iron with Hanratty almost without a break. His nerves hummed like the straining cables.

Hearing the edge in his son's voice, Ford put down the phone one evening and called for his car and chauffeur. The quiet of the Sands Point winter had suddenly begun to seem like the last exile of a tired old man. He felt a rush of need to be back on a major site, alive with men and trucks and building. Especially did he miss the jolt of excitement that came with handling a situation that might come apart at any moment.

There was also, behind it all, a touch of guilt at the way he had utterly abandoned Ronald in this brutal undertaking because it was not the sort of thing he himself favored. Not that he would be of any use with his age and different expertise, but, damn it, there was too much in this family of people turning their backs on one another.

"Anne, I'm going into Manhattan to look in on Ronald at the building."

They lived in different parts of the big house now, but still went through some of the motions of other married people. "Now? It's down to freezing out there. And he'll be up high where it will be worse."

She didn't care, of course, but she always said and did the correct thing. Getting into his heavy clothes he looked at her standing on the stairs, many years younger than he and still every inch the society beauty. Even the wearing years with her distastefully tainted husband had not been able to grind that down. As old as he was, there were still nights when he would have liked to go to her room. "I'll tell Ronald you were asking for him."

"Why would you do that when I most certainly was not?"

Knowing she felt neglected and abandoned by the son she had worked so hard to make like herself, he was not surprised by these little darts.

"Good night, Anne. I'll be back tomorrow."

"If you'd like."

Sometimes he wondered if she knew about his will, and that life would not be nearly as wonderful as she thought when he was dead.

Ronald was amazed to see Ford crossing the planking, leaning against the wind that whipped across the groaning, floodlit ironwork. Ford felt good at seeing the big grin cross his son's face, and liked seeing him in the trenches, dressed like the workmen. It was important for a builder to remember that this business wasn't all banks and briefcases.

"What in hell's this about, Dad?"

"Letting the wind blow the cobwebs out for a while. And I wanted see all those marvelous tricks of yours they're all talking about. How about the four-bit tour?"

Ronald walked him slowly around the entire floor, steering him between hustling crews and the giant trucks chugging up the ramps in dead-low gears.

To Ford, whose idea of a great strain in construction was a ten-penny nail binding two-by-eight headers, the principle of Laird Hanratty's cabling was awesome. He kept after Ronald until he understood it enough for it to make him nervous.

Ronald kicked one of the great winches. "Until we pour a lot more floors, these babies are holding up the whole erector set."

"I don't like where you've got them set very much. Right at the bottom of the ramps."

"Neither does Laird. But that's the way it all worked out. Don't worry. Those drivers know what would happen if they ever piled hard into one of those cables."

"Get back to work. I've bothered you long enough. Let me just wander around for a while."

"Okay. We've got a tarp shelter in the center there, with a heater and coffee for when you're tired."

"Good. Hey, Ron."

"Yeah?"

"I guess there might be something interesting in these big sons-of-bitches after all."

Ronald feigned a faint and left him free to explore.

As Ford trudged, missing nothing, he felt a huge, bursting pride in the son who had brought the genius of this together.

A measure of youth flowed back into him. He reveled in the bustling uproar and thought he could smell the honest sweat of building right through all the layers of the men's thick clothes. He longed to bawl orders again and almost sent a foreman to straighten out a crew that was showing confusion around one of the forms.

After a while he made his way out near the open edge of the flooring. Where the big construction lights no longer fell, he was able to look outward on some of the works of Victor Oakhill and, for all his contempt for such heartless structures, felt part of a grand, honorable continuity.

The gusts picked up and he placed a hand around one of the huge, taut cables where it left a winch. His hand could hardly span the strands, and he could feel them stirring with the numberless tons held checked.

One of the immense trucks, its diesel clattering deafeningly, emerged like a giant, gray snail from the floor below and made its tight, ponderous turn. The driver gunned again and Ford watched the vehicle begin to crawl upward on the tilted ramp. Standing behind it he watched it go, the end of the turning drum pointed squarely at him as he stood at the winch.

Near the head of the ramp, the truck lurched and slowed as a rasping, grinding clank reverberated from the engine. There was another moment of coughing growls followed by a gnash of gears, and the diesel died completely. The truck began to slide backward before a frantic hiss of brakes arrested it.

The cab door popped open and a black driver, swearing and stomping, climbed from the heights and came huffing down the bowing planks. "Hey, man," he said to Ford. "Can you keep an eye on that lump 'til I get the mechanic up here? Don't let *nobody* get up in that cab and fuck with her, okay?"

"Uh, sure. Okay."

The man made his way toward a phone. Ford stood there until the wind began to draw too much heat out of him. He thought that moving around some might help, so he headed up the ramp toward where the hulking concrete truck sat.

It was as he was walking near the rear wheels, impressed by the brutal chest-high tires, that he heard a high, squealing hiss from the bowels of the vehicle. It soon lowered itself a note and became louder, rising above the clamor of the site.

The metal interstices of the truck gave out a lengthening creak, its frame shuddered and slowly it began to inch backward in short lurches.

Ford looked fearfully backward to where the winch bulked at the foot of the ramp, it's thick cable stretching far out into its place in the critical web that stabilized the soaring steel. It was a dead certainty that the truck was a cannonball aimed squarely at the squat cylinder and what it held, and that such a hit would sweep it away as though it had been a slender vase on a table.

The hiss expanded and lowered itself to a roar. The lurching ended and the truck began a smooth roll, very slow at first, then getting its bulk into the acceleration.

Stepping back out of its way, Ford turned and yelled as loudly as he could between cupped hands. *"Runaway . . . Runaway on the ramp—"*

Nobody was looking his way and the thunder of two pounding jackhammers tore away his words.

When he spun around again, the rear wheels had moved away past him. The door to the cab still stood open, and he had started to duck beneath its approach when it came to him what he must do.

Shifting his weight, he sprang up for the high step of the cab and the grab bar. He made it, but the truck's momentum was already enough to pivot his body hard into the big steering wheel. Something exploded painfully in his shoulder, and his left arm would no longer move. He quickly switched the grip of his good hand from the grab bar to the wheel. One last glance to the rear before he pulled himself onto the seat showed him that the truck's front wheels had not been left cocked. The weight of a full load of concrete was already a quarter of the way down the ramp, heading hard for the building's ghastly vulnerability and just beginning to gather speed.

Ford had been in the cabs of enough heavy trucks to know the rudiments of operation, and he tried to run through all the stopping procedures he knew. But his dead arm hindered him. He couldn't get the gears to do anything but slip and screech. The brakes seemed disconnected from their operating pedals and levers. Through the windshield he watched the long ribbon of ramp lengthening rapidly as he shot backward. In the sideview mirror he saw the empty night rushing closer.

He began to throw his weight into spinning the wheel hard with one arm.

"Overgrown piece of shit," Ford screamed furiously at either the truck or the building that was killing him.

He felt the rear wheels leave the side of the ramp. The truck's nose tilted crazily upward for a second, then leveled off with a horrendous bump as the juggernaut found the flooring, righted itself as it came off the ramp completely and then went crashing out over the edge. As it did so, Ford was able to glimpse the winch, untouched and intact, still clutching its stabilizing load. He yelled happily.

Nobody in the steel heard the truck hit Broadway or felt the rush of the dark wings that had just gone by.

New York, with its astounding ability to digest and forget the most spectacular tragedies, made brief note of the heroic end of Ford Stryker, the legend who had given America its own home.

Working in shock, Ronald got all the way through the inquiry before he caved in to the enormity of his loss. He flew alone to Nassau for a full two days so one would disturb his memories or see him weep. He suddenly despised himself for having let his mother pull him away to the life and values of a rich snot. He hated every day that he might have been at his father's side but had gone instead to ski at Gstaad or sail at Newport. And most bitterly he regretted not having stood against Anne as she destroyed all the spontaneous warmth and joy that might have grown between her husband and son.

Ronald visited Ford's grave just once, where he placed his flowers and said to the cold, empty air, "I wasn't there for you at the beginning. And I wasn't there for you at the end. But I loved you, damn it, and I wish I could have found the way to tell you how much."

The terms of Ford's will almost killed Anne Bennington Stryker. She took to her bed for the best part of a month, keeping the room dark and avoiding mirrors so that neither she nor anyone else would read the fury and shame she felt.

Ronald knew Anne hoped that he would come to her unasked and outraged, and himself make the proper transfer of the estate to her, but that was not to be the case. Ronald carefully respected his father's last wish, making no effort to probe its origin. Her look told him that she would die before he had that answer.

Anne did not try to overturn the will in a lawsuit because it was beneath her dignity, and no one knew for certain how completely she had been cut out. She only spoke to Ronald about it once, when her bitterness could not be contained.

"I suppose he couldn't bear that he was never quite accepted in our family after I let him get in."

"I thought *our* family was the *Stryker* family, Mother."

"*I* never thought of it that way."

"Why not?"

"The Benningtons were colonial aristocracy when the Strykers were quite properly chained to a slaver's deck."

"Where does that leave me, Mother? Tap dancing at the cotillion?"

"Truthfully, I've wondered for a long time about where you felt you belonged—with us or with them. Thank you for clearing it up for me in these last weeks."

She left him then, and he didn't hear from her for a long time.

When she reappeared their relationship was entirely correct, with no mention of what had been. And that left very little to exchange.

Through the seventies and into the eighties Fiona watched Ronald Stryker become a preeminent builder in New York. The innovative financing and fast-tracking that he had pioneered made Stryker and Oakhill the place to look for a prestige building and an occasional wild bit of fiscal daredeviltry. There were huge losses once in a while when he pushed too far and too hard. And people who knew how to look through a company's statement could see that Stryker and Oakhill was not as solidly underpinned as an organization of its fame should be.

But it was far from sure that Ronald cared. He had become a media celebrity as much as a builder. He and the eye-filling Snugge Gustafsen, together for as long as most married couples of the day, more than ever filled the pages of *Architectural Record, Vogue, Gentleman's Quarterly* and *Yachting* with their suites, homes, clothes and boats. There was no fund-raiser, no opening of a new restaurant or club, no cultural jewel at which they did not match their blinding competition sparkle for sparkle. Nicholson, Streep, de Kooning and all the others were never quite as centered in the picture as Ronald and Snugge.

"Good Jesus," Justin had said, "I thought I was a ham. Next to this guy I was a Franciscan monk."

The centerpiece of Ronald's fame was the Silver Spire, a major media wonder and the hot place for the bi-coastal, bi-continental names to live. Apartments above the soaring, chromed, pink-marbled shopping atrium sold for $325,000 per room. An afternoon of shopping in the atrium's dazzling stores could have brought several houses in the old Strykertown.

While the exterior architecture received plaudits except for its excess glitter—sometimes pinpointed as a danger to blinded street traffic—its lobby, garish and overdone, became something of a joke in the architectural community even as it knocked the breath out of tourists. It was widely known that the design had sprung from Snugge Gustafsen, who had wanted to reestablish some respect after the costly failure of the Gustafsen Express clothing line Ronald had financed for her.

As old as Justin now was, his legs were still spectacularly solid, and Fiona took him to see the maligned lobby. "Great balls of horseshit, Fi. With all those waterfalls and that marble it looks like the men's room at Versailles."

"I hear you, Jus. I don't get it. The Ronald Stryker I remember wouldn't let this in the same city where he was building."

"Well, damn, what the hell does he care about building anymore? He's all wrapped up in his Vegas casino and his baseball team and his muscle movies with that gorilla from Hungary, what's his name—?"

"Zoltan Weissflusser. Don't laugh at him too much. Those no-brainer films of his are burning down the box offices."

"Wish Ronnie-boy'd take grandma's name off his damned company. She wouldn't want to be tied together with a prick like him."

Fiona knew well what Justin meant. Even in a business filled with rough and tumble practitioners not especially concerned with niceties, Ronald was overstepping the permissible. In such an elegant city there were unwritten laws governing even the most savage negotiations, and to violate them was to invite bitter animosity.

Ronald had torn down a row of buildings one night without proper permits and with a near-total disregard of legalities because they were to become protected by landmark status the next day. His lawyers had squirmed him out of it with fines that were trifling compared to what he would get for unencumbered property, and the other builders had writhed under the ensuing civic crackdown on all of them.

The dust from that demolition had hardly cleared when he matched it with one even more infamous. An acquired property, otherwise undistinguished, had a treasury of classic Art Deco statuary on its facade. When several art preservation groups threatened to hold up his renovation of the building until homes for the works could be found in suitable museums, he had the works sledgehammered to bits before a horrified lunchtime crowd. The enraged public outcry was more than offset for him by the publicity gained for the building, which he rented out at top dollar.

Even dirtier was his alleged treatment of holdout tenants in a building he was trying to empty. Investigative reporters filled pages with stories of terror tactics. Empty apartments, they said, were purposely filled with dangerous squatters, addicts who had been encouraged to defecate and urinate in the halls, stairways and elevators, and to blast radios and brutally intimidate.

Ronald had this time vehemently denied knowledge of the tactic. He cooperated enthusiastically in the prosecution of the guilty management company and in the advantageous relocation of the tenants. But his reputation for callous arrogance grew to match the one he already had for florid, pretentious display.

"I remember," said Justin, "that you were kind of chummy with him back when you were doing that Museum building together. Was he always like that, Fi?"

She remembered back, the hurt at least partially dulled by the years. "No," she said, "not at all. Something changed him, and I bet it wasn't any fun."

"Why should *he* have any fun? I don't have any."

Justin had never gotten over being bumped off the big stage, even though Oakhill and Keefe was doing handsomely and he still worked on it at home. Fiona kissed him energetically on his lined cheek, their old romance now just a memory that they occasionally laughed about.

"You have plenty of good times," she said.

"The only thing that's given me any satisfaction since Liza came back was outliving Ford Stryker."

As she walked with Justin back to the car, she thought about the terribly eligible American Airlines executive who would shortly arrive at her apartment to take her to dinner. Fresh from a divorce from a much younger woman, he was still pathetically vulnerable and wouldn't know whether he should ask to spend the night. She though she might invite him, because he was sweet and genuinely liked her. Either way, it was of no real importance. The end of an evening never bothered her the way the beginning did. No matter how hard she tried not to, when the bell rang she always hoped that when she answered the door it would be Ronald standing there, dressed to take her away.

"You look like you're on the moon," Justin said to her.

Right, she thought. Cold and floating away.

Ronald Stryker was as unhappy as a man standing at the center of his own party, in a four-million-dollar penthouse in his own building, could be. Which was considerably.

He had roused himself from a state of animated unconsciousness only once. That was when he saw a straight, flowingly graceful girl through the crush who looked enough like Fiona to propel him forward three steps before he realized that it could not be her. This girl was in her middle twenties, and Fiona, like himself, had stepped across forty in the years since she had sent him away to Snugge Gustafsen.

Not that those years had hurt Fiona. He saw her in trade magazine pictures all the time and in person more often than she knew. Many a ticket he had bought to a dismal testimonial in order to catch a glimpse of her far across a room, contemplating going to her as if nothing had happened to separate them. And as many times he had walked away, unseen, perhaps just ignored, feeling worse than before as her date covered her like an NFL cornerback. Which, come to think of it, was the way that Snugge covered him.

"See the Thayers, darling," she said, gliding by in a silver Balenciaga, her accent rigorously maintained. "They gave four thousand last time."

This reminded Ronald that technically speaking he was not a host at all, but a Foundation Head. Snugge, who could have achieved a Ph.D. in parties, had taught him the angle: You start your own foundation—his was The Stryker Foundation for Urban Youth Medicine. Then you gave "benefits," and all the people to whom you gave, or who wanted from you, had to come. You could write off the expenses and the foundation administrators served as your social organizers.

It was more effective and efficient than having to sweat for a special super-guest to draw the others, and having to send a limousine to provide transport.

"You should never have dumped Gambretti, Ron. There's no shortstop who hits like that."

"But he fields like Quasimodo."

"C'mon, Ronnie. You know it's because he snotted off to your majesty."

Ronald turned away scowling because he knew the man was right. Why did every sonofabitch in the world think he could run a baseball team? Just like himself.

He could tell first-time guests by the way they lingered over the study's flocked red-velvet walls edged in green *faux marbre*, and hungrily fingered the Second Empire chairs and various Napoleon III appointments.

"Did Bray-Schaible do anything here?"

"No, dear. Snugge thinks minimalist decorators are risky." She also thought that the decorator she used enjoyed a better relationship with *Architectural Record*, in which her rooms had twice been featured.

Ronald tried to hide himself in a bank of Ronaldo Maia Rothschild lilies and tuberoses as he watched Snugge work the room. The simple Norwegian maiden, with a grade-school education and twenty-three Vogue covers to her credit, never made a mistake in her adopted world.

She schussed at Taos and Wengen and belonged to the Maidstone in Easthampton. Palm-Aire and La Costa held fat at bay, and she had gone to Silver Hill for a "breakdown" simply because so many of her friends were there and the stories would be so good.

Her fling with art had been strictly by the rules, with the carpentry costing almost as much as the paintings. (Only by turning closets into storage racks could you possibly be seen as a serious collector.)

He had never married Snugge. First it had been mostly her, at the zenith of her fame and beauty, afraid that some passing oil minister who had learned some manners at Cambridge might want to put her into the yacht-with-a-seaplane class. Then it had been Ronald, who had decided that he admired her most for the straightforwardness of her cheerful greed and ambition, and that this was sometimes amusing but not a great foundation for a marriage.

In many ways Snugge had served him better than a wife. She ran the precise and rigorous social circus that his position demanded, and did it with flawless panache. Her determination to be a queen had much to do with his recognition as a king of international New York.

"How is your house coming, Ronald?" a borough president asked as he shouldered by.

"Check it with Snugge. I don't get to the Hamptons much this time of year."

"Who's doing it for you? One of the scratch-builders, I'm sure. Charlie Moore? Bob Stern? Mike Graves?"

"It changes a lot," Ronald said wearily. "Somebody she commissioned through the Castelli Gallery."

"Can't wait to see it."

I'll bet, Ronald thought as the man edged to a table covered with a thousand dollars' worth of Italian cashews.

A tall, silver-maned man with a Mediterranean shading to his eyes leaned over Ronald's shoulder. Except for the broken knuckles above the beautifully manicured nails, no one would have picked him out as the security man that all parties such as this must have.

"How is it going, Carmine?"

"Pretty well, sir. Not perfect. That woman in the green sequins has taken the smaller of the Mayan bronzes from the vanity in the small guest bedroom upstairs. It's in her purse. Shall I speak to her?"

"I don't see the purse."

"Under her coat in the closet."

"Just slip the bronze out when you can. Put it right back where it was. That will make the point. What else?"

"The man in the Armani sharkskin has a monogrammed cigarette box from your study."

"It's only silverplate. He wants to have it at home to show people he's been here. I buy them by the dozen and chalk it up to advertising. How about drugs?"

"More than I'm comfortable with, Mr. Stryker. Mr. Sewell has at least a quarter kilo. I'm sure he's trying to sell it."

"Uh, huh. That divorce is picking his pockets. Don't let him peddle. And keep the sniffing reasonable."

"Those people are in the library, sir. Small groups in and out. And the bathrooms, of course. You really shouldn't keep those hand mirrors available on these occasions."

"Hospitality, Carmine. Make sure one of the maids keeps them clean between snorts."

"Yes, sir. One more thing. There was a delivery from the exterminator."

"That'll be the fumigating bombs." Ronald caught the man's bewilderment. "That's right, Carmine," he said laughing. "Roaches in a four-million-dollar apartment. One of the maids let a big delivery from one of the supermarkets sit here for a weekend when we were in the Hamptons. It must have been loaded with the little bastards. By the time we figured it out, they'd decided they like the address. Tried everything. No dice. Now we fumigate. They'll do it while we're in L.A. next week."

"Won't the gas ruin the apartment, sir?"

"They say not. They just light off those bombs after they seal the place up. That gases the buggers out, and by the time we get back we won't whiff a thing."

"I pulled the boxes into the first closet off the entryway. Mr. Weissflusser was good enough to help me."

"He's useful for that, at least," Ronald said, observing the yard-wide shoulders of the former Mr. World Physique across the room.

"My kids enjoy those movies he makes for you," Carmine said as he left to begin circulating again among the guests. "Especially the one where he blows up the Kremlin and strangles the General Secretary with his bare hands."

It had been Snugge's idea to invite Zoltan Weissflusser. He was a fad celebrity and a fine womanizer, just the thing for a small party of a hundred and fifty.

As handsome and overblown as a character on a comic book cover, he was enchanting an entire corner. He had placed the jacket from his six foot three, two-hundred-and-forty-pound frame over Snugge while she squeaked with laughter and held her arms straight out sideways to attempt to fill the huge shoulders. Weissflusser had contrived to be wearing a short-sleeved shirt. The nineteen-inch biceps had the anticipated effect on those assembled, with Snugge trying unsuccessfully to span them with both her hands. Then she tried to get her arms completely around his chest, hugging as hard as she could to get her hands to clasp behind him. He chuckled and raised her off the ground with one arm, kissing her nose, after which she kissed his.

"If you broke it, you bought it, Zollie," said Ronald as he passed.

"Hey, boss," said Weissflusser, fighting the consonants in his standard German hash, "I didn't hear that you two got married."

"No. And you won't."

"Ronald," said Snugge, still suspended, "Zollie says he can take you to his gym and train you. In two years you can look like him."

"And sleep hanging by my tail."

"You're getting soft," she called after him.

"Where?" he heard Weissflusser chortle. "It's not that soft half-inch in the middle, is it?"

Arriving at the bar, Ronald was pleased to see the burly figure of Laird Hanratty. The bulky construction manager looked seriously uncomfortable in an expensive suit that was a size too small.

"Good to see you, Laird," said Ronald, meaning it and giving him a rough hug. "I thought you made it a principle not to come to my parties."

"I show up once in a while to remind myself why." He knocked back a water glass half-filled with Glenfiddich. "And also to remind myself what you look like. You know we've got some buildings ready to go up. It'd be nice for us to see you once in a while, chief."

"I've been in Rome negotiating a package for Zollie's next epic. *Ragnar III, The Plunderer.* There's a great deal on European TV rights there, too."

"Does he talk in this one?"

"Hell, yes," grinned Ronald. "We're trying multiple sentences for the first time. Like, 'Stay your lance, Bokhtar. The stripling fights well.'"

"And that's where all your time goes?"

"There's the team, too. Got an eye on a couple of pitchers in an Arizona instructional league. One of em's another Bob Gibson. And I've got to get rid of the throw-ins in the Gambretti trade."

"Don't you have a general manager for that?"

"I'm canning him."

"That's the third one in four years."

"They don't shape up, Laird. Hey, you look like you're smelling shit."

"I think I am. What the hell is wrong with you, Ron? You used to be worth something. A few years ago you wouldn't have pissed on these people from a girder."

Ronald shrugged and poured a jolt of Chivas. "I'm in a different world now. Different values."

"Oh, right," said Laird drily. "Is letting some steroid-stuffing kraut jam his weiner schnitzel into your woman part of that?"

Ronald turned to where Weissflusser was leading Snugge out of the crowd. "You heard something I should know about?"

"I can sniff thirty tons of concrete and know I'm getting a bad pour. And if I had a lady that looked like that, I wouldn't have to do more than look across this room to tell you what's coming off. Namely her scanties."

"Let's see, Laird. Should I take a swing at you or at him?"

"Both bad ideas if you enjoy breathing in and out. How about her? I think that with the shape you're in you could get to her by the fifth round."

"I think maybe you're in the wrong bar."

"Damned right I am. Only five blocks toward the river is Irish Freddie the Turk's. There's puke on the mirrors and always a dozen honest drunks who would sooner pursue pederasty than movies or baseball. Come on down with me and let's talk about things that don't make a man blush."

Down upon them swept three top executives from Bloomingdale's. One of them spun Ronald around and bawled, "Tell these assholes how you're going to turn Miller into a third baseman so you can move Alvarez to short. You know. The way you talked about it at Le Cirque last week—"

Ronald mumbled the things he had to as quickly as he could and turned the men away. When he looked behind him for Laird, the construction manager and the bottle of Glenfiddich were both gone from the room.

Laird's contempt stung him. He saw clearly what he had become and tried to make it right in his mind.

He sometimes blamed Fiona for his chronic dissatisfaction. Anne's domination of his social upbringing had taught him the immense advantages of not caring for people or honor or too much dedication. The pleasure of power, the power of wealth were all. He had grown up comfortable with that and made himself good at all the games, even when Ford had sometimes caused him to slide backward.

But then there had been that time of illusion with Fiona. And her sweet, rough way with him had at first made him unsure and then begun to undo his family-wrought defenses. She had lured him into a place in the heart where he had never been. He had opened to her in a way he had not before known, and he thought he had felt the same warmth glowing in her.

The joy he had known with Fiona had struck him as one who had never known the happy virus. He had no resistance. And when she had gone, its fever remained in his blood, recurring periodically and painfully.

Without Fiona as a center, his distractions—like Snugge—had been able to carry him for only so many years. Then he had let himself succumb again to the numbing, comfortable games his mother had taught earlier and Snugge had later revived. Ronald looked at the sea of posed faces around him, seeing all the eyes darting nervously over shoulders to try to pick out someone more important than the present conversationalist. He heard the babble of maneuvering for a position one scintilla higher, smelled the low-pitched stink of fear, boredom and drift.

Why weren't they screaming their dissatisfaction instead of battling for ways to find more of it? He hurried to the library.

In the light of a single lamp, he saw six people, couples, he supposed. They were crouched about a rosewood desk at whose center lay a red Gucci scarf scattered with tablets and capsules of many sizes and colors. There was also a glass picture frame, taken from a bookshelf and now laid flat. On it a woman was just finishing laying out cocaine lines. The way they jittered or looked out of stunned eyes told Ronald that this group had been here for a while.

The picture frame and the scarf were held out to him simultaneously.

"Join us. Please," a man said.

"My doctor made these up by hand," a woman said. "They're really special. Usually he makes them just for his own family. Try the orange ones."

Like a dying man grasping at any medicine on hand, he took a capsule and swallowed it with a glass of wine that stood half-empty on the desk. Then he made his way to a chair in a dark corner and tried to drift away from his growing nightmare.

Time soon grew plastic. The shadows of the room became slowly swimming colors. His bitter unhappiness did not leave, but changed shape so that he could see it more clearly from all its horrible angles.

The shapes of new people came and went, the faces smeared masks. Their voices took on a screeching, obsessive rhythm and their words became darts of pain that peppered his churning mind. A short, miserable sleep without rest, dreams of immovable imprisonment in an ice-cold tomb began to overcome him.

When he came out of it, his mind had the clarity said to come to comatose patients at the moment before their death. He suddenly knew he must move to somehow take command and return to the life he was losing. But now his body was as heavy as softly rotten logs.

Pushing hard against the arm of the chair he managed to lurch to his feet, but felt about to collapse backward. At the desk, a bald man was pouring cocaine out of a vial onto the picture frame, whose surface was now so powdery that the picture beneath was no longer discernible. The man saw Ronald and offered him a rolled hundred-dollar bill.

"Come on, Stryker. It will get you moving again."

"You said the magic words." Ronald took the bill and dragged a line of powder up each nostril. He waited for the jolt to hit him before he took the vial away from the man. Now he was becoming taller and stronger. "Look, Mister, I've got a lot of tough things to do tonight and damned little oomph to carry me. So I'm going to take your little white helper here to get me through."

"Hey—"

Ronald jabbed him in the solar plexus just hard enough to drive the breath out of him and let him feel how hopeless any objection would be. "There's a guy out there who looks like Rossano Brazzi with muscles. Ask him to give you whatever it costs to square it. Then get that chemistry set on the desk picked up and haul ass out of here before I have you tossed off the terrace."

He sailed out of the library, more and more ready for the rest of whatever he must do.

Almost two hours had slipped by since he had taken the pill, but the crowd was as dense as ever. He prowled about for Snugge so he could tell her he was leaving, but found no sign of her.

"I thought I saw her going upstairs with Zollie," somebody offered. "They're probably grabbing a breath on the upstairs terrace."

"Thanks," Ronald said. "Let me go see if that's what they're grabbing."

He glided up the steps and checked all the terraces. Nothing. "Laird, my boy," he murmured to himself, "let me now apologize for my behavior."

Walking gingerly down the row of bedrooms, he saw one, small and meant for a maid, that had a weak light showing under the door. The illumination was reddish and shimmering. That would be a Lava Lamp he knew to be in the room, left by a woman with raffish tastes. There was also a fine, soft bed in there.

He switched off the corridor light and pushed the door open just enough to peer inside.

What Ronald saw was the great, V-shaped wedge of rippling beef that was the back of Zoltan Weissflusser. Spread above each bare and mighty shoulder showed the perfect calves and wriggling pink toes of Snugge Gustafsen. Her still-perfect buttocks, gleaming redly and squirming in the moving diffusions of the Lava Lamp, were handsomely visible beneath the kneeling perfection of Mr. World Physique.

Weissflusser's organ was hidden, plunged into the pink pudding of Snugge.

Ronald's approach from behind was thoroughly hidden by a vast barn door of latissimus dorsi, and he tiptoed carefully forward on the thick rug.

Perhaps it was the surging cocaine, perhaps it was just the way things had become for Ronald. He felt no twinge of jealous rage at this indiscretion by his old companion under his own roof. He was as suddenly sick to death of her as he was of everything in this whole wretched tower. But, of course, what Weissflusser was doing was a total violation of party decorum and the guest-host relationship even in this society, and there would have to be a rebuke.

Ronald darted forward and caught Weissflusser's testicles from behind, feeling the scrotum pull up spasmodically in a primordial reflex of protection. He did not yet squeeze but maintained an iron circle just at the edge of pain. "Ah, ha, Zollie. Complete control of the Mr. World Physique. Sorry to interrupt your cock development routine, but that's my exercise mat you're using."

Snugge and Weissflusser piped shrieks in exactly the same pitch. The giant tried to withdraw from Snugge, but Ronald held him firmly down so the copulators remained neatly locked in their jackknife pose.

Sweat poured off Weissflusser as though he had begun to bench-press five hundred pounds. "Oh, Jesus. Oh, God. Ron. Please. Be careful. Ow! *Ow!* Please. Don't. *Ow!* Oh."

"Ronald," Snugge said tearfully. "We were drunk. We didn't know what we were doing. This never happened before."

"It won't happen again, Ron—*Ow!* . . . Don't do tha—*Ow!*"

Ronald had not yet begun any serious twisting. "Aw, c'mon kids. No need to apologize. Fact is, you two can go on dorking for the next twenty years without worrying about me. I'm firing you both. Zollie, I've got a fresh five-year exclusive picture contract with you, based on participation. I'll just sit on it while the musclehead fad passes and your pecs start to sag. Snugge, you have no contract at all, but I won't forget all those good decorating jobs, not to say the blowjobs. But get your penetrated ass out of here tonight."

"Ronald, we meant something to one another after all these years—"

"That's why I never once dipped my jumbo into anybody else's jampot, sweetness."

She attempted to weep. "Who gets the new house?"

"The lawyers. One of us may see it again in twenty years or so."

"*Ow!* Watch it, Ron—That's too tight—*Ugh!*"

"A couple of things you should know, Zollie. After she gets to know you she farts fit to blow the covers off. She also cunt farts—but you must know that—and seldom flushes the pot."

"You are a *penis,* Ronald," she squeaked.

"There's not much I can tell you about Zollie, Snugge, except that I'd worry about two hundred and forty pounds of dynamite with a four-inch fuse."

"You *cocksu*—"

Weissflusser's attempt to turn and swing came to a quick end as Ronald applied a violent and crushing twist to the entrapped testicles. Like one of the great Roman statues of gods beset by overwhelming torment, Mr. World Physique rolled headfirst off the bed and writhed upon the floor.

Snugge was so surprised that she forgot to close or lower her legs. "Ron—"

"Thanks anyway, Snugge," Ronald said as he backed out of the door, "but I've got a million things to do."

The cocaine was still short-circuiting through his brain, and ideas tumbled over one another.

He stepped into his study and ransacked an oaken file cabinet until he found a large, thick envelope that he kissed as if it were a newfound love. "You and I are going places, baby. If Laird doesn't piss on my foot."

There was one more thing before he left.

He slipped through the tumultuous party to the closet near the entryway and then tore open the boxes that had been left there. Selecting two medium-size fumigation bombs, he took one under each armpit beneath his jacket and made his way to the utilities room. The auxiliary air-conditioner was not on, but the ventilating fans were humming full blast against the party smoke. It took only a moment to find an access panel beneath the main duct, and he quickly removed it. It then remained only to drag up a short stepladder and set the insect bombs on it under the duct opening.

His gold-ribbed Ronson lighter touched off the two wicks. He slipped quickly from the room, stopping only to address Carmine. "Take a pizza break, Carm. Unless you want to get caught in a stampede of hundred-and-eighty-pound roaches."

They rode down in the private elevator and took up a position on a corner opposite the Silver Spire. It took them five minutes to see results. Fifty stories above the street, where slashes of horizontal light marked the Stryker penthouse, a line of people suddenly appeared. They were far too high for their cries to be heard, but their weak waving recalled the sagging despair of the first-class passengers on the stern of the tilting *Titanic*. Ronald mischievously wondered whether he should have locked the terrace floors and whether Snugge and Zollie had time to hide their dangling charms.

He waited until the front doors of the gleaming tower opened to send a mob of wheezing, coughing, swearing guests scurrying in chase of the few late-night cabs.

"There will be trouble, sir."

"No, Carmine. Roaches never complain. They just get back to reproducing and trying to get into your house."

"Yes, sir. I've got the car right here. Can I drop you someplace?"

"Yeah. There's a bar. Irish Freddie the Turk's."

"I know it. It's not a safe place."

"I'm real tired of safe places, Carmine."

Laird was still there, seated at a table in the deepest corner of the saloon. He wore his necktie around his forehead in the manner of the headband he wore when he was in the high steel. His suit jacket was being worn by a seventyish man with a chest-length beard who had collapsed over the adjoining table.

Ronald knew that although Laird would have been drinking steadily, he would not be drunk beyond the operational. He had long ago established a workable level of inebriation and had learned to hold himself precisely at it for entire days.

He did not appear pleased to see Ronald. "Don't tell me I forgot to tell you to go fuck yourself?"

Ronald threw down the thick envelope in Laird's lap. "Throw up on my shoulders, flatten my nose, kick me in the kneecaps and whatever else it takes to get rid of your hard-on. I've got something here that's going to make them remember us."

"A home for people down to their last ten million? A twenty-five-story cabana for Asparagus Beach? Another insurance company tower designed entirely with a T-square?"

"I'm off that shit, Laird."

Laird looked hard into his face, all traces of drunkenness suddenly cleared away. "Okay. Now tell me what you *are* on that's got your eyes looking like homemade pearls."

Ronald took out the vial. "I needed a little help tonight—"

"Tough shit. I don't talk to people on other planets."

"Don't like 'em myself." Ronald uncapped the vial and poured the white powder into Laird's drink. "Now maybe we're ready for a talk."

"Maybe."

What they began in the saloon ended the middle of the next morning in the old Central Penn railyards on the West Side.

Stubbled, bleary and as rumpled as many of the street people collapsed against the building across the street, they looked out over the blocks-long expanse of rusty tracks sprawling below the level of the street.

"The International Banking City, huh?" said Laird. "Seemed a helluva lot easier in the saloon than it does looking at it. Now suppose you tell me how you happened to have that ten pounds of sketches and studies so handy?"

"This idea goes back a dozen years. I had it half worked out before the inflation took off, when I still had some lead in my pencil."

"You'd better be sure the time is right. This is a bet that could have you selling mobile homes in Dothan, Alabama if you lose it."

"It's time all right. Look, the world doesn't run on production anymore, it runs on finance. New York had that all wrapped up for itself. But look what's happened overseas. Tokyo, Frankfurt, London, they're all coming like a panzer division. It could all go bye-bye."

"We've *got* a financial center, Ron. It's called Wall Street. Maybe you've heard of it?"

"No good anymore. Goatpath streets that throttle traffic. Growing fragmentation of operations. The big financial companies are overflowing into a dozen buildings and creating a communications disaster, not to mention paying rents that could retire the Mexican debt. Then there's the workers. They can't get good people because it takes two coronaries and a cerebral to get to and from the office. You can't park a car without blowing the City Council first, and you can't get a train where your feet touch the floor. At noon you've got to bribe the maître d' at Burger King to get a stool for four minutes.

"It's worse for the foreign companies, because they're coming in late, and the shit facilities left are overloaded and spread all over the map. Those guys are going to stay home or go somewhere else. Right time? The Almighty is ready to come down and command it."

"Easy, pal," said Laird. "I'm on *your* team. Remember?"

Ronald unrolled the master sketch for the fiftieth time since they had begun to talk the night before. Coming down off the drugs, he was talking as much to jack himself up as he was to convince the already-sold Laird. "Just imagine it. As big as any of the old wacko plans from Justin."

"A city within a city, he used to say."

"Hell, I'm the first one to say there are a lot of his ideas here. Believe it. Living spaces coordinated right in with the commercial complex. Enough underground parking to take care of the whole thing. Traffic routed underneath tunneled-out building to take pressure off the streets. Shopping promenades to service the entire center and strengthen the neighborhood around it. Special highway connections and our own air service—"

"Shit, maybe you should call it the Oakhill Banking city."

"Justin was just a master salesman and manipulator. A deal maker. When it came time to make it happen, he was an unguided missile. Sure, he built a lot and owned a lot more, but he never got one of the big ones flying."

"I dunno, Ron. There are a lot of big hitters who said he was the only one in the world who could organize on the scale his ideas needed. The backers were just too small for him, maybe."

"Well, we're never going to know that, are we? Because it's Stryker's turn at the plate now. I'm going to keep this country on top in at least one place. This is going to make us the axle of the world, my friend, with big American silver dollars for wheels." The drugs were not quite through talking.

"Maybe we shouldn't get so pumped," said Laird. "Even with the yards in hand, we need the waterfront and a lot of land from the city. And there are blocks we need on all sides for the highway work, and a ton of easement okays. The private people will rob us, but the city could kill us . . ."

"That's sure, with all the financial hot water they're in. The bridges and main roads are going fast, the subways are in worse repair than the pyramids and the water tunnels were old when

Moses was young. And that's not talking about a welfare population the size of a Super Bowl crowd, and homeless in every other doorway on Park Avenue."

"I hear that S & O isn't in the greatest financial shape in the world, Ron. And you've got a lot going up already."

"The fast-tracking got us run over a couple times. And we had an eighteen-million-dollar overrun on *Ragnar II* that was going to be made up for in *Ragnar III*, which is not going to be made anymore. Also, there's a shaky ball club without a shortstop and without enough people who will buy tickets to see balls going through into left field."

"Then I hope you've got a lot of credit cards, boss."

"I'm going to pull out of what we're putting up."

"The penalties will be killers."

"I can unload most of it for a bearable loss. I've got to get my credit freed up."

"Maybe you should sleep on this."

"I just woke up, Laird. If I can't get my thumb out of my ass for a big one, now's the time to find out."

"Sure. I always liked Dothan, Alabama. What do you think of cinder-block foundations under those double-wide fifty-five foot trailers?"

The beginning was maddeningly slow and filled with mistakes and difficulties.

It took far longer than anticipated to disengage from the ongoing projects, and in one case it was not possible.

The retrenchment resulted in so many rumbles about the soundness of S & O that Ronald was forced to expose some of his grand plan before he really wanted to. So the city began to rub its hands gleefully and the holders of property surrounding the railyards began to put up their prices unconscionably.

With no major financing put in place and no perfected architectural plans to show the sweep and utility of what was to be,

Ronald had no choice but to watch helplessly as the vast forces of greed and the municipal bureaucracy took aim at an unmoving target.

Not that the breadth of the project did not get respectful attention. The City of New York and the downtown financial community immediately expressed hot desire for Ronald's International Banking City. All across the globe, in dozens of languages, the monetary powers heard sketchy and compelling accounts of the miracle laboring to be born.

All agreed that it would carry New York, if not the entire United States, into command of the financial heights. But was Stryker and Oakhill a company to trust with it? Although they had been efficient, even brilliant, in putting up impressive single-structure projects, the scale of this seemed wrong for them.

Perhaps the unspoken additional difficulty was Ronald Stryker's character. He had hung up some nasty incidents for the public to see, and that public had been quick to write its legislators. And the building industry had not forgotten the trouble those legislators made or the man who had brought it upon them.

"Stryker's on the phone, huh? Hang up and have it cleaned."

But the money was there to be made, and so it was finally, somewhat grudgingly, loaned. It was not quite enough, with various completion clauses making fast, hard work necessary if more was to be obtained. After a lifetime spent mocking Justin for mortgaging himself too far over the edge, Ronald followed him to the same place. Everything, including the Silver Spire, was pledged to the preliminary work on the International Banking City.

"We're in trouble on cash flow," Ronald told his assemblers. Get what you can on options. We'll make the buys on the next transfusion."

The railyards at least were his. The rails came out. True to his fast-tracking heritage, the foundations started to go down when there was nothing more than a ground plan. Steel and concrete deliveries were locked up in massive amounts.

Plans were made to make use of the rotting Hudson River piers in order to deliver material from huge barges, avoiding street traffic tie-ups and piecemeal truck deliveries. The barges were leased and the tugs contracted for. But now Ronald realized that he still did not control the riverfront or the city-owned properties he would need to complete his assemblage so he could go to work with the loans which they would release.

Negotiations with the city became especially brutal when Garvey Kitsworth became involved. A former borough president and present power in the Bronx political machine, he was now chairman of DEPEND, a militant coalition of social and welfare crusaders. Quite properly, he saw the coming goldmine as a deep pocket that the impoverished city must tap to the absolute limit to make up lost federal funds.

He was as tall, fierce and handsome as his Watusi ancestors and spoke pure Back Bay Boston in a voice of rolling thunder. He was as sensitive as a landmine and sorely burdened by a distressing honesty, a great handicap in his political work.

"My people are sinking along with this city, Mr. Stryker. And you're sailing a fat treasure galleon down the river, the first we've seen in a long time."

"If you sink it, Mr. Kitsworth, there won't be anything for anybody."

"I understand the point. But I just want to warn you that there won't be any sweetheart arrangement with the city like the Grand Admiral Hotel job. We are going to make sure those politicians get every cent out of you they can, because it's the only way we can get ours."

"Sounds fair," said Ronald warily.

Weeks became months. There was no more money flowing into S & O. Dates of delivery and payment fell into jeopardy. Ronald felt as though he should have taken a room at City Hall.

Finally, with many great creaks and explosions, the logjam of politicos showed signs of breaking. Smiles and handshakes were exchanged at last. There were nits to be fine-combed, but the lawyers were certain they could get to them as they drew the contracts. The word around town was that the piers, adjacent properties and legal razorwire holding up Ronald Stryker's International Banking City would all be cleared as obstacles by the end of the next month.

The banks felt good enough at what they were hearing to begin at once to start their money flowing almost without reservation. In days S & O would be roaring forward full throttle, and Ronald was relieved that he had pushed so far forward on his own funds.

As a pleasant surprise, Anne Bennington Stryker apparently caught her son's elevated mood. They had been having one correct but chilly dinner a month at her home, where he brought her up to date on his life and work and she at least pretended interest. These meetings satisfied a sense of family duty for each of them and kept the spark of natural affection from growing even dimmer than it was.

Anne had never again talked about the terms of Ford's will. It was possible for Ronald to believe that the wall it had put between them had at last crumbled beneath her tart and proper exterior. Except for her breaking down unexpectedly at George Oakhill's funeral—in contrast to her later cool control at Ford's, Ronald recalled—he had never seen her grieve or give way to any hearty emotion. Until now.

He supposed she had been much more concerned than she had seemed at his extravagant gloom over the delays of the International Banking City. As the project had strung out, she had actually dropped by the office during her periodic shopping trips to the city and inquired how things were going for him. Sometimes she even wandered about waiting for him when he was in a meeting.

Happy for her interest after all the years at arm's length, he was pleased to keep her up to date, unburdening himself of many hopes and worries. And when he had called to tell her of the breakthrough, she had hurrahed as happily as he and had insisted on coming in that very day to buy him lunch at Lutèce.

For every minute of the delectable meal she questioned him as eagerly as if she had been a partner herself. It wasn't until they were over cognac and coffee that she completely relaxed.

She covered his hand with hers. "I might not have shown it, Ronald, but I've worried about you always."

"I'm glad of that, Mother, because I always wanted you to care about me. I hated it seeming so stiff between us. Especially when I knew so much of it was my fault."

"Your father and I didn't set much of an example."

"May I tell you now that I've always loved you very much, Mother."

Anne kissed his hand and his cheek. "Oh, that's so good to hear at last. Now I'm going to give you a chance to prove it."

Ronald tried not to let her feel the slight tensing of his hand. "Any way I can."

"I want you to promise me—no, to swear—that you're going to take next week off for a vacation. Every *second* of it."

"Gee, I don't think—"

She pulled an airline ticket folder out of her purse. "This will get you down to Marina Cay in the Bahamas tonight. It's a lush, beautiful little island that goes way up into the sky. A friend of mine has an empty house there, almost on the highest spot. You can look out over almost every island in the chain. No resort, no golf course, no tourists. No telephone in this place and no TV. Just sun, tennis, pools, cloudless skies and the relaxation you desperately need. The housekeeper is the best cook in the Caribbean, and the wine cellar would make a Rothschild drool."

"God, it sounds so wonderful. But how can I go now when it's all starting to happen?"

"Didn't you just tell me that nothing much can happen for a week, until all the papers are ready? If you miss this you won't see the sun again for years. You've been under murderous pressure. How much more will your body stand? I'm your mother, damn it, and I *care.* Please go, sweet. For me."

He took the ticket out of her hand and tucked it into his briefcase. "Consider me sunburned. And thank you, Mother. With all my heart." He squeezed her with both arms. "Hey. You want to come? We can catch up on a lot of things."

"I'd have loved that, Ronald. But I have so much to catch up on myself right back here. I'll send a good sun-block."

On Marina Cay, Ronald let the strength and optimism come flooding back into him. Sometimes new ideas for the International Banking City came tumbling out of him so fast that he wished he had brought a secretary. But mostly he luxuriated in the sun under cloudless blue skies, looking out upon a silvered sea sprinkled with skimming white birdwings that were the sails of distant yachts. He floated in the pool, snorkeled among gaudy schools of fish and listened to the best record collection he had ever heard.

It was almost, but not quite, perfect. He didn't want Snugge back, but at least she had always been there as a woman. Her shallowness had never grated much on him because she kept him too preoccupied with her distractive nonsense of parties, travel and buying. And she had kept him from being so dismally lonely.

Sometimes, as he went round and round on his raft in the slow circulation of the azure pool, his eyes closed behind his sunglasses and he pretended it was the sixties again and Fiona was with him. She would be floating on another raft just the way he was, and when they bumped together in their random spinning they would reach out their hands to one another and talk sleepily of a candlelit dinner later, and of the wide bed with brandy and breezes.

He considered what might happen if he were able to find a phone and call her to come down to him right here, right now. She would probably, he thought, notify the police that she was receiving unwelcome calls from a voice she remembered but couldn't quite place.

"Damn it, Fiona," he said aloud into the faint sea breeze. "Goddamn it to hell."

The Bahamian sun burned down on him, but now could not quite warm him through.

What Ronald found when he returned, bronzed and exploding with energy, was that something was going desperately wrong.

The city suddenly appeared not a single day closer to having the deal worked out for signing, although some lower functionaries reported they had seen the papers all prepared. The municipal lawyers appeared subdued and uneasy, answering the sharp inquiries of Ronald's legal staff with inspired evasions. Some were apologetic. "Hey, Ronald, I thought we had a deal, too. Something's happening high up. I can't get at it. The mayor knows. Kitsworth too, I think. But not me."

"Is it anything under the table they want? If they do, let's hear it straight. I can't hold out much longer."

"Naw. They're straight arrows as politicians go. But something's starting to stink."

Things were disintegrating elsewhere, too. The assemblers came to Ronald angry and confused. "We had these properties ninety-nine percent sewed up, Mr. Stryker. Now, without any warning, they're reneging on the deals. The ones we had on a handshake while they waited for a couple more thousand have stopped talking to us. The guys that had our binders are giving them back, and anybody who can still wiggle out is doing it, even when we threaten them with suits and penalties."

"They've gotten together to hold us up."

"No, sir, there's no sign that they're organized."

"Offer some of them all you can, just to see where they cave in."

"I already did. Not interested. Even in prices we could never pay."

"They must have given you some reason."

"It looks to me that someone gave them an awfully good excuse not to talk to us."

Very quickly, all the benefits of Ronald's vacation vanished. He flung himself against the silent city bureaucracy with all his influence. Kitsworth might have had the answer, but he was in Nairobi for an intra-African congress. The mayor was lying low, emerging only for an occasional ribbon-cutting.

Ronald called the steamroom attendant at the New York Racquet Club, a retired army sergeant whom he tipped outrageously at Christmas. "His Honor come by for a broiling anymore?"

"Fridays, Mr. Stryker."

"What time?"

"No schedule. Anytime from real early to real late."

"Okay, Reggie, lay me in a couple dozen magazines that won't fall apart in there. I'm going to be your first customer on Friday. And maybe your last."

He sat in the swirling steam for four hours, the wet pages dissolving in his restless fingers, the Perrier barely holding off death by dehydration, before the mayor of New York walked unawares into his trap.

His Honor Irwin Block made his way through the fiery billows looking for a chair. Carrying his towel, he looked like he had been carved out of giant marshmallow.

"Hi, Win. How are they hanging? Never mind, I can see for myself."

Block peered over his huge, shapeless nose with the eyes of a beagle too old to play with the kids anymore. He groaned when he recognized Ronald, and let go with the pugnacious nasal whine that made him an impressionist's dream. "Mother of Moses, you caught me with my circumcision down. Ronnie, I love you like I loved your father, but you're the last—the very last—sonofabitch I want to see in the whole world. I should run for my life." But he flopped down next to Ronald and slapped him on the knee. "Yes. I am a treacherous and revolting shitpig of a political roundheel."

"No. You're a ballbuster, but none of those other things. Otherwise you'd have hunted me up and pelted me with handcrafted bullturds instead of just skulking away."

"So you think I'll let you tickle it all out of me, huh?"

"Yep. I think you'll feel so slimy about letting them dork me like this that you'll hold me down and make me listen to every last word."

"How do you know I'm not in on it?"

"You are in on it, Win. But you'll tell me how, why and with whom because your father the rabbi is watching from a heaven where ten thousand angels are ready to piss down guilt on you."

The mayor sighed and eased his chair to the horizontal. "Fifteen years with my shrink makes it easier for me to spill from the reclining position."

"What am I facing?"

"Japs. You're facing Japs, Ronnie."

"As in Japanese?"

"Nope. Japanese are tough but polite little geniuses with codes of honor, who run things by consensus after they sing the company song. Japs are guys who are still mad as hell that they missed the carriers at Pearl, and who run things by making banzai charges up your ass. These are definitely Japs."

"Which ones?"

"The Kawanagi Corporation."

"Shit. They're *big*."

"And mean, Ronnie. Mean. Even the other Nip tough guys consider them outlaws."

"But they're cars, heavy machinery, ships, computers. Why in hell are they sneaking around kicking my insignificant balls? And why are *you*?"

"For them, you're going to have to ask their boss, old Akita Fukamara. But if you do, tie your head on. They say that back home he warms up for a tough day by whacking out a couple of hogs with one of those Samurai choppers."

"Are you saying he's here?"

"Yes. He wants this one bad. That's why he's offering half of Hokkaido for the city property."

"And he figures he can use you to stall me out of business and get my railyards at a firesale from me or the bank."

"Hey, you should have been in building."

"I didn't figure you to fuck me like this, Win."

"I wouldn't have, I swear on St. Levy. But whoever filled in Fukamara really did some homework. They sent him to Garvey Kitsworth and the DEPEND lobby first. Told 'em that it would cost the city and their people boxcars of yen if we sold to you. Then he got Kitsworth to lean on me to jerk you along until you went bust. So the Japs could put the money they saved on your land into ours. Guilty."

"How could they know so much? They got to every single person we had lined up for the assemblage, and they negotiated knowing the exact dollar figure we offered each one. That's more secret than the Pope's flamenco lessons."

"Worse than that, Ron. You'd think they were sitting in the meetings you and I had alone. I actually went back and had my office checked for bugs. How many people in your office were in on what we did?"

"Two lawyers and an executive vice president. But I know those guys. They don't even say good morning to anyone because they're afraid our rivals might make use of the weather report."

"Bullshit. It's one of them. Fire 'em."

"What's the dollars Fukamara's talking?"

Mayor Block wrote a number in the condensation on the arm of his chair. "I can't say it out loud. It hurts my jaw when I try to get in all those zeros."

"This doesn't make sense," said Ronald, stunned. "How could they make any money off what they built?"

"What an interesting question."

"Win, I guess it would kill you if they found out you told me all this."

"Kill me? No. Kitsworth would merely have his black, brown, homeless and sick brethren vote me back to my hot little law office on Pulaski Street. Where I could enjoy suing the city on behalf of people who trip over the white line in the middle of Fifth Avenue."

"Ratshit. Then I can't confront Fukamara with this."

"With what? And why bother? He's already on his way to having your nuts. In a couple of weeks you won't need that towel around your waist."

"I want to tell him I'm going to stop him."

"Why would you tell him a lie like that?"

"Right. But I sure as hell can't stop him if I can't understand what he's doing."

"Even if I didn't care about him and Kitsworth knowing I finked, the Jap wouldn't see you. Why should he?"

"Remember those news pictures from the fall of Corregidor? The grinning faces holding up the captured American flags?"

"Who could forget? Yeah. They wouldn't have missed it for the world. Some of them do like their little gloat."

"It could be the same with Fukamara, Win. Tell him I know. Set it up for me."

"Why the hell should I? I *like* this job. Why *should* I? Give me a reason."

"Because your daddy didn't buy enough war bonds. And your

shitty eyes kept you at Camp Dix. Because you're sixty-six years old and you've kissed all the asses in North America. It's too late to work your way through Asia."

"In other words, no reason at all."

The hours in the debilitating steam appeared to get to Ronald all at once. Block saw him rapidly wilting. "Help me play my two deuces, Win."

The mayor lay with his eyes closed for some minutes. "Can it be that I always wanted to be John Wayne? Okay, Ronnie. I'll try him. Maybe two million southern Democrats will move into New York and save me before Election Day."

"Irwin Block, I don't believe I've ever kissed a man in a Turkish bath before now."

"Then you're going to have a helluva hard time getting into office in this town. I'll let you know."

The New York office of Tokyo-based Kawanagi was the former headquarters of a bankrupted five-and-dime chain, an ancient pile of ugly masonry on upper Third Avenue. Its interior had been gutted and replaced with more glass and stainless steel than Ronald would have believed possible. There were none of the lovely, traditional prints of old Japan, or the charming Japanese potted plants that might have softened the decor for the scurrying hordes of Orientals that he had passed on his way to the office of the chairman. The people looked frightened. The story abroad was that working for Kawanagi was terrifyingly different from working for any of the other Nippon mastodons. The paternal contract of a lifetime job and a comfortable retirement, standard in Japanese industry, were here replaced by a promise of ruthless dismissal for work that was anything short of outstanding.

Fukamara's office, huge and high, featured no wood, no fabric and no decoration. There was only chrome, glass and mirror, with the floors of slab marble and the tall windows bare of drapes and blinds. The chair behind the vast expanse of glass-topped desk was straight, upright and armless with no padding, a duplicate of an old Midwest kitchen chair in hard, black plastic. The chair, opposite, the only other place in the room where one might sit, looked slightly more comfortable, having some leather upholstery at least.

Akita Fukamara did not rise or offer to shake hands. He merely waved at the empty chair. "I am going to call you Ronald, and you are going to call me Akita. Not because we are to become old friends, but because it is your custom to use first names and I like to do business in the manner of my adversaries."

"We are adversaries, then?"

"More than you could ever imagine."

Ronald's anticipation of an enigmatic Buddha figure grunting convoluted evasions, proverbs and inscrutable pronouncements in Mister Moto accents was not to be met. Nor were the expectations of a wearing series of Oriental courtesies.

Unlike his affable counterparts who ran other automotive and electronic giants in Japan, Fukamara did not grant interviews where he might be seen as a gentle philanthropist and philosopher, working among his beloved bonsai and doting on kimonoed grandchildren with bowl haircuts. Nor did his Kawanagi Corporation sponsor Masterpiece Theater and shows featuring migrating caribou. With all its size and power, his organization kept a presence as flat as the Inland Sea, and its inner workings were as shrouded in secrecy as the personal life of its chairman.

Only when it moved to devour another company or industry somewhere in the world was there a news story on Kawanagi, and the details were always thin and filled with reporter's guesswork. Such was the overwhelming force of the pounces that there was never a prolonged fight or negotiation, which held public examination down still further.

There was nothing other than an elaborate tea set on the desk, and Fukamara poured two cups, pushing one toward Ronald. The phone on the desk rang and the chairman of Kawanagi took it without apology, speaking in rapid Japanese. As he spoke he stood and slipped out of his suit jacket and English shoes, replacing them with a short kimono and thong sandals that had been lying on the credenza behind him.

Ronald estimated that Fukamara stood four inches taller than he did. And although the Japanese was every day of twenty-five years older, Ronald did not question that the box-jawed man with the gray, closely cropped hair could have taken him apart in hand to hand combat.

In Japanese the chairman had a voice rough enough to sandpaper mahogany. In English it had been gentler, and except for an excess of hisses and gutturals, Fukamara had appeared perfectly comfortable with the language.

He banged down the phone and impassively swallowed tea hot enough to have hospitalized Ronald. He had sensed what Ronald was thinking. "I find it odd that Americans find my behavior abrupt and rude, when all I do is ape them after much careful study."

"There's always something to be said for coming straight to the point."

"Yes, one of the few useful things you still have to teach us. May I tell you at once why I have acceded to Mayor Block's request to see you?"

"I'm all ears."

"A useful idiom, that, but terribly dated, don't you think?" Now the chairman stood up and bowed deeply and formally to Ronald. "From the bottom of my heart I salute your ancestors, Strykers and Oakhills both. Some honored lessons have come from them. They have my most reverent respect. I wished to tell you that."

"That's nice."

"When I wish for Kawanagi to become supreme in some industry, I carefully study its great people. Not so much for their technical methods, which my people have begun to surpass in all ways, but for their basic wisdom. For example, Mr. Carnegie didn't discover steel or the Bessemer process. But he saw that steel could not be cheap and widespread until it was made in the midst of the enormous coal resources needed to manufacture it, and near the rivers and rails to ship it in bulk. His great invention was not steel, it was Pittsburgh."

"Sounds good, Akita. What about my people?"

"Your Hannah Oakhill showed that one could not settle the land until one had first settled the imagination of the buyer. Your Victor Oakhill showed that the sky could be bought and sold like land itself. And your father demonstrated that the character of an entire nation could be changed in short years by changing the way it was housed. But I think that Justin Oakhill has been my favorite teacher."

"I can't say the same."

"Successful or not, he has always thrust toward one great point: Only the most gigantically daring and frightening plans can really make a difference in a world of congealed thinking. Such projects break loose the entire structure of society. The people who originate them reorder the basic structure of power. Each is a successful revolution against the established order."

"You would have loved his Palace of Tomorrow idea."

"I have copies of the plans for that framed on the wall of my office in Tokyo. Alas, he was too much ahead of his time. And mine."

"But the International Banking City is just the thing for you, is that it?"

Fukamara was not too Oriental to allow strong emotions to show. "That is exactly it, Ronald. It's much more important to us than it is to you. We really can't let you have it."

"I can't believe it's worth what you seem ready to pay. Hell, you're not even in the building business."

"Building? Kawanagi doesn't have the faintest interest in building. As with our other interests, our end product is always *control*." As he said it, one of the fine teacups broke in his clenched hand, producing a trickle of blood on the glass of the table. He worked on it with a handkerchief as he talked. "Yes, I have to be prepared to bid too high, because I know you will move to match me. It makes little sense for a corporation, you're thinking. But consider what it will mean to a *country*."

Ronald's brows knitted. "Japan, Incorporated?"

"If you like. Your newspapers turn phrases cleverly."

"You're saying that the Japanese government is the ultimate money behind this?"

"Sadly, I am not yet able to. At the moment. But it will finally have to be so. I am, as your saying goes, sticking my neck out here. I do so joyfully as an act of the highest patriotism. With this effort I can make the highest officials of my country see the shining hope I extend for our crowded, rocky little islands, which otherwise would become the narrow coffin of our happiness and prosperity. Soon perhaps, our slow leadership will be most pleased to fully back the efforts of companies like Kawanagi and gratefully take our gifts."

"Akita, have you ever thought about hanging a balcony off the front of this place? There was a politician in Germany—"

"I accept your mocking, Ronald. But once we come into the greatest city of the richest country in the world on this scale, you will never dislodge us. We will expand on this base, economically and politically, until we become your landlords. The one thing we can't out-manufacture you in is land. So we will have to use yours."

"The Arabs thought they might try something like that, too."

"Ah, but they did not have this opportunity. What better place to begin than a stupendous International Banking City, open to the financial institutions of all nations ostensibly, but ultimately controlled by us. Our financing mechanisms and leverage in place right on your doorstep. The equivalent of a Soviet port on the Mediterranean, I would say. And please don't look so distressed. It's an international world now. This city is already more than half non-white and foreign. I'm sure you would rather have us than the blacks, eh?"

"Here's another useful idiom, Akita. I'm going to fuck you up."

"Do you think I would have shared all this if I thought you could do anything about it, Ronald?"

"As a matter of fact, I think you might be a little worried about what I might do since Irwin spilled the sushi about you. What is it you want?"

"How quick you are. Yes. I want something that you will be quick to give. That is, once you realize the advantage of a small interest in an enormous undertaking over a total interest in a bankruptcy. For sentimental reasons, I would like to see Stryker and Oakhill survive. As I said, we are not interested in the building. We would come up with the plans and you would execute them through your company. Huge fees for you. A huge payroll for American workers."

"I don't think the guys swimming in the *Arizona* would be fooled by that."

"Ronald, you should all get what you still can. The days of American giants in building or anything else are over. We'll both live to see the day when the Japanese-made flag on top of the White House will be the only thing left to remind you of when you had everything your way."

"Well, nobody can say you've been evasive."

"It was a mistake, I came to see, to be devious in the beginning. I am not in the least bit angry at your Mayor Block. His violation of my confidence—in the name of honesty—made me see that putting you out of business gave me far less than offering to have you at my side from the beginning. The greed of the black thief, Kitsworth, has been too expensive for both of us. From here on, if you will not come along, I will operate openly."

"Thanks for your time. This has been enlightening, in a revolting kind of way."

"My door will remain open to you, Ronald."

"*Sayonara,* motherhumper."

As Ronald whirled to leave, his eye caught an odd flare in the large mirror opposite. Good old open Akita, he thought. Whoever had lighted that cigarette while standing too close to that one-way glass had been watching and listening the whole time.

Boiling, he slammed through the outer office and brushed away the Japanese girl who tried to show him out. In consequence he made a wrong turn. By the time he looked up to realize his mistake he was well around the corridor on the far side of Fukamara's office. He stopped and was about to retrace his steps when a door opened shortly in front of him. A tall woman slipped out and hurried in the opposite direction without a backward glance.

The sable coat and imperious strut were as familiar to him as the short, lovely, blonde bob. Anne Bennington Stryker was quickly gone around the turn of the corridor, never having seen him.

Astonished as he was, he almost called out and followed her. But it took only a split-second more to realize what a mistake that could be.

The corridor was now empty. Quickly he slipped into the darkened room from which Anne had come and locked the door behind him. He flicked on a switch that activated a sign above the door outside, reading, *In Use—Do Not Enter.*

The room was small and painted black. There was a double row of swivel chairs with writing arms. They faced a window twelve feet wide and five feet high. Through it he had a full view of the office he had just left. Fukamara sat where he had left him, speaking into the phone again, his eyes apparently right on Ronald. But of course he saw nothing, because the gaze of anyone in the office was thrown back by the mirror.

The overhead speaker had been left on. Ronald could hear the static of Japanese as plainly as if he had been in the room.

He sat down in one of the chairs and waited, picking the butts of several of Anne's special Turkish cigarettes out of the ashtray. In less than two minutes a smiling secretary, chatting with Anne as though they had met many times before, showed her into the office.

This time Fukamara was off his chair, bowing and smiling to usher her to the seat Ronald had occupied. "You are not to be upset, Anne. We could have expected no more. But the offer was made in good faith and remains open to him."

She was agitated, appearing pulled between regret and anger. "I feel like a goddamned . . ."

"—Jap," Fukamara finished with a frosty smile. "I have heard it many times before and regret its use is denied to me. You must not forget that this is all to his good, Anne. As useful as you have been to us since we came to you, we would have found other ways —less subtle—to vanquish him."

"I understand that very well."

"You were not just thinking of yourself and what was due to you, Anne. You were thinking of the preservation of a great and venerable business. One whose roots I greatly honor. I did not deceive your son when I told him of my worshipful respect for Justin Oakhill. To meet him in his full years would fulfill a long dream. To work with any Oakhill organization would be a great happiness for me."

"Of course I would share Stryker and Oakhill with him fully, and it would be his to guide," Anne went on, twisting her hands nervously. "All the operational details could stay with him. He shouldn't mind that much. If Ford hadn't kept such a dreadful hold on him and hadn't executed that vicious will, it's the way it would have been anyway. The Bennington family is only claiming its proper rights."

"Those rights will be fully protected in any reorganization, Anne. But there cannot be a reorganization if he drives the company out of business first."

From behind the mirror Ronald could see her fear. "Hold on. You said you'd put the company back together even if there was a bankruptcy. It's why I'm helping you."

"You are helping me mostly to help yourself. And I might have been too hasty with my promise. My directors assure me that our stockholders would not understand an expenditure to acquire a company so hugely in debt."

Angrily, Anne was on her feet. "Those directors would lick the soles of those ridiculous sandals if you ordered them to."

Fukamara smiled placidly. "I can see where your son gets his unfortunate temper. But there is no need to think now of unpleasant possibilities. As the old Irish song says, 'The cares of tomorrow must wait until this day is done.' Your intercession with Ronald—done with secrecy and delicacy—will be most important to both of us. Now, shall I get us some fresh tea?"

She seized one of the cups and went to throw it against the wall, but he had her wrist in his hand in an eyeblink. "Those are six hundred years old," he said as he removed the delicate porcelain from her grip, "and I have already lost one of them today."

Ronald got to the elevator before she did and got down to the street, walking in the grasp of anger and hurt. He thought bitterly of how much better it would be if people who could not love one another unreservedly would not love at all. If he had faced Anne at this moment, he doubted whether he could have kept the tears out of his eyes.

He had already decided not to confront her, though. He told himself that it was because it was better to cover what he knew and use her as he could. But it was more likely because there would have been just too much pain.

Back at the office he made a fast check of sensitive files and sign-out sheets and saw that Anne had made good and clever use of her visits with him. There was very little of value that Fukamara had not seen. He imagined that much of it had been set up during that wonderful week at the home of Anne's friend on Marina Cay.

Their regular monthly lunch was on the next day, and by that time he had managed to compose himself and begin to look for ways out of the closing jaws.

Anne was brilliant in her surprised anger as he told her of what he had learned from Mayor Block, receiving every detail of the meeting with Fukamara with a new expression of distaste.

Ronald thought that he did not do badly himself. He showed all the appropriate despair and foreboding of defeat and left no doubt that the Kawanagi offer was slowly becoming more attractive to him.

Even above the bustle of the busy restaurant he could almost hear the sign of relief from Anne. She lighted one of her fragrant Turkish cigarettes and leaned over to straighten his tie, the perfect picture of the doting mother.

"Ronald, sometimes it takes an unpleasant push to force us down a road that's going to be better for everybody. With just a small bending of that steel backbone you're going to get out from under something that would have crushed you and a company that traces back over a hundred and fifteen years. Sometimes things we don't know about are looking after us, and we don't find out until later."

"I know exactly what you mean, Mother."

That evening, in the S & O conference room looking down on the rushing, moon-drenched Hudson, Ronald laid out all the awesome obstacles for Laird Hanratty. Fueled by a dozen steaming mugs of powerful coffee, they hit a brick wall every way they turned.

Finally Laird sprawled out in the center of the big, round table, his head pillowed on a mound of files, and defined their ugly position as he saw it. "You have maybe two months before you go under. The banks won't extend because there's no guarantee that the city will move for you in the next hundred years. If you don't go in with Fukamara, he'll pick up everything you have cheaper, pay the city the big bundle he promised, and we might as well move the Statue of Liberty to Yokohama."

"I hope you see a solution as clearly as you see the problem, old friend."

"God, if we only had a pipeline into Kawanagi the way he had one into us. We don't have one damned piece of dirt to throw at them. Can we get inside?"

"Kawanagi is guarded like the Bank of Japan. They've got their own building and it's wall-to-wall Orientals. Round eyes in there would be picked up as hostile pretty fast. And we also don't know what we're looking for, where they hide it or how to break into it."

"I sure as hell know where I'd like to start. With the architect's plans. I've been to Tokyo, and let me tell you that half of what they build looks like my dog designed it. If what they're going to do on all that space isn't going to set right in what's gotten to be a pretty fucking beautiful city, we should know about it. There's enough civic chauvinism in high places to give us a couple of burrs to put in their jock while we're trying to get the city to forget all their money."

"My mother's the only one he lets see anything at all."

"There must be somebody else he'd let by. Some skirt you know who could reach for his *negamaki* and look around? One of your ballplayers? Jesus, he'd have loved Gambretti if you hadn't traded him."

Ronald put down his cup and straightened in his chair. "My God. I have it. He's so perfect I don't believe it. But . . ."

"But what?"

"He'd rather be dipped in bat sweat than help a Stryker."

"Who is it? *Who?*"

"Justin. Old Justin Oakhill. Fukamara thinks the old boy lives with the gods on Mount Fuji. He'd show Justin his collection of boy-and-goat pornography if he got asked the right way."

"Whoa, Ronnie. Old Oakhill's got to be crowding ninety now. Has he got the steam?"

"You heard him speak at the architects' dinner last year. He's a fucking wonder. He went up the steps two at a time, blew out everybody's eardrums and fried the ass off a lot of things he didn't like. Sharp as a used-camel dealer. And the way he and Liza were squeezing one another on the way out, I think he's still interested and operational."

"Sounds like he might be strong enough to pick you up and toss you straight down the stairs when you ask him."

Ronald slumped back in the chair. "Yeah. I can't approach him straight. All the people I knew he respected are dead. There's only—"

"Uh, hun. Fiona."

"I can't do that. You know why."

"Sure. Because you're not drunk." Laird bounced off the table and scuttled happily to the liquor cabinet. "But I have here, in the person of my dear uncle Jack Daniels, the cure for that."

The shock of hearing Ronald's voice on the phone at five in the morning was such that for a time Fiona was certain it was part of a dream. She had bolted quickly upright and was glad that there was none of the occasional sleepovers alongside to wonder at her fluttering.

She knew he had been drinking by the carefully measured

cadence of his words, and also by the call coming at an hour when no sober person would dare intrude.

"You understand, Fiona, that I wouldn't be calling you now if it weren't terribly important," he had said after an awkward greeting and some sketchy details.

All the arrogant assurance that had made him a figure of such dislike was gone. She had the impression that if he had not called at just that moment, when the whiskey still had some hold on him, he would never have dialed. She thanked God for the whiskey and kept her voice steady. "Of course. Let me put myself together and meet you. Six o'clock at the Plaza? We can get some breakfast and talk."

"Good. I can use some putting together myself."

"See you there."

"Fi?"

"Yes?"

"If I forget to say it later . . . It's awfully goddamned fine to hear you again."

Fiona, remembering with an ache how she had had to hurt him for Justin, could hardly believe that his anger had faded, even after all the years. "It's fine to hear you too, Ronald."

So fine that she caught herself crying while she fumbled with her makeup.

Walking all the way from 79th Street so she would have time to think and prepare herself for the often fantasized reunion, she saw no way back to him. His quick, steadfast switch to Snugge Gustafsen had been proof enough that his supposed love had not survived her own atrocious behavior. Even so, her mind persisted in comparing Ronald's switch to another with her own desperate seeking to lose herself after Justin's return to Liza. She hesitated to judge his long relationship with the Norwegian to have been as empty as her short, tragic marriage to the Marine, but she could not help hoping.

Although she saw no outcome for that hope, she was intensely aware that Snugge was gone and Ronald as free as she herself.

How stupid she was, she thought as she hurried, to be looking for more than the business he had sketched out on the phone. But the vibrating excitement she felt at the thought of being near him again, touching him, if only to shake hands, threatened to undo her. She struggled to slow her walk in the last block to the Plaza, so she would not appear flustered and breathless.

Ronald's head thumped and his vision had only begun to clear. Superficially, after new clothes, a shower and a shave, he looked as fresh as any of the other early-morning breakfasters in the Oak Room, but inside he felt like a train wreck. With the fortification of the Jack Daniels fading, he found himself groaning over the sheer gall of his early-morning call to Fiona. If he had found the nerve later on he would certainly have called her back to cancel. Sure, she had sounded nice enough on the phone after his callow sentiment, and had agreed to his outrageous request for a meeting, but he had learned long ago how quick and cruelly she could turn.

. . God knew, he was not afraid of being attacked, even crushed. Every heavyweight negotiation he attended involved caustic men determined to dominate or humiliate. He handled them with force or subtlety, as the occasion demanded, and came out with every hair in place. But he had not loved any of them for half his life.

He had just decided he would be all right so long as he kept the meeting strictly business and stayed entirely away from what they had been, when she walked into the room. And then that decision broke his heart, because he would never possess this cool, lovely embodiment of the only happy time of his life. She crossed through the tables toward him, the dreamily remembered smile subdued, but as haunting as ever.

He went to her and they shook hands. He didn't want to let go.

"Thank you so much for coming. I'll be brief. I guarantee it."

"I have time, Ronald."

His resolve broke for a moment. "I'm trying to find a way to tell you that you've gotten even prettier, without making it sound like a crock of syrup."

"Most people just say I've gotten to look a little more like Mother. Shall we order?"

As they did, they exchanged the minimum of required civilized small talk for the long-separated, each exhibiting a perfect, humorless composure. They were through with this quickly, and Ronald, scarcely able to believe what he was asking of this woman who had spurned him, and of a man who detested his family, told her what he needed. With few questions, her eyes mostly held firmly on his, she heard him through to the end.

"Fiona," he finished, "I can't think of another reason on earth that I've brought this to you other than that I'm so damned desperate and Justin is the only one I can turn to. I can't count on the couple of drops of blood we share to overcome all that's gone before. Especially when this is about the railyards he thinks I stole from him. For a million bucks—which I need badly—I couldn't tell you why you should throw in with me, or what arguments to use with Justin. I'm not a bit sure why you came, except for a laugh, and I'm a little surprised that I'm not wearing the scrambled eggs by now. But there it is. Do you want to think about it, or will you tell me to go diddle myself right now?"

Fiona's look had not changed since he had begun his request. He thought her attention to the subject might have wandered a couple of times, although her gaze had never moved.

Now at last she dropped her eyes and put aside her napkin. "Ronald, there was much more unsaid than said this morning. Maybe that's the best way to handle a thing like this. So I won't say very much about why I think I owe you something. There's no way of knowing how Justin will take this. He can't be forced, you know. Only intrigued. But you have my word that I'll do my very best for you."

At that she rose and offered her hand again, and he jumped to his feet to take it.

"I hope I can find a way to thank you someday."

"I hope there will be a reason for that. I'll be in touch with you."

"It's still the same number, Fiona. I'll give it to—"
"I remember it."
"I remember yours, too."
"But I'm not there anymore."
"Yes. I know."

Although they had been sitting quietly, there was something strangely breathless about their exchange, as though they had been making intense and vigorous love.

Chapter 16

WHILE OTHER MEN felt with dread the heavy hand of old age, Justin Oakhill almost wished that it would lay upon him harder. There was no longer even the subdued satisfactions of Oakhill and Keefe to sustain him. He had left the business mostly in Fiona's hands somewhere in his early eighties, more because of tedium than infirmity. Year after year he had grown more restive as he watched younger men seize the giant opportunities that had always filled his dreams. His expectations that his restlessness would pass with time were mocked by an energy and imagination that would not fade.

It amused him that the industry that had jeered, feared and deplored his plans now made him an object of veneration, a cult figure for young architects and magnates. Whole university classes came to him on what amounted to pilgrimages. For the few times he still spoke, places in the halls were sold out weeks before.

His old plans, complete with the logistical procedures he had plotted to carry them through—all once derided as hopelessly deluded dreams—now appeared in coffee table books and Public

Broadcasting specials. Although, to be sure, no one undertook to build their grandiose like.

By every right this vindication, late though it was, should have been enough to bring some peace to his last years. But it had been the reverse. For whole hours he would storm back and forth before the huge, horizon-spanning windows in his high apartment, trying to take solace in all he could see that he had built, trying not to let his anguish at what he had not built crush him.

Only Fiona, as attuned to his business heart as Liza was to his emotional one, fully understood his purgatory and attempted to bring him out of it. It was only natural that she would be the one to bring the hope he had long abandoned.

"Faster, Fi. Tell it *faster."*

Like someone who has prepared to lift a box thought to be filled with a giant anvil and found the load to be feathers, Fiona contemplated Justin's lightning acceptance of the scheme.

He had listened to the entire story of Ronald's deadly problem with Fukamara with an enthusiasm that would have sent others of his age to a recovery bed. Now she watched the years drop from him as lightly as the ashes of his cigar as he circled relentlessly on the rug.

With every word she waited for the explosion of rage and dismissal that would send her into the elaborate system of defending arguments she had planned. When he did not quickly detonate, she continued to think he might be too greatly enjoying the news of Stryker discomfiture to break into vituperation too soon. But then, incredulously, she could see his lips moving and eyes darting as he contemplated a sudden flood of plans and possibilities.

And slowly, simply, it came to her. The despised vermin of yesterday made the delectable meal of today when the hunter had starved long enough.

When she had hurried through as directed, she watched him come back into command as though the clock had whirled back to the days before The Hole.

Not that old times were entirely forgotten.

"I knew that pusillanimous, Norwegian-fucking little baseball brain would fall on his ass as soon as he tried to build something more ambitious than a highrise masturbation center for billionaires. Sure, Fukamara decided to move in on him. I've had my eye on that thieving, sneaking mob at Kawanagi for years. India, the Philippines, Malaysia, Australia, Spain, everyplace there's been land to steal, they've gone in. Europe's been a little too smart for him with their laws, so he had to come after the dummies. Boy, oh boy, he must have slavered on the *tatami* mats when he heard what a virgin like Ronnie Boy Stryker was getting ready to try."

"Hey, Jus, you better sit down before—"

"Nothing that Fukamara told him comes as any surprise to me, Fiona. Only Ford could've raised anybody dumb enough not to have spotted it himself."

"That's why he needs you so bad—"

"Fuck *him* needing me. This *city* of mine needs me. This *profession* of mine. Jesus, Fi, my goddamned *country*—"

At risk to limb she jumped in front of him, bumping him to a wheezing halt and producing a thick cascade of white hair over his eyes. "*Justin!* What's the first *move?*"

He looked mildly surprised. "The first move? Ronnie hit it right on the nose. I've got to get inside Kawanagi. I'm going to play my greatest role, and Liza, for once, is going to have to settle for supporting player."

"When?"

"*Yesterday*, if I can arrange it. Hey, I've got a ton of things to figure out. Tell Ronnie to stand by for a meeting to find out what he's got to do."

"I don't think he's expecting you to take *charge*—"

"Where's that guy with my vitamins? Doesn't anybody here realize how fucking *old* I am?"

With Fiona supporting him on one side and Liza on the other, Justin was able to totter down the gleaming corridors of

Kawanagi with the help of two canes. He kept a properly fixed and vacant smile on his face, and used the quaver in his voice he had practiced for a good part of the previous evening. "So awfully good of you, Akita. So awfully good. Are you sure it's all right to call you Akita?"

Akita Fukamara was two steps behind Justin, his ordinarily harsh face gentle with concern and respect, prepared to catch the wobbling figure if it should unexpectedly topple. "Of course, Mr. Oakhill. Are you sure I cannot get you a wheelchair from our clinic? I had not heard of your recent ill health."

"No, no. The doctors say that sitting produces the clots that are slowly killing me."

"My sorrow for your trouble is immense, Mr. Oakhill."

Justin smiled weakly. "It at least gives me a chance to be close to Fiona and Liza."

"You are blessed, sir, to know such loveliness. I must confess to you, Mrs. Oakhill, that your movie *Katie of Kentucky* had a profound effect on me during my early youth in Nagoya. I would sneak into the movie houses of the occupying forces."

"I'm so glad you liked it, Akita," said Liza, the best-looking woman in her sixties in the entire world and making the most of it. "Mr. Oakhill never thought much of it, I'm afraid."

"I bow to Mr. Oakhill in all opinions but that. This way, please. Through these doors." Fukamara waved away the security men after they had set the electrical controls to let the slow-moving party through.

"Are you sure that it's all right that we see these plans, my friend," Justin trembled. "As much as this would be the high point of my last years, I wouldn't want to violate—"

Fukamara patted his shoulder reassuringly. "For you to have been impressed with our project when the good Mayor Block spoke of them to you is more compliment than I ever hoped to earn. When you called with your kind offer to honor us with your opinion of the drawings, we were quite overwhelmed."

"It was the sort of dream that I could never get past those who could not see the future, Akita."

"Actually, sir, there is a something owing to Mr. Ronald Stryker."

Justin coughed and staggered in a wonderfully done rage. *"Ronald Stryker?* He stole every damned basic idea in the project. And anyway, it's as far beyond him as the rings of Saturn. He's an idiot and bumbler. A vandal. A fitting son for the father." Now Justin contrived to appear to catch himself, and looked back to Fukamara contritely. "I suppose it's obvious that our families never got on."

"Rifts in families are always regrettable. I have been aware of your old trouble."

They resumed their progress into a large inner room.

"You can't imagine what joy it will give me to see my sort of vision actually coming to life. I've told Fiona here a dozen times that if such a thing is ever done, a Japanese corporation that understands how to get through obstacles will do it. Isn't that so, Fiona?"

"How could I forget?"

The Japanese beamed, motioned two technicians to leave and began to gather the needed material together with his own hands.

The room was as white and spotless as any hospital operating room, with its walls a four-tier expanse of vertical drawers. Tapping information into a computer terminal, Fukamara brought up a slowly scrolling screen of information and made several selections. He hit the return and several of the drawers overhead slid slowly outward, pivoted to horizontal and lowered themselves to waist height. Fukamara, obviously proud of his ability to operate capably at the lower levels of his company, chose which of the mass of four-foot square drawings that he wanted. Then he set them in sequence on a table that ran for twenty feet down the room's center.

The chairman bowed twice and smilingly indicated that Justin might see what he would. "I await your pleasure."

Fiona thought that Lord Olivier in his most overwrought hour could not surpass the performance Justin now proceeded to give.

He passed along the rows of drawings, clucking and exclaiming, muttering and chuckling, running from surprise to amazement, from astonishment to cataclysmic awe. He erupted praise and lavish congratulation the way Fuji once sent forth rivers of lava. "May I tell you that New York City will divide its history, from the moment before to the moment after this absolutely unique vision."

"This has indeed been an unforgettable moment."

Justin leaned forward so enthusiastically to reach for Fukamara's hand that he overbalanced himself, upending heavily onto his back despite the frantic grabs of Liza and Fiona. Although they seemed to break his fall for the most part, the ancient man called out pitiably. "Oh! . . . *Oh!* . . . My back. My damned back's popped out again . . . Oh!"

When the distressed Fukamara knelt to help he found himself seized by the lapel in a desperate and unbreakable grip. "Please, sir," he said. "How badly are you hurt?"

"Not badly at all except for the back," said Justin, suddenly much more in command of himself. "It happens all the time actually. Any good chiropractor can snap it back in a jiffy."

"But I should call a doctor. We have an excellent clinic here."

His attempt to get to a phone was thwarted by Justin's steely grip.

"Don't get people rushing down here, Akita. Embarrasses the hell out of me. Lost face. Old man's pride."

"But we—"

"Just hoist me up, you and Liza. You're strong and she knows just how to wrestle me around. Then I can navigate enough for you two to get me to the clinic."

"Well, if you insist, sir. And we do have an excellent manipulator up there."

"Superb," said Justin, beginning to pull himself erect with just the right mixture of distress and assurance. "Fi, you can take care of things back here, perhaps—"

"Yes, please," said Fukamara as he and Liza brought the still considerable heft of the old man upright. "Miss Keefe, will you call Mr. Ozira on extension six-five-two and ask him to secure the room, please?"

"Yes. Of course I will," said Fiona, her voice heavy with concern as they helped Justin away. And when they had disappeared from sight she did exactly what she had said she would.

But not until she had withdrawn from her purse three tiny Minox cameras, each loaded with seventy-two frames of high-speed, high-resolution eight-millimeter film, and quickly photographed every square inch of the drawings before her.

Fiona thought that Ronald and Justin might have continued to circle one another, wary and growling in the center of Justin's living room, for the rest of the day if the blown-up and assembled Minox pictures had not finally arrived. Ronald, hugely grateful for what Justin had done for him, had tried to be warm and civil, but Justin's never-ending jabs had finally worn him down.

"Out in the bushes is where your old man always belonged. He would have lasted two minutes in the streets of New York. In fact, he fell off just about the first thing taller than a henhouse that he ever climbed up on, didn't he?"

"He's got his name on some of the finest communities in the country," Ronald said testily.

"You couldn't pay me enough millions to put my name on prairie-dog towns like that."

"If you'll look out that window, Justin, you'll see an awful lot of buildings the Strykers put there."

"They're not buildings. Buildings are what you get when you know what the second floor is going to look like before you build the first. Airplane crashes, I call 'em. Nobody knows where the parts are going to come down."

"We've won big architectural awards."

"Who gave them out? The Mud Men of New Guinea?"

"Hey, why the hell did you help me?" Ronald snapped.

"Because I'm senile," bawled Justin.

The drawings for Fukamara's version of the International Banking City ended the argument for good. No sooner had Fiona pushed back the furniture and spread the plans over the rug than both men were on their knees crawling among them.

Almost instantly they were crying out as one, more dismayed with every glance.

"Holy suffering shit, they've *raped* us," groaned Ronald.

"What's this supposed to be? The Nagoya skyline? They can't bring this felonious assault into New York," spluttered Justin.

"Shoeboxes. Some giant cleaned all the old shoeboxes out of his closet and tossed them in a pile."

"I've seen wider streets in Khartoum."

"And more green space in San Quentin. Where are the plazas?"

"Where's the shopping? The social interaction? Their *robots* wouldn't want to work here."

"How could they get the *colors* wrong? Puke is coordinated better than this."

It went on this way for many minutes more before Fiona finally dropped to her knees to join them. "Just carrying on about it isn't going to change anything or get us moving. Will this help us or not? What are we going to do?"

The red-faced men collected themselves. Ronald helped Justin to his feet.

"The trouble," said Ronald, "is that plain old ugliness and thoughtlessness isn't a crime. I'm sure that every line is going to be legal and right up to the codes."

"They're not stupid or unable to make beautiful things," said Justin. "This is a deliberate choice by Fukamara. The whole project is designed by accountants, not architects. The idea is to maximize the space and slash costs to the bone and beyond. Maybe they've got to do that with what the land is going to cost them. Anyway, he probably figures what the hell do Americans care what their cities look like. The people who build them, anyway. If you attacked him on this he could haul out pictures of two dozen of our so-called major metropolises and show you that his design is better-looking."

"But for the love of God, Justin, this isn't some chaos that grew up over half a century, or a new microchip mecca on the plains of Hokkaido. It's going into a big chunk of New York, by plan, and in one gulp. People will sail up that river for the first time and think *we* put that sonofabitch there. They'll think it's the packages the other buildings came in."

Justin looked startled and actually smiled at Ronald. He stepped closer and looked straight into his face, as though a stranger had come into the room. "Sweet mother. Can it be that you actually give a shit about more than saving your own incompetent nuts?"

"Yeah. Maybe."

"Sorry what I hollered about your old man. I know what Ford did, you can bet your ass, and how well he did it. Maybe that's what always set my hair on fire. He wasn't a barrel of fun, but he had a lot of sand. I know, because we went back an awful long way. I pulled him out of a river once. Wish I'd been around to pull him out of that truck."

"I sort of figured that," Ronald said.

Fiona interceded before Justin could think of something nasty and new to say. "If you guys aren't going to punch one another out, talk about what happens next."

Justin jumped quickly back into his previous scathing growl. "No need to talk. I had it as soon as I saw this shit on the rug. Ronnie, you got your own plans for the project here?"

"Not all. But enough for an idea."

"All I've seen are a couple of renderer's dreams. Get the real stuff. Throw it down on top of these."

For the better part of the next hour they studied what Ronald's architects had done. Justin grimaced and talked much, but it was all to himself, almost completely under his breath. "Not a chance . . . Nope . . . Uh, uh . . . Can't be done . . . Not good enough . . . No . . . Not nearly . . ." After a bit more stumping about he put his hands on his hips and faced Ronald.

Fiona saw that he was preparing himself to handle the younger man, and knew from experience that Ronald would have very little chance.

"Ron, there's nothing terribly wrong with this stuff. It's loaded with all the good ideas I've always loved, God knows. Building by building, even group by group, it's just fine. Good individual things. But for something this size, you need some unifying concept. Some genius. And, bluntly, it ain't here."

Ronald's child had been insulted, and he couldn't quite keep his hurt from showing. "Are you going to sketch the brilliant solution on the back of a napkin?"

Justin fired up another cigar and resumed his crabbed, rapid pacing. "I couldn't design a bread box. Now hear me out. I'll lay it out step by step for us." The billows of cigar smoke stood out behind him as from the funnel of an accelerating locomotive. "We know we can't stand up to Kawanagi dollar for dollar. But there are ways we can come a lot closer with our offer, and we make up the rest of the distance with *emotion.*"

"Whose?" asked Fiona.

"The most unlikely bunch of bastards in America. The steel-headed, stone-hearted builders of New York. And if you think that's not ridiculous enough, their bankers, too."

"Sit down, Justin," Ronald said. "Better yet, lie down."

The old man blew a cloud into his face as he steamed past. "We're going to call a secret meeting. Only the giants. Maybe twenty people who can whisper into fifty major ears in the city government and the financial centers."

"And then?"

"Show them the churlish, incongruous, stultifying thing that's about to be thrust upon us. Churn them up. Tie a cinch around their gray balls and jerk it. Get them screaming that this thing has got to be stopped."

"How, for Christ's sake? *How?"*

"First they lean on good old Mayor Block for a few things. He knows that without these power-hitters' support this city is ungovernable, unlivable and unfinancable. Besides which, the old hack is practically honest, almost sensitive and loves his city nearly as much as I do."

"Block can't buck Kitsworth and the social services group," said Fiona. "Especially when they've got a helluva good point about needing that money like they never have before."

"Take it easy, Fi. Nobody's trying to starve anybody. Remember, if we can persuade enough financial movers to help us buy that land because they don't want Kawanagi to have it, there may not be that much difference in money. And we'll have something that will be worth a lot more to New York and all its people than the project's sale price."

"Kitsworth can't feed today's hungry with the intangibles of five years from now."

Ronald exasperation was mounting. "And what can we do in the two months we've got left, anyway?"

"That's my next point," said Justin, turning so quickly that Ronald almost ran him down. "Our strongmen hustle Block and the banks to string us out for six months. Then we have a competition. The city makes its decision. The winner gets the land and the International Banking City. The loser goes away."

"Competition?" Ronald said, looking at Fiona.

"Competition?" Fiona said turning to Justin.

"Yep. Their collection of egg crates against the design that replaces your nice try, Ron. The design that architects are going to be looking at a hundred years from now the way they look at the Parthenon today."

"Uh, will you tell us who does this design for the ages in what is not enough time to whip up a decent McDonald's in Topeka?"

"An army. All ours. Every major builder and architect in New York putting in his best. We'll pick them at the meeting we're going to have. I've got to get the list together. Beligman of Stone Kreider. Tony McGarahan of McGarahan and Sons. Brilliant architects on those staffs. And they can pull strings getting Ramjak and Bellefontaine. They're the best of the independents. Did you see the tower they did for that textile conglomerate in St. Louis? Wow! . . . I should probably see the bankers separately, but I won't. I want the enthusiasm to feed on itself. Let's see, Jess Blaine of New Amsterdam Trust, Bella Harkness of Padgett Guaranty. Chase and Citibank will respect anything they do—"

"Back *up*, will you?" Ronald finally shouted. "That whole bunch has been cutting one another's throats every day for twenty-five years. Under all those silk suits and hundred-dollar hair bobs, they're biting, scratching, kicking Neanderthals. And if I asked them to knock it off so they can save their city while they bail out somebody they loathe, they'd run out and buy me a hat to shit in."

"Of course, they would. They think you're a real dick. That's why I'm going to have to do it myself."

"*You?*" Ronald said, flopping into a chair. "What makes you think I'd let you put any part of your hammy hands on the International Banking City?"

"Which sits on my railyards, you pipsqueak, with my ideas covered with the slime of what you mistake for design."

"This isn't helping," Fiona protested.

"You're an *antique*," Ronald said.

"And you've got the charm and persuasiveness of a Gila monster. You couldn't convince—"

"Well," said Ronald jumping up. "It's time to go—"

Fiona stepped in front of him. "Listen to him, damn you. He's *got* something. If he's old it *works* for us. He's not a rival anymore, he's a legend. Also, they know he understands a job on this scale better than anybody ever born, and how to organize it and push it. Nobody ever dreamed so big. You copied him, and you know it. They'll listen to Justin where they wouldn't listen to anybody else in this world. And once they listen to him they're lost. He can persuade the rocks to go soft—".

"Let me pass, Fi—"

"Ronald, please," she said, letting him see the great, melting violet eyes. "For me if not for him. For you if not for me."

She realized that she was calling on something she had no right to expect to be there. But it was. Her arms had gone around him to hold him there. Now his crept hesitantly around her, if only for a moment.

"Call your meeting in the shark tank, Justin," Ronald said. "And don't ask Jesus to help you. He's too smart to go into that room."

"Too bad," said Justin. "He might learn something. I'm going to make the Sermon on the Mount sound like it might have needed a little more eloquence."

* * *

It took Justin just three days to round up the people he wanted. On the evening of the third day, Fiona and Liza watched from a doorway down the block as the long, black cars rolled up in turn in front of the Oakhill apartment building. The two had been sent away. Ronald had not been permitted to come either.

"It's got to be just me and them," Justin had said. "When I'm working I don't want anybody thinking what an insolent bastard Ron is, or how they used to stroke over *Katie of Kentucky*, or how juicy Fi's legs look. In fact, I don't want to be thinking about any of those things myself. And anyhow, the way the blood's going to be flying around up there, I wouldn't want to stick you with a big drycleaning bill."

"Suppose the blood is yours?" Fiona had asked.

"You can come up and blot me later."

The meeting had been scheduled for nine, and Fiona ticked off the arrivals. In every case they arrived alone, their thoughts and character standing out unhidden in their faces. Even from where she was, Fiona could see the pitiless, glacial set of the features, marking long years in one of the most brutish and unsentimental businesses that had ever been practiced. They had come out of respect or curiosity, but it was going to take breathtakingly more than that to bring together personalities that would not ordinarily have consented to be in the same room together except for a foreclosure.

Last to arrive was Mayor Block, who had apparently slipped away in a taxi to throw off any newsmen who might have gotten a hint of the meeting. There was none of the usual good-natured ethnic clown to be seen in him as he glanced up and down the street and hurried inside.

"This is going to be savage," Fiona said to Liza. "We'll get hauled for loitering for lewd purposes if we stay here. That hotel over there has a splendid spot to buy alchoholic beverages."

"This is worse than waiting for reviews," Liza said. "Especially when bad ones might kill the star. God help that old ham."

They waited, sipped, fretted, said little. The late cocktail crowd became the dinner crowd and then the after-dinner crowd. Soon after that there was the after-theater flood and, close to closing time, the problem drinkers who could believe they had no problem so long as they were taking their liquor out of the home.

Several groups of admirers stopped by to talk with Liza, some being allowed to sit for a while as the women sought to tear their minds away from what might be happening in the penthouse apartment down the block.

At two-thirty, the lights in the plush room dimmed and the tables around the women almost empty, a flamboyant figure sailed through the entrance, weaving with fatigue.

Fiona picked him out as he headed for the nearby bar, and shook Liza's shoulders. "That's Jackson Bellefontaine. He was there. It's *over*."

Bellefontaine was an international figure as an architect and as a longtime lion of New York's underground night life. He was a proudly prominent figure in the gay rights organization, a frequent cover on *Gentleman's Quarterly* and the owner of a much-quoted tongue unsurpassed for its vitriol.

Though far from young, he fully maintained the explosive enthusiasm of youth and had not the faintest use for reserve. His heart lived nowhere but upon his sleeve, while his emotional excesses were worth long columns.

But now he seemed shaken, introspective, almost completely removed from the man Fiona remembered from a score of conversations at heavy-caliber social and business functions.

His elegant profile had gone from its usual haughty tilt to a frightening, forward-looking concentration. When he turned to see Fiona and Liza staring at him from their table, they could see that his bright-blue eyes glistened. Some of his makeup had run as far down as his delicately undershot jaw. He ordered a double Beefeater martini to be sent after him, then flew to the women, covering them with kisses before he threw aside his coat and flung himself down half on top of them.

At other times his metallic and unrestrained baritone filled an entire room, but now he spoke in something close to a whisper, the words choked with fervor. "Fiona . . . Dear Liza . . . Forgive the way I am. I'm exhausted . . . drained . . . torn to bits inside.

I can't believe I've let myself be taken advantage of so. Neither can any of the others. But let me tell you, Liza Hayborn Keefe Oakhill, that your husband has just made some sort of history up there. It was the equivalent of walking into the Colosseum and getting the Christians, the lions and Nero to agree to go on a picnic together for the benefit of Rome."

"What did Justin *say?*" begged Fiona.

"Don't ask for words. I don't remember any. He went past those. Every time he opened his mouth another passion came flying out to knock us flat or turn us upside down."

"Did they fight him hard?" Liza wanted to know.

"Some of them . . . me, too, I think . . . ran up to him as though they were going to murder him where he stood. But he thundered back without giving an inch, and they crawled away with wounds you could put your fist into."

"Will they ever forgive him?"

"*Forgive* him? They *love* him. He was the first eighty-nine-year-old man I ever wanted to make a pass at. I don't know how long it can last, but right now Justin Oakhill is George Washington, Patrick Henry, Henry the Fifth, Napoleon and Genghis Khan."

"Good God. They *agreed?*"

"Amsterdam Trust actually hugged Padgett Guaranty. Stone Kreider kissed Scaglione Cement. And, heaven help us all, *I* promised to buy out Le Cirque for a party for all of us if we won."

"Will . . . *you* work on the design, Jackson?"

Bellefontaine preened for them. "I will *lead* the most brilliant task force of designers ever to come together for a single project, and I do include the Great Wall. Can you imagine Angelo Zoretti being willing to listen to me? And can you imagine Jackson Bellefontaine giving up a chance to do a new San Diego Symphony Center—for zillions—so I can work with a gang of assassins for peanuts and promises? Although I must admit the others gave up a good deal, too. I'm sure we are all headed for a place where we will be permitted to design only with crayons."

Liza gave him a huge kiss on the lips. "You have amazed us, Jackson."

"Mercy, Liza. If only you had balls." His martini came and he poured it down with three quick gulps and ordered another. "Actually, my sweet, the Kawanagi Corporation is going to be the one to be amazed." He let the drink steam down into him, then caught his breath and spoke with suddenly narrowed eyes and an intensity that they had only seen before in Justin. "If it leaves us dead we are going to come up with an International Banking City that blazes out this country's spirit and brilliance. We're going to be so much better than that Kawanagi desecration that no amount of money in the solar system will let them give the heart of our city away for the Mongol horde to heap with their contemptible insults."

As he plunged on, whipping himself near hysteria, Fiona heard Justin's rolling phrases knifing through and almost cheered with the pride she felt.

"The mayor has come in on it, then?" Fiona said when Bellefontaine paused for breath and another martini.

"Old Irwin? He tried to slither away at first, intimidated by that Kitsworth man, but he's been around long enough to recognize a steamroller going over him. Actually, once he got a look at those Oriental nightmares he was as pissed off as the rest of us."

"Did Justin get the whole six months for you?"

"Every day of it. Block said it would be war with Kitsworth and the City Council, but he could call in all his IOUs to swing it."

Fiona cut loose with a cowboy yip that jolted the few remaining drinkers at the tables. Liza grabbed Bellefontaine's latest martini and knocked it back like Derrol Keefe had once done. "Sorry, Jackson."

"Only your liver should be sorry, my sweet. Just one trouble with all of this. It's the most exciting thing that's happened to me since that afternoon in the shooting blind with the Nizam of Kawashoram, and I'm not allowed to talk about it. This is going to be a little Manhattan Project for secrecy. Well, if Angelo Zoretti can button those big, wet lips of his, so can I."

"Will you excuse us, Jackson?" said Liza, gathering her things. "There's a man we have to see."

"And what a man," Bellefontaine, said. "Look after him. He looked much too tired at the end."

"Yes. Now go make us something we could never imagine," Fiona called back to him as they half ran from the room.

There were still some long cars scattered in front of the apartment when they arrived, with several excited, still-chattering people in front of the canopy. The excitement in their voices had not diminished as they attempted to outshout one another in the formulation of the work that would have to begin the next day. One of them spotted the women and raised his hat, grinning. The others were too engrossed to notice.

Upstairs they found an apartment that looked like a fight had been staged between a dozen particularly vicious heavyweights while they drank and smoked.

Justin, still wearing his suit, was sprawled out on a bed, awake but pale and sweating. Whatever his discomfort, it could not keep the smile off his face as the women ran to him. "I'm not dying, appearances to the contrary," he breathed wearily. "Not for the next six months, anyway."

"We saw Bellefontaine," said Liza.

"He told us," said Fiona.

"That's good, ladies, because I don't have enough left to tell you anything. Ronnie's got a few major partners now that he didn't know he was getting, because those people would die of shame if anybody found out they were working for love. And the city is going to own an important bit, too. But it's nothing to frighten the horses. Tell Ron we're due at the mayor's tomorrow afternoon at four to lock up a couple of things."

"No, damn it. You've got to rest a couple of days at least," pleaded Liza.

"We've got so little time that I'm going to have to hire somebody to fart for me. Now give me a kiss and let me grab a snooze."

"I'll call Ronald," said Fiona as she led Liza away. She was almost out of the room when Justin beckoned her back.

The old man put his hand on her cheek. "Listen to me, beauty. Talk about more than business with Ron. I've been watching you with him. Can you believe that it's taken me until now to figure out what there was between you two? And how important it was? He wouldn't be my dream of paradise untrammeled, but I recognize a kind of bold feistiness that might not be all bad. If the business is going to eat you guys up like it did all the rest of us, it might be nice to get swallowed together."

"I love you," she said squeezing his hand, wanting to cry.

"Let's not start that again," said Justin, asleep almost before his wink ended.

At City Hall, Mayor Block was a grizzly in its lair. Comfortable, fearless, in complete command. He was unaffected by either the dark, distrustful looks and murmurs of Kitsworth or the slyly victorious bearing of Justin and Ronald. He ignored them all for a while as he sipped coffee and watched the autumn colors of the park outside his window.

"This is collusion," Kitsworth was saying. "This is an insult to the minority groups of this city. And its poor, its sick, its homeless and its old. None of our representatives was consulted for your secret meeting."

"Which we didn't have to tell you about," Ronald said. "Except that we respected you enough to believe you'd understand how this postponement could help all of us, and the city, too."

"Stop blowing smoke up my giggy. And let me tell you that I'm not going to let a lot of rich men and honky dealmakers screw the helpless people of my town out of one dollar that might be coming to them."

"This will give us time to raise our offer to the city," said Justin gently. "And if that makes Fukamara raise his in turn, how can that hurt you?"

Kitsworth had no good answer for that, but his mood was too bad to admit it. "Don't talk to me like some sort of monetary moron. I have two degrees in economics. And don't make it sound like I'm a moneysucker who doesn't care about his town. My family was here putting this place together when yours was busy in Europe riding out on pogroms against the mayor's family. I dig this place, but by Jesus, we're going to have our rightful due from it."

Block now turned to them. "I'm not going to discuss it any more, my friends. I'm in a couple of thousand other pockets besides yours, and I can't—and won't—give any preferences from here on. Now here it is one last time.

"On April first we're going to get together to hear two presentations for the granting of the city's permission to purchase the waterfront and the city properties surrounding the old Penn Central railyards. This property will be for the construction of the project known as the International Banking City. The presenters will be Stryker and Oakhill Corporation, represented by Ronald Stryker, and the Kawanagi Corporation, represented by Akita Fukamara.

"The finance commissioner of the city, the city council, the zoning and environmental-impact people, representatives of Mr. Kitsworth's constituencies and any other concerned folks, including my Aunt Minnie and her gerbil, will be present. We will listen to one speaker—one, count 'em, one—from each side, covering his position as generally as possible. The city will say as little as it can and trust that Mister Kitsworth will do the same."

"When does the decision come?" asked Kitsworth.

"Not that evening, obviously. The two groups will leave behind with the appropriate people a written summary folder with details that cannot fit into their show. And, of course, you will be asked to deliver full details in volume to the proper agencies. I promise you that the city's final decision will come in exactly one week from the presentation day. I also promise that no amount of further appeal will change that judgment. Use any visual aids that you want."

Ronald stirred uneasily. "Is one week enough time—?"

"Not enough to go over every detail. But plenty of time to see the big things, right and wrong, and take our vote. There it is. Questions?"

"Did you tell Fukamara?"

"Yeah. Right in that chair. He was far from pleased. Thought he had it wrapped. But then he got over it real fast."

"What does that mean, Mayor?" asked Justin.

"After a while he got to love the idea, it looked like. Decided he could make a real World Series out of it. Spectacle. Drama.

Says he'll foot the bill for everybody to come up to the Windows On the World for the shootout. Highest spot in the city. Major swank and glamor. Big news coverage. Why not?"

"I see," said Ronald.

"I daresay he expects to win," Justin said.

Kitsworth picked up his hat. "And I daresay that expectation will be met. Goodbye, gentlemen. I don't expect any of us will be seeing much of you until then."

Justin's unlikely strike force started its work. On the surface the world of New York building and heavy finance had never been more quiet. Underneath it hummed with an energy and excitement it hadn't known since the explosive days following the end of the Depression and the Great War.

Under Justin's inspired goading, swearing, prying and mediating, gigantic egos that had not bowed to anyone for decades and had quite forgotten how, were made to grudgingly, then willingly, then cheerfully bend. It quickly, incredibly, became a race to see who could contribute the most in energy and ideas.

"The last time I felt this good," one of the architects shouted out into the turmoil around him, "I was driving a tank with the Third Army on my way to Bastogne."

The secrecy with which they worked was part of the fun, with laborious misdirection practiced every day. Inside the companies, job numbers were given out for phantom clients. Key men left for "overseas efforts" that were in fact undertaken in the middle of Manhattan, shuttling between meeting rooms, drafting rooms and late-night hotel rooms.

Somehow, a patriotic theme crept into the work, and American flags sprouted in lapels and appeared on walls and desks. Tape decks and speakers boomed out Sousa marches at any moment when energies appeared to be flagging.

While there were some epic arguments, and exhaustion sometimes cut tempers short, outsiders arriving for deliveries had no trouble identifying the disparate personalities caught up in this frenzy as happy men.

Not the least of the mighty people subordinated in the giant task was Ronald Stryker. Justin made the younger man his arms and legs. Along with Fiona he carried Justin's tastes and commands to the workers and helped in the mediations.

Fiona watched Ronald carefully for the signs of rebellion one might have expected from a man of such brazen swagger. But he had understood that his humbling was part of the payment expected by Justin.

Ronald was seeing a thousand new kinds of brilliance. It came out of people from whom he had always resolutely believed he had nothing to learn. He drank eagerly from all of them, but mostly from Justin.

"It scares me to think of all my father and that man might have done together if they weren't so busy breaking one another's stones," Ronald told Fiona. "Both not giving a sweet damn what went before. Both big thinkers. One trying to change the way a country lives family by family. One trying to do it city by city. Can you imagine Ford's attention to detail together with Justin's balls-out dash?"

"Too bad we can never see it."

"Can't we, Fi? I've come to Justin kind of late, but a job like this can teach more lessons in a month than any of the others could in five years. If I get all the old rocks out of my head and get my eyes and ears open twice as wide as I ever did before, I think I can get those worlds together. If Justin could go from a Florida wild man to running something like this in a mere sixty years, there's some hope I can go from high-speed glitz merchant to somebody who might build things that make a difference."

He was so eager and boyish, so unlike his old, superior self, that Fiona reached over and mussed his hair without thinking. She blushed and pulled her hand away, but his look told her unmistakably that he hadn't minded.

It was the beginning of their growing comfortable together again. While they were too busy to explore mending what had gone before, the difficult and exhilarating days slowly brought back the old friendship.

After several weeks, Fiona began to permit more small hopes

to stir in her, and prayed that what she saw in Ronald was the same.

At one point, after a succession of hectic days, he gave her the key to his apartment. "It's a helluva lot closer than yours for showers, naps and changing. And it's big enough so you won't have to worry about running into me very much."

Actually, that was the last worry she had in the world. And on some days when she had dropped on his couch so exhausted that she thought she might never move gain, she always woke when he came in. If he had wanted to disturb her, she knew, she would have been very fast to find new strength. That he didn't was sad testimony to how badly she had injured him that last time. He was taking no chances. But when the competition was done, she began to think, she would bring him back, gradually and with great care.

Akita Fukamara became slowly aware that not only was Ronald not coming to him, but he had somehow assembled potentially dangerous forces. His attempts to learn exactly what they were met unaccustomed rebuffs. The traditionally loose security of the American building business tightened to high Japanese standards. Even the reliable Anne Stryker was not as useful as she should have been, although she would press on.

His former allies, Mayor Block and the sullen black, Kitsworth, were clearly no longer committed to him alone. They had presented no satisfactory explanation of the decision to go to a competition, although it was obviously a way to drive the price higher.

At one point he had decided that it might be a bluff, and with his bid already uncomfortably high he had wondered if he might threaten to walk away. But this pot was too big to take chances, and he made a decision to push the stakes even higher, although it would thrust even the massive Kawanagi to the limit.

The first inkling that the force arrayed against him might be even stronger than he imagined came when he tried to go deeper into the American banks. The money was there, but not the welcome and not the special terms he wanted. Those terms would have been more than good enough for them ordinarily, but they were hanging back, evidently doing so in concert.

Fukamara recognized the tactic and respected it. It was a staple of Japanese commerce to gently but stubbornly freeze out foreigners whose business threatened a significant national interest. That a tactic almost never employed in America was being used against him caused him to realize the competition might not be the automatic win he had counted on.

Already far into the Japanese banks, he went to West Germany and Switzerland where the New York shadow did not fall, this time meeting success.

He now had a package behind him of the size usually reserved for bailout packages to small sovereign nations. The chairman of Kawanagi made sure that Ronald Stryker knew this.

Justin showed no sign of panic when he sat with Ronald and Fiona for their regular Friday morning review of the project's progress. But he saw that it would be wise to lay in extra ammunition. "Victor always said that you could never jolt the Japanese away from an idea they were driving toward. That you had to somehow poison the idea for them. Let's think about this, children."

The next morning, Fiona arrived at the bustling headquarters of Kitsworth's DEPEND. It was efficiently staffed with a tough, experienced cadre of dedicated professionals, as well as scores of enthusiastic volunteers of all races. The turnover of these latter from day to day was high and Fiona knew it. She also knew that Kitsworth, the only one in this connected series of storefronts who was likely to remember her, was gone for the day.

"Good morning," she called to nonexistent friends across the room as she arrived with the first crush of volunteers. Then she removed her coat and rolled up her cuffs to make herself indistinguishable from any of the others. Busily she shuttled between work stations, going hard at her envelope stuffing and duplicating until everyone assumed she belonged.

During the lunch hour she found it easy to enter one of the executive cubicles and look about.

"Can I help you, miss?" asked a young Asian girl walking past with a sandwich and a glass of milk.

"Yes. Please. We need a few sheets of executive letterhead and some envelopes for some duplicating. If it wouldn't be too much trouble."

The girl set down her tray and reached under a desk calendar for some keys. "The way they lock that stuff up you'd think it was worth a billion dollars a sheet." She opened a drawer and handed the stationery over with a conspiratorial wink.

Fiona left for her own lunch and never returned, surreptitiously leaving a hundred-dollar bill in the donation box to assuage her lightly bruised conscience.

Anne Bennington Stryker was enjoying the sixty-dollar angel's-hair pasta with caviar sauce at Giambelli's—her son was paying—when Ronald threw a torn-open envelope alongside her plate. He had been sounding more irritable than usual as he rambled on to her about his dogged battle to prevail against Kawanagi. Anne did not understand that for many weeks these lunches had been a leading weapon in that battle.

"What is that filthy thing you're throwing on the table?" she said as he watched her read the return address to DEPEND. The envelope was addressed to the Kawanagi Corporation, and the attention of Akita Fukamara.

"That is the kind of crap we come up against every day. I told you how Kitsworth's guys are supposed to stay neutral and wait for the decision, right? Well, I have a big hunch that money's being passed around. Probably not to Kitsworth, but at some lower executive level."

"And this is the evidence, I take it."

"You take it right, Mother. We're damned lucky we've got a man at DEPEND who pulled that out of the mail before it went out. It's one helluva good idea. The kind of thing that could kill us if things got really close."

Ronald watched Anne making sure there was no unseemly haste in her taking up the envelope. She was perfect right down to the discreetly suppressed yawn as she withdrew the letter and glanced at it.

The opening was the important part.

> My Dear Mr. Fukamara:
> Those of us who have hidden our distress at Mr. Kitsworth's determination to play into the hands of New York's business power structure will be heard. We would like to share with you our idea of a crying, desperate requirement for our city and its cruelly underprivileged.
> Incorporated as part of your construction, it would instantly give you the support of the rank and file of DEPEND and other caring organizations. Such support would be close to irresistible in the decision.
> You realize, of course, that it would be fatal to the writers if Mr. Kitsworth knew of this communication. Whether or not you wish to make use of the proposal attached, there is no need for contact between us.
> Now to the point—

Anne slipped the letter back into the envelope and replaced it on the table. Much closer to herself than to him, Ronald noticed, and behind a vase and a tall pepper grinder. "Do you mind, dear, if I don't read it all at this moment? It's all such a mystery to me, and angel hair and caviar is really very ordinary when cold."

She chatted on about other things, telling him that he really must take his mind off the project once in a while. Even though he told her so little about it, she said, she knew it was grinding him down. As she went on, her napkin fell across the envelope, almost obscuring it. So it was natural that when Ronald had to go, leaving her there over a Green Chartreuse, he forgot his letter entirely.

As he hurried back to the office he prayed that she wouldn't forget it, too. Fat chance.

* * *

"Hello, Miss Keefe. Mr. Stryker is in Washington, you know," said Max, the white-haired doorman at the Silver Spire's special penthouse entrance. "He won't be back for a couple of hours."

"I know that, Max," Fiona said. "We've been working together. I'm just going to stop in to freshen up. Like always." A doorman without a memory is in trouble, she thought.

"Yes, ma'am. Right you are."

As she passed through the lobby she caught a glimpse of Max in the mirror in front of her. He was reaching to ring the penthouse phone. Force of habit.

It had been a gruelling afternoon for Fiona. The tension and stuffiness of the meeting rooms had left her feeling clammy under her clothes. And then one of the bankers had stumbled behind her chair and showered her yellow blouse with coffee. With a dinner meeting scheduled with the traffic experts, she had to clean up and change quickly. There were enough of her things in the room Ronald let her use. She could pull herself together satisfactorily.

This not being a cleaning day, and with Ronald having been away for most of the week, there would be no help on duty. Fiona stepped off the private elevator into the entrance foyer and made straight for her room, peeling off her jacket and blouse as she went.

The double doors to Ronald's bedroom were standing open as she passed, and what she saw inside stopped her cold.

Snugge Gustafsen was there. She was seated in a lounge chair alongside the turned-down bed, a long, golden vision looking up from the book she had been reading. There was a champagne magnum in a cooler nearby. "Excuse me for not being there to greet you, Fiona," she said silkily, the accent more charming than ever, "but I don't think it's ever right to receive outside the bedroom in one's nightwear."

Snugge put the book and her glasses aside and uncurled from the chair. The pajamas were of green silk, the top long-sleeved and low cut, the trousers culotte-style, with a slit to the hip up one leg. As Snugge came forward showing magnificent flashes of thigh, Fiona felt like a poor shepherdess who had stumbled upon Olympus.

Without the slightest warning a great, nauseating twist of jealousy hit Fiona. Wanting to rage or weep, and with no right to do either, she swept her eyes around for Ronald.

Snugge read it all. "Oh, he's not here, darling. This is a marvelous surprise for him. Since Max was too stupid to turn you away —even after all the nice things I gave out to convince him that Mr. Stryker would be pleased to see me—I thought you might as well have *your* surprise now."

"Tell me just what that is, please."

"I'm coming back to Ronald. And he will be extremely happy to come back to me after he sees me. Your neat little dream to have him drop into your pocket—or was it your pocketbook?— isn't going to happen after all."

"I wouldn't be so sure that he wants this, Snugge."

The Norwegian feigned surprise. "And why not, Fiona? Has he let you into some deep, secret place in his heart where he never let me? Has he made you an undying promise that I just don't know about? Since I left, has he turned to look into your eyes and said, 'Fiona, I'm in love with you?' Please tell me if he has. That would certainly make a difference."

Fiona could only set her teeth. "It sounds like you made damned sure he hadn't."

"I might have asked some people to keep their eyes and ears open."

"Why? You were gone, just as you both wanted."

"Fiona, I wasn't away a day before I knew we had done a silly, self-indulgent, childish thing. I do confess that I was more wrong. Do you know that Ronald was absolutely true to me during all those years together? He told me, and of course I'd had him watched, too. But I myself had only a few bedtime tosses. Zoltan Weissflusser was the stupidest. Too visible. Too big-mouthed. And, very sadly, too short-cocked. The tax shelter people, it turned out, had fleeced him nicely out of his movie money, and Ronald's contract kept him from earning more. So it turned out he had only royalties from his workout books, his pectorals, his barbell and his mini-IQ. He'd hang around the house all day moaning softly and sucking either his thumb or my pussy."

"Gee, Snugge, Ron probably loved you for that crazy streak of sentimentality."

"We had a lot of good things, Ron and I. I gave him what you never could. I put him into the kind of world he has to have. Could you have put together the houses, the furnishings, the best of the golden people for him? Christ, he hasn't given a party since I left. He hasn't bought a painting or flown to Cortina for a weekend. Way down in his veins he's got some of the African villager in him. He's got to be kept away from low tastes."

"He's changed, you know. Maybe you wouldn't like him anymore."

"I could survive that. As long as he remembers what he liked about me. We always had a very good time in bed, you know. Especially in the first years. My tastes are lower than his, but I got very good at dragging him down, and finally he loved it. It would have been better if he had never known you, of course. He wouldn't talk about you to me, but I found out in other ways. I wish I could have learned how you made him love you so much and for so long. I'd have made use of that."

With these last words Fiona's heart bounded violently upward. "I think you're talking about a problem you never had."

"I'm talking about a problem I'm getting rid of now. You'll find I've packed what clothes you left here. They're in a very good alligator suitcase with Ronald's initials on it. You can keep it as a remembrance."

"You don't really think you can fuck him into staying with you."

"I wish you could stay and watch me do it, dear. Now please be a good girl. Go take your shit and march it out of here right this second."

"Or what?" said Fiona, feeling some ancient and unquenchable possessiveness rising inside her.

Snugge read the emotion, and her Viking blood surged to meet it. "Or I'll throw you into that elevator with my bare hands, Fiona."

"You're not big enough."

Actually, Snugge was more than big enough. She stood a head taller than Fiona, and all her hard loveliness hung on wider, stronger bone. "I've been through Packy O'Rourke's twelve-thousand-dollar course," Snugge said ominously.

Packy O'Rourke gave a rigorous, very fashionable introduction to the martial arts in a million-dollar studio in the Trump Tower. Part of its chic was its emphasis on the sudden and nasty.

"I've had the Derrol Keefe short course myself," said Fiona, laying her jacket aside and kicking off her heels. Her father had told her, *"If you ever get in a mixup, Sunshine, introduce every sharp edge you have into every soft cranny and dangle they have and repeat until symptoms of life subside."* She had watched Derrol practice this homey philosophy in the Polo Lounge against three abusive UCLA footballers, and it seemed to work.

"Okay, cocklicker, here it comes," said Snugge. She was very good and appeared to want to end things before the results of many hours at Georgette Klinger and the hairdresser could be undone. Unfortunately, she selected as the all-important opening blow a kick that she had learned as part of a series that defended against rape.

Her pale thigh flashed beneath the green culotte as an instep shot out to land squarely and explosively against Fiona's groin. The expected devastation not taking place, Fiona was able to close with her.

From the first this was no typical woman's fight. There was no scratching, no biting, no hair pulling. Instead, they ran together, wrestling and hammering, each trying to do massive, disabling damage to bone and tissue.

The advantage of Snugge's training was rapidly evident. She fought out of the cat stance mostly, weight on one foot so she could launch straight or roundhouse kicks with the other. In between she unleashed a fearsome repertoire of chops to the neck, finger spears to the throat and palm drives to the chin.

But Fiona, despite some early awesome thumps that awarded her a gushing nose, a knotted eyebrow and swollen lips, was not to be overwhelmed. The sinews and reflexes of a man who had swung on a severed shroud through shiploads of celluloid pirates, cutlassing them left and right, were well represented in her. She dove inside Snugge's maneuvering area and in turn applied elbows, knuckle tips, heels, knees, shoulders and forehead.

"*I'd knot your tits if I could find them—*"

"*Your twat is all I'm worried about. If I fell in there, you could crush me—*"

"*That's your mother you're talking about—*"

"*Butt fucker—*"

"*Mouse—*"

The battle was too big to occupy only one battlefield. They rioted from room to room in their advances and retreats, scattering furniture that truck drivers might have found difficult to tumble.

Snugge's decorating tastes, which Ronald had let stand after her departure, ran to sculptured treasures displayed upon spindly stands. Items that had survived the sack of Rome and Constantinople now went in great numbers to their violent fate.

As victory continued to elude her, Snugge went to throws calculated to snap bones and separate joints, to chokes that could easily rupture a windpipe.

Fiona realized belatedly that she was no longer just fighting for a man, but for her life. "Snugge, for the love of—" A leg sweep knocked her onto her back, her head snapping against a stretch of marble floor that brought flashes dancing in front of her eyes. When her vision cleared, Snugge was standing above her, ice-blue eyes wild, a glass tabletop held above her head, edge down and angled at the enemy neck.

With a gasp Fiona jackknifed out of the way as the gleaming guillotine shattered an inch beyond her scalp. Seeing that she could not survive against such an uncaring assault, she tried to scramble away on hands and knees, kicking backward to break the attempts of the frenzied Norwegian to haul her back.

"*I'll maim you, you home-wrecking whore—*"

As Fiona leaped to the closed top of the Baldwin grand piano, Snugge began to come up over the keyboard, gathering into her hand a hefty bronze of Franz Liszt. The nose of the sculpted maestro being lethally long and hooked, Fiona reacted dramatically.

In the finest tradition of her late father, she seized the base of the brass lamp that hung suspended above the piano on a swagged chain. When Snugge, now a glaring witch covered with bloody abrasions and blue bruises, reached just the right altitude, Fiona drew back on the lamp and swung it forward with an all-out grunt. The arc was perfect. Although Snugge turned her face away quickly enough to avoid the ranks of the formerly beautiful, the square, metal base clouted her loudly above the ear. There was a decisive spray of blood through the golden hair and she rolled off the piano sideways, bouncing noisily on the middle octaves before she hit the bench and then the rug.

Fiona sagged down on the lid where she was, sure she was breathing harder than anyone ever had. Everything hurt. Nothing moved. She was aghast at what she might have done to Snugge, but unable to crawl over and look down.

Finally, with enormous relief, she heard gasping as great as her own from below. After a while Snugge wobbled up, her back to Fiona, a bloody hand clapped to the side of her head. She staggered away to another room, her still-handsome rump showing blue bruises through a tear in the green pajamas.

Snugge didn't reappear until long after Fiona had dragged her aching body into a chair, holding a napkin filled with ice cubes against her bruise-covered brow. The Norwegian had dressed herself, after a fashion, and probably looked very little worse than some of the inebriated unfortunates who slept on sidewalk grates on cold nights. Her fallen hair was matted around the handkerchief that stopped the flow from her wound. She took no further step toward her late adversary, but hung a purse on her shoulder and continued toward the elevator.

Not until the car came did Snugge manage a few garbled words out of a damaged mouth and a jaw that might have been partly unhinged. What Fiona thought she might have said was "Keep the sonofabitch. You want him more than I do."

When Ronald burst into the room fifteen minutes later, Fiona had not stirred an inch. The sight of her appeared to destroy a composure already badly shaken. "Oh, my God. You look like the Unknown Soldier." He squatted alongside the chair and held her. "I caught the early plane back and saw Snugge on the street trying to get a cab. Between the screeching and the dirty words I got an idea of what went on."

"Do you think she's all right?" Fiona breathed through swelling lips and a tongue that felt like she had bitten it halfway off.

"Maybe a couple of stitches in the scalp. Nothing that'll keep her from calling on ten different lawyers in the morning."

"If you'd gone with her you'd get something a lot more fun than a lawyer."

"She mentioned something about that," he said, now trying to blot her up with a handkerchief and not knowing where to start. "Oh, you poor guy," he said, as though looking for a way to take the pain on himself. "Snugge's a killer, Fi. You had no business taking her on. Why in hell didn't you just walk out?"

Fiona was too weak to dissemble. "Because I wasn't going to let that big Norse iceberg melt all over you."

"What's that suppose—"

She held him hard. "I'll bob my nose. I'll get silicone. A tuck in my butt. I'll even get real tall—"

He tried to kiss her but couldn't find a place without damage. "How can I show you how much I love you when there's nothing I can touch?"

"Oh, there must be something. There *must*."

"Maybe the doctor can find it."

"Not tonight, he can't."

"Fi, you should really—"

"Draw me the hottest bath anybody ever ran. Then put me in it. Then rub my back. Then cancel my meeting. Then—"

"Hey, look. The soles of your feet look okay."

"What a nice place to start."

He reached into the chair and gathered Fiona into his arms, standing up with her in the shambles of the room. "Thank you for redecorating, darling."

"I just thought, Ron. The night with Fukamara's only a little bit away. I'm going to look like poop."

"We might all look like poop. But maybe you'll enjoy being married to a man living in a four-million-dollar apartment who's worth a cool eighty-five cents."

"Let's hurry, sweet man. Before they turn off the hot water."

If invitations to the Windows On the World had been tickets, they would have commanded four figures.

Fukamara had bought out the entire evening, so there was space for considerably more than those who would be involved in the final decision. Consequently, for several weeks before the competition there evolved a vicious jockeying among the city's predominant.

To this sliver of ruling caste, the merest waft of change in the direction in which power and money were to flow excited a pheromonic rush. No Super Bowl or World Series final could raise as many tremors of anticipation.

Osmotically, without knowing all of the underlying stakes for certain, they knew failure in the contest would be catastrophic for Stryker and Oakhill, and they sensed the length of the odds.

"S & O is like the bull in a bullfight," an investment banker confided. "Prominent on the program, but not expected to win."

In recognition of the expected fatal outcome, the evening in the restaurant 107 stories above Manhattan was dubbed Death in the Sky.

No amount of persuasion could tell the wives of scheduled attendees that this was a strictly business occasion, an event of municipal government at which spousal attendance was superfluous if not ludicrous. But they had wind that Fukamara was hosting a magnificent pre-presentation dinner, and that there was to be music before the theatrics. And so gowns were bought, and then there was no turning back. Men sweated over obtaining invitations as they did over ten-million-dollar deals, and knew they were slowly being pushed into formal wear.

As the terror of not being invited mounted in power circles, the insistence that all attendees be at least tangentially involved in the decision or its impact decreased.

Fukamara, Ronald heard, was more than ever pleased. Let the Americans provide the circus. He would provide the lions. The publicity would lend unimaginable impetus and prestige to the winner, and that would finally be worth billions. And a fine little island between the rivers, too.

The evening of April Fool's Day featured a sunset as spectacular as any that had been seen since the start of the gray and glowering winter. The sun had suddenly cracked away the chill and marched all day across a blue vault of flawless sky, asserting its first exhilarating power. Now it fell slowly into the great harbor, stirring blazes of crimson and glinting gold into wind-flung clouds for the delectation of early arrivals at the Windows On the World.

Descendants of the society orchestra that had performed at the wedding of Anne Bennington Stryker, tonight present, played discreetly against the tense chatter and the clink of glasses. It had been announced that the observation decks would be kept open until the final departure, and some went there and watched, quiet and awed, as the night swept purple and majestic over Brooklyn, carrying the first cold, brilliant stars.

Akita Fukamara was a miracle of relaxation and congeniality, considering that he had chosen himself to present the Kawanagi design. He might have selected a smoother representative—someone speaking perfect, colloquial English—even an American employee. But since he expected that Ronald Stryker was going to be delivering the S & O case, his sense of Bushido—the warrior code—would let him do no less.

The Kawanagi chairman was circulating charmingly among people at the tables when yet another flood of newcomers entered the spectacular room. The panorama of floor-to-ceiling windows giving out on the heartstopping sweep of New York, its sparkling bridges, it rushing rivers, captivated even the most jaded. Most thoroughly held by the sight was Justin Oakhill, whose entrance with Liza and Fiona brought a ripple of applause.

Justin thought that Fukamara would be wondering if this old man had decided to sit and pull for his countrymen or against his despised kinsman.

The Japanese went to where Justin was making his way slowly around the windows, drinking in the splendor. The canes were gone. When Justin turned to him, Fukamara bowed. "Soon we will be adding new diamonds to that beauty, Mr. Oakhill."

"Yes. Choosing the right jeweler will be important."

Fukamara personally escorted Justin and his party to a table near his own, well removed from where Ronald sat between his mother and Laird Hanratty.

"I hope you will be able to see everything, sir," the chairman said as they were seated.

"I will have a commanding view," Justin assured him.

The air tingled with a turbulent impatience throughout the magnificent meal.

At the key table, the largest and with the best view, were seated Mayor Block and all the city functionaries to be involved in the ultimate decision. Uneasily, Ronald saw, Garvey Kitsworth was also at this table, as was a powerful phalanx of the social services lobby. These men brought no wives and wore no frills. They drank no wine and made no jokes. They were hard men present to make unsentimental decisions.

Whatever facade of calm presented itself at the competitors' tables—Fukamara with the impassive samurai of Kawanagi, Ronald with the top men of Stryker and Oakhill—there was turmoil offstage. On the floor below, in separate spaces, both teams had their technicians adjusting the last touches on the dramatic props of their presentations. There were plentiful screams, and curses in two languages, with wrists threatening to become lamed by excessive glances at wristwatches.

Along with coffee came the thick folders, red for Stryker and Oakhill, blue for Kawanagi. These were placed before every man at the key table and contained the detailed particulars of what was to sketched by the speakers.

The audience began to look expectantly toward the wall against which was set a high speaker's platform, banked with microphones and backed with a multiplicity of viewing screens. Technicians pulled lights, stereo speakers and switching equipment quickly into place. A considerable space was kept clear in front of the platform.

There was a flurry of moving chairs and tables as people tried to maneuver for an advantageous view of what boded to be an event long retold.

While waiters cleared what remained on the rearranged tables, the standard room lighting went down and that installed by the Kawanagi technicians took over, compellingly dramatic.

Fukamara was to present first, as he had requested. Ronald recalled an interview where he had called the first blow the most decisive.

Mayor Block mounted the speaker's place with no introduction. He quelled a rustle of applause with an impatient wave and spoke in the ugly flatnesses of his native Bronx. "This isn't a party, appearances to the contrary. It's a place of critical decision for our city. What we're about to decide will affect the way we and our grandchildren will live, because this project will key much of what follows. Beyond the obvious advantages of the International Banking City for New York will be its direct and indirect impact on those in need. Not everybody in this town is an international banker. I like the idea of an open hearing, and you know I like a little show business as well as the next politician. But I urge you to look for the substance. Each side will present its building design. We'll then take a short recess for expert examination of the financial proposals. A closing statement will be allowed for each side. Thanks. Now Mr. Akita Fukamara will begin for Kawanagi, and I wish everybody the same luck."

The spectacle was on.

The Kawanagi presentation had been prepared by masters and brilliantly rehearsed. Rather than trying to play down their foreign affiliation, they made subtle and splendid use of it. The specially written and recorded score was cued perfectly to the action, powerfully symphonic but with distinct echoes of the ancient East. Among the woodwinds and brasses ran the plaintive strings and flutes of the beautiful Orient.

The multi-screens behind featured an exquisitely choreographed slide show, every shot the work of a towering painter or photographer. Traditional Japanese graphics—prints and *sumi-e*—blended with modern Western themes and added peace, softness and sophistication.

To Ronald's astonishment, Fukamara was able to remove almost all the rough vocal edges and slurring accents from his speech. Obviously he reached for a level of English minimal to the needs of his immediate audience. Ronald deduced that the chairman had thought him not terribly important. For now he was purring forward like a Japanese James Mason.

Fully aware of the shortcomings of his austere intentional design, he was careful to sell the sizzle and aroma before he brought forth the steak.

"As the great European designers of the Bauhaus School taught us, form takes beauty from its function. On a land-starved island, the space-eating frivolities of the past are a criminal thing. Here, where landmarks need not be of consideration, we can shape the inevitable rebuilding of Manhattan. Someone must lay down the mold from which the others will build outward. We are proud to claim that honor."

Not forgetting the awe in which the knowing audience held the growing Japanese dominance, he did not neglect that theme.

"You must not sit here, a brilliant people like yourselves, and lament the Japanese economic engine while you neglect its lessons. As a nation poor in natural resources and infinitely poorer than you in space, we have learned to maximize what we construct. Above all, we have learned not to become excessively attached to what we build or to the quaint mistakes of the past. For the day must come quite quickly when it is time to revise it or pull it down for more necessary things. The Pyramids and the Louvre are examples of building for the centuries, but is there a man here who would care to run a Manhattan business—or International Banking City—out of one of them?"

By the time the Kawanagi plan for the project began to appear on the screen to the lovely music, with highly fanciful artist's renderings hiding much of the work's stark nature, the viewers had been well prepared to receive it.

"Like a brilliantly designed dynamo, the beauty of our design radiates from the commercial power packed into it, not from obsolete references to great but dead civilizations. And we can assure you that every inch of this structure is meant to extract the maximum economic force for the project's occupants and for the people of this great city. In five years we will be pouring taxable wealth into New York through this complex at a rate that will make Wall Street—if there is a Wall Street left except as a curiosity—hide its face."

He gestured to the rear and several men in spotless white coveralls wheeled forward a large, square table whose lumpy top was covered with a sheet of white silk. This table was placed before the speaker's platform in the space reserved for it.

With a sure sense of drama Fukamara stepped down from above carrying a hand microphone, and moved into the powerful spotlight that now focused on the table as the other lights went down.

"With great pride, we the servants of Kawanagi present to you your new International Banking City." He drew aside the sheet with a flourish and a bow, revealing a sprawling, carved model of his project as it fitted into the surrounding island.

Ronald saw immediately why Justin had been so delighted to learn that Fukamara had decided to add a model to his presentation. Even though the programmed music crescendoed to an impressive finish, the spell of the fine presentation was instantly lost in the unhideable banality now uncovered in three brutal dimensions. The complex looked like an alien spaceship come to rest on the Manhattan shore preparatory to devouring the surrounding buildings and all in them.

Fukamara heard his mistake before he saw it. The wave of applause from the front row audience, coming off the good momentum generated by the words, slides and music, started to fade before it became anything like impressive. To try to save something of the moment, he called for everyone to pass by for a close look. All pressed forward curiously. But the tide would not turn.

Those who knew nothing of architecture found little to excite deeper instincts or match the sparkle of the show. And those who made architecture their lives were as apathetic as well-bred people could politely be. A few could not hide outright pain.

As far away as Ronald was, he could not miss the furious disappointment that tugged at the corners of Fukamara's smiling face. The man had pulled the door closed and then let it swing open again. The expression of some of his underlings said that their leader might well have gone against their advice in estimating his audience.

Ronald was close enough to the model to hear Justin speak to Fukamara as he filed past. "It's every bit of everything you said it was, Akita."

The orchestra played briefly while the Kawanagi lighting and audio equipment were removed. The model was left in place for later examination.

The Stryker and Oakhill materials were starkly simple in comparison to what had gone before. There was a standing light on each side of the platform to illuminate the speaker, one square of screen behind, and no audio other than the room's own hookup.

Ronald met Fiona's smile from across the room, and his joy in her almost made him forget the monstrous stakes.

Anne couldn't quite hold her composure. "Damn it, Ronald, I can never tell how it's going. How did they do?"

"They did a strong job. It might have been enough if they didn't push their luck and show that collection of Darth Vader lunch boxes."

"Still, you should have given the man what he wanted. I know it."

"Well, if he gets it, the place is going to need a night watchman. I might have the inside track."

"Are you nervous about going up there?"

"No, Mother. Not at all. Because Justin's going to do the job."

"Oh," Anne said, confused and then startled. "Why is that?"

"Because the people in this room who know building think he not only walks on water, but tap dances on it. And because he's probably the greatest salesman of outsize ideas and the things he believes in since Moses."

"Excuse me while I freshen up, Ronald," Anne said.

He caught her stopping to speak briefly to Fukamara as she passed him. The chairman of Kawanagi looked less happy than ever.

"Ladies and gentlemen," Justin heard Ronald say from the platform, "I thought Stryker and Oakhill should be getting more mileage out of the second part of our name. With great pleasure I announce to you that Mr. Justin Oakhill has been a major part of our effort. What you will see, and what magnificent people were gathered to execute it, were in great measure due to his immense efforts. It's only proper that he be the one to present the S & O position. Justin. Please."

Justin was not surprised at the warm applause and surprised cries of delight that washed over him as he made his way forward from his table. But he was aware that much of it was the sort of thing given to doddering old stars at baseball old-timers' games. And a couple of creaking swings and a roller to the pitcher were not going to be enough this time. He could see that in the impassive faces of the Kitsworth group.

As he went by Fukamara he nodded, suppressing a smile at the chairman's amazement when he saw the transformation of the teetering wreck he had received at his office.

The audience watched Justin charge up the steps and embrace Ronald, who looked more surprised than anyone as he returned to his table. The ending of a famous family war was a ceremony that needed spectators.

Still squat and broad, white hair still thick and flying, almost unbent by the years, he leaned forward and spoke unquaveringly, with the same bounding urgency some in the room remembered from his glory years.

"I'll thank you for that nice welcome by keeping this short and straight. Our work will speak for us, mostly."

He motioned down to the Kawanagi model below the platform. "You have seen a work of the highest efficiency, powerfully presented. I must tell you now that what you will see from us will not surpass it—surely will not even match it—in the function of an International Banking City."

Even against the lights Justin could make out an exchange of surprised glances, and Ronald's concern.

"Dollar for dollar, brick for brick, Mr. Fukamara's inspiration is every bit the brilliant machine he described. A tool whose every inch is crafted to maximize its economic impact. Mr. Fukamara is to be congratulated." Here he bowed with sincerity to the Japanese table. The flustered chairman rose for a moment to acknowledge the salute with a bow of his own.

"There is another compelling argument he makes: Holding to the structures of the past with a sentimentality enforced by zoning and landmark commissions confounds the changes needed to make more efficient dwelling machines. The inability to destroy the past cripples the future to a definite degree."

By now Ronald looked like a man who had made a hideous misjudgment. He was sitting half out of his chair, prepared to accept a call to the platform. But Justin rolled on.

"As Mr. Fukamara has said, we have an inexplicable inability to follow the superbly effective and admirable examples set forth by Japanese industry, and are thereby much to blame for our own difficulties.

"So widespread is this failure at the highest levels of our industrial society, that I had no trouble assembling a group of these misfits, men as deluded as myself in their philosophy. All we will show you this evening will bear the imprint of their shortcomings. May I take a moment now to have these miscreants stand and let themselves be seen plainly with their red hands. Until yesterday they were hidden all over town, working in shameful secrecy for our ends. I believe they are all known to most of this audience. Gentlemen. If you will."

At Justin's signal, some twenty-five men got to their feet, grinning. The craning people around them saw the cream of the city's architects and builders, the most subtly powerful of the financial men. It was superb theater, taking only a moment and assigning an awesome pedigree to whatever Justin would show.

"Now I will appoint myself the confessor of our crimes."

No opening night hit had every engaged spectators more quickly. They were already pressing forward.

"All of us New Yorkers have an enormous affection for extended families. Ancestors. When at a reunion we see those familiar old jug-handle ears and that irrepressible family nose that rambles on for too long, we are no more offended than when we see the bloodline's strong shoulders or good, square hands. We're most comfortable knowing where we came from and who we belong to. We look for something of ourselves in the children."

He saw enough nods in the crowd to know he could move on.

"Not surprisingly, we feel the same way about this city, whose generations of buildings grew up with our own generations. It's not all pretty, it's not all practical, effective, productive or even competitive, God help us. There's a hell of an argument to be made for replacing most of them with things that work better for the needs of today. But think about this. A few years ago, in the great tragedy of a war, grand and ancient cities were bombed flat. Terrible. But the people, at least, were able to start almost from scratch, correcting all the old mistakes and incorporating all the new efficiencies and conveniences. And do you know what? Not one of those remade cities ever approached the glories of what they once had. Their new citizens will tell you that as quickly as the old. Am I right in that, my architect friends?"

The answers came back from all over the room.

"You couldn't be righter."

"Berlin."

"Leningrad."

"Frankfurt."

"Dresden."

Justin nodded and continued. "Now we could whip out our flags and make a cry for keeping New York good old American.

But that cry would be false. Because the fact is that New York is as great as it is because it's the most un-American of the American cities. The people from across the sea came here in waves, from the Dutch, to the English, to the Germans, to the Irish to the Asians and dozens more. And every wave brought some building customs and talents and wants and needs to this skyline. From Astor to Woolworth, from Zeckendorf to Tisch, from Trump to Stryker and Oakhill, we put our ancestry and our history into our buildings. Those foundations going down into the bedrock of Manhattan are our own roots."

Now he signaled with a wave of an arm. The lights went down and the single screen behind him glowed with not just the S & O logotype, but that of every organization that had contributed to their project. Meanwhile, a second rolling table, covered in the same way as Fukamara's had been, was trundled in and placed alongside the Kawanagi model.

"No matter what the decision, it has been the proudest time of my life to work with the toughest, meanest, most contentious bunch of geniuses who ever came so willingly together on one job. But let me tell you now what they did."

The slides began to run, the sequence carefully calculated to slowly, majestically build the master concept. Like a conductor working a magnificent Philharmonic to successively higher plateaus of grandeur, he worked the listeners toward his destination. He didn't force them beyond themselves, only interpreting for them when they had the basic shape of the thought.

"I think you're beginning to see it now," he was finally able to say with certainty. "The architecture of our International Banking City is crafted to mirror and retain the history of a city more fabled than Baghdad—New York. And we've worked not just with the designs of the past, but with the colors, the heights, the textures and the mix. It's all new, mind you, and set up with traffic flows and interior designs that should be in the vanguard through the next century. But if the rest of New York ceased to exist, this mighty center alone would hold our architectural past for the children of the future."

At this point the slides moved away from the detailed and on to the distant perspectives that began to reveal the whole breathtaking unity.

"Along the waterfront, in the dark and colorful masonry of the eighteenth century, are rows of beautiful three-story residential buildings which, while modern and spacious, powerfully suggest the earliest Dutch and English cities. Rising behind, framing those, is a second series of structures, again fully advanced technologically, but cut off between nine and twenty stories. They're tapestried with glorious stone and replete with the classical and gothic forms of our ornamented nineteenth-century skyscrapers."

A final wide-screen panorama slid into place.

"And above all of what you're seeing is the shimmering city of the *next* century. It goes beyond where Mr. Fukamara has so capably paused. It soars in sheer, shining glass, compound curves and glittering steel. Its windows capture the reflections of the older echoes we've created and hold it forever like an eternal memory."

Justin noticed happily that he could hardly be heard above the exclamations of wonder below him.

"Efficient as it could be? No. Does it realize every last dollar of potential? Absolutely not. It's hard to grind money out of these sweeping parks and boulevards done on the old scale. You can't obtain that useful Japanese bulk when you're breaking up the mass to the sun and sky and using broad belts of trees to make the whole flow together in air and sunshine."

As the applause was starting to gather, Justin charged down from the platform and snatched the white cover from his model city.

It would have been an astoundingly dominating thing in itself, but placed alongside the Kawanagi model it gave the sweeping contrast between earthbound blocks and a flight of soaring gulls. For what had been announced as a hardheaded business meeting, the cheers and applause and the rush forward to marvel at the model were quite moving.

Things became much grimmer for S & O in the recess, as the participants sat with officials in their examination of the thick folders detailing the financial bids.

Ronald could see Fukamara beginning to regain some of the composure he had lost at the reception of the rival design, although an aide was seen slipping him three fresh handkerchiefs against the sweat he could not stem.

"We've got him leaking," Ronald said to Justin.

"Maybe not as much as he's got us leaking. I thought we'd lined up enough new money to bid only a length or two behind, so we could make up the difference with pizzazz. But he must have hocked the Ginza."

"The city guys loved our stuff. We've got a week to work on them before the final word."

"They're going to go out of here tonight with their minds made up. Bet all your baseball cards on that."

They managed to capture Mayor Block on his way to the men's room.

"What do you think, Win?" asked Ronald, fearing the answer.

"I think that Justin here did with building what that other guy did with loaves and fishes. I'll tell you right now that if you put it to anybody in this room with a six-figure bank account and twenty credit cards, you'd be home by twenty lengths. That editor from the *Times* Sunday Magazine said he'd give it a whole issue if you won."

"Look, Win, everybody owes you their eyes. Push on them. It would make it a contest. Nobody poor will lose a damned nickel in the end."

"Kitsworth isn't ready to wait. And I wouldn't have been nominated last time without him."

"The party isn't split anymore. If you still wanted to run you wouldn't need him."

"I don't work that way, Ron. He delivered when I was sliding down. I won't go against him. Besides that, even though he's an epic pain in the ass, he's as much a friend as you are."

"Did you talk to him, Irwin?" asked Justin.

"Sure. He hated Fukamara's item and loved yours as much as I did. But there's so much difference in the offers. His people have real needs."

"God knows they do. But that kind of money is a one-shot. In five, six years it's gone, and that dog's breakfast is standing for a hundred."

"Kitsworth knows that."

"So, Irwin? So?"

"For one thing, five, six years' eating ain't bad. And for another, I hear Fukamara's going to sweeten his deal in the closing statement."

Ronald grimaced. "Well, I guess maybe that's the letter edged in black."

"Sorry, guys. I'll be thinking very sadly about the beautiful thing this city is losing for the whole time I'm pissing. I'll try *not* to think of bankruptcy."

When he had hurried away, Justin wrapped an arm around Ronald. "Stiffen up. For every time your opponent's big idea destroys you, it saves you five times."

"Oh, yeah?"

"Sure. Especially when his big idea is yours."

Fukamara was a man not used to having things go against him, however temporarily. Justin put on his most long-range glasses and watched him impatiently shrugging off his staff as they tried to offer him written notes for his closing. He scattered these with an agitated swipe and prepared to do what had gotten him where he was. He clearly intended to face his enemy and deliver all the firepower at his disposal in the straightest, easiest language possible.

With an inward smile, Justin remembered that such bluntness was something like he had promised to this audience himself. But, of course, he had then been too smart to do anything of the kind.

Now the chairman mounted the platform with one small index card in his hand. He looked as if he were a conquering general, perhaps about to express his displeasure to the defeated garrison that had dared by its resistance to hold up the advance of his armies.

He had apparently decided that what he was about to add could be shown adequately by the simple screen Justin had left in place. There was no music and the lighting stayed as it was.

"We were not to dwell on small details in our spoken presentation, but I have decided that this addition is not a small detail after all. It was conceived a bit too late to make your booklets, gentlemen, or to come to a finished state. But I am sure you will discern the full intention."

He snapped his fingers and a view of a long, low concrete building appeared. It's small, high windows gave it some of the appearance of the sort of a shed found housing heavy equipment on a large farm, although its color revealed it to be part of the Kawanagi project. The rough degree of finish of the sketches showed the plans to have been done rather hastily and without the degree of interest visible in the rest of the Japanese work. One might have supposed that they had hoped this would never see the light of day, either on this screen or in stone.

"It came to us that it would be insensitive not to recognize the distressing plight of your city. Indeed, the troubles of New York are standard features in much of the international press, with Japan a leader in the growing concern."

Justin heard Ronald's whisper to him. "That's what he sounded like when I went to see him. Like he was gargling with razor blades."

"Yes," said Justin softly. "And why do you suppose the gentlemen at Mr. Fukamara's table look as though they might be getting ready to duck under it?"

The chairman went on. "Is there a foreign schoolboy not aware of the problem of your army of the homeless, of your streets full of the mentally impaired who were driven from institutions by an unfeeling government? Can there be from Hokkaido to Kyushu a heart so stony that it does not go out to New York people failed by their federal government? Have I myself not walked your streets and seen your hungry, your sick, your uneducated, your unemployable lying and living in the filth of the streets?"

An annoyed voice muttered behind Justin. "What the fuck is he describing? Ethiopia? Afghanistan?"

Fukamara, plainly pleased at how quickly and concisely he had outlined the problem, rushed to the solution. "The Kawanagi House of Hope will not be some hidden-away, backstreet shelter scrambling for funds. It will enjoy a place of prominence in the

International Banking City, symbolizing the need for affluent business communities to be in the forefront of helping the wretched and hopeless. In the House of Hope will be found a hot meal any hour of the night or day. There will be dormitories for up to two hundred people a night, and space for a paramedical and social clinic."

Justin kept his eyes roving. Kitsworth and his followers did not look as pleased as might have been expected. But they were not missing a word.

The Japanese glanced at his index card. "Some of our own projections show that at the rate of growth of your underclass, as many as ten percent of your city's population will be permanently homeless by the twenty-first century. As many as fifteen percent may be unemployable, and twenty-five percent, welfare-dependent permanently. And as you are overwhelmed, an ungrateful world that has forgotten the generosity of the American people at the time of the destruction of other nations finds it convenient to ignore you. To ignore people like many in this city who can never rise. The illiterate. The indigent and socially injured."

He had the bone in his teeth, proud that he could show these haughty leaders that the day of the fawning, discursive Japanese businessman moving through consensus for torturously slow decisions was emphatically ending. If these people respected directness, indeed had invented it, then he would show himself as a most apt pupil.

Justin was quite proud of judging the man so well from Ronald's description.

"Best of all," Fukamara was saying, "our House of Hope will take the pressure off your city's budget. I intend to lead all the major corporations of Japan who may come here in giving thanks for our own present and growing prosperity. By sharing it with your less fortunate. More than that, we will lead our people in contributing to a special Brother City Fund. Yearly contributions by both corporate and private citizens of Japan will remind us of our responsibility to the deprived. We are extremely confident that the Kawanagi House of Hope in New York may one day represent a pinnacle of international caring and help for the helpless. I thank you very much, ladies and gentlemen of New York."

The clapping that splattered weakly around the room as Fukamara stepped down was so sparse and so soon ended that Justin was tempted to help keep it going himself to alleviate the chairman's suddenly blossoming embarrassment.

Those of the the gathering who were most offended glared without shame. The gentler, more polite souls just drooped their eyes and examined their hands and shoes.

No one at Fukamara's table was able to meet his gaze. A red flush spread from his collar and rose until it could be seen on his scalp through his closely cropped hair. His bewilderment held him between uncomprehending fury and unaccustomed terror.

With some measure of guilt, which he found himself able to control very well, Justin walked forward quickly to take his turn on the platform. His heels rang in the awful silence. The Japanese appeared hugely grateful when he began because it lifted the attention from them.

"Again, Mr. Fukamara points the way. His call for attention to an immense, continuing problem in our city is well taken. So much so that I feel compelled to call the attention of Mayor Block and others in the city family to page four-fifteen of the folder, where our own plan, which we fortunately did have time to detail, is described."

There was a vehement turning of pages at the Mayor's table. This was done noisily, in the manner of people venting anger at something indirectly.

"You will see there a determination to permanently divert a quite substantial portion of the complex's income to a fund for scholarships for the disadvantaged. Sending them to major schools of finance, engineering and architecture. These are professions that produce leaders. Going beyond that, we will insist that those who take leases make substantial commitments to training and giving preference to the employment of those for whom the doors have remained closed. I commit Stryker and Oakhill to placing a dramatic part of our fees in an endowment to this end in the name of the International Banking City Bootstrap Fund. We can't speak for the rest of the city, much less the rest of the world, but S & O means to build something here that makes inclusion of the disadvantaged as second nature as exclusion is now. And, with thanks to all others, we think we should do this for ourselves and by ourselves."

If Fukamara had been hoping that his own performance would be quickly forgotten, he was getting that wish.

"We've been getting away too long with dropping off a few alms to keep the helpless going day to day. And all the while doing essentially nothing to find their gifted and to bring them up to levels that we seem to regard as sacrosanct to ourselves.

"If we're going to have an International Banking City to attract the envy of the world, let's make sure that we can be as proud of the people we put in it as we are of the buildings we put them in. It will be a pleasure now to put this decision into the hands of the city I love."

Sweeter even than the renewed thunder of approval was the hint of a smile he caught from Garvey Kitsworth.

Nobody heard much of Mayor Block's closing remarks thanking the participants and promising a prompt decision in the allowed time. But such was the business instinct of this audience that none doubted the decision been already handed down. And they liked the outcome.

Fiona was squeezing Ronald, and Liza was kissing Justin in the congratulatory crush.

Having expected a victory to relish, Fukamara had early in the evening commanded further music and drinks after the competition, and now the orchestra again piped up.

Laird Hanratty, his tie pulled loose and a smile as wide as the River Shannon on his apple-cheeked face, pulled Ronald aside. "In case you're deaf and blind about what Justin's pulled off here, I just heard the clinch. One of Fukamara's smoothies came at Block and Kitsworth and tried to deal a new hand, and they leveled him."

"Spare me no detail, no matter how painful."

"Well, leaving out all the cusses and splutters it gets pretty short. The mayor told him he'd rub snakeshit in his hair before he'd let some kelp-eater set up the world's most advertised soup kitchen in a city that was great when the mayor of Tokyo was still painting his behind blue."

"What about Kitsworth?"

"He was a little more polite. Before he finally lost his temper, I mean. Then he said that the next time anybody from outside talked down like that to his people, his city or his country, he'd better have a couple of Ninja to back him up."

They whooped and whacked each other joyfully. Justin appeared with Fiona. He crushed Ronald's hand. "Sonofabitch. I'm finally in a *big* one. I'll never find time to die now. Uh, oh."

Akita Fukamara was there before them. With the inner strength that had made him the commercial terror that he was, he showed calm in the inevitability of personal disaster. For one last time he bowed to Justin, showing as much reverence as a man like him ever could. He allowed a long-hidden likability to gleam through for an instant. "Oakhill-*san*. The wisdom I saluted in our first meeting was but a shadow of what I salute now. I am grateful to you for releasing the arrogant fool in me to run among these honored guests. Now there is hope that he will never return."

Justin stuck out his hand. Fukamara shook it firmly, nodded to the others and turned away. He then found himself face to face with Anne. They stared at one another for a moment, and then he was gone without a gesture to her.

As soon as she looked at Ronald she saw that he knew. Stricken, she could only twist her purse awkwardly, trying to keep her head high. "Ronald—"

"It's all right, Mother," he said to her as softly as he could. "I didn't use you very nicely either."

"I'm sorry—"

"Me, too. Come with us, will you? It's over."

She nodded brokenly, and he couldn't make out the emotion that brought the tears to the corners of her eyes. He suspected he never would.

Laird clapped his hands loudly for attention. "Hey, let's lift a glass to what all this is about." From the bar he grabbed a bottle of champagne with one big hand and five long-stemmed glasses with the other. "Upstairs, everybody. Under the stars," he said as he herded them to the elevator.

They were alone on the observation deck, the trillion diamonds of the brilliant city rising beneath them shaming even the glories of the heavenly jewels above. The wind was gentle and oddly warm for the date, ruffling the women's hair like a passing lover. Beneath a white, blazing moon, transparent wisps of cloud curled and marched.

"Like ghosts," Fiona said, watching them go.

"I wonder if any of them is Hannah, or Jack Grant," said Justin. "Proud of how their work turned out."

"Or Victor or Ford," said Ronald. He waved his filled glass toward the Brooklyn Bridge. "I remember you told me how Victor climbed one of those towers while they were building it."

Liza looked about her, the gleaming wonderland around them reflected in the great violet eyes. "Do you think we could stand here and count all the ones we did? And the ones the rest of them did before us?"

"Of course," Justin said. "Show a father a million children from any distance and he'll pick out his own."

Laird raised his glass. "To more."

"To more," said Fiona, as close to Ronald as she could get.

They drank, glorying in the glittering, soaring miracles rising about them.

Justin felt the old ones in the air all around him, calling him out with them to be young once more and fly among the towers they had sent to challenge the stars.

"Look at all our beautiful children." He said it so softly that the high breeze took it away unheard into the bright, wisping clouds at which his city pointed.